COMPANIONS
MORE THAN SIXTY YEARS OF DOCTOR WHO ASSISTANTS

Philip Bates
&
Andy Frankham-Allen

CANDY JAR BOOKS · CARDIFF
2025

The right of Philip Bates and Andy Frankham-Allen to be
identified as the Authors of the Work has been asserted
by them in accordance with the Copyright, Designs
and Patents Act 1988.

Copyright © Andy Frankham-Allen & Philip Bates 2013, 2025
Editor: Shaun Russell
Editorial: Terry Cooper, Keren Williams, Hayley Cox,
Richard Kelly and Justin Chaloner

Doctor Who is © British Broadcasting Corporation, 1963, 2025

Published by
Candy Jar Books
Mackintosh House
136 Newport Road
Cardiff, CF24 1DJ
www.candyjarbooks.co.uk

ISBN: 978-1-917022-63-7

Printed and bound in the UK by
4edge, 22 Eldon Way, Hockley, Essex, SS5 4AD

Dedicated to the memory of...

William Russell
Jacqueline Hill
Adrienne Hill
Jackie Lane
Michael Craze
Deborah Watling
Caroline John
Richard Franklin
Elisabeth Sladen
Ian Marter
Mary Tamm
Gerald Flood
Nicholas Courtney

Companions forever gone,
but always remembered.

'I only take the best.'
The Doctor (The Long Game)

Foreword

When I was very young I fell in love with *Doctor Who* – it was a series that 'spoke' to me unlike anything else I had ever seen. And of course, my main way of entering its weird, scary, thrilling, subversive worlds was through the eyes of the Doctor's friends, his assistants, his companions.

So what is the companion there for? Somewhat accurately, but cynically, pointing out a flaw in the show's format back in 1971, the writers described the companion as someone who was there to pass the Doctor his test tubes and tell him he was brilliant. However this is a rather unfair generalisation and had the people responsible for that swipe subsequently shaken up what they perceived as the status quo and done something to change that conception, one might be more forgiving of their little piece of whimsy.

Because the companion is far far more important than that. Yes, of course they are a sounding board, someone to pat him on the back, or get into trouble and need rescuing, or point out the bleedin' obvious when he gets all spacey and alien and misses the little details. But above all else, the companion is there to be his best friend. And, as a result, the viewer, especially the under tens, become the Doctor's best friend by default. Because they identify with the companion. More than anything else, if I was in any way the 'typical' viewer back in the 1960s and 1970s, I wanted to *be* the companion. We aspire to be the companion, we want to find our own magical Police Box and be whisked off into space and time, fighting Daleks, stopping Cybermen, facing down the Weeping Angels. Because that's exactly what we'd do to help the Doctor.

That's why this show so captured the imaginations of generations, yes generations, of children. The need, and the love the viewer has for the companion, is as valid and true now as it was on that foggy night in November 1963.

My first 'best friends' were Ben and Polly. My first tears shed when a companion said goodbye was for Jo Grant. My first 'blimey she's sexy' was Leela. My first 'I don't like this companion' was K9 (sorry, but I cannot abide cute robots and much as I respect the little mutt now, back in 1977 I wanted to punt him into outer space). Yes, the middle-aged *Doctor Who* fan I am now can look back and say 'that one worked well' and 'that one wasn't really that well developed as a character' and 'what were they thinking?' – but the pre-teen inside me who fell in love with this madcap, insane and brilliant show, still looks at each and every companion, from Susan to Ruby, via Jamie, Sarah Jane, Tegan and Mel and all the others, with affection, admiration and of course a huge amount of jealousy. Because they got to do what I never did. They found their madman with a box.

Which brings us neatly to this book, and this guide to each and every one of those companions (and a few other friends that don't quite count as companions but were of equal importance to the Doctor at any given moment). Of course there have been books about companions before – but few of them going into this amount of detail, display this amount of in-depth knowledge and above all, this amount of love. As a celebration of everything that makes the Doctor's (and therefore our) best friends unique and special, this book is essential.

Whether you were there through the days of Ian and Barbara, Victoria and Zoe, Liz and the men of UNIT, the two Romanas, Adric and Nyssa, Peri, Ace and Grace – or whether you only discovered your Doctor through the eyes of Rose, Martha, Donna or Amy and Rory, this is the book for you.

So step aboard your own Police Box and take a trip through the Doctor's outer-space Rolodex and get reacquainted with old chums, or discover some fantastic new ones. It's good to know who these guys are – because if you do find that Police Box of your own, you might just need to know what they did to ensure you don't get exterminated in the first five minutes!

Gary Russell

What Makes a Companion?

Finding a topic for *Doctor Who* fans to argue about is like shooting Fish People in a barrel. Are you allowed to have a favourite Doctor? Are the Virgin New Adventures 'canon'? Who's the best showrunner? And one of the most prevalent questions is surely: what makes a *Doctor Who* companion?

In considering this, you have to take note of all those the Doctor became friends with, and question if they can really be seen as 'companions'. Some are obvious: Ian and Barbara, Amy and Rory, Ben and Polly – all travelled in the TARDIS and fought monsters side-by-side with the face-changing alien. Others muddy the water, including one person many think of as the very first companion: Susan. Actress, Carole Ann Ford doesn't class her as the Doctor's companion; she's his granddaughter, not some fly-by-night human looking for an escape from earthly troubles.

The Brigadier falls into the latter category. Few can agree as to whether he should be classed as the Doctor's companion or not. He doesn't strictly adhere to the blueprint set out by the likes of Susan, Barbara, and Ian, but then, neither do River Song or Kate Stewart.

Twenty-first century *Doctor Who* further complicates matters. The 2009 Specials, for example, boast a succession of would-be companions like Captain Adelaide Brooke (*The Waters of Mars*), Lady Christina de Souza (*Planet of the Dead*), and Jackson Lake (*The Next Doctor*)… who has a companion himself!

So how do we separate the Wrights from the wrongs?

You have to analyse the Doctor's relationship with that person, and trust is a key part of any relationship. In travelling with him, companions become his representatives in some ways;

4

he must have confidence in them doing the right thing when he's not there. But there are numerous companions who can't be trusted.

When he first met her in *Silence in the Library / Forest of the Dead* (2008), the Tenth Doctor was sceptical of River Song, despite her assurances that she was someone he'd 'trust absolutely'. It took her to whisper his real name for him to realise their shared future. Nonetheless, he's keen to get away from River when they next meet, and her duplicity is highlighted when it's revealed she's imprisoned in the Stormcage facility. Whereas River gains his trust, the Doctor never holds any faith in Adam Mitchell – which proves just as well: Adam swiftly puts time and space in peril and is duly dumped back home, with a hole in his head for his troubles.

Some might be unsure about giving River Song and Adam Mitchell 'companion' status, but few can quibble over Kamelion's inclusion. The Doctor shows great confidence in him, yet, in *Planet of Fire* (1984), the shape-shifting android caves in to the Master. He's not the only Fifth Doctor companion who's not trustworthy.

'Turlough was an alien, so when you first saw him, you needed to be a bit suspicious of him: he shouldn't have looked quite right,' actor, Mark Strickson explains. 'People often say, "weren't you too old to play a schoolboy?" And I could throttle them! I was not a schoolboy; I was an alien who had landed *posing* as a schoolboy. It's just completely different. So if, when you first saw me, you thought, *Oh, he's too old to be a schoolboy, he looks weird* – that's exactly what you were supposed to think! Immediately be suspicious of him.' Vislor Turlough's backstory wasn't expanded upon until his last serial, and his *raison d'être* was as a mysterious companion whose motivations remained elusive. The Doctor learned to trust him, encouraging him to find his own titular prize in *Enlightenment* (1983). A far cry from the schoolboy who was going to cave the Time Lord's head in at the cliffhanger of his debut episode.

You might think a proclivity to violence would stop fans from classifying someone as a companion. In theory, the Doctor doesn't approve of militaristic or rash action. He definitely spends enough time scolding the Brigadier for using such means to attack enemies.

Except that's not entirely true.

In *Journey's End* (2008), Davros tells the Doctor that 'you take ordinary people and you fashion them into weapons'. The Doctor certainly uses people: Ace is a good example of this because he says he doesn't like her use of Nitro-9, though is happy enough to exploit her unhealthy obsession. Other companions are more than willing to get their hands dirty: Jack Harkness, Leela, and River Song all revel in combat. The Tenth Doctor is visibly disgusted to learn Jack works for Torchwood and at Jack's suggestion that he break the Master's neck in *The Sound of Drums* (2007). The Fourth Doctor frequently refers to Leela as 'savage' and attempts to educate her on the ways of pacificism. At least with River, the Eleventh Doctor admits that she 'has her own gun, and unlike me, she really doesn't mind shooting people. I shouldn't like that. Kind of do – a bit.' The Doctor uses all these companions' less-desirable attributes for his own purposes while also decrying them. He's a hypocrite, but we forgive him for that because he tries to be better. A brief glance over the list of people associated with the Doctor disperses the notion that adherence to violence excludes anyone from being a companion.

It's not this which excludes Captain Mike Yates and Sergeant Benton, whose statuses, like the Brigadier, are ambiguous. Many see them as recurring characters, in a similar fashion to Jackie Tyler, Sylvia Noble, and Professor Travers. Osgood is perhaps the nearest example: as with Yates and Benton, she's part of the UNIT family, so doesn't travel with the Doctor but remains a regular face working on Earth's defences.

Do companions have to travel in the TARDIS to qualify for companion status? If so, *The Three Doctors* (1973) would elevate the Brigadier and Benton to this distinction. However, it would also qualify Eldrad (*The Hand of Fear*), Courtney Woods (*Kill the Moon*), and a large array of characters throughout the 1980s, including much of the cast of *Earthshock* (1982). It would further discount Liz Shaw, the Third Doctor's co-scientific advisor during the period when the TARDIS wasn't working. Surely no one can question whether she's a companion or not.

Harry Sullivan occupies an interesting place in *Doctor Who*. He's part of the UNIT family and travels extensively with the Doctor, both with and without the TARDIS. And while he joins the Doctor and Sarah in something of a whirlwind, even before that he demonstrates an intuition and independence that marks him apart from some fellow UNIT employees. This could be because he's employed as a surgeon rather than a soldier, allowing him some flexibility due to a different degree of expertise. Nonetheless, it remains paramount for anyone under the employ of the military to obey orders.

Ian Marter had auditioned for the part of Harry when it was thought an older Fourth Doctor would be cast, hence his being written out in *The Android Invasion* (1975), when it became clear Tom Baker didn't need someone else to do physically exhausting scenes. *Doctor Who*, as a programme, demands some action-adventure traits, so it becomes a necessity to cast characters perfect for this part. William Russell, Peter Purves, and Michael Craze were all taken on as 'action heroes' as William Hartnell couldn't fulfil that role on the show.

Ultimately, what makes a companion is the intent of the production team.

Someone like Katarina, although having much less screen time than Sara Kingdom, is regarded as a companion because she was created to be so; yes, even Kamelion, who only appeared in two adventures, since he was intended to be a companion. Grace Holloway falls into the grey area, half companion, half almost companion, because the intent was that she'd apparently become the Doctor's companion had a series been picked up on the success of *The Television Movie*. No such series materialised.

It's inevitable, then, that we all have different criteria in mind when classifying companions – and that's okay. Much like the TARDIS, *Doctor Who* fandom is infinite in its view, and no one view is better than the other.

After all, *Doctor Who* tells us to keep an open mind. One common theme in the series is that companions can be found anywhere and everywhere. Look at the people who have travelled with the Doctor, at the diverse cultures and times represented on the TARDIS. Jamie and Amy might share an accent, a love of fried food, and a place in the Time Lord's hearts, but their lives are poles apart otherwise.

But it's not all about people. *Doctor Who* tells us that we all have companions, and they're often more intangible than we initially think. Take *Listen* (2014) for example, in which Clara Oswald tells a young Doctor: 'Fear is like a companion. A constant companion, always there. But that's okay. Because fear can bring us together. Fear can bring you home. I'm going to leave you something just so you'll always remember: fear makes companions of us all.'

Clara's sentiment echoes one expressed by the First Doctor in *An Unearthly Child* (1963). 'Fear makes companions of all of us, Miss Wright,' he tells Barbara. 'Fear is with all of us, and always will be. Just like that other sensation that lives with it... Hope.'

If we define the term 'companion' as something that accompanies us throughout our life – or even something that accompanies us through a substantial amount of time – we're surrounded by companions. That could mean people: for the Doctor it does, and similarly it's the TARDIS.

It's art too, in all its mediums: screen, theatre, dance, and music. The ear-worms the Twelfth Doctor mentions in *Before the Flood* (2015) underscore our lives. In this sense, companions are an expression of self. It's that ELO song you're humming, that person you can't get off your mind, or the programme you love so much, your house is brimming with associated memorabilia.

The First Doctor
William Hartnell

*'It all started out as a mild curiosity in the junkyard
and now it's turned out to be quite a spirit of adventure.'*
The Doctor – *The Sensorites*

Susan – Carole Ann Ford (*An Unearthly Child* to *The Dalek
Invasion of Earth* and *The Five Doctors*)

Space Oddity (David Bowie); *Grandad* (Clive Dunn).

If there is one main character in *Doctor Who* we know less about
than the Doctor, it's Susan. For a start, we don't even know
her real name. Susan Foreman is almost certainly a fiction; the
surname we know she took from the name painted on the doors
of the junkyard in which we first see the TARDIS – IM Foreman.
Even in the second episode, Ian and Barbara question this. In
all likelihood, her forename is incorrect too, given what we later
learn about her home-world (however, the events of *The Legend
of Ruby Sunday / Empire of Death* suggest otherwise). For not only
is she an alien, but she heralds from the same world as the
Doctor; indeed, she is his granddaughter, a bond that proves to
be the linchpin of Sutekh's revenge plan throughout the 2024
season. We only see her on screen for a year, and in that time
we learn so little about her that when she remains on Earth in
the twenty-second century, we feel as if we barely know her.

In the very first story, we learn only a bit (which seems
curious given *An Unearthly Child* is named after her): she is from
'another time, another world', a place where the children would
be insulted if they were compared to human adults like Ian and

Barbara. Her home is far in advance of twentieth century Earth, confirmed by her technical and scientific knowledge: she is dismissive of Ian's experiment with the litmus paper, and is baffled by the notion that there are only three dimensions.

But for all her knowledge, for all her supposed alienness, she is still a child. In some ways, she is more child-like than her 'peers' at Coal Hill School. This ought not be much of a surprise, really, when one considers that Gallifreyans are a long-lived people, and fifteen must be extremely young – the Doctor explains in *The Sound of Drums* that, 'Children on Gallifrey are taken from their families at the age of eight to enter the Academy' (perhaps Susan somehow escaped that fate?). And, in *The Stolen Earth*, states that ninety is young. Susan's reactions tend to be of someone much younger than fifteen years of age, seemingly living in a heightened emotional state (maybe there's a reason the children of Gallifrey are rarely seen). Yet that isn't to say she is not brave.

Witness her mission to find a cure for the radiation sickness that has struck her and her travelling companions in the second story. She is clearly horrified to discover that she's the only one able to go, but more than anything else, it is the sight of her grandfather deteriorating that urges her to swallow her fear and press on. This fear of the unknown; of being on her own, is her constant companion during her mission through the radiation-soaked jungle of Skaro, yet still she goes. And later, when she is travelling in Marco Polo's caravan across China, she displays an impressive level of bravery. After all the dangers faced on that journey, the travellers manage to gain entry to the TARDIS once again, and so can finally escape. Susan, however, insists on saying goodbye to Ping-Cho. This puts first herself in danger, and then her friends, as she is used against them. It shows the foolish level of bravery Susan excels at: brash, impulsive, and contradictory, often without much thought as to how it may affect others, but also considering how her sudden absence might impact a new pal.

Another minor thing we learn about Susan in *The Sensorites* is that she is telepathic, although this doesn't appear to be a well-developed ability. The Doctor is surprised to learn that Susan has this gift, which begs the question: why? It is later established that all Time Lords are telepathic to some extent (to the point where the Doctor states in *Logopolis* that in some ways they all 'have the same mind'). The Doctor suggests she will be better trained when they return home; could this be because she is developing early, a consequence of her travels in the TARDIS? Or is it, as he acknowledges in *Heaven Sent*, that she's 'young and telepathic', as if the two attributes are linked and the latter has to be practised in order to be maintained into adulthood?

It is also interesting to note that, in *An Unearthly Child*, Susan states she 'made up the name TARDIS from the initials Time And Relative Dimension In Space'. In the context of the series as a whole, this implies a lot about Susan, since we later learn that all Gallifreyan timeships are called TARDISes. Although when you consider that in the early days of the show the Doctor most often referred to the TARDIS as 'the ship', is it possible that the name Susan used caught on after they left Gallifrey? As with most things related to Susan, we are only given a tantalising hint, but few firm facts.

Susan, it would appear, is out of her depth a lot of the time. She was taken out of the comfort of her home... Or did she choose to go with her grandfather? One can assume she did; after all, when talking to Ping-Cho in *Marco Polo,* she expresses her frustration at being stuck on Earth, when she should be out among the stars. We never properly know, although she seemed willing enough to accompany him when we glimpse the pair in *The Name of the Doctor*. Much has been revealed about her in other media, but on TV all we ever get are intriguing hints of a character that could have been so much more.

The Doctor himself forces Susan to leave in *The Dalek Invasion of Earth* after seeing her grow closer to freedom fighter David Campbell. It's a subtle romance – never quite believable, it almost comes as a surprise to the viewer when Susan considers remaining on Earth. But she is fearful of leaving her grandfather, thinking he needs her, when in truth it is perfectly obvious that she is dependent on him. That she should end up settling on Earth makes a certain sense, however, considering how much she enjoyed her time in 1963, and considering the five months living in the twentieth century were the happiest of her life.

We see Susan once more, almost twenty years later when she is taken to Gallifrey and reunited with her grandfather. And, although she is clearly older, it does not appear she has changed at all. As ever, we are given nothing new with which to work; she is simply the Doctor's granddaughter, although as soon as she spots the Dark Tower, she realises that she's on Gallifrey thus confirming that she is definitely *from* there.

Susan's fate remains unknown. In *The Empty Child*, the Doctor tells Rose, 'My entire planet died. My whole family.' After Doctor Constantine mentions he used to be 'a father and a grandfather. Now I'm neither, but I'm still a doctor,' the Doctor points out, 'Yeah, I know the feeling.' He later confirms, in *The Beast Below*, that it's 'just me now,' but alludes to unseen adventures with Susan in *The Rings of Akhaten*, noting that he visited the bazaar 'a long time ago with my granddaughter.'

But things get considerably more complicated in the Fifteenth Doctor era. The Doctor mentions having family a few times – so often that his companion, Ruby Sunday, jumps to the conclusion that the mysterious Susan Triad could, in fact, be the Doctor's granddaughter (*The Legend of Ruby Sunday*). The Doctor sees this as a possibility, despite previously ruminating that the Master might've killed her after he found out the truth of the Timeless Child (*The Devil's Chord*). Susan's parentage is further muddled. In *The Legend of Ruby Sunday*, Kate Stewart says that her father, UNIT's Brigadier Lethbridge-Stewart, never mentioned the Doctor having a granddaughter (which is especially curious, considering the events of *The Five Doctors*, not to mention a photo of Susan being in UNIT's Black Archive); the Doctor says he hasn't got children 'yet'. When Kate questions how he can 'have a granddaughter before a daughter', the Doctor passes this off: 'Life of a Time Lord'. This at least hints that there's plenty more about the species, about these complicated space-time events, that we still don't know.

What we do know is that the Doctor regrets leaving Susan behind. In *Empire of Death*, the Doctor promises he'll come back for Ruby, but she counters that he never went back for his own granddaughter. He concedes that he made a mistake: 'Maybe I'll find her again, one day...'

Compared to Susan, the rest of the Doctor's companions were pretty straightforward – at least during the initial twenty-six year run of the series, although some were more fleshed out than others. Some with well-defined back-stories, others less so...

Ian Chesterton* and Barbara Wright – William Russell and Jacqueline Hill (*An Unearthly Child* to *The Chase,* *plus *The Power of the Doctor*)

Ticket to Ride (The Beatles); *December, 1963 (Oh What a Night!)* (Frankie Valli & The Four Seasons).

Suspicious Minds (Elvis); *I Have Confidence* (Julie Andrews).

Along with Susan, we are introduced to two of the most defined companions: Ian Chesterton and Barbara Wright. Unusually for *Doctor Who* – indeed, it has only happened three times (arguably four if we include Rose and Mickey) – Ian and Barbara become synonymous with each other. It almost becomes impossible to separate them. They start together, they finish together, and even when mentioned in the 2010 episode of *The Sarah Jane Adventures* episode, *Death of the Doctor*, they are still together. They are as much defined by their relationship to each other as they are as individuals. Both were teachers at Coal Hill School, Ian teaching Science and Barbara teaching History, and both had their curiosity piqued by the mystery that was Susan. These two are, in some respect, more important than either the Doctor or Susan during the first year of *Doctor Who*. While Susan was the child who would always get in trouble, it was Barbara who often proved to be the voice of reason, always ready to challenge the more alien aspects of the Doctor's reasoning. Ian is the man of action, displaying a broad range of skills one might not expect from a comprehensive school teacher. Barbara is also the very first person in *Doctor Who* to meet a Dalek. Make no mistake: these two ordinary teachers are the key players in a series of extraordinary adventures.

It is through their eyes that we see the initial adventures. They take us into the Doctor's strange world; forcing their way into the TARDIS, all the way to Skaro and the historical first encounter with the Daleks. Neither expected what was to follow, but both had to assuage their curiosity and followed Susan home, to a junkyard in London. Worried for Susan's safety they both force their way into the old Police Box, and immediately find themselves challenging their own perceptions of everything they have ever known. Both are equally incredulous and unbelieving, but while Ian tries to reason things with science, Barbara attempts a more common sense approach, certain that it is just an elaborate illusion created by Susan's grandfather.

Although an unwilling adventurer, Barbara's compassion often overrides her own fear, as seen in the very first journey in *An Unearthly Child* when Za, a caveman on pre-historic Earth, is attacked by a tiger. Even though Za was willing to sacrifice them a short while earlier, Barbara cannot leave the wounded man unattended. This trait continues. Even after being sold as a slave in ancient Rome (*The Romans*), Barbara still helps her fellow prisoner, rather than worrying about her own safety. Such is her compassion that Ian remarks that she probably has stray cats in her flat in London.

Barbara is not only compassionate, but also full of passion, which comes out in anger and frustration. It's notable that, when the travellers are all trapped in the TARDIS (*The Edge of Destruction*) and the Doctor accuses Ian and Barbara of sabotaging the ship, it is Barbara who confronts him with a verbal slap that would've had the most callous of men reeling in shock: 'How dare you?! Do you realise, you stupid old man, that you'd have died in the Cave of Skulls if Ian hadn't made fire for you? And what about what we went through with the Daleks? Not just for us, but for you and Susan, too, and all because you tricked us into going down to the city. Accuse us? You ought to get down on your hands and knees and thank us. But gratitude's the last thing you'll ever have, or any sort of common sense, either.' Such is the power behind her words that the Doctor ultimately apologises to her.

Her passion for history is also a driving force during their travels, most notably when she is mistaken for the reincarnation of the Aztec High Priest Yetaxa (*The Aztecs*). She is convinced that she can prevent the human sacrifices, and brings the Aztecs out of their superstitious ways so their society can flourish. She fails, of course, but she learns a valuable lesson. Although they are travellers in time, they cannot affect history on a big scale. This lesson stands Barbara in good stead when they later visit such periods as the French Revolution (*The Reign of Terror*) and the fall of Rome (*The Romans*). That's not to say that Barbara doesn't get involved; an unwilling adventurer she may be, but she was never going to be a quiet one too.

On the other hand, Ian adapts to adventuring relatively quickly. His National Service prepares him for the challenges ahead, and he displays a remarkable set of useful skills, including horse riding, sword fighting, and how to disable an opponent with pressure points. On Earth, he's a man of reason, but he soon learns that reason alone is simply not enough when travelling to dangerous times and places. Such is his level of bravery and courage that he is even knighted by King Richard the Lionheart as Sir Ian of Jaffa in *The Crusades*.

An interesting, and not often explored, trait of Ian's is his familiarity with popular youth culture, in particular music, and his ease with children. National Service may have prepared him for adventuring, but his understanding of young people prepared him for the varied people he was to meet on his travels.

Ian and Barbara were always close, at least close enough initially that it was in Ian that Barbara confided her doubts about Susan in *An Unearthly Child*. This obvious closeness develops through their travels, as Ian becomes something of a protector for Barbara. The most obvious hint at the level of intimacy between the two comes when they are alone at the villa on the outskirts of Rome (*The Romans*). The familiarity they display with each other, both physically and verbally, hints at much more. It is never expressly stated, but to consider some kind of romantic interest between them isn't much of a stretch.

Consistently throughout their travels is the thought of returning home. Although they become less vocal about it over time, when presented with the first opportunity, Barbara takes hold of it without question. Ian is a little more cautious, but he soon comes around. The Doctor, clearly upset by their departure, responds obstinately, almost point blank refusing to help them. But they win him over, as they often do. Because of them, this grumpy alien softens, becoming almost kindly in his dealings with others. Through Ian and Barbara, the Doctor learns compassion.

They leave in *The Chase*, using a Dalek time machine to get them back to contemporary London, 1965, something they're overjoyed about. Importantly, the Doctor checks they got back safe and well using the Time-Space Visualiser, showing their fondness for him is certainly reciprocated.

Ian and Barbara were such a huge part in establishing *Doctor Who* as a success, and defining the future relationships the Doctor has with his travelling companions and, ultimately, his friends and extended family. It's only natural, then, that the show drops hints about what happened to them after they left the TARDIS – although not during its initial twentieth-century run. Ian almost returns in the 1983 adventure *Mawdryn Undead*, but due to William Russell being unavailable, it never came to pass. In 2010, we finally get a clue about what happened to them. Sarah Jane Smith had looked up the Doctor's old companions, and she learned that there were two professors in Cambridge, Ian and Barbara Chesterton, who, according to rumour, had not aged since the 1960s. Ultimately, however, it all comes back to Coal Hill School: in *The Day of the Doctor*, an 'I. Chesterton' is named as the Chairman of the Board of Governors.

We next see Ian attending a companions' support group in *The Power of the Doctor*; while Barbara isn't with him, there is a laptop open on a nearby chair, so we might infer that she simply couldn't make it that day so is joining the get-together digitally. After all, it feels right that they remain, as they began, together.

With the departure of Susan, there was a void in the Doctor's life. He'd grown close to his granddaughter, so it was unsurprising, although convenient (at least so it seems, but in *The Doctor's Wife* the TARDIS explained that she always took the Doctor to where he needed to be, and this may well be a case in point), that the next destination brought the Doctor, Ian, and Barbara to the planet Dido, and the young orphan, Vicki.

Vicki – Maureen O'Brien (*The Rescue* to *The Myth Makers*)

Only the Young (Brandon Flowers); *Cassandra* (ABBA).

Almost immediately Vicki forms a close bond with the Doctor, both having lost the most important people in their lives. When the Doctor asks her to join them on their adventures, Vicki jumps at the chance. It's interesting to note that Vicki is the first person the Doctor asks to go with him, the next being Victoria Waterfield (also an orphan).

Vicki's mother and father died following the crash of the *UK-201* on Dido. Her only companion on the desolate world is a man called Bennett who, it transpires, is quite insane and has murdered all the survivors of the crash.

Vicki comes from an Earth where the children are taught advanced academic subjects at a young age; she herself claims to have studied medicine, physics, chemistry, and various other subjects when she was only ten, a fact that she shares when Barbara explains that she taught using the three Rs – at which point Vicki exclaims that she didn't realise Barbara taught at a nursery. This shows that either Vicki liked to tease Barbara, or was simply being naive at her own rudeness.

This yearning for adventure grows during the month they all spend at the villa on the outskirts of Rome. This isn't the life Vicki had been expecting, and she convinces the Doctor to take her to the city. As their travels continue, we see much of this spirit of adventure; an outlook that brings Vicki and the Doctor closer together, developing a very gentle relationship. It's this closeness that allows her to convince the Doctor to do things he might otherwise resist. A good example comes in *The Chase*, when Ian and Barbara realise they could use the Daleks' time ship to return home; the Doctor refuses to show them how it works. But Vicki gets through his anger and convinces him to let them go – even though she doesn't want to see them leave either. After all, along with the Doctor, Ian and Barbara became something of a foster family for her.

Vicki's sharp and deductive brain comes into good use on Xeros in *The Space Museum* when she enables the subjugated Xerons to override the Moroks' computer, and later on in *Galaxy 4* when she works out that the Chumblies only respond to movement directly in front of them. She also fixes the meaning of the name TARDIS when she tells Steven that the D stands for 'Dimensions', possibly recognising the equational and grammatical inaccuracy in the acronym when it was told to her as 'Dimension'.

Vicki has a habit of giving the aliens they meet strange

names: she calls the beast on Dido 'Sandy' because it lives in the sand and the little robot servants of the Rills she calls 'Chumblies', due to the way they move. This inclination could well be an indication of the loneliness she feels as she seeks to find a place to call home once again. Her loneliness is evident in the way she quickly draws close to the Doctor, and later with Steven with whom she develops a sibling-like relationship.

Vicki's desire for a family again becomes obvious when the TARDIS brings them to Asia Minor just before the Fall of Troy (*The Myth Makers*). She finds her way into Troy on her own and is immediately taken in by King Priam, who is equally impressed by her. She even accepts the new name of Cressida from Priam. During the course of the siege, she starts responding to the affections of Priam's son, Troilus, and realises she will be quite happy settling there with him, even though he is only seventeen and she sixteen (when Troilus tells Vicki how old he is, she says, 'That's barely older than me' – the first time her age is inferred). We never get to see exactly how the Doctor reacts to Vicki's news, as this happens off-screen, but he doesn't seem to oppose it. He appears to be more concerned with Steven's wound suffered during the battle between the Greeks and the Trojans. The last we ever see of Vicki is shortly after the TARDIS departs and she finds Troilus watching the destruction of his people; he thinks she has betrayed them, but she convinces him otherwise. And from there, they pass into history, through tales by Chaucer ('*Troilus and Criseyde*') and Shakespeare ('*Troilus and Cressida*'), from which we can, at least, infer something of Vicki's later life...

As with Susan and Vicki, a replacement was waiting in the wings once Ian and Barbara returned to their own time. This new companion joined the Doctor's travels by what would become the most popular method of all: stowing away in the TARDIS.

COMPANIONS

Steven Taylor – Peter Purves (*The Chase* to *The Savages*)

Rocket Man (Elton John); *Barnacle Bill* (Royal Philharmonic Orchestra).

When the Doctor, with Ian, Barbara, and Vicki, first meet him, he introduces himself as Steven Taylor, Flight Red Fifty. He has already spent two years as a prisoner of the robotic Mechanoids on the planet Mechanus, in an undisclosed period of Earth's future. Steven is an astronaut, his ship having crashed on that planet; his only companion his stuffed panda, Hi-Fi. Despite two years of captivity, he is a man of good humour, grateful of some human company at last. He happily assists the Doctor and company in escaping the Mechanoids' city, but at the last minute returns for Hi-Fi. He manages to escape the burning city himself, and stumbles through the jungle, disorientated, and into what he describes as a door.

'I went through it,' he says. 'I must have flaked out. I remember registering that, well, it didn't look like a ship – it was very small. I must have been delirious.'

After his initial incredulity, and mocking of Vicki's explanations, Steven soon adapts to time travel. Granted, his scepticism is supported when he discovers a wristwatch in a small woods in Northumbria in 1066 (*The Time Meddler*), but events reveal the truth. Steven is prone to natural sarcasm and bouts of frustrated anger, but to counter these less positive attributes, he also has great courage and resourcefulness.

He becomes very close to Vicki, and develops a strong bond with her, displaying the typical bickering one would expect to find in an older brother/younger sister relationship, most notable when they are both imprisoned in Troy and Vicki becomes the object of Troilus' affections. Both are determined in their mindsets, and often butt heads over the simplest of things, but ultimately they stand by each other. His relationship with Dodo is, in contrast, merely that of two friends. Steven's natural cynicism is often contrasted by Dodo's enthusiasm for everything they encounter, and she tends to bring out the child in him, as shown during the games of the Toymaker (*The Celestial Toymaker*) and Steven's joy at being in the 'Wild West' of American legend (*The Gunfighters*).

By the time they arrive on the 'Ark', a space craft taking the survivors of Earth to the world of Rufusis, Steven's good humour has already been sorely tried by his experiences in Paris and the Massacre of St Bartholomew's Eve. He spends most of the time without the Doctor's company, getting embroiled in the political and religious strife that is plaguing Paris, despite the Doctor warning him not to, and becomes greatly angered by the Doctor's refusal to involve himself in events – an act that, in Steven's eyes, means the death of a young woman he's befriended, Anne Chaplet. This anger is compounded by all the other deaths he's witnessed recently, including those of Katarina and Sara Kingdom, both of whom died during the Doctor's effort to prevent the Daleks from gaining control of the Time Destructor (*The Daleks' Master Plan*). Such is his anger that, as soon as the TARDIS arrives on Wimbledon Common in the 1960s, he storms out of the ship, intent on leaving the Doctor for good. It's only the presence of police officers that changes his mind, and he returns to warn the Doctor to move the TARDIS. He is immediately concerned about Dodo, who has just happened upon the TARDIS, too. He wonders what her parents will think of her disappearing, but that concern soon fades when he realises that Dodo is a likely descendant of Anne Chaplet, suggesting that the young French girl has survived the massacre after all. Even with this positive news, Steven carries an angry undercurrent with him. This erupts when he's put on trial by the humans on the Ark and he expresses his distaste for humanity and the fear that always seems to drive them.

Despite his growing dislike for his own race, Steven remains the compassionate man he has always been and is willing to sacrifice his freedom for both the Doctor and Dodo when faced with the dilemma of how to escape the Toymaker's celestial domain.

He learns much during his journeys, and when asked to help

the Elders and the Savages find a way to live together in peace, he initially resists, not wanting to walk out on the Doctor and Dodo. But the Doctor insists he take up the offer, a position he is now ready for. Steven agrees, but only if both sides wish him to (which they do). He takes his leave of the Doctor and Dodo, and we never hear of him again.

Katarina – Adrienne Hill (*The Myth Makers* to *The Daleks' Master Plan*)

Houdini (Dua Lipa); *Cello Suite No. 1 in G Major* (Brooklyn Classical).

Katarina, the handmaiden of Cassandra of Troy, was one of the shortest-lived companions of the Doctor, and the first to die.

Cassandra, fearful of the false prophetess, Cressida, sends Katarina to spy on Vicki. During the battle between the Greeks and the Trojans, Steven is wounded by a spear in the shoulder, and Katarina is tasked with caring for him. She helps him back to the TARDIS and is still aboard the ship when the Doctor quickly leaves the troubled land.

She has no understanding of the strange world she has entered, and believes the Doctor to be the Greek King of Gods, Zeus, and the TARDIS his temple. She is, in her mind, on a journey to the Palace of Perfection – the afterlife. Out of her depth, she remains by Steven's side, practically worshipping at the Doctor's feet. Such is her devotion, that when the criminal Kirksen holds her hostage to force the Doctor to return the *Spar*, stolen from the planet Kembel where the Daleks are waiting, she understands enough to know that it cannot be. She sacrifices her life, by blowing the airlock in which she and Kirksen stand, and the two of them are swept out into the depths of space.

Dorothea 'Dodo' Chaplet – Jackie Lane (*The Massacre* to *The War Machines*)

Good Try (Cloves); *Be Young, Be Foolish, Be Happy* (The Tams).

Dorothea 'Dodo' Chaplet was one of only two companions to find herself inside the TARDIS after mistaking it for a real Police

Box. Having witnessed an accident on Wimbledon Common, she rushed to it to get help...

Dodo adapts quickly to TARDIS life, although with the usual level of incredulity to the idea that it's a time machine. Due to the police officers rushing towards the TARDIS, the Doctor has no choice but to leave Wimbledon Common, and when Steven voices his concerns about leaving with Dodo, she points out that she doesn't care. She has no parents and no reason to stay in London. One suspects that it is not just the arrival of the police that causes the Doctor to take Dodo away with them, but rather the fact that he thinks she looks a bit like his absent granddaughter, Susan.

During the initial journey, Dodo finds time to root through the TARDIS' wardrobe, something she continues to avail herself of throughout her short time as a companion. When arriving in a jungle, Dodo refuses to accept it might be an alien world, instead believing it to be Whipsnade Zoo, and shows a keen awareness and liking for nature. She is rather smug about her knowledge, presenting a 'know it all' attitude. Of course, she is soon proven wrong when they discover the jungle is just a small part of a space craft taking refugees from the dying Earth. She dubs the ship 'the Ark', and accidentally infects all its inhabitants with her cold – something that has not existed on Earth for centuries. She feels terrible for causing so much trouble and does everything she can to assist the Doctor in finding a cure, especially when Steven, who has no antibodies to combat the cold, also succumbs to it.

While pitted against the dolls created by the Toymaker, Dodo takes the view that they are as much victims as she and Steven – even arguing her point about free will, although she never convinces Steven of her stance. This is another example of her contrary nature and her single-mindedness. As she points out when they land on the world of the Savages and Elders (*The Savages*), she never did like guided tours and preferred to wander off the assigned route. Or, as Steven once said, 'If it wasn't allowed, Dodo would be first in line.' This is evidenced a lot during their visit to Tombstone (*The Gunfighters*). Dodo is a big fan of the Wild West and has always wanted to meet Wyatt Earp, so she throws herself into the period, giving herself over to every 'western' cliché. She even seems to enjoy being forced to play the piano at gunpoint! Steven is more perturbed, but Dodo encourages him to sing, and shows an ability to not only play but also read music. She is also taken in by Doc Holliday's charm, barely batting an eye at his propensity for killing almost everybody they meet, even though she is, ultimately, his captive.

She is upset by Steven's sudden departure, and wonders if she will ever see him again. The Doctor explains how unlikely it is, and is proven to be correct when they next land back in London, 1966 (*The War Machines*). Glad to be back in familiar surroundings, Dodo bonds with Polly, a secretary who takes her to the Inferno nightclub where they both meet Able Seaman, Ben Jackson. WOTAN, an intelligent machine, brainwashes Dodo in an attempt to remove the Doctor, but the Doctor sees through the conditioning and breaks it. He sends Dodo to a house in the country to recover, and she is never seen again.

After showing such enthusiasm for her travels, and growing attached to the Doctor, it is very odd that she doesn't return to at least say goodbye to him. Instead, she passes on a message to him through Ben and Polly, saying that she has decided to remain in London. What is the reason for such a drastic shift in her character? We never find out on television, but several other reasons have been offered up in the *Doctor Who* Expanded Universe.

As with Ian and Barbara, the next companions came as a 'couple' – they joined together, they left together and, according to Sarah in 2010, they are still together.

*

THE FIRST DOCTOR

Ben Jackson and Polly – Michael Craze and Anneke Wills
(*The War Machines* to *The Faceless One*s)

My Old Man's a Dustman (Lonnie Donegan); *All the Young Dudes* (Mott The Hoople).

Sunflower (Tamino and Angèle); *We Are Young* (fun feat. Janelle Monáe).

Polly is the secretary of Professor Brett, a young 'dolly bird' with an active social life, enjoying the night life of the Inferno club. When Polly meets the downhearted Ben Jackson, she takes it on herself to cheer him up, with mixed results. Despite this, Ben defends Polly against the attentions of an unwanted admirer, a trait that continues throughout their time together.

Polly has a tendency to tease those she likes, Ben in particular. He soon gets used to this and takes to calling her 'Pol'. After assisting the Doctor in defeating WOTAN and the War Machines, it's Polly who is curious as to why the Doctor enters a Police Box. Ben is less bothered, more concerned about returning to his own ship, but Ben remembers the key that had fallen out of the Doctor's pocket earlier. At her urging, Ben joins her and they enter the Police Box mere seconds before it dematerialises.

Both are somewhat sceptical of the Doctor's claims about the TARDIS, but Polly adapts a lot quicker than Ben, who is, upon arriving on a beach in Cornwall, sure that the Doctor is a hypnotist or something. Throughout their harrowing adventures in the seventeenth century (*The Smugglers*), Polly finds herself enjoying the notion of time travel, while Ben is more worried about getting home, back to his ship. Even when the Doctor insists they must stay and sort out the problem with the pirates and the smugglers, it takes both him and Polly to convince Ben that it's the right thing to do. Polly's humour is also something Ben takes a while to get used to, coming across as positively miserable next to her cheekiness. But he does take some pleasure in her horror at seeing a rat, despite them both being imprisoned at the time and facing a likely death sentence, a fact that doesn't seem to bother Polly too much. The humour soon infects Ben too; he begins to turn on his own cocky charm, even to the point of quipping, 'Polly, put the kettle on' when he has to leave her for a short while.

By the time the TARDIS brings them to the South Pole some twenty years after their own native 1966, both seem to have adapted nicely to travelling with the Doctor. Faced with the emotionless Cybermen (*The Tenth Planet*), it's Polly who first challenges them, while Ben tries to hold his 'duchess' back, fearing for her safety. Ben also stands up to the Cybermen, making inventive use of a projector to blind one, and then using its own weapon against it. It's an act Ben is not proud of – but he knows it's necessary. His courage is never far away, and when the Cybermen intend on taking Polly prisoner, Ben soon stands forward, insisting he go in her place.

Ben and Polly are the first companions to meet the Cybermen, but also, at the end of *The Tenth Planet*, they're on hand to witness the most remarkable thing about the Doctor. His body wearing thin, the Doctor staggers back to the TARDIS, and it's there that a concerned Ben and Polly see him collapse mere moments after setting the time machine in motion. They pull him over to check on him, and watch as his face begins to blur and change...

The First Doctor
Expanded Universe

Once again, we start with Susan, a character we know so little about from TV; the stories contained in the Expanded Universe, then, aim to address this, exploring her origins and character in some extreme (and often conflicting) ways.

There are four distinct 'origin' stories for Susan. In one account (written by 1980s *Doctor Who* script editor, Eric Saward, and published in the *Radio Times 20th Anniversary Special*), she's the Lady Larn, whom the Doctor rescues when he escapes from Gallifrey. Larn is a descendent of Rassilon (the 'greatest single figure' in Time Lord history), and the last of Gallifrey's royal family. This draws from Anthony Coburn's original draft of the first episode, in which he describes Susan as being of royal blood; an idea that never made it beyond that first draft.

A second origin is presented in the tongue-in-cheek radio broadcast, *Whatever Happened to... Susan Foreman?* This suggests that Susan's parents dispatched her to Earth with her grandfather because she's failing such subjects as French on Gallifrey, French being a common language in most galaxies, but she's fine with subjects such as thermodynamics. It's full of contradictions and is not meant to be taken seriously.

A third, much more complex idea is put forward in the 1997 novel *Lungbarrow*, which doesn't completely contradict established facts at that time (though is arguably affected by the Timeless Child revelations of the Thirteenth Doctor era). In this, Susan is the last child born on Ancient Gallifrey, and granddaughter of the mysterious Other – a mythical being said to form a triumvirate with Rassilon and Omega, and thus is one of the founders of Time Lord society. This Other, in this account, is reincarnated centuries later as the Doctor, who, when escaping Gallifreyan life, finds himself in his planet's past where both Susan and he recognise each other. She then joins him on his travels. This fits in with some hints from stories late in the classic era's run, such as *Remembrance of the Daleks* and *Silver Nemesis,* both of which imply that the Doctor was present at the birth of the Time Lords. What gives this account some credence is that it was written by a TV script writer, Marc Platt, using the so-called 'Cartmel Masterplan' – a name given to the long-term plans of script editor, Andrew Cartmel – which informed much of the final two years of *Doctor Who*'s original twenty-six-year run on TV. This origin story has been acknowledged by many of the novels that follow, though has never been acknowledged otherwise on screen. He's confirmed he was 'a dad once', and, in *The Rings of Akhaten*, tells Clara that he once visited the Tiaanamat market with his granddaughter. It might also fit in with the Fifteenth Doctor saying he's not had children 'yet' (*The Legend of Ruby Sunday*).

Susan's origins are further expanded upon in the novella *Frayed*, set before the first TV story. We learn that the name 'Susan' was given to her by an Earth colonist called Jill, after her mother. And a short story published in *Doctor Who Magazine* #214 reveals Susan's real name as Arkytior, High Gallifreyan for 'rose' (an interesting link between the first companions of twentieth and twentieth-first century *Who*; even more so when you consider the short story was published in 1994), though nowhere is this confirmed. In the audio story, *The Shoreditch Incident*, part of *Susan's War*, her real name is said to be a closely-guarded 'state secret', implying her importance to Time Lord society. A final jigsaw piece slots into place in the short story, *Ash*, wherein the Doctor says that Susan's parents entrusted her care to him.

Little more is added to Susan during the period she travelled with Ian and Barbara, despite the many Expanded Universe journeys written. However, one area people seem keen to explore is her life after she left the Doctor. As one might expect, the accounts are contradictory.

Only one thing has been consistent in these accounts: Susan and David marry and have children. In the novelisation of *The Five Doctors*, author Terrance Dicks mentions that she has three children, an idea revisited in John Peel's *Legacy of the Daleks* which sees a reunion between Susan and her grandfather, now in his eighth incarnation. She and David had helped rebuild England after the Dalek invasion, and adopted three war orphans, who they named Ian, Barbara, and David Junior. The reason for the adoption is that Susan is not able to conceive with David. She also ages slower than humans, and often has to wear make-up to disguise her younger appearance. During the course of the story, she's taken captive by the Doctor's nemesis, the Master, and brought to the planet Tersurus. She leaves that planet in his TARDIS, believing she's killed the Master.

This interesting, grittier side of Susan has never been further explored, since she never returns to the novels. However, the audio production company, Big Finish, offers its own version of events, post-*The Five Doctors*. Again, she reunites with the Doctor in his eighth incarnation, and is a mother. Only this time, she and David have their own biological child, a son called Alex. He's only got one heart, and Susan asks the Doctor to take Alex to Gallifrey to be better educated. She helps the Doctor repel a second Dalek invasion of Earth, which costs Alex his life in *To the Death*. She's left alone to deal with her son's death. The audio, *All Hands on Deck*, picks up with Susan still helping to rebuild, and living in what used to be Coal Hill School: though since converted into flats, the area had survived the Daleks' assaults. At the end of this story, Susan decides to venture into the Time War. This leads into *Susan's War*, which firstly regales how she reunited with Ian Chesterton when they were acting as diplomats between the Time Lords and the Sensorites, so that the Gallifreyans could benefit further from their telepathy in their battle with the Daleks. This fits in nicely with *The Sensorites* establishing Susan having telepathic abilities of her own. Sadly, she doesn't meet with Barbara again here (obviously due to Jacqueline Hill's untimely passing), though it's clear she and Ian are still together: Susan drops Ian home, but has to rush off to return to the war; as she does so, Barbara comes home and Ian happily teases her about who he's just had a visit from. *The Shoreditch Intervention* also reunites Susan with the Eighth Doctor, as they try to stop the Daleks taking the Hand of Omega from 1963, it having been revealed in *Remembrance of the Daleks* that hiding the interstellar weapon was one chief reason the Doctor and Susan were there when we met them in *An Unearthly Child*.

She meets the Eighth Doctor again in Big Finish's sixtieth anniversary event, *Once and Future*. *The Union*, however, puts her heritage into question: she and River Song (who she'd previously met in the 2019 audio story *An Unearthly Woman*, when the Doctor's future wife taught at Coal Hill School) are immune to degeneration energies that have affected the Doctor. River explains that it's because she's not fully a Time Lord, but what does this mean for Susan? Is she not wholly a Time Lord either? Or could it be that this is Susan's first body so she *can't* degenerate?

Susan clearly takes an important role in the Time War: at the end of *Susan's War*, she's invited into the War Room to discuss how she can further advance the Time Lords' agendas. Many years have passed, but Susan has managed not to even regenerate in all that time. Indeed, we learn a curious detail about her when she tells the story, *Here There Be Monsters*. She claims that at the time of her travels with Ian and Barbara, her actual age was more than theirs combined, even though she was still a baby by Gallifreyan standards – and the Doctor only a child.

In a further account, the universe is rewritten by a planar shift, an event so catastrophic that it destroys Gallifrey and rewrites the Doctor's entire timeline. In *Matrix Revelation*, written by Dale Smith in 2006, it's revealed that Susan was copied into the Matrix, the repository of all Time Lord knowledge, when Earth's history was rewritten. There, she's eventually reunited with her grandfather, now in an alternative fifth incarnation.

It's fitting that, as the Doctor's first acknowledged companion,

Susan displays wonderful foresight, as demonstrated in *Press Play*, a Thirteenth Doctor short story published on the BBC website in 2020. Before being forced to leave, she predicts that the Doctor travelling with Ian and Barbara will set a precedent, but also that there will be times when they're on their own. Knowing they suffer from loneliness, a recording of Susan reveals that she's built a message bank and retrieval system into the TARDIS data core, meaning all the Doctor's adventures are recorded, telepathically linked to the Time Lord. 'So if you're ever feeling bored, or lonely, or sad, all you have to do is access the data bank, and retrieve a favourite memory,' she says. 'It'll keep on recording until you tell it to stop. All your adventures, all your stories won't go to waste. They'll always be here, waiting for you, like an archive. Alive for eternity.'

The rest of the First Doctor's companions are dealt with in a more straightforward manner in the Expanded Universe, mostly filling in the back-stories of characters who, on TV, tended to have a past that was largely a blank slate. Writers of the apocryphal material also liked to ask what had happened to people after they left the Doctor, with varying degrees of success.

Like on TV, Ian and Barbara's Expanded Universe appearances are mostly coherent. We learn more about Ian's past than Barbara's, discover some new information from their journeys in the TARDIS, and find out that they do get married – long before it's confirmed in *The Sarah Jane Adventures*. They even have a son...

Ian was born in Reading, and grew up during the London Blitz, with a brother and a sister. He loved Jules Verne and HG Wells as a child, and was inspired by them to become a science teacher. He served in the British Army as a private for two years, confirming what we know about his National Service from the television series. *The Eleventh Tiger* tells us that his great-great-grandfather, Major William Chesterton, looks a lot like an older Ian, when Ian was mistaken for him. Of Barbara's early life, we learn very little – other than that she once dated a boy who carried a knife; that she has an aunt named Cecilia; that, when she was a student teacher, she had a flat in Cricklewood; and that Ian and Barbara first met in a little tea shop on Tottenham Court Road.

Extra information about these two is a little thin on the ground, despite the amount of Expanded Universe adventures they've had. We discover in *The Sorcerer's Apprentice* that Barbara has a fear of heights, something she's not aware of until she soars high into the sky on a broomstick. At one point (in the short story, *Set in Stone*), they spend four months living in 1950s Shoreditch, believing that is the closest they will ever get to their own time. And, most curiously, there are two different accounts of the month between the opening scenes of *The Romans* that lead up to their moving into the villa on the outskirts of Rome – accounts that are hard to marry (in the short story, *Romans Cutaway*, and the novel, *Byzantium!*).

But the oddest reveal of all is in *City at World's End* when Ian believes the Doctor and Susan to be human – even though he knows otherwise from *An Unearthly Child*!

There are also confused accounts of when Ian and Barbara first realise their love for each other. There are moments in the book, *Venusian Lullaby*, when Ian's true feelings are hinted at. The loss he feels when he believes Barbara has died in a spaceship explosion is crushing, to the point where he ponders suicide. In the later book, *The Plotters*, Barbara is quite comfortable posing as Ian's wife. Further books set before *The Plotters* reveal that both have confessed their love for each other. In *Romans Cutaway*, Ian admits that he loves Barbara, but is unable to tell her. Barbara finally tells Ian that she loves him in *The Eleventh Tiger* and Ian reciprocates. It's at this point that they agree to get married when they return home. However, the later audiobook, *The Rocket Men*, has Ian realising he loves Barbara, even though this is set some time after the events of *The Eleventh Tiger*.

In the 1991 novel, *Timewyrm: Revelation*, we get the first mention of singer Johnny Chess (or Johnny Chester), who is idolised by future companion, Ace, at the age of fourteen. Johnny is the son of Ian and Barbara born in 1967, his full name being John Alydon Ganatus Chesterton, named after two Thals encountered in the television story, *The Daleks* (the full name isn't revealed until *Byzantium!* in 2001). Information on the events that lead to their marriage are not revealed until 1996 with the release of the novel, *Who Killed Kennedy?* After returning to Earth, Ian and Barbara excuse their two year absence by claiming they have been missionaries in Central Africa. Barbara takes up a position at a university lecturing, specialising on the Aztecs, while Ian gains a professorship within a year (which at least backs up the reference to Professor Chesterton in the novelisation of *The War Machines*, set in 1966) and begins writing papers on astronomy.

In 2005's *The Time Travellers*, we're treated to a scene set straight after *The Chase* in which Ian takes Barbara home to see her mother, Joan. More information is revealed when Ian and Barbara finally return to *Doctor Who* fiction in the 1998 novel, *Face of the Enemy*. Set during the 1970s, Ian is in his late 30s and teaching at the RAF college in Farnborough, while Barbara is teaching at a local comprehensive school. They are called in to assist UNIT, thus helping the lifelong friend of the Doctor, Brigadier Alistair Gordon Lethbridge-Stewart, and work alongside the Doctor's enemy, the Master. We learn a bit more about their life post-Doctor – how they eloped on the first anniversary of their return home and how Ian had to sell everything he owned to get a new place, while Barbara stayed with her parents. They also have plans to leave a journal for Susan, who they know will end up on Earth in 2167. During the course of the book, Ian believes Barbara has died in a car crash, and again considers suicide as a way to end his pain.

In *Byzantium!*, we're given a peek into the life of a thirty-two year old Barbara in 1973. She apparently gave up teaching probably around the time of her son's birth (although she's still a teacher in *Face of the Enemy,* almost certainly set in the early 1970s).

From Ian and Barbara's point of view, the first story to feature them post-*The Chase* is the comic strip, *Hunters of the Burning Stone*, the fiftieth anniversary story published in *Doctor Who Magazine* #456 to #461. They're kidnapped by the Prometheans and placed in an illusionary world that looks like Coal Hill School. The Eleventh Doctor finds them there, but they've forgotten all their adventures with him. Eventually, he's able to jog their memories, but Ian is not as willing to be convinced that the young man before them is the Doctor; as per *An Unearthly Child*, Barbara keeps a more open mind. Along with the Doctor, they find themselves up against the Tribe of Gum, the cavemen primitives they encountered in the first *Doctor Who* story, now a group of Hunters scouring the galaxy, having been given psychic metal by the Prometheans. At the end of this comic strip, the Doctor finally attends the wedding of Ian and Barbara, and we finally find out why the TARDIS' chameleon circuit broke in 1963.

Their later lives aren't touched upon until a *Brief Encounter* in which the Seventh Doctor bumps into an old Ian outside a conservatory in Greenwich. The Doctor says he's in the area visiting an old friend who is, unfortunately, out. Once home with his wife, Barbara, Ian is handed a present which has been delivered earlier that day; a Coal Hill School tie to replace the one destroyed on the surface of Vortis in the television story, *The Web Planet*.

An older Ian is reunited with Steven Taylor in the 2011 audio play, *The Five Companions*; neither has seen the Doctor since ending their travels. When Ian first meets the Fifth Doctor, he believes him to be a younger version of the Doctor he knew, but later learns about regeneration (at odds with *Hunters of the Burning Stone*). He explains that, for thirty years, he was a researcher, and, after a bout of retirement, he returned to teaching, which Barbara isn't happy about; then again, she's started writing a new book. Sadly, Ian gets an adventure with Susan that Barbara doesn't: she picks him up in *Susan's War* to act as a diplomat between the Time Lords and the Sensorites during the Time War, and drops him back just seconds before Barbara comes home.

These encounters indicate that the 'rumour' Sarah Jane Smith heard about Ian and Barbara – that they had not aged since the 1960s – was just that: a rumour. Of course, like everything above, until it's confirmed in the TV show, it remains merely a possibility.

No Expanded Universe mention of Ian and Barbara would be complete without a mention of *Doctor Who in An Exciting Adventure with the Daleks*, the novelisation of the television story of the (almost) same name, published in 1964. It's the first Expanded Universe appearance of Ian and Barbara, and the book that begins *Doctor Who*'s sixty-year publishing history. It presents a truly apocryphal introduction to *Doctor Who* by having Ian, apparently older than on television, relate a story that's basically the same as its TV counterpart but with a few important differences: he's after a job as an assistant research scientist at Donneby's (a big rocket component firm) who happens upon Barbara on Barnes Common, after she and Susan are involved in a car accident. Susan has mysteriously gone missing, and Ian and Barbara meet the Doctor, who's as evasive as on television. They follow him to a Police Box on the common and, as per the show, they push their way in. It's interesting that Ian and Barbara don't know each other, and he often refers to her as a 'girl in her early twenties', while Barbara is Susan's private tutor. It makes one wonder what might have happened if this narrative were continued in all Expanded Universe versions of *Doctor Who*.

The first truly alternative look at *Doctor Who* came in 1965 with the first ever *Doctor Who* cinematic release, *Dr Who & the Daleks*. Essentially a re-telling of the first Dalek serial from 1963 to 1964, the film differs in many key ways. Both Susan (most often called 'Suzie') and Barbara are the granddaughters of Earth inventor, Dr Who, while Ian is Barbara's new boyfriend (the first occasion in which these two characters get romantically paired, perhaps even the origin of their perceived television romance, even though the film was released the day before Ian and Barbara left the TARDIS in *The Chase*). Susan is a little scientist, and the apple of Dr Who's eye, his protégé, while Barbara and Ian are very removed from their television counterparts, not a teaching credential between them. For the following film, *Daleks: Invasion Earth 2150AD* (1966), things were changed a little and two new companions were introduced. First is Louise, Dr Who's niece and Susan's cousin; then there's police constable Tom Campbell (played by Bernard Cribbins, who would go on to play Wilfred Mott, the grandfather of future companion, Donna Noble), who stumbled into *Tardis* thinking it's a real Police Box.

Vicki has appeared in comparatively few Expanded Universe stories; it's not surprising, then, that we don't learn much that's new. The 2001 novel, *Byzantium!*, reveals that she left Earth in 2493 and was only fourteen (an age contradicted by *The Myth Makers*). Her mother died when Vicki was eleven, and she wanted to call Vicki 'Tanni' (a name originally devised by the production team for Vicki) while her father preferred 'Vicki'. She thought it a stupid name, which ties nicely in with her willingness to change it in *The Myth Makers*. Most importantly, we're told that her surname is 'Pallister', a name used in most of her Expanded Universe appearances. And in the 1996 novel, *The Plotters*, we learn that, when she was five, she was inoculated against many diseases by medical laser injection.

Vicki finds herself conflicted, having grown used to Ian and Barbara's company, yet wishing they would find their way home. Her historical knowledge has as many gaps as it does on television: she confuses singer Dido with Sister Bliss, and has never heard of Plato, Archimedes, or Socrates, although she is dimly aware of Charles Dickens. She also thinks Shakespeare is good, but prefers the works of Lynda La Plante – ironic, given she'd end up meeting a young William Shakespeare a few years after leaving the Doctor.

She finds herself the unwilling object of King James' affections in *The Plotters,* when she's posing as a boy called 'Victor', and in *The Empire of Glass* an alien Greld wants to mate with her.

Some stories visit Vicki, or Cressida as she is known by then, a few years after *The Myth Makers*. First, we have *Apocrypha Bipedium* which has the Eighth Doctor and his companion,

Charley, arrive some time after the Fall of Troy. They are en route back to England, returning a young Shakespeare home. Vicki recognises the Doctor as a younger version of the man she knew, and so goes to great lengths to ensure that neither she nor her husband, Troilus, reveal any future knowledge of him. Eventually, the Doctor explains things to Vicki and advises her and Troilus to move to Cornwall, as he's worried that she may end up becoming one of her own ancestors.

The 2007 audiobook, *Frostfire*, features an older Lady Cressida in 1164BC (confusingly twenty years before the traditional date of the Fall of Troy), when she's living in Carthage. There, she tells a story of when she, Steven, and the Doctor meet Jane Austen during the frost fair of 1814. During this adventure, she witnesses the death of a phoenix, a cinder from which finds its way into Vicki's eye – and there it remains until Cressida and Troilus settle in Carthage many years later. One day, missing her old life and feeling so alone Cressida cries and the cinder escapes her eye. It's still alive and able to communicate with her. She keeps the cinder in an oil lamp and often talks to it, since it's the only thing that knows anything of her life with the Doctor. This changes by the time of *The Storyteller*, a 2022 mini-episode released to publicise *The Collection: Season 2* Blu-ray set. In this, Vicki is regaling her tales to a young girl called Sophia, who, it's implied, is related to her; it's likely Sophia is her granddaughter.

The 2018 audio, *The Crash of the UK-201*, gives us and Vicki a tantalising glimpse into what might have been: when she's given the chance to stop the crash of the titular ship, she finds herself enjoying a life without the Doctor, with Steven popping in and out of her timeline. She still has to face up to many tragedies, but she has children and lives an unusually-long, generally happy life. It becomes a necessity to undo this existence, however, to beat cloaked creatures that feed off the paradox. It's nonetheless a chance to enjoy an elderly Vicki – an idea also picked up in the 2024 audio, *Fugitive of the Daleks*, in which an older Vicki finds herself on the TARDIS once more alongside the First Doctor.

Steven has managed a much better Expanded Universe life, with many appearances in short stories and audio books, though he's only been in three novels.

We discover in the short story, *Ash*, that he was given learning pills as part of his education, and in *The Empire of Glass*, that he spent most of his adult career in cramped quarters, with the first new smell for him being the burning forest on Mechanus at the end of *The Chase*. Also in *The Empire of Glass*, Steven flirts with Christopher Marlowe, so we may infer Steven could've been the first gay companion in *Doctor Who*. During his time in space, Steven pilots a streamlined Terran ship made of modified Dalek technology, and at one point, while on shore leave on Roylus Prime, he witnesses a woman being savagely beaten yet doesn't help her. This guilt tortures him for some time, resurfacing in *Salvation*, and compounded by the deaths of Katarina and Sara.

In the novel, *Bunker Soldiers*, Steven is still smarting from the conclusion of the TV story, *The Massacre*, and initially sides against the Doctor, in favour of interceding and saving lives; the Doctor convinces him why it would be wrong to do so. We also learn that he doesn't believe in heaven, despite claiming to be a Protestant in *The Massacre*, since in all his travels he's seen nothing that convinces him otherwise. Indeed, he's learned to expect a rational explanation for everything, even if he cannot understand it.

In a touching short story, Steven and the Doctor accidentally ruin the future of a young boy called Bobby Zierath; with more than a little guilt for his part in events, Steven gives Bobby his panda, Hi-Fi – which is never seen on TV after *The Time Meddler*.

We meet Steven again in the audio adventure, *The Five Companions*, set many years after he last saw the Doctor. At first, he's reunited with Ian, followed by the Fifth Doctor, who, like Ian, he believes to be a younger version of the Doctor he knew, until the Doctor explains about regeneration. Steven is surprised to encounter an older Sara, having witnessed her death many years before. Sara never really explains to him the reason for her survival; only that even the Doctor never could quite understand it, either. Nonetheless, he's happy to see Ian, Sara, and the Doctor again, though, like the others, is convinced that the Doctor will not return to look them up, despite his promises to the contrary.

Still, Steven and Sara spend a fair amount of time with each other in various audio stories including *The Anachronauts*, in which Steven confirms he'd spent a long time in solitary confinement as a prisoner of the Mechanoids in *The Chase*; *The Sontarans*, during which Steven explains that he'd found himself on Mechanus after he was shot down by the Krayt, a species at war with Earth in the twenty-fourth century (as established in *The Empire of Glass*); and *The Little Drummer Boy*. The latter suggests Steven was indeed born in the twenty-fourth century, something contradicted by the Target novelisation of *The Chase* (which implies the twenty-sixth century), and again by the 2016 audio, *The Ravelli Conspiracy*, in which Steven fondly recalls the 2784 Olympics. Considering we don't know which century he hails from, it's something of a surprise that *Return of the Rocket Men* goes as far as naming the day and month Steven was born: 10th February.

The Secrets of Det-Sen establishes that Steven was close to his grandmother as a child, but that she died when he was a teenager. This is indicative of the tragedies Steven faces throughout his life. The 2014 audio, *The War to End All Wars*, catches up with Steven long after he's left the TARDIS, finding him the deposed king of the unnamed planet from *The Savages*, and telling his granddaughter, Sida, about his visit to the planet Comfort with the Doctor and Dodo; the Doctor telling Steven that he had to leave its citizens rebuild themselves without Steven's assistance informed his decision to leave the TARDIS, intent on unifying the Elders and Savages. The story establishes that Steven had three daughters: Sida's mother, Raleigh, and Dodo Taylor. The latter – naturally named after his travelling companion – was his favourite, but she was assassinated and his other daughters wanted their share of his kingdom, ultimately forcing Steven's abdication.

Despite these horrors, Steven recalls his time with the Doctor with fondness, and he at least enjoyed some brief respites, notably in *An Ordinary Life*, set during *The Daleks' Master Plan*, in which he and Sara settle into 1950s London for a short time; and in *Mother Russia*, in which Steven befriends Count Grigori Nikitin and Semion Borisovich Stasov, while the Doctor tutors Nikitin's son. Steven spends this time reading, fishing, hiking, and learning to hunt. He's even best man at Stasov's wedding.

Since Katarina literally went from Troy to Kembel and then sacrificed herself, there's no time for other adventures. Regardless of this, the short story, *Scribbles in Chalk*, tells of a 'missing adventure'. We're told that Cassandra chose Katarina as her handmaiden because she'd predicated Katarina's death. We also learn that, although she likes Steven, Katarina finds him arrogant.

Something interesting happens in the 2003 short story, *Katarina in the Underworld*. We follow Katarina as she journeys to the Elysian fields of the afterlife. She doesn't have the coins to pay her way across the River Styx, so an old woman summons the Doctor to help her. Before Hades, she explains how she sacrificed her life to save millions. Persephone vouches for Katarina and she's allowed into the Elysian fields. As she enters, she ponders that this may have been just a dream, but even so, she's convinced that the Doctor inspired her to achieve her destiny.

Poor Dodo! On television, she had a pretty rum deal – joining the Doctor without preamble or an introductory story, and then cast aside for no real good reason, and thus denied a final adventure. She fares little better in the Expanded Universe prose.

Salvation, a novel published in 1999, attempts to give her a good introductory story, but only succeeds in messing up things further. On TV, it's clearly stated that she ran into the TARDIS because she witnessed an accident on Wimbledon Common, but *Salvation* tells us otherwise: she's fleeing an increasingly insane alien metamorph called Joseph, one of six extra-dimensional beings who came into light as a result of the beliefs of those they encountered. This book also goes to great lengths to explain why

Dodo's accent changes so drastically between scenes at the opening of *The Celestial Toymaker*.

'Dodo' starts out as a horrible nickname in school, because of her inferior North London accent; she later takes the nickname on to spite her peers, and uses one accent as Dodo in everyday life, and the other as the 'proper schoolgirl' Dorothea. Her mother died in 1962, while her father was institutionalised shortly after, which led to Dodo living with her aunt, Margaret, a tyrannical woman if ever there was one. These background details are contradicted in *The Man in the Velvet Mask*, in which we're told that she grew up in one of the poorer parts of London, and her parents died when she was young. She then moved in with her aunt, a wealthy social climber. Dodo had trouble marrying her previously poor existence with this new life, and tried reinventing herself depending on each situation, explaining that her accent was 'situational' at best.

Audio adventures cast more doubt about Dodo's past: she says in *The Miniaturist* that she might have family in Yorkshire, and, in *The Incherton Incident*, even suggests she's from there.

Just to make her life a little bit worse, the Doctor implies in *Bunker Soldiers* that her remark to Dmitri in Kiev, 1240, may have been the inspiration for the Black Death over a hundred years later. After Dmitri orders his food is thrown to the pigs, Dodo tells him, 'You can't just throw something away because you don't like it,' which leads the half-mad Dmitri to order the plague-ridden bodies hurled over the walls of Kiev at the Mongol horde – a tactic that would be remembered and passed on.

The Expanded Universe novelists aren't finished with her yet. In 1996's *The Man in the Velvet Mask*, Dodo loses her virginity to Dalville, an actor in an alternative Paris in 1804, but is infected by a virus created by the mad Minksi. This virus infects all her future lovers and possible children. We also find out that she spent most of her French lessons learning how to kiss behind the gym.

The worst addition to Dodo's life, however, is saved for when she leaves the Doctor. The novel, *Who Killed Kennedy?*, details

Dodo's life after the Doctor palms her off to recover in the country. She spends several months there, then returns to London to get a job. It doesn't work out too well for her as she starts experiencing blackouts and memory loss, a result of the conditioning from WOTAN. She goes to a series of psychiatric hospitals, and even undergoes fourteen months of electro-shock treatment. She's interrogated by the Master, once he learns she used to know the Doctor, who then wipes her memory of said event. She lives in a halfway house for homeless people and, after reading an article about mind control eventually gets in touch with journalist, James Stevens, who's on a mission to expose UNIT and the cover-ups of alien invasions. They end up becoming lovers and she falls pregnant. While James investigates the Glasshouse, a special UNIT-funded hospital (secretly run by the Master, who was goading James to be a thorn in UNIT's side), she's shot in her home. Dodo is buried in South London and either the Second or Seventh Doctor attends her funeral, carrying a white rose.

Other media gives Dodo a more favourable outcome. The *Brief Encounters* short story, *Ships*, sees a slightly older Dodo recalling her trips in the TARDIS and bumping into Sarah Jane Smith; and in the 2020 webcast, *Farewell, Sarah Jane*, Dodo attended the titular character's funeral at some point in the early twenty-first century, averting Dodo's *Who Killed Kennedy?* fate.

The Tenth Doctor gives a final salute to his early companion in the 2007 novel, *The Last Dodo*, affectionately naming the historically-important bird 'Dorothea'.

There's no real gap to fill in the short time Ben and Polly travelled with the First Doctor, yet they do appear in a few stories, both in prose and on audio. Understandably, we learn little, though more when they're later paired with the Second Doctor.

In the 2002 novel, *Ten Little Aliens*, we find out that Ben has an older brother who taught him how to swear when they were in school. He's a little conscious of his height, since Polly is a good inch taller than he is. Polly tends to think of people as either cat or dog people: she considers Ben a dog person, whereas she's a cat person, due to her independent nature. She's had a rather privileged upbringing, being more used to Beaujolais Nouveau parties, and having attended a finishing school in South Kensington, London. When Polly becomes the object of Trooper Matthew Shade's affections, Ben is a little jealous, even though he's getting close to Trooper Mel Narda. The Doctor reminds Ben of his father, who had a knack for fixing things haphazardly.

Sometimes, narratives accommodate for the lack of wriggle room in the pair's time with the Doctor. A timeline distortion in the 2017 audio, *The Bonfires of the Vanities*, explains how they end up in Lewes in the 1950s at the end of *The Smugglers* instead of immediately arriving in Antarctica in 1986 for *The Tenth Planet*. The Time Lords apparently try to fix this distortion (ostensibly caused by the Time War, far in the Doctor's personal future), but cannot interfere too much as it occurs so close to the First Doctor's regeneration; this leads to further adventures for the trio, including *The Crumbling Magician*, in which the Doctor and Polly swap minds, and Polly even gets a little Time Lord DNA; *The Plague of Dreams*, featuring a psychoactive virus that causes Ben to have a nightmare about pirates; and the 1994 comic strip, *Food for Thought*, the first Expanded Universe story to use Ben and Polly as the First Doctor's companions.

Finally, there's *Falling*, a *Short Trip* from 2017 which segues between different periods of Polly and Ben's lives. Polly is now Polly Jackson, and as she roots around a box of curios, she recalls her travels with the Doctor, specifically the time she, Ben, and the First Doctor all had the same, ominous dream – just as the TARDIS materialises at the South Pole, ahead of his regeneration.

As with all incarnations of the Doctor, the first has several companions that are exclusive to Expanded Universe. The first of these were introduced in 1964: Dr Who's two grandchildren, John and Gillian. They travelled with Dr Who (during the 1960s comics, he was always referred to as such) for four years in total, until the first episode of *Invasion of the Quarks* in 1968, by which time they were travelling with the Second Doctor. There's no discernible moment when they leave and return; indeed it's strongly implied that they never did leave their grandfather and were, thus, with him for his regeneration in the comic-verse.

In the *Doctor Who Annual*, Dr Who is joined by several companions, first in the 1966 annual story, *The Monster from Earth* (released in 1965). Playing hide and seek, brother and sister, Amy and Tony Barker, decide to hide in a Police Box and find themselves off on an adventure with the Sensorites (who barely resemble their TV counterparts), before the Doctor, after feeding them, takes them back home. The following year, a whole plethora of prose companions are introduced to readers, first in the novella-length release, *Doctor Who and the Invasion from Space*, and later in the 1967 annual. Other than annoying Dr Who, the Mortimer (some sources say Mortimore) family does little except take up space and get into trouble. They are George and Helen, and their two children, Ida and Alan, who, at the beginning of the story, are fleeing the Great Fire of London and run into the TARDIS before it dematerialises. In the annual story, *The Devil-Birds of Corbo*, we're introduced to Harroll Strong, an Earth-maker looking for minerals on the planet Corbo, alongside his twin children, Jack and Dot. The Doctor rescues them from the Devil-Bird of the title, as well as three other astronauts, Shelly, Chertzog, and Hill. They return in the follow-up story, *Playthings of Fo*, and at the end of that tale, they set course for Earth. Other than John and Gillian, none of those Expanded Universe companions are heard of again.

The next Expanded Universe-only companion, Oliver Harper, comes along in 2011. A city trader from 1966, Oliver joins the Doctor and Steven in the audiobook, *The Perpetual Bond,* and is killed two stories later, in *The First Wave*. His mind continues to exist, and he remains with the Doctor (who's completely unaware of his presence) for the rest of his first incarnation until fading out when the Doctor regenerates.

The last Expanded Universe companion is one of the most interesting, in that she was created for television, but was never intended to be an ongoing companion. Sara Kingdom appeared in the twelve-part story, *The Daleks' Master Plan*, and was killed in the closing moments. Terry Nation and Brad Ashton explored Sara's back-story in the 1966 annual, *The Dalek Outer Space Book*, and Nation had further designs on the character, intending to feature her, the Daleks, and the Space Security Service in their own spin-off series which ultimately never came to be (though was adapted into a *Lost Stories* tale by Big Finish as *The Destroyers*). Her position as companion has been hotly contested by fans for decades – a debate ratcheted up in 1989 when John Peel adapted the story into two books, fixing a very definite six month gap between episodes seven and eight. During that time, Sara continues to travel with the Doctor and Steven, as seen in several audio books and short stories, namely *The Little Drummer Boy*, *The Anachronauts*, *The Drowned World*, *The Guardian of the Solar System* (which considerably adds to several *Master Plan* threads, involving Mavic Chen and Sara's brother, Bret Vyon, and paradoxically results in Sara's past promotion and assignment to Earth), *An Ordinary Life*, and *The Sontarans*. The latter was meant to close this period in Sara's life, but in 2018, the audiobook, *Men of War*, slotted into this time too. Most notably, in the 2008 audio, *Home Truths*, we learn that Sara's mind is copied by a house, and she's later reincarnated as an older woman. It's this Sara who appears in the audio play, *The Five Companions*.

And Sara's legacy lives on in her niece, Anya Kingdom, who's inspired to join the Space Security Service, then becomes an audio companion, first to the Fourth Doctor – in *The Sinestran Kill* (as WPC Ann Kelso) and *The Perfect Prisoners*, before spying on him throughout *The Dalek Protocol* – then to the Tenth Doctor in the *Dalek Universe* box sets.

The Second Doctor
Patrick Troughton

> *'Our lives are different to anybody else's.*
> *Nobody in the universe can do what we're doing.'*
> The Doctor – *The Tomb of the Cybermen*

With the change of Doctor, a radical shift in the companion dynamic occurred. Up to this point, the majority of the Doctor's companions were contemporary (and even when they weren't, very little was made of the 'out of time' aspect of their characters), with a nice balance between male and female. But along came the Second Doctor, and off go Ben and Polly. Their replacements were three very distinctively different types of companions – and not one contemporary character among them – a fact that was tailored to the stories' benefit, and, indeed, the Doctor's.

Ben Jackson and Polly – Michael Craze and Anneke Wills – Continued... (*The War Machines* to *The Faceless Ones*)

During the rest of their travels with the Doctor, we learn very little about Ben and Polly, even though they continue with him for a further six adventures. We don't even find out Polly's surname during this time.

It's a curious thing that from the start, despite having seen the Doctor's 'renewal', Ben refuses to accept that the Doctor is indeed who he claims to be. Once again, Polly is the voice of reason, willing to accept what she has seen, even if she cannot really understand it. Throughout their adventure on the human colony on Vulcan (*The Power of the Daleks*), Ben continues to be irritable and highly strung, while Polly opts for calmness. It is only when a Dalek recognises the Doctor that Ben finally accepts this strange man in the frock coat is the same old man he had come to trust.

Throughout his travels, Ben complains a lot and often responds with aggression, but, at his heart, he is a good man; a hero of sorts, although not always the sharpest of travelling companions. His lack of historical knowledge is proven when the TARDIS takes its occupants to the Battle of Culloden in 1746 (*The Highlanders*), but he displays an unexpected level of scientific knowledge on the Moonbase when helping Polly find a way to combat the Cybermen. He reveals himself to be a little ignorant of other cultures when he points out that Polly can speak 'foreign' and continues to be protective of Polly, calling her 'Duchess' on many occasions. When separated for some time, Ben's first thought on seeing the Doctor is always, 'Where's Polly?'

With the arrival of Jamie, Ben finds a kindred spirit – another young man who is not shy of taking action. There's an apparent brotherly bond between them, which almost come to blows when Ben suggests that Jamie 'cracks up' while on the Moonbase. Ben's will is easily overcome by the Macra (*The Macra Terror*), who turn him against his friends, but the brainwashing is eventually fixed by the Doctor, who has already prevented Polly from succumbing to the same conditioning techniques.

Polly maintains her usual level of optimism while travelling, although the horror of the events she's witnessed continues to affect her. She is sickened by the Daleks' slaughter of the human colonists on Vulcan, but despite her revulsion at witnessing the death of Gascoigne (*The Faceless Ones*), she still goes to check his body. Regardless of her outward 'dolly bird' appearance, and her well-to-do upbringing, she remains a strong and determined person, not ashamed to use her feminine wiles to gain the assistance of British soldier Finch, while on the Scottish highlands of 1746, as well as dominating the much weaker Kirsty McLaren, daughter of the Laird of the clan McLaren. She considers Ben a 'real man' and never loses hope that one day the Doctor will take her home (she thinks of Chelsea in *The Underwater Menace*, which suggests that is where she is from). She is partly responsible for Jamie joining the Doctor too – she suggests he should come with them, rather than be left to fend for himself on the highlands.

Much like Dodo before them, during their last adventure set in London (*The Faceless Ones*), Ben and Polly are sidelined. In this case, both disappear by the end of the second episode; Polly is replaced by an alien Chameleon in the first episode, calling itself Michelle Leuppi, while Ben is last seen in the second episode being frozen by the Chameleon, Spencer. The Doctor never gives up looking for them and eventually frees them at the end of episode six, in which they return for a final brief scene. Ben is the first to realise that the date, July 20th 1966, is the exact same day the pair joined the Doctor in *The War Machines*. Ben and Polly want to remain in London for a while, glad to be in a normal place again, away from monsters. They both decide it's time to stop travelling, but only if the Doctor doesn't mind. The Doctor is sad to see them go, but makes Polly promise to look after Ben, which she does.

We never see them again on television, but in 2010, we discover in *The Sarah Jane Adventures* that Polly made good on her promise: she and Ben remained together, running an orphanage in India.

James Robert McCrimmon was quite unique in *Doctor Who* history. Not only did he appear in more episodes than any other companion (not counting any return appearances), but he also travelled with the Second Doctor for all but one of his on-screen adventures (the only companion who came close in twentieth century *Doctor Who* was Tegan Jovanka, who travelled with the Fifth Doctor for all but two of his stories).

It was, therefore, no surprise to learn that, even today, the Doctor regarded Jamie with great affection, having mentioned him several times in later incarnations; he went so far as to use Jamie's full name as an alias when the Doctor, in his tenth incarnation, encountered Queen Victoria on the moors of Scotland (*Tooth and Claw*).

THE SECOND DOCTOR

Jamie McCrimmon – Frazer Hines (*The Highlanders* to *The War Games,* and *The Two Doctors*)

Man on the Moon (R.E.M.); *There'll Never Be Peace Till Jamie Comes Home* (Canterach).

The Doctor first encounters Jamie in the Scottish highlands during the aftermath of the Battle of Culloden in 1746 (though Jamie later explicitly states he comes from 1745 when being questioned by the Security Chief in *The War Games*). It's a violent first encounter, in which Jamie holds a dirk to Ben's throat, but the Doctor convinces the highlanders that he and his friends are not English spies. At the time, Jamie is a piper for the McLaren clan. Surviving death at the gallows, Jamie helps the Doctor, Ben, and Polly across the glen, suspecting they'll become lost if they try to find their way on their own. Realising the danger, Polly convinces the Doctor to let Jamie go with them. Jamie is a little uncertain at first, wondering what he has 'come upon', but soon enters the TARDIS to be spirited away to Atlantis (*The Underwater Menace*).

The first thing to change about Jamie is his accent, which softens almost immediately. One might attribute this to travel, except it happens too quickly. The harder accent returns, however, when his features are temporarily changed in the Land of Fiction (*The Mind Robber*), but the soft familiar tones continue once his normal features are returned. It's interesting that once he is sent back to his own time, his original accent resurfaces, confirming his travels with the Doctor 'no longer happened for him'.

A product of the eighteenth century, Jamie's knowledge base is somewhat lacking, and he is constantly exposed to new things which he can barely understand. To cope, he often equates such things with his own time period; calling a plane a 'flying beastie', for instance, or in the case of a hovercraft, a fairytale. He is initially fearful of flying in a helicopter in *The Enemy of the World*, despite having previously flown in an aeroplane sometime before in *The Faceless Ones*, but by the time he is next in a helicopter, in *Fury from the Deep*, he is perfectly comfortable – just one instance in which Jamie displays his amazing adaptability to new situations. This lack of knowledge should never be mistaken for stupidity; he shows an amazing level of intelligence, resourcefulness, and common sense throughout his travels, quickly learning to read and how to tell the time. Note, for example, how he finds a way onto the Chameleon Tours plane, despite previously never having been in an airport.

It seems that, at first, Jamie doesn't quite know how to act around women; horrified by the notion of being pampered by a group of women on the leisure colony of *The Macra Terror*, and flustered by the attention of Samantha Briggs in *The Faceless Ones*. He soon learns to adapt to her bolshy attitude and does his best to charm her. This experience leaves him in good standing, since in the next adventure (*The Evil of the Daleks*), he is quite happy to question the 'lassies' in a London cafe, and rather enjoys the experience, getting the required information with ease. When he is later transferred to 1866, he easily charms Maxtible's maid, Molly. These all prepare him for the arrival of Victoria Waterfield.

Jamie's relationship with his travelling companions tends to be mostly affectionate, especially with the Doctor, Victoria, and Zoe. He is competitive with Ben, often responding with bravado and aggression at some perceived insult.

Nonetheless, Jamie is disappointed when Ben and Polly leave: they had taken him under their wing and treated him much like a younger sibling (possibly it was them, in particular Polly, who encouraged him to learn to read). He promises to look out for the Doctor, a pledge he takes very seriously over the course of the next two years. As he and the Doctor become close, a strong relationship of trust and respect is built.

This relationship is almost brought to an abrupt end when the Doctor appears to ally himself with the Daleks (*The Evil of the Daleks*), putting Jamie through a series of dangerous tests as the Daleks attempt to define the 'human factor'. When Jamie discovers the Doctor's apparent betrayal, he is angry and calls him callous and uncaring. Uncharacteristically, he appears to want to leave the TARDIS, but the Doctor manages to win him over. Jamie is later devastated when he believes the Doctor to be infected by the 'Dalek factor'. He is not entirely convinced by the Doctor's insistence that he is still actually himself. This presents a shift in their previous dynamic and Jamie continues to display a willingness to call the Doctor out when he believes him to be wrong. Still, despite that shift, they remain close, with Jamie considering himself responsible for the Doctor's safety.

Outwardly, he treats new companion Victoria as a little sister, adopting the role of protective big brother. Jamie seems to hold a torch for her, as most clearly seen in *The Enemy of the World*: after Victoria makes a disparaging remark about the future fashion of women's clothing, Jamie suggests that she would look good in such garb herself, with a solicitous smirk. This on its own could be a case of Jamie's typical playfulness with those he is close to, but when coupled with his sadness when Victoria elects to remain on Earth in the 1970s (*Fury from the Deep*), it suggests something a little more. He tries to convince her to remain, and has a difficult time expressing his sadness to the Doctor, instead appearing gruff, until the Doctor points out that he too will miss her.

After leaving Victoria behind, the Doctor and Jamie find themselves in the twenty-first century (*The Wheel in Space*). It is in this story that Jamie first attributes the name 'John Smith' to the Doctor, having read it on a piece of medical equipment. While the Doctor is rendered unconscious, Jamie is introduced to astrophysicist Zoe Heriot. It takes Jamie a while to warm to Zoe. He finds her too intelligent for her own good; with her 'big brain', she often laughs at his lesser intelligence, calling his kilt a 'skirt' and making other snide comments. Zoe and Jamie soon settle into a friendly bickering relationship, characterised by Jamie's usual protectiveness and Zoe's bossiness. His more simple thinking often wins out over Zoe's logic.

During his travels with the Doctor, Jamie grows a lot, both emotionally and intellectually. By the time of *The War Games,*

Jamie is quite willing to work with a redcoat, the one-time sworn enemy of the highlanders, to escape the prisoners' camp. After some years travelling together, Jamie remains convinced that the Doctor hasn't betrayed the rebels, even though he appears to have allied himself with the War Chief, an old Time Lord acquaintance in *The War Games*. At the end of this adventure, the Doctor is left with no choice but to call his own people, and is ready to part company with Jamie and Zoe, fearing for their safety if the Time Lords catch up with them. Jamie doesn't care about the danger – he will not leave the Doctor's side.

Such is his loyalty to the Doctor that Jamie insists they attempt an escape from the Time Lords. He is angered by the Time Lord's insistence that he and Zoe must leave. It is only the Doctor's sad certainty that convinces Jamie that his adventures truly must end. A sombre farewell follows, in which Jamie states that he will never forget the Doctor, not knowing that his memory is soon to be wiped by the Time Lords.

Jamie appears to return in *The Five Doctors* in 1983, although he, like Zoe, is only a phantom, an illusion created by the force of Rassilon's will. His appearance serves to help the Doctor solve a problem, since Jamie remembers the Brigadier, which is clearly impossible since his memory was wiped. How the Doctor could remember this wasn't going to be explored for some time, although the 1986 adventure *The Two Doctors* would provide some clues.

Although Jamie is returned to his own time, with only the memory of his first adventure with the Doctor remaining, he does return – *sixteen* years later! In *The Two Doctors*, Jamie and the Doctor appear to still be travelling together, both having aged considerably. The Doctor is seen to be working for the Time Lords, a fact fully known to Jamie. The familiar loyalty is evident, and now they have become firm friends, much more so than they ever were when they were originally travelling together. There is no indication of how long they've been travelling together or indeed why (such explanations are bountiful in the Expanded

Universe material). It is, however, clear that the Sixth Doctor remembers his extra journeys with Jamie since he shows no surprise at his older appearance, or at the fact that his own second incarnation has grey hair. While stranded on Station Camera, believing the Doctor to be dead, Jamie reverts to a feral state, to the point where he attacks Peri – like an animal protecting its lair. He accepts the Sixth Doctor with ease. Even though the explanation makes little sense to Jamie, he doesn't question it any further. He enjoys a good rapport with the Sixth Doctor, and becomes a little protective of Peri, much like he had once had been with Victoria and Zoe. He is last seen departing in the TARDIS with the Second Doctor, but not before giving Peri a quick peck on the cheek.

Victoria Waterfield – Deborah Watling (*The Evil of the Daleks* to *Fury from the Deep*)

Just A Girl (No Doubt); *Flou* (Angèle).

The teenage daughter of wealthy scientist, Edward Waterfield, Victoria was from 1866 and was very much a girl of her time, well educated both academically and in the subject of manners and propriety.

Victoria meets Jamie while the Daleks are holding her captive (*The Evil of the Daleks*), to ensure the continued assistance of her father and his associate Theodore Maxtible. She is understandably almost hysterical with fear, isolated with only the occasional appearance of a Dalek for company (it comes in barking orders at her, asking her to repeat her name constantly; an abject lesson in creating terror in a person). Even through her fear, she continues to feed the birds that land on the sill of her cell window, despite orders not to do so. It's as if she considers them the only contact she still has with a world she *does* understand. Her fear is not helped once Jamie and Kemel rescue her, since they are, for a time, barricaded in the cell. Later, she and Kemel are transferred to Skaro in the distant future, which Victoria has some difficulty accepting, but not as much as when Kemel is killed. Death seems to follow her a lot and her father is also killed by the Daleks on Skaro, but not before he asks the Doctor to take care of Victoria for him.

Victoria accepts the Doctor's offer to join the TARDIS crew, albeit with little other choice, since she is now an orphan, cut off and far from home. She is somewhat surprised by the TARDIS, and laughs at the idea that it's a time machine, having no knowledge of the experiments in time travel her own father conducted. Her laughter soon turns to worry when she realises just how old the Doctor is. This concern becomes even more evident when she tells him he probably needs rest, being 'so old'. The Doctor, however, rebuffs this as he is quite sprightly really.

Victoria changes into clothes she considers far too short, until the Doctor points out that Jamie's kilt is not much different (by *The Enemy of the World*, however, she dons an even shorter skirt and calls it 'elegant', showing some acceptance of her new life). This nineteenth century mindset continues with her for some time, but she still maintains an inquisitive mind, no doubt encouraged by her father (as witnessed by her knowledge of science in *The Abominable Snowmen*) and evident in her dealings with the crew of the rocket that brings the archaeological team to Telos (*The Tomb of the Cybermen*). She talks down to them a lot, probably in the same manner she would have adopted speaking to servants back home – it's telling that she doesn't show the same attitude to the archaeologists themselves.

Although a product of her time, Victoria does demonstrate a surprising level of bravery: even when being held at gunpoint, she holds her own and later stands up to Donald Bruce, the thuggish head of security for the World Zone Authority in *The Enemy of the World*. It appears she's been trained in firearms, or is a very lucky shot, since she manages to hit a Cybermat with her first shot.

She often demonstrates a wide knowledge of academic subjects, including the sciences and geology, but she hasn't heard of the London Underground, despite it existing in her native time. She is not afraid to lie if the situation requires it; for example, when she professes knowledge of cooking, when it's clear she has never cooked in her life, spouting ingredients which she has most likely heard being mentioned before.

Victoria draws a great comfort from the Doctor's presence, looking upon him in something of a fatherly way. She learns how to cope with her own loss by following his advice. With Jamie, she develops a sibling-like relationship, and is often amused by his lack of knowledge and view on women, in particular the way they dress.

Victoria is known for her screaming – indeed, her reaction to any monster she meets is to scream. However, in *Fury from the Deep*, it's discovered that the weed creatures are susceptible to high-pitched noise and so the survivors on the oil refinery hit on the idea of recording Victoria's screams and using them as a weapon. Ironically, she discovers she simply cannot do it on command, but upon seeing a weed creature again, she fortunately manages to scream anyway.

She becomes resigned to the random travels early on, but by the time of *Fury from the Deep*, she's come to realise that she's tired of the endless travelling and longs for peace and happiness. She decides to remain behind in the 1970s with the Harris family, a decision the Doctor completely understands, although he does insist he remain for another night just so she can be sure. Jamie has a harder time letting go, to the point where he tries to convince her to continue to go with him and the Doctor, but she knows she cannot. Leaving them is hard, but she must do it. The last we see is an image of her on the TARDIS scanner as she waves goodbye.

We never hear of Victoria again, save for a mention in *The Two Doctors* when an older Doctor explains to Jamie that she is off studying graphology for a short time, implying that somehow she resumed her travels with the Doctor and Jamie for almost another twenty years.

Zoe Heriot – Wendy Padbury (*The Wheel in Space* to *The War Games*)

The Sounds of Science (Beastie Boys); *Don't You (Forget About Me)* (Simple Minds).

An astrophysicist from an undefined point in the twenty-first century (*The War Games*), Zoe Heriot states quite specifically that she was *born* in the twenty-first century, although in *The Mind Robber* she explains how she read *The Hourly Telepress* from the year 2000.

Zoe meets the Doctor and Jamie in *The Wheel in Space* while she is working as a librarian. Highly trained in logic (which, the Doctor points out, only allows people to be wrong with authority), she is considered to be 'all brain and no heart' by her colleagues, especially Leo Ryan. She realises this is true and wants to feel more and not be like the students usually produced by the parapsychology teachers.

Her need to 'feel' expresses itself straight away upon meeting Jamie. She is fascinated by his 'girl's' clothing, having never seen a kilt before. This immediately annoys Jamie, and Zoe realises he's an easy target, setting the scene for much teasing and bossiness for the rest of their association. Her logical approach is called into question as she spends more and more time with the Doctor, who is the most illogical and instinctive person she has ever met. The Doctor intrigues her greatly, and when she learns about the TARDIS, her curiosity is taken to a whole new level. So, after being refused entry, she stows away as soon as the Doctor and Jamie's backs are turned. The Doctor spots her, and gives her the choice; no doubt because he is still weary of the reasons behind Victoria's departure.

Despite witnessing the Doctor and Jamie's previous encounter with the Daleks by way of the former transmitting his thoughts to the TARDIS scanner (*The Evil of the Daleks*), Zoe elects to remain and thoroughly enjoys her first trip to the planet Dulkis (*The*

Dominators). She is more than happy to assist the Dulcians, encouraging them to resist the oppressive Dominators, although she does make the usual first-traveller mistake of giving away too much information about the TARDIS and how they arrived on the planet.

When the TARDIS is removed from regular time to escape an exploding volcano, Zoe has to explain to Jamie the danger they are in, and the concept of 'nothing' being outside the ship is something she has no problem understanding (*The Mind Robber*). While there, she sees an image of her home city – a sprawling futuristic metropolis quite unlike anything ever seen on twenty-first century Earth! This image is soon swept away when she finds herself alone in the Land of Fiction; she reacts with sheer terror at being removed from everything she finds familiar. Her knowledge of history is not very good, but she is aware of some classic tales, like Theseus and the Minotaur, Perseus' battle against the Gorgon Medusa, and *Gulliver's Travels*. She's also a fan of the Karkus' adventures in *The Hourly Telepress*. She displays some basic self-defence training, and is temporarily turned into fiction by the Master of the Land of Fiction. Her photographic memory comes into play when she corrects a mistake the Doctor makes as he reassembles Jamie's face, thus altering his appearance for a short time.

Upon arriving in the 1970s (*The Invasion*), Zoe is enticed into a brief stint of model work by fashion photographer, Isobel Watkins, and through the subsequent friendship, she discovers a much more normal, fun-loving side of her character. In particular, she thinks posing for the camera is 'great fun', yet she finds it hard to relax while the Doctor and Jamie are off finding Isobel's father and can't help but sense that something is wrong. Isobel and Zoe encourage each other to visit International Electromatics and come up against the robotic secretary. Frustrated by its unwillingness to help, and refusing to be beaten by a 'brainless' box, Zoe sets it an unsolvable puzzle by use of the computer language ALGOL, a chance for her to prove that she is better than a machine. It's actually Zoe who computes the attack patterns needed to defeat the Cybermen's spaceships, which leads to one UNIT soldier remarking that she is 'so much prettier than a computer', a comment that pleases Zoe greatly. Her total recall (and expertise in space flight) comes in useful when learning to fly Professor Eldred's rocket in *The Seeds of Death* too.

On the planet of the Gonds (*The Krotons*), Zoe displays knowledge of geology. She recognises the mica rocks and likens the Gond city to those built by the Incans. The Doctor admits that Zoe is something of a genius, which can be irritating at times, while Zoe believes the Doctor to be 'almost as clever' as she is. This appears to be proven when she initially gets a better score on the Krotons' teaching machine; she is, however, trumped as soon as the Doctor realises his mistake.

Like Jamie, Zoe is returned to her own time by the Time Lords, and her memory of the Doctor is erased, save her initial adventure with him (*The War Games*). She doesn't want to leave him and hopes that they will one day see each other again. It's sad that, once returned to the Wheel, all that she learned and experienced is taken from her, and so she reverts back to the 'all brains and no heart' Zoe we first met – although for a moment she can't help but think that she has forgotten something.

We never see Zoe again, except as a phantom, alongside phantom Jamie, produced by the mind of Rassilon in the Dark Tower on Gallifrey in *The Five Doctors*.

The Second Doctor
Expanded Universe

What happened to companions after they left the Second Doctor? That seems a primary focus for Expanded Universe writers who pick up the stories of Ben and Polly, Jamie, Victoria, and Zoe...

One thing is certain in the minds of most of *Doctor Who* fandom: Ben and Polly end up together and most likely get married. Much like Ian and Barbara, writers of the books and comics seem intent on bringing these two characters together.

First of all, there's the little matter of Polly's surname. In the original character outline, she's Polly Wright, sharing the same surname as Barbara. It never makes it to television screens, but is confirmed as her surname in the 1995 novel, *Invasion of the Cat-People*, by Gary Russell. In this story, we also learn that both Ben and Polly were born in 1942, a point later contradicted in the 2009 audio, *Resistance*, which tells us that Polly was born in 1943. Her father is Doctor Edward Wright and her mother the former Miss Bettingham-Smith. Polly considers that she took them both for granted, spending so much time away from home enjoying herself. Another important point is mentioned: Polly and Barbara aren't related; they simply share a common surname.

As for Ben, we find out that, when he was fourteen, he snuck aboard his father's ship, and, as a result of his interest in the vessel, the captain promised him a job when he turned fifteen. *Doctor Who and the Cybermen*, the 1975 novelisation of *The Moonbase*, indicated that a young Ben had his eye set on spaceships, rather than convention sea-faring ships, as he wanted to be an astronaut. Nonetheless, the naval life seems to be in Ben's blood: the 2016 audio story, *The Mouthless Dead*, reveals that his uncle served on the *Lion*, and fought in World War I's Battle of Jutland. It was an experience that soured Ben's uncle to the Royal Navy, describing those who'd died as 'the lucky ones.' Ben's year of birth is also backed up by the audio books, *Lost and Found* (during which he recalls finding bodies during the Blitz), and *The Forsaken*, in which we meet Ben's father, Private James Jackson – who, after being convinced that he'd make a great father by the TARDIS crew, intends to name a prospective baby 'Polly'! Understandably, Ben is particularly protective of Private 'Jim', making sure no harm comes to him. Sadly, Ben's father later died of a heart attack, as revealed in 2015's *The Yes Men*, and Ben didn't get along with his mother's next beau, Alfred.

During *Lost and Found*, the Doctor, Polly, and Ben meet a younger Polly as she wanders through Henrik's, the department store that Ninth and Tenth Doctor companion, Rose Tyler, would eventually work in. This six-year-old Miss Wright didn't find out the significance of the trio.

Polly is also one of a select bunch of companions who meet their doppelgängers: for Polly, this is Tatiana Kregki, an ambitious Russian fighter pilot who serves during World War II (as per 2017's *The Night Witches*). Though Tatiana is initially keen to escape the war and take Polly's place in the TARDIS, she's instead inspired to lead the fight against the Nazis when they attack a Soviet Air Force base. The 2004 short story, *The Thief of Sherwood*, reveals she apparently also looks like Maid Marion – this is contradicted by *Robot of Sherwood*, but reinforced by Joseph Lidster's short story, *That Time I Nearly Destroyed the World Whilst Looking for a Dress*. Published in 2004, the latter tale puts Polly's later life under the microscope. Described as something of a music mogul, Polly regularly features in *OK!*, *Hello*, and *Heat* magazines, and has been married several times. Her first husband, Simon, is dead and she also, at some point, marries a gay boy-band member. As a result, she suffers a few bouts of excessive alcohol dependency and bulimia. She has a son, Mikey, and by the end of 1999, she fears she will mess his life up too. She goes on a rather bizarre journey through time and encounters the First Doctor, Ian, and Susan in Sherwood, and later the Fifth Doctor, Tegan, Peri, and Erimem (and has a fight with the latter). Eventually, as 2000 comes to pass, she encounters the Second Doctor and Jamie once again. The TARDIS crew take her to Ben, who is now running a pub in Sydenham, and the two finally admit their love for each other. Indeed, in the 2005 *Doctor Who Magazine* comic, *The Love Invasion*, there's a brief moment where the Ninth Doctor and Rose Tyler rush by at the top of the Post Office Tower in 1966 and witness Ben proposing to Polly. In *The Five Companions* Polly takes Ben home to meet her parents, much to their horror. But Ben and Polly each go on to marry other people. However, in the 1998 short story, *Mondas Passing*, the estranged couple meet up in 1986, but separate as friends after reminiscing about their time with the Doctor and Jamie.

A special note must be made of the 1968 *Doctor Who Annual*. In this collection of stories, we see a different side of their journeys. These are at odds with their television counterpoints, especially the characters inter-personal relationships. In one tale, the Doctor favours Polly over Ben, considering her sensible and smarter than Ben. This may explain why, in another story, Ben and the Doctor have a very contentious relationship. In yet another, Polly manages to operate the TARDIS, something she never does on television, although it does correlate with some audio adventures, notably *The Yes Men*, in which the Doctor attempts to teach Ben, Polly, and Jamie how to pilot the ship.

Before meeting the Fifth Doctor again in *The Five Companions*, Polly searches online to find other companions of the Doctor. Brigadier Lethbridge-Stewart has erased all such information, but they communicate via email and are joined by companion of the Fifth Doctor, Thomas Brewster (*The Three Companions*). This somewhat leads into the 2012 play, *The Five Companions*, where she finds herself in an alternative version of the Gallifreyan Death Zone, coming into contact with several past companions and the

Fifth Doctor. She admits to him that she feels useless, but he reminds her of how she stood up to the Cyberleader in 1986. She parts company with the Doctor once more, certain she'll never see him again, but not before she tells him that she and Ben are, indeed, married. This expands upon Sarah's saying they run an orphanage in India (*The Sarah Jane Adventures: Death of the Doctor*), resulting in the pair attending her memorial service in the webcast special, *Farewell, Sarah Jane*.

Jamie's Expanded Universe appearances often jar with his TV counterpart, most notably his 1968- 69 solo adventures with the Doctor in *TV Comic*. Trying to place these adventures has been a bone of contention among fans for decades, but Jamie does appear to be older than he is on television, muddying the waters somewhat. For an unknown reason, he's initially living in 1960s Scotland, working at a tracking station in #872. His final appearance is in #898, though nothing is said about where he goes; he's just not there the following issue and never returns.

To explain away the obvious age difference of Patrick Troughton and Frazer Hines in the 1986 adventure *The Two Doctors*, Season 6B was created by the authors of *The Discontinuity Guide* (first published in 1995 by Virgin Publishing). It suggests that before the Doctor was forced to regenerate and exiled by the Time Lords, he was used as their agent. This isn't confirmed beyond the guide until the 2005 novel, *World Game* by Terrance Dicks, in which the Time Lords indeed set him up as such – the alternative is his execution (a change from the television series, wherein he's solely threatened with exile). At the end of the novel, the Doctor demands assistance on his missions. Consequently, the Time Lords agree to return an older Jamie to him, albeit with his memory altered to include an awareness of their mission and the 'knowledge' that Victoria is absent studying graphology (as established in *The Two Doctors*). It's distinctly possible that this older Jamie is the one seen in *TV Comic*. Various short stories have been written, seemingly set during this Season 6B, but mostly they see the Doctor travelling alone, with a few exceptions like the 2007 audio, *Helicon Prime*; the audio anthologies, *Beyond the War Games* (2022) and *James Robert McCrimmon* (2023); and *The Annihilators*, part of 2022's *The Third Doctor Adventures* box set, in which Jamie meets future companion, Liz Shaw, and the Third Doctor but doesn't believe him to actually be the Time Lord. The latter is arguably at odds with the 1997 novel, *The Dark Path*, which says that Jamie knows all about the Doctor's regeneration from Ben and Polly, meaning he should know the Doctor can change. As Terrance Dicks' final *Doctor Who* work, published posthumously, the short story, *Save Yourself* (in *The Target Storybook*) effectively brings this era to a close, establishing that the Time Lords wiped the Doctor's mind after each mission.

It's curious, then, that the 2015 audio, *The Black Hole*, offered up another explanation for the events of *The Two Doctors*, i.e. that the Meddling Monk sent the Doctor and Jamie on that quest so they wouldn't prove a distraction while he conducts research.

An older version of Jamie continues to appear in other Expanded Universe material including a Jamie some forty-two years after he left the Doctor. He appears in *The Glorious Revolution* in 2009, visited by an agent of the Celestial Intervention Agency of Gallifrey, who removes the memory block placed on Jamie by the Time Lords. At this point, Jamie is happily married to Kirsty McLaren (who appears in the television story, *The Highlanders*) with at least eight children and an unmentioned number of grandchildren. Once the Time Lord agent solves the problem of Jamie's past, Jamie asks for his memory block to be restored since he doesn't want the knowledge of his travels with the Doctor to threaten his happy life.

In another possibly contradictory tale, the Sixth Doctor and Peri reunite with a man the locals call 'Mad Jamie', who claims to have travelled to the moon and beyond. In *The World Shapers* (*Doctor Who Magazine* #127-129, published in 1987), it's revealed that Jamie, some forty years after he left the Doctor, remembers his travels. Following an adventure against the Voord, Jamie sacrifices himself to stop the Worldshaper from evolving the Voord into Cybermen.

His relationship with the Sixth Doctor develops on audio too, specifically in an audio trilogy produced by Big Finish in 2012: *City of Spires*, *The Wreck of the Titan*, and *Legend of the Cybermen*. The Sixth Doctor arrives in the Scottish highlands in 1780 and comes across Jamie who, posing as Black Donald, is the ruthless leader of rebels fighting the Redcoats. Jamie has no memory of the Doctor, but still agrees to travel with him. They discover they're in the Land of Fiction, now run by its Mistress, and become involved in a series of adventures which leads them to Zoe, who Jamie doesn't remember either. Zoe is able to release the Time Lord's block and later discovers that he's not the real Jamie at all, rather a work of fiction created by the Mistress of the Land. Fictional Jamie isn't keen when learning that the Doctor never returned to the real Jamie. It's eventually revealed that this Zoe is also a work of fiction, and the Mistress of the Land is actually the real Zoe. At the end of the adventure, fictional Jamie makes the Doctor promise that he will one day seek out the real Jamie. The actual Jamie enjoys another adventure with the Sixth Doctor when the Second Doctor switches places with this future incarnation and they, with Zoe, must stop an archaeologist from reactivating the Cyber-Planner in *Last of the Cybermen* (2015).

But what do we learn about Jamie in the Expanded Media while he's travelling with the Second Doctor? We find out out that Jamie was twenty-two when he joined the TARDIS (according to the 2013 audiobook, *Shadow of Death*); that he enjoys the smell of a new world (*The Story of Extinction*); and that Ben and Polly helped him understand much on their travels, including, as *The Mouthless Dead* details, how trains work.

Indeed, the friendships he makes with his travelling companions are added to. In 2011's *The Forbidden Time*, for example, we learn that Ben and Polly consider Jamie a 'little brother', with the trio often winding each other up: Ben jokes about Jamie fancying Jemma Morton in *The Morton Legacy*, and

Polly describes the Scotsman as 'brawny and reckless but lovely' in *The Three Companions*. Jamie is even brainwashed by the Master into thinking he's married to Polly in the 2019 audio, *The Home Guard*! Though he has an obvious attraction to Victoria on TV (and he admits to missing her in 2018 download, *The Last Day at Work*), audio stories highlight a sibling-like dynamic with Zoe too, with him saying she's a 'nice enough lassie' in *The Edge*, but also that her intelligence and confidence sometimes irritates him.

Finally, much later on, we meet a comic Tenth Doctor companion: Heather McCrimmon, a descendant of Jamie's...

Victoria Maud Waterfield, as the 1996 novel *Downtime* reveals, was born in 1852, meaning she was only fourteen during her travels with the Doctor. Her mother, Edith Rose, died in November 1863 when Victoria was eleven. And she was once photographed by Charles Dodgson, implying she was the physical model of his heroine Alice while writing under the pseudonym Lewis Carroll.

Her travels with the Doctor, despite being covered in many novels, short stories, and audios, remain largely unaffected, although a few authors are keen to explore the fallout of her father's death. She's understandably deeply affected by his passing, with her being haunted by hallucinations of him in the 2019 audio, *The Elysian Blade*. In 2010's *The Emperor of Eternity*, she reveals to Jamie that she's forgiven the Daleks for killing her father, and in the novel, *The Dark Path*, Koschei (later revealed as the Master) offers Victoria a chance to change the past by destroying Skaro, rewriting the events of *The Evil of the Daleks*. Faced with such a decision, she wants to do so, but fortunately the Doctor's very presence prevents this from happening. A further link to the Daleks comes in the comic strip, *The Bringer of Darkness* in a *Doctor Who Magazine Special* published in 1993. In this, Victoria is appalled at the way the Doctor destroys the Dalek force and realises she will leave the Doctor and Jamie soon.

Her life in the twentieth century, after leaving the Doctor, has been explored by several authors to varying degrees. In a prelude to the 1993 novel, *Birthright,* published in *Doctor Who Magazine* #203, the Seventh Doctor visits Victoria when she's with her adoptive parents (presumably the Harrises) and takes her back to 1868 to take care of her father's fortunes before returning her to twentieth century life. This comes back to haunt her in 1980 (in the video drama and novel, *Downtime*) when she's visited by a lawyer with her father's will. At this point in her life, she still feels displaced, despite a stint working at the British Museum. Haunted by the voice of her father, she returns to Det Sen in Tibet, and once again comes under the influence of the Great Intelligence – manipulating her through the body of her old friend, Professor Travers (from the television stories, *The Abominable Snowmen* and *The Web of Fear*). With her fortune, she founds New World University. She hires journalist Sarah Jane Smith, unaware that Sarah was once a companion of the Doctor, to investigate the cover up of the Intelligence's previous invasion attempt. This attracts the attention of retired Brigadier Lethbridge-Stewart, who once met Victoria during the last invasion attempt (*The Web of Fear*), and eventually helps UNIT to overpower the alien, Victoria escaping in the confusion. It's only later that Sarah realises who Victoria is, having been told about her by the Doctor in the TV story, *Pyramids of Mars*. At the end of *Downtime*, Victoria is visited by the Third Doctor who apologises for not checking up on her sooner. He gives her a letter of recommendation for UNIT, as well as asking her to travel with him again. She refuses, and refuses again when the same offer is made by the Fourth Doctor.

By 2008, she's married and expecting her first grandchild. She's never told any of her family about her adventures or that she was born in the nineteenth century (*The Great Space Elevator*).

Victoria, now over sixty years old, is reunited with the Doctor in the 2012 audio play, *Power Play*, albeit his sixth incarnation. She curiously knows nothing of regeneration and it takes both the Doctor and Peri to convince her that he is the same man she once knew. Not unlike Jo Grant, here Victoria is shown to be fighting for Earth in her own way, by protecting the environment.

*

Zoe alters little in the books and audios, though we do learn more about her time before and after her travels with the Doctor. Various tales disagree about when she was born: 2013's *The Dying Light* audio pinpoints 2063, while the 2004 novel, *The Indestructible Man*, suggests some time after 2084. Either way, *The Uncertainty Principle* (2012) digs into her harsh upbringing: at a young age, the Company forced her through mental and physical conditioning as part of the Elite Programme, but she found joy in memorising stories (presumably including the Karkus from *The Mind Robber* and, as revealed in *Echoes of Grey*, the work of Oscar Wilde).

Events that take place after the Time Lords return her to her own time, with only the knowledge of her initial adventure intact, are difficult to put into chronological order, especially as much is contradictory. For instance, in the 2003 short story, *The Tip of the Mind,* Zoe is seen to be working on Space Station XZ49 for UrtiCorp. Although she doesn't remember her time with the Doctor, she can access her memories unconsciously. The Third Doctor visits the station, believing that Zoe holds the secrets to the dematerialisation codes he needs to help him beat his Time Lord-imposed exile. Fearful of the damage such a recall may have, the Doctor knows he must tread carefully, but a spiteful supervisor working on the station intentionally brings Zoe into contact with the TARDIS. This opens the floodgates: she remembers everything, causing her to fall unconscious. Yet when she wakes, she's forgotten every single memory of the Doctor, permanently.

In the later *Companion Chronicles*, released by Big Finish, we are told in several stories that Zoe remembers her journeys as detailed dreams and often talks about them with a psychiatric counsellor. In *The Uncertainty Principle*, she's targeted specifically because of her buried memories by a race who wish to unlock them for their own nefarious reasons.

In 2012's *Legend of the Cybermen*, we discover that only a month after returning home, Zoe had somehow aged two years. From this, she deduces that she must have had further adventures with the Doctor that she couldn't recall. An attack by the Cybermen leads to surprising developments: they realise she has above average intelligence and could be a suitable Cyber-Planner (she'd been considered for normal cyber-conversion much earlier, in 2016's *The Isos Network*), but this unblocks all her memories of her travels. Only partly converted, Zoe takes control of the Cybermen's ship and takes them all to the Land of Fiction. She uses the Land's damaged control computer to create fictional characters to fight the Cybermen. She realises she needs the Doctor to truly defeat them and, unable to create an accurate fictional version, she draws the TARDIS into the Land. It materialises far off course, and Zoe creates a fictional Jamie to protect the Doctor (now in his sixth incarnation, one she'd also met in *Last of the Cybermen* when the Second and Sixth Doctors switched places) as he finds his way to the control centre. The three manage to defeat the Cybermen, and the Doctor returns her back to the Wheel, but her removal from the Land causes her to lose her memories of the Doctor once again.

Her damaged memories result in her feeling isolated and struggling to form meaningful relationships as she approaches her late fifties; the Company tracks her down, trying to obtain her knowledge of time travel. Their continued efforts (in the audio tetralogy, *Echoes of Grey*, *The Memory Cheats*, *The Uncertainty Principle*, and *Second Chances*) result in her again regaining her memories, albeit fleetingly; her defence attorney, Jen, promises to help her smooth out disparities in her mind.

The Second Doctor also has exclusive Expanded Universe companions: his comic grandchildren, John and Gillian. They travel with him into their teens, making no mention of his change of appearance. The role of grandfather in the First Doctor strips in *TV Comic* doesn't take with the new impish Second Doctor. John and Gillian are soon written out in #872, when he abruptly enrols them into Zebedee University to keep them safe from the Quarks (even though they had fought the Quarks several times already), before he visits Scotland and reunites with Jamie.

John returns for a cameo appearance in a later issue, now as Professor John Who. And slightly different versions of them are seen later, first in the 1994 novel, *Conundrum*, in which they're fictional characters from the Land of Fiction, travelling with a man called Dr Who. They meet the Seventh Doctor, who has never heard of them.

In a further and final appearance, they appear in the Eighth Doctor's dream in *The Land of Happy Endings* printed in the pages of *Doctor Who Magazine* #337.

The Third Doctor
Jon Pertwee

> '*A straight line may be the shortest distance between two points,
> but it is by no means the most interesting.*'
> The Doctor – *The Time Warrior*

For the first time in six years of *Doctor Who* history, the Doctor encountered a new type of companion. While the only carry over from the Second Doctor era was UNIT, led by Brigadier Lethbridge-Stewart – a familiar element to reassure the audience that it was still the same show – the Doctor's companions were purely contemporary characters, with not a single male voice amongst them. From a fully-fledged scientist, to a wannabe secret agent, all the way up to an investigative journalist, the Third Doctor was challenged by a very independent kind of companion.

Liz Shaw – Caroline John (*Spearhead from Space* to *Inferno*)

Sweet Caroline (Neil Diamond); *Disco Inferno* (The Trammps).

We meet Liz as she is being driven from Cambridge to London at the start of *Spearhead from Space*, much to her obvious irritation; she is far from impressed with her drafted position as scientific advisor for UNIT. She has important research programmes going on at Cambridge and is an admired member of the scientific community (known, for instance, by Professor Lennox in *The Ambassadors of Death*), an expert on meteorites with degrees in medicine, physics, and a dozen different subjects. She takes a while to warm to the Brigadier, initially finding him irritating and bemusing, not believing a word he says: 'An alien who travels through time and space in a Police Box?'

She takes pleasure in belittling him in front of General Scobie, UNIT's liaison with the regular army and, technically, the Brigadier's superior. When he questions the presence of the TARDIS in Liz's quickly assembled lab, she points out, much to the Brigadier's annoyance, 'It's not just a Police Box – it's a space ship.' Nonetheless, she gets on with the job at hand, and starts examining the space debris, which she realises aren't meteorites at all. But it takes the presence of the Doctor to reveal that they're actually containers for an alien intelligence called the Nestene Consciousness.

She finds the Doctor both amusing and charming, and soon sides with him in his dismissal of the Brigadier, smirking when the Doctor tells him to go away and let him and 'Miss Shaw' get on with their work. She finds the idea of the TARDIS incredulous, in particular the supposed size of the interior. When the Doctor states that he has an entire laboratory in there, she laughs at him like he is an imaginative child: 'Yes, I'm sure you have.'

Under the pretence of needing specialist equipment, found only in the TARDIS, to further study the Nestene container, Liz agrees to ask the Brigadier for the TARDIS key. The Brigadier pays her no attention and she cheerfully steals the key off his desk, reasoning that it is, after all, the Doctor's property. When the Doctor then attempts to escape in the TARDIS, leaving Liz behind, she refuses to accept the Brigadier's assertion that they will never see him again. When the Doctor does return, Liz berates him for tricking her. At the end of this first adventure together, the Doctor requests the continued assistance of Liz, who notably doesn't resist – a sign of her growing affection. That's not to say that this leaves her blind to his inaccuracies: she is quite willing to confront him if she thinks he's wrong, and is especially happy to mock him over Bessie, the Edwardian roadster the Doctor insists on as a part of his agreement to work for UNIT.

She's not above employing a bit of manipulation to get her own way either. When she wants to enter the caves beneath Wenley Moor during *Doctor Who and the Silurians*, she threatens to tell the Brigadier about the Doctor's planned expedition if he doesn't comply. The Doctor relents easily enough, suggesting he had every intention of letting Liz join him in the first place.

Similarly, she will not be ordered about. She's not a soldier and doesn't believe she's required to follow the Brigadier's orders or indeed the orders of Reegan when he holds her captive in *The Ambassadors of Death*.

Her scientific background is often used to great effect. While working with the Doctor in the lab at the Wenley Moor research centre, very little is said – the Doctor is confident in Liz's abilities to help find a cure for the Silurian virus. And when kidnapped by Reegan, she works with disgraced Cambridge professor, Lennox, to keep the alien ambassadors alive, and help him create a device to communicate with them. Once again, the Doctor demonstrates his faith in Liz when, once the ambassadors are safe, he leaves her and Professor Cornish with the task of returning them home.

Liz's doubts regarding the TARDIS continue in *The Ambassadors of Death*. When the Doctor accidentally shifts her fifteen seconds into the future, she is very sceptical, believing he simply vanished. We never see her inside the TARDIS, mainly because the console has been moved into his UNIT lab (but we're not exactly sure how). Later, it makes an appearance in a shed at the Inferno drilling station. By this point, Liz has learned enough about this alien technology to monitor the Doctor's experimental test flight and return him and the console. When the Doctor disappears completely (in reality to a fascist parallel Earth where he meets Section Leader Elizabeth Shaw), Liz remains in the shed, confident he'll somehow find his way back. When the Doctor does finally return, she cares for him, railing against the Brigadier's assertion that a medical doctor should look at him. She checks both his hearts – the first companion to know that he has two, knowledge she presumably gleans from the reports made by Doctor Lomax in *Spearhead from Space*. As the Doctor wakes, he is almost in a rage having seen the result of the Inferno project destroy one world. Everyone, including the Brigadier, thinks he's mad – but Liz believes him and sides with him against the Brigadier once more.

Liz remains unique among the Doctor's companions. She never travels in the TARDIS, be it to another world or another time. She is also one of the rare few who are able to hold their own against the Doctor's scientific knowledge: although never his equal, she knows her stuff. We last see Liz as she laughs at the Doctor, who after storming off in a sulk, accidentally lands the TARDIS in a rubbish dump. Before leaving he does, however, make a point of saying to her, 'I will miss *you*.'

In the next story, *Terror of the Autons*, we discover that Liz, for reasons unknown, has returned to her research at Cambridge, never to be seen again. However, in 2010, we finally learn that she's still alive and well, working on the UNIT moonbase (*The Sarah Jane Adventures: Death of the Doctor*).

Jo Grant, in most ways, was the complete opposite of Liz. She had no scientific background: though she took general science at A-level, she didn't pass. She was clumsy and often got herself into the kind of trouble that tested the Doctor's ability to conduct a safe rescue. In some ways, then, she was a continuation of the type of companion seen throughout the 1960s.

Josephine Grant/Jones – Katy Manning (*Terror of the Autons* to *The Green Death*, and *The Sarah Jane Adventures: Death of the Doctor*, plus *The Power of the Doctor*)

Devil Gate Drive (Suzi Quatro); *Wouldn't It Be Nice* (The Beach Boys).

After Liz leaves, the Doctor asks the Brigadier to find him a new assistant. Enter Jo: barely twenty years old, she's a recently trained civilian agent who's dumped on the Brigadier by her uncle, a high ranking civil servant pulling some strings to get her assigned to UNIT. Unsure what to do with her, and knowing the Doctor needs an assistant, the Brigadier reaches the obvious conclusion.

Initially the Doctor thinks Jo is a tea-lady, and is far from impressed when she botches his experimental work on the TARDIS' dematerialisation circuit. She introduces herself as his new assistant to which the Doctor can only respond, 'Oh no.' He later takes the Brigadier to task over this. The Brig is happy to 'sack' her but only if the Doctor tells her himself. In the event, the Doctor finds he can't do it, and so he has no choice but to welcome Jo.

Determined to prove herself, Jo goes off to investigate on her own. Her inexperience and clumsy nature means she becomes subject to the Master's incredible hypnotic powers. He sends her back to UNIT headquarters to eliminate the Doctor which she almost does, but is prevented in the nick of time by Sergeant Benton. The Doctor initially finds it difficult to bring Jo around, but eventually succeeds, leaving her traumatised by the thought of being forced to do something against her will. But this is not the last time she is hypnotised. In *The Curse of Peladon*, she's accidentally hypnotised by the Doctor when she stumbles in and prevents his attempts to placate the royal beast of Peladon, Aggedor. This susceptibility to hypnotism is finally overcome in *Frontier in Space* when the Master attempts to hypnotise her and she reveals she's learned mental techniques to prevent such a thing happening again.

Jo develops an early fondness for the Doctor, as seen when she mothers him while he's held at Stangmoor Prison (*The Mind of Evil*) but she doesn't really believe his stories of adventures in space and time, especially when he talks of historical figures in a matter-of-fact way. However, her fondness and loyalty is not absolute for a while. She is easily convinced that he's betrayed Earth and his friends when he appears to ally himself with the Master, leaving Earth to the mercy of Axos (*The Claws of Axos*). As it turns out, the Doctor is merely using the Master to get to Axos so he can trap the space vampire in a time loop for eternity. The Brigadier is certain the Doctor won't return, but Jo hopes he will, and she's validated moments later when the TARDIS does indeed come back – although not by the Doctor's choice, since the Time Lords wired the TARDIS to return to Earth to prevent him from escaping his exile. His need to travel is still stronger than his connections to his UNIT family.

Jo finally learns firsthand the truth of the Doctor's claims about time travel when she enters the TARDIS in *Colony in Space* and is whisked off five centuries into the future. She is, as were so many before her, amazed by the TARDIS' interior, but doesn't really believe they're heading to another world. As she thinks about it, fear kicks in, and she only tentatively steps out onto Uxarieus with the Doctor, not willing to stray too far from the relative safety of the TARDIS. Even though she's on an alien world, Jo's still not convinced they've travelled in time until Mary, a human colonist she befriends, tells her that the year is 2471.

Jo is a rather superstitious girl, despite the Doctor's attempts at making a scientist of her, and believes in both magic (*The Dæmons*) and ghosts (*Day of the Daleks*). She doesn't hold to the Doctor's thinking that science can explain everything, despite learning that the satanic creature feared by the inhabitants of Devil's End is actually an alien called a Dæmon and that black magic is just the remnant of the Dæmon's old science. Later, when confronted by 'ghosts', Jo discovers that they are merely echoes of future and past times or timelines crossing over – for instance, she and the Doctor see slightly older versions of themselves in the UNIT lab, a result of the Doctor's playing with the time mechanism of the TARDIS console.

She's quick to form opinions, often seeing things in black and white. She considers Anat's time travelling guerrilla force to be criminals (*Day of the Daleks*), even though the Doctor tries to make her see the truth. And she's easily taken in by the Controller's story of future Earth, despite the Doctor's assertion that twenty-second century Earth is not a free and prosperous society; as Jo later discovers first hand, humanity has, by then, been conquered and enslaved by the Daleks again.

With the Doctor convinced he has the TARDIS working, and Jo dolled up for a night on the town with Captain Mike Yates, the Time Lord persuades her to join him on a quick joyride. This takes them to Peladon *(The Curse of Peladon)* and she's introduced to King Peladon as Princess Josephine of TARDIS. She catches the king's eye, and is quite taken by him, until she realises he's looking for a political ally; she simply fails to see that he's clearly attracted to her. Once again, her simplistic view of life interferes with her thinking. She's not, however, above using his interest in her to get him to spare the Doctor's life. Over the course of her stay on Peladon, Jo warms to the king and freely admits she would love to remain behind with him, but she can't and is upset when it's time to leave. She starts to become used to TARDIS travel, and insists on accompanying the Doctor on his next mission for the Time Lords to the planet Solos in *The Mutants*, claiming that he needs her to look after him. While there, she discovers the state of the Earth Empire and how bad things have become on the planet by the thirtieth century. It's a key moment for Jo, awakening in her a concern for her home; the first seeds of her eventual departure from the Doctor are planted.

Although charmed by the Master while he's imprisoned in *The Sea Devils*, Jo never forgets what he's capable of, and is further insistent on going with the Doctor to Atlantis when he pursues the Master in *The Time Monster*. During this adventure, the Doctor appears to die, having been cast out into the time vortex; such is her grief that she doesn't care what the Master intends to do to her. Later, to defeat the Master, she is more willing than the Doctor to sacrifice them both and forces the Doctor to ram his TARDIS into the Master's. As a result of this 'time ram', they end up in a netherworld created by the Chronovore, Kronos, somewhere Jo believes to be heaven – a place she considers groovy. This isn't the last time she believes they are in heaven: when she and the Doctor are later transported to Omega's anti-matter world, she believes it to be the afterlife too.

In *The Three Doctors*, she's initially confused by the idea of more than one Doctor, until Benton explains who the Second Doctor is, and she learns about regeneration. She's also infuriated by the Doctors' inability to work together, and when they're faced with the might of Omega's will, she convinces them that, as two Time Lords, they should be able to combat him. At the end of this adventure, in thanks for saving them, the Time Lords finally lift the Doctor's exile. Seeing the delight on the Doctor's face, Jo worries he'll leave her behind. Of course, he tells her otherwise and promises her a trip to Metebelis Three to break in the new dematerialisation circuit.

They never quite make it there, however, instead ending up in the Miniscope – a kind of intergalactic zoo (*Carnival of Monsters*) containing a variety of life forms including humans, Ogrons, and Cybermen. By this point, she's becoming an old hand at time travel and takes most things in her stride, but upon meeting the horrifying Drashigs, a new fear is born. It's a terror that the Master attempts to use against her with his fear-inducing device in *Frontier in Space*; other fears that manifest include a Sea Devil and a Mutt, but Jo is able to combat the device, impressing the Master no end.

Such is her experience with the Doctor that she expects trouble when the Draconian ship docks with the Earth ship that the TARDIS has landed on, despite knowing nothing about the political cold-war happening between the two planets. Her instincts serve her well. She ends up stranded on Earth, a 'guest' of the Earth Empire while they decide what to do with her; meanwhile, the Doctor is carted off to the Lunar penal colony. She's rescued by an unlikely ally, the Master, but she's not afraid to stand up to him, even though she needs his help to get off Earth and rescue the Doctor. It's a strange alliance, but she's not so easily charmed this time. At the end of *Frontier in Space*, the Doctor is gravely wounded, and Jo helps him into the TARDIS. Her concern for him is so considerable that she appears to have forgotten that he sent a message to the Time Lords to guide the TARDIS to the secret Dalek base on Spiridon (*Planet of the Daleks*).

While on Spiridon, Jo meets a group of Thals, and bonds with one in particular, Latep, with whom a slight romance develops. After the Dalek army is destroyed, Latep asks the Doctor's permission for Jo to go back to Skaro with him. The Doctor first wants to check 'if that's what she wants', but Jo declines Latep's offer, preferring to return home where she has her own life, a life she cannot leave behind.

This decision is fortunate: when she's back on Earth, she meets a young activist, Professor Clifford Jones (*The Green Death*). Jo has been following the exploits of Global Chemicals in the Welsh mining town of Llanfairfach. In particular, she's interested in the happenings at the Wholeweal Community run by Cliff Jones, who is creating a new fungus-based protein. Jones reminds her of a younger Doctor and she's determined to go to Llanfairfach and assist them against Global Chemicals (even threatening to resign from UNIT in the face of the Brigadier's apparent opposition to her trip). The Doctor tries to entice her to come with him to Metebelis Three, certain he can get there this time, but Jo is so fired up about Jones' work that she's not really listening. She heads to Llanfairfach with the Brigadier, and the Doctor decides to take a trip to Metebelis Three alone. Before he does, he ponders the truth of the situation – 'the fledgling flies the coup'. He knows, even before she does, that Jo is going to be leaving him soon.

Jo's first meeting with Cliff is not the most auspicious, and she ends up messing up his experiments through a mix of absent-mindedness and clumsiness – much like when she first met the Doctor. She's quickly charmed by Jones and a very strong romance develops between them: she simply can't get enough of his company, and won't stop talking about him. She's completely enthralled by his stories of the Amazon and confesses to him that, when she was first assigned to the Doctor, she expected to be holding test tubes and telling the Doctor how brilliant he was – but it didn't quite work out like that. In some ways, she treats Jones much like she does the Doctor. Cliff insists she does nothing, just stay safe at the Nuthutch, but she instead goes to collect samples of the giant maggots for him to run tests on, seemingly keen to impress him. He's furious, but still goes after her and comes to her rescue when she's trapped by several of the huge creatures. Later, when Jones is infected by the chemical waste, Jo maintains a vigil, and is still there when he finally recovers. He kisses her hand in appreciation.

When it's time to return to UNIT, Jo explains to the Doctor that she's not going with him, but is staying with Jones to explore the Amazon. Jones is very happy about this and reveals they will probably get married along the way – this comes as a surprise to Jo, but she readily accepts the offer. Before leaving, Jo and the Doctor talk one last time, and she says she hopes to see him again. He tells her to save him a piece of wedding cake, suggesting that they will indeed meet again. He gives her a blue crystal from Metebelis Three as a wedding gift, and leaves, heartbroken. Jo is clearly sad to be leaving the Doctor, but also overjoyed about her forthcoming adventures with Cliff Jones.

Many months later, in *Planet of the Spiders*, the Doctor hears from Jo when she returns the blue crystal to him in the post as it was offending the natives of the Amazon. In *The Sarah Jane Adventures* story, *Death of the Doctor*, Jo reveals that, after she returned from the Amazon, she called UNIT to speak to the Doctor, only to learn that he had left and never returned (which suggests this is some point after *Terror of the Zygons*). Jo continues to wait for him, but he seemingly never returns to see her.

We discover in the interceding thirty-plus years that Jo and her husband continue a life of political and environmental activism; she lives in huts, climbs trees, tears down barricades, flies kites on Mount Kilimanjaro, and sails down the Yangtze River in a tea chest. At one point, she even chains herself to Robert Mugabe. By 2010, she and Cliff have seven children and twelve grandchildren, with a thirteenth on the way.

In *Death of the Doctor*, when she's invited to the Doctor's funeral at a UNIT installation at the base of Mount Snowdon, she brings one of her grandchildren, Santiago. They arrive late, interrupting the service, and much like her initial meeting with the Doctor, the first thing Jo Jones does is trip up, smashing a vase of flowers she brought with her to commemorate the Doctor.

Despite the sombre atmosphere, she's thrilled to meet the vulture-looking Claw Shansheeth, having not seen any aliens in such a long time. At the funeral, she finally meets Sarah Jane Smith, who joins the Doctor shortly after Jo leaves. They have both heard of each other; Sarah, no doubt, from the Doctor, and Jo presumably from someone at UNIT. She's surprised to learn that Sarah has met the Doctor again and is a little hurt, explaining that the Doctor never returned for her. Sarah's explanation that it was an accident the first time only makes Jo sadder: discovering that Sarah and the Doctor have seen each other several times since 2007 obviously affects her. Neither is willing to accept the Doctor's death, believing that, should the Doctor die, somehow they would just *know*. As it turns out, the Doctor is indeed alive, and Jo is finally reunited with a very young looking Eleventh Doctor – who she thinks looks like a baby. The Doctor responds that it is odd for him too: when he last saw Jo, she had been either twenty-two or twenty-three and now she looks as if someone has baked her.

On an alien planet, the Wasteland of the Crimson Heart, Jo sits watching the banter between the Doctor and Sarah. This, in her eyes, only serves to emphasise how useless she must've been for him to never have returned. She's also saddened to hear that the Doctor now travels with a married couple since she only left him because she got engaged. They have a heart to heart, and she asks him if she was stupid since he never came back to see her: 'I thought... he wouldn't just leave, not forever. Not *me*. I've waited my whole silly life.' The Doctor admits he couldn't keep up with Jo's life; she moved about so much that he could never hope to find her, but before his last regeneration, he had tracked her down, and watched her entire life unfold. Their peace made, she visits the TARDIS one last time (she loves the new look console room and, despite numerous modifications, notes that it still smells the same). Jo admits she is very tempted to carry on travelling with him, but doesn't want him getting into trouble with the Time Lords (not aware that the Time Lords are all dead at that point). Finally able to say goodbye, Jo returns to her life of activism, but not before suggesting to Sarah that she try and find herself a fella.

We see Jo again in *The Power of the Doctor* when numerous companions meet up to discuss the Doctor. After Melanie Bush asks how many incarnations of the Doctor there are, Jo, having seen the first three Doctors, plus the Eleventh, jokes that they're 'going to be here quite some time'...

If Jo was an ideologist, then Sarah was a realist. Jo, although independent, is very much a girl with an eye for the men and developed a familial relationship with the Doctor. He was the affectionate uncle, she the doting niece. With the arrival of Sarah, a new shift occurred. For the first time since Jamie, the Doctor made a new friend – someone who became his best friend.

Sarah Jane Smith – Elisabeth Sladen (*The Time Warrior* to *The Hand of Fear*, *K9 & Company: A Girl's Best Friend*, *The Five Doctors*, *School Reunion* and *The Sarah Jane Adventures*, plus *The Stolen Earth* to *Journey's End* and *The End of Time*)

Paperback Writer (The Beatles); *The Best* (Tina Turner).

It is important to note from the outset that, certainly according to Sarah, her full name is *not* 'Sarah Jane'. The only time she is seen to use 'Jane' is when introducing herself as 'Sarah Jane Smith'. We learn that her family seem to always call her 'Sarah Jane', including her Aunt Lavinia (*K9 & Company: A Girl's Best Friend*) and her parents (*SJA: The Temptation of Sarah Jane Smith*), which might suggest why she later calls herself 'Sarah' – a sign of her independence or maybe to distance herself from her loss. The Doctor occasionally refers to her as 'Sarah Jane', a term of affection from him (used, most notably, moments before he 'dies' in his lab at the end of *Planet of the Spiders*). Once her time with the Doctor comes to an end, Sarah takes to calling herself 'Sarah Jane', and doesn't allow anyone, except the Doctor, to call her 'Sarah'. It seems that 'Sarah' is a name that she associates with him and him alone. It says much about her mindset, and the influence he has on her life.

Sarah was just a baby when her parents died; she was raised by her father's sister, Lavinia Smith. When Sarah meets the Doctor, she is only twenty-three-years-old (it is later revealed that she was born in 1951, dating *The Time Warrior*, at least in regards to her, as 1974). However, in *Pyramids of Mars*, she states categorically that she comes from 1980, suggesting that she travels with the Doctor for over six years.

Sarah is a journalist working for *The Metropolitan* magazine, investigating the strange disappearance of scientists. She poses as her Aunt Lavinia to get into the UNIT-controlled research base, where she meets the Doctor (calling himself 'Doctor John Smith'), who is still working for UNIT – his friendship with the Brigadier the only thing keeping him on Earth. He finds her story amusing, concluding that 'Miss Lavinia Smith' must have been only five when she wrote a paper on the teleological response of a virus. Sarah, accepting she's been found out, admits the truth, and introduces herself. A strong believer in Women's Lib, Sarah is incensed when the Doctor promises not to give her away as long as she makes the coffee. Sarah initially finds the Doctor patronising and believes him to be a spy. She doesn't trust him, quite certain that he is hiding something. It's only when she stows away in the TARDIS that she discovers the truth. She's transported to Medieval England and finds her way to Irongron's castle. Sarah refuses to accept the authenticity of her surroundings – convinced that she has walked into some kind of pageant or film set – and will take none of Irongron's bile.

When confronted by Linx, a Sontaran warrior who determines that she's from the future, Sarah begins to accept the truth. Sarah is rescued by Hal the Archer who takes her to the castle of the Earl of Wessex. She impresses all of them with her fire and her plan to kidnap the Doctor, who she now believes is working for Irongron. Once back at Wessex castle, the Doctor explains the truth (that Linx is kidnapping scientists from the future to fix his crashed spaceship) and Sarah admits she *might* have been wrong. She's bewildered when the Doctor explains he is a Time Lord and his people are keen to stamp out unlicensed time travel ('intergalactic ticket inspectors'). Before leaving the Middle Ages, the Doctor tells Hal that he's not a magician at all, but Sarah's no longer sure of this.

En route back to Earth, Sarah gets herself a new haircut, presumably in the TARDIS since it's stated clearly that they have only just left the Middle Ages. Faced with a largely deserted London in *Invasion of the Dinosaurs*, she's not entirely convinced that they have returned to her own time. After being arrested for looting, they have their mug-shots taken. Sarah is amused by the Doctor's frivolity and soon joins him in making light of the situation. It's the first real sign of affection she shows for him. To help discover the truth behind the strange appearances of dinosaurs in contemporary London, Sarah makes use of her own journalistic contacts, despite the danger. She has great interpersonal skills and twists people around her little finger with ease, notably Yates, Benton, and General Finch, with a mix of easy charm and forthright cheek. She does, however, have a tendency to allow her enthusiasm to blind her to what's staring her straight in the face – like Sir Charles' duplicity. The idea that the world is a bad place is an alien concept to her; she is a constant optimist and loves the chaos of life. Sarah is quite happy to remain on Earth, but the Doctor entices her with tales of Florana and so the stowaway becomes a chosen companion.

But they never make it to Florana, even though Sarah has her water wings ready ('I can sink anywhere'). Instead, the TARDIS lands on the barren plains of Exxilon and she encounters her second alien species (*Death to the Daleks*). At first, she's understandably both scared and untrusting of them; that is, until she meets Bellal, a friendly Exxilon who wins her over with his gentleness. Conversely, she's less fearful of the Daleks, thinking them mere machines, before the Doctor shows her otherwise. Here, we also learn that Sarah's natural defence mechanism for dealing with her fear is to make jokes. During their time on Exxilon, the Doctor and Sarah draw closer together, a consequence of his determination to save her from being sacrificed by the high priests. When the Doctor realises he must go to the ancient Exxilon city (from which he may not return), the two travellers share a tender moment – more tender perhaps because he is still mourning the loss of Jo.

Sarah's gradual acceptance of aliens continues when they land on Peladon and she meets a whole host of creatures, most notably the Martian Ice Warriors and Alpha Centauri, whom she initially finds repellent until she, once again, learns that not all aliens mean her harm. It's in *The Monster of Peladon* that Sarah once again demonstrates her strong sense of self when, on seeing how Queen Thalira is constantly undermined by the men around her, she teaches her about Women's Lib and how she needs to stand up for herself. Similarly on Peladon, Sarah is confronted by the idea that her travels are far from safe when it appears the Doctor has died. She finds it very hard to accept, not because she is stranded on an alien world, but because of her emotional attachment to the Doctor. She has to carry on without him, working with the Ice Warriors and making the most of a bad situation. She cries over the Doctor's supposedly dead body... which wakes him up. This is not the last time she thinks him dead.

Although travelling with the Doctor, Sarah still manages to hold down her job whenever they return to Earth, and is often found to be working on a story. She develops a very good friendship with Mike Yates, mostly off screen; so much so that he calls her in to help when he suspects dodgy goings-on at the monastery he lives in following his dismissal from UNIT after the events of *Invasion of the Dinosaurs*.

On Metebelis Three, in *Planet of the Spiders*, she once more faces the Doctor's apparent death. She's also convinced that he can help the human colonists of Metebelis Three (the 'two-legs') against the giant spiders that rule there; she doesn't know how, but she has complete faith in the Doctor. She is at the monastery when K'anpo, an old Time Lord hermit and former guru of the Doctor's regenerates – an event that helps her to deal with what happens to the Doctor.

For what nonetheless must've been a gut-wrenching three weeks, the Doctor goes missing, having returned to Metebelis Three to face his biggest fear. Sarah continues to return to UNIT HQ, but despite the Brigadier's reassurances, she succumbs to the belief that the Doctor has died and will not return. Just then, the TARDIS materialises and the Doctor staggers out – his body all but destroyed by the radiation of the cave in which the Great One of the spiders resides. Sarah attempts to comfort him, but her ministrations prove fruitless. Before he dies in her arms, he feels her tears fall on his face: 'A tear, Sarah Jane? No, don't cry. Where there's life, there's...' he says, giving up his last breath, repeating a phrase he previously spoke to her on Peladon. Sarah is devastated, but barely has time to breathe before K'anpo arrives, floating mid-air in the Doctor's lab. Things become too much for her, but she accepts the hope K'anpo brings and watches in amazement as the Doctor regenerates...

The Third Doctor
Expanded Universe

The writers of the Expanded Universe generally regard the Third Doctor's era with a lot of affection; they just don't want to tamper with it. Most stories hold true to the television series, but unfortunately when they do add to them, they often find themselves contradicted by later television episodes – in large due to *The Sarah Jane Adventures*, which frequently reveals new information about UNIT-related stories.

On TV, Liz never travels in the TARDIS. She always seems a little disdainful of the notion that it could do even half the things the Doctor claims. However, one of the most common things in the other media is to see Liz travel in space and time. Most notably, in *The Wages of Sin*, she joins the Doctor and Jo Grant on an adventure in the past, solving the mystery of Rasputin, and later, in *The Sentinels of the New Dawn*, she travels to the year 2014. It's suggested that she even travels alone with the Fourth Doctor for an unknown length of time: *Down to Earth* (*Doctor Who Magazine* #210) sees the Fourth Doctor visit to apologise for having never said goodbye to her – in an attempt to make amends, he offers to take her off in the TARDIS, an offer she accepts.

Liz's departure is also the topic of many stories, with several conflicting reasons behind it. In *Reconnaissance*, a short story published in the 1994 *Doctor Who Yearbook*, Liz is visited by the Master who then hypnotises her to discover all she knows about the Doctor. Once he leaves, she's left with no memory of his visit and decides it's time to resign from UNIT. But in the previous *Yearbook*'s *Country of the Blind*, she's offered a position at CERN, a research centre. In that story, unable to get to the Doctor to say goodbye, she quietly slips away. Several years later, in the 1996 novel, *The Scales of Injustice,* it's after another disastrous encounter with the Silurians that Liz decides she's had enough and quits. These accounts, on the surface, seem to be contradictory, although in 1997's *The Devil Goblins from Neptune,* Liz mentions that she's 'always leaving', which suggests that her involvement with UNIT is not as straightforward as it seems.

Some audio stories suggest Liz is pretty indecisive about leaving: facing up to the Cybermen in 2007's *The Blue Tooth* makes her conclude that she should resign; realising what she offered the organisation made her reevaluate this decision in 2012's *Binary.* *The Hidden Realm* (2016) reveals that she spent her time at UNIT further compiling a list of mysterious happenings in Great Britain across half a century.

Liz's Expanded Universe life scores a first. With the advent of the short-lived *PROBE* series of videos produced in the mid-1990s, Liz becomes the first companion to star in her own live action spin-off series, long before *Torchwood, The Sarah Jane Adventures,* and *K9.* In this series, Liz heads an organisation called the Preternatural Research Bureau (or PROBE), created at her behest to investigate paranormal activity. Dealing with issues like psychiatric trauma and possession, this series shows us a harder edge to Liz than ever seen in *Doctor Who,* as well introducing her new habit of smoking pipes (something she's also seen to do in the novel, *Who Killed Kennedy?*).

In *Shadow of the Past,* an older Liz is aware of other versions of the Doctor, knowledge she likely gets from the short story, *Girls' Night In* (1992's *Doctor Who Magazine Holiday Special*), in which she responds to an advert placed in *Time Out* by Jo and Sarah. She enjoys a night of wine and shared memories alongside future companions, Tegan and Ace. Alternatively, she could've learned about the Doctor's other faces from the Brigadier or from River Song, who Lethbridge-Stewart drafts in as a Scientific Advisor (much to Liz's annoyance) when the Doctor is indisposed in the 2021 box set, *The Diary of River Song: New Recruit.*

Liz's ultimate end is a mystery in the Expanded Universe: in the novel, *Eternity Weeps*, Liz dies on the moon in 2003 from Agent Yellow, a biological weapon; yet in the audio story, *Faithful Friends*, Liz attends a Christmas meal arranged for the Brigadier at some point after his wife, Doris, dies in 2012. She's also there are Sarah Jane Smith's memorial, likely in the early- to mid-2020s. What we do know, from a 2007 short story, *Fable Fusion*, and the 2012 audio, *The Last Post*, is that Liz is survived by two children, and at least one granddaughter, Elizabeth Holub, who assists the Seventh Doctor in Prague, 2050.

A few background details are also revealed. She was born in 1943, in Stoke-on-Trent, to Reuben and Dame Emily Shaw, and had one sister, Lucy, who by the time of Liz's association with the Doctor, had two daughters. Emily, a former ambulance driver during World War II, even met and briefly travelled with the Fourth Doctor and Leela in 2015's *The Cloisters of Terror*.

In *The Sarah Jane Adventures* story, *Death of the Doctor*, the Eleventh Doctor reveals that he last saw Jo Grant (i.e. in *The Green Death*) when she was twenty-one or twenty-two. The Expanded Universe instantly contradicts this. *The Doll of Death* states that she was eighteen when she started working for UNIT, and in *Carpenter/Butterfly/Baronet*, we're told that she was born in 1951, suggesting that *Terror of the Autons* is set in 1969. The 2015 audio, *The Other Woman*, pinpoints her year of birth as 1961 instead. Not only is her birth covered in the Expanded Universe, but so is her death; she dies in a house fire in 2028, at the age of seventy-seven. At this point, she is still a Jones, even though in the novel, *Genocide*, she's going under the name of Grant again. It's heavily implied that, by this point in the 1990s, she's no longer married to Cliff, although they did have a son, Matthew, and a daughter, Lisa (*Once upon a Time Machine*). As we've come to expect, the Expanded Universe gives contradictory evidence. In *The Doll of Death*, she's still happily married in the 2000s. Indeed, this is the likelier outcome: in *Death of the Doctor*, she speaks happily of Cliff, explaining that he's picketing an oil rig in the Ascension Islands, and that they have seven children and thirteen grandchildren together, including Rio de Janeiro (*Farewell, Sarah Jane*) and Santiago, their first-born grandson, according to 2022's *The Turn of the Tides*, in which Jo is reunited with Rani Chandra. Jo and Cliff are also seen together in 2019's promotional mini-episode, *Hello Boys!*, in which they return to Llanfairfach (something Jo does again in the 2019 *Torchwood* audio, *The Green Life*), and the following year's *Return of the Autons*. However, he's passed away by the time of 2023's follow-up, *Defenders of Earth*, in which Jo witnesses the birth of a Sea Devil and vows to protect all life on the planet as part of Cliff's legacy. In *Supernature*, part of the same year's box set, *The Return of Jo Jones*, it's established that the pair were married for fifty years before he lost his life helping civilians after a landslide in Nepal.

In terms of her time with the Doctor, several writers attempt to explain threads that weren't followed up on TV; for instance, the never-quite-romance with Captain Mike Yates. In *The Curse of Peladon*, Jo's all set to go on a date with Yates, but it never comes about and isn't mentioned again. However, in the novel, *The Speed of Flight* it's revealed that Sergeant Benton and Corporal Bell set up a blind date for Jo and Mike. The Doctor gets wind of this and offers to take them both to the planet Karfel (which also solves the mystery brought about in the TV story, *Timelash*, where we're told that the Third Doctor once visited there with Jo and a mysterious second person – even though he never travelled with Jo and another person on TV). In the short story, *The Switching*, Yates asks Jo out on a date after receiving what he believes to be the Doctor's blessing – he doesn't know that it is, in fact, the Master who's switched bodies with the Doctor.

One further, unusual bit of continuity is apparently cleared up in *The Touch of Nurzah*: Jo watches the Doctor undergo an almost-regeneration and sees a glimpse of his fourth incarnation. She later explains to the Doctor that he would become all 'teeth and curls', a phrase the Third Doctor says in *The Five Doctors* when he later meets Sarah who mentions his future face.

The social conscience that leads her to leave the Doctor is explored in the short story, *Come Friendly Bombs…*, as Jo requests to participate in the original CND (Campaign for Nuclear Disarmament) march of the 1960s, so she can learn why it's so important that such weapons are banned.

But UNIT isn't done with Jo just yet, even after she officially leaves. In 2017's *Tidal Wave*, Kate Stewart enlists Jo to investigate Project Charybdis, an experimental tidal energy generator, alongside Petronella Osgood. Jo is perfectly placed for this mission as she manages to convince the Sea Devils to go back into hibernation until they can reach a peaceful accord (and she shows off her lock-picking skills, freeing herself and Osgood from the project's base before it explodes). Kate puts considerable trust in Jo, putting her, Benton, and Yates in charge of the situation with the Sea Devils and Silurians in *United*, part of the same audio set. Jo clearly made friends in this new era of UNIT too: at the start of *The Sacrifice of Jo Grant* (a story which also sees Jo reunited with the Third Doctor when she's sent back in time to the 1970s), she's on holiday with Osgood, a partnership which is further rewarded when Petronella and Kate find instructions from the Doctor on how to save Jo from being trapped forever in the Time Vortex.

On television, Sarah spends only a season with the Third Doctor, so it's little surprise that her time with him doesn't take up a wealth of material in the Expanded Universe.

The biggest curiosity of Sarah's Expanded Universe is that she meets the Brigadier for the first time in a story that contradicts their first meeting on television. The radio play, *The Paradise of Death*, was written by the producer of the Third Doctor's television run, Barry Letts, but it just adds to the confusion. While she interviews the Doctor for *The Metropolitan*, she's sceptical of his stories about travelling in the TARDIS, despite having experienced such travel herself – a fact the Doctor himself draws her attention to.

It's established in stories set after Sarah leaves the Doctor that she ends up writing books. The first instance of this is in another radio play, *The Ghosts of N-Space*, when an exasperated Sarah decides that a career as a best-selling author is better than that of a hardworking journalist, but her attempts at writing don't work out too well for her. She's joined in both these stories by Jeremy Fitzoliver, an inexperienced office boy from her paper. In many ways, their relationship is a template for what will later develop between Sarah and Harry Sullivan (though certainly frostier).

In the short story *Separation Day*, the Doctor reminisces to Sarah about Jo, completely oblivious to how it makes Sarah feel. In a nice echo, we see shades of these feelings many years later when Sarah and Jo finally meet in *Death of the Doctor*. Sarah even comments that she has heard so much about Jo. *Defenders of Earth!* reveals that Sarah left Jo her sonic lipstick after she passed away.

Playtime, a short story from 1992's *Doctor Who Magazine Holiday Special*, reveals that a very young Sarah snuck into a junkyard in Totter's Lane in 1963, where she not only saw the TARDIS but Susan as well (who, of course, she didn't recognise at the time). Interesting as it is, it's hard to reconcile this moment with all that's later established in *The Sarah Jane Adventures* – she would've been twelve in 1963. Another thing mentioned in a novel that's later contradicted is her father's locality: in *Island of Death*, he's from Liverpool, yet when he appears in *The Temptation of Sarah Jane Smith* he's clearly a Londoner.

One thing from the TV show that's not contradicted is the Doctor's attempt to get Sarah to Florana in *Death to the Daleks*. In the short story, *Neptune*, the Doctor is still attempting to fulfil this promise; so too in the 2022 audio, *The House That Hoxx Built*. They make it there in the year 5968, in the short story, *The Hungry Bomb*.

Additional stories are typically slotted in just after *Invasion of the Dinosaurs* and either side of *The Monster of Peladon*, often foreshadowing events, like Sarah's meeting the Cybermen (in the 2021 audio download, *Scourge of the Cybermen*); adventures with Harry Sullivan (the following year's *Kaleidoscope*); and the

TARDIS being able to tow a planet, something which the Third Doctor, in 2021's *The Gulf*, tells Sarah she might be lucky enough to see one day (and she does, in *Journey's End*).

A major alteration does occur during Sarah's time with the Third Doctor in the Expanded Universe, although in this instance it's intentional. In the two-part novel, *Interference*, Sarah witnesses the Doctor getting shot and, upon dragging him into the TARDIS, she can do nothing but watch him regenerate. Many years later, Sarah's memory of the events on Dust is confused: she remembers the Doctor both regenerating and dying. In the event, it's a deliberate alteration of the timeline by the Faction Paradox, which is ultimately restored in the novel, *The Ancestor Cell*.

The Third Doctor has a few one-off companions in various *Doctor Who Annuals* and *TV Comic* issues, and even, in the 1990s, in a stage show (Jason and Crystal became bona-fide Expanded Universe companions via the Big Finish adaptation of *The Ultimate Adventure* and its sequel, *Beyond the Ultimate Adventure*).

The first non-TV companion to remain with the Third Doctor for more than one story is a young boy called Arnold. Introduced in *TV Comic*, he remains with the Doctor for fifteen issues (#1133-1148), i.e. just over two stories. On a world run by children, the Doctor is sentenced to imprisonment, and one of his jailers, Arnold, is convinced to free him and help him overthrow the regime of Oswald (*Children of the Evil Eye*). He joins the Doctor, having a further adventure against the evil Spidrons in *Nova* before he's returned home at the start of *The Amateur*.

Jeremy Fitzoliver is introduced in the 1993 radio play, *The Paradise of Death*. Although never intended as a companion, his later appearances in two anthologies, *Short Trips: Repercussions* and *Short Trips: The Solar System*, show him travelling alone with the Doctor. Jeremy's an office boy at *The Metropolitan*, the paper at which Sarah works, and is sent along as a photographer at the grand opening of Spaceworld on Hampstead Heath. It's clear that Sarah doesn't think terribly highly of Jeremy, who's definitely *not* a photographer; Clorinda, Sarah's editor, sends Jeremy as a kind of joke. Poor Jeremy is the comic relief in both radio appearances, only accidentally joining the Doctor, Sarah, and the Brigadier on Parakon: he carries some equipment onto the TARDIS and the Doctor forgets he's on board. Jeremy is always polite, constantly amazed and horrified by the events unfolding around him, and, like Harry, likes to play the role of gentleman for Sarah – not something she appreciates, especially since she proves herself braver than him. His mettle is sufficiently stronger when he returns in 1996's *The Ghosts of N-Space,* although he's still a 'wimp and a wally. And if you can think of anything else that begins with a "w", then you're probably that, too,' as Sarah puts it. Nonetheless, he's keen to prove himself and smuggles aboard a boat owned by the gangster Max Vilmio; when found out, and faced with physical violence, he tries to stand up to Vilmio, with horrible results.

In the short stories, *The Dead Man's Story* (2004) and *Sedna* (2006), Jeremy is clumsy and adept at getting himself into trouble. At this point, he's travelling alone with the Doctor, although perhaps not at the Doctor's request. In the former, Jeremy's clumsiness leads to an explosion that throws an innocent bystander, Jake Morgan, into an altered state of being – essentially turning him into a ghost. In the latter, after landing on Sedna and meeting the Siccati, a race of intergalactic artists, it's Jeremy's ineptitude at pottery that saves the day. The Siccati are more impressed by Jeremy's imperfect vase than the Doctor's amazing painting, a fact the Doctor is less than impressed with. Jeremy also finds a way to end the war and save Sedna and Neptune.

Jeremy returns one final time, in the novel, *Instruments of Darkness,* as the amnesiac villain, John Doe. During the intervening years, Jeremy's memory was wiped after he messed with the Doctor's IRIS machine (seen on TV in *Planet of the Spiders*), and he's later used psychically by a race of aliens. Unfortunately, 'John Doe' is killed before he comes face-to-face with the Sixth Doctor, and so any chance of redemption is lost.

The Fourth Doctor
Tom Baker

*'I have the advantage of being slightly ahead of you.
Sometimes behind you, but normally ahead of you.'*
The Doctor – *Pyramids of Mars*

Sarah Jane Smith – Elisabeth Sladen – Continued… (*The Time Warrior* to *The Hand of Fear*, *K9 & Company: A Girl's Best Friend*, *The Five Doctors*, *School Reunion* and *The Sarah Jane Adventures*, plus *The Stolen Earth* to *Journey's End* and *The End of Time*)

Although clearly worried about the Doctor (*Robot*), who has a bout of rambling madness, Sarah keeps herself busy with work, visiting UNIT from time to time to check up on him. The Brigadier finds himself confiding top secret information in Sarah, simply because the Doctor is not around to be told. After meeting the new UNIT doctor, Harry Sullivan, who's assigned to look after the Doctor, she decides he's a bit old fashioned, a view that continues when he joins Sarah and the Doctor on their travels – she doesn't care for his insistence on calling her 'old girl'. When the Doctor attempts to abruptly leave, it's Sarah who convinces him to stay and assist the Brigadier, which he does while Sarah continues her own avenue of investigation with the Think Tank organisation – actually a front for the Scientific Reform Society. When confronted with the experimental robot, K1, Sarah's experiences with the Doctor prove valuable as she entertains the notion that the robot is alive. Her compassion for it puzzles those around her, especially Miss Winters, but these concerns are proven well-placed when it's forced into performing functions against its prime directive – to serve and never harm humanity –

and as a result kidnaps Sarah. After the robot is killed because of the risk it poses to humanity, Sarah is very glum and isn't even cheered up by the idea of travelling in the TARDIS. That is, until the Doctor rants about the Brigadier's insistence that he talk to the Cabinet and write seventeen reports in triplicate: she points out that he's being childish and he agrees, 'There's no point in being grown up if you can't be childish sometimes.' After he offers her a jelly baby, Sarah agrees to join him again (she rather likes this new incarnation of the Doctor), but she fails to stop the Doctor teasing Harry, who doesn't believe a word about the TARDIS. She does, however, sympathise with Harry when the TARDIS arrives on Space Station Nerva in *The Ark in Space*; he finds it hard to understand the inside dimensions and the fact that the TARDIS has moved: 'That's how I felt the first time.'

Despite her objections to Harry's old fashioned way, she strikes up a very easy friendship with him during their few travels together, and develops a lot of affection for him, clearly loving the way he fusses over her. Throughout their journeys, there's a lot of gentle ribbing and banter between them – indeed, decades later, her affection for Harry is confirmed when she explains that she always loved him, albeit not in a romantic way (*The Sarah Jane Adventures: Death of the Doctor*). After nearly suffocating on Nerva, she's accidentally placed in suspended animation for a short time and upon her revival, she has an unusually strong and adverse reaction to the Wirrn. And when she gets stuck in a conduit, she exhibits the symptoms of claustrophobia. It's only the Doctor's goading that forces Sarah to drag herself out. She calls the Doctor a brute for being horrible to her, but soon realises she has been had and jokingly hits him.

Later, on a war-torn Skaro in *Genesis of the Daleks*, Sarah is the first person to see Davros, secretly observing him test a Dalek gun. Whilst a captive of the Kaleds, she learns she's being exposed to distronic toxaemia – which will kill her and her fellow captives after only a few hours. She organises an escape, which ultimately fails, but it does reveal her fear of heights (something we see again in *The Five Doctors*) and her suffering of vertigo, which is also exploited by Styre in *The Sontaran Experiment*. She and Harry are tortured by Davros, who uses them against the Doctor to learn secrets of future Dalek defeats; despite the intense pain, Sarah demands that the Doctor doesn't give in, knowing full well what such knowledge could mean in the hands of a man like Davros. She has a very clear view of the Daleks, believing them to be the most evil race ever created, and urges the Doctor on in his mission to wipe them out before they can spread across the universe.

In Scotland, in *Terror of the Zygons*, Sarah once again uses her investigative skills to discover the truth behind the mystery of Tulloch Moor, by which time she is so used to Harry that she easily spots something wrong when she encounters a Zygon duplicate of him (one who tries to kill her with a pitchfork after she gives chase). Once the mystery's solved, the Doctor asks if she's going to continue travelling with him: both Harry and the Brigadier refuse the offer – and she says only if they go straight back to London. She knows it's unlikely, but still goes with him.

Her journalistic background surfaces again when they arrive in the Old Priory, the building upon which UNIT HQ was built, and she explains to the Doctor that the Priory was burned to the ground – presumably she researched the site after spending so much time there in recent months. When the Doctor is moody in *Pyramids of Mars* about returning to Earth, she suggests if he's tired of being UNIT's scientific advisor, he can always resign, and tries to cheer him up by wearing a dress that once belonged to Victoria, only making him more sullen. Fortunately, arriving in 1911, the mystery presented there does lift the Doctor's spirits somewhat. Cheered on by this, Sarah embraces the unexpected stop-over, and is heavily bemused by Marcus Scarman's incredulity over her telling him that she's from the future, and enjoys his bewilderment of the TARDIS interior which he claims is like something by HG Wells. When confronted with the unimaginable power of Sutekh, Sarah asks the Doctor to just take them home – after all, she knows that Sutekh did not destroy the world in 1911, as she's from 1980.

The Doctor shows her the barren ruins that Sutekh would leave; it would take someone with the power of Sutekh to make such a drastic alteration to the future. That's why they have to stay. Sarah never forgets her encounter with Sutekh, the last of the Osirians: in *The Sarah Jane Adventures: The Vault of Secrets* (2010), with the help of her computer, Mr Smith, she interferes with a NASA probe on Mars to prevent it from transmitting an image of the Osirian pyramid on Mars; she knows the danger should NASA discover such an 'ancient and deadly civilisation'.

Knowing how loyal the Doctor is, it's especially curious that, in *The Android Invasion*, when the TARDIS automatically dematerialises from the ersatz village of Devesham created by the Kraals (having gone on to the real Devesham on Earth), Sarah's convinced the Doctor has simply left her. It's an unusual reaction from Sarah, who tends to display unwavering faith in her relationship with him. Indeed, such is their bond that he later states that Sarah is his best friend (*The Seeds of Doom*). Then again, she appears somewhat out of sorts in this story: when she re-meets Harry, who appears to be working against her and the Doctor, she doesn't even consider that he may, once again, be a duplicate.

(She also has an apparent strong distaste for fizzy drinks; in *The Android Invasion*, she doesn't like ginger pop, and later in *The Sarah Jane Adventures: Invasion of the Bane*, she's one of the two percent of Earth's population who doesn't like Bubble Shock!, a new fizzy drink and the front of an alien invasion.)

Once the attempted Kraal invasion is thwarted, Sarah jokingly says she's going home – by taxi this time – but in the next breath agrees to go by TARDIS. Despite the constant visits to her own time, it becomes increasingly clear that neither Sarah nor the Doctor intend to sever their contact with each other. Such is her influence that, when they arrive on Karn in *The Brain of Morbius* and the Doctor's in a funk because he believes the Time Lords are manipulating him, Sarah teases him to no avail. But upon discovering a graveyard of crashed spaceships, she easily gets the Doctor's interest when she finds the detached head of a Mutt.

When temporarily blinded by Maren's ring, Sarah maintains her usual level of sarcasm, although her sudden return to full vision produces something of a shock when she comes face-to-face with the hastily assembled body of Morbius – one of the rare occasions in which Sarah is seen to really scream in terror. The Doctor's love for Sarah is on full display when he walks into an obvious trap in the hope that he can procure some of the Elixir of Life to restore Sarah's eyesight. And when she's taken by Scorbie in *The Seeds of Doom*, the Doctor's anger is palpable.

Like most of the Doctor's companions, Sarah doesn't question how she can understand all the aliens and non-English speakers they've encountered; that is, until they're in fifteenth century Italy in *The Masque of Mandragora*. The fact that she does alerts the Doctor to the influence that the Mandragora Helix temporarily has on Sarah. His explanation, that it's a Time Lord gift he allows her to share, is later explored in *The End of the World* when the Doctor tells Rose that the TARDIS' telepathic circuits get inside their heads and translates languages for them. When they next arrive on Earth in 1976, Sarah is convinced the quarry in which the TARDIS has materialised is an alien planet, having seen so many similar planets in her travels. Her extensive travelling means she takes much in her stride by now: even being possessed by Eldrad doesn't seem to faze her too much; indeed, she makes a joke about it, having become so used to such occurrences. When the Doctor heads off into a dangerous situation, she sticks by his side, telling him that she worries about him, and he confesses that her concerns are mutual.

At the end of *The Hand of Fear*, Sarah expresses her frustrations, but the Doctor's not really listening to her, more intent on fixing the TARDIS console. She gets in such a strop that she storms off to her room and returns with her things, determined that it's time the Doctor returned her home. Of course, it's an empty threat, but when the Doctor explains that he does actually have to return her, she's certain he's joking. But, alas, he's been summoned back to Gallifrey and, although Sarah wants to see it, humans are not allowed. The Doctor sadly says that they have to say goodbye. Sarah tries to put on a brave face when the Doctor tells her that they have arrived in Croydon, but she's clearly hurting. She tells him not to forget her, and he responds with, 'Don't you forget me. 'Til we meet again, Sarah'. Sarah watches the TARDIS dematerialise, and then realises she's not on her street after all – she suspects she's not even in Croydon. When she finally does meet the Doctor again, some twenty-seven years later, she reveals that he left her in Aberdeen.

We meet Sarah again, just over a year later from her point of view, in Christmas 1981 in the spin-off episode, *K9 & Company: A Girl's Best Friend*. We learn she once lived with her Aunt Lavinia in Croydon. Lavinia moves to Morton Harwood and Sarah eventually follows her there, but, as Lavinia says, she's so hard to pin down; much like a butterfly, she's never in one place for long. Once settled in at her aunt's house, Sarah discovers a large box addressed to her. She opens it to find K9 Mark III: a gift from the Doctor (delivered to Croydon in 1978). K9 has a message from the Doctor: 'Give Sarah Jane Smith my fondest love. Tell her I shall remember her always.' Never before has such an expression of love come from the Doctor, and Sarah whispers, with a smile, 'Oh, Doctor, you didn't forget'.

She eventually returns to London with K9, and it's from there that she's scooped to Gallifrey to take part in the Game of Rassilon, where she re-meets the Third Doctor (*The Five Doctors*). She's confused at first, wondering why he looks the way he did when she first met him, and his explanation that maybe he has changed, but he hasn't yet, doesn't help her one bit. During the Game, she encounters the Cybermen again, meets Tegan Jovanka, companion of the Fifth Doctor, and is briefly reunited with the Brigadier. Between them, they attempt to work out which order the four Doctors come in (the first, second, third and fifth incarnations), but ultimately, it comes to nothing: when Sarah's returned home, her memory of that adventure is wiped clean. This is revealed in 2007 – she meets the Tenth Doctor and confesses she believed him to be dead, since he never ever returned for her, and in 2010, she mentions that, 'I can't be sure, but there's a Tegan,' suggesting she doesn't know Ms Jovanka.

For a short while, the Doctor and Sarah are joined by Harry Sullivan, the first male companion since Jamie in 1969. At the time, it was possible that the Fourth Doctor might've been played by an older actor, so Harry was created to carry much of the action, in much the same way as Ian did at the beginning of the series. But in the event, Tom Baker was cast and Harry arguably seemed surplus to requirements. He lasted only six stories, plus one return appearance, but during his time there he certainly helped create a memorable team, alongside the Doctor and Sarah.

Harry Sullivan – Ian Marter (*Robot* to *Terror of the Zygons*, and *The Android Invasion*)

I Am the Very Model of a Modern Major-General (The D'Oyly Carte Opera Company); *Following the Leader* (Bobby Driscoll and Paul Collins).

Harry is quite distinctive as companions go. He only travels in the TARDIS a couple of times (twice more than Liz) and he's mentioned in a story previous to his introduction. When the Doctor briefly falls into a coma in *Planet of the Spiders*, the Brigadier puts in a call to Doctor Sullivan, but cancels it as soon as the Doctor is revived by a cup of tea brought in by Benton. Surgeon Lieutenant Harry Sullivan is called in some weeks later, in *Robot*, to attend to the newly-regenerated Doctor.

Harry's baffled by his new charge, and attempts to humour him before the Doctor strings him up in a nearby utility cupboard like a pair of old boots. For reasons unknown, despite being the medical doctor at UNIT HQ, seconded there from the Royal Navy, Harry's completely unaware of the Doctor's alien physiognomy, as shown when the Doctor tests his own hearts'

100

rate; 'I say, that can't be right', Harry says, shocked at the double heartbeat. He keeps close to the Doctor during the investigation into Think Tank, and even suggests he should be a spy ('a real James Bond,' as Sarah puts it), which he does rather successfully, posing as a man from the Ministry of Health, until he's making a report over the phone and is coshed unconscious. When Sarah's also taken captive by the Scientific Reform Society, she finds Harry held at gun point and mocks him with 'James Bond'. It's the first of many such moments of light mockery and banter which soon come to characterise their relationship. Once Think Tank is defeated, Harry pops by to see the Doctor and Sarah who are planning a trip in the TARDIS. He scoffs at the idea, thinking the whole concept of the TARDIS is absurd. The Doctor asks him inside, just to prove that it is indeed absurd, and Harry agrees. Upon entering, his only response is, 'Oh, I say'. The Doctor and Sarah follow him in, and while the TARDIS dematerialises Harry decides to play with the helmic regulator, sending the TARDIS far off course.

At the beginning of *The Ark in Space*, he staggers out of the TARDIS, 'burbling', telling the Doctor that he could make a lot of money from the time machine by selling it to the police; the space inside could contain a lot of bobbies in Trafalgar Square. Harry's sceptical of the idea that they're in the distant future, but soon learns otherwise when confronted with the cryogenic bay of Nerva Station. His twentieth century knowledge of medicine puts him on the back foot for a while, having never encountered anything like the advanced medical techniques of Nerva, but he soon works out the basic principles and is able to perform the resuscitation process on his own. From the moment they arrive there, Harry starts addressing Sarah by her first name, not as 'Miss Smith', but begins to fuss over her a lot, taking on a chivalrous attitude that's not entirely appreciated by her. During their time aboard Nerva, the Doctor claims Harry's improving – that's entirely down to the Doctor's influence, of course; Harry mustn't take any of the credit.

Understandably, being a doctor, Harry's a strong believer in the sanctity of life: when Vira asks if Sarah (having been accidentally placed in cryogenic suspension) is of value, he responds quite abrasively with, 'Of value? She's a human being!' His lack of experience with the Doctor leads him to suggest that they could use the TARDIS to ferry the revived humans down to Earth to begin the repopulation of it; the Doctor balks at the idea, but agrees to go ahead of the humans to make sure the transmat relays are safe. His companions go with him, and Harry particularly enjoys the sensation of transmitting his atoms across space. When he finds a man tortured by Styre in *The Sontaran Experiment*, his Hippocratic Oath comes into play and he does his best to save the man, albeit with little success. Such a wilful loss of life incenses him intensely. Later, on Skaro, Harry shows an amazing level of bravery when the Doctor accidentally places his foot on a landmine in *Genesis of the Daleks*. Despite the Doctor's insistence that there's no sense in them both being blown up, Harry refuses to leave and manages to steady the landmine enough for the Doctor to safely move his foot away.

His humour is demonstrated throughout his adventures; he takes most things in his stride, and keeps up a playful banter with Sarah. He observes much, and learns quickly. Just from watching the Doctor, he figures out how to operate the transmat controls. He thinks in practical terms, but can be clumsy, at one point causing a rock fall that knocks the Doctor unconscious. Seeing the prone Doctor, with something strapped to him, Harry attempts to remove the strap. Unbeknown to him, releasing the strap will cause the bomb to go off. The Doctor stops him in the nick of time and shouts, 'Harry Sullivan is an imbecile!' Of course, Harry could have no idea about the bomb, so the Doctor's claim is rather unjust. Harry proves time and again that he's far from an imbecile, but rather a brave man with a good head on his shoulders, often thrown into situations far beyond his comprehension.

After returning to Earth in *Terror of the Zygons*, Harry elects to take the train back to London, rather than continue travelling in the TARDIS. It's unclear why he would make such a decision, since he clearly learns a lot during his short time with the Doctor, and the trio clearly get on especially well. Perhaps it's his duty to UNIT: after all, he's standing next to the Brigadier when the offer is made and the Brigadier is Harry's commanding officer. We see Harry once more, several stories later in *The Android Invasion*, when he's stationed with UNIT at the Devesham Space Defence Station, and his knowledge of 'space medicine' is of special use. During the course of the story, however, we learn that no one in Devesham is real – they're all android duplicates created by the Kraals, inhabiting a fake Devesham on the planet Oseidon, a testing ground for an eventual invasion of Earth. When the Doctor and Sarah get to Earth to warn the administration at the real Space Defence Station, Harry is there, serving the same role his android double did. However, we don't see much of the real Harry since he's soon captured and replaced by his android duplicate.

Like Dodo, Harry never gets a proper goodbye scene. Still, he at least gets a goodbye in *Terror of the Zygons*, although it's somewhat voided by his inconsequential return in *The Android Invasion*... and then that's that. The question, therefore remains: what happened to this strong, but often forgotten, companion?

In *Mawdryn Undead*, when the Brigadier reunites with the Fifth Doctor in 1983, the Brigadier says that the last he heard of Harry was that he'd been seconded to NATO and was doing something 'hush hush' at Porton Down. 2015's *The Zygon Invasion* implies that, at that military base, Harry – described simply as a 'naval surgeon' by the Brigadier's daughter, Kate – developed the nerve gas, Z67, which affects the Zygons, 'unravels their DNA; basically turns them inside-out.' That seems out of character for a doctor who values life so greatly; then again, perhaps being replaced by the Zygons had a bigger impact on Harry than initially thought (or that UNIT used his expertise to develop the gas without his knowing exactly how it might be used).

Harry is fondly remembered by Sarah, who considers naming her adopted son after him (*SJA: Invasion of the Bane*). In 2010, she mentions Harry in the past tense, suggesting that he may be dead; she does, however, tell her friends, Clyde and Rani, that Harry went on to do great work developing vaccines and saving thousands of lives (*SJA: Death of the Doctor*). Now that sounds more like it.

Sarah's departure saw another shift in the companion/Doctor dynamic. Enter Leela, a character who, in some ways, harkened back to Jamie. Leela appeared to come from an uneducated and superstitious culture, primitive in many ways. But to think of Leela as stupid was a big mistake.

Leela – Louise Jameson (*The Face of Evil* to *The Invasion of Time*)

Two Tribes (Frankie Goes To Hollywood); *Everybody's Changing* (Keane).

Leela comes from an unnamed planet in the distant future and is a descendant of a human expedition that settled there. She's a warrior of the Sevateem, a tribe living in a jungle wilderness, one half of a long-term eugenics experiment conducted by the mad computer, Xoanon. Like all her people – and like the Tesh, the advanced second half of Xoanon's test – she knows nothing of her history. She has been brought up to believe Xoanon is a god. When she is cast out from the Sevateem for heresy, she bumps into the Doctor and believes him to be 'the evil one' with whom he shares a resemblance. With the Doctor, she discovers that her ancestors were a Mordee expedition; the Sevateem being descended from the survey team sent out to explore the planet and the Tesh from the technicians, who remained behind in the ship. The Doctor had previously repaired the Mordee computer, but forgot to remove his own personality from it, and in doing so, caused an imbalance between Xoanon's personality and his own, resulting in split-personality madness. From the moment we meet her, it's clear that Leela has a hunger for knowledge. She may be uneducated, but she has a sharp brain and soaks up information with the sponge-like mind of a child. However, she's prone to using weapons to solve her problems, notably a knife and her trusty Janis thorns which cause paralysis and then death. The Doctor warns her to stop using them; Leela doesn't agree, but the Doctor takes her silence as such anyway (a fact he mentions when Leela later kills a Chinese coolie in *The Talons of Weng-Chiang*). Once the Doctor's solved the problem with Xoanon, he's all set to leave on his own, but Leela pushes past and rushes into the TARDIS. The Doctor barely has a chance to close the door before Leela plays with the controls of the time ship and they dematerialise.

In *The Robots of Death*, the Doctor is busy teaching Leela that there's no such thing as magic, merely misunderstood science. She believes making a yo-yo go up and down helps the TARDIS fly – that it's part of the magic. Still not understanding, she asks him to explain why the TARDIS is bigger inside than out, and he tries to explain using a large and small box. He places the large one at a distance and brings the smaller up to Leela, making it appear bigger. He tells her that if you can have the large box at that distance *and* in the same place as the small one, then the large can fit inside the small. Leela calls this silly, which amuses the Doctor, and when the TARDIS materialises inside the sandminer (a large mobile ore processing vessel), Leela asks how one box, i.e. the TARDIS, can fit inside another (the sandminer), the Doctor reminds her of his previous explanation, which Leela still doesn't think is clear. As she goes to leave the TARDIS for the first time, she picks up the laser gun (a Tesh invention), but the Doctor tells her to leave it behind. She shrugs but keeps her knife in its sheath anyway – a fact that the Doctor doesn't comment on (her knife proves useless when they come up against the murderous Voc robots). Leela displays a sixth sense about danger; she can almost predict or feel something is wrong with no external evidence. Having spent a life surrounded by little or no technology, Leela feels uncomfortable around the Voc robots, who she calls 'creepy mechanical men'. She's already fiercely protective of the Doctor, as Borg learns when he foolishly attempts to attack the Time Lord, receiving a gut punch from Leela that floors him. She's also very adept at reading body language, no doubt something that makes her such a good hunter, being able to spot at first glance that Pool is not what he seems.

The Doctor and Leela's next trip is to Victorian London (*The Talons of Weng-Chiang*), as if he's showing her the vastly different worlds she can expect to see on her travels – an echo of the smaller world inhabited by the savage Sevateem and the technologically advanced Tesh. She finds knickerbockers very uncomfortable, but she surely chose them herself when the Doctor insisted she get out of animal skins – knickerbockers enable a huntress like Leela to hide her blowpipe and Janis thorns – since walking around in skins in London would 'frighten the horses'. She believes the Doctor's trying to annoy her, having no interest in the historical teachings he's trying to impart. She's somewhat indifferent to learning about her ancestors at this point, but, in *Image of the Fendahl*, she at least doesn't like the Doctor insulting them. She has very little concern for the intricacies of nineteenth century police procedure, and when a coolie, who attacks the Doctor, is being questioned unsuccessfully, she steps forward, growling, 'make him talk', quite intent on doing so herself. The idea of Victorian propriety is lost on her. She's not even slightly fazed by the autopsy conducted by Professor Litefoot and is amused by the deference he shows her. The Doctor attempts to explain Leela away by saying he found her 'floating down the river in a hatbox'. She's fascinated by Litefoot's pipe smoking, wondering why he makes smoke from his mouth. The Doctor says they don't have tobacco where Leela comes from, a fact Litefoot finds to be rather dull yet he soon becomes fascinated by the savage girl. He's fascinated when she attacks a joint of meat with a knife and uses her fingers. But it's actually her relationship with Litefoot that teaches her about her own femininity – she loves the dress he buys for her, and clearly enjoys being treated as a lady, even though she does still happily jump through a window to give chase when Mr Sin steals the time cabinet from Litefoot's house.

It's a great shame that, when they arrive on Fang Rock, much of what she learned from Litefoot is either forgotten or discarded. She starts out in period clothing, but soon changes into more practical clothes (trousers and a jumper) at the earliest opportunity. This she does in front of the young lighthouse keeper, Vince. He's obviously embarrassed saying that such clothes are not made for ladies. 'I'm no lady, Vince,' she tells him.

Once more, she demonstrates her fierce belief in the Doctor; when he attempts to explain the situation to survivors of a ship wreck, but they don't listen, she warns them to pay attention or she'll cut out their hearts. After Vince tells her about the mythical Beast of Fang Rock, Leela admits she once believed in superstition, but the Doctor has taught her to believe in science. 'It is better to believe in science,' she affirms. At the end of *Horror of Fang Rock*, after witnessing the explosion of a Rutan ship, Leela's eyes turn from their natural deep brown to blue – due to pigment dispersal.

The Doctor's education of Leela seems to end at this point, for no discernible reason, as she was clearly developing, both intellectually and socially. So when we next see her in *The Invisible Enemy*, she's back in her animal skins, and both her and the Doctor seemingly accept that she will always be a savage at heart. Nonetheless, she has somehow learned to operate the TARDIS controls, despite never having seen the 'new' console before (up to this point she has only been in the mahogany-based secondary control room, and is introduced to the original – now redecorated – console room in *The Invisible Enemy*). This suggests that considerable learning happened off screen, and later, in *Underworld*, she's still learning how to operate that TARDIS' controls. By the time they return to Earth in *Image of the Fendahl*, Leela has developed an odd bloodlust, and seems to want to kill everyone, including the guards at Fetch Priory and even a man from the council. This new over-aggressive streak extends to firearms, which she's now adept at using, despite having barely touched them before in *The Talons of Weng-Chiang*. She, more than the Doctor, initially responds to K9 favourably, referring to the mobile computer as 'he' before the Doctor does.

Leela does score a first in the history of Gallifrey, being the first 'alien' to be allowed there (a sharp contrast to Sarah's departure). The Doctor's acting very out of character, even to the point of telling K9 to shoot Leela if she questions him again, but despite this, she's convinced he has a plan and trusts him, even when, as President of the Time Lords, the Doctor casts her out of the Capitol into the wilderness of Gallifrey. Leela's loyalty to the Doctor convinces Rodan – the first female Gallifreyan to be seen on screen since Susan – to join Leela in the wilderness. Rodan is out of her depth among the Outsiders, who are not unlike Leela's tribe, but Leela protects her and teaches Rodan how to survive. When the Doctor reveals his plan (a trap for the Vardans), things get complicated: the Vardans are unveiled as dupes for the Sontaran invasion of Gallifrey. To remove the Sontaran threat, the Doctor has to assemble the ultimate Gallifreyan weapon, the DeMat Gun, and trusts Leela with the Great Key of Rassilon, an almost mythical Gallifreyan artefact. The Doctor's trust in her is a source of disconcertion for others, but shows how much stock the Doctor places in his 'savage'. At the end of *The Invasion of Time*, Leela abruptly elects to remain on Gallifrey, having chosen Andred, captain of the Capitol Guards, to be her mate. Andred doesn't seem surprised by this, despite the fact that there's no previous indication of any such feeling between them. K9 also chooses to remain behind with his 'mistress', leaving the Doctor to continue on his own (or not, as it turns out, since the Doctor has already started building K9 Mark II).

Nothing is ever heard of Leela again, except a mention in *Arc of Infinity* when the Fifth Doctor returns to Gallifrey and enquires after her, having missed her wedding. We learn nothing, save that she's still married to Andred.

It's interesting that, in *Resurrection of the Daleks*, the Daleks create an android duplicate of the Doctor to assassinate the High Council of the Time Lords. The duplicate needs the memories of the real Doctor, and during this memory extraction, images of *all* the Doctor's previous companions are shown on a screen, except for Leela, the only companion who would be on Gallifrey when the duplicate arrives. We never see this attempted assassination, however, and so never learn why the Doctor failed to remember Leela. An intentional omission?

The next companion was completely different to any featured before; a mobile computer in the shape of a dog called K9. There have actually been five versions of K9 in *Doctor Who* and associated spin-offs, but they all had the same basic character. Mark I was destroyed in the first episode of the spin-off series, *K9*, in 2009, only to regenerate into a more advanced (and for the first time ever, physically different) model. Mark II was left in E-Space with Romana. Mark III was given to Sarah in the 1981 spin-off episode, *K9 & Company: A Girl's Best Friend* and destroyed in the 2006 episode *School Reunion,* and replaced by a newly built Mark IV. Since neither Mark III nor Mark IV ever travelled with the Doctor, however, they are not considered companions, even though they both refer to the Doctor as 'master'.

K9 Mark I – John Leeson (*The Invisible Enemy* to *The Invasion of Time* and *K9*)

Old King (Neil Young); *Together In Electric Dreams* (Phil Oakey).

K9 is an advanced computer-shaped dog created for Professor Marius, to help him conduct advanced medical research at the Bi-Al Foundation in the year 5000 (*The Invisible Enemy*). Unable to bring his own dog with him from Earth due to weight restrictions, Marius constructs K9 himself, and considers the dog his best friend. Leela particularly takes to K9, and he soon becomes very protective of her, rarely far from her side. Unable to return to Earth with K9, again due to the weight restrictions, Marius offers K9 to the Doctor, but the Doctor's uncertain about the prospect, although Leela is keen on K9 joining them. The decision is, however, taken out of their hands, when K9 trundles into the TARDIS of his own accord.

Due to the often impractical conditions of their adventures, Leela is regularly forced to leave K9 in the TARDIS, but that doesn't stop him from exiting the time ship if he believes his help is needed. He's smug in his attitude, believing himself superior to the TARDIS, and the Doctor never seems to quite get on with him. The Doctor appears to tolerate K9 for the sake of Leela (or in light of the revelation in *The Invasion of Time* that the Doctor has been making the Mark II while travelling with the Mark I, it might be that the Doctor merely thinks he can do a better job creating a K9 unit). Leela looks on K9 more as her pet than that of the Doctor's. For a machine who claims to have no emotion, he shows a surprising amount of it, including sulking when Leela shouts at him. K9 is equally loyal to both of them, but his mood will often alter the level of his loyalty, sometimes favouring Leela over the Doctor and vice versa.

It's unsurprising that, when Leela chooses to remain on Gallifrey, K9 decides to stay with her. As soon as the TARDIS leaves Gallifrey, the Doctor unveils a box containing the Mark II, which, as suggested by the following story, *The Ribos Operation*), he simply needs to assemble.

It's unknown how long the Mark I remains on Gallifrey, but he clearly leaves before the Time War: he ends up in the year 50,000 and meets Zanthus Pia, the head of the Galactic Peace Conference. He witnesses the murder of Zanthus by the Jixen, who escape to London in 2050. K9 follows them there and self-destructs to defeat them. Revealing a previously unknown ability, K9 uses a 'regeneration unit' (which is inscribed with symbols that are said to be the Doctor's Gallifreyan name – suggesting the Doctor installed this unit at some point prior to K9's remaining on Gallifrey) to transform his remains into a, confusingly named, Mark Two body (*K9: Regeneration*). He still remains on twenty-first century Earth, working for the Department as part of the K9 Unit, defending the planet with Professor Gryffen and his friends, Starkey, Darius, and Jorjie.

K9 Mark II – John Leeson and David Brierly (*The Ribos Operation* to *Warriors' Gate*)

The Mark II is more advanced than the original version; understandably so, the Doctor having built it. His personality, although essentially the same as before, takes on a few more of the Doctor's values, as well as a much more obvious ironic wit. As a rule, this version doesn't kill – he'll only stun with his nose laser, but will kill in defence if necessary. He responds to a dog whistle, and has the ability to sense danger and the Doctor from a distance. Technologically, the Doctor has made some improvements, including the ability to hover. This is not seen on screen, however, but the Eleventh Doctor, in *The Power of Three*, mentions that he had a robot dog that could hover – presumably it's the Mark II model since he was built by the Doctor.

At one point, in *The Pirate Planet*, K9 remarks that Romana is prettier than the Doctor, which means she is more likely to receive help than he is. The Doctor is not convinced, but K9 is proven right moments later. As with his predecessor, the Mark II insists he feels nothing, but his actions and responses often belie that assertion, as seen when taking pride in correcting the Doctor in *The Ribos Operation*. He finds organic life forms unpredictable, and is glad to have a conversation with the super-computer, Mentalis, in *The Armageddon Factor*. For a short spell, he's turned against the Doctor by the Shadow, an agent of the Black Guardian, but the Doctor's able to restore him to normal. K9 assists the Doctor and Romana in tracking down the Key to Time, after which a very strange thing happens to him. K9, a robot, contracts laryngitis! Whether K9 actually possesses a larynx or not is explored until later: in *The Creature from the Pit*, Erato, the

Tyhthonian ambassador, uses K9 as a medium by which to speak – Erato doesn't possess a larynx and can only communicate verbally by using the larynxes of others. So K9 must have a larynx! As a consequence of his laryngitis, K9 is temporarily grounded in the TARDIS (*Destiny of the Daleks* and *City of Death*), unable to speak, but when his voice returns, it has changed. His usual voice eventually returns in *The Leisure Hive* for reasons unknown, although he doesn't get to use it very much as his lack of waterproofing causes him to malfunction when he chases a beach ball into the sea at Brighton Beach.

Mark II K9 remains in E-Space, the Exo-space/time continuum, with Romana. Damaged by the time winds, it's revealed that, if K9 were to return to N-Space, the Normal-space/time continuum, he would no longer function, so he remains with Romana to help free the time-sensitive Tharils. It's assumed that both Romana and K9 eventually escape E-Space since K9 is left with a complete knowledge of how to build a TARDIS. There has, however, never been any indication of their return shown, or hinted at, on screen.

While one companion remained on Gallifrey, the next came from there. The Doctor still had K9, and for a further three seasons, they were joined by another member of the Doctor's own race: Romanadvoratrelundar, a young Time Lord (or Lady, depending on the story) who had never left Gallifrey before. For the first time in *Doctor Who* history, the TARDIS was over-crowded with intelligence – two Time Lords and a brilliant dog-shaped sentient computer. Who was going to ask the questions the audience needed answering?

Romanadvoratrelundar – Mary Tamm and Lalla Ward (*The Ribos Operation* to *Warriors' Gate*)

I'm Outta Time (Oasis); *Time in a Bottle* (Jim Croce).

Romanadvoratrelundar doesn't want to travel with the Doctor; she's quite content to continue her academic life on Gallifrey, but her presence is requested by the President of the High Council of Time Lords, later revealed to be the White Guardian, posing as the president (*The Armageddon Factor*). She's assigned to assist the Doctor in his search for the Key to Time, an ancient artefact that has to be assembled to restore the universal balance of good and evil. After some initial sparring – her haughty attitude conflicts with the Doctor's bohemian outlook on life – the Doctor decides he doesn't like her name; it's too long. He suggests shortening it to Romana, but she doesn't like that. 'It's either Romana or Fred,' the Doctor insists. She prefers the latter. That settled, the Doctor calls her Romana. (Curiously, the Time Lords refer to her as Romana in *Arc of Infinity* even though the Doctor came up with the name: we must assume that this name change was transmitted to them at some point – perhaps just before *Full Circle*, when she's ordered back to Gallifrey?)

Whereas much later, Missy refers to herself as a 'Time Lady', Romana initially calls herself a Time 'Lord', and does so on several further occasions. Only once does she refer to herself as a Time Lady, in *City of Death*; in *State of Decay*, Aukon calls her a Time Lord, yet in the same story, Adric says she's a Time Lady (but then again, how would Adric know either way?).

During their Key to Time mission, Romana mellows slowly. She starts off with a massive superiority complex. Having graduated from the Time Lord Academy with a triple-first, she's easily irritated by K9, believing academic knowledge is better than field experience, and is rather smug in her ability to land the TARDIS better than the Doctor. For a long while, she's bossy, and loves ordering the Doctor around. The one time she goes off on her own to locate a Key segment, she does so in record time, not distracted by the Doctor's usual habit of getting involved in the adventure of their travels (*The Androids of Tara*). But her encounter with Professor Amelia Rumford and Vivian Fay on 1970s Earth in *The Stones of Blood* helps to ground her – she learns to favour the quaint things of life, bringing her down from her lofty ways. Her sense of superiority comes in useful on the planet

Tara, where she's forced by Count Grendel to play the part of Princess Strella, Romana's physical twin. This isn't the first time we've seen Time Lords sharing their likenesses with others: notable instances include the First Doctor, the double of the Abbot of Amboise in *The Massacre of St Bartholomew's Eve*; the Second Doctor and Salamander in *The Enemy of the World*; and the Twelfth Doctor, who got his face from Caecilius (*The Fires of Pompeii*).

The idea of being a princess seems to appeal to Romana on a certain level: when she later regenerates in *Destiny of the Daleks*, she intentionally takes on the appearance of Princess Astra who she met on Atrios in *The Armageddon Factor*.

Romana enjoys dressing up, and is often seen selecting clothes suitable for the location in which they land. She particularly enjoys the fashions of Tara and Earth, although in the latter instance the Doctor does point out the impracticality of her shoes.

Although she eventually comes to trust and respect him, in *The Stones of Blood*, she's enticed to a cliff-edge by a vision of the Doctor, who then pushes her over the edge. When the real Doctor rescues her, she's very wary of him, but such doubt soon passes and they develop a relationship of mutual respect. Almost.

It's never established on screen the reason behind Romana's regeneration – or indeed which regeneration it is. It's always been assumed that it's her first, but there's nothing in the official canon to back this up. She undergoes a most peculiar regeneration, doing so off screen; it's only when she enters the console room that the Doctor realises she has regenerated (although at first he confuses her for Princess Astra). He tells her she can't go around wearing someone else's body – a point he later ignores in his sixth incarnation when he's walking around wearing the body of Commander Maxil, who he'd met in *Arc of Infinity* – and she has to change it. She does, going through a selection of options before returning in the guise of Astra, now wearing a pink and white version of the Doctor's clothes. The Doctor highly approves of her attire, and eventually gives up on convincing her to change her appearance again. It's only many years later, in stories like

The Christmas Invasion and *Let's Kill Hitler*, that we discover that a Time Lord's body remains in flux for several hours after a regeneration, allowing some to continually alter their form to fit their personal ideal. This explains, in part, why Romana is able to control her regeneration in such a way (albeit somewhat more extreme than shrinking the arm length or growing a new hand).

The new incarnation of Romana is much more flighty, with a buoyant personality. Witty and relaxed in equal measure, it seems that in some ways, she's fashioned herself on the Doctor, even to the point where she often lies about her age. When she first arrives on the TARDIS in *The Ribos Operation*, she states that she's almost 140, but in *City of Death*, now quite settled into her new persona, she says she's 125, then, in *The Leisure Hive*, she decides she's 160. The previous friction between them seems to have fallen by the wayside; it's quite clear throughout the remainder of their time together that they greatly enjoy each other's company, to the point where, when she is summoned back to Gallifrey in *Full Circle* (having only been assigned to the Doctor for the Key to Time mission), she spends some time sulking in her room, unwilling to give up her life with the Doctor. On the surface, there seems to almost be romantic overtones to their relationship; they're flirty and complimentary with each other: in *State of Decay*, when the Doctor tells her, 'You are wonderful', she responds with, 'Am I? I suppose I am. Never thought about it.' And when she leaves, the Doctor tells her that she is the, 'Noblest Romana of them all.'

Despite all this, she maintains her superiority to most people she meets, but is scared witless by the Daleks, whom she claims to know nothing about – a clear lie. This fear is often evident when she's alone with the monsters, without the Doctor to support her, or others to lead, notable in such stories as *The Horns of Nimon*. In *City of Death*, she, like the Doctor, is aware of time fluctuations and, in *Meglos*, is aware of the time loop they become trapped in. She prefers the computer pictures of Gallifrey over the hand drawn and painted pictures of Earth, to the point where she states that the

Mona Lisa is only 'quite good'. At some point before *The Horns of Nimon*, she builds her own sonic screwdriver, which is better than the Doctor's (not that he will admit it, of course), but he still tries to palm it and switch it with his own.

In *State of Decay*, she's horrified by the idea of vampires, and knows nothing of their Great War against the Time Lords. She's endlessly irritated by Adric, who stows away in the TARDIS at the end of *Full Circle*; she is very dismissive of him, constantly casting him dirty looks – possibly an indication of her subtle romance with the Doctor, finding the boy an unwanted intrusion of her perfect set-up with the Doctor and K9. This is backed up somewhat when she starts thinking of leaving the Doctor shortly after Adric becomes a permanent fixture aboard the TARDIS in *Warriors' Gate*. Indeed, she strongly disagrees with the notion of taking Adric back to N-Space with them.

When Adric learns that Romana is thinking of leaving, he doesn't believe her. This only exasperates her more, so she shows an even stronger irritation at his constant questions and smug attitude. He simply fails to earn her respect. Initially, she's terrified by the appearance of the wounded Tharil, but later shows concern for the way they're being treated by the crew of the *Privateer*; being a time-sensitive race, the Tharils are enslaved and used to help pilot through time winds. Her concern is so great that she decides she will not leave them – a big factor in her eventual departure. Her goodbye is abrupt, leaving the Doctor with no choice but to accept it. It's possibly for the best: it seems likely that it would've been a painful goodbye for both of them if it'd been a more drawn-out affair.

Indeed, her departure is as abrupt as her arrival, which adds a nice symmetry to her time aboard the TARDIS. Since K9 has been damaged by the time winds, so cannot return to N-Space, he remains with Romana to help her free the Tharils. Adric, showing concern for her despite her treatment of him, asks the Doctor if she'll be all right. The Doctor beams, his smile belying his sadness: 'All right? She'll be superb!'

Up to this point, the Doctor had only ever travelled with humans or, in two instances, people from his own world (Susan and Romana). With the introduction of Adric, a new run of non-human companions began, continuing up until the Fifth Doctor's penultimate story, *Planet of Fire*.

Adric was the first male companion since Harry left in 1975, some five years previously. He was also one of the most contentious companions in *Doctor Who*'s sixty-year history.

Adric – Matthew Waterhouse (*Full Circle* to *Earthshock* and *Time-Flight*)

American Pie (Don Mclean); *Disintegration* (The Cure).

Following his introduction in *Full Circle*, there's no mistaking Adric's two most dominant character traits: immaturity and arrogance. He wants to be one of the Outlers, a small band of teenage rebels on Alzarius (one of whom is his brother, Varsh), even though he thinks himself superior to them. He holds a position as one of the elite, but has seemingly turned his back on his roots. Arguably, Adric is comparable to characters often seen in 1960s kitchen sink dramas – wanting to better themselves, but not having the capacity to achieve their absolute goals. His arrogance is slightly more complicated though; he wants to be accepted for his mathematical excellence, but also be one of the 'gang'. Adric agrees to steal river fruit, just to impress his brother, for instance. He fails miserably. However, when the Outlers threaten Romana, he stands up to them, showing an unusual level of loyalty and bravery. On the other hand, in *State of Decay*, he betrays the Doctor and Romana to the Three Who Rule and later claims it was a deliberate ploy. This conflicting self-serving attitude continues throughout his run in the series.

Nevertheless, Adric is very clever. When Romana is possessed after being bitten by the Marshspiders, he and the Outlers scarper into the TARDIS, with Adric managing to pilot the time ship into the Starliner – a skill worthy of the Doctor. Adric is not very emotional; his scientific mind doesn't let him shed a tear when he witnesses his brother die at the hands of the Marshmen. He just takes Varsh's string belt, the badge of the Outlers, as a keepsake. However, as he faces his own death in *Earthshock*, he clings tightly to Varsh's belt, as though this is his final act of bravery.

We never discover much about Adric's family life, beyond his brother. It's not made clear if his parents are still alive in *Full Circle* or if they are actually dead. One can assume they're dead, since in *Earthshock*, he states there's nothing for him to return to on Terradon (the ultimate destination of his people following the events in *Full Circle*). But then again, considering the lack of consideration Adric often displays for others, it could just be that he doesn't consider his parents reason enough to return home. Either way, he never once mentions them.

K9 is the first to discover Adric after he stows away in the TARDIS. K9 is immediately keen to stun him, but Adric convinces K9 that, since he's a stowaway, he should be allowed to leave the ship. Such logic can't be argued with, so Adric follows the Doctor and Romana onto an unnamed planet in E-Space. He arrives at the village sometime later, and is caught stealing food by Marta, a local resident who has recently lost her son to the vampire lords, the Three Who Rule. Adric wilfully plays on Marta's sadness and gets himself settled with food, having forgotten about the Doctor and Romana. Despite his forceful and selfish nature, Adric's not as strong-minded as he likes to believe. Aukon, one of the vampire lords, easily enthrals him and takes him back to the castle. At this point, Romana is still rather fond of Adric, or at least feels some kind of duty to him; when she discovers he's been captured, she refuses to leave the castle until she's found him. She needn't have bothered – he's very ungrateful for the rescue and betrays her to Aukon the moment she finds him. He later states that he only pretended to want the eternal life offered him, but Romana isn't convinced. All the evidence suggests that Adric is serious about taking the offer, and only changes his mind when he realises the danger he is in. (This is compounded much later when he's equally entranced by another offer of eternal life, this time as an android in *Four to Doomsday*.) As a result, the Doctor's determined to return Adric home.

However, when we next see them, the Doctor wants to leave E-Space. Romana questions the wisdom of taking Adric with them, especially back to Gallifrey. The Doctor suggests to Adric that he flips a coin. He does so and the decision is made. The TARDIS then materialises near the Gateway, a stone structure that intersects E-Space and N-Space.

Here, Adric's selfishness comes into play once again. At one point in *Warriors' Gate*, he's happy to leave the Tharils as slaves as long as he, the Doctor, and Romana can return to N-Space. Both Romana and the Doctor verbally slap him down for this and he learns a valuable lesson about the right of freedom. Once Romana leaves, Adric becomes a faithful student, even slightly mocking the Doctor for not making a lot of sense. He does find it difficult to be around strong women – note that he develops a very easy friendship with Nyssa, who he considers just a 'girl', but clashes a lot with Tegan, who is very sure of herself and is quite a powerhouse of a woman.

Despite experiencing the awesome power of the Keeper of Traken, Adric is still surprised by the science of Traken, clearly taken in by the tranquillity of this idyllic planet. Adric responds well to Nyssa, working with the young scientist while on Traken to discover the truth behind the Melkur (revealed to be the Master's TARDIS), and find a way to interrupt the source manipulator, the secret of the Keeper's power. When Nyssa is later brought to Logopolis by the Watcher, Adric is delighted to see her again.

In *Logopolis*, Adric learns the basics of block transfer computations, a method of mathematical calculation that shapes reality. He helps the Doctor map the exterior dimensions of a real Police Box in preparation for repairing the chameleon circuit. Adric is less bothered about the sudden arrival of Tegan than the Doctor, although he does clearly take a dislike to her, preferring the company of Nyssa. However, all three work together to distract the guards at the Pharos Project, in order to give the Doctor and the Master time to stabilise the CVE (a Charged Vacuum Emboitment, akin to a door between different pockets of space). They all watch the Doctor's tragic fall from the radio telescope and rush to his side. Adric's voice actually pulls the Doctor out of his shocked state (during which the life of his entire fourth incarnation flashes before him); similarly, the Fifth Doctor sees Adric during his regeneration, and calls out his name (*The Caves of Androzani*). Having already met the Master's newly regenerated form, Adric isn't terribly surprised to watch the Doctor regenerate before his eyes...

Nyssa of Traken was never intended to be a companion. She was merely one of several characters in *The Keeper of Traken*, the daughter of Consul Tremas. However, she returned in the following story as part of the official companion line-up to oversee the change of Doctors.

Nyssa – Sarah Sutton (*The Keeper of Traken*, and *Logopolis* to *Terminus*)

I Wanna Know (Patrick Martin and Adé); *Wake Up Time* (Tom Petty).

Ultimately, Nyssa is something of a tragic figure. When we first meet her, she's already lost her mother, and within two stories she loses both her father and her entire planet to the machinations of the Master. One more orphan for the Doctor to take under his wing...

She's the loyal daughter of Tremas, a consul of Traken, one of the much revered ruling body who guides the Traken Union via the wishes of the Keeper. Everybody seems to know and love Nyssa, including her step-mother, Kassia, although their relationship deteriorates rapidly when the Melkur exerts his influence upon the latter. Nyssa is incensed when Kassia usurps

Tremas' position as Keeper-elect, but is still upset when Kassia dies as a result of the Melkur taking over the Keepership.

On the surface, Nyssa appears a gentle soul, always polite and friendly; a great mediator, trying to understand all points of view. But inside, she's a strong young woman. When she needs to get into the Grove, she's not above bribing Proctor Neman, and she single-handedly breaks her father and the Doctor out of prison. She's also very intelligent and gifted, an expert in bioelectronics with a good understanding of general scientific principles.

After her father appears to go missing, she contacts the Doctor for help, and the Watcher (an echo of the Doctor's fifth incarnation) brings her from Traken to Logopolis. There, she's reunited with Adric and finally finds her father – who appears to be younger and a lot paler. In truth, as she later learns, it's no longer her father: it's the Master who possesses Tremas' body with the stolen power of the Keeper – effectively killing him. She's easily taken in by the Master's lie, and doesn't question his obvious physical change, accepting his lacklustre excuse that it's because Logopolis is a cold place. She bonds quite quickly with Tegan, but remains with Adric when the Watcher pilots the TARDIS outside of space and time. It is there that she, with Adric beside her, watches as Traken is consumed by the entropy caused by the destabilised CVE, a direct result of the Master's meddling. It's Nyssa who makes quite the deductive leap, working out that the Watcher was the Doctor all the time, as he merges with the Fourth Doctor's damaged body to regenerate.

The third in the trio of companions brought in to smooth the transition between the Fourth and Fifth Doctors was Tegan. And she was certainly different from any who had come before. She would turn out to be one of the longest serving companions, continuing for almost the entire run of the Fifth Doctor's adventures (bar the final two, although she still makes a cameo in the very last moments of *The Caves of Androzani*). She was also the first Earth-based companion not to be British, and the first companion to have various family members appear in the show – in this case an aunt, a cousin, and her grandfather (something that would become very commonplace in *Doctor Who* from 2005).

Tegan Jovanka – Janet Fielding (*Logopolis* to *Resurrection of the Daleks,* plus *The Power of the Doctor)*

Come Fly With Me (Frank Sinatra); *Brave Heart* (Animelmack).

We meet Tegan on the first day of her new job as an air hostess (*Logopolis*). At this point, February 1981, Tegan is living with her Aunt Vanessa in London. Both of them come from Australia, though, after meeting her maternal grandfather in *The Awakening*, we later discover that Tegan's mother's family is English. This suggests that Vanessa is the sister of Tegan's Australian father.

Aunt Vanessa is driving Tegan to Heathrow when her car breaks down on the Barnet Bypass. While her aunt waits by the car, Tegan goes to a Police Box beside the road to phone for help, only to find the door open. Seeking aid, and amazed by the interior of the TARDIS (which is apparently deserted, the Doctor and Adric now being trapped inside a series of recursive TARDISes), she explores beyond the console room, eventually becoming lost in the labyrinthine corridors, discovering another Police Box deeper inside (in reality, the Master's TARDIS). By the time she finds her way back to the console room, she's almost hysterical and directly confronts the Doctor – who is somewhat stunned by her sudden appearance. He has no idea what to do with her, but it's too late: the TARDIS is already en route to Logopolis.

While she's on Logopolis, Tegan learns that her aunt has been killed by the Master and receives very little comfort from the Doctor; as far as he's concerned, he has bigger problems than the grief of one human. When the Master insists on her help, she refuses until he threatens to kill both Nyssa and Adric. Thrown in the deep end, Tegan has little option but to deal with her current situation. She remains very close to the Doctor (who is, after all, her ticket back home), and is just as concerned as her fellow companions when he's seemingly trapped in a shrinking TARDIS. Even when the Doctor forces them all back in the ship to be taken away to safety by the Watcher, she sneaks back out and follows the Doctor, displaying a huge degree of loyalty from the off. She travels back to Earth with him and the Master, and finds herself having to rescue Nyssa and Adric from the Pharos Project guards. Alongside her new found friends, she watches the Doctor drop from the radio telescope gantry, kneeling by his side when he regenerates into his new, younger body...

The Fourth Doctor

Expanded Universe

If Sarah's appearances in the Third Doctor's Expanded Universe are contentious, then her time with the Fourth Doctor, and life beyond the Doctor, ends up becoming pretty much irrelevant, to a point, due to the continuation of Sarah's story on TV from her return in the 2006 episode, *School Reunion*, onwards. Though largely at odds with Sarah's TV adventures, her appearances in other media still give interesting insights into what might have been, had Sarah *turned left* and followed a different path.

As on television, her name shifts between 'Sarah' and 'Sarah Jane' depending on the author of any given story (occasionally, the name even alternates *within* some of the stories; for instance in the prose stories found in 1983's *K9 Annual*). However in the pages of *TV Comic*, she's consistently referred to as 'Sarah-Jane'. It seems her given name will always remain a mystery.

Despite the amount of Expanded Universe material covering her time with the Fourth Doctor, there's little new to be gleaned, except for a few instances that serve to explain some of her post-Doctor appearances. She's kidnapped from her adventure in Takhail, 2086 (in the 1996 *Doctor Who Magazine* #238-242 comic strip, *Ground Zero*) by the Threshold and trapped in a collective consciousness with future companions, Peri and Ace. There, she meets the Seventh Doctor, who wipes her memory of this time, and returns her to Takhail where she continues with the Fourth Doctor and Harry to Loch Ness (*Black Destiny*, *Doctor Who Magazine* #235-237). Later, she encounters further incarnations of the Doctor, notably the First, Second, Third, Fifth, Sixth, Seventh (again), and Eighth in the 2004 short story, *Categorical Imperative*. She also observes, briefly, fellow companions Susan,

Jamie, Jo, Tegan, Turlough, Peri, Ace, and Charley Pollard. (This knowledge of other companions is expanded on in the 2003 short story, *Balloon Debate*, when, sometime after leaving the Doctor, she writes a short story featuring every TV companion in an attempt to defeat writer's block.)

One of the strangest things to happen to Sarah during her Expanded Universe journeys is in the *Doctor Who Annual 1978* story, *The Sands of Tymus*, when the entire planet is repopulated by copies of her. Another curious incident happens in *The Return of the Daleks* (*TV Comic* #1217), in which, contrary to later events in the television series, Sarah visits the planet of the Time Lords – called Jewel for the first and only time in any medium.

Regardless of what we learn in *School Reunion*, Sarah encounters the Doctor several times after finishing travelling with him. Naturally, such accounts conflict in various ways, but chronologically she first re-meets the Doctor (still in his fourth incarnation, and now travelling with Romana and K9) in 1979, in the short story, *Suitors, Inc.* Here, she and Harry are investigating a company called Wildthyme Unlimited, which is in the process of making DoctorBots, robotic copies of the Doctor. Not only does Sarah meet K9 three years before *K9 & Company: A Girl's Best Friend*, but at the end of this story, she, Harry, and the Doctor disappear into the Time Vortex, closely followed by Romana and K9, one presumes to have further adventures (still untold). At some point after *The Five Doctors*, the Fourth Doctor pays Sarah a visit, to give her a proper goodbye, as per *Farewells*, a short story published in the *Doctor Who Yearbook 1993*. Sarah says that the Doctor is 'the you you', quoting herself from *The Five Doctors* and the Doctor agrees that yes, he's all 'teeth and curls'. In a conflicting account, the Seventh Doctor visits Sarah in 1990, again to apologise for not saying goodbye properly in *The Hand of Fear*, in the *Doctor Who Magazine* #159-161 comic, *Train-Flight*. Sarah is still very hurt by his abrupt departure, but eventually forgives him with a hug of reconciliation. She meets the Eighth Doctor in 1996 in the two-part novel, *Interference*, where she reveals she doesn't know if she was ever on Dust with the Third Doctor at all, and can't quite remember his third regeneration properly (all part of the Faction Paradox's war on the Doctor). At the book's conclusion, Samantha Jones, the Eighth Doctor's companion, elects to remain with Sarah. By the year 2000, Sarah is married to Paul Morely (actually sometime between 1996 and 1998 since they're married in *Christmas on a Rational Planet*, set in 1998), and Sarah and Sam are still best friends at some further point in the future. The biggest shift in Sarah's expanded timeline occurs in 1997's *Bullet Time*, wherein she becomes involved in a complex plan set up by the Seventh Doctor, shooting herself to avoid being taken hostage. Although it's unclear whether Sarah survives, the 2004 novel, *Sometime Never...*, reveals that Sarah's maybe-death was one of many (others included future companions Harry, Mel, Ace, and Sam) orchestrated by the Council of Eight, an organisation created to replace the now-destroyed Time Lords.

Sam isn't the only one of the Doctor's Expanded Universe companions who Sarah befriends. In *Vortex Butterflies*, part of Titan Comics' *Tenth Doctor* series, the Tenth Doctor asks Sarah to check in with Gabby Gonzalez and Cindy Wu, two friends he's had to temporarily leave in Willesden in 2009. The three bond over their adventures in time and space, and specifically over their encounters with Sutekh; while Sarah is impressed by Gabby's artistic skills, both Cindy and Gabby are wowed by Sarah, who helps them realise just how amazing their travels have been. Cindy even suggests Sarah could be in charge of Earth, such is her wisdom, but she counters that she knows exactly where she's needed: defending the planet. They spend at least a few weeks together, with Sarah giving the two New Yorkers a proper tour of London, and helping Cindy realise her true feelings for Gabby. When it's time to say goodbye, Sarah tells the Doctor to hold onto Gabby and Cindy because they're special; the Doctor affirms that all his companions are special.

Even if we ignore the times she met the Doctor again, her life after leaving him is nothing less than complicated. Following on from *K9 & Company*, many prose stories deal with Sarah and K9's further adventures, some involving the cast of the television story, most notably in the stories found in the *K9 Annual 1983* and the novelisation of the television episode – which curiously changes the location of the drama from Moreton Harwood to Hazelbury Abbas. Sarah's reputation has developed quite considerably: she's something of a celebrity. Aunt Lavinia continues to pop up from time to time. She even sends Sarah to Egypt in 1983 in the comic, *City of Devils* (*Doctor Who Magazine Holiday Special 1992*), where she and K9 encounter another tribe of Homo Reptilia, i.e. Silurians. Sarah continues to work with K9 for a while, including the time she and Mike Yates investigate a haunted house and find themselves up against the Master in the short story, *Housewarming*, and in the novelisation of the straight-to-video drama, *Downtime*. During this, she encounters Victoria Waterfield, not realising Victoria was a former companion of the Doctor's until a later conversation with the Brigadier, comparing notes. In a perfect example of the Expanded Universe contradicting itself, Lavinia dies twice: first, in 1998, according to the novel, *Millennium Shock*, and then just before the start of 2002's *Comeback*, the opening story of the *Sarah Jane Smith* audio series, which begins with Sarah back in Moreton Harwood, attending Lavinia's funeral.

The fate of K9 Mark III is also different to what's later revealed on TV. In the short story, *Moving On*, Sarah accepts that she must put the Doctor out of her life and move on – and so, she orders K9 to shut down. Later, in the finale of the first audio season of *Sarah Jane Smith*, we discover that K9 is in pieces, his parts having been salvaged by Hilda Winters in *Mirror, Signal, Manoeuvre*, who was involved in a personal vendetta against Sarah for her part in Winters' downfall in the television story, *Robot*.

Sarah's friendship with Harry Sullivan carries on for many years after she leaves the Doctor, such as in the novel, *Harry Sullivan's War*, and the novel-duology, *System Shock* and *Millennium Shock*. In the 2006 season two opener for *Sarah Jane Smith*, we discover that Sarah and Harry meet once a year to talk about their time at UNIT and with the Doctor – just to remind each other that it all happened. But in *Buried Secrets*, Harry fails to turn up, leading Sarah to wonder what's happened to him, especially when his step-brother, Will, turns up in his place. At the end of this season, Sarah is left alone, orbiting the Earth in the space shuttle *Dauntless*, a bright light fast approaching. The outcome of this cliffhanger has never been followed up, due in part to the commissioning of *The Sarah Jane Adventures* and the unexpected death of Elisabeth Sladen in 2011.

Rather wonderfully, *The Sarah Jane Adventures* has its own Expanded Universe content, namely a run of audio stories released between 2007 and 2011, the lion's share of which were read by Sladen herself. In these, we meet a couple of Sarah's neighbours on Bannerman Road (Doris at #54, for instance, according to *Deadly Download*, and John O'Brien and his parents at *The Ghost House*, i.e. the temporarily time-displaced #39), and learn more about Sarah's Aunt Lavinia, including that she took a young Sarah to the Natural History Museum (*The Time Capsule*), and, as per *The White Wolf*, that she was friends with clinical pathologist, Dr Eddison Clough, who lived in the Dorset village of Wolfenden. When she was eight, Sarah had lived there with her aunt too, though their memories had been wiped of this time by the alien fugitive, Mrs Hendrick. When her aunt died, Sarah had written lovingly about her for the *Metropolitan*.

In comparison, Harry Sullivan's Expanded Universe is fairly straightforward. His TV appearances largely run in such a tight consecutive order that they don't really allow for other adventures – not that it stops the 1976 and 1977 *Doctor Who Annuals* from depicting various adventures for Harry, Sarah, and the Doctor. Neither does it stop Christopher Bulis from writing *A Device of Death* and setting it in between the television stories, *Genesis of the Daleks* and *Revenge of the Cybermen*. The only gap that works is before the TARDIS crew arrive in Scotland in *Terror of the Zygons*, which is when the comic, *Black Destiny* (*Doctor Who Magazine*

#235-237) takes place. However, the 2019 novelisation of the unmade *Doctor Who Meets Scratchman*, written by Tom Baker and Ian Marter and adapted by Baker with James Goss, opens up a world of possibilities for Harry, affirming that he went on to travel more with the Doctor and Sarah after *The Android Invasion*.

The character was referenced before his actual first appearance during *Planet of Spiders*. The Expanded Universe establishes an even earlier involvement with UNIT during the 1998 novel, *The Face of the Enemy*: we see Harry, while in the Royal Navy, assist UNIT while the Doctor is visiting Peladon (as per the television story, *The Curse of Peladon*). In 2022's *London Orbital*, part of the *Sullivan and Cross – A WOL* audio set, we learn that it's actually the plague of *Doctor Who and the Silurians* that inspires Harry to quit the Navy, having felt useless at sea, unable to help fight the virus on land. While applying for a hospital job, he learns that someone from UNIT cured the plague and, as he investigates a massacre, he comes into contact with the Brigadier, who offers him a job. During an early assignment, he sees the TARDIS for the first time (*Kaleidoscope*), though naturally doesn't realise its significance.

As mentioned on-screen in *Mawdryn Undead*, Harry goes on to work with NATO; one of these adventures is chronicled in the *Companions of Doctor Who* book, *Harry Sullivan's War*. It seems that some years later, Harry would work with MI5, and by 1997, he's a Deputy Director at MI5 (*System Shock*), finding himself working with the Fourth Doctor once more, as well as Sarah – both of whom have only recently seen Harry some twenty-plus years earlier in the TV tale, *The Android Invasion*. He's reunited with the Fourth Doctor two years later in *Millennium Shock*; having returned Sarah to Earth after his unexpected summons to Gallifrey, the Doctor is now travelling alone. By 2005, Harry has returned to NATO, now holding the rank of commodore, and is called upon by the Brigadier during the audio play, *The Wasting*.

The Doctor and Sarah meet Harry's great-grandparents, Athena (daughter of Odysseus James) and Albert Sullivan (who bears a striking resemblance to Harry) in the 2016 Titan comic,

Gaze of the Medusa. Albert was a lieutenant in the Royal Navy, serving as a surgeon. He and Athena are so impressed by the Doctor and Sarah that they invite the pair to their wedding! Titan's *Ninth Doctor* series also shows Harry meeting the Ninth Doctor, Rose, and Jack Harkness (*Official Secrets*) at some point during his career at UNIT, likely after he left the TARDIS. Harry further encounters the Sixth Doctor, of sorts, the Third Doctor having 'degenerated' into his older incarnation during the sixtieth anniversary audio, *Once and Future: Two's Company*. Arguably in an alternative timeline, Harry travelled with this Doctor and Peri, in 1986's choose-your-own-adventure book, *Doctor Who and the Rebel's Gamble*.

Harry's later years become slightly more complicated. *The Sarah Jane Adventures* implies that Harry has died by 2010; indeed, the novelisation of *The Wedding of Sarah Jane Smith* notes that he died sometime before 2009. It's possible that he's instead gone missing: the 2006 *Sarah Jane Smith* audio, *Buried Secrets*, establishes that Harry and Sarah meet up every year to discuss their travels, but that he didn't turn up at their last scheduled meeting. His implied passing contradicts the 1996 novel, *Damaged Goods* (written by the executive producer and creator of *The Sarah Jane Adventures*, Russell T Davies), which mentions Harry living until at least 2015 where he discovers a possible cure for HIV.

Big Finish's audio adventures muddy the water further: he and fellow UNIT employee, Naomi Cross, travel in the TARDIS for a while, but the Fourth Doctor drops them off in the 2010s, some thirty years after their own time (*London Orbital*). They work with a contemporary UNIT under Kate Stewart, investigating Ice Warriors (2021's *UNIT: Between Two Worlds*), the Dominators (the following year's *Agents of the Vulpreen*), and the Axons (*Objective: Earth*, also 2022).

When they come into contact with the Seventh Doctor, he promises to take them back to the twentieth century – eventually.

It's unsurprising that most of Leela's Expanded Universe life focuses on the time after she left the Doctor. She appears in several short stories, comics, and prose tales in the pages of *Doctor Who Magazine* and *TV Comic*, as well as a handful of original novels, all set during her time with the Doctor. Throughout these, she's the same as she is on TV, although more in keeping with the character-arc seen in the television stories, *The Face of Evil* through to *Horror of Fang Rock*, with the Doctor continuing her education. There also seems to be a trend in taking Leela through Sarah's 'greatest hits': in the Big Finish audio dramas, she encounters Daleks and Kraals as well as visiting Space Station Nerva (from *The Ark in Space*); plus returning monsters in *Zygon Hunt* (2014), *The Exxilons* (2015), and *Kill the Doctor!/ The Age of Sutekh* (2018). The net is cast wider when she meets Weeping Angels in 2023's *Stone Cold*; various iterations of the Master; and the scaredy titular alien in *The Tivolian Who Knew Too Much* (2022), a species seen later on TV in *The God Complex* and *Under the Lake/ Before the Flood*. *The King of Sontar* (2014) foreshadows *The Invasion of Time* too.

In the 1998 novel, *Eye of Heaven*, we discover much about Leela's past. Her father was named Sole, and her mother, Neela. She also had an older sister, Ennia, who died at the age of three before Leela was born. The knife that Leela carries is the same one her mother used to defend Ennia. In this story, we learn that Leela won't swear on her mother's grave – suggesting that perhaps she's still alive. However, in the 2008 audiobook, *Empathy Games*, we learn that Neela died while protecting Leela, doing what she couldn't do with Ennia.

As revealed in several stories across the Expanded Universe, Leela's life on Gallifrey covers several hundred years, during which time she ages very slowly, due to the influence of living in the Gallifreyan environment; the *Gallifrey* audio series tells us she lives on Gallifrey for over five hundred 'spans' (possibly 'years').

The first time we see Leela's life on Gallifrey is in 1997's *Lungbarrow*; she's still married to Andred and now has an official Gallifreyan name: Leelandredloomsagwinaechegesima. We further discover that she's pregnant, carrying the first child to be born on Gallifrey for millennia. We never find out what happens to this child.

We next encounter Leela in the Big Finish audio play, *Zagreus* (the fortieth anniversary adventure), when she receives a telepathic call from Rassilon and breaks into the presidential suite to see Romana – her successor in the Doctor's long line of companions, and now President of the High Council of Time Lords. Romana initially considers her a 'savage', but over the course of both *Zagreus* and the following series, *Gallifrey*, a respectful and trusting friendship is built up between the two former companions (both of whom have a version of K9 with them). Leela has previously advised another of the planet's presidents: the Fifth Doctor in *Time in Office* (2017), who she accompanies on a diplomatic mission while Andred and K9 are clearing up the Death Zone following the events of *The Five Doctors*. She later enlists the Fifth Doctor herself, in a mission for the Time Lords in 2020's *Wicked Sisters*.

During *Zagreus*, she encounters, and ultimately plays a part in saving, the Eighth Doctor. As a result of her strength and loyalty, she becomes Romana's personal bodyguard during the early chapters of *Gallifrey*. Although clearly not a political animal, Leela finds herself more and more drawn into the politics of Gallifrey, not always seeing eye to eye with Romana. Her husband, Andred, goes missing at one point, and she later discovers he's been killed – though the person who imparts this information is later revealed to be a regenerated Andred. She never forgives him for his deceit, not even when he does finally die. Nonetheless, in the 2022 audio, *Tenth Doctor, Classic Companions: Splinters*, she's still sad about his passing.

During the course of a civil war on Gallifrey, K9 is destroyed (thus contradicting the *K9* television series) and Leela refuses a replacement unit; she's unhappy with the loss of her final link to the Doctor. In *Gallifrey: Fractures*, she's blinded for the second time (she was temporarily blinded in the TV story, *Horror of Fang Rock*), and her sight isn't returned until a while later in *Annihilation*, by which time she and Romana are stuck moving from one alternative version of Gallifrey to another. Her sight is restored by the blood of a vampire, but not before she's tortured by an alternative version of herself. On another version of Gallifrey, she meets an alternative Sixth Doctor, now called the Lord Burner (*Disassembled*). She and Romana finally settle on a version of Gallifrey that hasn't mastered time travel; while Romana seeks to bring some time travel ability to the people of that world, Leela finds herself leading the Outsiders (as she did in *The Invasion of Time*) who were once slaves to the Regenerators of Gallifrey.

At some point, Leela is sent to London in the 1890s by Romana to investigate 'time breaks'. It's unclear at which point in Leela's timeline this occurs, but based on the evidence of her being able to recognise the Sixth Doctor (living in 1890s London under the disguise of Professor Claudius Dark), it must take place after Leela and Romana return to the original Gallifrey (in series six), as Leela uses the time ring technology previously seen in season twelve of the TV show. While in London, she teams up with Henry Gordon Jago and Professor George Litefoot (whom she befriended in *The Talons of Weng-Chiang*), and remains working alongside them for some time – from the end of series two of *Jago & Litefoot* (*The Ruthven Inheritance*) right through the following two series until *The Hourglass Killer*. The Sixth Doctor initially hides his true identity from Jago and Litefoot, although Leela knows, while he works to fix the time break, repair the damage made by Payne's time experiments, and defeat the Sandmen. Leela returns to Gallifrey after the Doctor fixes the time ring.

So, having been left on the seemingly doomed Gallifrey, what happened to Leela during the Time War? This period is explored through a number of *Time War*, *War Rooms*, *War Doctor*, and *The War Doctor Begins* audio sets. These detailed her initial secondment to the War Council, where she was able to place Earth behind a quantum field to minimise the damage to it caused by the war. However, she's disgusted to find out the Council's plans to resurrect dead Time Lords, as per 2018's *Celestial Intervention*. Romana then asks Leela to keep an eye on the Master, who ultimately abandons her in the Time Vortex (the same year's *The Devil You Know*). After being saved and taken into another dimension, Leela meets Sholan, her possible son in that alternate universe, though he sacrifices himself in the 2020 episode, *Mother Tongue*. Following a stint with the resistance, a group set up to oppose both the Daleks and Time Lords, Leela is conscripted by Rassilon to fight in the Time War; however, she goes missing at the Battle of the Pillars of Consequence, believed dead by the Time Lords (*The Lady of Obsidian* and *The Enigma Dimension*, both 2017). Actually, a specialised Disruptor Dalek displaces her in time and space, and she's only saved by the War Doctor. Though not travelling with the War Doctor during the events of *The Day of the Doctor*, she survives Gallifrey's apparent destruction, as confirmed in a trilogy of *Companion Chronicles* (*The Catalyst, Empathy Games*, and *The Time Vampire*) in which an older Leela narrates a few past trips in the TARDIS. At the end of the trilogy, Leela, after living for hundreds of years, finally dies and moves on to the Great Hereafter. 2012's *The Child* acts as a coda to this: her soul is reanimated in a young girl called Emily, who hears of Leela's many adventures with the Doctor.

K9's Expanded Universe stories diverge quite significantly, given that there are various versions of the robotic characters scattered around. K9 Mk I – that is, the original built by Professor Marius and seen in *The Invisible Enemy* – left in *The Invasion of Time*, staying with Leela on the Doctor's home planet, so he accompanies her on many of her adventures in the aforementioned *Gallifrey* audio series. However, there are a number of stories featuring K9 Mk I that bookend this period.

One Man and His Dog, a story in the 2015 book, *The Essential Book of K9*, significant for being written by Bob Baker, K9's co-creator, expands on Marius' motivation for making K9, i.e. that he had to leave his German Shepherd, Kelso, with a friend called Grace when assigned to the Bi-Al Foundation medical facility. This contradicts the *Brief Encounters* tale, *Tautology*, published in *Doctor Who Magazine* #194, which calls Marius' dog Toby, and suggests the professor based K9 on old design for a robotic dog; that is, the K9 the Doctor left for Sarah, based on Marius' K9 Mk I – an ontological paradox.

While travelling with the Fourth Doctor and Leela, in the 2015 two-part audio, *The Fate of Krelos/Return to Telos*, K9 reveals a vulnerability to the Cybermen: after declaring 'you belong to us,' he pilots the TARDIS to Telos, where the Doctor discovers a Cybermat inside K9's systems. Later, in the 2022-23 iOS and Android game, *Lost in Time*, we learn that K9 can pick up signals from vortex manipulators, immediately recognising River Song's in the vicinity of the TARDIS. K9 Mk IV, himself fitted with a vortex manipulator circuit and Temporal Positioning System, to allow him to travel in time with the Thirteenth Doctor, is also in this same period. The Mk IV was left to Sarah at the conclusion of *School Reunion* and was seen throughout *The Sarah Jane Adventures*. *Farewell, Sarah Jane* reveals that, following her passing, K9 Mk IV was left to Ace, who was already working with K9 Mk II to detect fallout from the Time War (as per *Quantum of Axos*, part of *Tenth Doctor, Classic Companions*). K9 Mk II left the TARDIS with Romana in E-Space, so, according to the audios, eventually found himself back on Gallifrey, where he often worked alongside the Mk I (though he found his predecessor 'inferior', likely due to his retaining all his data and memories). He acts as President Romana's aide, and travels with her as she and Leela are forced to visit alternative versions of Gallifrey (and even meet an alternate Sixth Doctor).

K9 Mk III's timeline is far more linear. This unit is left with Sarah in *K9 & Company*, though before that, he appears in a few prose and comic strips with the Fourth Doctor and Adric in the *Doctor Who Annual 1982*. The 2014 audio story, *Psychodrome*, tells us that Adric missed K9 Mk II, so we might infer that the Doctor decided to ease the Alzarian's transition into N-Space by letting him spend some more time with the robot dog before sending the Mk III to Earth. This K9 then has several adventures with Sarah and Brendan Richards in the *K9 Annual 1983*. K9 Mk III's decline is touched upon in *A Dog's Life*, a short story in the 2006 book, *Doctor Who Files 6: K9*, in which we learn that Sarah simply can't get the parts to repair his batteries and self-repair systems, meaning he's left powered down in her lounge. When burglars try to steal him, he fights them off then alerts the police, depleting the last of his energy. At some point between this and *School Reunion*, then, Sarah takes to bringing K9 with her on car journeys, perhaps due to his being dismantled and analysed by a vengeful Hilda Winters in the audio episode, *Mirror, Signal, Manoeuvre*, indicating he could be a security risk to Sarah and Earth.

But that's not the end for K9. Despite K9 Mk I apparently being obliterated in the *Gallifrey* story, *Imperiatrix*, the *K9* TV spin-off, which ran from 2009 to 2010 and was co-produced by Bob Baker, suggests he survived the Time War, and travelled back from the year 50,000 to 2050 through a Space-Time Manipulator. This Mk I self-destructed to get rid of the turtle-like warrior Jixen race, but activated his own regeneration unit (implied to have been fitted by the Doctor) to create *another* K9 Mk II, which features in a few tales in *The Essential Book of K9*.

Romana, especially the second incarnation, has been a popular topic in the Expanded Universe, and no matter which series you follow (be it the BBC Books or the Big Finish audios), all writers agree on one thing: she escapes E-Space and ascends to the august position of President of the High Council of Time Lords. Russell T Davies, showrunner of *Doctor Who* from 2005 to 2010, then 2023 onwards, states in the *Doctor Who Annual 2006* that Romana was president during the Time War, even though, in *The End of Time*, we saw Rassilon as president. In the comic, *The Forgotten*, the Tenth Doctor says that the Time War didn't end well for Romana, and this is explored in Big Finish's stories about this period in *Doctor Who* history. But before that...

Romana first escapes E-Space in the 1994 novel, *Blood Harvest*, with the aid of the Seventh Doctor and Bernice Summerfield.

She's given a seat on the High Council by the time of *Goth Opera* and is president by *Happy Endings* (by this time, K9 Mk II has also been freed from E-Space). It's from this point that the timelines seem to diverge, since Romana's time as president in the novels is different from in the Big Finish audios. In the novels published by BBC Books, Romana returns in *The Shadows of Avalon*, newly regenerated into her third body, and sets about hunting down the Doctor's companion, Compassion, who's evolved into the first fully sentient TARDIS. There's a war between the Time Lords and an unknown Enemy, and Romana intends to be ready for it. In *The Ancestor Cell*, the Doctor destroys Gallifrey and retroactively erases the Time Lords from history, but Romana is implied to be one of the very few survivors, in the novel *Tomb of Valdemar*.

Things run in an almost parallel way in the Big Finish audios, with Romana making her first appearance as president in *The Apocalypse Element*, having spent some time as a prisoner of the Daleks. Upon her escape, she and the Sixth Doctor work together to repel the Daleks' first attempt at invading Gallifrey. She returns heading the Time Lords' battle against the Neverpeople, wishing to kill the Eighth Doctor's companion, Charley Pollard, who's a gateway between this universe and the Never-universe. Like the books, Romana is pitted against the Doctor, and the story ends with the latter fleeing. She continues on in the series, *Gallifrey*, alongside Leela, where we discover that Romana, in her first body, was corrupted by an ancient evil entity called Pandora. She regenerated to free herself of the taint, but in the *Gallifrey* series, Pandora returns in the body of the First Romana and claims herself Imperiatrix of Gallifrey, provoking a civil war. Romana succeeds in destroying Pandora, but is deposed of her position and has to escape Gallifrey. She ends up travelling through various alternative versions of the planet with Leela, but eventually they find their way back, and Romana is even reinstated as president! Holding this position, she orders the Seventh Doctor to collect the Master's remains from Skaro (revealed in both the novel, *Lungbarrow*, and the audio, *The Eleven*), leading into *The TV Movie*.

This is where Big Finish's stories diverge from Davies' assertion that Romana was president during the Time War: according to *Gallifrey: Enemy Lines* (2016), Romana resigns, naming Lady Livia Caralis as her successor, and appointing herself coordinator of the Celestial Intervention Agency (CIA), with Narvinectralonum, aka. Narvin, as her deputy. She and Narvin are suspicious of their own species during the early days of the Time War, and she's arrested for treason; fortunately, and rather surprisingly, she's pardoned by the newly-resurrected Rassilon in *Havoc*, part of the 2019 set, *Time War: Volume Two*. Still, Romana and Narvin continue to see red flags, including Rassilon announcing any planet that doesn't stand with Gallifrey is automatically an enemy, and his erasing the planet Ysalus from time as a show of strength. Romana attempts to assassinate Rassilon, but this only results in her and Narvin being exiled, and joining the resistance. During this time, Romana reveals she's heard tales of the War Doctor – who she describes as 'you know who' – and believes he's changed for the worst (2021's *Beyond*). Rassilon catches up with Romana in *Homecoming*, imprisoning her in a pocket dimension, archiving her own adventures in space and time, though not before inspiring Leela to defend Gallifrey.

What happens to Romana next is a mystery: in one timeline, she regenerates again and lives through a war that leads to her being the last of the Time Lords; this universe was erased, however, apparently on the orders of Romana herself in *Enemy Lines*. Nevertheless, Leela likely believes she's dead – or at least 'gone', as she tells the Tenth Doctor in *Splinters*.

But long before the darkness of the Time War, there are numerous stories that explore happier times for both incarnations of Romana, including sequels to *Warriors' Gate* like *Stolen Futures*, part of 2022's *Protectors of Time* set, and the 2021 BBC audio, *The Kairos Ring*, written by the TV serial's scribe, Stephen Gallagher. Mary Tamm's incarnation of Romana enjoys further stories too, either slotted in between episodes of the *Key to Time* season or set just afterwards. *The Auntie Matter*, for instance, finds the Doctor and Romana relaxing in the 1920s, while the TARDIS, with K9 inside, leads the Black Guardian on a wild goose-chase across the universe following *The Armageddon Factor*. During this 2013 run of audio stories, Romana meets the Daleks, as well as Jago and Litefoot, while a previous 2011 *Companion Chronicles* instalment, *Tales from the Vault*, sees her taken in for questioning by UNIT. Other mediums – notably novels like *The Shadow of Weng-Chiang* (1996) and short stories in the *Doctor Who Annual 1980* – tell of further diversions from their mission.

We don't learn a great deal more about Romana's history, but some details creep out in books like the 2018 adaptation, *Doctor Who and the Krikkitmen*, which says that Borusa was one of her tutors at the Academy, and in 2017's *A Brief History of Time Lords*, in which we discover that, much like the Doctor, an eight-year-old Romana ran away when she looked into the Untempered Schism, a 'gap in the fabric of reality' which allows Time Lords to see into the Vortex itself.

Adric doesn't have many Expanded Universe tales with the Fourth Doctor, but he does appear in the *Doctor Who Annual 1982* alongside K9 Mk III, as well as in some audio adventures.

The Invasion of E-Space, a 2010 *Companion Chronicles* tale, opens up a lot of potential for Adric travelling with the Fourth Doctor and Romana: it's set before they escape E-Space in *Warriors' Gate*, but establishes that Adric has been with the pair for around two months already. In the 2003 *Short Trips* story, *O, Darkness*, Adric is troubled by the idea that Time Lords with such expansive lives might not consider spending months is one place a waste of time.

Indeed, *A Full Life* (2016) details a parallel version of Adric's life, where the Doctor and Romana die and he's trapped on the planet Veridis. There, he marries Asun, and they have two sons, Varsh and Neegat. Nonetheless, knowing this isn't how his life is supposed to turn out, he creates a time machine using TARDIS crystals and rewrites his past, bringing the two Time Lords back to life and paving the way for his continued travels in N-Space.

The Fourth Doctor and Adric meet further parallel versions of themselves in the 2003 short story, *Mauritz*.

Perhaps the most notable Fourth Doctor companion exclusive to the Expanded Universe is Sharon Davies, who has the honour of being the first black companion in any *Doctor Who* medium.

She first appears in *Doctor Who and the Star Beast*, the basis for the sixtieth anniversary special with the Fourteenth Doctor; both stories have the Wrarth Warriors chasing Beep the Meep, a seemingly sweet creature that's actually a psychotic killer. This comic was adapted by Big Finish in 2019, with Davies voiced by Rhianne Starbuck. At the conclusion of the strip, the Doctor says he'll take Sharon back to her home, Blackcastle in Yorkshire, but naturally, the TARDIS doesn't play ball, instead taking them to the Spacehog space-freighter (*Doctor Who and the Dogs of War*). The Doctor clearly cares for her, refusing to put her in even greater danger when he learns the Daleks are involved in the attack on the Spacehog. She, however, has a lot of fun – so much that she decides to stay on in the TARDIS for a time. Her travels see her lost in a blank dimension with the Doctor (*Doctor Who and the Time Witch*), meet the Sontarans (*Dragon's Claw*), and briefly return home in *The Collector*; she's apprehensive about going back to Blackcastle since she's grown into an adult during her journeys, and feels like a different person. She needn't have worried: during a trip to Unicepter IV in *Dreamers of Death*, she falls in love with Vernor Allen and leaves the TARDIS to start a new life with him. She makes the Doctor promise to return, and he cheekily replies, 'I'll try, Sharon... but you know the TARDIS... If I set the controls for Unicepter, it'll probably put me in Blackcastle!'

We do see Sharon again, however. In *Star Beast II*, a story from the *Doctor Who Yearbook 1996*, we learn that she and Vernon did indeed get married, and by the 2012 strip, *The Stockbridge Showdown*, she's a TV journalist for the Galactic Broadcasting Corporation. She's open about her travels with the Doctor, telling viewers in *Mistress of Chaos* (2019-20), 'I was a girl when I first met the Doctor. Trust me when I say that the name means many things to many people: A warrior... Healer... Scientist... Clown... But I think most of all, an example.'

Fenella Wibbsey, played by Susan Jameson in all her audio appearances (and all written by Paul Magrs), is the most unusual Expanded Universe Fourth Doctor companion.

Introduced as the Doctor's housekeeper in *The Stuff of Nightmares*, this kicked off three seasons of stories connected to Nest Cottage, the Doctor's 'vacation home'. The Doctor takes Mrs Wibbsey from her hometown of Cromer in 1932 to the cottage in Surrey in 2009 in order to escape the influence of the Hornets, insectoids that could possess others, including Wibbsey. With the help of former UNIT captain Mike Yates (who arguably becomes a Fourth Doctor companion through this run of audios), they fight off the Hornets. Unfortunately, while trying to repair the TARDIS, he disassembles part of his ship, and Wibbsey accidentally sells a component at a church rummage sale (*The Relics of Time*). Their quest to get it back takes them to Montmatre, 1894 (*The Demon of Paris*), where they meet Henri de Toulouse-Lautrec, and New York in 1976 (*Starfall*), before Fenella is kidnapped by the Demon who hails from the shadow dimension. *Sepulchre* reveals that Wibbsey has been under the influence of the Hornets the whole time; the Doctor cures her, and she recalls recent events only as a bad dream.

Mrs Wibbsey is a warm and thoughtful sort, though the Doctor is rather selfish: he dismisses her feelings about going home to 1932, telling her that there's nothing left for her there, despite her clearly having a job that she seemed enjoyed, i.e. curator of the Cromer Palace of Curios. Conversely, the Doctor's attitude likely comes from his fondness for her, despite or perhaps due to there being a steeliness behind her 'grandmotherly' exterior that means she stands up to the Time Lord whenever she needs to; not to mention her ability to sniff out trouble. Still, there's a sadness to her, partly because she's out of her own time, and partly because she's so often at the whims of alien beings, whether they be the Hornets or the Doctor.

And yet Fenella obviously likes the Doctor's company and misses him when he disappears for a couple of months in 2011's *The Hexford Invasion*. During this adventure, she's reunited with Mike Yates who seemingly brings with him the Second Doctor – actually a clone created by the Fourth Doctor. *Survivors in Space* brought the *Nest Cottage Chronicles* to an end, but what makes Wibbsey so unique is that she appears in a spiritual successor series, *Baker's End*, this time as Fenella Frimbly. This four-part 2016-17 run of audio stories obscures whether Tom Baker plays the Doctor or whether the Doctor is Tom Baker…

Granted, the Fourth Doctor's Big Finish companions are rather unusual too, seeing as both Ann Kelso and Naomi Cross also travel with other incarnations of the Doctor.

In fact, WPC Ann Kelso doesn't even exist. This is an alias, a result of her being sent deep undercover by the Space Security Service; she's even implanted with false memories, though her subconscious is strong enough that, after meeting the Doctor in *The Sinestran Kill* (2019), she tries to use the TARDIS to complete her mission to track down a criminal gang from the forty-first century known as the Syndicate. They largely succeed, with Kelso concealing her brutal side: unbeknown to the Doctor, she kills any criminals she can then covers up their deaths. In *The Perfect Prisoners*, the Doctor find out that Ann is really Anya Kingdom, and that her boss is secretly the final Syndicate member. They defeat him, but when Anya asks to travel more with the Doctor, he refuses: he liked Ann too much, and Anya is a pale imitation.

While Kingdom's better associated with the Tenth Doctor, Naomi Cross mostly travels with the Seventh Doctor. Working for UNIT with Harry Sullivan, Naomi stars in a number of Fourth Doctor tales like *The Storm of the Sea Devils*, *Matryoshka*, and *The Face in the Storm* (all 2024), before being mistakenly left in the 2010s, instead of their native 1980s (*London Orbital*).

The Fifth Doctor
Peter Davison

'*There's always something to look at if you open your eyes.*'
The Doctor – *Kinda*

Adric – Matthew Waterhouse – Continued... (*Full Circle* to
Earthshock and *Time-Flight*)

Almost immediately after the Doctor regenerates, Adric is
kidnapped by the Master. For a long while, neither Tegan
nor Nyssa realise this, as the Master forces Adric to create a block
transfer computation of himself. This fake Adric helps them
dematerialise the TARDIS and guide the Doctor towards the Zero
Room, a tranquil space in the TARDIS that helps the Doctor
recover from his regeneration. The ersatz Adric is quite
knowledgeable about regeneration: this might be because the
Master is feeding him the information, or that the Doctor
explained regeneration to him at some point after Romana left.

As a prisoner, Adric's mathematical genius is used to create
Castrovalva, another block transfer computation – in truth, a
complex space-time trap used to destabilise the Doctor further.
Adric shows an amazing amount of will power in his attempts to
resist the Master's control, creating several images of himself to
communicate and warn Tegan and Nyssa. It's almost certain that
Adric gives Shardovan (a denizen of Castrovalva, and so, also a
block transfer computation) the free will to help the Doctor defeat
the Master. As the fake city starts to collapse, only Adric can see
the way out as he created the place. The strain on him is obvious;
by the time they reach the TARDIS, Adric is almost green, looking
quite sick.

Once more, Adric's fickle and inconsiderate nature comes into play when the TARDIS arrives on the Urbankan ship in *Four to Doomsday*. He's easily taken in by the promises offered by Monarch, i.e. being transferred into an android body that will never wither and die. This is the first real crack in his relationship with the Doctor, something that never quite heals. It gets to the point where the Doctor calls him a 'young idiot', yet acknowledges that some might deem him gullible but he is, instead, 'idealistic'. By itself, that's no bad thing, but mixed with Adric's naivety, it makes for an unfortunate combination. He often speaks overly freely, revealing too much information to anyone who asks, usually with no thought as to the consequences. This could be his need to be accepted; as an outsider, Adric is always trying to find a place to belong. Unfortunately, his desire to impress often fails and comes across as arrogance.

Adric's impulsive too: on Deva Loka (*Kinda*), he closes the Total Survival Suit (TSS) before the Doctor can warn him not to touch it. As a result, they're marched to the dome of the Earth expedition. Still, he's shrewd enough to play along with the unhinged Hindle to get a key to free the Doctor from his cell (though the rescue attempt ultimately fails). He later panics as he enters the TSS and ends up almost killing Aris, one of the Kinda people, but the Doctor is eventually able to release him from the metal suit. In *The Visitation*, the Doctor strongly berates Adric for his carelessness on Deva Loka; such arguments punctuate their relationship from hereon in, leading to their biggest falling out in *Earthshock*. Adric is insistent on returning to Terradon and plots a course through a CVE, even though the Doctor is certain he will kill himself if such an attempt is made. The Doctor's clearly upset at the thought of losing Adric, despite their abrasiveness, and playfully hits him on the head when Adric admits he doesn't really want to go back to E-Space, even though his calculations are correct. 'Well, it proves a point,' Adric retorts.

Despite his alien origins, Adric does come across as a typical teenage boy at times. At the party in Cranleigh Hall in *Black*

Orchid, he would rather stuff his face with food than join in, until Nyssa forces him to dance. Every now and then, he does display some playful cheekiness, which Tegan warms to, even though verbally they spar a lot. Often, it's Nyssa who proves to be the calming influence, since the Doctor just seems to be irritated by the continual arguing. Tegan's concern for Adric comes to the fore when he's forced to remain behind on a space freighter that is heading on a collision course with Earth. She struggles against the Cybermen as they drag her away, and in response, Adric can only offer a sad smile. Despite his outward attitude, it seems that Adric does indeed have a fondness for Tegan. Adric is almost saved from his fate by Captain Scott; however, at the last moment, as the doors to the escape pod close, Adric jumps out – certain he's worked out the final course correction. He begins inputting the data, unaware that a damaged Cyberman is in the vicinity. Before he can see if his computations are correct, the Cyberman destroys the console. Adric can only stand by and watch as Earth rapidly approaches. He twists Varsh's Outler sash in his hands, bravely accepting his fate. His arrogance (or maybe pride) seems to win out: 'Now I'll never know if I was right.'

Adric's death affects the Doctor, Nyssa, and Tegan in very different ways. Tegan is the most vocal, vehemently insisting the Doctor take the TARDIS back to save Adric, but the Doctor angrily says he can't break the laws of time. He swiftly calms down, acknowledging their grief is shared, and finds some solace in the fact Adric died trying to save others.

In *Time-Flight*, a phantom of Adric briefly appears to warn Tegan and Nyssa away from Kalid's domain, but they spot his badge for mathematical excellence which the Doctor had used to destroy the Cyber Leader, and realise it's not really Adric. The trio do seem to move on quite quickly, by necessity perhaps, but his passing hits them all hard enough for Adric to be a pressure point for the Master (as Kalid) to exploit.

It seems the Doctor carries a lot of guilt with him over Adric's death. This is probably what drives him to such extremes to save

Peri's life in *The Caves of Androzani* and explains why the very last word to pass through his mind before regenerating is 'Adric.'

And when Tegan is reunited with the Doctor many years later in *The Power of the Doctor*, she believes he's largely forgotten her; to prove himself, she asks the Doctor what she's thinking after 'seeing all these Cybermen.' His reply is simply, and apparently correctly, 'Adric.'

Nyssa – Sarah Sutton – Continued... (*The Keeper of Traken*, and *Logopolis* to *Terminus*)

Nyssa's scientific knowledge comes into play in *Castrovalva* when she shows an understanding of the Zero Room – a place that's cut off the outside world, allowing Time Lords to recover from difficult regenerations. And when the room is accidentally jettisoned from the TARDIS to save them all from Event One, i.e. the creation of the universe, it's Nyssa who hits upon the idea of building a Zero Cabinet (in which the Doctor can safely recover) from the room's remaining wall. She also shows a good understanding of recursion, where ideas and concepts fold back on themselves. Though she can't pilot the TARDIS, she is able to understand many of its controls merely by deduction. She later claims she's an expert in bio-engineering and cybernetics, indicating the level of advancement Traken had reached before its destruction. Initially, she understandably finds it very difficult to look at the Master: after all, he is walking around with her dead father's face (yet it seems she's forgotten this the next time they meet in *Time-Flight*).

Nyssa is always sensible; there's a marked difference between her maturity and Adric's, even though they were supposed to be similar ages and have advanced scientific knowledge. The Doctor certainly has great faith in her technical abilities. She develops a very strong relationship with Tegan during their initial travels together and is clearly upset by the idea of Tegan leaving at the start of *The Visitation*, although this departure doesn't happen, since the TARDIS arrives in the wrong century.

THE FIFTH DOCTOR

In *Black Orchid*, they meet Nyssa's doppelgänger, Ann Talbot, and the two girls play a joke at the fancy dress ball by wearing the same outfit. Her playfulness with Ann brings Nyssa out of her shell somewhat (she even learns the Charleston from Tegan), and she's rather bemused by the initial attention she receives as people try to work out if Nyssa is a member of the extended Talbot family. She's kidnapped by Ann's former fiancé, George Cranleigh, who's been demented and disfigured by a tribe of Indians, but she's eventually released to the safe arms of the Doctor once George realises his mistake. Despite him having taken her captive, Nyssa is nonetheless disturbed to see George fall to his death.

She's almost transferred into an android body on the Urbankan ship in *Four to Doomsday*, an experience that obviously hits her hard as she collapses from the stress. The Doctor builds a delta wave augmentor, which induces her into a deep level of sleep so she can recover (*Kinda*). She wakes up four days later.

Adric's death leaves Nyssa more subdued and she spends some time helping the Doctor rescue the survivors of the space freighter in *Earthshock*. The loss is made worse when, after returning the passengers of Concorde from prehistoric Earth (*Time-Flight*), she and the Doctor rush off in the TARDIS to avoid official questions, accidentally leaving Tegan behind.

It's unclear how long Nyssa travels alone with the Doctor, but when we next see them in *Arc of Infinity*, they do appear a lot closer. Nyssa has even become more outspoken – almost as if she were filling in for Tegan – pointing out the problems with the TARDIS quite brazenly. Nyssa has become extremely protective of the Doctor, her one last link to her lost life. Her impassioned plea to the High Council of Time Lords on Gallifrey to intercede and save the Doctor's life brings her to tears, and she resorts to violence to try and save him. Like on Traken, she doesn't use a lethal weapon, merely a taser on stun, until the Doctor stops her. She can do nothing but watch as the Doctor is seemingly killed. She's distraught and retires to the TARDIS, unwilling to talk to anyone for a while, but she's easily persuaded that the Doctor is

147

still alive, taking any bit of hope offered to her. When she discovers that the Doctor, via the Matrix of Gallifrey, has been in contact with Tegan (who's in Amsterdam), Nyssa is very pleased at the idea of seeing her again; sure enough, when they're reunited, the women immediately bond. Once again, Nyssa has the two most important people in her life with her – Tegan, her best friend, and the Doctor, the man who reminds her of her father. Her affection for Tegan is further shown in *Snakedance*: after learning Tegan's still infected by the malignant entity known as the Mara, Nyssa insists she put on a device to keep her free from its influence.

In that serial, Nyssa makes a big deal about changing into new clothes, supporting all on-screen evidence that, other than the fancy dress party in *Black Orchid*, she's worn the same clothes since leaving Traken. Perhaps continually being in the clothes from her home has helped her deal with her loss. If so, changing out of them could be an indication that she's finally coming to terms with the loss, and is able to start moving on. This notion is backed up when she departs the TARDIS a couple of stories later.

In *Mawdryn Undead*, Nyssa meets a school boy named Turlough, and decides he seems 'quite nice', despite Tegan's initial distrust of him. Like Tegan, she's convinced that Mawdryn is the Doctor, albeit in a badly mutated regenerated state, even though there's little physical evidence for this. He's clearly not wearing the Doctor's clothes, and has a strange brain mass erupting from his head. The Brigadier – who is teaching at Turlough's school some six years earlier (in 1977) – gives Mawdryn the benefit of the doubt, but is less sure than either Nyssa or Tegan. For reasons not fully explained, both Nyssa and Tegan become infected by exposure to Mawdryn and his ship, and cannot leave without being aged to death or regressed to babies. The Doctor, no doubt still suffering from the guilt of Adric's death, decides that he will sacrifice his remaining lives to cure them. Such a course proves unnecessary since the meeting of two Brigadiers (one from 1977 and one from 1983) results in the Blinovitch Limitation Effect, curing Nyssa and Tegan instead (again, it's not explained why the meeting of the two Brigadiers does this).

We never get to see Nyssa develop a relationship with Turlough. In *Terminus*, she becomes infected with Lazar's disease. But as she deteriorates, Tegan and Turlough are not around to offer her comfort. Resourceful and clever, she eventually finds a way to cure her illness, and believes she can do the same for others suffering from the disease. Having learned the importance of self-sacrifice from the Doctor (and possibly Adric), Nyssa initially tells Tegan about her decision. Tegan is very upset by this – the two of them having only been recently reunited after their unexpected separation – and tells the Doctor to convince Nyssa to remain with them. Although he clearly doesn't want to lose Nyssa, the Doctor knows that she's doing what she feels is right, and he cannot fault her for that. It's a sad, but final farewell, as Nyssa tells her friend, 'Like you, Tegan, I am indestructible.'

The last we see of Nyssa is during the Doctor's regeneration in *The Caves of Androzani*, amid a swirling hallucination of talking heads: this vision of Nyssa asserts, 'You're needed. You mustn't die, Doctor.'

Tegan Jovanka – Janet Fielding – Continued... (*Logopolis* to *Resurrection of the Daleks,* plus *The Power of the Doctor*)

The Doctor barely has time to get to know Tegan in *Logopolis,* but still places a large degree of trust in her (arguably out of necessity) when he assigns her the job of 'co-ordinator' in *Castrovalva.* While he recovers in the Zero Room, Tegan begins to organise the crew.

She quickly learns how to reconfigure the TARDIS, with a few hints from the Doctor, and is quite pleased that she's able to pilot it to Castrovalva – although she's later disheartened to learn that it would've ended up there anyway, since the Master used the captured Adric to pre-set the co-ordinates.

Tegan is very determined to return home and to her job, despite the constant disappointments with false landings, and insists on wearing her stewardess uniform throughout her initial journeys, only changing once, to attend the fancy dress party at

Cranleigh Hall. In *Four to Doomsday*, the Doctor offers her a TARDIS key, which she doesn't accept immediately, still annoyed at the Doctor's inability to return her to Heathrow. She does take it eventually – if only to stop Adric having it.

When she explains to the Urbankans about modern day Earth fashions, she proves herself to be an exceptional sketch artist. She also understands the Aboriginal dialect spoken by Kurkutji, even though the language he speaks almost certainly would've changed over the intervening twenty thousand years (presumably the TARDIS' rather selective telepathic circuits help Tegan to do this). The idea of being immortalised as an android horrifies her, but her main concern is always for Earth; whenever Earth's in danger, most other concerns become secondary to her. Even in her panicked state, she manages to pilot the TARDIS a short distance, showing considerable aptitude for it after all.

She's temporarily possessed by the Mara on Deva Loka (*Kinda*), after it works its way into her unconscious in the 'place of shared dreams'. She's freed after the psychic parasite transfers to Aris, and for a while she remembers almost nothing of the possession. Her curiosity gets the better of her when the Mara is contained in a trap of mirrors: she wants to see what possessed her, and, unbeknown to her, a small portion of it escapes into her deep unconsciousness. The horror of having her mind controlled by anything remains with her, as witnessed by her response to the Terileptil's attempt at mind control in *The Visitation*.

By the time the Doctor tries to return her to Heathrow again in *The Visitation*, Tegan is close friends with Nyssa, and expresses sadness at having to leave; nonetheless, she's determined to get on with her life, and is annoyed when the Doctor fails to get her back to her own time: 'Call yourself a Time Lord? A broken clock keeps better time than you do. At least it's accurate twice a day, which is more than you ever are!'

The Doctor considers her bad-tempered. When they later arrive in 1925 (*Black Orchid*), Tegan decides she wants to remain with the TARDIS, yet she continues to wear her uniform, perhaps clinging to her old life. She enjoys her time at the party in Cranleigh Hall, mixing with the guests, calling it a 'hoot', and demonstrating her dancing ability by taking part in the Charleston.

Like the companions before her, and despite their earlier differences, she assertively supports the Doctor. When he's accused of murder, she point blank refuses to accept such an accusation and strives to prove him innocent in her usual argumentative way. In *Earthshock*, she's more than willing to take the fight to the Cybermen, showing courage and a will to back up the Doctor. Still, she's devastated by Adric's death, even though she didn't particularly like him, and is furious when the Doctor refuses to go back in time to save him, regardless of his reasoning.

The Doctor finally brings the TARDIS to Heathrow in *Time-Flight*, prompting her to question if she wants to stay there. It's curious that, for the first time since entering the TARDIS in *Logopolis*, she leaves *with* her handbag (which no doubt contains her personal documentation) – as if she expects to remain behind, which is exactly what happens. By the time she returns to the TARDIS, it's gone. The Doctor and Nyssa have left without her.

The next time we see Tegan is in *Arc of Infinity*. She's visiting Amsterdam to spend time with her favourite cousin, Colin Frazer, who's backpacking with his friend, Robin Stuart. Colin and Robin arrive a day earlier than Tegan, and can't find a hotel, so spend the night in the abandoned Frankendael mansion. That's when Colin is kidnapped by the Ergon. We never discover how much time has passed since the TARDIS dematerialised without Tegan, although we do learn that she lost her job and returned to Australia. We can infer, however, that since her grandfather is unsurprised to see her in *The Awakening* (set in 1984), her visit to Amsterdam is not too long before this, most likely at some point in 1983. Upon arrival, she meets Robin who tells her about the disappearance of Colin, and his later zombie-like behaviour. She's annoyed the local police will do nothing to help, and investigates the mansion herself, coming face-to-face with the Time Lord legend, Omega. He uses Tegan as leverage against his old adversary, the Doctor. Tegan gets a message to the Doctor, telling him that she's in Amsterdam; although her main concern is for her cousin, this is quickly replaced by her need to help the Doctor. Eventually, she telephones Colin to see how he is, before explaining to the Doctor that he's now stuck with her, since she has no job. Nyssa is delighted, but the Doctor appears less so.

She probably should've stayed on Earth.

Almost immediately, Tegan comes under the influence of the Mara and she unknowingly alters the TARDIS co-ordinates for Manussa (*Snakedance*). The Doctor creates a device to prevent the Mara from taking hold, but it's removed, and the Mara consumes her. Eventually, the Doctor frees Tegan from the Mara, but she's still concerned that it exists within her. The Doctor places an arm around her when she starts to break down: 'Brave heart, Tegan.'

Following this ordeal, she decides she wants to return to Earth – not to leave, just to be surrounded by familiar things. The Doctor obliges, but the TARDIS becomes trapped in a warp ellipse and materialises aboard Mawdryn's ship (*Mawdryn Undead*). She immediately takes an active dislike to Turlough; she doesn't trust him at all, but she does warm to the Brigadier when she encounters him in 1977 and discovers he knows the Doctor. Nevertheless, she finds it difficult to take orders from the old military officer, thinking him a chauvinist. When the Doctor agrees that Turlough can join the TARDIS crew, Tegan is unhappy about the addition.

On *Terminus*, she and Turlough become trapped together in a ventilation shaft, but despite this time together, they don't strike up a friendship. Though Turlough tries to smooth things over with charm, Tegan remains abrasive and untrusting of him, and Nyssa's departure further puts her on the back foot.

In *Enlightenment*, the TARDIS arrives on *Shadow*, apparently an Edwardian racing yacht, at the behest of the White Guardian. The Doctor takes Turlough with him to explore, asking Tegan to remain in the TARDIS in case the White Guardian attempts to make contact again. She wants to go with them, but realises the Doctor is placing a great trust in her, so does as asked. She's quite charmed by Marriner, the first mate, but is later repulsed by his probing her mind (the taint of her experiences with the Mara lingers). She's also very uncomfortable with the room he's prepared for her, littered as it is with things from her mind, including her air hostess uniform and a picture of her Aunt Vanessa – two things that surely remind her of what she's lost. As she says, it's a strange mix of her room in the TARDIS and her room in Brisbane. She experiences the symptoms of sea sickness, and with the departure of Nyssa finds herself drawing closer to Turlough, although she still doesn't quite trust him. Once Turlough chooses the Doctor over Enlightenment, Tegan begins to become more relaxed around him.

But she's less than impressed by their brief stay in thirteenth century England during *The King's Demons*, and discovers her knowledge of British history isn't as good as she thought it was – despite her historian grandfather's teachings. This visit ends with the addition of a new travelling companion, the shape-shifting android, Kamelion. Once more, Tegan's unimpressed by the idea of the android joining them. This at least explains why she never refers to him again, happily forgetting that he's in the TARDIS.

Later, while they enjoy a well-deserved rest in the most tranquil place in the universe, the Eye of Orion, Tegan's alarmed when the Doctor starts to lose his temporal cohesion (*The Five Doctors*). In the Death Zone on Gallifrey, she's surprised by the arrival of the First Doctor, recognising that his former incarnations shouldn't exist in the same time and space (possibly recalling the last time the Doctor's lives overlapped, i.e. the ethereal Watcher in *Logopolis*). She's determined to explore the Death Zone with her Doctor and is joined by Susan, the Doctor's granddaughter. It's never clear if Tegan is made aware of this familial connection, but they do share time chatting over food, so it's likely Susan would've mentioned it; either way, Susan stops calling him 'grandfather' as soon as she meets Tegan, Turlough, and the younger-looking Fifth Doctor.

Both watch in shock as the Doctor and the Master are attacked by a squadron of Cybermen and the Fifth Doctor transmats away. As a result, Tegan joins the First Doctor, who heads to the Dark Tower. She finds him a little miserable, but clearly enjoys his company, calling him 'Doc'. This is unusual as she has never really used such a nickname before – perhaps this is Tegan's way of distinguishing the two Doctors in her mind. In the Dark Tower, she feels something oppressive, but the First Doctor simply explains it's fear being transmitted from the mind of Rassilon, so she should simply ignore it. Once in the Tomb of Rassilon, she's reacquainted with the Brigadier and meets Sarah, as well as the Second and Third Doctors.

At the end, she, like Turlough, is convinced the Doctor is about to say goodbye after being asked to become President of the High Council, but the Doctor explains that he has no intention of returning to Gallifrey. Tegan is amused that he's willing to go on the run in a 'rackety old TARDIS', but the Doctor points out that 'that's how it all started.'

Following the slaughter at the seabase in *Warriors of the Deep*, it's Tegan's turn to question whether it's time to say goodbye. She asks the Doctor to return her to Earth to visit her grandfather, Andrew Verney, in 1984. And so, for the first time ever, the Doctor actively sets the TARDIS to take one of his companions to visit a member of their family. Upon arrival in Little Hodcombe in *The Awakening*, they see a man in seventeenth century clothing. Tegan is, once again, convinced the Doctor has got the destination wrong, even though Turlough insists otherwise. When she and Verney finally meet up, he doesn't seem surprised to see his granddaughter, nor is he too shocked by the TARDIS – this might imply that she has told him all about the Doctor during her return to Earth after *Time-Flight*. Tegan forces the Doctor, with the help of a few locals, to remain there for a while, so she can at least spend some proper time with her grandfather, instead of solely dealing with temporal problems and war games.

While on the human colony of *Frontios*, she comes under the scrutiny of the alien Tractators, but the Doctor attempts to convince them that Tegan is an android. 'I got it cheap because the walk's not quite right. And then there's the accent, of course,' he says, before admitting, 'when it's working well, it's very reliable: keeping track of appointments, financial planning, word processing; that sort of thing...' She knows this is just the Doctor trying to keep her safe, but she's still a little affronted.

During a return to Earth in 1984 (*Resurrection of the Daleks*), Tegan witnesses many people being killed by Daleks and android duplicates – including an innocent man who she calls to for help when being chased by duplicate policemen. No doubt she blames herself for his death, and is greatly disturbed by the needless slaughter. It's here that she realises she can no longer carry on; too many good people have died. In a sudden moment, just as they're about to leave, Tegan tells the Doctor that she's not going with him. Tegan doesn't blame him for all the deaths. She does, however, take comfort in what her Aunt Vanessa once said: that if you stop enjoying something, you should give it up. 'It's stopped being fun, Doctor.' She bravely shakes Turlough's hand and dashes off, unable to contain the hurt of leaving any more. She returns seconds after the TARDIS dematerialises, and tells herself, 'Brave heart, Tegan', then adds: 'I am going to miss you, Doctor'.

That feeling appears mutual: when the Doctor's regenerating, it's Tegan that he sees first in his mind's eye. She reminds him: 'What is it you always told me, Doctor? "Brave heart"?' Tegan stayed with the Fifth Doctor longer than anyone else, which might account for her face being the first that bubbles up from his subconscious; or perhaps it's a sign of his guilt over why she left.

Travelling nonetheless seems in Tegan's blood. After she leaves the TARDIS, Tegan spends some thirty years 'living like a nomad.' In 2010's *SJA: Death of the Doctor*, Sarah tells her friends that Tegan now lives in Australia fighting for Aboriginal rights, but in *The Power of the Doctor*, Tegan shares that, while trying to help people, she's faced land mines, coups, hijacking, and near-death from drowning. 'I've seen off two husbands, and somewhere out there is an adopted son who hasn't called me for six weeks,' she adds.

It's not until 2022 that Tegan meets the Doctor again. While investigating the disappearance of seismologists in Romania, she finds a box addressed to her, apparently from the Doctor. Inside is a 'toy' Cyberman, which understandably seems to put Tegan in a bad mood. When the Thirteenth Doctor asks how she and Ace have been, Tegan counters, 'Like you care'. Still, she appears to have been counting the days since she left the TARDIS, acknowledging that thirty-eight years have gone by. She also seems strangely perturbed by the Doctor looking so young (though not that the Time Lord is now a woman, having been told this information by Kate Stewart, head of UNIT).

Fortunately, her cold exterior is broken when she sees a hologram of the Fifth Doctor and the pair admit they've missed each other. It's sad, then, that Tegan doesn't get to say a proper goodbye: Thirteenth Doctor companion, Yasmin Khan, drops Tegan off on Earth while the Doctor is unconscious, on the verge of regeneration. At least Tegan catches up with Yasmin at the companions' meet-up, checking that the Doctor will be okay.

With Turlough, we had the last male companion until 2005, and the only one to be introduced with the express intention of killing the Doctor.

Vislor Turlough – Mark Strickson (*Mawdryn Undead* to *Planet of Fire*)

Paint It Black (The Rolling Stones); *Fox on the Run* (Sweet).

There's something a little off about Turlough. He looks a bit older than the other schoolboys, has curious eyebrows, and is hugely intelligent. Like many young boys, however, he's cocky and a bit of a troublemaker, happy to shift the blame of a post-joyride car accident to his 'friend', Ibbotson. Indeed, Turlough's used to talking his way out of tricky situations. It's only when he's lying unconscious beside the car that we learn he's actually an alien.

The Black Guardian promises him a way off Earth if he does one thing for him: kill the Doctor!

At this point, it seems Turlough will do almost anything to break free from Earth, a planet he finds beyond tedious. We don't discover exactly why he is on Earth, what planet he's really from, or his first name until *Planet of Fire*, but when he does meet the Doctor and foolishly demonstrates an awareness of transmats and alien technology, the Doctor doesn't question it – almost as if the Doctor is wiser to the situation than he lets on. The Doctor isn't surprised by the appearance of the White Guardian in *Enlightenment* either, so could it be that the Doctor has been warned already? It would certainly explain the Doctor's distrust of Turlough, despite welcoming him on board the TARDIS at the end of *Mawdryn Undead*.

Turlough quickly warms to the Doctor, and starts questioning the Black Guardian, but his will is nothing in comparison and he discovers there's no way out of their deal. Still, his attempts at killing the Doctor are, at best, lacklustre. He initially finds his way into the TARDIS in a scene that's almost echoed in the closing moments of his introduction story, and is very evasive of Tegan and Nyssa's questions, sticking to the Doctor's side. The Doctor notices, but lets it slide. Once the threat of Mawdryn is removed and the two Brigadiers are returned to their proper times, the Doctor suddenly remembers Turlough, who he believes is still on Mawdryn's ship, set to self-destruct. They rush into the TARDIS to find Turlough there waiting for them – he asks if he can join them, and the Doctor agrees. He derides his peers at Brendon School, glad to be free of the 'children', and is unimpressed at being given Adric's old room, which he considers a kid's room.

But Tegan is very weary of him. From the moment she meets Turlough, she's instinctively untrusting of him. He tries to smooth things over with her, but he's not having any of it; instead, he tells her that he finds her own way of communicating to be more like a sledge hammer. It's wonderfully ironic that, shortly after arriving at *Terminus*, he finds himself trapped with only Tegan for company. Ultimately, he has no one but himself to blame: he sabotaged the TARDIS at the behest of the Black Guardian, and forced it to merge with the leper ship that docked at Terminus. He initiates a conversation with Tegan about killing, wondering if she could do such a thing, clearly trying to work through his morality. His conscience pricks at him, mostly because he genuinely likes the Doctor, but he's a natural liar and deflects Tegan's own questions.

He knows he hasn't completely gained the Doctor's trust and cheerfully joins him in exploring the Edwardian racing yacht, Shadow (*Enlightenment*). Initially, he's out of his depth with the rowdy sailors, but soon adapts, donning a straw hat and engaging them in loud and raucous conversation.

Rather astonishingly, his bargain with the Guardian drives him so insane that he does something no previous companion (and only two since) has: attempted suicide. He jumps overboard, seemingly at odds with his rather selfish attitude seen in the previous two serials. Turlough, then, reveals himself to be a surprisingly moral character, who'd rather sacrifice his own life than that of his new-found friend. Nevertheless, he's rescued by an Eternal called Wrack, captain of the *Buccaneer*, also an agent of the Black Guardian. She reads his mind but finds it hard to do so, since it's divided and confused. She does recognise that greed is dominant though. Turlough is on the winning ship when it crosses the line and is thus offered the prize of Enlightenment, where he is confronted by both the Black and White Guardians. The former goads him, reminding Turlough of their bargain – he can now either give up Enlightenment or the Doctor. He casts the Enlightenment diamond at the Guardian, his choice made. Tired, Turlough strangely wants the Doctor to take him back to his home planet – even though, as we later discover, he's a political exile and cannot return there.

As it turns out, the TARDIS crew ends up back on Earth (*The King's Demons*). Whether Turlough has changed his mind or not is unknown, but he doesn't seem too impressed to be there again.

It's fairly uneventful for him, although he is almost given over to the iron maiden (the medieval torture device, not the rock band). He's somewhat surprised by the Doctor agreeing to take Kamelion with them; he seems to forget about the android almost immediately, preferring to focus on helping the Doctor rebuild the TARDIS console while at the Eye of Orion (one can infer this by the fact Turlough's familiar with the controls of the radically altered control console in *The Five Doctors* even though it's brand new and the Doctor is only finishing work on it at the beginning of the story – fortunately, Turlough already showed some aptitude for the TARDIS console in previous stories).

Being at the Eye of Orion seems to be a changing point in the Doctor and Turlough's relationship. There are still occasions when the Doctor doubts him, but the two are more relaxed around each other. They're certainly happy in each other's company, with Turlough drawing and the Doctor enjoying the vista. Turlough is very comfortable with the concept of regeneration: he doesn't bat an eyelid at the appearance of more than one Doctor and delights in heightening the tension with Susan as they spot Cybermen planting a bomb outside the TARDIS. One of the most curious incidents in the Dark Tower is when Turlough steps out of the TARDIS, joining the team of companions who are watching the Doctors' activities with interest. Among these old friends is the Brigadier, one of Turlough's teachers from Brendon – yet they don't acknowledge each other's presence, even though Turlough went missing from the school, and there'd been tension between the pair after Turlough crashed the Brigadier's car.

At the end of *The Five Doctors*, Turlough is convinced that the Time Lords will send him home, which surprisingly doesn't seem to bother him. The Doctor says he's no intention to go back to Gallifrey, and it's around this point that Turlough says he doesn't want to return to his home planet either: he'd rather remain with the Doctor, since he still has a lot to learn. The Doctor is a little doubtful, thinking that Turlough will change his mind again.

Not only are the Doctor and Turlough getting on better, but

so are Tegan and Turlough; they are slowly developing a friendly bit of rivalry, with Turlough's cynicism proving to be a nice foil for Tegan's passion. At the beginning of *Frontios*, he rather enjoys disturbing her when reading about the 'doomed Earth': she cares so deeply for her planet, whereas Turlough doesn't feel that pull for Earth. His confidence is undermined, however, when he hears stories of the ground eating people and he delves into the tunnels beneath the colony. Turlough regresses into a primal, almost feral state, the race memory of Tractators turning him into a gibbering mess. It would be easy to dismiss him as a deserter, but that assertion would be wrong. 'Don't torture yourself,' Norna, one of the colonists, says to him. 'Nobody expects you to go back down there.' Turlough replies, 'No, of course they don't. I'm Turlough.' He overcomes his fears and goes back into the tunnels after his friends. Far from being a coward, in truth, he's a survivor, something further enforced in *Resurrection of the Daleks* when he's forced to take up arms rather than die.

He's sad to see Tegan leave, and finds himself missing her in *Planet of Fire* (though not as much as the Doctor is). When the TARDIS picks up a distress signal, Turlough recognises its origin and instantly disconnects it. Even though Kamelion is responsible for reprogramming the TARDIS co-ordinates, the Doctor grows a little suspicious of Turlough, and isn't convinced by his pleas of innocence. Their relationship has progressed, but the Doctor still reserves a certain level of doubt. While the Doctor explores Lanzarote for the source of the signal, Turlough does everything he can to cancel it out, including shorting out Kamelion, but is soon distracted when he sees a woman apparently drowning. He's exasperated, but still goes out and rescues her, bringing her into the TARDIS for safety. In her bag, he discovers an artefact from Trion, his home planet, and the source of the signal. The signal takes them to the planet Sarn. Turlough ventures out and discovers a younger man called Malkon – his brother!

When Malkon is hurt, Turlough's aggressive side comes to the fore and he threatens to kill the one responsible. The Doctor's suspicious when his companion won't confide in him, and warns Turlough that, if his secrets should end up aiding the Master, then their friendship would be over. Turlough eventually reveals that his family were political prisoners after a civil war on Trion and he was exiled to Earth. After contacting Trion, he learns that the war is over and he, and all his people, are now free to return. Turlough is torn. In some ways, he doesn't want to leave the Doctor, but he knows he must. Before leaving, he asks Peri, the girl he saved from drowning, to look after the Doctor for him.

An image of Turlough appears to the dying Doctor in *The Caves of Androzani*, telling him, 'You must survive, Doctor. Too many of your enemies would delight in your death.'

It had been some years since K9 was booted out of the TARDIS, but he wasn't the last robotic companion. Enter Kamelion, a shape-shifting android found on Xeriphas. An android that could turn into anyone seemed like a wonderful idea, but the reality was somewhat different. Introduced in one story, he isn't seen again until six stories later when he is destroyed – the worst treatment of a companion ever in *Doctor Who*.

Kamelion – Gerald Flood (*The King's Demons* to *Planet of Fire*)

Karma Chameleon (Culture Club); *The Man Who Can't Be Moved* (The Script).

While trapped on Xeriphas, the Master discovers an android called Kamelion. Although sentient, Kamelion is susceptible to strong personalities, and so the Master, something of an expert at controlling others, uses Kamelion to pose as King John in an attempt to prevent the signing of Magna Carta (*The King's Demons*). A battle of wills ensues between the Doctor and the Master; ultimately the Doctor wins. He frees Kamelion and allows the android to travel with them. After this, Kamelion seems to just vanish – we must assume he's still in the TARDIS somewhere, but there's no logical reason for everyone to simply forget about him. Turlough is surprised by the Doctor's decision, and Tegan's certainly not happy about him being there. If a deleted scene from *The Awakening* had stayed in, Tegan's distrust of Kamelion would've been highlighted when she walks in on him fiddling with controls in a TARDIS roundel. He tells her that he's just learning, and assures her, 'You forget, I'm benign.' Tegan counters, 'So the Doctor says.' She admits part of this uneasiness is due to him still using King John's voice, and Kamelion doesn't help the situation by mimicking the Doctor and Turlough. No matter how he makes them feel, the fact that none of them mention Kamelion again is odd to say the least. In *Frontios*, the TARDIS is torn apart by the force of the Tractators, and scattered throughout the planet. But what happens to Kamelion?

The next time we see Kamelion (*Planet of Fire*), he's being manipulated once more by the Master, but this time, it's not only the Master whose mind is powerful enough to do this. Peri, distraught after almost having drowned, starts to affect Kamelion, to the point where he takes on the form of her step-father, Howard Foster. The Master and Peri mentally spar for dominance. The former finally gains complete control, but briefly relinquishes it; that's when Kamelion begs the Doctor to destroy him, not wanting to be used again. The Doctor reluctantly agrees.

Unfortunately, due to his lack of screen time, and the fact that when he is on screen, he's primarily being controlled by someone else, we never see any real growth in Kamelion.

That said, the Doctor clearly never forgets him since he appears to the dying Doctor in *The Caves of Androzani*, encouraging him to not give in.

By the mid-1980s, *Doctor Who* was becoming popular in America, and to that end a decision was made to introduce an American companion. She was also to serve as the transition across Doctors, since the end of the Fifth Doctor's run was drawing near...

Perpugilliam 'Peri' Brown – Nicola Bryant (*Planet of Fire* to *The Trial of a Time Lord*)

Only Happy When It Rains (Garbage); *Kings & Queens* (Ava Max).

A young student of botany, when we meet Peri, she's on holiday in Lanzarote with her mother and step-father. She seems to have a close relationship with her step-father, Howard, but not so much with her mother. She's a bit flighty when we first meet her, opting to cash in her travellers' cheques to travel to Morocco with a bunch of people she has only just met. When Howard asks her how she hopes to pay for her ticket home, she simply says, 'I'll get a job', indicating she hasn't really thought about it at all. Howard isn't keen on this idea, and so purposely strands her on his boat to ensure she cannot leave until they can have a long talk about it. Peri reacts in a spoiled way, and chooses to steal one of Howard's artefacts to get some money to fund her trip. The only problem she has is getting to shore.

As it turns out, Peri is not a strong swimmer and is soon rescued by Turlough, who takes her into the TARDIS to recover. Her dreams about her recent argument with Howard are so realistic that she accidentally influences Kamelion, who takes his form. When she wakes up, she's no idea where she is, and stumbles into the console room to find Howard there with the Doctor and Turlough. The time travellers go out to explore, leaving the confused Peri with her apparent step-father. Here, she learns it's not really him; it's Kamelion being controlled by the Master. Unusually for a companion, the Master is quite impressed by Peri's force of will, being able to wrest control of Kamelion from him. Despite her whining, she proves to have a strong sense of self, and is willing to be convinced that they're on another planet. In her short time on Sarn, Peri becomes fond of the Doctor and agrees to look after him when Turlough realises it's his time to return to Trion. The Doctor isn't so sure about having her join him, but she explains she still has three months of vacation left, and he almost reluctantly agrees that she can travel with him.

Their first port of call is the planet Androzani Minor – a place Peri is initially impressed with. While exploring, she demonstrates her sarcastic wit, which helps build up a nice sense of friendship between her and the Doctor. For the first time, the Fifth Doctor seems to be relaxed with his travelling companion. But she's impatient to move on once she tires of talk about fused silica – the Doctor's in full exploration mode so she has no choice but to follow him: '"Is this wise?" I ask myself…'

The adventure becomes less fun when they're arrested as suspected gun runners, and are scheduled to be executed. Peri has a particularly hard time on Androzani: she narrowly avoids death by firing squad; is infected by Spectrox Toxaemia, a fatal infection with only one cure; and reluctantly becomes the muse of Sharez Jek, an insane genius who's obsessed with her beauty. The Doctor is protective of Peri in Jek's company, but his flippancy can't quell her fear. She tries to keep her humour, but finds it very difficult in the face of such horrendous company. The Doctor literally risks his life to find the cure for his young companion (probably as a result of his guilt at the loss of Adric, Nyssa, Tegan, and Turlough). Determined to save Peri, the Doctor holds back his regeneration, as he too is infected and near to death.

By the time he returns, Jek is dead. The Doctor carries Peri back to the TARDIS, dodging blasts of primordial mud, and accidentally spills the cure for Spectrox Toxaemia – he only has enough to save Peri. Peri wakes to find the Doctor lying on the TARDIS floor, dying. She can do nothing but cradle him in her arms. She's understandably upset, and terrified that she's being left alone in a ship she doesn't understand. 'Don't give up. You can't leave me now!' she tells him. Too late. The Doctor warns her that he might regenerate; she's no idea what he means. With no clue what's happening, Peri crawls away as the Doctor begins to change. And not a moment too soon…

The Fifth Doctor
Expanded Universe

The Fifth Doctor's companions are a disparate group, often arguing with each other while frustrating the Doctor. Did this change in the Expanded Universe, or did the authors take the opportunity to delve deeper into the characters to find out why they were so aggressive towards each other? And what of Kamelion, the most wasted 1980s companion?

In *Divided Loyalties*, the 1999 novel in which the Doctor, Adric, Nyssa, and Tegan battle the Toymaker, we learn that pizza is a mystery to Adric. He also doesn't appear to know what hygiene is as both Nyssa and Tegan suggest to the Doctor that he have a chat with Adric about his reluctance to bathe regularly; a chat doesn't take place. Never one for tact, Tegan also thinks that Adric is lazy and generally loathsome, although in *The Sands of Time*, she discusses the emotional impact of his death with the Doctor and the reasons why Adric cannot be saved using the TARDIS.

We also get a glimpse of Adric's earlier years in *Divided Loyalties*; his childhood friend Jiana, with whom there may have been a romantic link, flees when Adric joins his brother Varsh's rebel forces as they fight against the elite. The Toymaker traps Adric in an illusionary dreamscape and uses Jiana's image to try and turn Adric against the Doctor, reminding him of the numerous times the Time Lord has placed his life in danger while fighting against such foes as the Master and the Terileptils.

There's little exploration of his family life beyond this mention of Varsh, but we do find out that Adric's parents are named Morell and Tanisa. The audios, *The Invasion of E-Space* and *A Full Life*, affirm that they died during a forest fire, while the *Short Trips* story,

165

A Boy's Tale, suggests they were killed in a farming accident.

Adric's adeptness at chess is touched upon in *Divided Loyalties* (as is his mastery of astrometrics); he also repeatedly beats Nyssa at the game in *Hearts of Stone*, a short story in the *Short Trips: Companions* collection. The 2014 audio, *Psychodrome*, details Adric's fears: primarily, letting people down, but also encountering a mathematical problem he can't solve! The former fear is slightly ironic, given that he does sometimes let people down, chiefly by not considering the consequences of his actions. In the *Short Trips* tale, *The Immortals*, the Doctor is concerned when Adric introduces the longbow to a tribe in Eastern Europe before they should have such a strategic advantage. He's determined to learn how to fly the TARDIS too, despite the Doctor running simulations for him in the 2017 audio story, *The Star Men*, which always results in Adric accidentally killing his travelling companions. It's brave of Tegan to ask him to pilot the TARDIS to Heathrow two stories later, in *Zaltys...*

Following Adric's death in *Earthshock*, he's remembered by Nyssa, Tegan, and the Doctor in the novels, *Zeta Major* and *Fear of the Dark*. Unsurprisingly, Tegan finds it easier to deal with his death than the others but not for the reasons you'd think: in *The Sands of Time*, she says it's because she didn't see him die. His passing certainly sticks with Nyssa; the 2011 audio, *Heroes of Sontar*, reveals that she named her son after the lost Alzarian.

It's following his death that Adric makes his strangest appearance in the Expanded Universe. In *The Boy That Time Forgot*, the 2008 audio drama, the Doctor and Nyssa are looking for the TARDIS after its theft by Thomas Brewster (following *The Haunting of Thomas Brewster*) and their search leads them to an Aztec jungle pocket-dimension packed with insects and giant scorpions. There, they find that, during a séance, the Doctor unintentionally saves Adric by sending him subconscious Block Transfer Computations. However, the Adric they encounter is not the boy they remember: alone and isolated for centuries, he has become quite insane and seethes with bitterness. The Doctor makes repeated attempts to show him that he has become essentially a very old and resentful teenager.

Curiously, the Celestial Intervention Agency believes the Master rescued Adric before he died, at least according to *The Cyber Files*, a 1986 tie-in to *The Doctor Who Role Playing Game*. But *Seb*, a short story in 2021's *Doctor Who Magazine* #560, shows Adric's mind being uploaded to the Nethersphere after death (i.e. giving more back-story to the TV story, *Dark Water / Death in Heaven*), with Missy apparently eager to see him again.

Either way, Adric's death continues to haunt the Doctor. In the 2019 audio, *Conversion*, the Doctor admits he was harsh on Adric because he reminded him of himself as a youngster (a theory previously put forward by Waterhouse in the 2013 documentary, *The Doctors Revisited – The Fifth Doctor*); while various antagonists lord his passing over the Doctor, often in comics like *The Forgotten* (2008-09), *Tesseract* (2010), and *Planet of the Dead* (1988).

In the Expanded Universe of *Doctor Who* novels it appears that Nyssa, the aristocratic daughter of Traken, is often being turned into a monster of some kind. *Goth Opera*, a 1994 *Virgin Missing Adventure* and Big Finish audio, sees her changed into a vampire; she even bites the Doctor. In *The Sands of Time*, she's chosen to become a host for Nephthys, the sister and wife of Sutekh (encountered by the Fourth Doctor in *Pyramids of Mars*) and for most of the book is wrapped up as a mummy, spending four thousand years comatose. This gives her chance to rest, before becoming a feral monster in *Zeta Major*, a *BBC Past Doctor Adventure*, after being implanted with anti-matter – her Trakenite body gives her only partial protection from radiation. Nyssa at least manages to remain herself through *Divided Loyalties*, a book which provides some more information regarding her character; for instance, that she has a working knowledge of bioelectronics, in addition to biology.

According to Big Finish, there's a large gap between seasons nineteen and twenty, and Nyssa spends quite some time travelling alone with the Doctor before Tegan rejoins them in *Arc of Infinity*. During this time, her latent telepathic powers are explored, most notably when she visits Traken's past. She witnesses the creation of the Cybermen on a battered Mondas in *Spare Parts*, and is later joined in her travels, firstly by Thomas Brewster, then by Hannah Bartholemew, and (after reuniting with Tegan) by Marc.

In *Autumn*, part of *Circular Time*, we meet Nyssa's first kiss: Andrew Harper (originally Andrew Wittaker), an engineering student and waiter in the village of Stockbridge. Their first date is at a restaurant in Traken Village, situated a little under an hour away from Stockbridge. Nyssa draws a star map to show Andrew where she really comes from: though her home has been destroyed, its light is still visible in the night sky. She briefly considers leaving the TARDIS for him, but they split up, leading Nyssa to be wary of the village. In *Castle of Fear*, they choose to visit Stockbridge in 1899 and 1199, and the forty-fifth century in *Plague of the Daleks* (all 2009), so they avoid meeting Andrew again.

Accounts differ slightly as to what happens immediately after *Arc of Infinity*: the 2003 novel, *Fear of the Dark*, says they go to Akoshemon's moon, 2382; *The Elite*, a 2011 *Lost Stories* audio, says they're inspired by the tulips of Amsterdam to visit the beautiful planet, Florana; and the 2016 audio, *The Waters of Amsterdam*, says they spend some time in Holland, exploring the Rijksmuseum.

In *The Darkening Eye*, Nyssa's subjected to the Dar Traders' cataloguing process which is halted so that the Dar Trader can inform her that, as a Trakenite, death is attracted to her but she should be able to master and calcify it. Before the process stops, she has a vision of Tegan cradling her in a field of leaves. Later, Nyssa is stabbed and dies for three minutes before being brought back to life by the same Dar Trader. She wakes to find herself in a field of leaves, being held by Tegan, as prophesied.

During the same story, Nyssa claims she has a familiarity with dimensional transcendentalism that predates her travels with the Doctor. She adds that she probably understands it better than the Doctor, once again displaying a knowledge that extends beyond her specialist subject of biology. This is explored further in another audio story, *The Deep*, in which she fixes the chameleon circuit. The Doctor claims to have a TARDIS repair manual and is bewildered as to how Nyssa could've repaired the circuit without it. It takes her a while to master the TARDIS, though, as she fails to get Tegan back to Heathrow in *Iterations of I* (2014).

Her travels with the Doctor, knowledge of the Time Lords, and her mourning her home prepare Nyssa for the Time War, during which she helps planets affected by the conflict, operating out of a hospital ship called the Traken (2017's *A Heart on Both Sides*); meets the Tenth Doctor and K9 in 2022's *The Stuntman*; and is manipulated by the War Master (*The Orphan* in 2021).

Like most people of Traken (often called Trakenites), she's no knowledge of her planet's history as she wasn't taught this as a child (mentioned in the audio drama, *Primeval*). Its destruction naturally haunts her as does the death of her father, and the Master's taking her body: the evil Time Lord taunts and hypnotises her in the 2013 AudioGO tale, *Smoke and Mirrors*; while she has nightmares about him in *The Toy* (2015). In the *BBC Past Doctor Adventure*, *Empire of Death*, Nyssa considers asking the Doctor to take her to Traken before its destruction. She actually does so in *Cobwebs*, but it's a while before he can. In this audio tale, an older Nyssa, years after she left in *Terminus*, rejoins the Doctor, Tegan, and Turlough on their travels. In *Heroes of Sontar*, she confides in Tegan that she's married to a man called Lasarti and has three children: Adric, Neeka, and Tegan. She asks Tegan to keep this from the Doctor, to protect the Web of Time as it isn't until shortly before his regeneration that he finds out that she's married (in *Winter*, in which Nyssa enters the Doctor's mindscape seconds before he regenerates in *The Caves of Androzani*). During this period, Nyssa and Turlough spend more time together, notably a year in Reykjavik, working to bring down Magnus Greel, as per 2012's *The Butcher of Brisbane*.

In 2012's *The Emerald Tiger*, Nyssa's youth is remarkably restored, so she now looks like she did before *Terminus*.

Though we may infer she travels more with the Doctor, Tegan, and Turlough after she's been rejuvenated, they soon find themselves in E-Space, where she's robbed of her youth as she's affected by entropy (as per *The Entropy Plague* in 2015). Nyssa stays in E-Space, sealing an unstable portal to N-Space after helping her friends return to their own universe. She stays there at least a decade and, despite the Doctor's concerns that entropy would collapse the pocket-sized continuum, sees the birth of a new star in the sky. At some point, however, she does get back to N-Space and finds Tegan; by the time the pair attend Sarah Jane Smith's memorial in *Farewell, Sarah*, the two are a couple.

'Tegan, has anyone told you how nice it is to have you around?' the Doctor asks Tegan in *Divided Loyalties*.

She replies, 'Not recently, no.'

'No?' the Doctor retorts. 'Hmmm, I wonder why that is.'

This gives you an idea why Tegan, irascible, outspoken, and, in her own words, 'downright bolshie' (from the audio, *The Children of Seth*), is such a popular companion with both fans and writers of the Expanded Universe. She's referred to as 'the shrieking hell cat' by Dawson in *The Emerald Tiger*, the first in a 2012 audio trilogy, and as 'an Antipodean harpy' by Major Haggard in the same story. In 2011's *The Lions of Trafalgar*, she freely admits to having a big mouth. Being so strong-willed works to her advantage at times, such as in *Goth Opera* where her temperament supplies her with enough resilience to make her immune to the vampires' attempts to hypnotise her. Rather than religion, Tegan's beliefs lie in the writings of Primo Levi, Quantas, Australian musician James Reyne, and the Australian republic.

Tegan's biographical details are covered quite extensively in the Expanded Universe, most notably in *The King of Terror* (a *Past Doctor Adventure* novel), *Divided Loyalties*, and *Cradle of the Snake* (a 2010 audio story). Tegan, a Cornish name meaning 'lovely little thing', grew up in Caloundra, around seventy miles from Brisbane (*The King of Terror*). Her father, William (*Divided Loyalties*), owned a sheep farm and two thousand head of merino. One of Tegan's most treasured memories is flying with him in his Cessna Skyhawk over the farm (*The Cradle of the Snake*). He understood that Tegan wasn't cut out for farm life. When she was seven or eight, her mother, Joy, took her to see Aboriginal cave paintings in Arnhem Land and the corroboree aboriginal ceremony, but she got lost in the caves and was freaked out by the dancing, leaving her with recurring nightmares (*Psychodrome*). Other family mentioned are her mother's brother, Richard, and sister-in-law, Felicity. She has two cousins, Colin and Michael, and Serbian grandparents living in Yugoslavia named Mjovic and Sneshna Jovanka. However, the thirteen-year-old Tegan hated her 'mad cow' grandmother, who died of coronary thrombosis. 2019's *The Kamelion Empire* establishes that her maternal grandfather was Albert Jovanka (who shared with her his experiences of serving in Gallipoli in World War I), while she mentions an Uncle Roger in *Devil in the Mist*, and, in *The Contingency Club* (2017), cousins who work as blast-miners in Australia. In the 2015 short story, *The Constant Doctor*, she realises the Doctor has a wider family too, after she watches a play about the First Doctor and Susan saving the planet of Lemaria (in which the First Doctor is played by the Twelfth!).

The young Tegan was a John Lennon and ABBA fan, listening to their records with her friends Fliss, Dave, Susannah, and Richard (*Divided Loyalties*).

Scandal shook the family when Tegan's father had an affair with a twenty-year-old woman who worked in a typing pool. They moved up the coast to try and escape the repercussions of this and Tegan's mother sent her away to a boarding school, where she was expelled after only a few terms. At just fifteen, she ran away and headed for Sydney where she ended up squatting in King's Cross. Eventually, her father tracked her down and sent her to England, to stay with her Aunt Vanessa (*The King of Terror*).

The teenage Tegan didn't have a boyfriend. Tegan was, as she admits herself, overweight and extremely sensitive about this. A boy named Gary Lovarik was the only one she had any interest in but her supposed best friend, Felicity Spoonsy, moved in on him first (*The King of Terror*). According to *Divided Loyalties*, she'd passed through this difficult period by the age of eighteen and she certainly seems more at ease with herself and the opposite sex by the time she embarks on her journeys with Doctor. In *The King of Terror*, she flirts with Captain Paynter, who she seems to be both attracted to and infuriated by. They kiss but the relationship doesn't really go anywhere. In the 1996 novel *Cold Fusion*, Chris Cwej (companion of the Seventh Doctor) gets amorous and makes advances but she drenches him with champagne. An inebriated Tegan is supported by Police Sergeant Andy Weathers in the novel *Deep Blue*, later going on a date with him. She even ruminates on what life with Andy would be like if she were to stay on Earth.

Tegan's character offers the writers of the Extended Universe a chance to have a little fun: this is no more evident than in her repeated references to western popular culture. In the 2011 audio story, *Kiss of Death*, she asks Turlough if his parents inherited the planet of Enid Blyton; later, in *The Emerald Tiger*, she comments on a three-piece suit he's wearing, saying it makes him look more mature. Tegan also mentions Tigger from *Winnie the Pooh* and calls Dawon – the one who dubbed her a shrieking she-cat – Pussy Galore, referencing the James Bond novel and film, *Goldfinger*. In *Cobwebs*, a 2010 audio drama, she refers to Loki, Nyssa's robot, as R2-D2, the iconic droid from *Star Wars*. Keeping up with popular culture can come in very handy when you are time travelling; in *Cold Fusion*, Tegan is able to deal with the idea of transmats because of what she has gleaned from *Blake's 7,* the cult 1980s TV show from Dalek creator, Terry Nation. However, it's not only this that makes the character fun; there's also her wonderful sense of mischievousness as evidenced in *The Sands of Time* when Tegan tries to make a minor change to history just to see if the Doctor's insistence that it cannot be changed is correct. Then there's her repeated use of the word 'rabbits' as an expletive, something she does in *The Emerald Tiger*.

A series of audio adventures see Tegan warming to her time on the TARDIS, and in *Smoke and Mirrors*, she finally tells Nyssa that she actively enjoys it (leading up to her telling the Doctor that she doesn't want to go back to Heathrow just yet in *Black Orchid*) – she even turns down an offer to stay with Joe Mazzini, a teacher in the 2018 audio, *Serpent in the Silver Mask*, despite the pair having feelings for one another.

The 2016 audio, *The Waters of Amsterdam*, explores her time away from the Doctor after he leaves her in *Time-Flight*, detailing her being fired in her first year as an air-stewardess after assaulting a troublesome passenger; she gets into a relationship with an android called Kylex-12, but she breaks it off as he's about to propose. The 2003 novel, *Fear of the Dark*, sees her having nightmares related to the Mara (which ultimately returns in *Cradle of the Snake*), and she goes to travel the world.

Tegan makes her choice to leave the TARDIS in 1984 – a decision compounded by deaths in *The Auton Infinity*, part of the 2022 set, *Forty: Volume 2* – but *The Gathering*, a 2006 audio story, sees her reunited with the Doctor twenty years later, on her forty-sixth birthday (incidentally Tegan has the same birthday, 22nd September, as Billie Piper, referenced in the story on a radio show heard in the background). She's taken on the job of running Verney Food Supplies, her father's stock feed company, likely inherited from Tegan's maternal grandfather, Andrew Verney. It's one of the more poignant outings on audio as she and the Doctor explore their past as travelling companions. Having been diagnosed with a fatal brain tumour while at the same time struggling with a number of relationships, Tegan undergoes a process of reconciling herself with the decisions she's made. Her recovery for *The Power of the Doctor* has yet to be explained.

Turlough's trustworthiness is a matter of ongoing debate between the Doctor and Tegan, most notably in the audio story, *Cobwebs*, when Tegan comments that her Aunt Vanessa always said, 'Once a wrong 'un, always a wrong 'un.' They argue over Turlough's loyalty, and his alliance with the Black Guardian is repeatedly brought up by Tegan in an attempt to change the Doctor's mind.

Indeed, Turlough has always kept secrets. In the 2009 audio, *Ringpullworld*, we discover that he didn't keep a diary as a child in case someone learned all his secrets; this is revisited somewhat in the following year's IDW comics, *Tesseract* and *Final Sacrifice*, in which Tenth Doctor companion, Matthew Finnegan, seemingly finds Vislor's journal of adventures on the TARDIS, but Turlough confirms it's fake when the Doctor visits him on Trion. In *Freakshow*, Turlough strongly believes that the Doctor mistrusts him due to his involvement with the Black Guardian, and is testing him in order to ascertain where his loyalties lie. Still, he places a lot of confidence in the Time Lord: in *Devil in the Mist*, the Doctor's trusting Kamelion is enough for Turlough to stand by the android when Tegan accuses him of stealing her purse.

Freakshow is also notable for the Doctor's observation that Turlough and Tegan are like a pair of bickering siblings, a fractious relationship which plays out on both television and in the Expanded Universe. During the story, Turlough gets annoyed with the Doctor for failing to knock before entering his room, pointing out that he wouldn't dare treat Tegan in the same manner. (Turlough also dons a Stetson, predating the Eleventh Doctor in *The Impossible Astronaut*, when the TARDIS lands in Buzzard Creek, Arizona, in 1905.)

Turlough's time at Brendon Public School on Earth gets a few mentions in the Expanded Universe. In the 1999 audio drama, *Phantasmagoria*, Turlough mentions his enjoyment of studying history there (and the Doctor gifts Turlough his 1928 Wisden Almanac) and in *The Heroes of Sontar*, we learn that the Brendon Public School scroll of honour is inscribed with the Latin phrase, *Dulci et decorum est pro patria mori* ('it is sweet and fitting to die for one's country'). This is dedicated to all the school's former students who've died in wars. Turlough actually outranks some of the Sontarans on Samur as he's a Junior Ensign Commander. In *The Emerald Tiger*, Turlough reveals he hated studying Shakespeare, and the Doctor tells Turlough that he should talk the Brigadier into emphasising the importance of playing sports more at the school – though Turlough showed some disdain for PE, dumping the sports' trophies in a pond while he was there (*The Memory Bank*). He did make friends at school, including, as seen in *Mawdryn Undead*, Hippo Ibbotson, with whom he visited Weston-super-Mare; and Charlie Gibbs, who, unbeknown to Vislor, was a fellow native of the planet Trion (*Eldrad Must Die!*).

In *Turlough and the Earthlink Dilemma*, the first *Companions of Doctor Who* novel (1986), Turlough gets a story of his own – one of the only times we see his life after parting company with the Doctor. In the book, he alters history to erase the annihilation of Trion, New Trion, and Earth, and in doing so thwarts the plans of evil dictator, Rehctaht (read it backwards!). But this results in him being unable to return home in case he creates a temporal paradox and he ends up in an alternative timeline, replacing a dead version of himself. On encountering his older alternative self with long hair, Turlough is warned against the folly of blindly trusting his Time Lord friend. The story also reveals the extent to which Turlough has developed as a scientist: through close study of the TARDIS' temporal control mechanisms, he has an astounding grasp of time travel (in the 2004 short story, *Observations*, he can operate the TARDIS with enough accuracy to pilot it six months forward in time to collect the Doctor). He's more than efficient in the fields of physics and quantum mechanics and is also in the possession of an almost perfect memory.

This is contradicted by *Gardens of the Dead*, a 2016 *Short Trips* audio, in which we find an elderly Turlough still on Trion, looking back fondly at his time on the TARDIS. He wishes he'd been better friends with Tegan and Nyssa, but other audio tales highlight their closeness: he and Nyssa spend two years together in *The Butcher of Brisbane*; Tegan starts to warm to him, admitting he's braver than he looks after delving into his past in *Kiss of Death* (2011), and they prove an efficient team in adventures like *Nightmare Country* (2019); and the foursome grow closer when they're reunited with an older Nyssa in *Cobwebs*, kicking off a season of stories that runs for five years, until 2015's *The Entropy Plague*. Turlough even meets two further companions, Constance Clarke and Charley Pollard, in 2021's *The End of the Beginning*!

*

Kamelion gets a raw deal on television, but in the Expanded Universe, he's treated a little better. In *The Crystal Bucephalus*, a 1994 novel, we learn that he and the TARDIS have probably been chatting for a while (and he gains access to the ship's information system via its telepathic circuits in *Devil in the Mist*). Kamelion reveals that he finds free will hard to negotiate and is more comfortable following orders. Being designed for war, this is hardly surprising.

It's not only the TARDIS that the android can hear: in the 2000 novel, *Imperial Moon*, Kamelion is able to sense the Time Lord's thoughts, due to their complexity; and he fell under the influence of the Mara in the 2017 short story, *Mark of the Medusa*. He also struggles with ethics and compassion, being affected by a widow's grief in the audio, *Black Thursday* (2019), taking on the dead man's face and seeking revenge. Kamelion clearly feels guilty for this, and apologises to the Doctor, suggesting that he should leave; instead, the Doctor appreciates that he's going through a considerable learning curve.

This character arc is expanded upon in the following month's Big Finish release, *The Kamelion Empire*, which establishes that Kamelion is one of many – an army created by the Kamille, a race of beings who'd uploaded their consciousness into a super-computer; they intended to experience the universe through their android avatars. As such, the Kamille sent Kamelion and his peers to wipe out the Xeraphins, i.e. the same species seen in *Time-Flight*, but the command signal was fortunately lost, meaning Kamelion lay dormant. It was in this state that the Master found him. Kamelion gets some form of payback on the evil Time Lord in the 2021 box set, *Masterful*, in which he infiltrates a meeting between incarnations of the Master and undermines their plans, a scheme which leads to Kamelion meeting Jo Grant, and taking the form of the Third Doctor. This timeline is rewritten, however.

Despite being killed in *Planet of Fire*, he returns in the follow-up novel, *The Ultimate Treasure*, his personality having survived due to his interfacing with the TARDIS. The natives of Gelsandor give him a new body (hence his being described in UNIT's Black Archive as 'Creation of the Galsandorans' in *The Day of the Doctor*) but he again has to sacrifice himself for the Doctor and Peri. Later, in *The Reproductive Cycle*, we discover the android had a child with the TARDIS, which is raised by Peri and the Sixth Doctor.

Seventeen-year-old Erimemushinteperem (meaning 'Daughter of Light') – Erimem, for short – was the first Expanded Universe companion created by Big Finish for the Fifth Doctor in 2001, introduced in *The Eye of the Scorpion*. Erimem's father was the late Pharaoh Amenhotep II and her mother, Rubak, one of his sixty concubines. Erimem's three elder half-brothers died the previous year and there's some suspicion surrounding these deaths. It transpires that the one thing Erimem regrets after stepping into the TARDIS is that she never said goodbye to her mother.

Erimem is adamant that she doesn't believe in Egyptian gods; however, by 2006's *The Kingmaker*, she informs Peri that she now believes in an afterlife. As an ancient Egyptian, she reveres cats and *The Church and the Crown* sees her getting a pet cat named Antranak. In *No Place Like Home*, it turns out that the Fifth Doctor isn't a cat-lover and the feline addition to the TARDIS becomes the subject of a running joke between the Doctor and Erimem, and remains so until Antranak's death in *Nekromanteia*.

As with Turlough and Peri, Erimem gets her own story in the 2005 novel, *The Coming of the Queen*. It's a pre-Doctor adventure which shows the Pharaoh's daughter, who's lived a protected and luxurious life in her father's palace in Thebes, approaching her sixteenth year, a period that'll plunge Erimem and her three half-brothers into a dark world of death, betrayal, and tragedy.

Erimem's departure from the TARDIS comes in the 2008 audio outing, *The Bride of Peladon*, in which she makes a decision to stay with King Pelleas. Erimem has a signet ring bearing the emblem of Sekhmet which she uses as a talisman to protect her from the gods, once again revealing that she has moved away from her previous agnostic leanings.

*

The Fifth Doctor gets a number of short-lived companions on audio too. First is Amy, later called Abby to distinguish her from the Eleventh Doctor's TV companion. She's a tracer given human form to help the Doctor track down the Key to Time in 2009's *The Judgement of Isskar*. During her travels, she becomes fully human. She later enters the Time Lord Academy, and joins Zara (her 'twin sister') on further adventures in *Graceless*. In the 2020 box set, *Wicked Sisters*, the Doctor and Leela are sent by the Time Lords to arrest the pair, but, after the the Doctor is killed and Abby and Zara resurrect him, they let the siblings get away, though not before the Doctor warns them to be careful using their powers, lest they attract attention from more than just his own people.

The Fifth Doctor travels for a time with Thomas Brewster, a street urchin from Victorian London who debuts in *The Haunting of Thomas Brewster*. He remains on Earth in 2008 to pursue a romance with Connie Winter in *A Perfect World*; however, she's hit by a car and falls into a coma. He re-enters the Doctor's life when the Time Lord is in his sixth incarnation.

In 2014, Hannah Bartholemew joins Nyssa and the Doctor at some time before *Arc of Infinity*, having stowed aboard the TARDIS. Hannah has a natural fascination in the unusual and the alien: when she's invited to the private hunting grounds of Nathaniel Whitlock in Suffolk, 1911, Hannah is rather taken with the titular *Moonflesh*, a crystallised rock said to have the power to call spirits from another realm. At its conclusion, the TARDIS' doors malfunction, meaning the adventuress is able to follow the Doctor; he doesn't learn this until near the end of *Tomb Ship* after she saves Nyssa from the insect-like Arrit-Ko.

Hannah asks to travel with them further, but the Doctor sets coordinates for 1911 – though he explains that the ship rarely takes them where they want to go. Sure enough, they instead find themselves near Paris in 1770 (*Masquerade*), and Hannah indeed leaves the TARDIS, albeit in sad circumstances: she's left devoid of emotions on SORDIDE Delta, a space station linked to France through a experimental Shadow-Space. She at least saves the

Doctor, Nyssa, and billions of others – her last human act.

Erimem isn't the only historical Fifth Doctor companion. In 2019's *Tartarus*, we meet Marcipor, better known as Marc (played by George Watkins, Peter Davison's nephew), slave to the Roman politician, Cicero, in 63 BC. Marc is clearly an intelligent man, having taught himself to read and write, and possessing an impressive memory. Despite his societal status, there's a mutual respect and friendship between Marc and his master – who frees him at the end of the tale so he can take up Nyssa's offer to travel with them in the TARDIS. He's both amazed and freaked out by their adventures, showing equal wonder at seeing the stars as he does at learning about sliding doors (*Interstitial*).

He and Tegan grow closer during a brief spell away from the Doctor and Nyssa in *Feast of Fear*. It's this connection which ultimately leads to Marc's demise. After seeking glory in gladiatorial-like games in *Warzone*, Marc is badly injured, and Tegan allows the medical bay on Samotis to fix him, not realising this means partial conversion into a Cyberman. Though Marc gains control over his own body, it badly affects both him and the Doctor, the latter leaving his companions so they could take a vacation on the sentient planet, Callanna (*Conversation* and its 2020 follow-up, *Madquake*). They fight alongside Steppa Westma Cotter-Thatch Slitheen, a member of the Raxacoricofallapatorian race who'd rejected her family's criminal leanings, while Marc tries to come to terms with his cyber-conversion: he no longer needs to eat or sleep; his heart is now a CPU; he's stronger than ever before; but he still wishes the Cybermen had simply killed him, admitting in 2021's *The Lost Resort* that he sees himself as a robotic slave.

The trio are understandably cross at the Doctor when he finally returns for them. This doesn't stop Marc essentially sacrificing his life for the Doctor in *Nightmare of the Daleks*, in which Marc takes the Doctor's place in the Daleks' neural command network, the Pathweb, to keep them all asleep and stop a full-scale invasion of the fifty-first century. It leaves Marc questioning whether his real life actually did happen, though he maintains that he had three best friends who he'll never forget.

The Fifth Doctor's shortest-lived companion, though, is likely Brooke. Played by Joanna Horton, Brooke is a Proto-Time Lord created from River Song's DNA by Madame Kovarian (a recurring Series 6 threat on TV) as part of a second batch of would-be assassins. Though she's both introduced and dispensed with in the 2018 box set, *The Diary of River Song: Series Three*, Brooke travels with the Doctor and River for a short time after being sent to kill him. Instead, River shoots Brooke, forcing her to regenerate into a body that physically resembled River's second incarnation, i.e. the one introduced on TV as Mels in *Let's Kill Hitler*. This Brooke had a taste for killing, even murdering her sibling, H-One – all the DNA duplicates having names derived from water – and turning on Kovarian. She at least saves the Doctor and stays behind with another sibling, H-Two, to keep their creator in check.

Big Finish isn't the only company to create non-television companions for the Fifth Doctor; no sooner had he appeared on TV, he receive his first 'exclusive' companion: Sir Justin, in the pages of *Doctor Who Magazine*. A knight from medieval England, Sir Justin gives his life to stop Melanicus, who he thought to be Satan (*The Tides of Time*). In that same comic strip, we meet another part-time companion created for the comics: Shayde, a Gallifreyan construct placed in the Doctor's TARDIS without the Doctor's permission. He returns on occasion to assist the Doctor, later appearing with the Eighth Doctor and merging with future companion, Fey Truscott-Sade.

The Sixth Doctor
Colin Baker

*'In all my travelling throughout the universe, I have battled
against evil, against power-mad conspirators.'*
The Doctor – *The Trial of a Time Lord*

Perpugilliam 'Peri' Brown – Nicola Bryant – Continued...
(*Planet of Fire* to *The Trial of a Time Lord*)

From the moment the Doctor sits up, fresh from his
regeneration, one thing is clear: he's not the man that saved
Peri's life. As she later states in *The Twin Dilemma*, she finds him
rude, self-obsessed, and ignorant – it's a wonder she remains with
him really, since it's obvious she no longer likes him. This isn't
surprising; she is distraught and confused by his change of
appearance, but the new Doctor is very dismissive of her
emotional state, saying she'll get used to it. Gone is the man she
considered sweet, replaced by a dangerously unstable stranger.
One who even attempts to kill her! He tries to strangle her,
apparently in a fit of confusion. His regenerative amnesia kicks
in, and the Doctor finds it hard to believe that he would even think
of something like that; when she cowers away from him in fear,
however, he realises she's not making it up, and that something
has gone dangerously wrong with the regeneration (likely a
consequence of the Fifth Doctor having actually died before the
regeneration kicked in).

A short time later, when Peri believes the Doctor has died in
a safe house explosion on Titan Three, she breaks down in tears.
That might just be due to her heightened emotional state (since
leaving Lanzarote, she's gone through a lot), but on the surface,

it doesn't entirely make sense as she has shown nothing but distaste for him following his regeneration – and with good reason. Even the Doctor doesn't understand why she would be so upset. She explains it away as compassion, but it fails to ring true. It's more likely that Peri's more distraught than she realises, being stuck with a man who might kill her at any time and unable to get home to Earth without him. Nonetheless, she remains defiant and refuses to be bullied by the unstable Doctor. Just as they leave Jaconda, the Doctor tells Peri that he is now fully stabilised, and Peri points out that he could do with a crash course in manners. But when he adds, 'I am the Doctor, whether you like it or not', Peri finds his smile infectious and cannot help but return one of her own. And that is all it really is, an infectious reaction: between then and the next time we see them in *Attack of the Cybermen*, things haven't improved much. They've spent much time in the TARDIS, although what Peri's been doing to occupy her time is unclear, and she is clearly bored out of her mind while the Doctor goes about repairing systems. She's finding it hard to relate to the Doctor now, and doesn't think he understands her, a far cry from the closeness that had been developing with the Fifth Doctor.

She's clearly worried about his state of mind; he's called her a number of names, including Tegan, Zoe, Susan and, at one point, Jamie. He calls her Susan once again while they stand outside the junkyard on Totter's Lane, although Peri fails to understand the reason for this slip up. She's merely frustrated that he forgets who she is. Again. She bemoans the fact that her first visit to London is to search for a distress call the TARDIS picked up, and wishes she could just visit like a regular tourist, which is perfectly in keeping with the reason why she remained with the Doctor in the first place. She spends most of her time in London on edge – not helped by the appearance of the Cybermen, or their threat to kill her if the Doctor doesn't take them to Telos. Still in a state of distress, Peri is initially horrified by the Cryons, but soon overcomes such terror when she realises they're peaceful, although fighting for their own survival. She learns that Lytton, a man they all thought was working for the Cybermen, is really working against them on behalf of the Cryons. It takes her some time to convince the Doctor that Lytton is actually one of the good guys. After Lytton sacrifices himself to save the Doctor, Peri's surprised, although heartened too, to see the Time Lord's remorse. Perhaps there is some hope for this Doctor after all. If nothing else, it's a hint of the man she once knew.

Peri appears to be something of an anglophile, fitting into London very well, seemingly something of an expert on British slang. It may be that she learned key phrases in preparation for travelling to the UK at some point, but it's curious that she rarely uses American slang – actually, more often than not, she tends to use British pronunciation. For instance, when the Doctor talks down to her, she tells him to not '*pat*-ronise' her, instead of saying '*pay*-tronise' as would be expected from an American.

When the TARDIS is out of Zeiton-7 ore in *Vengeance on Varos* and the Doctor explains that they have barely got enough power to reach the titular planet, she tells him she would rather be stuck there than in the TARDIS, since unlike the Doctor she doesn't have many lives to live; she only has one and doesn't want to spend it alone with him. This is perfectly understandable, since their level of bickering would only worsen after endless hours of being in each other's company. On Varos, she meets Sil, a slug-like alien from the planet Thoros Beta, and finds him as repulsive as he finds her. When she's put under the transmogrification beam, Sil is delighted to see her start to turn into some bird-like creature. She recovers from the ordeal, but the Doctor jokes much later (in *The Trial of a Time Lord*) that after leaving Varos, she cost him a fortune in birdseed – a joke Peri doesn't appreciate. When the Doctor appears to die in the punishment zone, Peri expresses real grief, almost guilt, at his passing, and wonders what she's going to do if she's stuck on such a horrible world. Although they still bicker and squabble, during their time on Varos, there are a few moments of levity between them that suggests that somehow they are bonding.

When the TARDIS takes them to the mining town of Killingworth in the 1820s, Peri expresses an interest in ecology, a perfect companion to her botany studies. On the short walk from the TARDIS to the town itself, there is actual banter between her and the Doctor, showing a steady growth in their friendship, even if they still quarrel. Indeed, at the end of *The Mark of the Rani*, when asked what it is he and Peri do in the TARDIS, the Doctor replies, 'Argue, mainly'. She's shocked by the Master's return, having witnessed his death on Sarn. As you might expect, the Master wishes her dead too. Nonetheless, he still has a lot of respect for Peri, referring to her as 'Miss Brown'.

She's saved by the Rani, another Time Lord, but not out of compassion; rather because she wants to use the chemicals in Peri's brain. After both the Master and the Rani are defeated, it's nice to note that the Doctor and Peri walk away together, with the Doctor putting his arm over her shoulders – a level of closeness not seen between them before. They still have a long way to go though, as shown when they're fishing in *The Two Doctors*, but by this point, Peri's giving as good as she gets, a tact that begins to have an effect on the Doctor. There have been several times she could've left him, yet Peri clearly thinks it's worth sticking it out.

Having already heard of Jamie, Peri gets to meet him and is rather charmed. Initially, Jamie is not completely on form, having been stranded alone on the deserted Space Station Camera. Peri doesn't quite understand how two Doctors can be in one period, nor how the TARDIS can be in two places at one time.

Despite seeing a holographic image of the Second Doctor on the space station, she fails to recognise him. Evidently, when in danger, Peri thinks of the Doctor, as witnessed when she's confronted by Chessene, who she feels is a threat. As they leave Spain, the Doctor decides that from now on (after the cannibalistic nature of the Androgums), it's a strict vegetarian diet for both of them. That appears to carry on at least until they arrive on Necros much later in *Revelation of the Daleks*, at which point Peri's 'enjoying' one of the Doctor's nut-roast rolls.

After these recent events, at the start of *Timelash,* Peri simply wants to go somewhere to relax and the Doctor suggests the Eye of Orion. But Peri wants to go somewhere else, somewhere fun. The Doctor offers to take her back to 1985 but Peri insists she doesn't want to go back; despite everything, she appears to enjoy her travels, or, at the very least, is not ready to give up on him yet. She doesn't care much for Karfel, and is especially not impressed by the Borad, yet another mutated creature who wishes to make Peri his mate. But she's particularly impressed when she learns that Herbert is the young HG Wells.

Although she's heard of the Daleks, by the time they arrive on Necros (*Revelation of the Daleks*), she can't have seen one as she doesn't identify a Dalek on sight. We also learn that, while on her travels, she's been collecting exotic alien plants, since she has to wow her teachers with something as her grades certainly will not – either suggesting she's been away longer than the planned three months, or that she has little faith in her academic ability. When a mutant, the result of Davros' experiments, attacks the Doctor, Peri accidentally kills it in her attempts at a rescue. It's the first time she's killed anyone, and she feels overwhelming guilt, especially since the mutant thanks her before dying. During their long walk to Tranquil Repose, the Doctor and Peri engage in a lot of banter which includes such topics as the American's monopoly on bad taste, and the Doctor's weight. While scaling a wall, she unintentionally breaks the Doctor's much treasured fob-watch too. She promises to buy him a new one, but the Doctor brushes it away with sarcasm, leaving Peri feeling more than a little guilty. When the Doctor is apparently crushed by his own gravestone, Peri is 'consoled' by the grotesque Jobel. She finds him both repellent and weird, and is comforted when the Doctor climbs from beneath the gravestone unharmed. While the Doctor exposes a plot to create a new army of Daleks by Davros, he leaves Peri in Jobel's care, thinking she'll be safer with him than whatever else is on Necros. Peri's not so convinced and gives him the slip at the first opportunity, instead enjoying the company of the DJ.

At first, she thinks he's really from America, and is a little disappointed to discover that his accent is false (indeed, that he has never even been to Earth). Nonetheless she does find him amusing, and is horrified when he is later killed by a Dalek. After the slaughter at Tranquil Repose, she decides she needs a holiday, and the Doctor agrees to take her to...

Something very strange has happened by the time we next see the Doctor. He arrives at a space station controlled by the Time Lords and is put on trial (*The Trial of a Time Lord: The Mysterious Planet*). Peri isn't with him, and he has no idea where she is. He soon finds out, but not before he's shown a couple of recent adventures. The first is set on Ravalox, and it's immediately clear that quite some time has passed for both the Doctor and Peri since they left Necros. Peri's hair is much longer, and they now have a close and quite tactile relationship. They think nothing of walking through a damp wood arm in arm, under an umbrella. Even their banter, once snippy and derisive, is now light and good natured.

Finally, Peri has found her Doctor again.

She's uneasy on Ravalox, unable to shake the feeling that she has been there before. The Doctor remarks on the similarities it has to Earth, and he wonders why. Peri is less interested in the mystery, until they come across the remains of Marble Arch Underground Station. She's very upset to discover that somehow the Earth was almost destroyed in a fireball and then shifted halfway across the galaxy, and reminisces about how London should be, as if she has been there before (not in *Attack of the Cybermen*, since the things she describes do not match what she experienced during her brief visit there in that story). The Doctor attempts to comfort her, explaining that this is over two million years in her future, the Earth she knows is still there, just as she remembers it. But this doesn't help and she simply wants to leave, but the Doctor can't until he discovers what happened to Earth – why was it almost destroyed and shifted half way across the galaxy?

When captured by the Tribe of the Free, Peri's promised several husbands by Queen Katryca, but it's not an idea that amuses her. She is, however, amused by intergalactic con-man Sabalom Glitz.

Her sadness over Earth's fate has a lasting impression on her because later, while on Thoros Beta (*The Trial of a Time Lord: Mindwarp*), she expresses a desire to return home, to be surrounded by people she loves – a nice bit of progression from the girl who was so willing to escape her home life when we first met her. But she doesn't get back. Or does she? Unfortunately, we learn about this adventure via the Matrix, which the Doctor later discovers has been tampered with, so much of the story didn't happen as we see it. This throws up all kinds of doubt as to what we see, but we can assume much of it is true, even if the attraction between Peri and warrior King Yrcarnos is a little odd. It's believable that Peri would be disgusted by the attentions of a 'dirty old war lord' on the planet Thordon, and that she would be disturbed to discover that Thoros Beta is the homeworld of Sil (even more so that the Doctor knew and didn't tell her). But what's hard to understand is the Doctor's betrayal of Peri. From almost any angle, it seems wrong and out of character. Had it happened shortly after his regeneration it might be accepted, but considering the development of their relationship, it just makes no sense at all.

For a while, the Doctor believes that Peri was killed on Thoros Beta, that her body was used to house the mind of Lord Kiv, Sil's superior, and that the Time Lords then used Yrcarnos as an assassin to destroy Peri's body and everyone involved in the unholy experiments being conducted on Thoros Beta. Later though, after he defeats the threat posed to him and Gallifrey, he's greatly relieved to hear that Peri survived after all, and has fallen in love with Yrcarnos.

We'll likely never learn how Peri felt at the Doctor's sudden disappearance (being taken out of time by the Time Lords to stand trial), but it's unlikely she'd have taken it well.

Peri's confused departure was a good indication of the behind-the-scenes upheaval in the series at time, and it continued with the introduction of Mel – the first companion since Susan to not even get an introduction story. She was simply just there...

Melanie Bush – Bonnie Langford (*The Trial of a Time Lord* to *Dragonfire*, plus *The Power of the Doctor*, *The Giggle* and *The Legend of Ruby Sunday / Empire of Death*)

Ice Ice Baby (Vanilla Ice); *Déjà vu* (Olivia Rodrigo).

While on trial, the Doctor shows an adventure set at some point in his own personal future (*The Trial of a Time Lord: Terror of the Vervoids*). At this point, he's travelling with an Earth girl called Mel. They've clearly been together for quite some time, since not only does the Doctor state that he would 'trust Mel with my life', but he has always envied her ability for almost total recall, suggesting a long association. They've an easy and lightweight friendship, with Mel looking to the Doctor with great affection. She's polite, bubbly, and always charming, clearly excited about the adventure she is on. We never learn how they meet, nor indeed where she is actually from (all this is mentioned in the character profile on official documents, but nothing is made of it on screen, so it has no bearing on the narrative). She's defiant and won't be cowed by anyone. She's also fiercely loyal to the Doctor, and will not tolerate anyone talking badly about him. During a moment of reflection, the Doctor points out that Mel isn't known for being subdued and thoughtful; she can only smile at this, knowing the Doctor's quite right. She places a high value on all life, and is saddened by the death of the Vervoids, even though she understands why it was necessary.

Mel is pulled from the Doctor's future and brought to his trial by the Master, as a witness, and the Doctor is not entirely sure what to make of her, especially when she enthusiastically calls him 'Doc' (*Trial of a Time Lord: The Ultimate Foe*). She's rude to Glitz, who has also been called as a witness, and treats him with total disinterest – clearly not as susceptible to his false charms as

Peri was. She admits she is 'truthful, honest, and about as boring as they come,' which is a little disingenuous since, although the former attributes are true, she proves in her encounter with the Vervoids that she is far from boring.

Once the threat is averted, the Doctor is once more offered the position of President of the High Council and again he refuses, leaving the Time Lord space station with Mel, a companion from his future that he hasn't actually met yet. You'd think that would confuse the timelines, but it's never really addressed on screen...

The Sixth Doctor
Expanded Universe

Probably more so than any other previous Doctor, the Sixth Doctor's Expanded Universe is primarily focused on fixing the perceived mistakes the television series made with both Peri and Mel; namely the former's very confused ending, and the latter's very confused beginning. Does the Expanded Universe fix this? Yes… and no.

The only child of Paul and Janine Brown, Peri was born in 1966 (her parents married on 21st November 1962). When Peri was thirteen, her father died in a boating accident, according to the 2004 novel, *Synthespians™*. Coincidentally, her parents and her stepfather are all archaeologists, and she travelled the world with them (2003's *Blue Box*). She was raised a Baptist, but didn't consider herself religious (the 2005 audio, *The Council of Nicaea*). Peri's prose stories typically adhere to the Fifth Doctor giving his life for someone he's really only just yet – indeed, the 2002 short story, *Five Card Draw*, from *Short Trips: Zodiac*, includes the Fifth Doctor meeting up with three of his past selves and telling Peri to stay inside the TARDIS as it doesn't feel right for this to be her first real trip in time and space; by the end of the tale, however, a future version of Peri is shocked to see the Fifth Doctor, instead looking for the Sixth. The Doctor deduces that his regeneration is just around the corner. But Peri's audio adventures go against this, adding much time to her travels with the Fifth Doctor. They battle Ice Warriors in *Red Dawn* (2000), get embroiled in a scheme between the Fifth and Seventh Doctors in *The Veiled Leopard* (2006) , and travel with Erimemushinteperem from 2001's *The Eye of the Scorpion* to *The Bride of Peladon* (2008). Perhaps most significantly in prose, the Fifth Doctor takes Peri to Karn, backdrop of the TV story, *The Brain of Morbius*, where she's kidnapped by the insane Time Lord (the 2002 novel, *Warmonger*); she escapes and becomes a guerilla leader fighting against Morbius.

Peri has a habit of leaving the Doctor in the Expanded Universe stories. After the events of *The Reaping* (2005), Peri leaves in tears, unable to deal with the deaths of her friends. She has barely departed the TARDIS when, in another tragic turn, her mother is killed, leaving her completely alone on Earth. When the Doctor comes back for her, she returns to his side, not wishing to stay on Earth alone.

In the 2004 short story, *Chaos,* included in the *Short Trips: Past Tense* anthology, Peri is homesick for 1980s America and leaves to pursue a life in New York City. However, she grows frustrated with her job and soon quits before rejoining the Doctor.

In *The Trial of a Time Lord*, we discover that Peri didn't in fact die on Thoros Beta, and this is explored in the Expanded Universe, in such stories as the 1996 novel *Bad Therapy* and audio play *Peri and the Piscon Paradox*. Peri and Yrcanos have three children; two sons and a daughter who go on to sire her at least three grandchildren, a few of whom would meet the Doctor and Frobisher in the 1994 comic *The Age of Chaos*. *Peri and the Piscon Paradox* goes into some detail about what exactly happens to Peri following the events of *The Trial of a Time Lord*. As a result of Time Lord interference in her timeline, there are five versions of Peri: one is killed in *The Trial of a Time Lord*; another becomes the wife of Yrcanos and a warrior queen on Krontep; while a third can only recall the events of her introductory story, *Planet of Fire*. The fates of the remaining two are somewhat vague although there's speculation that one returns to Earth in *Bad Therapy*. Another version, possibly the fifth, returns to twentieth century Earth with Yrcanos as depicted in the Target novelisation of *The Trial of a Time Lord: Mindwarp*, in which she becomes the manager of Yrcanos the Wrestler.

Bad Therapy shows a highly dissatisfied and stifled Peri, now

Queen Gilliam, on Krontep, as she makes a discovery while exploring the archaeological ruins of the first king of Krontep. It's an opportunity to escape, through time and space, by activating crystal globes left by Petruska, the first king's wife. Smothered by her own relationship with Yrcanos, who's obsessively in love, she uses the escape route to flee Krontep and return to Earth, where she comes into contact with the Seventh Doctor – it's not a happy reunion, what with Peri slapping him for never returning to her.

The 2022 webcast, *The Eternal Mystery*, released to promote the *Doctor Who: The Collection — Season 22* Blu-ray boxset, confuses things even more as another version of Peri invites a Krontep security guard called Rex to travel in the TARDIS with her and the Sixth Doctor. This establishes that Peri, now Warrior Queen, brought peace and prosperity to Krontep following Yrcanos' passing, and *Tales of the TARDIS* (2023) shows that she travelled with the Sixth Doctor again, on the understanding that she will return once a year to pay respects at Yrcanos' memorial. This is somewhat expanded upon in the 2024 audio, *The Trials of a Time Lord*, which shows Peri fighting various threats thrown at her by the Master until she is finally reunited with the Doctor and Mel. Though the former has some initial trouble marrying this battle-hardened queen with his ex-companion, they have a heart-to-heart during which the Doctor apologies for leaving her.

In the Marvel comic, *The Age of Chaos*, the Doctor travels to Krontep and finds himself on a quest to track down Peri's grandchildren (Artios and Euthys – her two grandsons who have plunged Krontep into civil war – and her granddaughter, Actis, who is very much like Peri in her temperament and taste for adventure). This particular outing is especially noteworthy as it's written by Colin Baker. His motivation was, according to him, because he felt somewhat responsible for Peri, and the mistreatment the character received during the making of *The Trial of a Time Lord*. An older Peri appears in the 2004 audio story, *Her Final Flight*, although this is a virtual-reality Peri created by an enemy to try and trick the Doctor into self-destructing the

TARDIS. Although she is illusionary, the story explores the relationship between the two and especially the Doctor's guilt on having to abandon Peri some twenty years before.

Yet another version of Peri finds her attacked by the mind parasite, Mandrake, which kills Yrcanos just a week after their wedding and inhabits Peri's body for some five years (2014's *The Widow's Assassin*). Once the Doctor fends the Mandrake off, Peri travels with the Doctor again, their first stop, in the 2014 audio, *Masters of Earth*, being the twenty-second century during the Daleks' invasion of Earth. Peri is also awarded an honourary degree in botany in *The Rani Elite* (2014). And by the time of *Conflict Theory*, a story in the 2020 audio set, *The Sixth Doctor and Peri: Volume One*, the Doctor and Peri have been travelling together for twelve years.

According to producer John Nathan-Turner in the 1987 reprint of his book *The Companions* (sound familiar?), the original plan for season twenty-four was to open with a story introducing Mel properly, having Mel meet the Doctor for the first time. However, this never came about due to the unfortunate removal of Colin Baker from the role in late 1986. As a result, we're left with a companion who never, technically, meets the Doctor. That is, until 1988, when Target released the novelisation of *The Trial of the Time Lord: The Ultimate Foe*. At the end of the book, we see the Doctor, directly after leaving the Time Lord space station, dropping Mel off on the planet Oxyveguramosa where his slightly older self is waiting for her. The post-*Trial* Doctor then heads off to his uncertain future, knowing that one day he'll not only meet Mel but also become the Valeyard.

This first proper meeting is chronicled in *Business Unusual*, a 1997 novel by Gary Russell, by which time the Doctor has been travelling both alone, and with various other Expanded Universe companions. The Doctor spends a lot of the novel trying to avoid Mel, knowing that to meet her means he's on the path that will lead to the Valeyard, but time conspires against him and the two are drawn together – although he has to go to great lengths to pretend he doesn't know her. That's in one version of events anyway. Big Finish gives us another possibility in the 2013 audio, *The Wrong Doctors*, in which the Doctor heads to Pease Pottage to meet Mel in the summer of 1987. This happens at the same time as an older Sixth Doctor is dropping an older Mel home after the events of *Trial of a Time Lord*. A younger Mel is back from university then, but is kidnapped by a time demon in the hope of using her photographic memory and two TARDISes to enter the real universe. Though the Doctor traps the time demon in its own dimension, it's at a cost: namely, that Mel is removed from time. The Doctor uses his TARDIS to save her, at the expense of her memories – probably for the best considering she's seen the older version of herself and the Doctor. In this way, we may marry *The Wrong Doctors* with *Business as Usual*, as well as hint at some timey-wimey interference in her home period, which is sometimes 1989 and at other times 1986 (as in the 1995 novel, *Head Games*, the 2015 audio, *We Are The Daleks*, and 2019's *Loud and Proud*, during which she encourages the Doctor to attend an anger management meeting at Pease Pottage).

We learn much more about Mel during her Expanded Universe travels with the Sixth Doctor; more than is ever revealed on television. When she meets the Doctor, she's twenty-five years old and not only a computer programmer, but a computer genius with a BSc (Hons) in Computer Science. Her full name is Melanie Jane Bush, daughter of Alan and Christine, and one account, the 2005 novel, *Spiral Scratch*, suggests she had a sister, Anabel, who died at the age of three; Mel has repressed this memory.

There is further biographical information to be gleaned in the 2005 audio story, *Catch-1782*, where we learn that Mel had a passion for science from an early age and was encouraged by her uncle, Dr John Hallam. She acknowledges his influence and views him as being largely responsible for her later success in academia at university. In 2003, Hallam tells a colleague, Professor David Munro, about Mel's gifted proficiency with computers. In *The*

Juggernauts (2005), we discover that she has an excellent knowledge of the computer languages BASIC, COBOL, and FORTAN.

Her home address, 36 Downview Crescent, is often used by Mel when she writes computer code to create a 'backdoor'. She uses it to great effect in *The Juggernauts*, efficiently overriding the Mechanoids' (the eponymous machines) programming. Mel, it seems, often gets separated from the Doctor. In *Catch-1781*, a freak accident transports her back to 1781, and it's some time before the Doctor is able to rescue her. In *The Juggernauts*, she is accidentally left on Lethe and it's three months before the Doctor can retrieve her. A testimony to Mel's strength of character and sheer pragmatism, though, is the manner in which she's successfully able to blend into, and become a part of, the societies in which she finds herself stranded.

In the 2001 novel *Instruments of Darkness*, Mel encounters Evelyn Smythe for the first time, and again, in a contradictory account, in the 2005 audio drama *Thicker Than Water*. In the audio drama, *The Vanity Box* she says it is her one wish to continue travelling with the Doctor: 'I love all this, our lives, racketing about the galaxy.'

The Sixth Doctor fares well with new companions in the audio plays. He's joined by companions from his past, in the shape of Second Doctor companions, Jamie and Zoe, plus Thomas Brewster who travelled with the Fifth Doctor previously. He also meets future companion, Charlotte Pollard, as well as two who have their own spin-off series, the eponymous *Jago & Litefoot*.

The first original-to-audio companion is Evelyn Smythe, played by Maggie Stables, the oldest travelling companion the Doctor's ever had. When the Doctor meets her in 2000, she is a fifty-five-year-old university lecturer, specialising in Tudor history and politics (*The Marian Conspiracy*). She's initially disdainful of the 'young' Doctor, waving away his concerns about her missing history, but she eventually accompanies him to 1555 where she meets Queen Mary I. She continues with the Doctor for some time, encountering Charles Darwin and Silurians on the Galapagos Islands in *Bloodtide*, the Brigadier in Cornwall in *The Spectre of Lanyon Moor*, and Daleks on Gallifrey in *The Apocalypse Element*. Up until this point, she shows immense joy and fun in her travels, but it is her encounters with Nimrod and the Forge that change all this. In *Project: Twilight*, she befriends the young Cassie who's been turned into a vampire, and with the Doctor they find a cure for her. But later in *Project: Lazarus*, they discover Cassie has been brainwashed by the Forge and watch as she's killed by Nimrod. This devastates Evelyn, but still she remains with the Doctor in spite of her developing heart condition and falling in love with Justice Rossiter on Vilâg in *Arrangements for War*. However, a return visit to Vilâg sees Evelyn leaving the Doctor for Rossiter. The Doctor reacts badly, and doesn't return for another two years, by which time he is travelling with Mel. The Doctor and Evelyn make their peace.

She is visited again, this time by the Seventh Doctor, Ace, and Hex, in *Death in the Family*, and dies of a heart attack but not before discovering that Cassie is survived by Hex, Cassie's son 'Little Tommy', first mentioned in *Project: Twilight*. The Doctor delivers a eulogy at Evelyn's funeral.

It's in 2011's *The Crimes of Thomas Brewster*, that Evelyn meets a future companion of the Doctor's. Philippa 'Flip' Jackson, played by Lisa Greenwood, is from 2010 London, and who slips through a temporal fissure, while on the Tube, onto the sentient world of Symbiosis. A year after those events, she and her boyfriend, Jared Ramon, find a crashed flying saucer in *The Curse of Davros*, and discover Davros inside – albeit a Davros whose mind has been swapped with the Doctor's! After defeating the Daleks, the Doctor offers to return her home, but temporarily leaves Jared, in favour of continuing with the Doctor.

Flip relates to many of her travels with pop culture references (which comes in handy when she's trapped inside a TV show in *The Fourth Wall*): she only knows the Battle of Waterloo thanks to ABBA; she seems to be a fan of *Star Wars*, *Die Hard*, and James Bond; and in *Stage Fright*, part of 2015's *The Sixth Doctor: The Last Adventure*, she likens the Prydonian Chapter on Gallifrey to the Hogwarts houses from Harry Potter.

One of her more harrowing adventures sees her nearly playing host to the titular space debris, *Scavenger* (2014), but ultimately left orbiting Earth in a space suit, utterly alone. Fearing she's running out of oxygen, she leaves a message for the Doctor before using thrusters to quicken the seemingly-inevitable, by sending herself plummeting towards the planet. Elsewhere, in *The Widow's Assassin*, the Doctor reveals he saved her using the TARDIS, bending space-time to slow her descent and save her; as such, she finds her way back to Jared and the pair get married. Though the Doctor thinks Jared is 'punching above his weight,' he obviously adores her, with Flip's wedding ring alone costing a week's wages. During their reception, Flip is kidnapped by the Zerith using a time-scoop. They intend to use her as a hostage against the Doctor during their war with the Vilal (*Quicksilver*). It's here that she meets another of the Doctor's companions, Constance Clarke, played by Miranda Raison; though both Flip and Constance intend to return to their respective lives, they're instead tempted into continuing their travels with the Doctor.

The Sixth Doctor met Constance – who prefers to be called 'Mrs Clarke' – in *Criss-Cross* (2015) at Bletchley Park in 1944, where Constance works as a WREN. As he's undercover there, she stands up to the Doctor for overworking a fellow WREN, the mathematical genius, Sylvia Wimpole. Constance married SubLieutenant Henry Clarke of the Naval Intelligence Division when they were both youngsters, but in 1943, he was called away for special duties abroad and she hadn't heard from him for some time. It's obviously something that cuts deeply, but she's still enthused enough with the Doctor's life that she agrees to travel with him a short time – that is, as long as she gets back soon as she doesn't want to be seen as a deserter. She soon meets the Daleks in *Order of the Daleks* (2016), as well as a slew of rogue Time

Lords, including the Rani (2015's *Planet of the Rani*), the Eleven (2021's *One for All*), and the Master in *The Last Adventure: The End of the Line* (interestingly, an anthology which had its release date pushed forward to August 2015, making it Constance's first appearance though audiences wouldn't get to learn how she met the Doctor until the following month).

She returns to 1944, only to find that her husband is lost in action. Wanting to learn about the mysterious circumstances of his disappearance, *Quicksilver* takes the Doctor and Constance to Vienna, only for the Doctor to be reunited with Flip Ramon, née Jackson, and Constance to learn that Henry has, in fact, absconded to marry and live with Ana Cook, who's pregnant with his child. Distraught, Constance laments that things always fall apart, and she finds solace in continuing her travels with the Doctor – this time, accompanied by Flip, who jokingly calls her 'Connie' (Constance gets her back by calling her 'Philippa').

The two have an almost sibling-like relationship, at times verbally sparring and at others showing how much they care about each other. Flip, for instance, is particularly keen to celebrate Constance's thirty-fifth birthday in *The Middle* (2017), a story which splits them apart and brings them closer together. Notably, a brief schism develops between them in *Scorched Earth* (2020) over their conflicting views on corporal punishment. Having experienced horrors during the Second World War, Constance is initially fine with French Allies treating traitors that way, but changes her mind and apologises to Flip by the story's conclusion.

Indeed, Constance's travels prove transformative in several ways. In *Static* (2017), Constance's body dies, but a duplicate is made and her mind is stored within. This results in her wanting to delay her return to 1944, and her enthusiasm for travelling in time and space leads her and Flip to meet the Ice Warriors (2020's *Cry of the Vultriss*), H.P. Lovecraft (in *The Lovecraft Invasion*, the same year) and Sontarans (in the 2024 boxset, *The Quin Dilemma*). And while Flip is in a coma due to a Pandorian Quill Spitter in 2021's *The End of the Beginning*, Constance is also introduced to other

Doctors (she takes a particular shining to the Eighth Doctor) and companions, i.e. Turlough and Charley Pollard.

As Constance is played by Miranda Raison, who previously appeared as Tallulah in *Daleks in Manhattan/Evolution of the Daleks*, another of the Sixth Doctor's companions, Hebe Harrison, is played by a fellow TV star, Ruth Madeley, who appeared in *The Star Beast* and *The Giggle*. Hebe befriended Evelyn Smythe while studying to be a marine biologist at Sheffield Hallam University. Evelyn left her with an SOS signal, to be used solely in extreme circumstances – as it connects to the TARDIS. She uses it in *The Rotting Deep*, part of the 2022 set, *Water Worlds*, as she investigates the effects an oil rig in the North Sea has on wildlife. Once the Doctor, Mel Bush, and Hebe solve the problem, the Doctor realises her connection to Evelyn and takes this as a sign that she should travel with them.

Hebe grows to have a teasing, playful relationship with Mel, even if they got off to a bad start as Mel berated peers on the oil rig for not helping Hebe, the latter being the first companion to use a wheelchair; this gets her back up as Hebe goes above and beyond to prove herself independent. The Doctor believes this anger to be a defence mechanism, and Hebe demonstrates that she's especially compassionate and thoughtful, hiding those qualities behind a veneer of sarcasm.

For her first trip in the TARDIS, the Doctor takes Hebe to the moon, which, some two billion years ago, is covered in water (*The Tides of the Moon*) – giving Hebe and Mel a chance to bond as the former saves Mel from drowning – and further adventures take them to Veludia, besieged by electromagnetic storms in *Maelstrom*; the moon Zoda-Kappa, where the Holomorph are imprisoned (*Interludes: The Dream Nexus*); and back to the university, where the Doctor and Mel meet the campus' most celebrated tutor, Professor Patricia McBride, in the 2022 boxset, *Purity Undreamed*. Though it seems she may become a companion, McBride's bigotry comes to light when the Doctor takes her to the twenty-sixth century, by which time McBride thinks they should've 'fixed' disabled people like Hebe.

Other companions are similarly shorter-lived as McBride: Joseph 'Joe' Carnaby, played by Luke Allen-Gale, was a Were Lord, a species of regenerating werewolves created by the Time Lords, accompanying the Sixth Doctor and Peri in the 2019 audio anthology, *Blood on Santa's Claw and Other Stories*. Joe's father was Lord Lycaon, the first Were Lord, who fled with his children to ancient Greece and lived among mankind for centuries, becoming the stuff of legend. When Joe learned of the Time Lords destroying his people in the fifty-ninth century, he studied the Doctor and hatched a plot to avert their extinction, including getting into a relationship with Peri, who invited him into the TARDIS. Their trip to the Ishtar institute is especially unnerving as the organisation genetically engineers Paul, Michael, and Janey, the potential offspring of Peri and Joe; when the children turn into were-creatures and disappear, Peri is understandably upset and deduces that Joe is a Were Lord who never really loved her.

Similarly, Grant Markham, a prose-exclusive companion, was created by Steve Lyons in the 1995 novel *Time of Your Life* and otherwise appeared in *Killing Ground* the following year. Grant comes from 2191 and is a computer programmer; although living in New Tokyo on New Earth, he's originally from an Earth colony on Agora. In his second appearance, he witnesses his father's death during an unsuccessful attempt at being converted into a Cyberman. He continues with the Doctor after this story, and a man who appears to look like him is featured in the linking material of the anthology *Short Trips: Repercussions* (2004). If it is him, then he ends up stuck travelling the time vortex in a temporal zeppelin with others who can no longer interact on the linear plane, such as Jake Morgan who encountered the Third Doctor and Jeremy Fitzoliver.

Strangely for *Doctor Who*, the Sixth Doctor only had one companion during his comic adventures in *Doctor Who Magazine* who was exclusive to the Expanded Universe: Frobisher. A wise-cracking Whifferdill, he first appears in *The Shape Shifter* (#88-89), having accepted the bounty placed on the Doctor by Josiah W Dogbolter (who is really more interested in the TARDIS – something that continues in *Death's Head* #8 when the titular Freelance Peacekeeping Agent also tracks down the Seventh Doctor), he infiltrates the TARDIS and makes the Doctor's life hell. At the time, he was living as Avan Tarklu, but upon joining the Doctor, he takes the name Frobisher because it sounds British and he thinks the Doctor will like it. He takes the shape of a penguin, and in *Genesis!* (#110) contracts mono-morphia which prevents him from shifting out of his penguin shape.

At some point, the Doctor and Frobisher travel with Peri. And Frobisher himself left the Doctor at least once, long enough for the Doctor to undergo his sixth regeneration since Frobisher appears in *A Cold Day in Hell*, a Seventh Doctor comic strip. It's in this story that Frobisher finally leaves, citing what happened to Peri as a reason (one assumes he was told about her 'death' in *The Trial of a Time Lord*).

Frobisher's popularity among fans is proven by his many return appearances, not only in the comics but in one novel, *Mission: Impractical*, and two Big Finish audio plays, *The Maltese Penguin* and *The Holy Terror* – all of which are set during his travels with the Sixth Doctor.

The other Expanded Universe companions to travel with the Sixth Doctor do the rare thing of crossing over mediums too; UNIT officers Colonel Emily Chaudhry and Lieutenant Will Hoffman appear in both prose and audio, while Jason and Crystal first appear alongside the Sixth Doctor (*and* the Third) in the stage play *The Ultimate Adventure* (1989). The play is later adapted into an audio adventure by Big Finish in 2008, with a sequel called, with great creative panache, *Beyond the Ultimate Adventure* in 2011. As if a stage play and audio adventures aren't enough, Jason and Crystal further appear in one prose story, *Face Value* in the 2000 anthology, *Short Trips and Side Steps*.

The Seventh Doctor
Sylvester McCoy

'Every great decision creates ripples.
Like a huge boulder dropped in a lake.'
The Doctor – *Remembrance of the Daleks*

Mel – Bonnie Langford – Continued... (*The Trial of a Time Lord* to *Dragonfire*, plus *The Power of the Doctor*, *The Giggle* and *The Legend of Ruby Sunday / Empire of Death*)

In *Time and the Rani*, the Doctor's regeneration goes unobserved by his companion (for the first time since the Second Doctor turning into the Third), because Mel is unconscious on the TARDIS floor. The tumultuous buffeting of the ship endures as a result of the Rani's attack not only knocks Mel out cold, but somehow causes the Doctor to regenerate. It's never clear at which point in Mel's journey we meet her again – although the Doctor's waistcoat and cravat suggest very little time has passed since *The Trial of a Time Lord*, so whether or not the Doctor returned Mel to her correct point in time and he finally got to meet her in the right order remains unclear on TV. When she leaves in *Dragonfire*, the Doctor says, 'You're going. You've been gone for ages. You're already gone. You're still here. You've just arrived. I haven't even met you yet. It all depends on who you are and how you look at it,' which suggests that Mel's timeline is as confused as it appears.

The Rani leaves her in the TARDIS, but she's later removed by the Lakertyan, Ikona. While being carried across the surface of Lakertya, Mel has enough sense to feign unconsciousness, until

Ikona is distracted, at which point she causes such a fuss that he loses grip of her and she's able to make her escape. Unfortunately, this ends in a shocking face-to-face encounter with another Lakertyan, Sarn, who runs away in shock and ends up dying in one of the Rani's bubbletraps – Mel's sadness at her death is only matched by Faroon's (Sarn's mother) who shuns Mel's sympathy. Despite Ikona's unwillingness to accept that Mel is innocent of what's happening on Lakertya (his people being enslaved by the Rani), she still saves him from one of the Rani's traps, and he accepts that she *might* be telling the truth. Away from the Doctor, who is being coerced into helping the Rani (at this point, his memory is affected by both his regeneration and drugs administered by the Rani), Mel seems to be in a state of total shock – quickly shifting from histrionic to just plain dumb. When Mel finds her way to the Doctor, she takes some convincing to believe the clowning oaf before her is the man she knew so well; such convincing includes her showing him some of the basic self-defence techniques she knows, throwing him across the lab. It's only when they finally agree to a truce and check each other's pulse that they realise the truth. Mel, who knows about regeneration from his trial, is fascinated by the Doctor's new appearance and personality, and responds favourably to it.

His presence gives Mel back her fire. She is all for the Rani getting a taste of her own medicine, after the callous way she has treated the Lakertyans. Before they leave, Mel points out that the new Doctor will take some getting used to, but he promises her that he will grow on her. And he is not wrong: when we next see them in *Paradise Towers*, they've settled into a nice playful banter, with the Doctor happy to indulge her wish to visit the Towers.

After the promise of the video brochure, Mel is distinctly unimpressed by the run-down Towers, and is even more unimpressed by the Kangs, young girls who live in the Towers. They are the polar opposite to Mel – abrasive, rude, abrupt, and violent. Later, Mel comes across two elderly residents known as the Rezzies, who are exactly the kind of people you would expect

Mel to like. Tabby and Tilda are welcoming, friendly, polite, and conversational. Mel responds, unsurprisingly, very well to them, but totally fails to see the undercurrent running through their conversation. She is, quite literally, being fattened up. It's ironic that the Kangs, who she doesn't take to at all, turn out to be less harmful to her and the Doctor than the Rezzies; it demonstrates Mel's blinkered world view, and this is only enhanced later when she is 'saved' by Pex – the would-be champion of Paradise Towers (in reality, something of a coward). Mel doesn't think much of Pex's bravado and will clearly dump him given the chance – indeed, when she does manage to free herself of his company, she finds her way back into the clutches of Tabby and Tilda, and still fails to see the truth of these two women, until they've trapped her and are all set to cook her. This time, she does welcome Pex's rescue, and develops some respect for him, not liking the way the Kangs later bully him. Throughout this adventure, her stubborn nature is on display; she's loyal and driven, determined to make her way to the swimming pool at the top of the Towers, where she agreed to meet the Doctor, and won't let anything prevent her from achieving this.

It seems Mel just doesn't learn to look beyond appearance, as shown in the South Wales holiday camp of Shangri-La in 1959 (*Delta and the Bannermen*). Despite the joyous atmosphere, she views the camp with disdain, although this might be disappointment at their failure to reach Disneyland. She soon adapts though, and throws herself into the swing of things, clearly enjoying the rock 'n' roll – joining in the dancing and the sing-song atmosphere. But her righteous side comes to the fore when Gavrok destroys a bus-load of innocent holiday makers in his search for Delta and her daughter, the last Chimeron princess. Despite the threat to her life, Mel can't contain her righteous fury and is smart enough to make Gavrok believe Delta was on the bus.

People find Mel to be trustworthy, as Delta demonstrates when Mel witnesses the birth of the Chimeron Princess. Her ability to make friends quickly is impressive, although she doesn't always seem to be a good judge of character (as proven by Tabby and Tilda). This is certainly true on Iceworld, the trading colony on the dark side of Svartos in *Dragonfire*. There, she and the Doctor are reunited with Glitz, who fobs them off with some story about how he lost his ship and crew, and procured a treasure map. Mel believes him, but when the truth comes out – that he sold his crew – she immediately turns her back on him. It's curious that she believes him at all, having seen how spendthrift he is on their previous encounter at the Doctor's trial. This shows how naïve and trusting she can be, even when she should know better.

Mel is paired with Ace, a sixteen-year-old Londoner who is stranded on Iceworld. Unlike the clean-cut, healthy living Mel, Ace is a rebel – a very strong-willed character who's out for some fun, regardless of the rules she has to break. Mel is easily led by Ace's excitement, coming across as a prefect being misled by the 'bad girl' of the class, brushing with danger for the first time ever – and developing a taste for it. This is no more evident than when Mel is throwing a can of nitro-9, a homemade glycerine-based explosive of Ace's design. There is a clear joy on her face as Ace eggs her on. But there are still moments of friction between them. When Ace takes Mel to her very messy quarters, Mel is clearly disgusted and struggles for a place to sit, until Ace insists she just perch on the clothes. However, when stuck with Glitz, she happily joins Ace in tag-teaming him with verbal abuse. Despite all this unexpected edginess to Mel, it still comes as something of a surprise when she decides to take her leave of the Doctor, especially as she decides to continue her travels with Glitz – keeping him on the straight and narrow instead, a prospect that doesn't fill Glitz with joy. She obviously doesn't care for Glitz at all, so why does she leave? The Doctor is sad to see Mel go, but realises he has no choice but to respect her decision. Before leaving, Mel suggests the Doctor take Ace with him – possibly realising the perfect fit they will be together.

In *The Giggle*, she tells the Fourteenth Doctor that Glitz died at the age of one-hundred and one, having fallen over a whiskey bottle (then was treated to a Viking-style funeral); Mel hitched a lift with a Zingo back to contemporary Earth. There, Kate Stewart offered her a job at UNIT, and she goes on to meet the Fourteenth and Fifteenth Doctors.

If Mel was one of the most under-developed companions, then her successor couldn't have been more different. For the first time in twenty-four years, we met a companion whose back-story was almost as important as the Doctor's.

Ace – Sophie Aldred (*Dragonfire* to *Survival, The Power of the Doctor*)

Firestarter (The Prodigy); *Ending* (Isak Danielson).

The first time we see Ace is just before the Doctor and Mel enter the cantina on Iceworld. Ace is right in the thick of it, arguing with Glitz, or 'bilge bag' as she calls him. She's immediately moody and argumentative, character traits that soften during her deepening friendship with the Doctor – her 'Professor'. She hones in on Glitz's conversation with the Doctor and Mel, and lets them know that Glitz won the treasure map in a game of cards. She's not convinced by the promise of treasure, but enthusiastically invites herself on the treasure hunt (a better alternative to working as a waitress in a space bar).

She finds herself teaming up with Mel, whom she calls 'Doughnut'. Ace often uses nicknames – usually derogatory – which isn't a surprise, given she refuses to accept her own real name and goes by a self-assigned nickname. She doesn't take too kindly to Mel's prim ways, but enjoys the challenge of corrupting such an obviously clean-living person, and finds herself opening up to Mel in a way that's clearly unusual for her. She tells Mel that she's sixteen and comes from Perivale (almost certainly from a time no earlier than 1987, as one of the many badges that adorn her bomber jacket says 1987; when they visit 1988 in *Silver Nemesis* she checks up on her football team, Charlton Athletic, which suggests that she is near her own time). She was studying Chemistry A-level and even developed her own explosive, nitro-9; during an experiment, a time storm whipped up in her bedroom and whisked her off to Iceworld. The origin of this time storm is later revealed in *The Curse of Fenric*.

Ace is certain her parents adopted her since her *real* parents would never have given her a 'naff' name like Dorothy. Ace is a young girl looking for somewhere to fit in. Consequently, she's almost seduced into serving Kane, the cold-hearted ruler of Iceworld; it's only Mel who stops her from giving in. Despite their obvious differences, Ace bonds with Mel. While the latter is horrified by the bio-mechanoid dragon that guards the treasure, Ace is merely in awe of it. At the end of *Dragonfire*, Ace is all set to go with Mel and Glitz, but at the behest of Mel, the Doctor offers Ace a trip around the twelve galaxies en route to Perivale. Ace is excited about the prospect, even willing to obey his rules, although the rule of calling him 'Doctor' and not 'Professor' doesn't last long at all. Of course, what neither Ace nor the viewer realises at the time is that the Doctor's actual reasons for taking Ace with him are much darker than anyone would suspect.

When we next see Ace and the Doctor, they have just arrived in London, 1963 (*Remembrance of the Daleks*), and it's obvious that some time has passed since they left Iceworld. Their bond is extremely well-defined, an easy student-mentor relationship that was barely hinted at in *Dragonfire*. But it's more than that. The Doctor clearly trusts Ace a great deal, and in return, Ace has great respect for him. Still, this is Ace's first journey into the past. She has a complete indifference to walking around the streets of 1963 London with a huge ghetto blaster over her shoulder, pumping out tunes that are over twenty years out of time. When she comes across a jukebox in a nearby cafe, she's amused by the music, and immediately takes to Mike Smith (a sergeant in the Intrusion Countermeasures Group, a pre-cursor to UNIT who are in the area investigating alien activity). Mike watches her in fascination as she tries to work out the coinage of the time. Later, while walking back towards Coal Hill School, he tries to teach her the pre-decimal system, and Ace has as much trouble understanding it as Susan did in *An Unearthly Child* (a wonderfully clever piece of continuity, since *Remembrance of the Daleks* is set in the same locations as that episode *and* only a month or so later). Once at the junkyard in Totter's Lane, Ace is itching to get in on the action, highly impressed by the weaponry used against the Dalek, even though she considers it unsophisticated. The Doctor is fully aware of Ace's nitro-9, including that she carries several canisters in her rucksack, despite his instructions not to. Ace uses it against the Dalek more successfully than the contemporary weapons used by the army presence.

Ace can drive, although she does have a problem with the choke (something cars in her day don't have), and is fascinated by the Doctor's history. Admittedly, she finds his explanation of Dalek history somewhat confusing, but instinctively recognises the Daleks' racist ideals, and is repelled by them. This resonates deeply with her: in *Ghost Light*, for instance, we learn she once burned down an old house because of her fury over a racist attack against her best friend, Manisha. This protective anger is often on display whenever she feels the Doctor is being attacked too, be it verbally or physically, as the headmaster of Coal Hill School discovers after he traps the Doctor in the cellar with a Dalek and Ace head-butts him.

She seems to have an instinctive understanding of most weaponry, easily handling the anti-tank rocket, with which she destroys a Dalek. One thing she doesn't like, though, is being left behind by the Doctor when he decides it's time to wander the streets of London to 'bury' his past. She wants to go with him, but he tells her, 'It's not your past; you haven't been born yet'. This statement pricks the curiosity of Professor Rachel Jensen, but Ace won't explain what he meant, revelling in the mystery as much as the Doctor. She's very possessive of the Doctor and doesn't like anyone who sees feels is trying to take her role in their partnership – indeed, in *Battlefield*, she states that protecting the Doctor is *her* job. She doesn't like being treated like a housewife either; when Mike suggests she cooks something nice for when he, the Doctor, and the others return, her response is to call him a 'scumbag'. Fortunately, the Doctor calms her down, asking her to trust him. Of course, she does and remains behind. But not for long. Boredom soon sets in, and when she spots the 'no coloureds' sign in the window, she's incensed and ready to verbally assault Mike's mother. But then she realises she can't blame them for being a product of their time, and goes out for a breath of fresh air instead.

Her earlier indifference to the web of time has unfortunate consequences for her: when she returns to the school to collect her ghetto blaster, she comes up against a whole Dalek assault squad. She doesn't shy from them. 'Who you calling small?' she yells, lashing out with her baseball bat (turned into a powerful weapon by the Hand of Omega). She's rescued by the Doctor and Gilmore's men, although her ghetto blaster doesn't come out in one piece – a fact the Doctor is glad about, since its existence could have caused incalculable damage to the timeline. The Doctor takes her into his confidence, explaining the importance of the Hand of Omega – a remote stellar manipulator – and how it played a part in the formation of Gallifrey and the Time Lords. He even hints that he was there at the beginning, although when Ace picks him up on his slip, he tries to cover it up. Ace's impulsiveness almost proves a problem when she and the Doctor go Dalek hunting; he has to hold her back several times, and when she discovers that Mike betrayed them to the Daleks, she takes it very personally: 'I trusted you. I even liked you.' His excuse of trying to keep the outsiders out repulses Ace; she's disgusted by his bigotry which she feels is no better than the viewpoint of the Daleks.

In *The Happiness Patrol*, we discover that Ace hates fake and phoney things – muzak, for instance – which is hardly surprising for someone with such raw emotions. She's initially unimpressed by the Happiness Patrol's 'fun guns', thinking them toys, but upon seeing their firepower, she soon tries one out. She cannot play the spoons (possibly explaining her disdain at the Doctor playing them in *The Greatest Show in the Galaxy*), and isn't great at telling jokes. She's not the performing type – for such a loud, outgoing kind of girl, she's not someone who likes attention. While on Terra Alpha she easily befriends Susan Q, an ex-member of the Happiness Patrol, finding in her a kindred spirit; like Ace, Susan Q isn't part of the team, and has never been one to fit in.

Ace isn't a fan of junk mail, and is against visiting the advertised Psychic Circus in *The Greatest Show in the Galaxy*. She reveals a fear of clowns – another demonstration of her hating fake things – but the Doctor, instead of simply understanding, coerces her into going with him to the circus, exactly so she can face this fear. (This isn't the last time he does such a thing either; most notably later in *Ghost Light*.) When the Doctor challenges her, she says that she's scared of nothing, but her reaction to the Chief Clown belies this. The Doctor is surprised to hear her call him 'Doctor'. 'Ah so, "Doctor", you *can* remember', but actually, she often refers to him as such – frequently when she's stressed or in danger. She doesn't even have her precious nitro-9 as an explosive failsafe, should she be backed into a corner; it's in her rucksack, which she's convinced the Doctor has hidden. (She finds it again by the time they reach 1988 in the next story, *Silver Nemesis*.)

Once the Doctor defeats the Gods of Ragnarok, who are responsible for corrupting the Physic Circus, Ace is impressed to discover that the Doctor had planned their downfall from the moment the junk mail arrived in the TARDIS. She's equally impressed by his plan to defeat the Daleks in *Remembrance of the Daleks*, and later when he wipes out the entire Cybermen fleet in *Silver Nemesis*. This awe and respect will wane somewhat, however, when he begins to interfere in her life later on.

Adhering to some rebellious clichés, Ace reveals she has a thing for bikes after seeing Nord the Vandal's on Segonax, the planet on which the Psychic Circus performs. And in *Silver Nemesis*, Ace, like the Doctor, has a great love of jazz; in particular, she's a fan of Courtney Pine and enjoys relaxing in a pub garden on a warm November day – that is, until the Doctor's alarm goes off. She finds this irritating, but not as much as when she learns that the Doctor somehow managed to forget that the world is due to end on 23rd November 1988.

She enjoys being in the Windsor Castle vault, but is a little worried about being arrested for treason. While running from security officers in the castle, she and the Doctor come across a painting of Ace in nineteenth century dress – from an adventure they are yet to have. For someone who seems so exposed to death during her travels, she's unusually freaked out when she and the Doctor find the dead mathematician in Lady Peinforte's study. As she did twenty-five years previously, as the chronometer flies, she learns a lot more about the history of the Time Lords and Gallifrey, and discovers that the Doctor was involved in some capacity during 'the Dark Time, the Time of Chaos' (echoing *Remembrance of the Daleks*). When Lady Peinforte attempts to use this knowledge against the Doctor, Ace is as unconcerned as he is: she trusts the Doctor implicitly – although at the end of the story, she wants one particular question answered: 'Professor? Doctor... Who are you?' She never does find out, of course.

The concept of the Cybermen disturbs her on a very visceral level, and she takes great pleasure in destroying one of their warships with nitro-9, also destroying her much-treasured rucksack in the process. She's similarly horrified when the Cybermen then kill the half-converted 'walkmen' simply because she blew up the ship. This anger fuels her later when she holds back a battalion of Cybermen with a catapult and bag of gold coins while the Doctor and the Nemesis statue prepare the final trap.

Once again, the time between seasons – in this case twenty-five (1988) and twenty-six (1989) – seems a lot longer on screen than in reality, since when we next see Ace she has grown up significantly. Her clothes show a new maturity, which develops gradually in her final four stories. It's notable that she rarely wears her bomber jacket through the twenty-sixth season, except when cold, but she still carries it with her. It's as if she's unwilling to let go of the 'Ace' identity she has created; the word 'Ace' is embroidered, in large letters, on the back of the jacket. Her age is now unclear, but one gets the feeling she's a long way from sixteen now, despite the Doctor not allowing her to drink alcohol in *Battlefield*. They have a new understanding about her use of nitro-9 and the Doctor actively encourages her to use it to uncover a secret entrance to an underground tunnel, after seeing Gallifreyan writing at an archaeological dig. She's aware of Clarke's Law – that any sufficiently advanced form of technology is indistinguishable from magic – and discovers the reverse is also true after encountering the magic of the parallel Earth, Avallion, a world in which the legend of King Arthur is closer to the myth. She pulls the alien sword, Excalibur, from the stone (in truth, part of a control mechanism for an organic spaceship hidden beneath Vortigen's Lake) and becomes the Maiden of the Lake. Mixing with the people of legend doesn't phase Ace too much, although she's confused by the idea that the Doctor will, one day, become Merlin. She also meets a legend of the Doctor's life: his lives-long friend, retired-Brigadier Alistair Lethbridge-Stewart. She doesn't respond well to the Brigadier initially, who refers to her as the 'latest one', one of many companions he has met over the years. She finds the Brigadier's closeness to the Doctor something of a threat to her position too. She does, however, warm to him gradually, and is especially affected by the Brigadier's apparent death, and the effect it has on the Doctor.

She's derisive of Bessie, the Doctor's old car, but as with the Brigadier, soon comes to love it and is seen to drive it at the end of the story. When protected by the force field from Excalibur, Morgaine tries to play mind games against Ace, but the racist attitude it brings out in her soon wakes Ace up, leaving Morgaine to muse that they 'breed their children strong' on Earth.

After telling him about her fear of haunted houses, the Doctor promptly takes Ace to the house in question, Gabriel Chase, in *Ghost Light*. Once again, while they explore Gabriel Chase, Ace carries her jacket like a safety blanket. She's no idea why they're at this house, with the Doctor conducting an 'initiative test', allowing Ace to work things out as she goes along. She's slowly introduced to the house guests, including a big-game hunter whose mind is clearly gone, and a butler who's the last surviving example of the extinct Neanderthals. Ace finds herself being more and more creeped out, and wants out – she thinks the house is an 'asylum, with the patients in charge'. She's not too fussed that her off-the-shoulder top incenses Reverend Ernest Matthews, though she later finds herself wearing a contemporary dress, which she initially finds uncomfortable, not to say restricting when she ends up in a brawl. She easily befriends Gwendoline, the supposed ward of the naturalist, Josiah Samuel Smith, and enjoys subverting her in much the same way as she did Mel, to the point where they both dress up in gentlemen's formal wear. She discovers that she's in Gabriel Chase and gets understandably angry at the Doctor: he's manipulated her, and when he tries to coax more information out of Ace, she resists for a short while, but eventually concedes – to a point. She wants to deal with her terrors on her own terms.

Much like in *Silver Nemesis*, the Doctor offers Ace the TARDIS key as a way out, but she refuses because it *is* the easy option. Eventually, she confesses all; that she burned down Gabriel Chase in 1983 when she was thirteen, after white kids fire-bombed Manisha's flat. She stumbled into Gabriel Chase which was full of the evil left over by the events of 1883, both haunted by the memory. She learns much about herself during her brief stay there, but admits she wishes she'd blown up the house instead. She is clearly joking, and the Doctor responds with a tongue-in-cheek 'wicked', a phrase Ace often uses.

Ace's trust, although mildly shaken by the events of *Ghost Light*, is severely tested when they arrive in Northumbria during World War II (*The Curse of Fenric*). Continuing her developing maturity, Ace chooses a contemporary hairstyle and clothes, although she's a little self-conscious about her appearance. Again, she carries her jacket with her, and adds a military issue rucksack to her ensemble. She understands logic diagrams, having really enjoyed computer studies in school – her mathematical knowledge impresses the genius Doctor Judson no end. She loves watching the sea, which makes her feel so small, but despite her usual bravery (shown during her rock climbing with evacuees, Phyllis and Jean), she's not stupid enough to go into the treacherous water – a fact that saves her from becoming a vampiric haemovore. However, Ace's level of intelligence is called into question somewhat when she meets WREN Kathleen Dudman, and her baby, Audrey. It seems almost unbelievable that Ace wouldn't recognise her own grandmother: didn't she ever hear stories about her grandfather who went missing in action? Yet, somehow, Ace doesn't see her link with Kathleen; Ace even states that she hates the name Audrey because it's her mother's name. This is compounded when Ace reads a telegram to Kathleen about her husband going missing. Even later, Ace sends Kathleen and the baby to Streatham, to the future home of her Nan (Kathleen herself!). One can only assume that, at some point, Kathleen remarried and Ace never learned about this. Ace is confused by her loyalty to both Kathleen and Audrey, and seems to care for the baby remarkably quickly. The Doctor is surprised by this turn of events too. When she discovers the truth about Audrey, Ace cannot understand how she can love the baby but still hate her mum – she's sure there's something wrong with her. Indeed, when she's lined up to be shot, she screams out, 'Mum, I'm sorry!' But when the Doctor questions her about this, she refuses to comment.

Amongst the drama with her mum, Ace finds herself attracted to Russian *Kapitän* Sorin. The feeling's mutual. Sorin finds in Ace the 'spirit of a fighter' and is impressed that she has the Russian Red Army emblem on her jacket. She tells him it's a fake, bought cheap in a market – so he gives her a real one, as well as his scarf. Angered by the death of Kathleen's husband, and that the Doctor knows what's going on but is reluctant to share, Ace confronts him and makes him tell her about Fenric, a creature he once trapped in the Shadow Dimension. But he fails to tell her everything: he later admits she's a Wolf of Fenric, a descendent of the Vikings who stole the flask in which the Doctor trapped the entity. She discovers that her whole life has been manipulated – sending Kathleen to Streatham and creating her own future is the start of this; her arriving in Northumbria in her own past is the endgame. Fenric was responsible for the timestorm that took her to Iceworld too, cementing her destiny. Sorin, also one of the Wolves, is possessed by Fenric and learns the Doctor's secret from Ace, who thinks she's talking to Sorin. Even then, Ace maintains her faith in the Doctor – in fact, it's so strong that it creates a psychic barrier which prevents the Doctor from closing his final trap around Fenric. For the Doctor to see his plan come to fruition, he needs to demolish Ace's faith in him. He does this in the most vicious way possible, calling forth every doubt she's ever had. He calls her an emotional cripple, a social misfit who he wouldn't have wasted his time on had he not had a use for her. It's all lies, and it's a testament to Ace's trust in him that she still forgives him afterwards. Nonetheless, the Doctor uses Ace for his own ends – a major departure for any *Doctor Who* companion.

Likely still hurt from being manipulated by both the Doctor and Fenric, Ace just wants to return home, so the Doctor takes her back to Perivale in *Survival*. However, she's not there to see her mother, but to catch up with her friends.

Sergeant Patterson recognises Ace, and tells her that Audrey has her listed as missing, but he's convinced that Ace doesn't care; otherwise, she would've called. He is, of course, right, but Ace ignores him and returns her focus to looking for her mates. One such friend, Ange, points out that people thought Ace was dead; either that or she'd gone to Birmingham.

Ace is quickly targeted by the Kitlings, under the guidance of the Master, and is transported to the planet of the Cheetah People. There, she meets a couple of her old mates, Midge and Shreela. It appears there's a lot of history between Ace and Midge – a rather aggressive history at that. Midge has spent three weeks skulking in the shadows, avoiding direct confrontation with the Cheetah People, but Ace's appearance brings out his aggression, and that later leads to his being possessed. Ace, too, ends up being influenced and possessed by the nature of the planet itself, which brings out her baser instincts. She connects with the Cheetah Person, Karra, who we later learn used to be human as well. Curiously, as the connection develops, Karra goes directly for the badge Sorin gave Ace, possibly sensing the deep feeling associated with the badge. The Doctor lets Ace's possession continue, knowing he needs it to return to Earth and track down the Master – who now shares a psychic link with Ace via the planet.

Upon returning to Earth, Ace asserts that the TARDIS is the only home she has now – her issues with belonging resolved. After seeing the Doctor apparently killed in a motorbike accident, she fights to hold back her rage, unconsciously calling on Karra, who promptly appears to scare off the gang who are about to descend on her. Karra is then killed by the Master and Ace finds herself weeping for all she's lost, clinging to the Doctor's hat and umbrella. However, when the Doctor returns unharmed, she shows no surprise, merely a smile of contentment. She knows that, with the Doctor, she'll always be fine.

At the end of *Survival*, she walks off with the Doctor, the promise of adventures ahead, towards the TARDIS. Her home.

Her time on the planet of the Cheetah People stays with her. When she sees the Master again in *The Power of the Doctor*, over thirty years later, she acknowledges that he was 'half cat.' He, meanwhile, teases her about an off-screen falling out she had with the Doctor, her 'Machiavellian maestro' who apparently ditched her. Still, it's Ace who tempered Tegan in preparation for them seeing the Doctor again when both are freelancing for UNIT. She's not phased by the Doctor now being a woman either, simply saying, 'That is a good look on you, Professor.'

Ace is recognisably the same, albeit with a more mature mindset. She carries her baseball bat with her (plus 'souped up' nitro-9), is eager to don her 1980s jacket again, and only has slight reservations about parachuting off UNIT HQ. And she's very enthusiastic about blowing up Daleks! She's not so possessive of the Doctor now: she brushes off the fact that Thirteenth Doctor companion, Yasmin, is allowed to fly the TARDIS, and gets on well with Graham O'Brien.

This perspective likely comes from her having left the Doctor so long ago, and by the companion meet-ups. She has more responsibility too: in *SJA: Death of the Doctor*, Sarah says Ace runs the business, A Charitable Earth (ACE), raising billions of pounds for good causes – backed up by the promotional mini-episode, *The Promise*, in which the Seventh Doctor visits her there – and is going by the name Dorothy (*something*, Sarah adds, drawing attention to that fact that we never learn Ace's surname). The Master has obviously been keeping tabs on her too, asking in *The Power of the Doctor* if he should call her Dorothy. Clearly, Ace is impossible to forget.

There were many plans for Ace had the series continued into the 1990s, but alas the show didn't return for many years. When we next see the Seventh Doctor in 1996, he's travelling alone. Ace didn't get a proper farewell, but in *The Power of the Doctor*, it's obvious she still means a lot to the Time Lord. Ace and the Seventh Doctor (as a hologram) reinforce their friendship, their falling-out seemingly having hung over them both. 'I was only ever trying to teach you good habits, Ace. Obviously, I failed,' he says; to which she replies, 'You never failed me, Professor. You made me the person I am today. I'm sorry we fell out. I'm sorry I judged you. I didn't understand the burden you carried.'

And so, on 6th December 1989, the original twenty-six-year run of *Doctor Who* ended.

Since the series returned in 2005, every companion associated with the Tenth Doctor has ended up becoming some kind of warrior – willing to do anything to protect Earth, to the point of destroying it, as revealed in *Journey's End*. As Davros says, the Doctor fashions weapons out of people. This wasn't always the case – all his companions pre-Time War have gone on to do their part, but in productive non-destructive ways; from running an orphanage, to developing an international charity organisation, or fighting for aboriginal rights and the planet's ecology, to developing vaccines that have saved millions. The Doctor's legacy continues on in his companions – the friends he leaves behind…

The Seventh Doctor

Expanded Universe

With the non-cancellation of the television series in 1989, it was only a matter of time before something was done to continue the Doctor's adventures. The comic strips in *Doctor Who Magazine* waited for no man and proceeded with companionless adventures, but what of Ace, who was last seen walking towards that big cup of tea in the sky?

Enter Virgin Publishing!

WH Allen, under the Target imprint, had been printing novelisations of the television stories since the early 1970s, and had often broached the idea of publishing original novels based on the series. Only two ever surfaced under the *Companions of Doctor Who* umbrella title: *Harry Sullivan's War* and *Turlough and the Earthlink Dilemma*. This all changed in 1991, by which time Virgin had purchased WH Allen, when they got the rights from the BBC to publish original *Doctor Who* novels – and so the *New Adventures* were born.

For several years, these were the only ongoing stories to feature the Doctor and Ace (interlinked with comic strips at one point), but Big Finish came along in 1999 and launched a new series of audio dramas featuring the Fifth to Seventh Doctors. At first, it was a simple matter of linking the two products together, but as time went on, it became quite clear that the tales of the Doctor and Ace in the Big Finish dramas no longer gelled with those published by Virgin, and latterly by BBC Books.

Over at Virgin, Ace was replaced by original-to-prose companion Professor Bernice Summerfield (a character who proved so popular that she continues to this day, having adventures with Big Finish, thirty years later). Bernice was the first new companion created for Virgin, while at Big Finish the Doctor and Ace were joined by their own brand new companion, Thomas Hector Schofield (Hex, as he was known).

As later companion, Amy, would go on to say, this is where it gets complicated...

As we saw in the Sixth Doctor's Expanded Universe, the character of Mel is well served, the writers enjoying developing her into a strong and well-focused character. They also enjoyed delving into how Mel joined the Doctor, and fixing the issue surrounding the final moments of *The Trial of a Time Lord*. The writers of the Seventh Doctor Expanded Universe take it upon themselves to explore what happens to make her leave so suddenly with Glitz at the end of *Dragonfire*.

Before that, though, there was a certain reticence over using her; she only appears in two novels then a handful of audios between 2000 and 2007. Fortunately, since 2013, Big Finish has stepped in and explored her adventures with the Seventh Doctor as well as some other companions like Ace (giving us a fun relationship we only got a hint of on TV) and the previously mentioned Hebe Harrison with the Sixth Doctor.

Mel's first full audio appearance is in a story that shares a lot of similarities with the 2008 episode, *The Fires of Pompeii*. *The Fires of Vulcan* was released in 2000, and like in the later television episode, it's set during the moments leading up to the eruption of Mount Vesuvius and the death of all those in Pompeii. Learning that they're stuck in a time paradox, the ash-shell of the TARDIS having been discovered in 1980, the Doctor realises they are destined to die in Pompeii. It's Mel who forces the Doctor to consider a way out of the paradox. In a short story called *Special Weapons* (1999), Mel meets a young man called Oliver during World War II. Still shocked by the death of Pex in the TV story, *Paradise Towers*, Mel tries to convince him not to fight the Germans, worried he'll die needlessly, but regardless of Mel's words, he still intends to join the army the following year.

In *Heritage* (2002), we discover that in another timeline Mel never left the TARDIS with Glitz, but instead stayed on Heritage where she died in the sixty-first century. However, in the novel *Head Games*, from 1995, we do meet Mel some years after she left with Glitz. She explains she parted company with Glitz after six months, and tried to hitch-hike across space, ending on the planet Avalone where she got stuck. The Doctor tells her that he knew she was there, but he thought she'd settled. In truth, she tried for Earth again, but got kidnapped by the evil 'Dr Who' who imprisoned her in the Land of Fiction. She's disgusted by the way the Doctor has changed since she left, and even though Ace attempts to explain why they've needed to get 'harder', she refuses to speak to the Doctor again. She discovers that he manipulated her to leave him on Iceworld because he knew she wasn't the kind of companion he needed. Ace agrees to get Mel back home using her time hopper.

In the two-part short story, *Missing*, published in 1999, we learn that Mel often sent her parents postcards whenever the Doctor brought her near her own time, and that they've missed her dearly. She talks to Detective Inspector Bob Lines (previously in *Business Unusual*), who offers to take her the rest of the way home. This, of course, contradicts her twenty-first century TV stories with the Fourteenth Doctor, in which she stayed with Glitz until his death then got back to Earth using a Zingo.

The audio stories explore how strong a character Mel really is: soon after the Doctor's regeneration, Mel still proves loyal in 2005's *Unregenerate!*, when she's stranded on Earth in 2007 and must find her way back to him, a man who is essentially a stranger to her; she shows off her computer skills and doesn't panic in the face of an horrific impending death in *Red* (2006); and in a series of adventures set after she leaves both the TARDIS and Glitz in *Dragonfire*, she gels with Ace as they travel together with the Doctor. The latter tales begin in *A Life of Crime* (2016), in which Mel demonstrates how much she's learned from both Sabalom and the Doctor – she's more scheming, more morally-ambiguous, but, just as vitally, remains devoted to the Doctor. Her relationship with Ace develops really nicely too, which makes it more shocking when we meet a Mel from an alternate timeline who's a staunch communist (*Red Planets* in 2018). In 2017's *The Blood Furnace*, we're introduced to Stuart Dale, who Mel dated for over two years while at university but who, in 1991, discovered the fantastical Dark Alloy. Dale offers Mel a job creating an IT system, a proposal she accepts, though this doesn't stop her travelling in the TARDIS. Indeed, she's learning more about the Doctor's ship than even he knows: she starts reading its manuals in *The Dispossessed*, and proved a more adept pilot than the Doctor in *The Quantum Possibility Engine* (both 2018).

No wonder he comes back for her in 2021's *A Business Proposal for Mel!*, a trailer promoting *The Collection – Season 24*, which shows Mel as the head of a health and lifestyle business named 24 Carat.

Ace, in the Expanded Universe, becomes one of the most storied companions ever. It seems she lives at least three different lives – certainly not easy to reconcile. Her first Expanded Universe life is in the Virgin *New Adventures*, and for four years in the comic strip of *Doctor Who Magazine* which ran concurrently with the novels (*Fellow Travellers* to *Cuckoo* in #164- 210), which see her becoming Time's Vigilante; while her second is in the comic strip *Ground Zero* that leads to her death; and the third is her audio adventures in which she teams up with Hex and goes through a different maturing process to that witnessed in the *New Adventures*.

Other than a multitude of short stories, the novel authors seem to be disinterested in exploring her journeys with the Doctor during the TV seasons, even though there are plenty of gaps to explore, notably between seasons. There are notable exceptions, however. *Relative Dementias* (2002) explains the two surnames Ace has. Throughout the *New Adventures* and the Big Finish audios, it's accepted that her real name is Dorothy McShane (first established in the 1995 novel, *Set Piece*); but in *Prime Time* (2000), her name is given as Dorothy Gale. To make some kind of sense of this, *Relative Dementias* has Ace explaining that her first and middle names come from *The Wizard of Oz* (as revealed in *Love and War*, this was her grandmother's favourite film), thus making her full name Dorothy Gale McShane. We're also shown that she's learned some basic TARDIS operational procedures, enough to cross her own timeline, and has already found out about regeneration. In *The Hollow Men* (1998), we discover that Ace suffers from hay fever and has a very strong dislike for the countryside (which follows, since in *Relative Dementias*, she says that at heart she's not a country girl). She carries with her some putty and a small metal disc which, when combined, form to make a powerful explosive. She also screams, when a scarecrow breaks through a door, for the first time since she was ten years old.

Much like *The New Adventures* and Big Finish, the BBC Books tend to explore her life post-*Survival.* This causes a problem in trying to marry them with the Virgin material, since the *New Adventures* begin after *Survival* and tell Ace's story in a way that allows for no other material. It's, therefore, probably easier to place the BBC Books with the Big Finish audios that lead up to the introduction of Hex. As such, we shall look at those books after the *New Adventures*.

Ace's First Timeline: The New Adventures

In *Head Games* (1995), it's explicitly stated that the only companions the Seventh Doctor travelled with are Mel, Ace, Bernice, Chris Cwej, and Roz Forrester, thereby setting this range completely apart from the Big Finish stories that introduce other companions. And the *New Adventures* presents a version of *Doctor Who* that's grown up with its audience, and explores her increasing mistrust of the Doctor, developing his manipulation of her life – first seen in TV stories such as *Ghost Light* and *The Curse of Fenric*, and it soon became a case of sex, guns, and lock 'n' load…

Ace's television journey makes it quite clear that there are some major issues between her and her mother. With so many hints, it's hardly a surprise that her past is explored in so much detail during the *New Adventures* – some might say in *too* much detail. Her mother didn't care much about Ace's school life, and was absent so much that the school arranged for her to get a social worker. Often, her mother's various boyfriends would look after her, which tended to mean Ace being around a lot of booze. She usually calls her mother by her name, Audrey, while Audrey tended to call the young Ace 'Dorry'. At school, she was called Dotty, the object of bullying from Chad Boyle (in one reality, he even kills her). Fourteen-year-old Ace idolised singer Johnny Chess (the son of ex-companions, Ian and Barbara Chesterton), and after he rejected her attention, she resolved to never like someone again without getting to know them first.

Following on from *Survival*, Ace is initially much the same as she was onscreen, fiercely loyal to her 'Professor' and always the first to throw herself into any adventure. Her love of explosives continues, and in *Timewyrm: Exodus*, she creates nitro-9a, much more stable than the previous brand, but half the weight and half the explosive quality. She also takes up arms for the first time, shooting guns and blowing several Nazis away to protect the Doctor. She considers the Doctor her best friend and only family, but in *Timewyrm: Apocalypse*, the first chink in their relationship appears, after Ace learns that the Doctor knew Raphael – a young man befriended by Ace on Kirith – would die, and did nothing to prevent it. She finds herself angry about this, certain the Doctor could've done something. It's the first of many such actions that will, ultimately, pull them apart. Nonetheless, she still trusts the Doctor, after visiting his mind in *Timewyrm: Revelation* and learning how tortured he is by his past lives. At this point, she's, apparently, in her early twenties, which possibly ties in with the obvious gap between seasons twenty-five and twenty-six. She's sure she's going to travel with the Doctor forever, but this changes in *Nightshade* when she meets Robin Yeadon in 1968.

She falls deeply in love with Robin, a proper innocent, deeply emotional love, and when she decides it's time to stop travelling and remain with Robin, the Doctor refuses to let her go. He *accidentally* materialises the TARDIS on an alien world instead of back on Earth. Ace later meets a much older Robin again in Cheldon Bonniface, 2010, in *Happy Endings*, and learns that he spent five months waiting for her before moving on to London. In an odd twist, by 2010, Robin is dating Audrey McShane, Ace's mother, and the two get engaged.

In *Cat Litter* (in *Doctor Who Magazine* #192), Ace finds her bedroom deleted by the TARDIS and a new room appears – she wonders why, and the Doctor warns her that something dangerous is coming. Not long after, on the planet Heaven, in *Love and War*, Ace meets a traveller called Jan Rydd. They fall in love, but unlike Robin, it's more of a mad, passionate love (one suspects it could be a rebound on Ace's part – certainly by *Lucifer Rising*, she doubts her love for Jan and thinks it was an act of rebellion against the Doctor) and they get engaged. Jan is killed by the Hoothi (supposedly mentioned in *The Brain of Morbius*, but it was misheard by author Paul Cornell, and should be the Muthi) – an act the Doctor had a huge part in. Ace is beyond unforgiving of the Doctor, even more so when she discovers he had always planned on sacrificing Jan. She accuses the Doctor of being jealous of Jan and how she was going to leave the TARDIS for him. She departs the Doctor's company, taking with her a device called a tesseract to remind herself of Jan. The Doctor keeps Ace's bomber jacket, knowing that she'll need it again one day.

For Ace, it's three years until she next meets the Doctor in *Deceit*, by which time she's become part of Earth's Spacefleet, Special Weapons division. She's hardened and bitter, violence and sex being her currency. She discovers that the Doctor psychically drove her away from him in *Love and War* because he was infected by a protoplasmic virus which infected him on Tír na n-Óg (*Cat's Cradle: Witch Mark*), and he left the tesseract with her so she could contact him when the time was right to remove the virus. She remains with the Doctor to keep him honest, but Bernice Summerfield (an archaeologist who joined the Doctor on Heaven) is unsure about her. Ace, while travelling with the Doctor, was infected with a virus that boosts her immune system and prevents her from getting ill. She now considers the twenty-sixth century her home. While visiting Haiti in 1915 (*White Darkness*), Ace is made to confront her violent tendencies. She shoots a man called Richmann in self defence and continues shooting, emptying her gun, angry and upset over her wounded friend. She throws the gun away in fear of her own future. The violence gets worse in *Shadowmind* when she wipes out the entire command crew of the *Broadsword*, who are possessed by the Umbra, and considers it the worst thing she's done.

Her nitro-9 is further advanced when she develops neo-nitro, small white spheres that are activated with saliva, and later the nitro-9a smart bombs.

In *Time and Time Again* (*DWM* #207) while searching for the Key to Time, Ace gets into a sword fight with the Third Doctor, and encounters Adric during a fancy dress party at Cranliegh Hall (from *Black Orchid*); Adric tries to make a move on her, and she warns him to stop or he'll end up limping away.

In *Birthright*, we see the template for what will become a regular feature in *Doctor Who* from 2006 – the Doctor-lite story. In this book, Ace and Bernice have an adventure in Victorian London while the Doctor is elsewhere. When they see the Doctor again, he claims to have spent the entire time in one of the TARDIS' rooms, but neither of the women trust him. This is potent enough to feed the Garvond in *The Dimension Riders*, a creature that lives off fear, hate, and suspicion. Ace realises how much the Doctor stood between her and Robin and then Jan, and remains only to one-up the Doctor. In *No Future*, she totally fails to charm Danny Pain, the front man of 1970s punk band, *Plasticine*, which frustrates her – she's not used to being rejected. They encounter the Monk (whose name is revealed to be Mortimus), and he offers to take Ace back and save Jan, trying to steal her from the Doctor. Ace refuses, siding with the Doctor despite her distrust of him. She cheats time and prevents the Brigadier from dying in 1976. We also learn that she often feels like killing herself and only drinks to make herself feel vulnerable.

In *First Frontier*, Ace finally gets to have her second round with the Master, who has used Tzun nanites to remove his corrupted Trakenite DNA (he's been living in a half-Trakenite body since he merged with Tremas in *The Keeper of Traken*) and restore his Time Lord regenerative cycle. Still infected by the Cheetah Planet (*Survival*), Ace is able to detect the Master, and she shoots him in the back, unintentionally causing him to regenerate – an act that wipes out the Master's connection with the Cheetah Planet. At this point, she's almost twenty-seven. In *Falls the Shadows*, the Doctor and Ace discuss the way she's become hardened since she left him, and he's worried about her; she tells him that nothing touches her, and he responds that 'it should'. Despite her bravado, Ace retreats to her room and cries for hours. We also discover that she was born in 1970, which means she must have left Earth fairly early in 1987, before her seventeenth birthday.

Ace finally leaves in *Set Piece*, and remains behind in 1870s France (as first revealed in the novelisation of *The Curse of Fenric*); it was during her time there that the painting found in Windsor Castle in 1988 (*Silver Nemesis*) was commissioned. She decides to remain to keep an eye on the time rifts, and defend the Commune to save more lives. She takes one of Kadiatu Lethbridge-Stewart's time hoppers. The Doctor, having taken a look at Ace's timeline, always knew this would happen. The Doctor, shortly after, meets a thirty-seven-year-old Ace who is being courted by Count Sorin, the grandfather of Captain Sorin from *The Curse of Fenric*. Ace's time hopper cannot take her any further than 2001; however, in *Happy Endings*, she visits Cheldon Bonniface in 2010, for Bernice's wedding to Jason Kane and sleeps with a clone of Jason (later leaving with him). She's reunited with her mother and Robin, and finally makes her peace with Audrey, promising to visit more often. By this point, she's known as Dorothée Sorina-McShane, although she and Count Sorin are no longer together, and they only pretended to be married. She's thirty-one, six years younger than in *Set Piece* when she was being courted by the count – an apparent contradiction. She returns one final time in *Lungbarrow*, the last *New Adventure* for the Seventh Doctor, and discovers that the Doctor originally wanted to enrol her in the Time Lord Academy on Gallifrey (a reference to the intent of the production team had *Doctor Who* continued on television in 1990). At this point, she hasn't seen the Doctor for a year, and still totally believes in him. They depart company as close as they ever were, although both a lot older and wiser.

Ace's Second Timeline: Ground Zero

This is an oddity in Ace's history. After years of featuring in the comic strips of *Doctor Who Magazine* in her *New Adventures* persona, she returns to the strip in a story called *Ground Zero*. Here, she's back to her television persona, travelling with an older Seventh Doctor, looking much as he did in *The TV Movie* (1996). This creates all kind of placement issues in itself, but none so much as the resolution of the story.

In the most dramatic moment of the entire five parts, Ace attacks the alien Lorbi with the Doctor's umbrella and a can of nitro-9. She destroys the Lobri, and in so doing kills herself for her 'Professor', leading to the tragic shot of the Doctor on his knees cradling the dead Ace in his arms. This obviously contradicts her further TV appearance in *The Power of the Doctor*.

Ace's Third Timeline: BBC Books and Big Finish

The loosely linked pentalogy of books comprising *Illegal Alien*, *Matrix, Storm Harvest, Prime Time*, and *Loving the Alien* cover a lot of ground for Ace, and it's quite clearly an Ace that has only recently lived through the television story, *Survival*. Indeed, the second book reveals that it's been several months since she and the Doctor left Perivale – immediately putting it at odds with the *New Adventures*. This incompatibility is later compounded when the Master, still heavily infected by his symbiosis with the Cheetah Planet, returns in *Prime Time*, flatly contradicting events established in *First Frontier*.

Throughout these books, and the other Seventh Doctor and Ace novels published by BBC Books, it's established that Ace has many sexual partners (including James Dean in *Loving the Alien!*), which doesn't tie in with the list of sexual partners she gives in *Happy Endings*, at which point we discover that Ace lost her virginity to Glitz (at some point prior to *Dragonfire*) and never slept with anyone else until Jan in *Love and War*. Placing these books alongside Big Finish's stories is relatively easy, because *Prime Time* references the audio *The Genocide Machine*, and *Dust Breeding* is an audio play set shortly after the novel, *Storm Harvest*.

In *Illegal Alien*, we see an Ace who still has her trust in the Doctor, and has never used a shotgun. This is also her first encounter with Nazis (contradicting *Timewyrm: Exodus*), and she still uses the ghetto blaster built for her by the Doctor in *Silver Nemesis*. The Valeyard, the Doctor's dark future incarnation introduced in *The Trial of a Time Lord*, pushes her to her limits in *Matrix*, when he mentally corrupts her into a semi-Cheetah Person. She becomes feral, eats raw meat, and drinks blood, and later confronts a full-Cheetah Person version of herself.

In *Storm Harvest*, she makes it clear that she's been travelling with the Doctor for three years; alas, in *Prime Time*, the Doctor learns that Ace is due to die at some point in the near future. He digs up her coffin to confirm that it is Ace as she appears now. Obsessed with discovering how she died, the Doctor and Ace visit 1959 in *Loving the Alien*, and she's shot in the head by a man called George Limb. The Doctor is unable to save her, and at her autopsy he discovers that she was pregnant with James Dean's baby. The Doctor ends up travelling with an alternative version of Ace who is hardly any different from the original – as later revealed, Ace's death (and that of Sarah in *Bullet Time* and Mel in *Heritage*) is a part of the Council of Eight's war against the Doctor.

In a 2000 audio adventure, Ace is willing to give her life for the Doctor; when she's convinced he's host to *The Fearmonger*, she would rather blow them both up than allow the Fearmonger to carry on turning the Doctor into something he isn't. But when she discovers it's actually inside her, enhancing her own fear and paranoia, she finds a way to control it and send it packing. She continues a trait she began in *Remembrance of the Daleks*, using her nitro-9 to dispatch several Daleks in *The Genocide Machine*. They create a duplicate of Ace to help them secure the Library on Kar-Charrat, but water-based inhabitants of the planet short out the duplicate before it can do any real damage. Once again, she's pitted against the Master in *Dust Breeding*, who has had his Trakenite body destroyed by a device called the Warp Core resulting in his returning to his skeletal form last seen in *The Keeper of Traken*, and further drifting from the *New Adventures* timeline.

She impresses the prisoners of *Colditz*, so much that they go on protests for her. Her loathing for Nazis comes to the fore again, but seeing the death of Kurtz inside the TARDIS shakes her up and she decides it's time for her to grow up and get away from the Ace persona. From this point on, she decides she's going to be known as McShane. Just as she is reeling from the deaths she's seen, and attempting to become an adult, the Doctor takes her to Ibiza and a fateful meeting with a young man called Liam McShane, in *The Rapture*. It's reinforced that Ace was born in 1970, only this time it was on 20th August (the real birthday of Ace actress, Sophie Aldred), which further suggests she left 1987 relatively early in the year. Liam is Ace's younger brother by four years – he was taken from her life by their father, Harry, while Ace was in playschool, after he discovered that Audrey was having an affair with Harry's best friend, Jack. This flies in the face of everything established in the *New Adventures*, where there isn't any mention of Ace's siblings, despite the sheer amount of background covered in those books. Ace promises to visit Liam again one day, after initially trying to deny him and their past.

A new companion is introduced in *The Harvest*: Thomas Hector Schofield, or Hex as he likes to be known. He's a nurse at St Gart's Brookside Hospital, London, in 2021. He and Ace immediately strike up a good friendship, and he refuses to call her 'McShane', preferring Ace. We learn that she always aced the multiple-choice tests at school (presumably where her nickname derived), and she's been with the Doctor for 'a surprisingly long time'. By *LIVE 34*, she's reverted back to being called Ace, deciding that it is the name that is 'her'. It also suggests that she's now in her mid- to late-twenties. Another titbit of information drifts through when we find out that her nan, Kathleen, died in 1973 when Ace was only three years old.

Hex, played by Philip Olivier, was born on 12th October 1998 to Cassie Schofield, who, as she was still at school, gave Hex to her mother, Hilda, to look after. Cassie left Liverpool for London, in order to get a good job to support herself and her son, but was reported missing on 23rd August 2001. She had actually been killed by a being known as Nimrod; though she was briefly resurrected, she then gave her life again to save her son (*Project: Twilight*, *Project: Lazarus*, and *Project: Destiny*). In *Dark Thoughts*, Hex admits that he thought Hilda was his real mum until the age of six. Hex was raised a Catholic – he wore a St Christopher necklace engraved "H.T." on the back – and his caring nature led him to idolise Florence Nightingale (*The Angel of Scutari*) and ultimately a career as a nurse.

By the time of *The Settling*, Hex has found himself drawn to Ace in a romantic way; if Ace notices, she doesn't reciprocate, though in *No Man's Land*, she considers the Doctor and Hex her only family. There's friction in that family too, as Hex argues with the Doctor about him repeatedly taking them to warzones (understandable, considering Hex was tortured there). Hex takes a short time away from the Doctor and Ace in *World Apart*, contemplating his feelings for Ace; there, he watches the sea, as he did with growing up with Hilda, something that made him feel both peaceful and insignificant. In *Enemy of the Daleks*, Ace shows an unusual amount of tactical and military knowledge, more in keeping with her *New Adventures* persona than the version that's been developing in the audio plays; Hex, meanwhile, is deeply shocked at seeing so many deaths.

Things come full circle for Ace in *Gods and Monsters* with the return of Fenric, who's been manipulating events for a while. Fenric reveals that Ace becoming one of his wolves was pure chance, a flip of a coin, and it could've easily been a 'lovelorn motorcyclist from Wales' (an allusion to Ray from *Delta and the Bannermen*, a contender for replacement companion in season twenty-four). Fenric takes Ace back to Perivale, to the day she originally left, and offers her a chance to change history, but she doesn't take it. In a final confrontation, Fenric possesses a dying Hex, but he's surprised by the faith Hex has in his dead mother. In turn, Ace has faith in Hex, further weakening Fenric's hold. Hex, intent on sacrificing himself to stop Fenric, asks Ace to open the TARDIS doors so he can throw himself into the time vortex. Ace will not do it, and has to be held back by fellow companion, Sally Morgan while Captain Lysandra Aristides complies. Ace is shocked by this, and refuses to be comforted by anyone; not even by the Doctor. 'Just... don't say anything, Professor. I don't want to hear another word.'

This isn't the end for Ace and Hex, though. She's horrified that the TARDIS is already deleting Hex's room and forces the Doctor to break the bad news to Hex's grandmother, Hilda, in *Afterlife*. It's revealed that Hex survived in the realm of the Elder Gods with Fenric and an Elemental named Koloon; from the latter, Hex won one year of life on Earth, which is where Ace finds him again. Using the TARDIS to jump them all forwards, they invalidate Koloon's offer of living an extra year, and in anger, Koloon wipes Hex's memories of his previous life with the Doctor. Still, Ace won't let go of him and encourages him to travel with them further, while also getting into a sexual relationship with him. They do eventually restore his memories in *Signs and Wonders*, memories stored in his St. Christopher's necklace, but he'd fallen in love with Sally Morgan and the two settle down in Liverpool in the 2020s.

She and the Doctor return to see Hex and Sally in the 2040s, fifteen years after they've left the TARDIS. Sally is pregnant with their second child – the first being Cassie, named after Hex's mother – and Hex thanks them both for all they'd done.

Sometime later, Ace and the Doctor are then joined by Mel.

*

In a separate Big Finish range, Ace returned in a short series of stories based on scripts that would've been part of season twenty-seven had *Doctor Who* continued into 1990. This season, called *The Lost Stories*, comprises *Thin Ice, Crime of the Century, Animal*, and *Earth Aid*. The range was overseen by Andrew Cartmel, script editor of *Doctor Who* from 1987 to 1989, and it followed the basic plan of the proposed season twenty-seven, by introducing a new companion in the shape of Raine Creevy, played by Beth Chalmers. Raine was a safecracker and thief in 1989, and in one particular safe, she found the Doctor. Though she and Ace initially butt heads, she accepts the Doctor's invitation to join them in the TARDIS, and her first journey takes her to Margrave University in 2001, where she and Ace go undercover. However, Raine finds out her father, with whom she had a fractious relationship owing to him betraying her mother by having numerous affairs, has died by that period, and she asks the Doctor to leave her there for a week to gather her thoughts.

This being the Doctor, he returned much later, and, in a nice reversal, found Raine in a safe, waiting for him while she investigated the curious circumstances behind her father's passing. Indeed, the Doctor was aware of her parents, Raina Kerenskaya and Markus Creevy, having met them in *Thin Ice* – and having delivered baby Raine into the world! At some point after Ace leaves the TARDIS, the Doctor and Raine continue to travel together, as per the 2012 boxset, *UNIT: Dominion*.

The only plot line not picked up for this series of audios, though, is the Doctor's intent to enrol Ace into the Time Lord Academy, which is how Ace would've been written out in 1990.

Instead, in *Thin Ice*, the Time Lords turn down his request, apparently as a way of getting back at him for his interfering; it turns out for the best, however, as Ace doesn't want to go there anyway and is, as ever, upset at his machinations.

And in yet another audio range, Ace is admitted to the Time Lord Academy, where, in *The Lights of Skaro* (part of the 2014 set, *The New Adventures of Bernice Summerfield: Volume One*), she learns that her mother died of cancer. During her time with the Time Lords, she's reunited with the Doctor and Benny; comes up against a vast array of enemies including the Daleks, Sutkeh the Destroyer, and Omega; and worked with other former companions, Romana and Leela. Big Finish reconciles these events by having Ace's memories of Gallifrey and the Time War erased in *Soldier Obscura*, part of *Gallifrey: Time War – Volume One* (2018), and she's returned to Earth. Later, however, in a story named *In Remembrance* (2018's *Class: The Audio Adventures – Volume Two*), she remembers her time on Gallifrey.

At some point after that, the Seventh Doctor enlists Ace to help in his battle against the mad Time Lord, the Eleven (2020's *Dark Universe*), a plan which ultimately backfires, leaving Ace and the Doctor to fall out – which does at least tie into *The Power of the Doctor*.

So how can we account for Ace's numerous timelines? It's easy to say these are merely alternate versions of the same character – indeed, that's what the 2020 novel, *At Childhood's End*, suggests. The book is notable for not only being written by Sophie Aldred (alongside Mike Tucker and Steve Cole) but for being the first time Ace meets the Thirteenth Doctor. And in doing so, it further muddied the waters.

After *Survival*, Ace comes into contact with the Quantum Anvil, a temporal possibility engine which shattered time streams into endless potentials, allowing her to see different splinters of her life. This includes travels with Bernice and Hex (Big Finish), dying in the Doctor's arms (*Ground Zero*), and living with Sorin's ancestor (the *New Adventures*). *At Childhood's End* says the Doctor's manipulating her to touch the Anvil made her leave him, and she goes on to set up A Charitable Earth, its headquarters next to the Tower of London so she can keep a watchful eye on UNIT.

But *At Childhood's End* itself is thrown through the Quantum Anvil, given that its events are made moot by Ace then being introduced to the Thirteenth Doctor in the TV episode, *The Power of the Doctor*. When Ace meets the Tenth Doctor in the Big Finish audio, *Quantum of Axos*, part of *Tenth Doctor Classic Companions: Volume Three* (2022) boxset, she says she's just met a future incarnation of the Doctor who is, we can infer, a woman.

As you might expect from a Doctor with such a long life, he has his fair share of companions exclusive to the Expanded Universe, including the aforementioned Hex and Raine, the first of whom is Olla, a Dreilyn aka heat vampire, who appears in the comic strips, *A Cold Day in Hell* and *Redemption!* She initially attacks the Doctor to obtain the heat she needs, after he and Frobisher find her on the planet A-Lux, which had been transformed into a chilly wasteland by the Ice Warriors. After defeating them, she asks to join the Doctor. Her past comes back to haunt her, though: she stole money from the Vachysian warlord, Skaroux, and went on the run; she intends to kill Skaroux, so the Doctor hands her over before she can, on the grounds that she's afforded a fair trial.

In the books, after Bernice joins, comes Chris Cwej and Roz Forrester, two adjudicators (i.e. policemen) from Earth in the late thirtieth century. They remain with the Doctor for the latter half of the *New Adventures*, joining in *Original Sin*. Following a murder, Cwej and Forrester unravel a conspiracy at the heart of their society, a civilisation corrupted by Tobias Vaughn (from the TV story, *The Invasion*), and the pair are framed, leading them to accept the Doctor's offer to travel with him. The pair get to flex their detective skills in stories like *Shakedown*; meet a plethora of antagonists like Daleks, Ice Warriors, and Sontarans; and are an interesting look at xenophobia, with Chris visiting a gay club in *Damaged Goods*, written by future showrunner, Russell T Davies, and Roz experiencing racism in *Toy Soldiers* – *Doctor Who* imagines such discrimination doesn't exist in the thirtieth century.

In *The Also People*, Chris falls in love with Dep, and she becomes pregnant with his child – though she doesn't tell him this and he leaves in the TARDIS. (It's revealed in *Happy Endings* that Dep has named their daughter, iKrissi.)

Chris questions how well-suited he is to life with the Doctor, but it's Roz who goes through a more harrowing time. She struggles to fit in, is wracked by grief when reflecting on the death of her first partner when she was adjudicator, and, in *Just War*, falls for George Reed, a British lieutenant serving in Nazi occupied Guernsey; the racism she's previously been exposed to, however, stops her from staying in 1941, so she instead leaves with the Doctor, albeit taking an engagement ring with her as a reminder of Reed. In *So Vile a Sin*, she's afforded a glimpse of an alternate life in which she settled with George. It's not a great comfort, though, as she dies on a battlefield, fighting alongside her sister, Lady Leabie Susan Inyathi Forrester. Roz is buried in the Umtata Reclamation Zone in Africa, on 1st September 2982.

Roz's death obviously deeply affects Chris, and, as more of the Doctor's schemes are unveiled, he decides to leave, deciding first to travel using a time ring given to him by Romana in *Lungbarrow* then being recruited by the Time Lords to retrieve Gallifreyan weapons (*The Dying Days*). He goes on to appear now and then in Bernice's own *New Adventures* series, and, in *Happy Endings*, he meets the twenty-year-old former-Timewyrm. The two have a daughter, Jasmine Surprise Hutchings.

Aside from Hex, the Seventh Doctor gets a few more audio-exclusive companions in Private Sally Morgan and Captain Lysandra Aristedes, respectively played by Amy Pemberton and Maggie O'Neill. Though Morgan joins the TARDIS before Aristedes, we meet the latter first, as she worked for the Forge in the 2005 novel, *Project: Valhalla*, though she was soon transferred to the Internal Counter-Intelligence Service. Meanwhile, Sally is involved in the Blue Fire Project, an attempt to develop psychic weapons; the Doctor ends the nightmarish trials and takes Sally with him in *House of Blue Fire*. At this point, there are two TARDISes, so when they invite Lysandra to travel with them, they're in the Black TARDIS while Ace and Hex travel with the Doctor in the White TARDIS. The two ships soon combine back into the normal blue Police Box, at which point Sally and Lysandra continue their travels alongside Ace and Hex, and are there when

Hex apparently sacrifices himself to stop Fenric. In *Afterlife*, Lysandra leaves to fight a war in the New African States, and Sally stays to look after Hilda, Hex's beloved grandmother. Following Hilda's passing, Sally goes travelling, but returns in time to learn Hex is alive and well, and the pair fall in love.

At some point after this, the Doctor is joined by Doctor Elizabeth Klein (Tracey Childs), a Nazi scientist from an alternative Earth who he'd previously met in *Colditz*. In the aftermath of the Second World War, Klein goes to South America, then Africa, where she's present during the Kenyan Mau Mau Uprising (*A Thousand Tiny Wings*). The Doctor insists she travel with him to prevent her causing trouble to established history, preferring to keep an eye on her. They travel together for a while, so long that Klein learns how to fly the TARDIS simply by observing the Time Lord, but she ultimately betrays the Doctor in *Survival of the Fittest*, escaping and using the TARDIS to try to restore her timeline. Instead, she creates a new one where the Third Reich is established in 1944; her justification is that they've stopped wars, invasions, and famine (but at what expense?). This all falls apart on her in *The Architects of History*, and she's tried, likely by the Time Lords, and the original timeline is rebuilt – a timeline where Klein works for UNIT for the good of mankind. Curiously viewing her as a loose end towards the end of his seventh life, the Doctor later asks Klein to travel with him again, briefly with stowaway, Will Arrowsmith, played by Christian Edwards, who is Klein's assistant at UNIT. Unusually for a member of the taskforce, Will is naïve, offering up sensitive information on a platter in *Daleks Among Us*, but is clearly intelligent, quick-thinking, and quiet.

Klein's strong personality pulls her through a few shocking revelations: namely that her past has been changed; that her biological mother was a high-ranking Nazi official; and that she was artificially grown to operate the Persuasion Machine, a device capable of instilling ideologies as genuine beliefs in society.

After the Doctor takes her back to her own time, Klein remains UNIT's scientific advisor through the 1990s (*Warlock's Cross*) and into the 2010s (*UNIT: Assembled*).

THE SEVENTH DOCTOR

The Doctor's most well-known and prolific Expanded Universe companion is, without a doubt, Professor Bernice 'Benny' Summerfield. Introduced in *Love and War* in 1993, she went on to travel with the Doctor – with Ace, and Chris and Roz – until *Happy Endings* in 1996. She returns several times after, most notably in *The Dying Days* and becomes the first companion to meet the Eighth Doctor; at the end the Doctor drops her off to the planet Dellah where she finally becomes a real professor and begins teaching archaeology in *Oh No It Isn't!* – that is, when she's sober enough. This series of *New Adventures* continues until October 1999 with the publication of *Twilight of the Gods*. But even the cancellation of that series doesn't keep Bernice down, and Big Finish picks up her story. They had already been adapting some of the books since 1998, but in December 2000, a brand new series of adventures began with *The Secret of Cassandra*. The series still continues today, occasionally featuring other *Doctor Who* elements, including the regular character of Irving Braxiatel, who's first introduced in the novel *Theatre of War* in 1994. (Braxiatel is noteworthy because not only is he a Time Lord, a younger version of him appearing in Big Finish's *Gallifrey* series alongside companions Leela and Romana, but he's mentioned in the TV series obliquely in 1979's *City of Death*.)

We first meet Benny at an archeological dig, where she shows first Ace then the Doctor remains of the native species of Heaven. Benny is no traditional archaeologist: she quickly proves herself a crack shot when defending herself and the Doctor by shooting an attacker in the arm early on; she's also not really a qualified professor – she confesses to Ace that she faked her degree from Heidelberg University so that she could gain access to otherwise locked-down sites. Benny is searching for her father, Admiral Isaac Douglas Summerfield, who went to fight the Daleks when Benny was seven and subsequently disappeared. (Though she gives up her quest, believing him dead, Benny finds her father, in *Return of the Living Dad*, on Earth in 1983, twenty years after he got stranded there when his ship, the Tisiphone, got caught in a transdimensional rift. There, he hopes to prematurely develop Earth's defensive and offensive capacities to such an extent that they'd be able to repel the Daleks' invasion in the twenty-second century. You can understand why the Summerfield family hate the Daleks so much, given that Benny's mother, Claire, was exterminated when the mutant race invaded Beta Caprisis, and Benny's childhood was marred by the Second Dalek War, meaning she was evacuated, put into foster care, and ran away.)

When Ace temporarily leaves the TARDIS in *Love and War*, the Doctor asks Benny to travel with him, as he needs someone to remind him to continue the good fight. And Benny's certainly a fighter: her first lover, Simon Kyle, betrayed her to the Spacefleet Academy she'd ran away from, leading her to escape by stowing away on a spaceship; she has to contend with both vampires (from the TV story, *State of Decay*) and the disbelieving locals while teaming up with Romana in *Blood Harvest*; she's tortured by Nazis in *Just War*; and has to stop a nuclear war in *Blood Heat*.

Benny's learned a lot from Ace in a very short time: when she joins the Doctor, she makes him promise not to manipulate her life in a similar way he did to Ace. Ace rejoins the Doctor and Benny in *Deceit*, but Benny nonetheless spends quite a lot of time split from her travelling companions, including being stranded in 1909 (*Birthright*), leaving the TARDIS for three months while leading a survey to Phaester Osiris (*Legacy*), and staying on the space station Orbos to catch up with an old friend in *The Dark Flame*. Still, she gets to know the Doctor intimately, both being submerged in his mind and meeting his first eight incarnations there, and, it's implied in *The Dying Days*, having sex with him!

In *Death and Diplomacy*, Benny meets, falls in love with, and gets engaged to Jason Kane, and they get married in the Norfolk village of Cheldon Bonniface on 24th April 2010, exchanging time rings gifted to them by the Doctor (*Happy Endings*) after Benny leaves the TARDIS. Theirs is a rocky relationship, however, so, despite Jason motivating her to complete her doctorate and the two of them travelling together for a time, they ultimately get divorced in *Eternity Weeps* and *Beyond the Sun*. During this period, Benny demonstrates how manipulative she can be, even lying to Jason about being pregnant. It's worth noting that Jason is just as cut-throat, with him later stealing Benny's time ring, and their pairing is toxic. Benny nevertheless does fall pregnant in *The Squire's Crystal*, albeit not with Jason's child and instead when her body is taken over by 'the soul sucker,' Avril Fenman. The half-human and half-Killoran Peter Guy Summerfield is welcomed into the universe in *The Glass Prison* (his middle name harking from the doomed Guy de Carnac, who Benny had fallen in love with in *Sanctuary*. Sadly, Peter is later manipulated into killing Jason (*The Wake*), something that does deeply affect Benny, but she soon forgives him and the mother and son go travelling.

Benny is finally reunited with the Doctor and Ace in the 2014 audio boxset, *The New Adventures of Bernice Summerfield*, then again after attending her son's wedding in *The Pyramid of Sutekh*; she further meets the Twelfth Doctor in the 2015 book, *Big Bang Generation*. Her travels then take her into a parallel dimension where she meets an alternate Doctor, played by David Warner (partner of actress Lisa Bowerman until his passing in 2022), an incarnation who's eventually elected President of the Universe; being the Doctor, though, he's more interested in running away and escapes his duties, only for the presidency to then be handed to the Master in 2017's *The New Adventures of Bernice Summerfield: Ruler of the Universe*. It's fortunate that this, too, is part of the Doctor's plan, resulting in him and his new companion getting back to Benny's universe.

As this Doctor doesn't belong in that universe, the two of them have to evade the Time Lords, and spend twenty-six days together in a cabin on a quiet planet before the Doctor's people nonetheless catch up with them. On Gallifrey, Benny is appointed his defender and studies Time Lord lore in detail to try to get him off; though events are tumultuous, she and the Doctor eventually get away together, their next stop 1930s Berlin (in 2022's *Blood & Steel*), where they fight the Cybermen.

By the time we next catch up with Benny, she's part of *The*

Eternity Club (2024), trying to deal with all manner of *Doctor Who* stalwarts including Sontarans, Draconians (from *Frontier in Space*), and Drahvin (from *Galaxy 4*).

Bernice Summerfield is to the Expanded Universe what Sarah Jane Smith is to the television series; the longest-running and probably most commercially successful companion ever.

More than three decades on, Bernice's adventures continue…

The Eighth Doctor
Paul McGann

> *'I love humans. They always see patterns in things that aren't there.'*
> The Doctor – *The TV Movie*

The next bona fide companion wouldn't appear until the series returned in 2005, although in the interim *Doctor Who* continued in novels, comics, and audio dramas, with a plethora of Expanded Universe companions introduced.

But, in 1996, there came an unconventional companion, one whose actual status as companion is debatable: Grace Holloway, who appeared in *The TV Movie*. Had a new full series been picked up, the studio hadn't planned to bring Grace back; a move that Paul McGann says he'd have argued against as he and Daphne Ashbrook got along so well. That's why she remains synonymous with McGann's time as the Doctor.

Grace Holloway – Daphne Ashbrook (*The TV Movie*)

Un bel dí vedremo (Maria Callas); *Disco 2000* (Pulp).

Grace's introduction to the Doctor is unlike that of any other companions: she meets him on the operating table!

We first see Grace at a performance of *Madame Butterfly*, immediately establishing herself as high brow, far removed from many more down-to-Earth companions before her (she has a framed Da Vinci sketch in her living room too, drawn, the Doctor informs her, when the artist had a cold); this turns out to be a crucial aspect of her character. She seemingly seeks out the finer things because, as the Doctor later says, she's 'tired of life, but afraid of dying'. Nonetheless, she's clearly empathetic, crying at the opera but tugged away by her sense of duty – or more accurately, her pager. Grace is a cardiologist at the Walker General Hospital in San Francisco, called away to perform surgery on the Seventh Doctor after he's shot.

As you might imagine, it's a day-to-day occurrence to her and doesn't stress Grace out – she even plays a CD of *Madame Butterfly* during surgery – but she panics when she can't properly navigate the Doctor's alien physiology. 'I got lost,' she says, shocked. Ultimately, it's her mistake that results in a fatal injury: she's actually responsible for killing the Doctor. She tries to marry her expertise with what she's just experienced, and immediately demands to see his x-rays, whereupon she realises it's not double exposure: he has two hearts. She orders a post-mortem, but is horrified both when the Doctor's body vanishes from the morgue (after regenerating, the Eighth Doctor is now wandering around the hospital) and when Dr Swift, her superior, suggests that they 'don't need to advertise [their] mistakes' and burns the x-ray. His sentiment about not being able to afford to lose her from the team backfires: seeing this blatant cover-up, Grace quits her job. She's obviously got strong principles, perhaps one of the things that made her take the Hippocratic Oath. Though acknowledging that it's all like 'a bad dream,' she doesn't seem to feel too much guilt over the Doctor's apparent death; instead, she rightly says that she couldn't have known about his binary vascular system, and expresses more concern over what they could've learned from his body if it hadn't have gone missing.

She's a big loss to the hospital because she ably demonstrates the right skills, ethical integrity, and intelligence that make her a great doctor. Indeed, Grace is smart enough to realise there's something fishy about Chang Lee, the guilt-ridden youngster who brought the Doctor in after being involved in his shooting.

It's no shock that she's cynical and scared as the Eighth Doctor gets into her car when she's on her way home. She's freaked out when he pulls a surgical probe out of his body – one she'd left there. She takes him to her house, a plush pad with a nice view; her job clearly paid well. She's angry but not overly upset that her now-ex-boyfriend, Brian, has taken all his stuff and left her, seemingly after she ditched him at the opera. His leaving, and the Doctor arriving, signals a turning point in Grace's life: not only has she turned her back on her profession, but her eyes are also open to more possibilities. She maintains that the Doctor's talking nonsense when he tells her about regeneration and scorns him for treating her 'like [she's] a child', yet she soon accepts his alien biology when listening to his heartbeats again. It's no narrative coincidence that this change occurs on New Year's Eve 1999, with the (atomic) clock ticking away to the new Millennium.

And she is very receptive to the Doctor. Despite thinking him deluded for a while, she's rather taken by him – metaphorically and literally, as she somehow finds herself going along with his crazy stories about a rival Time Lord called the Master trying to use the TARDIS' Eye of Harmony to steal his body.

By that point, however, something important has happened between them. The Doctor had previously been suffering from a post-regenerative amnesia, but the Master opening the Eye wakes his memories back up. In the rush of excitement, remembering exactly who he is, the Doctor kisses Grace – the first time he's ever kissed a companion on screen. This isn't just a spur of the moment thing: Grace tells him to 'do that again', and he does.

Nonetheless, this brief dalliance doesn't blind-side her. After his talk of the Eye of Harmony sucking in the Earth, she calls an ambulance, intent on getting him a bed in the psychiatric unit. She maintains her cynicism even after the Doctor demonstrates the planet's molecular structure breaking down by stepping through a glass window without breaking it. When the ambulance driver and his assistant turn out to be the Master and Chang Lee (the former of whom spits some burning bile at her), she comes round to the Doctor's way of thinking, if only for the night. Recalling her childhood wish to hold back death, the Doctor says he did just that and promises, 'I can't make your dream come true forever, but I can make it come true today.'

The Doctor has extraordinary foreknowledge of Grace, almost as if he's looked her up at some prior point for an unknown reason. He assures her that she'll 'do great things' and later warns that there's something she should know about her future – before she stops him. That's a departure from her earlier attitude: the Doctor explains that, 'The universe hangs by such a fragile thread of coincidences; it's useless to meddle with it, unless, like me, you're a Time Lord', but, fearing that Brian will move back in with her sometime, she still asks for 'some pointers.' The Eighth Doctor shows a remarkable aptitude for seeing personal futures – at the end, he tells Chang Lee to take a vacation next Christmas, just make sure he's not in San Francisco, and the Doctor also recognises the guard at the the Institute for Technological Advancement and Research (ITAR), and says, 'Gareth, answer the second question on your mid-term exam, not the third. The third may look easier, but you'll mess it up.'

The Doctor intends to pilfer a component from the Institute's beryllium atomic clock (which is counting down to the twenty-first century) to fix the TARDIS. Once more, the level of respect Grace commands is reinforced when it turns out she's one of ITAR's Board of Trustees. She even personally knows Professor Wagg, creator of the clock, and introduces him to the Doctor. It's here, during their escape when the Master catches up with them, that Grace also admits she has a fear of heights.

Their escape is short-lived, though: Grace, too, is possessed by the Master – surprising, given that, while we saw Jo Grant initially fall under his hypnosis, Peri's mind proved too strong, and you'd think Dr Holloway's would be similar. This somewhat overshadows something important Grace says when first entering the TARDIS: the Doctor mentions temporal physics and she immediately follows up, 'Oh, you mean like interdimensional transference. That would explain the spatial displacement we experienced as we passed over the threshold.' Grace makes the intellectual leap and figures out how the ship can be bigger on the inside, something few companions actually do.

The Doctor places considerable trust in Grace, both before and after her possession: he tells her his plan to essentially jump-start the TARDIS and shows her which buttons on the console she needs to press; similarly, after the Master frees her so he can use her to open the Eye of Harmony all the way (something that temporarily blinds her), she runs off to the control room to follow his previous instructions. Granted, the Doctor is at the mercy of the Master, so he doesn't have much choice except to have faith in her, but she's already demonstrated the intellectual aptitude to operate the TARDIS on a basic level – at least enough to put the ship into temporal orbit and more or less save Earth.

She goes back for the Doctor, breaking the Master's connection with him; in return, the Master kills her. She's the first companion of the Doctor's that the Master murders, though she wouldn't exactly be the last, and it doesn't stick: energy from the Eye resurrects both her and Chang Lee (who the Master had also killed). 'Hello, Grace,' the Doctor says as she awakens. 'Well? How does it feel to hold back death?'

It's a fresh start, with the TARDIS appropriately materialising in the first minute of the year 2000. Post-resurrection, she's not exactly a new person, but she certainly has an enthusiasm for life that was missing before. Her cynicism seems to have ebbed away. He offers to take her with him; she counters that he could go with *her*. Grace and the Doctor share one last kiss, then thank each other for all they've done. Off he goes to explore everything and everywhen, and off she goes into the new millennium.

Sadly, she's not referenced again, although UNIT is aware of her: her photo is in the Black Archive (*The Day of the Doctor*) alongside other companions to have visited the facility. Still, as the first companion to kiss the Doctor, the first to be resurrected, and the first to stake a claim on the twenty-first century (of sorts), Dr Grace Holloway is very much a bridge between the original run of *Doctor Who* and its 2005 revival.

The Eighth Doctor
Expanded Universe

The next bona fide companion wouldn't appear until the series returned in 2005. In the interim, *Doctor Who* continued in novels and audio dramas, with a plethora of Expanded Universe companions introduced. Notably, many of these companions are mentioned in the 2013 mini-episode, *The Night of the Doctor*: as the Eighth Doctor is about to regenerate, he makes a toast to 'Charley, C'rizz, Lucie, Tamsin, Molly – friends, companions I have known. I salute you.'

So let's meet them, and a few more besides…

In Prose

After *The TV Movie*, the BBC decided to take back the licence they'd given to Virgin Publishing in 1991. And so, from 1997 to 2005, they published an ongoing series of novels collectively known as the *Eighth Doctor Adventures*. Due to copyright issues, Grace Holloway was unable to be used (though she does appear in a few comic strips later on). Instead, the BBC had to create brand new companions for the Eighth Doctor – the first of whom was Samantha Jones. Four more companions followed. But this was only the beginning.

The initial three print companions demonstrate the differing extremes the Eighth Doctor was faced with. At the beginning of the Eight Doctor Adventures, there seems to be a trend to echo the origins of the television series. Sam Jones, for instance, bumps into the Doctor in the junkyard at Totter's Lane and goes to Coal Hill School, much like Ian, Barbara, and Susan in the very first television episode, *An Unearthly Child*. The next companion, Fitz Kreiner, comes from 1963, the year *Doctor Who* began. The third companion, however, breaks the mould, in more ways than one, and, intentionally or not, paves the way for concepts that will be seen in the revived series.

Samantha Jones (*The Eight Doctors* to *Longest Day*, and *Dreamstone Moon* to *Interference, Book Two*)

The first companion of the Eighth Doctor (in prose, at least; *Doctor Who Magazine*'s Izzy Sinclair beat Sam by eight months, appearing in October 1996), Sam first appears in June 1997 and departs in August 1999, featuring in twenty-five novels and designed by long-time *Doctor Who* VHS cover artist, Colin Howard. In many ways, she sets the bar for all female companions that will follow, especially those featured in *Doctor Who* since 2005.

Sam first comes to the Doctor's attention when she's trying to hide from school drug dealers who believe she's grassed on them; she hides in the junkyard at Totter's Lane and the Doctor arrives, saving her from the criminals. Before she speaks to him, he rushes off in the TARDIS, to appear moments later. Sam enters the ship to avoid questions from the police, and the Doctor tells her he'll take her on one trip only. At this time, Sam is only sixteen, and a bit of an activist, having taken part in campaigns to save whales, to stop animal experiments, and defend gay rights. She's also a vegetarian. A clean-living girl, she's initially a bit out of her depth in the Doctor's world, and he drops her off at a Greenpeace rally while he travels for a further three years with other companions. She remains with the Doctor for ten to eleven months initially, and is faced with the reality of war when she meets the Daleks in *War of the Daleks*, forcing her to re-think her own ideals: 'It's easy to be anti-war when you're not stuck in the middle of one.' Sam always maintains a strong sense of right and wrong throughout her early travels, but finds holding onto such ideals more and more difficult the longer she's with the Doctor. For example, in *Longest Day*, she beats herself senseless rather than shoot two rebels on the planet Hirath.

During her initial adventures, she finds herself falling in love with the Doctor – building on a concept initially hinted at with Grace in *The TV Movie*, and further explored by Big Finish in audios with Charley Pollard, and later in the revived television series, in particular with Rose Tyler and Martha Jones. In *Longest Day*, while performing CPR on the Doctor, Sam finds herself kissing him passionately. Worried about what might happen between her and the Doctor, Sam runs from him. She returns a couple of novels later, but misses the Doctor by a hair's breadth, and ends up on the planet Ha'olan in *Seeing I*. She spends three years there, working out her feelings for the Doctor. When they finally meet again, Sam, now aged twenty-one, kisses the Doctor but feels no passion or need to do it again – it seems that she's over him.

Nonetheless, they continue travelling together, first just the two of them, but later with Fitz Kreiner, who develops his own thing for Sam. She doesn't reciprocate, but in *Unnatural History*, this changes briefly when Sam is erased from history and replaced by 'Dark' Sam. It transpires that Sam was never meant to travel with the Doctor; indeed, she should've remained on Earth living a hard life from a London bedsit – a life of drugs, sex, and work, the complete opposite to the Sam the Doctor knows. This Dark Sam continues to live while Sam is off with the Doctor. A dimensional scar tears through San Francisco, a result of the events seen in *The TV Movie*, and when Dark Sam falls into it, the scar's biodata is split in two, rippling back in time to create another version of Sam. In effect, Sam creates herself.

Sam continues to have links to various other *Doctor Who* media. In the novel *Revolution Man*, she uses the alias 'Evelyn Smith,' which is curiously close to the name of Big Finish companion Evelyn Smythe, who doesn't appear for another year. Her contact with her parents is another interesting link, later echoed in the revived television series. For several years, she sends them postcards to reassure them she's okay and is simply travelling. And, in *Interference* she works alongside Sarah Jane Smith, eventually leaving to live with Sarah a year before she even meets the Doctor. It echoes, in some respects, Sarah's offer to Rose in the TV episode, *School Reunion*, only in the book series Sam and Sarah remain lifelong friends. Sam even attends Sarah's funeral at some point.

There's one final link between Sam and twenty-first century *Doctor Who*, in the shape of Martha Jones. Not only do they share the same surname, but when Martha goes undercover to the Pharm in the *Torchwood* episode *Reset*, she uses the alias, Samantha Jones.

Fitzgerald 'Fitz' Kreiner (*The Taint* to *Ancestor Cell*, and *Escape Velocity* to *The Gallifrey Chronicles*)

Fitz is the second companion of the Eighth Doctor, and features in fifty novels, from February 1998 to June 2005, making him the longest-serving companion of any medium. Between him and Sam, they cover all but six of the *Eighth Doctor Adventures*. Such is his popularity that he even appears in one Big Finish audio play in the 2009 collection, *The Company of Friends: Fitz's Story*.

When the Doctor meets Fitz, he's twenty-seven years old and working as a florist in his native period of 1963, having dodged National Service. In his spare time, he's a guitarist – apparently a very good one – and plays as Fitz Fortune, in an effort to hide his German ancestry (his father being of German descent). He plays the role of a struggling artist with a 'gammy' leg to gain the sympathy of his audience. Fitz is a heavy smoker, although he does give up once or twice, but never for long, and loves his tea and coffee. His mother, Muriel, lives in a care home, but dies as a result of the Benelisa programme, which the Doctor has a hand in. Fitz initially holds this against the Doctor, but eventually comes to terms with it and joins the Doctor and Sam, as he's now a fugitive wanted for a murder he didn't commit. When first meeting Sam, he tries to seduce her (which may account for her not being overly enthusiastic about his joining them), and his interest continues for some time until he's eventually able to bed Dark Sam in *Unnatural History*. His strong libido stays with him throughout his travels and he has many liaisons with several women, but only falls in love with one – Filippa in *Parallel 59*, who he always considers his one true love.

Fitz has little understanding of such things as quantum physics and matter transmitters. Very much a man of his time, he's often out of his depth when visiting the future, but doesn't find 2002 all that different; in fact, he's disappointed that it's a far cry from the future promised in the 1960s – there are no flying cars or moving pavements in the sky. Nothing like *The Jetsons* at all: just more of the same. This eventually turns into a blasé attitude, as he starts to consider himself a seasoned time traveller, a fact he likes to lord over Anji Kapoor, after she joins him and the Doctor in *Escape Velocity*. This mindset comes across as more patronising than the imparting of wisdom. Fitz is nervous around strong women, and is not interested in Anji. He's often looked down on by Anji, because he's from the 1960s and she's from 2001.

He leaves the Doctor's company for two years in *The Revolution Man*, and is brainwashed into becoming an agent for the Chinese Communist Army from 1967 to 1969. Although he overcomes this eventually, he faces a bigger problem in *Interference* when he's stored in The Cold in 1966 and removed from it on the colony world, Ordifica in 2593. With little choice, being so far from the Doctor, he and the survivors of Ordifica join the Faction Paradox. He becomes one of their agents, the Remote, after an attempted suicide at the age of thirty-three fails. He eventually teams up with a woman called Laura Tobin (not the weather forecaster of our time), who he nicknames Compassion. In return, he's given the name Code-Boy due to his affinity with computer systems. Before leaving Anathema, a planet-sized warship, he places his memories in a Remembrance Tank which creates a replica of him called Kode. Fitz becomes a Father in the Faction Paradox, and lives to become the oldest of the Remote. Father Kreiner, twisted and distorted after hundreds of years, hunts down and kills many Time Lords, and even tries to kill the Third Doctor on Dust. He's eventually trapped in IM Foreman's universe-in-a-bottle. After he's freed in *The Ancestor Cell,* he's convinced into helping the Doctor. The Doctor explains that he didn't mean to abandon Father Kreiner – he truly believed Fitz had died. He asks the Doctor to change time and stop Fitz from meeting him in 1963, but the Doctor (now travelling with a 'remembered' Fitz) refuses. Father Kreiner is brutally killed by Grandfather Paradox, the ultimate Faction-induced corruption of the Doctor.

Kode, one of the Remote, is recognised by the Doctor as a copy of Fitz, and with a mixture of persuasion and a link to the TARDIS, is 'remembered' back to his Fitz identity, who's just shy of thirty at this point (again). He retains much of Fitz's old memories, but with gaps, and as a result, doesn't always trust his memories. He finds it difficult to talk to Compassion, his old Remote co-agent, and misses both versions of Sam. Fitz becomes good at anagrams and puzzles, something he used to shirk from, and often wakes up uncertain of his identity. As a result of the TARDIS' part in 'remembering' Fitz, he has a great affinity with the ship, and often finds himself talking to her – she, in turn, talks to him through vibrations. He's understandably shocked when the TARDIS is destroyed in *The Shadows of Avalon*, and finds it somewhat awkward when Compassion later becomes the first fully sentient TARDIS. The prospect of travelling *inside* her takes a while to process. Sometime later, in *The Ancestor Cell*, when they discover the Edifice – in truth the TARDIS which has rebuilt itself – Fitz finds himself confronted with Father Kreiner, his real self. Kreiner lets Fitz live, to see the truth of the Doctor for himself. To stop the Faction Paradox, as well as his twisted self, Grandfather Paradox, the Doctor destroys Gallifrey. Fortunately, both he and Fitz are rescued by Compassion. The Doctor, now with no memory of who is or what he's done, is taken to the late nineteenth century to recover for a hundred years. Compassion takes Fitz to 2001, where he has to wait for the Doctor to find him again. While the Doctor lives through over a hundred years of history, for Fitz, it only takes a week to be reunited with the Time Lord. Fitz is somewhat unsettled by the fact that the Doctor still has no memory of what he has done. Until his memory is restored, Fitz is in the unusual position of knowing more about the Doctor than he does, and so goes to great lengths to protect him.

Fitz develops a deep love for the Doctor over the course of their journeys, becoming very like brothers, something Anji notes on many occasions. Such is the length of time that he spends with the Doctor, that by *Eater of Wasps*, Fitz no longer considers Earth his home, but rather thinks of himself as a 'citizen of the universe', echoing a description the First Doctor once used for himself in *The Daleks' Master Plan*.

He turns thirty-three in *History 101*, the age his original self decided to join the Faction Paradox, and doesn't believe he'll make it to forty due to his dangerous life with the Doctor. But he's okay with this. He is, at least, near thirty-five when we last see him in *The Gallifrey Chronicles*, by which point Anji has left and Trix MacMillan has joined. While travelling through various alternative realities and watching them be destroyed, Fitz makes a documentary in an effort to try and cope. We later learn that he's actively blocking out many of his pre-remembered memories.

Unfortunately, the *Eighth Doctor Adventures* prose series comes to an abrupt end in June 2005, when the final book is published, due to the revived series on television and an upcoming series of ongoing novels featuring the Ninth Doctor. As a result of this, we never reach the end of Fitz's story. We're left with him, now in a relationship with Trix (the first proper couple to live in the TARDIS, foreshadowing Amy Pond and Rory Williams in 2010), and they're both thinking of leaving the Doctor after he's defeated the Vore. Do they leave or do they die? Does Fitz make it to forty? We may never know. Although Fitz does return for a one-off audio adventure in 2009 and the 2019 short story, *We Can't Stop What's Coming*, the former is set during his travels with Anji, and the latter with Trix, still travelling together in the TARDIS, so neither tells us anything that we didn't already know.

But Fitz's influence on the Doctor is far-reaching, as the first proper male companion since Turlough, and the longest-serving companion in any medium – seven years! That alone assures his place in the annals of *Doctor Who* lore, and he should never be forgotten.

Compassion (*Interference, Book One* to *The Ancestor Cell*, and *Halflife*)

Never destined to be a straightforward companion, Compassion's influence on the future lore of *Doctor Who* is unmistakable. In many ways, she becomes the prototype for what we discover in *The Doctor's Wife* in 2011. Although the idea of fully sentient TARDISes is first introduced in *Alien Bodies* (1997), it's not until Compassion comes along that we discover the origin of these enigmatic machines...

Originally a woman called Laura Tobin from the human colony on Ordifica, Compassion is the result of Laura's personality and biodata being copied into the Faction Paradox's Remembrance Tanks. She joins the Doctor and Fitz because of her previous connection to Fitz, when he'd been her partner in the Remote as Kode. She's very resistant to the Doctor, and refuses to allow him to change her, believing that people can do without his interference. She doesn't believe the Doctor understands the concept of having friends, thinking he treats his companions as pets – ironic, since it's the Doctor who suggests she spends three months on Earth to learn more about humanity.

As a member of the Remote, Compassion always wears an earpiece through which she receives various signals and media. Upon joining the Doctor, the Time Lord advises her that she no longer needs it, but she continues to wear it nevertheless. This works out very badly for her, since over a short period of time the connection between her earpiece and the TARDIS has unforeseen effects on her biodata. In *The Shadows of Avalon* (2000), it's warped along Block Transfer Computations, which turns her into the first sentient TARDIS – a type 102. The President of Gallifrey, Romana, wants Compassion so that the Time Lords can breed a new race of sentient TARDISes for the forthcoming war, but the Doctor, Fitz, and Compassion go on the run. Without telling her, the Doctor fits

COMPANIONS

Compassion with a Randomiser in *The Fall of Yquatine* (2000), which causes her a great deal of pain initially. She eventually forgives him, and gets used to not being able to control her travels through the time vortex. Due to her chameleon circuit, she can take on the form of any species she wishes; however, more often than not, she appears in her 'default' form, the body of Laura Tobin.

Although she's now, technically, immortal, she feels she is dead since becoming a TARDIS. She only sticks with the Doctor and Fitz because she doesn't want to run alone, but that changes when the Doctor destroys Gallifrey and she's no longer hunted by the Time Lords.

She meets Nivet in *The Ancestor Cell* (2000), a technician from Gallifrey, and after he repairs her, she decides to travel with him, since she will need an engineer. She returns the Doctor to Earth, with his TARDIS, and deposits Fitz a hundred years in the future.

She continues on her travels with Nivet, and both reappear in *Halflife* (2004). Compassion goes under the guise of Madame Xing and restores a portion of the Doctor's memory, giving him a device that will do the rest of the job should he wish to. She's last seen just before she leaves Espero, disappointed and hoping for another chance to restore the Doctor's memories – perhaps so she can tell him what he did to her. Either way, as with Fitz, Compassion's story is never finished due to the termination of the *Eighth Doctor Adventures* in 2005.

Other prose-exclusive companions include the aforementioned Anji Kapoor, Trix MacMillan, and Bazima. The latter appears in only two short stories, *Nettles* and *Transmission Ends* (both 2008). She's a fashion genegineer and travels with the Doctor on a few adventures, before returning home. She works on a plan to alter the DNA of her own people so they can defeat the Gati, who occupy her planet.

Anji, on the other hand, appears in twenty-six novels (from 2001's *Escape Velocity* to 2003's *Timeless*, returning briefly in the 2005 novel, *The Gallifrey Chronicles*), and one short story, *Notre Dame du Temps* (2003). Born in Yorkshire in 1973, she's a stockbroker,

254

third-generation British-Asian, and a lapsed Hindu. Indeed, she left home at the age of seventeen partly owing to her family's views on feminism and her scepticism about religion. She joins the Doctor after her boyfriend, Dave Young, is killed during a Kulan invasion of Earth, and leaves when she becomes the legal guardian of Chloe, a young time-sensitive (and ex-Time Lord), now trapped in the body of a young girl.

Anji gets engaged to a journalist called Greg – though she apparently doesn't tell him about her adventures in time and space – and keeps in contact with her replacement companion, Trix, who feeds Anji stock tips. Her knowledge of the future informs her choices in a job she clearly loves.

Beatrix MacMillan, aka Trix, appears in fifteen novels from 2002's *Time Zero* to *The Gallifrey Chronicles* in 2005, as well as a short story in 2019's *The Target Storybook*. She's a con artist working for the Doctor's enemy, Sabbath Dei, so the Doctor understandably refuses to allow her into the TARDIS. Nonetheless, she stows away and remains undetected for some time. When she is found out, in Anjli's last novel, *Timeless*, the Doctor is surprisingly accepting of her, and she officially joins as a companion. She's still with the Doctor and Fitz, with whom she falls in love, when the Doctor restores Gallifrey, and she and Fitz agree that, after the Doctor defeats the Vore, they'll leave him. But they're still in the TARDIS by the time of *We Can't Stop What's Coming* (2019); whatever happens to Trix after her departure is unknown.

Either way, Trix is a troubled individual: *The Gallifrey Chronicles* reveals that her real name is Patricia Joanne Pullman, but she'd taken on a pseudonym while on the run from the police. The Doctor and Fitz, then, help ground her and help her find some peace.

That same novel lists a number of other Eighth Doctor companions: Lorenzo Smitt (who the Doctor met in 1935 while spending a century on Earth; 2001's *The Year of Intelligent Tigers* reveals that Lorenzo passed away at some point); Delilah; Frank; Claudia Marwood, a young widow from 1976; Deborah Castle, a teacher from the 1980s; Jemima-Katy (whose name comes from the 1995 comedy skit, *The Skivers*, starring Jon Pertwee); Nina; and Miranda Dawkins. Of these, the latter is the most significant, given that she might be considered the Doctor's daughter – her father is the tyrannical Emperor, one of the last survivors of a largely-destroyed Gallifrey, who just so happens to be a dark incarnation of the Doctor in the far future. On the night Miranda is born, her father is assassinated and the baby, heir to the throne, taken to the village of Greyfrith in the 1970s by Imperial staff going under the aliases John and Kim Dawkins. When they're killed, the Eighth Doctor adopts Miranda and raises her as his own until the age of sixteen, at which point rebels try to assassinate her too. She eventually returns to her own time and rules as Empress, according to the 2003 comic series, *Miranda*.

On Audio

Big Finish has been producing audio plays based on *Doctor Who* since 1999, but it wasn't until 2001 that Paul McGann made his first appearance as the Eighth Doctor, for the first time since 1996. Similar to his prose adventures, three stalwart companions form the heart of the Eighth Doctor's audio tales, and through them, we're introduced to peers. For a long period, his main travelling companion is Charley Pollard. In 2006, Big Finish made a new series of Eighth Doctor plays for BBC Radio 7, for which they created a new companion, Lucie Miller. Then, as Big Finish embraced boxset serials in 2014, the company brought back Liv Chenka, a character who previously met the Seventh Doctor in *Robophobia* (2011).

Charley Pollard – India Fisher (*Storm Warning* to *Blue Forgotten Planet*, plus various special releases and cameos like *Destiny of the Doctor: Enemy Aliens*, *Sontarans vs Rutans*, and *The Stuff of Legend*, as well as her own series, *Charlotte Pollard*)

Charlotte 'Charley' Elspeth Pollard is a self-professed Edwardian Adventuress, born on 15th April 1912 to Lord Richard and Lady

Louisa Pollard. Understandably, then, her upbringing is a privileged one – comprised of attending boarding school, sitting for family portraits (alongside her siblings, Peggy and Sissy), trips to the Old Vic theatre, and holidays to, for instance, Ostend, which may account for her having dreams of flying – though Charley always had a rebellious streak. (She also reveals herself to be particularly well-read, having enjoyed *Alice in Wonderland*, *Dracula*, *Treasure Island*, and the works of Jane Austen when she was younger.) This adventurous attitude led her to running away from finishing school so she could meet with a boy called Alex Grayle in Singapore on New Year's Eve, 1930. To get there, she takes the doomed airship R101, but she is saved from its destruction by the Doctor and joins him in the TARDIS. Their early adventures together see her fighting the Cybermen in 2503 during the Orion War (*Sword of Orion*); being introduced to Brigadier Alistair Gordon Lethbridge-Stewart in *Minuet in Hell*; meeting the Fourth Doctor and Leela in an alternate reality (*The Light at the End*); helping the Doctor when he's turned into a puppet by the Celestial Toymaker (*The Companion Chronicles: Solitaire*); and facing the Daleks in *The Time of the Daleks*. At some point after this, she also meets the Master while contending with the Daleks in *The Stuff of Legend*.

It transpires that Charley was meant to die on the R101, an event which would've resulted in the suicide of her beloved house cook, Edith Thompson. The pair were close, Edith being the only person Charley told of her plan to catch the airship. Due to Charley being a paradox, Edith and 22 Edward Grove, the house she was working at in 1906, are stuck in a time loop (*The Chimes of Midnight*). Though Charley is able to save Edith, she's haunted by the knowledge of her apparent fate. As a result of her supposed death, Charley becomes a temporal anomaly, and is used by the Neverpeople of the Anti-time Universe to break through into the normal universe. The Doctor refuses to sacrifice Charley in order to save existence, showing how highly he regards her.

For a time, she travels with C'rizz, played by Conrad Westmaas, a Eutermesan from Bortresoye in the Divergent

Universe. C'rizz joins the Doctor and Charley after he's forced to kill L'da, his wife, who's been genetically altered by the Kromon (*The Creed of the Kromon*). He's still with them when they finally break free into the real universe again, and stays with them for a further series of adventures, all the while seeking the Doctor's help in fixing his emotional wounds. Like all Eutermaseans, he's an emotional chameleon, and is subject to the moods of those around him.

Events in *The Next Life* – during which C'rizz is faced with the imprinted-memory ghost of L'da and Charley meets an elderly Simon Murchford (the man whose uniform she stole so she could gain entry to the R101) strain the companions' relationship, though Charley admits that this is partly due to her jealousy over anyone else growing close to the Doctor. Indeed, while Charley develops a deep romantic love for the Doctor, she learns to accept that these feelings will never truly be reciprocated. Still, Charley and C'rizz bond again during *Terror Firma* when they're imprisoned by the Daleks and meet Davros.

C'rizz's alien appearance and ideals somewhat limits his adventuring: while Charley and the Doctor get to experience the Great Exhibition of the Works of Industry of All Nations in 1851, C'rizz has to stay in the TARDIS (*Other Lives*). It's Charley's fault, albeit an accident, that C'rizz eventually ventures out, is captured, and forced to participate in Jacob Crackles' freakshow. Though Charley rescues him, we experience a little of C'rizz's more brutal side, as he blinds and cripples Crackles as revenge; we get a further taste of this in the short story, *Salva Mea*, part of the 2007 prose collection, *Short Trips: Snapshots*, in which C'rizz attacks a bystander, Luke Tillyard, who tries to stop the alien from hurting Charley.

It's around this time that Charley is temporarily separated from C'rizz and the Doctor by the malicious Time Lord, the Nine – otherwise known as the Multitude, a being suffering from regenerative dissonance, a mental illness caused by the personalities of a Time Lord's previous incarnations living on, post-regeneration, in their current body, akin to dissociative identity disorder. (It's rather telling that, when the Nine tells Charley to expect company, she immediately thinks of C'rizz, but the Nine shoots this notion down by calling the Eutermesan a 'maniac.') Charley helps fellow companions, Liv Chenka, Helen Sinclair, Bliss, and River Song, all of whom travel with the Doctor after Charley departs, to defeat the Nine and the latter, i.e. the Doctor's wife, who we meet on TV in *Silence in the Library*, gets her back to the Eighth Doctor (*Companion Piece*, part of the 2019 set, *Ravenous 3*).

Though the relationship between the Doctor, Charley, and C'rizz is rather unusual, they're nonetheless a very strong trio who clearly care a lot about each other. In *Absolution*, Charley finds and opens C'rizz's Absolver, a device that apparently contains the voices and souls of the absolved, i.e. those who are killed and 'saved' by the Church of the Foundation, the religious sect that C'rizz is part of. C'rizz's feelings towards death, then, are complicated, but he's still determined to retrieve the souls that were unleashed when Charley unknowingly opened the Absolver, and goes on to sacrifice himself to save Charley and the Doctor. On his deathbed, he affirms that he views his friends as, instead, his family, calling Charley his sister, and looking forward to being reunited with L'da.

Distraught, Charley asks the Doctor to take her home. However, she becomes stranded in the year 500,002, believing the Doctor to be dead. Despite this, she holds onto the hope that the Doctor will return for her, but when the TARDIS does finally arrive, it brings with it the Sixth Doctor (*The Girl Who Never Was*). To preserve the Web of Time, Charley has to pretend not to know him, though her somewhat blasé reaction to the TARDIS raises an eyebrow. While the Doctor is mistakenly arrested for murder, Charley is kidnapped, but the pair are soon drawn together again, and she feigns amnesia to dodge some awkward questions. (Curiously enough, the Sixth Doctor and Evelyn Smythe saw the Eighth Doctor, Charley, and C'rizz – as well as another future companion, Lucie Miller – in 2007's *The 100 Days of the Doctor*, but the Sixth Doctor fails to recognise Charley when he meets her again in *The Condemned*.)

The Sixth Doctor and Charley travel together for a while, during which time, she comes face-to-face with Dick Turpin (*The Doomwood Curse*), the Valeyard (*The Red House*, from the 2015 special release, *The Sixth Doctor: The Last Adventure*), and the titular antagonists in 2008's *Return of the Krotons* (in which she falls unconscious and the Doctor hears her muttering about C'rizz's death, showing how deeply it, and the Eighth Doctor's reaction to it, affected her). Things seem to come to a head in *Patient Zero* when Charley is infected with a virus which enables an entity called Mila to shift Charley out of phase and take her place by the Doctor's side. After Mila sacrifices herself to save Earth, Charley reveals her secret to the Doctor. Still believing that he'll ultimately die as a consequence of knowing her, she uses memory-altering technology to convince the Doctor that he only ever travelled with Mila, not Charley.

Charley's being cured by the Viyrans in *Blue Forgotten Planet* also sees her effectively becoming their prisoner and being held in stasis for an untold number of years. She eventually escapes to twenty-first century London alongside Robert Buchan Jnr, another Viyran captive. The pair have a flirtatious relationship which leads to them growing closer and sleeping together. Charley says she misses the Doctor and laments not settling down and having children, a statement that recalls her attachment to family and her mother gifting her a familial brooch on her sixteenth birthday that she intends to hand down to her own children (*Scherzo*). Sadly, it's not long before Charley and Robert are enslaved for some ten years, keeping fit in order to survive cullings carried out by a humanoid Proto-Viyran workforce. Their time in what is essentially a concentration camp brings them closer, but their time together ends in tragedy as they are seemingly both shot. She, however, is transported away before she can be killed, and she ends up alone in an unknown destination, desperately calling for help (*The Destructive Quality of Life*, concluding the 2017 set, *Charlotte Pollard: Series Two*).

And that is where we leave Charley – at least for now. As one of the best-loved and most important companions in *Doctor Who* lore, Big Finish is bound to pick up Charley's story at some stage and hopefully give her a happy ending, one which reunites her with the Doctor.

Lucie Miller – Sheridan Smith (*Blood of the Daleks* to *To the Death*, plus *Short Trips* and *The Further Adventures of Lucie Miller*)

Both Lucie's arrival and first scene are not too dissimilar to those of Donna Noble in the TV stories, *Doomsday* and *The Runaway Bride*. (An unintentional coincidence it turns out, as told by author Steve Lyons, who knew nothing of Donna's first scene until he saw *The Runaway Bride*, which was transmitted barely a week before episode one of *Blood of the Daleks* in December 2006.) Lucie appears suddenly in the TARDIS, with no idea how she got there. She thinks the Doctor's kidnapped her, although he claims himself innocent. But she does really know why she's there. She makes a slip by calling the Doctor a Time Lord before he reveals this fact to her, at which point the Doctor recognises a perception filter placed around her, to block out some of her memories (a trick Time Lords often use). She tells him that the Time Lords sent her to him for protection, because she saw 'something' that she can't remember. It takes a while for Lucie to warm to the Doctor, who she thinks is a 'patronising git,' and only stays with him because she has no choice. She promises him that she'll leave at the earliest opportunity, something the Doctor looks forward to.

Lucie is nineteen and from Blackpool, 2006. She doesn't smoke, although seems very knowledgeable about indoor ultra-violet lamps, of the sort used for growing cannabis. She's always been close to her Aunt Pat; when it's revealed in *The Zygon Who Fell to Earth* that the Pat she knew is in fact a Zygon, who used to be Pat's dead husband Trevor, the Doctor keeps it from her. This secret comes back to haunt both the Doctor and Lucie in *Death in Blackpool*, and it is the sole reason she leaves him.

The reason behind her placement in 'temporal witness

protection' is revealed in *Human Resources*, when Straxus, a Time Lord working for the High Council, explains that he's the one who placed Lucie in the TARDIS after having learned that the CIA (that is, the Celestial Intervention Agency of Gallifrey) has been manipulating her life, believing she'll eventually become a dictator in Europe. It turns out, though, that they're mistaken and it's actually Karen, another young woman who goes for the same job as Lucie. Once this is all revealed, Lucie isn't sure she wants to remain with the Doctor, but comes to the realisation that she actually enjoys his company and the somewhat irreverent relationship that they have. However, she only agrees to continue their travels after he first admits that he, too, enjoys her company.

Lucie parts from the Doctor for several weeks after he apparently plummets to his death from the balcony of Morbius' palace. She returns home, believing the Doctor to be dead, crying for days as she tries to accept this. She's targeted by an alien Headhunter, and meets the Doctor again on the planet Orbis. Six-hundred years have passed for him, so he's forgotten who he is. A slap from Lucie restores his memories, due to the chronon particles on Lucie's fingertips. They resume their travels, once again falling into their usual banter and mutual teasing.

On their travels, Lucie encounters many foes from the Doctor's past, especially those who encountered him during his first four incarnations, including Daleks, the Monk, Cybermen, the Fendahl, Morbius, the Krynoids, and the Giant Spiders of Metebelis Three. It's during this encounter that Lucie shows her real strength when her body is taken over by the Eight Legs' Queen (much like Sarah was in *Planet of the Spiders*). She struggles against the Queen and learns of her secret link to a Gallifreyan remote stellar manipulator, inside which the Queen has created a virtual space. Lucie is able to take her own mind there, and use it to contact the Doctor. To save Lucie and stop the Eight Legs, the Doctor transfers Lucie's mind into the TARDIS' telepathic circuits, before using a blue crystal from Metebelis Three to return Lucie's mind to her own body.

Lucie's faith in the Doctor is shattered when they spend

Christmas 2009 in Blackpool with her Aunt Pat. She finally discovers the truth about Pat. Although she understands the reason behind the deceit, after Zygon-Pat dies, Lucie finds she cannot forgive the Doctor for the lie and leaves him, deciding to travel around Europe for a time.

At some point in 2010, Lucie joins the Monk (last seen on TV in 1965's *The Daleks' Master Plan*), after responding to an ad he placed in a newspaper for a new companion for the Doctor. It's uncertain how much time they spend together, but she goes on record as saying he's a 'homicidal maniac' and he kicks her out after she refuses to allow him to retroactively kill someone by ensuring said person is never born. She joins the Doctor once more, but only because he promises to give her a better Christmas than the one she had the previous year.

They spend time with Susan, the Doctor's granddaughter, and Alex, his great-grandson, whom Lucie becomes particularly fond of. Lucie returns to Alex's native time, the late twenty-second century, and travels Europe with him to see how humanity has rebuilt following the defeat of the Daleks in 2164 (*The Dalek Invasion of Earth*). While in Thailand, a sickness breaks out, engineered by the Daleks. Lucie contracts the illness, and although it doesn't kill her, it does cause her to lose an eye and cripples her. Realising she needs the Doctor's help, she summons him back to Earth but he arrives too late: Earth is once again occupied by the Daleks and Lucie, Alex, and Susan have joined the resistance fighters. Alex is killed by the Daleks while placing a bomb, an incident that leads Lucie to commit herself to a suicide mission that will save the Earth. She flies a Dalek saucer to the core of the planet and destroys the Daleks' time warp engine – killing herself in the process. Her death drives the Doctor to realise that he has always been too easy on the Daleks, and is determined to take the war to them (possibly leading to the Last Great Time War, implied in *The Great War*, part of 2012's *Dark Eyes: Volume One*, in which he meets his next companion, Molly O'Sullivan). He vows that one day, regardless of the Web of Time, he will travel back and prevent Lucie's death...

*

This isn't the last we hear of Alex either, although the one who joins the Doctor in *Meanwhile, Elsewhere*, from the 2023 audio anthology, *Time War: Cass*, is from an alternate dimension. Nonetheless, this Alex Campbell (played by Sonny McGann, son of Paul McGann) apparently shares a lot with the one we met in *An Earthly Child* in 2009, at least according to a profile piece in *DWM* #609, which says, 'we can assume that the multiverse Alex has the same history as his prime reality counterpart – at least up to a point.' Their main differences, then, appear to be that the *Time War* Alex actively likes travelling with his great-grandfather (who he simply calls 'grandfather') and that this Alex was drawn into the battle between the Daleks and Time Lords by the Dalek Time Strategist who found the alternate version, and imprisoned him in cryogenic suspension, in an effort to coerce the Eighth Doctor into destroying Gallifrey. Fortunately, the Doctor recovered this stasis pod in 2020's *Restoration of the Daleks* (from *Time War: Volume Four*), so by the time of *Meanwhile, Elsewhere*, he's been travelling with the Doctor for some time.

Born to Susan and David in 2170, Alex – full name David Alexander Campbell – is only seven per cent Time Lord, meaning he has one heart and can't regenerate; he certainly has his great-grandfather's love of travelling, however, and read Business Studies in Bristol, the same city the Twelfth Doctor would call home for around seventy years while lecturing at St Luke's University (Series 10). Alex is an upbeat type which gives the Doctor some levity in the face of the conflict with the Daleks – this might, however, change when Alex learns his prime counterpart is dead, something the Doctor is reluctant to share.

Alex is also an outrageous flirt, chatting up their travelling companion, Cass Fermazzi, hinting that he'd rather enjoy getting to know Cass' brother, and even flirting with himself when he's displaced in time in *Meanwhile, Elsewhere*.

Cass fills a hole left in the TARDIS by Bliss, a companion the Eighth Doctor has on the edges of the Time War but who both he and Alex forget about. *The Starship of Theseus*, from 2017's *Time War: Volume One*, starts with the Doctor travelling with Sheena, played by Olivia Vinall, who we're told has had numerous adventures on the TARDIS before she suggests a holiday that takes them to the luxury space-liner, Theseus. Sheena is a positive sort, being particularly enamoured with seeing Jupiter as the starship leaves port, and she brings out the best in the Doctor, which makes her eventual fate a real shame. But as the Time War starts to affect space-time, the Doctor first starts calling her Emma then Louise, and can't recall how they met. Even Sheena struggles to hold onto the details of their relationship – before she's erased from time altogether and the Doctor recalls landing on the Theseus alone.

It's here that the Doctor meets Bliss (Rakhee Thakrar), a scientist studying quantum fluctuations in a temporal warzone, but who thinks the Time War is 'ancient history' (*Echoes of War*). She soon leads a group of rebels against invading Daleks and, with the Doctor and several others, uses a Dalek ship to find temporary refuge on a jungle planet before the Theseus is obliterated. She is further kidnapped by a high-ranking Time Lord called Cardinal Ollistra, but escapes to the TARDIS, where she joins the Doctor as his companion, the pair essentially on the run from the Time War itself, as well as Ollistra, who's intent on forcing the Doctor to join the battle.

Bliss is a postgrad in Applied Quantum Astrotech, having studied at the Luna University (the same place River Song specialised in archaeology), and as such, she is well-versed in complex concepts that make her the perfect companion for the Doctor. She's also an orphan of the Time War, her family having been erased by the Time Lords in a failed attempt to stop the Daleks (*The Lords of Terror*, in 2018's *Time War: Volume Two*), making her an anomaly, though the Doctor still hopes to restore her parentage.

We also learn that Bliss lived with her mother and grandfather in Central City on the planet, Derilobia, both of whom worked in factories there. In a possible pre-Time War past that Bliss learns of in *State of Bliss* (from 2019's *Time War: Volume Three*), using a quantum visualiser that shows alternate timelines, she studied robotics at Derilobia University because she didn't want to leave her home, but was eventually tempted to apply for the Luna University anyway. This Bliss is kidnapped by the Nine, a rogue Time Lord seeking out those who travelled with the Eighth Doctor, so she is forced to fight him alongside River Song, Charley Pollard, Liv Chenka, and Helen Sinclair, despite having never met the Doctor (*Companion Piece*, part of *Ravenous 3*). *State of Bliss* further reveals that Bliss' life is a trap: it's been reworked by Professor Deepa using quantum visualisers to draw in the Doctor so she can steal his TARDIS. Thanks to Deepa's meddling, the Doctor at least comes to remember Sheena/Emma, while Bliss is able to retain memories of her parallel paths; she agrees with the Doctor's assertion that they'd better not fix her history to one timeline, so they don't go back to Derilobia to find the truth about this timeline. Instead, she and the Doctor go on a series of adventures together in which they meet *The War Valeyard* (2019); visit Vespertine, the ship of explorer Hudson Sage (according to *Meanwhile, Elsewhere*); find the *Planet of the Ogrons* (2018); and confront the ghosts of the war in *Salvage*, from *Short Trips: Volume 12* (2023). In the latter, we learn that Bliss collected seashells with her grandfather, told secrets to a Gossip Stone, owned posters for films she only pretended to have seen as a child, and lost her favourite chequered scarf while celebrating her successful application to the Luna University.

Eventually, they encounter an alternate Davros who lives in peace on Skaro, the war between the Thals and Kaleds never having begun (*Palindrome*). Davros even has a Thal wife, Charn. As an expert in transdimensional engineering, however, he creates a portal that allows the N-Space Dalek Time Strategist entry into this parallel world, and the peaceful Davros is then corrupted by his multiversal counterparts. Her past having been wrecked by the Daleks, Bliss is all too keen to kill Davros, eventually leading the evil genius to see great potential in her (*Restoration of the Daleks*). It's through this that the Doctor and Bliss are forced back into the Time War, coming face-to-face with the War Council in *Dreadshade* (2020).

Sadly, Bliss is seemingly erased from time and the Doctor and Alex, who they rescue, forget her by the time of *Meanwhile, Elsewhere*, but the Doctor recognises that there's a curious space left in the TARDIS. When the Doctor suggests someone's missing from his ship in *Previously, Next Time* (2023), his new companion, Cass, implies some knowledge of who this is by saying they'll have to live in 'blissful ignorance.' As the Valeyard can remember Bliss from his past, it's possible that she'll be remembered and brought back into reality; then again, it's also possible that the Valeyard's memories will simply alter to accommodate her absence.

We first meet Cass Fermazzi in the TV minisode, *The Night of the Doctor*, which also sees the Eighth Doctor, on the brink of death, relenting to the Time War and regenerating into the War Doctor. In this story, Cass dies, refusing his help as she's disgusted as much by Time Lords as by the Daleks. As on TV, she's played by Emma Campbell-Jones for Big Finish.

Though growing up in a big family with several brothers, Cass was close to her father, being especially engaged with the stories of Hudson Sage. It's likely hearing about Sage's exploits that prompts her to venture out into the universe following her dad's passing. She becomes an engineer on the errand-class starship, EC-141, but on her first day, the vessel is affected by fractures in reality, leading her to meet first Alex, then the Doctor, then an older Alex, displaced by time. Though she helps save the ship and is offered a promotion, she instead seizes her opportunity to join the Doctor. Her first proper trip is to Station Twilight, a facility built to study the wreck of the Vespertine, Sage's ship which history says is never found. Cass excitedly tells an oblivious Alex that Hudson discovered the Scarab Nebula and has three elements on the Periodic Table named after him. But meeting Hudson, who's trapped in a time-locked level of the ship, is something of a disappointment to Cass, given that he turns out to have been involved in an illegal weapons smuggling operation and that his crew mutinied.

Cass demonstrates a willingness to learn, so after the Doctor tells her about the Daleks, she finds out more about them using the

TARDIS databanks – just in time for the trio to learn that the Daleks are creating a 'Retcon Bomb,' which can alter their past mistakes (*Previously, Next Time*). This explosive, however, activates before it's meant to, trapping themselves and a desert planet in a time loop. Though they're able to stop the Daleks, Cass, like Bliss before her, is seemingly wiped from existence, not even appearing in the TARDIS' logs. Unlike with Bliss, the Doctor can still remember her, so he vows to get her back.

(Interestingly, *Loose Ends*, a segment in *DWM* #609, suggests the prime version of Cass was brought back to life by Ohila using a spare soupçon of the elixir of life; Ohila says it was the Doctor's idea, and 'he begged us to try. He wanted to show he was... "one of the nice ones".' That Cass goes on to join the Sisterhood of Karn. This is in contrast to *Light the Flame*, from 2021's *The War Doctor Begins: Forged in Fire*, in which the Sisterhood holds a funeral for Cass.)

Molly O'Sullivan – Ruth Bradley (From *Dark Eyes* to *Dark Eyes 4*)

Bliss, Alex, and Cass aren't the only Eighth Doctor companions inexorably linked to the Daleks' meddling with time. Molly O'Sullivan, played primarily by Ruth Bradley and then by Sorcha Cusack for her final two episodes, *Master of the Daleks* and *Eye of Darkness*, features in the *Dark Eyes* sets between 2012 and 2015, coming shortly after Lucie's Miller's passing in *To the Death*.

Hailing from Ireland, Molly is a Voluntary Aid Detachment (VAD) nursing assistant in France during the First World War. Following an old running gag from television, Molly believes Gallifrey is in Ireland, and calls it 'Galilee'. She's initially put in charge of caring for the Doctor after he's affected by time winds and collapses in July 1917; the Doctor, however, has actually been sent there by the Time Lord, Straxus, Coordinator of the Celestial Intervention Agency, to find a mysterious girl who's key to a plan to destroy the universe. Correctly presuming this is Molly, the Doctor takes her into the TARDIS after they're attacked by Daleks.

There's some friction between her and the Doctor as the time winds also killed Molly's friend, Kitty, who saw her akin to a sister. Kitty was, in fact, the reason Molly joined as a VAD: before the war, Molly served as a chambermaid for the Donaldson family in London, but when Kitty signed up as a VAD, their friendship meant Molly followed her into the conflict.

Fugitives takes Molly on a tour around time as the Doctor can't pilot the TARDIS back to Gallifrey. They first materialise on the sinking HMS Grenade on the 29th May 1940; then a house owned by the Doctor in London, 1972; and then to the planet, Halalka, where anti-grav devices mean tourists can swim in waterfalls. They don't have much time to rest, as the Daleks are in hot pursuit.

Molly is indeed a mystery, having eyes darker than anyone on Earth, and, when she first boards the TARDIS, she says, 'I've been here before,' but can't remember when. She's also able to operate its controls without knowing how. We find out much more about Molly in the final two stories of the first *Dark Eyes* set, *Tangled Web* and *X and the Daleks*. She was born in 1891 to Patrick and Cathy O'Sullivan, and had seven siblings, though she survived them all: her three sisters and two of her brothers died before their fifth birthdays, while her soldier brother, Patrick, died on his first day fighting in France, and Liam was killed by an English sentry in Ireland. Most significantly, Molly went missing for a little while on her second birthday in 1893, kidnapped by the Time Lord, Kotris, working on behalf of the Daleks. Kotris doses Molly with retro-genitor particles, capable of devolving the Time Lords out of existence, and giving her the 'dark eyes' for which she was bullied throughout her youth. This further allowed her some subconscious knowledge of how to fly the TARDIS. Kotris was also responsible for unleashing the time winds that had affected the Eighth Doctor in No Man's Land, and killed Kitty. When Kotris is instead erased from time, Molly returns to the First World War after realising Kitty must be alive and well.

Molly's hard shell is understandable, given the tough period she grew up in. Nonetheless, underneath it all is a warm heart and a sarcastic, fun nature, hence her calling the TARDIS a Tardy-Box, and often referring to the Doctor as 'the Doctor' instead of simply 'Doctor' – much to his annoyance!

She's obviously very fond of the Doctor, which might explain her returning, in *The White Room*, to 107 Baker Street, the house owned by the Doctor which she'd previously gone to in *Fugitives* (and which other past and future companions, including Charley Pollard and Lady Audacity, Liv Chenka, River Song, and Helen Sinclair, visit at different times, most notably in the *Stranded* boxset range). This leads her to meet the Doctor again, and they go to the cryo-ship, Orpheus, in *Time's Horizon*. There, they find its crew, including Liv Chenka, hiding from the Daleks at the edge of creation and encounter the psychic Eminence. Despite Liv initially interrogating Molly, the two become good friends, and the Doctor leaves them at Baker Street in the 1970s in an effort to keep Molly safe, given she's still infused with retro-genitor particles (*The Eyes of the Master*). Ironically, then, she's taken by the Master, who brainwashes her into thinking she'd travelled with him, not the Doctor (revealed in *Rule of the Eminence*), as the Master tries to use those particles to give him control of the Eminence. When they turn the tide and instead defeat both the Master and the Eminence, the Doctor concludes that it's too dangerous for them to continue travelling together; they reluctantly leave each other, with Molly, returning to London, thanking the Doctor for showing her the universe.

The very next story, *A Life in the Day*, takes the Doctor and Liv to London in 1921, albeit, as it turns out, in an alternate timeline, where they meet Kitty Donaldson and her war veteran brother, Martin, the siblings who'd previously been under Molly's charge. In this parallel universe, Molly apparently left to get married, and she and her husband became missionaries in Africa, only for their camps to be attacked by invading Daleks. Molly keeps a low profile by changing her name to Mary Carter and likely spends some forty years treating Dalek victims (*Master of the Daleks*). By 1961, she's in Moscow, serving as a nurse in a Dalek labour camp under her

Sontaran superior, Rastel, seemingly waiting for the Doctor to return as she knows the Daleks shouldn't have invaded at this point in history. After finally reuniting with the Doctor and Liv, Molly helps put paid to the Daleks, the Dalek Time Controller, and the Eminence using the remaining retro-genitor particles in *Eye of Darkness*, but at the cost of her life. Liv says they'll take her body home to Ireland.

Molly departs this life by reminding the Doctor to make people better. His toasting her memory in *The Night of the Doctor* before he regenerates implies that her message stayed with him – and that his embracing the 'warrior' means ditching that ideology.

Liv Chenka – Nicola Walker (From *Dark Eyes 2*, plus *Robophobia*)

We first meet Liv Chenka, a Med-tech (that is, a medical technician) on a Kaldor cargo vessel called the Lorelei, in the Seventh Doctor audio adventure, *Robophobia*, a sequel to the TV story, *The Robots of Death*. Liv immediately shows she has an enquiring mind, as, when her friend, Tal Karus, is murdered, she uses her own initiative to investigate, even ignoring a call from Security Chief Farel so she can focus on the problem at hand. She and the Doctor find each other interesting, with the Doctor almost egging her on, seeing her potential; indeed, she soon notes, 'It's like he knows all the answers, but just wants us to find out for ourselves. He knew I'd look into this. I suppose that means that he has faith in me for some bizarre reason.' Despite them having clear chemistry and her having a solid template for a fantastic companion, not to mention her helping the Doctor stop a plan to crash the Lorelei, the Doctor leaves Liv on the planet Ventalis.

But she clearly leaves an impression on both the Doctor and the TARDIS: in 2012's *Black and White*, the Doctor experiments with the TARDIS by briefly going back to the Lorelei in the twenty-third century, something which seems to excite the TARDIS as the ship asks if they can invite Liv to travel with them. Given that the TARDIS exists throughout time and so can effectively predict the future, this is a substantial request, and the Doctor responds, 'Another time, perhaps, but not now.'

Though hailing from Kaldor, Liv always wanted to explore the wider universe as a child. It's not surprising, then, that when the Eighth Doctor sees her again, it's on a different planet: Nixyce VII, where she helps the Daleks by tending to their slaves' medical issues. Her peers see her as a sell-out so they give her the unfair nickname of *The Traitor* – something which Molly O'Sullivan rails against when she hears it, a fellow nurse recognising Liv's duty to look after people in any way she can. Liv has plenty of grit herself: she refuses to believe the Eighth Doctor is the same man she met on the Lorelei and she is stroppier with the Daleks than most of his other companions are, demanding that they give her supplies so she can do her job and then leave her alone. Still, it's clear that the years under Dalek rule have got to her, and she's further frustrated by the Doctor when he chooses to save the lives of the Daleks' slaves (and Liv) while having to let them keep the superweapon they've been building. Liv makes it clear she thinks he's made the wrong decision.

Unbeknown to her, the Eighth Doctor has already encountered Liv, albeit in her personal future, and his real reason for coming to Nixyce VII is to stop the Eminence.

The Reviled (2014) tells the next part of Liv's story: she escapes the Daleks in a cargo ship, but she is affected by lethal radiation poisoning. Believing she'll die, she becomes a Med-tech on the cryo-ship, Orpheus, where she's put in stasis, until the ship reaches its eventual destination – hiding from the Daleks at the edge of the universe (*Time's Horizon*), where they're possessed by the Eminence. When the TARDIS arrives, Liv orders the Doctor's arrest straight away, based on what he did in *The Traitor*, events that haven't actually happened for the Eighth Doctor yet. As such, it takes a lot for her to warm to the Doctor, though she's at least baffled yet happy that, when she's about to sacrifice herself for her crew, the Doctor saves her, and effectively welcomes her on board his ship. Still, it's largely her friendship with Molly that motivates Liv to get away from the Orpheus via the TARDIS. She then encounters the

Eminence again in *Eyes of the Master* while in London, 1972, and the Doctor leaves Liv and Molly at his Baker Street residence for a time while he goes to play out the events on the Nixyce VII and so that Molly is kept safe, he thinks, due to her being infused with retro-genitor particles. Liv obviously enjoys it there, revelling in the quiet life: hardly a surprise, given she's seen her friends being taken over and dying on the Lorelei and Orpheus, as well as living on a Dalek-occupied planet for so long. She says she comes from a thousand years in the future, making her native time sometime in the twenty-ninth century, and, in the 2017 *Short Trips* story, *The World Beyond the Trees*, she dreams of the Doctor and confesses to him that she'd like to see her father again – a sign that she's slowly learning to trust him, perhaps after hearing so much about him from Molly. (Later on, in *A Day in the Life*, Liv confirms, 'My life's not exactly been conventional. It's nice to do ordinary things with ordinary people.') Nonetheless, Liv is dragged back into the action when Molly is abducted, and Liv is able to fashion a rudimentary distress beacon that's intercepted by Coordinator Narvin, on behalf of Gallifrey's Celestial Intervention Agency. He sends her to Ramosa, amid the Eminence War, where she's reunited with the Doctor – though not before she has to take on her old role as medic to the inhabitants of the planet, caught in the crossfire of the war (*The Reviled*). All their good work ultimately amounts to nothing when Ramosa and its population are destroyed.

Understandably, the Doctor is so driven to avoid this war, but it still puts Liv on the back foot. Nevertheless, she goes along with his plans, and, her radiation poisoning in mind, is happy enough to once more sacrifice herself for the greater good in *Masterplan*. Instead, she's kidnapped by the Master who has Molly alive and not-so-well. With her friend suffering from the Master's mind manipulations and the effects of the retro-genitor particles, Liv cares for Molly, trying to nurse her back to health. Those particles cure Liv of her radiation poisoning, Molly's lasting gift to Liv as the Doctor has to leave Molly with Narvin (*Rule of the Eminence*). In that time, though, Liv and the Doctor have proven themselves to each other, defeating the Master and the Eminence, so Liv joins the Doctor as a proper companion, even getting her own TARDIS key in *A Life in the Day* (2015).

During this adventure, set in 1921, they meet Kitty and Martin Donaldson (played respectively by Beth Chalmer, who also played Seventh Doctor companion, Raine Creevy, and Barnaby Kay, who married Nicola Walker in 2006), who were once in Molly O'Sullivan's care. Liv and Martin get close, and when the former admits that she's not sure whether she 'does' fun, Martin retorts, 'But you seem so full of life.' They go on what are effectively dates, going to see the Elgin Marbles at the British Museum, eating together at a fancy restaurant, and watching Buster Keaton's *The Goat*. In fact, Martin becomes so attached to Liv that, when he's caught by a time grenade, reliving the past day, he willingly lives through a time loop so he can get to know Liv better. It's no shock that the pair are attracted to each other, given their similar experiences, Martin being a World War I veteran and Liv suffering for so long under the Daleks – creatures she meets again, plus the Master, in *The Monster of Montmartre*, *Master of the Daleks*, and *Eye of Darkness*.

Mired in sadness, Liv is nonetheless pleased to see an aged Molly again, although she does ruin the latter's alias Mary Carter as she quickly recognises her. She's knocked by Molly's death, but affirms that she and the Doctor will take her body home to Ireland.

The next time we hear from the Eighth Doctor and Liv in *The Eleven*, the opening episode of *Doom Coalition 1* in 2015, they're getting on like a house on fire, escaping the hungry inhabitants of the planet Destrana. *Absent Friends* (2016) later establishes that the pair have been travelling for some time, likely years. Leaving Destrana, the TARDIS is taken to Gallifrey where they're given the task of tracking down the mad Time Lord known as the Eleven, who has all eleven of his personalities chattering away in his mind. By this point, Liv is up to speed with the Doctor, knowing about his previous incarnations and describing his last body, i.e. who she met in *Robophobia*, as the 'hat and umbrella' Doctor.

The Eleven is so impressed with Liv that he considers taking her on as his 'companion'. Instead, the Doctor gets a new companion while tracking down the Eleven: Helen Sinclair, played primarily by Hattie Morahan. Helen joins the TARDIS in *The Red Lady* (2015), inspired by the first ever *Doctor Who* producer, Verity Lambert, notably both succeeding in a male-dominated industry. As such, Helen, a specialist in translation for the Department of Linguistics at the National Museum in London, 1963, sees her inadequate colleague, Timothy, being promoted ahead of her. Professor Garland argues that Helen's temperament (which he believes is shared by most women) puts him off. She slams the door on him when he suggests she should be starting a family. Helen isn't Garland's assistant: Professor Pritchett is her superior, and while he's sympathetic, he's just happy not to lose her as his assistant. It's possible that Helen is on secondment to the National Museum, as the sign on her door reads, 'Helen Sinclair, language scholar, British Museum,' though perhaps the two names are interchangeable. When the Doctor and Liv track a time anomaly to the period, thinking it's the Eleven, they meet Helen, who immediately calls security on them, and the pair leave for what will become their regular haunt: 107 Baker Street. While the Doctor is preoccupied with mulling over their search for the Eleven, Liv is more practical and refocuses their efforts on the mysterious tablet at the National Gallery. Helen is understandably affected by Pritchett's death, especially as she can hear his last gasps as she's trying to get into him. She soon takes the Doctor and Liv into her confidence, fortunately, so after Garland fires her when part of the collection goes missing (it was taken by the Doctor to save the world), she goes home to find them waiting for her in the TARDIS. The Doctor's impressed with her, but so is Liv, and their mutual respect is so great that Helen's joining the team feels like a joint decision.

The Galileo Trap takes the trio to Florence in 1639, where they meet Galileo Galilei and Helen is overjoyed at now being able to understand Latin, thanks to the TARDIS' translation circuits, when she reads the tombstone of a Roman called Gaius Julius Epilichus. She's further inspired by Galileo, who tells her to go and see the wonders of the universe; and so, when the Doctor offers to take Helen home, to Tooting, while he and Liv go on looking for the Eleven, she says she wants to go with them. She still defers to Liv's experience: when the Doctor wanders off and tells them not to follow in *Scenes from Her Life* (2016), Helen asks Liv, 'You've done this more than I have – what's the standard amount of time we leave it before we follow him?' Liv swiftly concludes it's about three minutes. In *The Satanic Mill*, in a quick run-down before they do indeed find the Eleven, Liv explains regeneration to Helen too.

In subsequent adventures, the Doctor, Liv, and Helen come up against the Weeping Angels and Meddling Monk in *The Side of the Angels* (2017's *Doom Coalition 4*); visit San Francisco, 1906, in *The Gift* (2016) while searching for another rogue Time Lord, Caleera, aka the Red Lady, otherwise known as *The Sonomancer*; and try for a holiday in Stegmoor, 2017, in *Beachhead*, in which Helen mulls over the possibility that she and her family are still alive during this period. The Doctor warns her of the dangers of tracking them down, but she nonetheless does so, facilitated by Liv lying for her, taking a taxi to London from Calcot in August, 1998 (*Absent Friends*). She's unhappy to find her childhood home replaced by a block of flats, and, while pretending to be her own daughter Ruth, she is more distraught when she finds her brother, George, living there, as he tells her he wishes she'd never come: Helen's apparent theft and firing from the National Museum, followed by her disappearance, had sullied the Sinclair name. Meanwhile, the Doctor and Liv investigate a series of calls made to people in Calcot from deceased loved ones: the Doctor is confused by Liv's angered reaction to hearing her dead father, Kal Chenka, over the phone, recalling their hikes together through the mountains of Kaldor. 'You just don't understand people at all, do you?' she lashes out at the Doctor, leading her to open up more about the circumstances of his passing, namely that she was away with work when Kal fell ill and didn't get the correct treatment as he was misdiagnosed. Liv wishes she'd been there to use her training as a Med-tech to save him. In London, after George tells Helen that their parents passed away shortly after Helen went missing, as did their other brother, Harry, she argues that their father always mistreated Helen and her mother anyway. When he learns of their deception, the Doctor angrily scolds Liv and Helen – 'I can't believe the pair of you could be so stupid' – but ultimately forgives them when both have heart-to-hearts with their fathers by phone, granted by the time distortion affecting Calcot.

Their travels with the Doctor also see Liv and Helen meeting River Song, the Doctor's future wife. Aside from her doctorate from Luna University, River, at this point, has five Master's from the Sorbonne in five alternative timelines, and an honorary membership of the Royal Society (*The Sonomancer*). River may be a genius, but even she can't crack a code of the mining capsule that she's locked inside, given it has seventeen-million, five-hundred and fifty thousand possible combinations. Fortunately, Helen rescues her with the Eighth Doctor's sonic screwdriver. River insists that she can't meet this incarnation of the Doctor just yet, so when she saves Liv from the Eleven using Venusian aikido (a practice the Third Doctor similarly specialised in), she goes by the name of Professor Melody Malone, then leaves them while setting up a 'pointer to another rendezvous' with the Doctor, Liv, and Helen. River flits back into Helen and Liv's lives in *The Eighth Piece* and *The Doomsday Chronometer* (2016), while dressed as a nun and calling herself Sister Cantica, and disguises herself using a psychic wimple that makes her look somewhat like Rita Hayworth. In fact, River travels a fair amount with Helen using the vortex manipulator, the twosome going to Leonardo da Vinci's studio in the sixteenth century, Rennes-le-Château in the seventeenth century, Temple Church in May 1941, the Louvre and below the Vatican in the 1960s. River's acknowledgement of the name 'Octavian' places these adventures, in River's timeline, after *The Time of Angels / Flesh and Stone*, given that she's 'engaged in a manner of speaking' to Father Octavian in that TV serial.

When River does meet the Eighth Doctor, she considers him

'idealistic' and 'naïve' possibly for, at that point in his history, refusing to take part in the Time War (*The Rulers of the Universe*, part of *The Diary of River Song: Series One* in 2015). Still, they get on well in *The Crucible of Souls* (2016), which adds the interesting caveat that the TARDIS won't always do as even River asks it to – perhaps a shock, given that she is a 'child of the TARDIS.' In *Songs of Love* (2017), the Doctor temporarily remembers meeting River before, specifically in his fourth, fifth, sixth, and seventh bodies. River also explores the Capitol of Gallifrey, and establishes that she, like the Doctor, has a binary vascular system.

When the duplicitous Padraculomar III (Padrac for short), Lord President of Gallifrey, ejects an escape shuttle containing the Doctor, Liv, and Helen into the Time Vortex, hurtling towards the end of the universe, Helen's anxiety leads her into admitting she often feels useless next to the Doctor and Liv's experience. This isn't helped by the Doctor immediately poo-pooing Helen's 'leap of faith' suggestion to get out of their predicament, which prompts a snarking Liv to urge him to apologise. 'I worry for that man sometimes,' Liv confesses to Helen in private. 'I really do.'

It's here that their conflicting attitudes to life really show. 'There's nothing you can say to me that I haven't said to a hundred grieving families,' Liv says. 'It's horrible every time. That's why I try and try until there's no hope at all, and then... I *keep* trying, hoping for a miracle.' When Helen argues that miracles don't happen, Liv retorts, 'Not if you don't make them.' Once the Doctor has said he's sorry to Helen, they find that her initial idea *does* work, helping Helen to realise her own worth and take stock in Liv's never-say-die mindset. Still, to further prove herself, Helen seemingly sacrifices herself in *Stop the Clock* (2017), but Liv's positive attitude rubs off on the Doctor as he considers the possibility that an artron trail hailing from the Battle TARDIS that Helen 'died' in means she's still alive. As the TARDIS works out where Helen's ended up, the Doctor and Liv are called to London, 27th and 28th August 1940, by Winston Churchill, in *Their Finest Hour*. Liv seemingly dies too, but the Doctor is certain she'll have found a way out; she's got an equally substantial faith in him as Liv tells the Heliyon during interrogation, 'The person you're after eats things like you for breakfast. Oh, you might have a big scary ship, but I've got the Doctor. You want to take him on? Go ahead. Bring me some popcorn.' Liv indeed escapes them, alongside Pilot Officer Wilhelm Rozycki, who then dies the following day: Liv is cut to the quick at hearing that, despite surviving alien forces, he passed away the very next day, killed by another human.

They're reunited with Helen in *World of Damnation*, on the prison-turned-asylum, Rykerzon, an artificial satellite in orbit around Colony 23, where Helen's been trying to help the Eleven recuperate and come to terms with his mental battles, and then fight off the Kandyman (from the TV story, *The Happiness Patrol*) in *Sweet Salvation* (both 2018).

Escape to Kaldor begins a new era for Liv, although not a welcome one for her as she reluctantly returns to her home planet – despite her admitting she no longer feels like she *does* come from Kaldor. There, she sees her sister, Tula (Claire Rushbrook), again; not that they particularly get on, as Tula didn't visit their father, Kal, when he was ill, instead favouring her career at the Kaldor City Company, causing a rift between her and her sister. Each also believed the other to be their parents' favourite child. Tula incorrectly thought Kal hated robots; in fact, he loved them, but not what they had done to society. Nonetheless, Tula has an altruistic side, going undercover to free humans at an exclusive complex owned by the Company – where she finds Liv and Helen, plus Kit Laver, who trained with Liv back in the day, but who dropped out of training. His meddling with the Robots on Kaldor led to his death, proving that Liv was right when she called him 'a bit of an idiot.'

Liv asks to stay on Kaldor to make amends with Tula, but only for a year: while the Doctor and Helen fast-forward by dematerialising and materialising again twelve months later, Liv takes this time to look into further troubles with the Vocs, Super-Vocs, and Dums, as well as getting a job at the Kaldor City Hospital, where she trained (*The Robots of Life*, the premier episode of 2019's *The Robots: Volume One*). Liv and Tula's investigations into the Sons of Kaldor, an organisation intent on returning power to the Founding Families, find them trying to connect with Toos and Poul, the survivors of Storm Mine 4 (from the TV story, *The Robots of Death*), and aiming to stop enhancement chips that ultimately lead them into a malicious Recovery Training Course in *Force of Nature* (from *The Robots: Volume Six* in 2023). Though things don't go according to plan, when the Doctor comes back for Liv in *The Final Hour*, he thanks her for helping him through one of the toughest periods of his life and Liv rejoins him and Helen. To cheer Liv up, he takes them to experience a classic European Christmas in 2018's *Better Watch Out/Fairytale of Salzburg*, but instead, the Doctor and Liv are condemned to 'hell,' leaving Helen to fix things. It takes her decades to learn to fly the TARDIS, so by the time she saves her friends, she's on the verge of death. Though the Doctor seemingly can't tell that Helen has now aged, Liv finds a way to restore her to her youth.

The trio repeatedly come up against the Ravenous, creatures that eat regenerative energy, i.e. a Time Lord's natural predator. *Deeptime Frontier* and *Seizure* (2019) see the Doctor, Liv, and Helen stranded on a planetoid and surrounded by the clown-like monsters, but they're rescued by an old friend of the Doctor, Under Cardinal Rasmus. Hearing he's a Time Lord and drawing on her experiences, Liv asks, 'Can I ask up front, are you evil? Because, usually...'

This mentality holds Liv in good stead, as she soon meets the Eleven again, as well as, in *Companion Piece* (2019), his earlier incarnation, the Nine. During this story, she teams up with the Eighth Doctor's other companions, plus River, who has attempted to retrieve the body of First Doctor companion, Katarina, from space, only for it to be stolen by the Nine. To learn more about the Ravenous, they're forced into an uneasy partnership with the Eleven, and in *Whisper*, tensions are high as Liv and Helen agree to keep an eye on the Eleven, certain he's lying about getting his previous incarnations under control. This must be especially hard for Helen, who attempted to rehabilitate him previously on Rykerzon, so it's Helen who tries to defend him. Liv, steely as ever, warns the Eleven that she's got a gun. She tells the Doctor, 'You need someone to pull the trigger.' Though their friendship is threatened, Liv considers leaving the TARDIS and Helen agrees to go with her. Helen, however, is soon kidnapped by Missy, and Liv has to pair up with the War Master, who she initially suspects is an incarnation of the Eleven; Helen never learns who Missy is, and the Doctor presumes she's talking about the Rani (*Day of the Master*). The Master naturally turns on Liv, shooting her – only for her to start regenerating. The Eleven has used the Crucible of Souls to spread regenerative energy, in an effort to feed the Ravenous, thus accidentally saving Liv. In return, Liv shoots the Master in the arm, and goes on to say that he really shouldn't test her, given that she wouldn't enjoy murdering most people but with others, she'd 'throw a party and put up balloons.' After being reunited with Helen, Liv saves the Doctor from the Ravenous, sacrificing her newfound ability to regenerate, but allowing the three of them to escape in a badly damaged TARDIS.

While Helen and Liv are clearly close, Liv is instead attracted to Tania Bell, a transgender woman played by Rebecca Root, in the *Stranded* series, from 2020 to 2022. During this period, the Doctor, Liv, and Helen are left in London, 2020, as the TARDIS undergoes repairs following the Ravenous, meaning they have to live at 107 Baker Street. Though still some half a century from her time, a lot rides on Helen as she has the most experience with staying on Earth, meaning she's the one who primarily deals with bills, asks Liv to get a job to support them further, and shows the Doctor the ropes as a landlord, giving him a crash course in letting agencies, parking permits, council tax, and liability insurance. In *Lost Property*, the Curator (ostensibly a future incarnation of the Doctor, seen on TV in *The Day of the Doctor*) seemingly remembers the burden Helen has on her shoulders, so when she follows him to the Under Gallery, he asks her to please keep an eye on the Doctor, before disappearing. Helen then becomes a History teacher, having to brush up on some recent events, seeing as she comes from the 1960s.

Now working at Sanjit's convenience store, Liv is adjusting to life on twenty-first century Earth surprisingly well, though a large part of this, Helen suggests, is her growing friendship with Tania. Unbeknown to them, Tania moved into Flat One, 107 Baker Street, to keep an eye on the Doctor in 2014, knowing he'd soon show back up – though knowing he can't know of the organisation until his tenth incarnation, Tania works for Torchwood, but can't tell anyone. Still, her relationship with Liv blossoms further when Liv is shot by a robber (who kills Sanjit), falls unconscious, and agrees to go on a dinner date with Tania when she wakes up (*Wild Animals*). In *Divine Intervention*, Liv then trusts Tania with the truth of who she, the Doctor, and Helen are, unaware that Tania's still reporting back, albeit begrudgingly given that she's grown to care for them all, to Andy Davison (Tom Price), formerly a PC as seen in *Torchwood* on TV, but now working for the alien hunters officially.

In *Dead Time* (2021), the Doctor thinks he's got the TARDIS working again so he takes Helen, Liv, and Tania on a test drive, accompanied by Andy who forces his way on board, and Robin Bright-Thompson (played by Joel James Davison, son of Peter Davison), a youngster who also lives in a flat in 107 Baker Street with his father, Ken. Robin idolises the Doctor, but as this is an experiment in a recovering TARDIS, the Doctor promises to take Robin on a trip 'next time'; instead, Robin stows away, and they all find themselves some six million years in the future, during mankind's Third Glorious Empire. Seeing a devastated London panics Andy, so Liv is charged with calming him down, her medical training once more coming handy. Robin goes missing, and the Doctor gives Tania a TARDIS key so that she, Andy, and Helen can wait in safety. The ship, however, doesn't let them in, which the Doctor later puts down to it wanting everyone to stay together; it doesn't really ring true, though, so the TARDIS seems not to trust Andy and Tania – sure enough, as Liv learns about Torchwood, Andy confesses to Tania that the organisation was disbanded months ago (following *God Among Us 3* in 2019). While in the far future, Robin is also scanned by Earth Endstation 6, and we later learn, in *What Just Happened?*, that it's considerably slowed down his ageing process. Robin's resentment for his father grows when they return to 2020, only to find that his father is dragging Robin away from his new-found friends by moving to Edinburgh.

Andy wins the Doctor round somewhat by telling him that he'll help track down parts to repair the TARDIS, leading them to visit the 1970s (*UNIT Dating*); Helen and Liv help them by adapting the TARDIS key and radio transmissions so they can send messages through time via Morse code. We also find out that Helen had a brother called Albert, who was arrested and shunned by their father for being homosexual. Helen later meets 'Albie' again when a Weeping Angel sends her back to 1963, and is shocked to find that he lives less than a mile away from her old place of work, the National Museum (*Albie's Angels*). Helen gets to know both her brother and his partner, Trev Bailey, a guitarist in a band; when both Albie and Bailey are sent to the 1890s by another Weeping Angel, they live with Professor George Litefoot, the pathologist best associated with Henry Gordon Jago and seen on TV in *The Talons of Weng-Chiang*. The Doctor leaves them with a tape recorder, so they can send messages for Helen through time – including a very special *Song for Helen*.

Further trips through time include to 1941 to investigate an unexploded bomb (*Baker Street Irregulars*); to 2050, experiencing an altered future, courtesy of Divine Intervention, a group responsible for the subjugation of mankind (*The Long Way Round*); and, for Liv and Andy, a possible future in which Liv is heartbroken to find Tania, deemed a 'non-conformer' by the Divine Intervention, dying in her arms (*Snow*). This brings Liv and Tania in 2020 closer, as well as Liv and Andy, who helps her deal with her grief.

It turns out that this isn't the right 2020, but one that's been corrupted and changed by the TARDIS' malfunctioning. They avert a disastrous future in which Robin, now going under the name Mr Bird, becomes a dictator and leader of the Divine Intervention (detailed throughout the *Stranded 4* boxset in 2022), and Liv, Helen, Tania, and Andy manipulate their TARDIS keys again to reset the timeline, leaving them all in the real 2020 (*The Keys of Baker Street*). This leads to their *Best Year Ever*, in which they work to reform Divine Intervention on Robin's suggestion, with Andy taking over as CEO. Liv and Tania spend the Covid-19 lockdown together, but, sometime in early 2021, when the Doctor announces the TARDIS is working properly again, their relationship, it seems, isn't enough to keep Liv there – though Tania and Andy turn down offers for more trips in time and space, Liv and Helen happily accept. From Tania's perspective, however, Liv returns just moments later, telling her she's going to stay. Andy is soon working for Torchwood again, being sent back to the 1950s using a vortex manipulator (*Torchwood Soho*), while, around a year in their future, Liv and Tania meet first the Ninth Doctor (*Flatpack*, in 2022's *The Ninth Doctor Adventures: Hidden Depths*) then the Twelfth Doctor in *The Audio Novels: The Chaos Cascade* (2024).

Yet in the time between Liv leaving and coming back, she and Helen have countless more adventures with the Eighth Doctor – including encountering the Daleks again (*Paradox of the Daleks*, in the 2022 *What Lies Inside?* set), getting invited to the funeral of one of the Doctor's old friends (*Here Lies Drax*, using the Time Lord grifter introduced in *The Armageddon Factor*), and meeting *The Love Vampires* (in 2022's *Connections* boxset). Though both Helen and Liv have links to the past, the lure of time and space are too strong for these much-loved companions to ignore for very long.

Other companions created for Big Finish audio plays include Gemma and Samson Griffin, Mary Shelley, and Lady Audacity Montague.

Gemma and Samson Griffin, respectively played by Lizzie Hopley and Lee Ingleby, only actually appear in one audio story (*Terror Firma* in 2005) and a couple of short stories. They meet the Doctor in Folkestone Library and follow him into the TARDIS. They have several adventures, and are left in 1816 while the Doctor investigates a distress call. They resume their travels with the Doctor after he journeys with Mary Shelley, until they arrive on the time cruiser, Nekkistani, where they meet Davros (who takes control of their minds). He attempts to use Samson against the Doctor, but once beaten, the Doctor frees Samson from the Daleks' control. The Doctor continues his travels with Charley and C'rizz after Samson and Gemma have been reunited.

Mary Shelley (Julie Cox) appears in four audio adventures (from *Mary's Story* in 2009 to *Army of Death* in 2011). She meets the Doctor in 1816, seeing him apparently coming back to life (no doubt inspiring aspects of *Frankenstein*), and joins him for an unknown period of time. She leaves him eventually after an encounter with the Bone Lord, and realises she is fearful of the Doctor's one constant companion, death. Her time travelling in the TARDIS is at odds with her appearance in the TV episode, *The Haunting of Villa Diodati*, opposite the Thirteenth Doctor, so we might infer that one of these versions is from a parallel world.

Tamsin Drew, played by Niky Wardley, appears in seven audio adventures (from *Situation Vacant* in 2010 to *To the Death* in 2011). She meets the Doctor by answering an ad for a new companion, which we later discover has actually been placed by the Monk. She fails in her audition, but is later saved since the other contenders want to join him for nefarious purposes. Their adventures together take them to Nevermore, a volcanic planet in the constellation of Cassiopeia with a culture inspired by the works of Edgar Allan Poe; The Abbey of Kells, Ireland, in 1006; and the Martian moon, Deimos, where she meets the Ice Warriors. She leaves the Doctor because he won't sacrifice Lucie to save thousands of humans on Mars; Tamsin then takes up travelling with the Monk who convinces her that the Doctor is evil. During the Daleks' second invasion of Earth, she discovers the part the Monk plays in the incursion and she sides with the Doctor, Lucie, Susan, and Alex. She's exterminated by the Daleks, and the Doctor berates the Monk for his part in her demise; the rogue Time Lord obviously grew close to Tamsin and so, despite her calling him despicable in her final moments, the Monk still mourns her.

2023's addition to the TARDIS brings Big Finish's Eighth Doctor audio stories full circle as Lady Audacity Montague, played by Jaye Griffiths, travels with Charley Pollard, most likely early on in Charley's journeys with the Doctor before meeting C'rizz. Audacity is a stargazer, deemed unusual for a respectable lady in 1812, and while looking at a shooting star through her telescope, she inadvertently makes contact with *The Devouring*, a mysterious creature that consumes everyone Audacity is close to. In order to escape it, and save Audacity's husband, Ignatius, the Doctor offers to take her away from her native 1800s in the TARDIS, and she soon meets his other current companion, Charley – that is, following her first trip into time and space, which finds her at the heart of *The Great Cyber-War* after they land on the Aurum, a space station apparently made of gold. Despite refusing to acknowledge that the Doctor is a Time Lord as she thinks it's too entitled and pompous, Audacity enjoys a privileged way of life, attending balls, reading voraciously, and having experience with horse riding, semaphore, and fencing.

In *The Scent of Blood*, a 2019 collaboration between the BBC and Penguin, the Doctor meets another on-off companion, James MacFarlane, a journalist in the 1890s investigating vampires in Edinburgh. James, like a few individuals before him, such as Molly, thinks Gallifrey is in Ireland. Together, they find a den of vampires, but learn that they're not the ones affecting the locals; instead it's a Gallifreyan Bowship, still waging the Time Lords' war on the species, following up on the TV story, *State of Decay*.

James' inquisitive nature takes him to Cardiff for *The Code of Flesh* (2022), and, meeting the Doctor again, he quizzes him about the TARDIS, though the Doctor is reticent to say too much. James proves himself to be considerably braver than most, following his instincts to get an invitation to an 'anaesthesia frolics' event after interviewing one of its victims who's been left with a hand and two fingers missing. 2023's *The Teeth of Ice* then finds James at the MacReady Base near the South Pole in the 1900s. The Doctor is the base's medic, and by now, the two are old friends; when the Doctor leaves, he comments that they're bound to meet again as they've been drawn together like magnets. They're at odds when the Doctor sets himself up to blow up a ship, but James takes this responsibility on himself, something which aggravates the Doctor. Understandably, then, James is concerned about meeting the Doctor again in *The Force of Death* (2024), when the pair reunite to look into zombies in County Connemara, Galway. This Doctor, however, seems to have moved on, and tells James he's had a change of heart – hinting perhaps that he's now aware of the oncoming Time War or that he knows something about James' future.

Unusually, James MacFarlane has so far been written solely by one person, Andrew Lane, who no doubt has a plan in mind for this intrepid journalist.

In Comics

Both the novels and audios have gone to great lengths to say that each range exists in parallel universes to each other, but the comic strip from *Doctor Who Magazine* which ran from 1996 to 2005 is lent some level of credibility, given that later showrunner, Russell T Davies, offered the creative team a chance to link it in directly with show's 2005 revival. They had to turn it down, but this ultimately led to the creation of the War Doctor, so it all worked out for the best. Nonetheless, those working on the comics for *DWM* gave us some of the most consistently strong Eighth Doctor stories – and even included a rare Expanded Universe appearance of Grace Holloway!

The exact behind-the-scenes details of Grace's appearances are unknown as she's co-owned by Universal Studios, makers of *The TV Movie*, so while she makes cameos and gets mentioned here and there, her showing up in tales that add to her character development is much rarer. Actress Daphne Ashbrook has been in Big Finish audios, for instance, but can't play Grace; similarly, the company can't use Chang Lee (though he was in *Observer Effect*, a short story in the 2004 collection, *Short Trips: 2040*, which tells us that Chang became involved in Chinese-American space projects, hoping to lead mankind beyond our solar system, and that his son, Chang Hu, was born in 2009). Grace does, however, appear in the Titan Comic story, *The Body Politic*, released in 2013 but set in February 2000 during the period when she's still working as a surgeon in San Francisco. She's shocked to see the Eighth Doctor on her doorstep and this time agrees to take a few trips in the TARDIS to 'see the sights.' Instead, she's overwhelmed by the experience and asks to go home. More significant are her appearances in *DWM*'s *The Fallen* and *The Glorious Dead*.

Throughout this run, the Doctor is accompanied by a plethora of companions, all of whose stories merge together to form one engaging narrative, including the first legitimate LGBT companion, Izzy Sinclair, introduced in 1996. (Like Fitz, she also appears in one audio play from Big Finish, in 2009's *The Company of Friends: Izzy's Story*.)

Izzy first appears in *Endgame*, this incarnation of the Doctor's debut in the *DWM* comic. The Doctor is immediately receptive to Izzy as she's a friend of Maxwell Edison, a much-loved *DWM* character who'd been introduced in the Fifth Doctor story, *Stars Fell on Stockbridge*. Edison is the town's local UFO hunter, extending the hand of friendship to alien visitors; Izzy, being a sci-fi fan and having created a fantastical fiction for herself after finding out she was adopted, is one of the only people in Stockbridge to believe Maxwell's stories. After saving Stockbridge from the Celestial Toymaker, the Doctor offers to take Max with him in the TARDIS once more, but he turns it down. The Doctor extends the offer to Izzy, but he can't finish the sentence before she gives out an enthusiastic 'you bet!'

Izzy's first trip takes her to Earth in the fifty-first century – a more dystopian time than what she's expecting. 'Doctor, you can't be serious,' she says. 'Where are the spaceships, the hovercars, the fabulous cities of silver and gold?' Things don't really let up for Izzy:

on the Satelloid, Icarus Falling, orbiting an artificial star created in *The Keep*, she meets the Daleks, who use the rift created by that sun to delete 'imperfect' Daleks from parallel dimensions. Of course, those alternative Daleks start to invade this universe (*Fire and Brimstone*). Izzy's already very protective of the Doctor, perhaps a result of learning about him through Max, and intends to steal a spaceship and save the Doctor from the Daleks herself.

There is nonetheless some friction between them sometimes, albeit somewhat light-hearted and cheeky. She trusts him, but isn't afraid to stand up to him either, wanting to do her own thing. In *By Hook or By Crook*, for instance, she wants to finish reading a history book called *Tar-Ka-Nom: A History of a City State* before they go explore the place; the Doctor leaves her to it... and is soon arrested for seemingly murdering seven locals. It's Izzy's quick thinking – realising that she'd actually read about this very murder case in the book – that saves them both from execution. She clearly takes to this life with some ease, likely due to her love and deep knowledge of sci-fi. In *Fire and Brimstone*, she's overjoyed to see 'top space people' and greets them with Spock's Live Long and Prosper salute from *Star Trek*. She further acknowledges the *Alien* franchise and Terry Pratchett's *Discworld* books. In the later *Beautiful Freak*, we see that she has a Darth Vader poster and a Thunderbird 2 toy in her room in the TARDIS, alongside a snow globe depicting Stockbridge. She starts off as an excitable character, often thrilled by her time travelling with the Doctor, and although she goes through considerable hardships and challenges, she's ultimately a hopeful and clear-thinking companion.

Her cultural intelligence further prepares Izzy for her meeting vampires in *Tooth and Claw* (the comic which shares a name with a 2006 TV episode starring the Tenth Doctor), but she's still understandably scared when the Doctor falls victim to the vampiric infection. He defeats the bloodthirsty alien spacecraft, Cucurbite, but nearly at the cost of his own life.

In a way, Fey Truscott-Sade, an undercover agent for the British government, is somewhat like Mel Bush: we meet her in *Tooth and*

Claw, but she's apparently already met the Doctor. When she encounters vampires in 1939, she actually calls the TARDIS for help using a Stattenheim Summoner, a device that looks like a whistle, implying that the Doctor quickly learned to trust her during their previous encounter(s), so much so that he gives her something akin to the Space-Time Telegraph he entrusted to the Brigadier during his UNIT days. She proves her worth especially quickly, piloting the TARDIS (using its Manual, which Izzy couldn't have read, as it's written in Gallifreyan) to Gallifrey in order to save the Doctor's life after he's infected by a bioweapon, and thus becoming a companion.

In *The Final Chapter*, Izzy has to come to terms with not only having to trust someone she doesn't know, but also the Doctor seemingly regenerating. Fortunately, *Wormwood* reveals that this is a deception – this new Doctor is, in fact, a Time Lord construct named Shayde and the real Eighth Doctor is disguised using a personal Chameleon circuit – and Izzy is overjoyed to carry on travelling with the Doctor. Fey leaves at the same time, albeit temporarily, as she merges with Shayde, to become Feyde, and departs the TARDIS so she has time to come to terms with her new life.

The Doctor and Izzy's trip to 2001, in *The Fallen*, is significant for reintroducing Grace Holloway, now working in London in conjunction with MI6, but all is not rosy between her and the Doctor: the latter finds out Grace is conducting experiments on the DNA that she scraped off her arm, i.e. what the Master spat at her in *The TV Movie*. The Doctor thinks this is dangerous and irresponsible, but it's partly the Doctor's fault for promising big things for her in her future, which she takes as something to do with her scientific curiosity; she deduces that she's destined to use the substance to splice together human and Time Lord DNA to create a regenerative ability in mankind. The pair part ways on better terms: the Doctor apologises for meddling and she vows to destroy all traces of the Master's alien substance. They kiss again before he leaves.

Grace very much represents what could have been, so much so that she appears as the Doctor's wife in an alternate reality in *The Glorious Dead*. In the story, the Master returns and reveals he's been manipulating events, thanks to his connection to the TARDIS as a result of *The TV Movie*, including pushing the Doctor into seeing Grace again and meeting Kroton. Kroton is one of the more unusual companions ever – a Cyberman who has retained his emotions. He first appears in a back-up strip of *Doctor Who Weekly* in 1979, returning once the following year. This soulful Cyberman is never forgotten, however, and he comes back again in 1999 in *Doctor Who Magazine* in a story that sees him battling Sontarans. He joins the Doctor and Izzy later that year in *The Company of Thieves*, after the pair help him fight off space pirates on the Qutrusian Cargo Freighter X-703. It's a good thing too, as, in *The Glorious Dead*, he and Izzy are forced to survive in the ravished world of Paradost alone, when the Doctor is taken into the Glory, the heart of the Omniversal Spectrum, an intersection of multiverses described as 'the ocean of reality' and 'the totality of existence.'

Izzy is even shrunk by the Master's Tissue Compression Eliminator, but she finds a way back to normal size, bypassing what's apparently killed many others. She then uses a mnemonic crystal to help Kroton remember his life pre-conversion, including his wife and childhood sweetheart, Shallia. Kroton becomes effectively immortal and stays to look after the Omniversal Spectrum, further saving the Doctor and banishing the Master.

It's not long before there's another new face on the TARDIS. Destriianatos, called Destrii for short, is a unique comic-exclusive companion, in that she was, at one stage, intended to witness the Eighth Doctor's regeneration into the Ninth Doctor, then travel on in the *DWM* comic with the latter incarnation. The BBC vetoed the idea of Destrii travelling with the Ninth Doctor before *Rose*, and the creative team behind *DWM* politely declined Russell T Davies' offer to include the regeneration in the comic strip on the grounds that they'd have to write out Destrii before her time. Apparently a fan of the comic, Davies reportedly completely empathised, and so instead, Destrii became the last *DWM* comic companion of the Eighth Doctor but also one without a definitive ending, instead walking off into the horizon with the Time Lord, echoing the Seventh Doctor and Ace's last hurrah in *Survival* (though there is a coda in the Twelfth Doctor tale, *The Stockbridge Showdown*).

You wouldn't predict Destrii's importance in *DWM* lore from her first appearance in *Ophidius*, nor that she'd end up as a companion at all. The Doctor and Izzy meet her on the titular snake that acts as a starship after it consumes the TARDIS. Destrii's had it pretty rough, having survived inside Ophidius while evading its controllers, the Mobox, who she saves the Doctor and Izzy from. She's obviously resilient and takes the pair to her hidden den where she bonds with Izzy over their desire to explore. Sadly, it's a lie and she tricks Izzy into using a machine that swaps their bodies; Destrii's plan is to escape with the Doctor while her pursuers are after her old body, which now houses Izzy's consciousness. Destrii can't bring herself to shoot her old body though, so even though it seems she's detached from it, she has some emotional attachment anyway. Still, she finds the Doctor and he's taken in by her deception for a very short time – that is, until she guns someone down without a care in the world. The Doctor realises something is up, just as a vengeful Mobox tracks Destrii down; the real Izzy watches in horror, from inside Destrii's body, as the Mobox disintegrates Izzy's real body.

Izzy really struggles with her new situation. In *Beautiful Freak*, she starts to suffocate, not realising her amphibious body needs to be submerged in water periodically. The Doctor takes her to the TARDIS swimming pool but she admits that she feels cold and ugly, telling him, 'I just want to die.' It's shocking to hear a companion talk this way (though she's not the first to consider suicide, as Turlough actually attempted it in *Enlightenment*). Though the Doctor feels helpless, he tries to console her as he too has felt like a stranger in his own body, and the experience brings them closer. Still, by the time they land in Coyoacan, Mexico, on 2nd November 1941, she holds back from exploring, scared that she still looks like an alien and admits to 'chickening out' for the first time in her life (*The Way of All Flesh*). Artist Frida Kahlo tries to help her accept herself by painting a portrait of Izzy in her old body, telling her that she also shouldn't forget where she came from. The Doctor then takes her to a marine research facility called the Argus on the planet Kyrol so Izzy can learn more about her body (*Children of the Revolution*).

Izzy's kidnapping leads the Doctor to contact Feyde again. In the intervening time, Fey returns to 1939, where she carries on the good fight against the Nazis, as revealed in *Me and My Shadow*. In *Oblivion*, the Doctor sends her a sub-ether summons so she can help find Izzy, who's been taken by Destrii's mother, the Matriax Scalamanthia, believing it's her daughter. While getting Izzy back, the Doctor and Fey find Izzy's original body alive and well, with Destrii's consciousness trapped inside: the Mobox keep and reconstitute 'patterns' of those they disintegrate, so the Doctor rescues her and locates Izzy. When Izzy and Destrii are returned to their respective bodies, they're afforded glimpses into each other's lives, so Izzy learns that Destrii was raised in arenas on Oblivion, repeatedly having to fight for her life but desperately trying to win her own freedom. Though an anger-fuelled Destrii kills her own mother, Izzy convinces her not to destroy Oblivion altogether, and Destrii gets away, alongside her uncle, Count Jodafra.

Having seen Destrii's fractious relationship with her mother, Izzy realises she wants to see her adoptive parents again, so she asks the Doctor to take her back home. Before both leave, Feyde encourages Izzy to accept her sexuality, and the pair share a kiss. This time, the TARDIS gets its space-time coordinates spot on and returns Izzy to just moments after she's left. When her parents ask how her day's gone, Izzy enthuses that it's been 'pretty busy. I went for a ride. I met a few people…'

The Doctor, it seems, isn't without a companion for long, as he meets Destrii and Jodafra again a few strips later, in *Bad Blood*. When the TARDIS lands in America, 1875, he soon finds that General George Custer and nineteenth century Native American tribal chief, Tatanka Yotanka, are being attacked by the Wendigo. Destrii is horrified to learn that Jodafra intends to feed local children to the creature and foils his plan, showing she's learned a great deal about the value of life and likely coming to terms with her own harsh childhood. In return, however, Jodafra beats her and leaves her to die – only for the Doctor to save her by taking her to a hospital called Hippocrates Base (*Sins of the Fathers*). After defending the space station from the Zeronites, the Doctor officially asks Destrii to join him on board the TARDIS, an offer she accepts with a kiss (something he's less than pleased about). 'We're gonna be great together, Doctor, you'll see!' she enthuses. 'We'll be just like Starsky and Hutch… or Butch and Sundance…' As it turns out, Destrii watched a lot of TV as a kid, absorbing much human culture. She also takes a holographic projector necklace with her so that she can appear human when they next touch down on Earth.

Their last regular *DWM* story, *The Flood*, takes them to Camden Market, London, in 2005, where they experience rain that makes people more aggressive. This is an experiment carried out by futuristic Cybermen, who use cloaking devices that means the Doctor can't see them; Destrii, however, can, and though she puts up a good fight, she's taken by the Cybermen as they're unable to convert her alien biology. (During the Cybermen's invasion, we briefly see Izzy, who's still joyfully recalling her time with the Doctor as something that 'seemed like a daydream' but she always 'held onto the truth.') After being separated for a short time, the Doctor and Destrii are reunited, and the Time Lord offers to sacrifice his life for her – or, more accurately, his *lives*, as he seems to be open to giving the Cybermen the key to regeneration. Instead, he discovers that these Cybermen from the future are using the Time Vortex to travel back to the twenty-first century, and absorbs it to destroy them. Though absorbing so much vortex energy should kill him (or force him to regenerate, as in *The Parting of the Ways*), he breaks free from the Vortex in order to save Destrii when she's almost killed.

The Doctor and Destrii head off for new adventures. When

they land on another planet, Destrii asks where they are, and he happily replies, 'No idea. Absolutely no idea! Isn't that fantastic? Anything could be over that hill, Destrii. Anything! C'mon – let's go and find out...'

That's not entirely the end of the story, fortunately. Izzy is mentioned in *The Stockbridge Child* (2008) by Maxwell Edison, who tells the Tenth Doctor that she's gone travelling, and shortly after that, she joins Médecins Sans Frontières. Aged thirty-six, Izzy meets the Twelfth Doctor in *The Stockbridge Showdown* (2016) as she knocks out recurring antagonist, Josiah W. Dogbolter, then celebrates Max's birthday on the ancient city of Cornucopia – alongside Fourth Doctor companion, Sharon Allen (née Davies); Frobisher, who travelled with the Sixth and Seventh Doctor, and, unbeknown to the two of them, met the Eighth Doctor in *Where Nobody Knows Your Name*; Tenth Doctor companion, Majenta Pryce; and, of course, Destrii!

Paul McGann's incarnation of the Doctor finds another comic-exclusive companion in Josephine Day, courtesy of Titan's *The Eighth Doctor: A Matter of Life and Death*. The Doctor's attire (and the introductory page mentioning the likes of Charley, Lucie, and Molly) places the five-issue run later on in his tenure. The Doctor finds Josephine squatting in a house that he implies was owned by his third incarnation; he returns there to find his copy of *Jane Eyre*, but Josie has rearranged his bookshelves alphabetically – by title, not author. Josie herself is an artist whose paintings miraculously include Krotons, Ice Warriors, and Witherkin, immediately attracting the Doctor's attention. Her talents are supported by the community, with Mrs Fellowes, the landlady of the local pub, the White Hart, proudly displaying one of her pieces for all her punters to see. There are other mysteries surrounding her though, notably why she's swimming in alien animae particles that temporarily bring her paintings to life and who wrote a 'to do' list featuring five-dimensional space coordinates, a theatre show in 1866, and a party at Briarwood House, 1932, and why they did so. All this is enough for the Doctor to invite Josie on 'a little trip.'

Josie's first journey is to Lumin's World, at this point an apparent war zone, where she proves herself a classic companion by tripping over, hurting her ankle, and being infected by a transmogrifying agent that slowly turns its victims into crystal. She keeps a cool head and, in the face of her own death as there's no cure, she connects with the seeming attackers, relaying her belief that 'everyone matters. No matter who or what they are.' Resigned to her fate, Josie returns to the TARDIS after helping to save two species and stop the war, and she effectively saves herself by reasoning with the crystalline Spherions who expunge her of the infection. The Doctor then shows her a special room in the TARDIS which consists of a realistic-looking outdoor landscape, complete with mountains, sea, and sunset – perfect for her to paint.

She finds further inspiration from a trip to a mirror-image world and the horrors of an upper-class party where the guests are taken over by vegetation, until they reach their final destination on the list: a Bakri resurrection barge, where the consciousnesses of dead people are imprinted on the brains of synthetic individuals who, as it turns out, have minds of their own and take issue with them being overtaken. Josie doesn't like it there, immediately calling the place 'sickening.' She likes it even less when her true identity is revealed: she's a living portrait of the egotistical Lady Josephine, whose personal items were sold at auction when she passed away. Josie was bought by the Twelfth Doctor who left her on Earth in the house owned by his earlier incarnation so that she could travel with the Eighth Doctor; he also left the list based on memories of their travels. Luckily, the Eighth Doctor recognises Josie as an individual removed from Lady Josephine (who tries to destroy her portrait when she's resurrected into a synthetic body on the barge, but whose new visage is then taken over by its native, emerging mind) and wants to carry on travelling with her. Josie is overjoyed – the Doctor is too, as the Twelfth Doctor and Clara Oswald watch on from outside, the former even getting a tear in his eye as he looks back fondly on the good old days.

*

Last, but certainly not least, are Stacy Townsend and the Ice Warrior, Ssard, companions who an arguably larger audience has met, seeing as they begin their lives in the pages of *Radio Times* between 1996 and 1997, and later feature in the 1998 novel, *The Placebo Effect*. Stacy meets the Doctor after the Cybermen have attacked her space haulage freighter and converted her fiancé, Bill in 2246. She joins the Doctor on his travels, and later meets Ssard on Mars in 3998, who, after dealing with the treachery of High Lord Artix, accepts the Doctor's offer of a holiday. Stacy and Ssard leave the Doctor at the same time, and eventually become engaged and have three children. Later, they invite the Doctor to their wedding, and he attends with Sam Jones.

The Ninth Doctor
Christopher Eccleston

'You were fantastic. And, you know what? So was I!'
The Doctor – *The Parting of the Ways*

Suffering from survivor's guilt, a battle-hardened Doctor returns after having disappeared during the Last Great Time War. Sad and lonely in ways he's never been before, the Doctor has lost touch with his emotions, along with the reason why he travels. He's in need of a new companion, someone who can remind him of what he used to be. Enter Rose Tyler...

Rose Tyler – Billie Piper (*Rose* to *Doomsday* and *Partners in Crime,* and *Turn Left* to *Journey's End,* plus *The End of Time)*

Don't You Worry Child (Swedish House Mafia); *Toxic* (Britney Spears).

On the surface, Rose appears to be a very different kind of companion from those we've been used to, but when you consider her character, she's essentially a combination of Tegan and Ace. Much like the former, she's given a TARDIS key; we learn about her family; and we see her leave and return. Much like Ace, she develops deep feelings for the Doctor; she's from a London council estate; and her back-story is almost as important as the Doctor's, driving much of the ongoing narrative of the 2005-2006 show. In the pitch document, partly printed in the *Series One Companion* (*Doctor Who Magazine Special*), we're told that 'she loves [the Doctor], and he loves her. Simple as that. Not a kissy-kissy kind of love, this is *deeper*'.

Rose actually meets the Doctor earlier than she knew. In *The*

End of Time, just after midnight on 1st January 2005, she's walking home from a party with her mum, Jackie, and notices the Tenth Doctor standing in the shadows. When he asks what year it is now, she confuses him for a drunken party goer. He tells her that it will be a fantastic year – knowing full well that, in March, they'll go travelling together.

When we first meet Rose in the eponymous episode, she's a sales assistant in a department store called Henriks, living at home with her mother and dating Mickey Smith (although judging by the dismissive way she is with him, it comes across as if she's merely making do, waiting for something better to come along). Upon finding the mannequins in Henriks' basement coming to life, Rose thinks she's become the victim of a student prank, until they start attacking her – at which point a hand reaches out and grabs hold of hers. She's immediately running with the Doctor, barely having a chance to find out who this mysterious man is, before he blows up her place of work. Rose resigns herself to losing her job very quickly and ends up loafing around the house with nothing better to do. That is, until the Doctor appears at her house, having followed the signal from an Auton arm there. She drags him into the flat, wanting to know more about the previous night, but his answers only confuse her more. She follows him out of the flat; the Doctor is impressed by her curiosity, and the ease with which she handles his answers, but he remains distant from her. She, however, cannot get him out of her head and tries to find out more about him on the Internet. This leads her to Clive, who collects stories about the Doctor, though she ultimately decides he's a 'nutter'. She becomes totally distracted and doesn't notice that Mickey now is very clearly a plastic replica. The Doctor reappears and, amidst the chaos, removes the Auton-Mickey's head. Rose realises that Clive is right: the Doctor is dangerous, yet still she follows him into the TARDIS (after a moment's hesitation), and is stunned by the interior. Despite her shock, she's worried Mickey may now be dead and she'll have to tell his mother. She's annoyed that the Doctor doesn't seem to care about this. The Doctor confronts the Nestene Consciousness, but it's Rose who actually saves the day. He then offers her the chance to travel with him, but she refuses, feeling obligated to look after Mickey, who's now a gibbering mess after his Auton encounter. The Doctor leaves, and Rose is left alone with Mickey, already regretting her decision. However, when the TARDIS returns seconds later, and the Doctor mentions it also travels in time, Rose runs full-pelt inside, no longer giving Mickey a second thought.

There's an immediate banter between them, with her mocking his show-off attitude; he decides to really put her on the back foot and takes her to Platform One, in the year five billion, to witness *The End of the World*. She initially appears to take the plethora of alien dignitaries in her stride, but she is obviously overwhelmed at the same time. While the Doctor goes off with the sentient tree, Jabe, Rose takes a bit of time out on her own to acclimatise. Her attraction to the Doctor is obvious here, with a hint of jealousy when the Doctor goes off with Jabe (a sign of things to come). Rose can be catty, making very bitchy and sarcastic comments when she feels under attack, notably verbally sparring with Lady Cassandra, the so-called last human. Without realising it, she also encounters someone who would go on to become important to her: the Face of Boe. At the end of this first journey, she's saddened to learn that no one noticed the end of her planet because of the machinations of Cassandra. To cheer her up, the Doctor returns to her own time to demonstrate the nature of time travel. He highlights how nothing lasts forever, that one day, it's all gone; 'even the sky.' Then he tells her he's a Time Lord and admits, 'My planet's gone. It's dead. It burned like the earth. It's just rocks and dust. Before its time.' She assures him that he's not on his own – that she's there for him. Summing up the absurdities of their existence, in the wake of Earth's destruction, they get some chips together; something Rose later refers to as their 'first date'.

After taking her to the future, the Doctor promises a trip to the past. Naturally, the Doctor gets the time and place wrong, but Rose doesn't care: she's simply amazed that it's Christmas Day,

1869, all over again. Upon stepping out of the TARDIS in *The Unquiet Dead*, after changing into nineteenth century dress (to which the Doctor responds that she looks 'beautiful'), she carefully places her foot into the snow, amazed by the idea of travelling into the past. With her usual bravery, she chases after Sneed and Gwyneth, who appear to be stealing a dead body from the Palace Theatre, but Sneed is really an undertaker and the body has been reanimated by a Gelth, a gaseous life form.

For her troubles, she's chloroformed and shoved into the hearse, only to later awake in the undertakers being menaced by another corpse reanimated by the Gelth. Although fearing for her life, she responds with sarcasm and gusto. She meets Charles Dickens, who's now assisting the Doctor, but she barely acknowledges him; although she's aware of him, she's clearly not a huge fan. She bonds quickly with Gwyneth; however, much like Ace in *The Curse of Fenric*, she displays a degree of social ignorance when talking about boys. Gwyneth thinks Rose talks like a 'wild thing'. Rose brings her out of her shell a little, but Gwyneth's psychic abilities (enhanced by the Time Rift running through the heart of Cardiff) enable her to see into Rose's mind and she gets more than she bargained for, including the knowledge that Rose considers her stupid. Gwyneth also sees in Rose 'the Big Bad Wolf', an allusion to her forthcoming encounter with the time vortex in *The Parting of the Ways*. Her own sense of morality comes into play later when the Doctor suggests that allowing the Gelth to use dead bodies to save them just might work. Rose tells him that this is wrong, until he confronts her with the analogy of a donor card: 'It's a different morality', the Doctor responds. Despite this, Rose insists Gwyneth shouldn't be used to mediate with the Gelth. As they're surrounded by the animated corpses, Rose tells the Doctor that she's glad she met him, and he returns the sentiment.

The Doctor takes Rose home in *Aliens of London*, promising she'll arrive twelve hours after she left. This amazes her – to think she's experienced so much in less than a day – but upon returning to the flat, she's met by a stunned Jackie, who bursts into tears. Rose doesn't understand such a reaction. Then the Doctor rushes in and explains that it hasn't been twelve hours, but twelve *months*. It's March 2006. Rose has been gone a whole year.

In the intervening months, Mickey has been accused of murdering Rose, and is now something of a pariah on the Powell Estate. The police arrive to question both the Doctor and Rose, who can only explain that they've been travelling together. Everyone suspects a sexual relationship, but this embarrasses Rose, though not as much as Jackie who slaps the Doctor. Later, when she finds out that the Doctor is nine-hundred years old, Rose comments that her mother is right; it's quite an age gap.

It's now becoming clear that the Doctor is also falling for Rose – her passion and enthusiasm reminds him of the man he used to be. Unfortunately, such a connection has a price, one that becomes more evident as time progresses. Considering that Mickey waited a year for her, Rose is incredibly dismissive of him; she's more concerned that the Doctor might've left her, even though he gave her a TARDIS key to prove that he'll return. Mickey calls the Doctor Rose's new 'boyfriend', but Rose says the Doctor is much more important than that. In a quiet moment in the TARDIS, while the Doctor observes the news of the supposed first alien contact, Rose admits that she did miss Mickey. Nonetheless, she doesn't seem to want Mickey to be involved: when he's explaining about the Doctor's past with UNIT, Rose throws him a look of derision. He's definitely not welcome in Rose's new world. Despite this, Rose's concern for others is on display when she reaches Downing Street and sees how upset Harriet Jones, MP for Flydale North (yes, you know who she is), is over witnessing a Slitheen kill and skin a man. After Rose suggests blowing up Downing Street to stop the Slitheen, Harriet points out that she's a very violent young woman, but Rose doesn't care: she has faith that the Doctor will do whatever is necessary to save them all, even if it means sacrificing them in the process. Rose is adamant that her life is unimportant. Once the

Slitheen are defeated, Jackie points out how infatuated Rose is with him. She denies it, but she's soon packing her bags to continue her travels. Once again, she leaves Jackie and Mickey to worry – they both know now how dangerous life with the Doctor can be.

In *Dalek*, we see how fickle Rose really is. She meets a young genius, Adam Mitchell, working in Henry van Statten's underground base in Utah, 2012 (six years in her future). Adam reminds her somewhat of the Doctor, and she draws close to him (*The Long Game*). Rose still isn't entirely certain about her feelings for the Doctor (or perhaps she thinks they're not reciprocated) and as a result she hooks on to the closest alternative. Again, she appears to be settling for second best. Such a mercurial trait is further expanded upon when she meets Captain Jack Harkness in *The Empty Child*.

Still, she's outraged and empathetic when she hears the sound of the 'Metaltron' being tortured, and demands Adam take her to see it. At this point, she knows nothing of the Daleks and their part in the Last Great Time War (but she soon discovers it all), and fails to realise that the Dalek is manipulating her when it talks of its pain. She reaches out to comfort it, and in so doing gives it the chronon energy (a safe radiation picked up through travelling in the time vortex) it needs to rebuild itself. When she's trapped by the Dalek, the Doctor blames himself, and Rose tells him 'it wasn't your fault', a further example of her concern for the emotional well-being of others. The Dalek gets more than it bargained for by sampling Rose's DNA, picking up some of her compassion, to the point where she's able to talk the Dalek out of killing, and even assists it in committing suicide, rather than live on as the last of its kind. When the Doctor confronts the Dalek, armed with a gun, Rose is shocked by what the Doctor has become the Dalek merely wants to feel the warmth of the sun on its skin (it opens up its casing to show the mutated Kaled form inside), but the Doctor is determined to kill it. Rose accuses the Doctor of becoming the monster. Her horror and shock snaps the Doctor out of his rage, and he's unable to express himself clearly, such is the emotional damage done to him by the Time War.

With Adam in tow, they arrive on Satellite 5 (*The Long Game*). Rose initially finds Adam's awe amusing, until he faints at the sight of Earth as seen from an observation window. The Doctor points out that Adam's *her* boyfriend, and Rose looks at the unconscious Adam. 'Not anymore,' she says, dismissively.

A curious thing happens at the end of this story. Adam is found to be using technology from the year 200,000 to profit himself when he returns to 2012. The Doctor is angered by this and returns Adam home, complete with a cranial port that opens a hole in his forehead to his brain. The Doctor says he only takes the best, a moment of pride for Rose. She seems uncertain about leaving Adam, but the Doctor's comment settles it for her, and she rather smugly returns to the TARDIS with the Doctor.

It's odd that the Doctor should treat Adam in such a way, since what Rose does in the next story (*Father's Day*) is arguably much worse than trying to make a quick buck. Rose tells the Doctor the story of her father's death in 1987, and asks him to take her back there so that he won't die alone. The Doctor's a little unsure, but he soon agrees – an unusual move for him, since it must be clear what's going to happen. In the first instance, Rose freezes, unable to do anything but watch Pete Tyler get mowed down by a car. But once she recovers from the shock, she asks to try again. The Doctor warns her against this. It'll be even more dangerous this time as there will be two versions of them there. Rose says she understands, but that doesn't stop her from running out and pushing her dad out of the way – watched by the earlier Rose and Doctor, who promptly vanish from existence. The Doctor is furious: she's made a radical alteration to the timeline, but Rose fails to see how having Pete alive is a bad thing. The Doctor confronts her, accusing her of planning this as soon as she learned the TARDIS was a time machine. She refutes this, of course, arguing that the Doctor just doesn't like the idea that there's someone more important to her than him; it's a scathing comment, born of anger and hurt, probably because the Doctor is right. Nonetheless, when he storms off, having taken the TARDIS key from her, Rose pushes aside her hurt in favour of the joy of being with her dad. Seeing the reality of her parents' marriage is a shock to her: they're not the happy, hopelessly in love couple Jackie always told her about, but rather two people who are lumbered with each other, constantly arguing, her mother bitter at Pete's get-rich-quick schemes. Pete's existence threatens the timeline and calls forth the Reapers, creatures who eat the energies created by the rupture in the timeline. The Doctor returns. Rose is so happy to see him and there's no doubt how much she loves him. It takes Pete a while to work out who Rose is, and when he does, Rose is overwhelmed at finally meeting her dad properly – just calling him 'dad' brings her to tears. Despite Rose pretending he's still alive in the future, Pete realises the only way to fix things is for him to die. The story she tells him is of a man he will never be, and so he runs out in front of the car, restoring space-time. Rose holds his hands while he dies, watched from a distance by Jackie who, we later learn (in *The Parting of the Ways*), doesn't remember any of the events of this story, save that a strange blonde girl held Pete's hand while he died.

Arriving in 1941 at the height of the London Blitz, having followed a Chula spaceship to Earth, Rose is disappointed that the Doctor will not give her a 'bit of Spock' by scanning for alien tech, instead of doing his usual hands-on kind of search (despite having seen how effective the Doctor's standard method is). Her maternal side comes out when she wanders away from the Doctor to follow the cries of a child, only to find herself hanging from a barrage balloon, with a Union Flag t-shirt on full display. Fortunately, she's saved by Captain Jack Harkness, a former Time Agent from the fifty-first century – and he's responsible for throwing the Chula ship at them in the vortex. She responds to Jack's easy ways with some outrageous flirting; she even unintentionally prints his psychic paper with '*very* available', even though she considers Mickey an occasional boyfriend. In this instance, it's easy to see why she's so fickle: Jack's charm bewitches her as they dance to Glenn Miller tunes atop Jack's invisible Chula ship which is tethered to Big Ben. Here, they discuss terms of sale – in truth, a con run by Jack, as he later admits once the Doctor explains to him the reality of what Jack's unleashed on Earth. When Jack uses his multi-purpose vortex manipulator to scan for alien technology, Rose is impressed: 'finally, a professional.' She's amused later when, after the Doctor and Jack meet, they argue over the Doctor's sonic screwdriver and Jack's sonic 'squareness' gun – sonic envy – but, with assailants coming towards them, it's Rose who takes the initiative and saves them, using Jack's gun to create a hole through which they can escape. The Doctor displays a little jealousy over Rose's appreciation for Jack, and he is annoyed that she assumes he doesn't 'dance', although he is amused by Rose's dismay at learning that Jack 'dances' with everyone, regardless of gender or species. Among all this innuendo and flirting, Rose shares a quiet moment with Nancy, a young woman who helps the homeless kids of London, and reassures her that the future will work out fine – that Germany will lose the war. It's a nice moment, reminiscent of a moment between Ace and Wainwright in *The Curse of Fenric*, also during World War II, when the latter worries about the outcome of the war. After saving everyone, the Doctor and Rose save one final person: Jack. They invite him to join them, which he does, standing aside laughing as the Doctor and Rose dance around the control console in the TARDIS.

When we next see her, in *Boom Town*, it's clear that some time has passed since they rescued Jack. The three of them have settled into a camaraderie that only comes from a great deal of time spent together – indeed, so strong is it that, when Mickey arrives at the TARDIS in Cardiff Bay, he's very much an outsider, out of his depth. Rose confirms the passage of time with stories of the places she visited with the Doctor (and possibly Jack), places we have never seen or heard about on screen. Mickey only comes to Cardiff because Rose has asked him to bring her passport, but she later admits that she wanted to see him. Once again, she keeps him on hold, the 'occasional boyfriend'. After listening to her rabbit on about the Doctor, Mickey blurts out that he's dating Trisha Delaney. Rose reacts as if she's been slapped and accuses him of lying. He would never be attracted to such a girl, she says. It seems Mickey is trying to make Rose jealous, but when it doesn't work out, he tells her that she 'makes [him] feel like nothing, Rose. Nothing.' Rose promptly confirms his accusation by running straight back into the TARDIS when an earthquake strikes Cardiff Bay – really the Rift becoming violently active. It's only after Blon Fel-Fotch Pasameer-Day Slitheen is defeated and the Rift is closed that Rose thinks of Mickey again. She rushes off to find him, but in the chaos around the Bay, she can't see him, although he watches her from a distance. He walks away, finally accepting the truth of the situation. For her own part, Rose realises Mickey deserves better than her, a fact that obviously upsets her.

After a couple more off-screen adventures, a transmat beam breaks through the TARDIS' defences and the three are separated (*Bad Wolf*). They end up at the Game Station, the former Satellite 5. There, Rose takes part in a distorted version of *The Weakest Link* wherein after the immortal line, 'you are the weakest link, goodbye' is uttered by the Anne Droid, the loser is apparently vaporised. After some initial confusion, Rose is amused to be on the game show, bombarded by questions she cannot possibly know the answers to. Her amusement continues, until the loser of the first round reacts in utter terror; Rose doesn't understand the problem, until she sees the loser vaporised before her. Horror soon sets in, but Rose has no choice other than to continue and manages to survive until the final head-to-head round with fellow contestant, Roderick. She loses. The Doctor, Jack, and a young woman called Lynda Moss join Rose, only to see her vaporised in front of them! The Doctor and Jack are convinced she's dead. The Doctor is shocked, while Jack responds with anger and rage, threatening to kill those responsible. In truth, Rose has merely been transmatted to the Dalek mothership, one of two hundred ships on the outer-most limits of the Solar System. The Daleks try to intimidate Rose with fear, but she's resolute that the Doctor will save her. The Daleks attempt to use her against the Doctor, and after a direct confrontation with the Emperor, Rose is stunned to see the defeat on the Doctor's face. She's disconsolate about Lynda; she sees her as a rival and is annoyed by Lynda's obvious enthusiasm for the Doctor. When the Doctor explains that he'll build a Delta Wave, and use the Game Station as a transmitter to wipe out the Dalek fleet, Rose is resentful of Lynda's response: 'What are you waiting for?' she says, a split second before Rose.

Later, the Doctor convinces Rose to get into the TARDIS and he returns her to 2006. She's angered and hurt by this apparent betrayal, and tries everything to stop the ship, but it doesn't respond to her; she finds herself stranded back home, 'enjoying' chips with Mickey and Jackie – both of whom are happy to be reunited with her. Rose finds it difficult to just sit there while the Doctor is fighting to save them all, recognising that it's 'happening right now' in the future. Mickey doesn't understand this, until she tells him that there's nothing left on Earth for her. Despite this seeming to be the final nail in the coffin of their relationship, Mickey's love for her means he still follows her back to the TARDIS to try to get her back to where she wants to be. Having a quiet moment with her mother, Rose discloses that she met her dad in the past. She also reveals that *she* was the unknown girl that Jackie remembers seeing by his dying body: 'That's how good the Doctor is'. Though Jackie is initially freaked out by this, it still convinces her to help Rose get back to the Doctor.

Fortuitously, Rose realises the true meaning of the words 'Bad Wolf'. She's convinced it's a link between her and the Doctor. Rose's guess is correct: staring into the heart of the TARDIS, she absorbs the time vortex and becomes Bad Wolf, scattering the words throughout time and space, creating a message that only she can decipher. Using the power of the vortex, Rose returns to the future and disperses the atoms of the entire Dalek fleet, thus ending the Time War. However, the pain burns in her mind – she can see *everything* that has ever happened. She defies life itself and brings Jack back to life (having been killed during the Dalek assault on the station). The Doctor removes the vortex from her by kissing her – saving her life and dispelling the vortex safely. As Rose awakes in the console room, she finds the Doctor talking about how he's going to change. She remembers nothing about being Bad Wolf; the last thing she recalls is looking into the heart of the TARDIS. Rose is then shocked to see the Doctor regenerate in front of her...

Adam Mitchell – Bruno Langley (*Dalek* and *The Long Game*)

American Idiot (Green Day); *Driftwood* (Travis).

Unlike every other *Doctor Who* companion, Adam Mitchell is designed to show why not everyone *can* work as a companion, to 'prove how wonderful Rose is. And how wise the Doctor is, not selecting his crew 'cos he fancies them' (from Russell T Davies' pitch document). He is set up to fail. Nonetheless, he's intelligent, inquisitive, and uses his initiative – all key elements of a companion. Still, he's not a natural time traveller, passing out when first seeing Earth suspended in space during his sole trip into the future.

His biggest crime, however, goes largely unacknowledged. When we meet him, Adam is working for Van Statten, and is very aware that his employer is torturing the Dalek, the only living alien in the museum (until the Doctor arrives). When showing off his technical prowess, Adam shows Rose that he's hacked into the collection's communications and can spy on the Dalek's cell. He's clearly unsettled by it, but his job obviously means more to him. He must be aware, too, that his boss has even found the cure for the common cold, but won't share it because 'Why sell one cure when I can sell a thousand palliatives?' Adam may be clever, but his morals are clearly dubious. Then again, it's easy to argue that he's in a difficult position: he's working for the most powerful man in the world, the man who owns the Internet, so he wouldn't want to jeopardise that. But seeing how quickly Van Statten's empire topples, you can't help but think that Adam could've put an end to it earlier using his considerable genius. Indeed, he boasts to Rose that, 'When I was eight, I logged onto the US Defence System. Nearly caused World War Three.'

Adam might be in fear of his boss too. He keeps a hidden cache of alien weapons, uncatalogued, and tells the Doctor, 'Mr Van Statten tends to dispose of his staff, and when he does he wipes their memory. I kept this stuff in case I needed to fight my way out one day.'

It could be the scientific research Van Statten facilitates that enables him to compromise on his own morals. Adam is at least interested in alien technologies and is in charge of cataloguing them, something he describes as the 'best job in the world.' He's genuinely in awe of the wider cosmos and tries to inspire Rose by telling her that he thinks the whole universe is 'teeming with life.' He's also visibly disappointed that Van Statten dismissively throws aside an alien musical instrument Adam's showing him – he initially thinks it channels fuel, before the Doctor corrects him.

Adam has a fractious relationship with the Doctor. They never really get on; they're trying to make it work because of Rose. There's certainly some verbal sparring. They start shouting at each other when it looks like Rose is trapped in the museum with the Dalek, each blaming the other – the Doctor is responsible for sealing the doors and Adam left Rose behind as she couldn't run as fast as him. The Doctor's anger is driven by guilt: he thinks he's killed her. Fortunately, their argument doesn't have time to develop, as the Dalek reveals Rose is alive, after all.

After the Dalek is destroyed, unnamed authorities intend to fill the base in with cement, so Adam is out of a job and intends to go home. To his credit, he runs off to find Rose and the Doctor, and it's Rose who convinces the Doctor to take him with them.

'On your own head,' warns the Time Lord.

They quickly realise they've made a mistake. In *The Long*

Game, Adam's greed gets the better of him: he intends to make money from the knowledge he's gained from Satellite 5 by accessing a data port and phoning home, relaying information about the history of the microprocessor from the standing of the year 200,000. (It's interesting to note that Adam himself is from the future, hailing from 2012, whereas Rose boarded the TARDIS in 2005. Still, he doesn't display any particular knowledge of the intervening seven years; he might've shared some details between adventures as they've clearly spent a little time chatting at some point off-screen, given that the Doctor later knows where Adam lives.) He even goes so far as being physically deformed by his need for cash: to fully access the space-station's archives, he needs to 'be the computer', i.e. have an info-spike hole in his head which would allow him to learn the full history of the human race. His interest could've been scientific too, of course, but it's too much data for the brain to process, so he wouldn't remember any of it. His hope is to record it to his mum's answer-phone then decipher the white noise when he's back home. He manages to learn some basic information and withholds this fact from the Doctor – which only serves to infuriate the Doctor more.

The Doctor and Rose are partially to blame. It's clear he's out of his depth, though to the Doctor's credit, he tells him to open his mind, and enthuses, 'Time travel's like visiting Paris. You can't just read the guide book; you've got to throw yourself in – eat the food, use the wrong verbs, get charged double, and end up kissing complete strangers. Or is that just me?' Still, he basically ditches Adam in favour of investigating the mysteries of Satellite 5. Adam tells Rose he's going to acclimatise by going back to the TARDIS and she just assumes he does. When the Doctor later says that Adam's 'given up,' they agree that it's a good thing because it's just him and Rose again.

Of course, Adam's bad decisions affects the two and could've had wider implications to space-time: the editor of Satellite 5 (Simon Pegg), and his boss, the Mighty Jagrafess of the Holy Hadrojassic Maxarodenfoe, learn about the TARDIS from Adam and try to take his key. Fortunately, another employee of the station turns the system against the Jagrafess, and Satellite 5 is seemingly shut down. Adam tries to pass off his mistake, but the Doctor immediately takes him back home, furious at his one-trip companion.

Adam is clearly disappointed, understandably so. He's screwed up his big chance, and the Doctor effectively drops him back in 2012 because he doesn't like him. After all, in *Father's Day*, Rose's actions almost destroy all life, but she gets a slapped wrist because she's too important to him. As a result, Adam's not so much the companion who couldn't; he's the companion who didn't get a proper crack at the whip.

The Doctor soon takes on another male companion, this time one who's somehow charmed both him and Rose, despite making such a considerable error that humanity might've been changed forever. Unlike Adam, however, Captain Jack Harkness is obviously gutted and hugely apologetic about what he's done. Jack is one of the earliest conceived characters for the 2005 revival of *Doctor Who* – according to *The Inside Story* (written by Gary Russell and published by BBC Books in 2006), he was conceived and cast before the outline of the series was even confirmed. He's the soldier, created to do things the Doctor will never ordinarily do. But his travelling days with the Doctor are slightly different to what was originally planned, due to the creation of spin-off show, *Torchwood*, for which he became the lead character.

Jack Harkness – John Barrowman (*The Empty Child* to *The Parting of the Ways*; *Utopia* to *Last of the Time Lords, Fugitive of the Judoon, Revolution of the Daleks*)

Moonlight Serenade (Glenn Miller); *Brandy (You're a Fine Girl)* (Looking Glass).

Jack is introduced into the series under an assumed identity, stolen from an RAF captain (as revealed in *Torchwood: Captain Jack*

Harkness). Jack is an ex-Time Agent from the fifty-first century, who for some reason had two years of his life stolen from him. No longer working for the Time Agency, Jack is now a conman using his knowledge of Earth's history for his own personal ends. Jack's happy to flirt with everyone he meets; it's often his way of saying hello. It's inferred that Jack is having a secret sexual relationship with Algy, a British Army Officer. Yet he is also very impressed with Rose, but mistakes her for a Time Agent, until he later meets the Doctor whom he calls 'Mister Spock' initially due to Rose's use of the name. Despite his sizeable knowledge of Earth history, it seems Jack has some curious gaps – popular television and terminology being most prominent. He has a carefree attitude, with a lot of joking and sarcasm, never taking anything too seriously. His biggest character flaw, as he mentions to the Doctor in *The Parting of the Ways*, is his cowardice.

However, as Jack spends time with the Doctor, he draws on bravery he didn't know existed. This is evident in his first story, *The Empty Child / The Doctor Dances*, when he discovers he's actually responsible for the plague spreading through London (in fact, a plague of nanogenes rewriting human DNA that escaped from a crashed Chula ambulance he sent to Earth). This shakes him, but he sticks around to help the Doctor and Rose. To make amends, he returns to his own ship and stops a bomb from falling on the Chula ship, the Doctor and Rose, and all the patients. But, as he heads away from Earth, he discovers there's no way for him to escape the explosion. He accepts his fate with dignity and good humour, enjoying an alcoholic drink and engaging the onboard computer in conversation. The Doctor and Rose arrive in the TARDIS to take him away from the bomb, and he accepts their invitation to join them on their travels.

He remains with the Doctor and Rose for an undefined period of time; when we next see him in *Boom Town*, he's opening the TARDIS door to Mickey. Jack has settled into a very easy, and highly flirtatious, relationship with both the Doctor and Rose. He's out of uniform, now dressed in contemporary clothes. He enjoys winding Mickey up, not unlike the Doctor. They seem to spend some time in Cardiff (long enough for Margaret Blaine's photograph to appear in *The Western Mail*), with Jack enjoying being the centre of attention, telling his tall tales of past exploits as a Time Agent. Already, elements of the Doctor's personality seem to be infecting Jack, something that develops even more when Jack takes over Torchwood, and he begins to model himself on the Doctor – from name dropping to his dress-sense, as well as some more altruistic attitudes. When they go to Cardiff Town Hall to confront Blaine, now Mayor of Cardiff, Jack automatically assumes command, giving out instructions, until the Doctor queries who's in charge. Jack apologises, but the Doctor points out that it's a good plan, so they proceed as Jack suggested. He's very excited by the pan-dimensional surfboard, and instantly recognises it as technology far beyond the inhabitants of the Slitheen planet, Raxacoricofallapatorius; Blaine (aka Blon Slitheen) has procured it by nefarious means. He seems aware of the Time Lords and their technology: he easily operates the TARDIS console, and is even seen fixing components while the Doctor chats with Margaret and takes her to dinner, implying the Doctor has great trust in this rogue former-Time Agent.

Like Rose, Jack is also hijacked by transmat and deposited on the Game Station (*Bad Wolf*). He finds himself in a version of *What Not to Wear* and is at the mercy of the robotic Trine-E and Zu-Zana. They instruct him to try on various clothes before deciding he'd be better without a face. Being naked in front of a television audience amuses Jack, but it doesn't prevent him from hiding a gun about his person. He uses this to destroy both robots.

He's outraged by the apparent death of Rose, but he is the first person to work out where she's really been taken. He assists the Doctor in rescuing her, and arranges the defence of the Game Station against the oncoming Dalek fleet, showing considerable tactical nous. He's heard of the Time War and knows the Daleks disappeared, but he is unaware that the battle involved the Time Lords. When the Emperor Dalek challenges the Doctor's resolve in using the Delta Wave, Jack's faith in the Doctor is absolute. 'Never doubted him,' Jack says, 'never will' (this stance changes slightly over time, but his belief remains largely steady, despite the Doctor in return not treating him especially well). Such faith is misplaced: in the event, the Doctor can't use the Delta Wave. The sacrifice of every life on Earth is too great a price.

While the Doctor is admitting defeat, Jack fights to the last man. Cornered, he accepts his fate and is exterminated by a Dalek. He's later resurrected by the Bad Wolf version of Rose; only, she gets it wrong. He's shocked to find himself alive, and rushes towards the sound of the TARDIS dematerialising. The last we see of Jack is on the Game Station, seconds after the Doctor and Rose leave, upset at being abandoned. From his point of view, he might presume they've left because they think he's dead; nonetheless, given how close they all became, it surely stings that they don't look for his body. Initially, it seems that they left Jack behind because the Doctor is about to regenerate, but it's not until *Utopia* that we find out the real reason the Doctor moved on so quickly.

Indeed, it's some time before Jack meets the Doctor again – for him, a *lot* of time passes. Over a hundred years...

The Ninth Doctor
Expanded Universe

With the regeneration of *Doctor Who* into the more marketing-savvy and brand-conscious world of 2005 and its reintroduction into mainstream popular culture, the Expanded Universe expands like, well, a Big Bang. There are the additions of spin-off shows such as *Torchwood* and *The Sarah Jane Adventures*; and the appearance of magazines such as *Doctor Who Insider* and *Battles in Time*, the latter comprised of collectible trading cards reinforced by a magazine containing a comic strip of the Tenth Doctor's adventures. Pitched at a much younger audience, *Battles in Time* had a colourful, stylistically simple, and easily accessible look, as did another magazine, *Doctor Who Adventures*. Then there was the short-lived *Doctor Who Storybook* and its successor, *The Brilliant Book of Doctor Who*; a role-playing range, *Decide Your Destiny*; the *2-In-1* collections; numerous anthologies, audiobooks, and *Quick Reads* titles; and online projects such as the *BBC Online* comics, a series of strips posted on the BBC website by professional *Doctor Who* writers.

Most prominently, however, are the *New Series Adventures*, or NSA, novels that began in May 2005 with *The Clockwise Man*, *The Monsters Inside*, and *Winner Takes All*, the first of only six fiction books released during Christopher Eccleston's time as the Ninth Doctor.

Rose's first visit to an alien planet, Justice Alpha, is the subject of *The Monsters Inside*. This is part of the Justicia system – mentioned in passing during the episode, *Boom Town* – a penal colony sprawled across seven planets, and Rose is quickly separated from the Doctor, both being arrested and taken to difference jails (humans on Justice Beta and aliens on Justice

Prime). Prior to this, Rose's adventures have either been Earthbound or to space stations. These three books take place early on in her travels, though all occur sometime after *Aliens of London/World War Three*, given that she mistakes rogue Blatbereen in *The Monsters Inside* as Slitheen, both families hailing from Raxacoricofallapatorius.

She appears in all of the first twelve New Series Adventures novels, the next of which, *Winner Takes All*, sees her back on Earth and more specifically back on the Powell Estate, where her mum, Jackie, is mugged, and Mickey reveals himself to be quite the obsessive gamer, talking about *Grand Theft Auto*, Sonic the Hedgehog, XBoxes, and Playstations. Another of his games is called *Bad Wolf*.

Mickey isn't the only man in Rose's life, however. In *Only Human*, she marries a Neanderthal man named Tillun. Marriage sees her dispensing with 'Tyler' and becoming Rose Glathicgacymcilliach. Technically though, she ends up a widow as Tillun remains in his own time where he lives out his life. (The later novel, *The Stone Rose*, alludes to this, as the Tenth Doctor asks Rose if she has ever come close to marrying anyone that she shouldn't have. Then again, this could be a reference to Jimmy Stone, an ex-boyfriend of Rose's to whom she was engaged.)

Probably the best source of biographical information about Rose can be found in an article called *Meet Rose*, included in the 2006 *Doctor Who Annual* and written by Russell T Davies. Here we learn that Rose's middle name is Marion and that she has always dreamed of travelling. However, a school trip to France at the age of thirteen was the furthest she had ever got and this didn't end well. But it did reveal an early taste for adventure: Rose, and Shareen Costello, her best friend, gave their teachers the slip and rode a train to Parc Asterix instead of visiting the Louvre. (She'd eventually see the Mona Lisa in the 2005 comic, *Art Attack*, and Paris in 1923, as per the 2015 comic event, *The Four Doctors*.) They were eventually found by the police and subsequently sent home.

Rose started dating Mickey Smith, who lived on the same

estate, when she was fourteen years old, claiming that it really wasn't anything special. At school, further trouble occurred when she managed to talk the school choir into going on strike, resulting in her being suspended for three days. Rose, despite her ongoing tendency for mischief, did reasonably well in her exams, getting an A, a couple of Bs, four Cs, and a D in science. Encouraged by this, she made plans to study English, Art, and French at A-Level. Sadly though, this wasn't to be the case.

Jimmy Stone was twenty, had the title of 'fittest boy' on the estate, and played bass in a local band called No Hot Ashes. Rose fell very deeply for Jimmy and, after dumping Mickey and leaving home, she moved into a bedsit with him. Only five months later, she was back at home, heartbroken and £800 in debt while Jimmy was in Amsterdam with a woman named Noosh. Mickey forgave Rose and they got back together. She then got a temporary job to try and pay off her debt before getting, with Jackie's help, a more permanent position in Henrik's, which of course, was destined to go up in flames.

And what of Jimmy Stone? He's mentioned in *Rose*, with the companion berating her lack of job and concluding, 'It's all Jimmy Stone's fault. If I hadn't left school because of him… Look where he ended up.' According to the Target novelisation of the episode, Stone wound up imprisoned for eighteen months, then briefly became a door-to-door salesman, before being killed by Autons while he was robbing his then-girlfriend, Abena. (A parallel version of Rose marries Jimmy in *The Rogue Planet*, part of the 2022 audio set, *The Dimension Cannon: Other Worlds*, and has a child with him, also named Jimmy.)

What kind of an individual would get stranded in the Ataline System with only a traffic cone? Captain Jack Harkness, of course, who joins Rose and the Ninth Doctor in the last three official novels of 2005. The Ataline incident is referred to in *The Stealers of Dreams*, set in a world where fiction is against the law. Jack references his connection with the Time Agency, telling the enemy that he's still a Time Agent and will summon a Time Agency warfleet should he be forced to. This is a highly significant threat to most alien races as the Time Agency is much feared.

The Stealers of Dreams is also notable in that Jack mentions knowing the Face of Boe, touching on a contentious subject since *The Last of the Time Lords*, which raises the possibility that Jack and the Face of Boe are one and the same. *The Stealers of Dreams* was released almost two and half years before that TV episode aired, and the idea of a connection hadn't yet been fully conceptualised. In this novel, Jack recalls the Face of Boe as being a local figure of some fame in his own time, which doesn't negate the Face being Jack, living through Jack's own pre-Doctor life.

The book includes Rose calling her mother and references the events of *Boom Town*, placing this after that TV episode; that goes against the Doctor's assertion in *Bad Wolf* that the trio had gone from Raxacoricofallapatorius then Kyoto in 1336 before being taken by the transmat beam at the start of the series one finale. While that story fills in a narrative hole that doesn't exist, various others naturally fill in ones that do. This includes *The Last Party on Earth*, part of the 2019 audio anthology, *The Dimension Cannon*, which tells us that her grandfather Prentice passed away when she was eight or nine years old and that his life was celebrated in a lively wake. *The Ninth Doctor Chronicles Volume Three* (2017) features *The Other Side*, which sees the Doctor attempting to take Adam Mitchell home after he joined them in *Dalek*, but instead being caught in a temporal tsunami; with Rose stranded in 1922 and the Doctor in 1894, the Doctor waits twenty-eight years to see her again. The Doctor then accepts Adam as a new companion, pre-*The Long Game*, after he helps them defeat the anomaly-creating Bygone Horde. And the short story, *The Red Bicycle*, from 2016's *Twelve Doctors of Christmas*, shows the Ninth Doctor acting as Father Christmas by leaving her a beloved red bike when she was twelve (mentioned in *The Doctor Dances*) in 1998; this also tells us that Rose is a fan of The Stranglers, as she bought one of their albums at a record shop in Piccadilly Circus in 1977.

We also find out that Rose is a fan of the Vengaboys,

according to the 2006 short story *Voice from the Vortex!* in *Doctor Who Magazine* (written in the style of 1960s comics), as well as the Erasure song, *Sometimes*, which she sings during *Opera of Doom*, included in the 2007 *Doctor Who Storybook*.

Arguably, *A Groatsworth of Wit*, the last Ninth Doctor *DWM* comic strip from 2005-06, contradicts the 2007 TV episode, *The Shakespeare Code*, seeing as it shows the Doctor and Rose meeting William Shakespeare, as well as his rival playwright, Robert Greene.

In a perfect example of how twenty-first century *Doctor Who* expands on companions' backstories more than ever before, the origins of the Powell Estate, where Rose and Jackie (and, for a time, Pete Tyler) live are explored. Notably, *The Love Invasion*, Rose and the Ninth Doctor's comic strip debut in *DWM*, starts off in 1966 with the pair visiting the future site of the estate. But what should be all fields is instead a housing development called Brandon Mews; after they unravel the plans of the alien Kustollon called Igrix, the Doctor uses his sonic screwdriver to activate bulldozers that destroy Brandon Mews and make way for the Powell Estate. The Target novelisation of *Rose*, though, says that it wasn't built until 1973, and is comprised of two towers of sixteen floors, with six flats per storey. These towers were unofficially known as 'Enoch' and 'Powell', as some thought they were named after MP Enoch Powell, whereas they were actually named after the developer's mother-in-law, Mary Jane Powell. *Wednesdays For Beginners*, from the 2017 audio boxset, *The Lives of Captain Jack*, shows that Trisha Delaney, Rose's rival in the fight for Mickey's heart as mentioned in *Boom Town*, lives on the Powell Estate; so too does the Doctor's future wife, River Song, in 2020's *R&J*, specifically at number twenty-three in 2007.

Further adventures for Rose and the Ninth Doctor include a trippy trip to Mars (*The Cruel Sea*); Rose being turned into a vampire in *Monstrous Beauty*, part of the *Time Lord Victorious* event in 2020, during which they also come face to face with Rassilon; and, for Titan Comics' 2017 event, *The Lost Dimension*, meeting

Vastra, Jenny, and Strax, aka the Paternoster Row gang introduced on TV in 2011's *A Good Man Goes to War*. The latter takes places during the period Rose is travelling alongside Captain Jack Harkness.

Before Titan Comics got the license for official tie-ins, IDW published many comics, though primarily featuring the Tenth Doctor. Nonetheless, in 2008-09's *The Forgotten*, Jack is mentioned by a soldier who talks about him surviving a bullet in the head. This is in keeping with Jack's TV timeline which suggests on a few occasions that he left Torchwood Three in order to enlist in both world wars. Nonetheless, it's fruitful to delve into *Torchwood*'s Expanded Universe for more development of Jack's character.

In the 2008 *Torchwood* novel, *The Twilight Streets*, the 1940s Jack is seen as being critical and disapproving of Torchwood's approach and methods and is persuaded by Greg, a former boyfriend, to become a freelance agent. The novel further explains that, during the events of *Boom Town* – in which a younger Jack arrives with the Doctor and Rose to refuel the TARDIS at Cardiff Bay – Jack puts a lockdown on all Torchwood activity to avoid a paradox involving his past self. *Trace Memory* and the anthology *Consequences* then see Jack still working as a freelance agent for Torchwood in the 1960s. He also remains distrustful of UNIT, expressing complaints about the organisation in *Something in the Water* and *Bay of the Dead*.

Jack enters into a number of liaisons, including having affairs with Alison and Miles, whose wedding he also attends in *The House That Jack Built*; when Miles drowns his wife, however, Jack is left wracked by guilt.

Rather pleasingly, in *Trace Memory*, Jack hides out in the Shangri-La hotel, formerly the Shangri-La holiday camp as seen in the TV *Doctor Who* story, *Delta and the Bannermen*; *Risk Assessment* reveals that he helped Torchwood foil an invasion of the Ice Warriors in the 1960s, then apprehended one of their sonic cannons; and *The Undertaker's Gift* implies he's met Sontarans and Silurians.

Much like *Doctor Who Magazine*, albeit with less frequency, the monthly *Torchwood Magazine* featured comic strips in which Jack made regular appearances. Perhaps most noteworthy is the 2009 story, *Captain Jack and the Selkie*, written by John Barrowman and his sister, Carole E Barrowman. This writing duo return for the 2012 novel, *Exodus Code*, which is set after the events of *Torchwood: Miracle Day*, and sees Jack dealing with more consequences of his immortal life, brought down somewhat by becoming mortal in *Miracle Day*. He is no longer convinced he will remain immortal. The book reveals that Jack's aware of the Mandragora Helix, having been told by Sarah Jane Smith about its exploits (in the TV story, *The Masque of Mandragora*).

Jack's also had many audio adventures – most significant of these being *Month 25*, the fourth story in 2017's anthology, *The Lives of Captain Jack*, which tells us Jack's real name: Javic Piotr Thane.

In the same boxset, *The Year After I Died* shows what happened to Jack after *The Parting of the Ways*, namely that he's hailed as a hero but shuns the attention by becoming a recluse. He only starts integrating himself back into the world when aspiring reporter, Silo Crook, tries to interview him and instead draws him into the mystery of Trear Station, a place reconstituted from the Game Station. Not knowing he's immortal at that point, Jack is electrocuted and revived, which he puts down to the universe liking him; we might infer that his more positive attitude, spurred on by Silo's new agenda to rebuild the irradiated and largely-destroyed planet following the Daleks' attack, inspires him to travel back to twenty-first century Earth. His vortex manipulator's burning out leaves him stranded in 1869, as established in *Utopia*, meaning he spends a lot of time working for Torchwood: during this period, he meets Queen Victoria (*The Victorian Age*); shuts down Torchwood India (*Golden Age*); and is frozen in a temporary time bubble by Yvonne Hartman in *One Rule*. She recognises that he doesn't have Torchwood's best interests at heart – for her, that means acquisitioning the Doctor on behalf of 'Queen and country.' Jack also sets up a deadlock seal on his office at the Torchwood Hub, as per 2016's *Outbreak*, which effectively means even the Doctor can't use the sonic screwdriver to get in, should he ever wish to.

Jack does meet the Doctor again before *Utopia*, albeit the Sixth Doctor who seemingly dies in Jack's arms in 2019's *Piece of Mind*. Jack even dresses up as this Doctor... while the real Doctor pretends to be his companion, Captain Jack Harkness! The Sixth Doctor later falls into a healing coma during which he edits his own memories so his future self won't recognise Jack.

Night of the Whisper, part of the *Destiny of the Doctor* fiftieth anniversary audio series, shows that Jack has a second sonic blaster, his first having been destroyed in 2015 comic, *Weapons of Past Destruction*. That comic run explores the time Jack travelled with the Ninth Doctor and Rose: they track down Time Lord technology on the intergalactic black market in the aforementioned story; defeat rogue Raxacoricofallapatorian, Gleda Ley-Sooth Marka Jinglatheen, with the help of Slist Fayflut Marteveerthon Slitheen in *Doctormania*; meet Brigadier Alistair Gordon Lethbridge-Stewart, Harry Sullivan, and Sergeant Benton of UNIT in *Official Secrets*; and attempt to get Jack's missing memories back – only for them to encounter an assassin Time Agent taking the name Joshua Hughes in *Secret Agent Man*, who, of course, turns out to actually be Jack.

The comics further explore the companion who couldn't cut the mustard – Adam Mitchell, whose TV arc began in *Dalek* and ended in the very next episode. Before this, his story was foreshadowed online, via shorts on the site, Who is Doctor Who?, modelled after that seen in *Rose* run by Clive Finch, then expanded afterwards in *Welcome Home*, part of the 2015 book, *The Time Lord Letters*. That tome says his parents are Sandra and Geoff Mitchell, and he lives in Manchester, though this is contradicted by the online story, *Essay Competition*, which says their house is in Nottingham. The latter includes a thesis by fourteen-year-old Adam, in which he details why he wants to meet aliens – specifically that he wants to learn from them. This nicely explains his motives in *The Long Game*, notably his wanting to cure problems like arthritis, which his father suffers from. This essay won him (Adam) Geocomtex Hardware offered as a prize by his future employee, Henry Van Statten.

This is where IDW's comic picks up the story: *Mystery Date* shows that, after being dropped home, Adam grows resentful of the Doctor when his mother dies of a brain embolism, something Adam might've saved her from if the Time Lord hadn't have interfered with his plans. As he later tells the Doctor, 'It wasn't fair! I only made one mistake!' He has a point. Adam decides to take revenge and excavates Van Statten's vault in Utah, before stealing a vortex manipulator from a Time Agent. Now able to travel in time, Adam kidnaps many of the Doctor's companions during the *Prisoners of Time* event, including Susan, Ian Chesterton, Barbara Wright, Sara Kingdom, Jamie McCrimmon, the Brigadier, Sarah Jane Smith, K9, Frobisher, Grace Holloway, and Rose; as well as (to him) future companions, Jack Harkness, Mickey Smith, Martha Jones, Donna Noble, Amy Pond, Rory Williams, and Clara Oswald. With the help of the Master in *Façades*, Adam appears to kidnap Peri Brown too, but it actually turns out to be the shapeshifting Frobisher.

With all his companions in stasis, Adam gives the Eleventh Doctor a choice: he can only save one (*Endgame*).

The companions are rescued by the Doctor's previous ten incarnations, with Frobisher's help, before the Master springs his ultimate trap, to use their TARDISes to destroy the universe. Realising he's been used, Adam turns on the Master and dies stopping him. In his last moments, he apologises for what he's done. In turn, the Doctor apologises, by burying Adam outside his fortress located in the Time Vortex, his grave inscribed with 'Adam Mitchell – A Companion True.'

*

Meanwhile, Titan Comics' *Ninth Doctor* series is significant for introducing a new companion, Tara Mishra, a rarity for this incarnation of the Time Lord.

Born in Sri Lanka, Tara is a nurse-turned-UNIT soldier who meets the Ninth Doctor, Rose, and Jack at Blaise Castle in Bristol in *Official Secrets*. (Due to the UNIT dating controversy, it's not revealed whether Tara comes from the 1970s or 1980s.) There, she's investigating Albion Defence, a rival taskforce intent on undermining UNIT by creating attacks by monsters. She's clearly gutsy and values the safety of the country more than her career, as she sacrifices this by appearing on a chat show pretending to work for Albion Defence in order to publicly bring them down. At the end of the story, she sneaks on board the TARDIS. Tara and the Doctor quickly establish a bond, one which Rose is clearly jealous of.

Tara's first trip is to Brazil in 1682 (*Slaver's Song*), where they learn Zloy Volk (Russian for 'Bad Wolf'), someone who Jack was supposed to have assassinated when working for the Time Agency, is still alive, leading Jack to briefly leave the TARDIS to search for answers on his own. They catch up with him in *The Bidding War*, just in time to be attacked by the Cybermen, who Tara reveals she, alongside UNIT, has fought before, when they'd converted half the town of Halifax. Tara stays behind on the technology-haven of Nomicae, circa 5324, to help its population recover from the Cybermen. Jack's bond with Tara is so great that he goes back to find her in *The Lost Dimension*, but after his vortex manipulator fails him, they're eventually left on a planet likely to be Skaro. Tara's fate is left unanswered, but we know Jack makes it back to the TARDIS at some point.

The Ninth Doctor's audio-exclusive companions are similarly short-lived, though understandably so. The first is Nova, played by Camilla Beeput in Big Finish's *The Ninth Doctor Adventures: Series One* (2021). An intergalactic chef at the *Sphere of Freedom*, Nova is an eleventh-generation human refugee from the outer colonies, and so she has never even heard of Earth. She meets the Doctor as he's investigating time eddies, and though she's initially distrustful of him, she is soon won over – albeit mainly due to his agreeing to help her escape her life, which consists of fourteen-hour shifts in return for food and grubby sleeping quarters. As such, she follows the Doctor's orders to the letter, and is frustrated when the Doctor accidentally disappears into the TARDIS for three weeks.

Before she can join him in his ship, she's taken away by a time eddy and ends up on a planet covered in massive plants (*Cataclysm*). The Doctor finally rescues her in the TARDIS, and the pair find themselves on the planet Tarlishia, where they hope to learn why Sphere of Freedom CEO, Audrey Mohinson, is manipulating the time eddies.

It's a good thing that Nova likes science fiction, as she's quickly swept up in talk of time particles and teaming up with a ragtag group of time-eddy-displaced individuals including the former leader of the Roman Empire, Marcus Aurelius Gallius (*Food Fight*). Her former distrust of the Doctor comes back, however, when that timeline is aborted and the Ninth Doctor meets her again; this time, though, he befriends Mohinson, who agrees to give her enough credits to start a new life. Nova and the Doctor then bond over drinks, with the former explaining her love of sci-fi and gaming comes from her father; when the Doctor offers her one trip in the TARDIS, he says he already knows exactly the right place and time.

In 2023's *Red Darkness*, the Doctor meets Callen Lennox and his guide dog, Doyle, on Solis Kailya. Callen suffers from poor eyesight due to macular degeneration and red-green colour blindness, so Doyle is his 'seeing' dog; more than this, however – Doyle can also talk, using a neural relay! The Border Collie, voiced by Harki Bhambra, doesn't immediately like the Doctor, perhaps borne from not trusting outsiders given that colonists have been going missing, and the fact he's supposed to look out for Callen, who's still young (voice actor, Adam Martyn, being in his twenties at the time of recording) and adventurous.

Helpfully, Doyle can detect the real threat to the colonists – that is, Vashta Nerada, as seen on TV in *Silence in the Library/ Forest of the Dead*, combined with the malicious waveform, Vermine, to create the Red Darkness – but that's not enough to save Iona Lennox, Callen's mother, an optics specialist who was studying the unique light properties of the planet and the Red Darkness. After defeating the Vashta Nerada and Vermine, Callen feels displaced from his home, so the Doctor takes him and Doyle with him in the TARDIS. They travel together for a short time, though Doyle annoys the Doctor by asking for frequent toilet breaks. Nonetheless, Doyle's natural herding instincts come in handy on the spaceship Greenwood when he helps round up giant maggots (*The Green Gift*, a sequel to *The Green Death*). Though Callen is a keen explorer, the Ninth Doctor isn't quite ready to travel with anyone long-term, still suffering from the Time War, and is looking for an appropriate place for his new companions to settle down. Sure enough, Callen and Doyle stay to make a new life, having become emotionally attached to bio-habitat guardian, Tay Lothlor, and her dog, Lyrka.

The Tenth Doctor
David Tennant

'*Once upon a time there were people in charge of those laws, but they died. They all died. Do you know who that leaves? Me!*'
The Doctor – *The Waters of Mars*

Regenerated and healed, the Doctor finds himself drawn ever closer to Rose, to the point where he starts to lose much of the man he used to be – the distant traveller from Gallifrey is becoming more and more human. And not always the best example of one. The consequences of this humanisation follows him throughout his tenth incarnation, with devastating results...

Rose Tyler – Billie Piper – Continued... (*Rose* to *Doomsday* and *Partners in Crime,* and *Turn Left* to *Journey's End,* plus *The End of Time*)

She was so sure she knew the Doctor, but as his new face is presented to her, Rose realises she knows very little. Despite witnessing the change, she can't believe it at first, and is convinced an imposter has replaced the Doctor, suggesting it's some kind of body swap, a teleport, or somehow a Slitheen in disguise, despite the obvious lack of zip on the forehead. He insists it's him, but Rose wants him to change back. In spite of her distress, she still asks about Jack, and the Doctor simply says he's remained behind to rebuild Earth (it's a lie: the Doctor actively ran away from Jack – or, more accurately, what Bad Wolf-Rose did to him). She's scared when the regeneration begins to fail, and the unstable Doctor sends the TARDIS crashing towards Christmas 2006.

The TARDIS seems to alert both Jackie and Mickey to its

imminent arrival – they both hear the engines long before it materialises mid-air, not something that typically happens – so they're both on hand at the beginning of *The Christmas Invasion* to help Rose with the Doctor. Jackie is understandably confused, and intrigued by the notion of the Doctor having two hearts, but Rose is in no mood to humour her and responds with irritation, although she's curious as to why there are a pair of men's pyjamas and dressing gown at her mother's flat (they belong to one of Jackie's male 'friends'). Rose sits vigil over the Doctor as he recovers in the spare room, finding it difficult to explain what has happened. The more she looks at him, the more her heart breaks: on some level, she's convinced that she's lost the Doctor. Worse, that he's *left her*. As a distraction, she goes Christmas shopping with Mickey, who offers his support once more, even though he's tired of hearing about the Doctor. It's not long before they're being attacked by robot Santas and have to rush back to the flat. 'They were after us,' she tells Mickey. 'What's important about us? Nothing, except the one thing we've got tucked up in bed: the Doctor.' It's an interesting step for Rose: she acknowledges that he's still the Doctor, but also reveals her own estimation of herself has dropped, no longer considering herself important.

When a Christmas tree attacks them in the flat, tearing through the door and wall into the spare room, it's only a whisper from Rose that wakes the Doctor; he instantly disposes of the tree and confronts the Santas, which he calls pilot fish, signalling the arrival of something much more dangerous. That something is the Sycorax, and when they appear on a news programme, Rose realises how much trouble they really are in – even she cannot understand what they are saying, as if somehow the Doctor has damaged the circuit in the link between her and the TARDIS. Things become more desperate when the Sycorax ship hovers over London and they take control of a large percentage of the Earth's people. After hearing a plea from Prime Minister Harriet Jones, who begs for the Doctor's help, Rose breaks down. Now, to her mind, the Doctor really has gone. She knows she cannot cope without him: the only thing she can think to do is hide in the TARDIS with the Doctor. This she does and, along with Mickey, is transported to the Sycorax ship. She attempts to use knowledge gained from her travels against them, speaking for Earth, but she's mocked by the Sycorax who call her bravado 'borrowed words'. As soon as she starts to understand the Sycoraxic language, she works out what it means: with nervous anticipation, she looks to the TARDIS where the Doctor is standing in his dressing gown. Watching him face the Sycorax convinces her that he's still the Doctor, even though he's rude to her. Rose realises that she does still want to travel with him – she still thinks it's weird that he can change his face and grow a new hand, however.

They appear to remain on Earth for a while longer (the Doctor at least moves the TARDIS between stories, but it's implied that they're only now setting off on their travels again – perhaps Jackie convinced them to stay for the New Year), but they soon head off and travel further than they ever have before – to *New Earth*. While resting on the cliff's edge looking out towards New New York, Rose shows how much she now totally accepts the new Doctor – she states that she loves travelling with him, and together, they're much more tactile than before, holding hands and hugging on many occasions. She finds it difficult to get her head around the notion of the Cat People, and when she comes face-to-skin with Cassandra, who survived their previous encounter in *The End of the World*, she thinks that Cassandra deserved to die. This is a radical change of view: when Cassandra apparently died before, Rose was shaken up by it and even asked the Doctor to help her. But she's very aggressive to Cassandra this time around, perhaps because she's lured into a trap, without the Doctor by her side, and Cassandra gets her own back when she steals Rose's body, suppressing Rose in the process. Rose is aware of what's going on, but can't affect anything. Cassandra draws much from Rose's mind, including her obvious attraction to the Doctor, and enjoys snogging him. She thinks Rose is a chav. It's not only Rose who has developed an aggressive streak: the Doctor has too, as seen when he realises that Rose has been possessed by Cassandra. It seems that, since his regeneration, he's become closer to Rose, both emotionally and in attitude, almost as if her proximity to him when he changed has affected him.

The most obvious example of this can be seen when they arrive in the Scottish highlands in 1879. In *Tooth and Claw*, they meet Queen Victoria, and go on to Torchwood House, with the Doctor's psychic paper telling the queen that he's James McCrimmon, a doctor assigned by the Lord Provost as her protector. The Doctor passes Rose off as a feral child he 'bought for sixpence in old London Town. It was either her or the Elephant Man'. Rose can't believe she's meeting Queen Victoria, and makes a bet with the Doctor that she can get the queen to say, 'I am not amused'; still, Rose seems to have a considerable lack of respect for Queen Victoria. Such questionable actions are compounded by the Doctor actively taking part in the bet – although he at least has the decency to look embarrassed from time to time. This doesn't stop him from laughing and cheering with Rose, *in front* of Her Majesty, when Victoria finally says, 'and I am *not* amused' for which she gives them both a proper dressing down before banishing them both from the British Empire. At least she knights them Sir Doctor of TARDIS and Dame Rose of the Powell Estate, for saving her life from a werewolf. She tells them she sees a bad end for them if they continue 'straying from all that is good'. Unfortunately, neither takes any heed of what she tells them.

They're called back to 2007 by Mickey, who has heard reports of possible alien activity at a local London school in *School Reunion* (Rose thinks he has called her back just because he wants to see her, but he tells her no). Investigating the school proves to be an eye-opener for Rose when she meets the Doctor's old companion, Sarah Jane Smith, who hasn't seen the Doctor for some twenty-seven years (assuming he dropped her off in her own time of 1980 in *The Hand of Fear*). Rose is threatened by Sarah's presence, and is very jealous of the bond she shares with the Doctor. As Mickey points out, it's like Rose is meeting the Doctor's ex. As a result,

Rose constantly makes snide comments relating to Sarah's age and tries to undermine her experiences. She's confronted with what the Doctor calls the 'curse of a Time Lord': although she may live her entire life with him, he can never live his whole life with her. She'll grow old and die, but he will simply regenerate and carry on. Rose doesn't like the idea that the Doctor may one day leave her, like he did Sarah, since once they were obviously as close as he and Rose are now. She remains competitive with Sarah until they end up arguing over the things they've seen and Sarah trumps her by announcing that she met the Loch Ness Monster! They burst out laughing and bond by mocking the Doctor over how he tends to explain things at such a high speed that they can never keep up, and how he strokes bits of the TARDIS. In the end, Rose seeks Sarah's advice – should she continue travelling with the Doctor? Sarah says that some things are worth getting your heart broken over (a sentiment reinforced in the following episode). The Doctor asks Sarah to go with them, but she refuses, feeling she's too old for it; however, she suggests he take Mickey – the Doctor needs a Smith on board. Rose is less than impressed and mouths a 'no' to the Doctor, but he appears not to notice and agrees to let Mickey join.

Rose's view on Mickey's presence totally shifts in the time it takes them to reach the space station, *SS Madame de Pompadour*. From the beginning of *The Girl in the Fireplace*, Rose enjoys having Mickey around, and teaches him the rules of travelling with the Doctor, now the expert in a way she'd tried to be to Adam in *The Long Game*. In some ways, the camaraderie between the three of them is reminiscent of that which existed between the Doctor, Rose, and Jack at the beginning of *Boom Town*. This would normally suggest a lengthy passage of time between stories, except Mickey explicitly states that this is his first journey. As is to be expected, Rose is not impressed by the Doctor's preoccupation with Reinette (or Jeanne-Antoinette Poisson to use her given name, i.e. Madame de Pompadour) and Mickey takes great pleasure in this, quoting Sarah and Cleopatra as further examples of the Doctor having a 'girl in every fireplace'. Rose insists it's not like that, protests that come across as quite hollow. Unusually for Rose, she's impressed when she meets Reinette and shows the woman some respect – more than she showed Queen Victoria anyway. After the Doctor appears stranded in the past, Rose is obviously upset, realising he has no way back and she can't pilot the TARDIS to him (any knowledge she had was removed when the Doctor took the vortex out of her in *The Parting of the Ways*). Naturally, the Doctor finds a way back. After receiving a letter written for him by Reinette before her death, Rose doesn't know how to reach him through his pain, and it takes Mickey to lead her away, allowing the Doctor to grieve on his own.

The Doctor and Rose are back to their old selves again in the following story, *Rise of the Cybermen*, ganging up on Mickey as they share stories. They even leave him with his finger pressed down on a button on the TARDIS console for no reason, the Doctor forgetting he'd asked him to do this for half an hour. He's the spare part and realises this. They arrive on an alternative version of Earth (Pete's World, as it becomes known), where Rose discovers her father is not only alive, but is rich and still married to Jackie. The Doctor tries to warn her that the Pete of this world is not her father, but she *has* to go and see him. She walks off, leaving the Doctor torn between her and Mickey, who heads off to explore London on his own; Mickey points out that the Doctor knows nothing about him: 'There's no real choice is there? It'll always be Rose.' Rose doesn't actually exist in this reality, although Jackie does have a dog called Rose – a fact that amuses the Doctor endlessly. Rose is less impressed. She explains to the Doctor about Mickey's past, how he was raised by his gran who died some years ago (she's alive on Pete's World), and begins to realise that she's always taken him for granted. It's a realisation that comes too late, since Mickey has discovered his gran (or rather Ricky's gran – Ricky being the Pete's World version of Mickey, who dies at the hands of the Cybermen) and Mickey finds a place for himself on the alternative Earth.

Jealousy rears its head after the Doctor and Rose disguise themselves as waiting staff to gatecrash Jackie's birthday party. The Doctor tells her what he learned from Lucy, another waitress, and Rose responds with typically scathing comments. She talks to Pete, who finds himself opening up to her, though he can't understand why since he's only just met her. Later, when told who Rose is, he can't deal with the idea that she's his daughter, and walks away from her. He is not her father. This crushes her, as the Doctor warned her it would. Her conversation with Jackie is even worse. At first, Jackie chats happily to Rose, but when Rose starts to offer advice on Jackie's troubled marriage, Jackie looks at Rose as though she's nothing. To her mind, Rose is just staff. It's a particularly nasty exchange, demonstrating that Jackie can dish out harsh comments just as effectively as Rose can.

Rose finds it hard to believe that Mickey is going to remain behind, and tells him that she needs him – perhaps realising that her relationship with the Doctor is ultimately doomed and, when that happens, only Mickey will be there for her. Mickey doesn't agree, saying that she has the Doctor, but on Pete's World, he has his gran, and she *does* need him. Still upset, the Doctor returns her promptly to Earth Prime (the main Earth seen in *Doctor Who*) to her mother and she cries in Jackie's arms.

As ever with Rose, she soon bounces back and throws herself into the 1950s rock 'n' roll lifestyle during preparations for Queen Elizabeth II's coronation (*The Idiot's Lantern*). She surprises the Doctor with her knowledge of the contemporary dialect, a result of watching endless repeats of Cliff Richard movies when she was a child – the Doctor laments that he should've known Jackie would be a Cliff fan. When they invade Eddie Connolly's house, Rose takes him to task over the incorrectly positioned Union Flags (and points out to him that it is only the Union Jack when flown at sea). She heads off to investigate Magpie's Electricals on her own, but she finds herself out of her depth when confronted by the Wire, who steals Rose's face. The Doctor's anger at this act propels him to defeat the Wire and restore not only Rose but all those who have lost their faces to the alien. When Eddie's kicked out of the house by his wife (he's the one who snitched on his mother-in-law and their neighbours), his son Tommy is glad to see the back of him, because he's 'an idiot'. Rose agrees but says that he's still Tommy's dad, and send him after Eddie, probably as a result of her own relationship with her deceased father. This shows the softer, sympathetic side of Rose, though sending the boy after a father who is threatening, and has likely abused him and his mum shows questionable judgement. It seems both Rose and the Doctor extol forgiveness.

This sympathetic side of Rose is seen once more shortly after she and the Doctor arrive on Sanctuary Base Five, on the planet Krop Tor (a planet impossibly orbiting a black hole) in *The Impossible Planet*. She doesn't understand why the Ood are so willing to serve humanity, and wonders when humans needed slaves anyway. She's polite and respectful to the Ood, in contrast to the way the Sanctuary Base personnel take them for granted. When they think they've lost the TARDIS, Rose wonders what they'll do in 432K1 (the forty-second century). She suggests settling down together, a prospect the Doctor doesn't seem happy about (could it be that seeing Sarah again was the wake-up call he needed? Note that later, in *Fear Her*, when Rose mentions she'll always be with the Doctor, he quickly changes the subject). She builds up a good rapport with pretty much everybody on Sanctuary Base, and is as fearful as the rest of them at the notion that deep within the bowels of Krop Tor lives a creature claiming to be Satan. She wonders if the Devil is real, and the Doctor assures her that there's no such thing. Such a belief is shaken later when he meets the Beast, possibly the source of the myth.

The Beast tells her that she'll soon die in battle, a revelation that shakes her up, but the Doctor explains that the Beast is merely playing on her fears – on *all* their fears, in fact. As it turns out, in *Doomsday*, Rose does die (after a fashion) as she's listed among the dead after the Battle of Canary Wharf ends.

When the Ood become possessed by the telepathic field

emanating from the Beast, Rose's rapport with the crew comes in useful: she has to motivate them into taking a stand, finding a way to remove the threat. Before falling down the pit, being on the verge of a 'leap of faith', the Doctor realises he could die and expresses his absolute belief in Rose (though she doesn't hear any of this exchange), and he struggles to find the right goodbye message for her, deciding that she will *know* how he feels about her. After learning from Ida that the Doctor has gone, Rose refuses to accept that the Doctor is dead despite Ida's assertion that no one could've survived that fall. Such is her belief in the Doctor's survival that Rose won't leave the base, even though the whole planet is about to fall into the black hole. She's rendered unconscious and dragged to the escape rocket; when she comes to, she freaks out. She has little choice but to accept her fate. Despite her grief, she's the first to notice that Toby Zed has been possessed by the Beast, and uses a bolt gun to break the screen in the rocket cockpit, sending him into the black hole. She's understandably elated when the TARDIS latches on to the rocket and prevents it from following the Beast into the black hole. She subsequently shares a happy reunion with the Doctor in the TARDIS.

In *Love & Monsters*, we get a rare look at what it's like to be left behind, seeing life through Jackie's eyes for a short time. Her sadness and fear for Rose is palpable, never knowing where her daughter is, or if she's ever going to return home again. She sometimes gets a phone call, but it's never enough. Nonetheless, she's fiercely loyal to both Rose and the Doctor when she discovers that Elton Pope has only befriended her to find out more about the Doctor. When Rose next rings her mum, Jackie tells her all about Elton; Rose then tracks him down to give him a piece of her mind. Despite her anger, Rose realises how upset Elton is over losing the woman he loves, and she sits and comforts him, once again showing her compassionate side.

Soon, Rose finds herself alone again. In *Fear Her*, she has to solve an alien problem without the Doctor after he's turned into a drawing by a girl called Chloe Webber (who's been imbued by the reality-altering Isolus). Rose isn't very good with children – she calls them 'little terrors' at one point – and is shocked to learn that the Doctor was a dad once. Nonetheless, she proves herself capable of stepping into the Doctor's shoes, but panics and breaks down when everyone else reappears but the Doctor doesn't. She's overjoyed when he does show up, first at the London 2012 Olympic opening ceremony then when he comes back for her.

Rose says she's going to stay with the Doctor forever at the beginning of *Army of Ghosts*, but she soon learns that it's not going to be that easy. Like so many teenagers living away from home, she still brings her washing to her mother whenever she and the Doctor return to see Jackie. While Rose is operating the TARDIS console, helping the Doctor track the source of the 'ghost shifts' happening throughout the UK, Jackie expresses concern that Rose is becoming like the Doctor. She's convinced that one day she'll not be 'Rose' anymore, but an unrecognisable stranger with no remaining ties to Earth. Rose isn't so sure that's a bad thing at all.

On finding their way to Torchwood Tower (in real life, One Canada Square, also known as Canary Wharf), the Doctor passes Jackie off as Rose after Yvonne Hartman, director of Torchwood One, points out he's known for travelling with a companion. Rose remains inside the TARDIS as it's moved into a storage area, and decides to investigate the place herself. She uses the psychic paper to enable this, showing some of the brazen-like qualities the Doctor often uses (or, as the Seventh Doctor once said, 'act as if you own the place'). She's a lot more confident this time around, having learned much from her moments without the Doctor since *The Christmas Invasion* when she failed so miserably to impress the Sycorax. Unknowingly, she's guided to the Sphere Room by Mickey, who has already infiltrated Torchwood under the name Samuel. When he reveals himself, just as the Sphere becomes active, Rose is very pleased to see him, noticing a change in him since *The Age of Steel* (for him, it's been three years, since time on Pete's World moves faster than on Earth Prime).

While the Cybermen invade elsewhere, having passed through

the void between realities following the Sphere (a Void Ship, as the Doctor later calls it), Rose and Mickey find themselves facing four Daleks who are hiding in the Void Ship, safe from the Time War. These four, led by Dalek Sec, are the Cult of Skaro, a specially bred Dalek group tasked with thinking of new and unconventional ways to continue the Dalek Empire. Rose uses her knowledge of the Daleks to keep herself and Mickey alive, but when they continue to threaten her, she takes great pleasure in pointing out that she destroyed the Emperor. The Daleks have something called the Genesis Ark, later revealed to be a prison of Time Lord design, housing millions of Daleks. It can only be opened by the genetic imprint of someone who's travelled through the time vortex – which includes both Rose and Mickey. To save Mickey, who she calls the bravest human she knows, Rose agrees to open the Ark. As it turns out, Mickey accidentally provides the genetic imprint when he stumbles during a rescue by the Doctor and a combined army of Torchwood militia and Cybermen. Pete also returns, and Rose is there to witness the reunion between him and Jackie. It's a deeply emotional moment, tinged with humour when Jackie discovers Pete is rich ('I don't care about that… How rich?' Jackie asks. 'Very,' is Pete's response. 'I don't care about that… How very?' Jackie then wants to know).

The only way to defeat the Daleks and the Cybermen is to return them to the Void, but to do so will drag in anyone else who has crossed realities. This includes Rose. The Doctor realises that she has to return to Pete's World, but she refuses to go, even when Pete tricks her into travelling there. She immediately returns to Torchwood One, leaving Jackie and Mickey heartbroken in the knowledge that they'll never see her again. But in the moment, Rose seems not to care: all that's important to her is being with the Doctor. While the Daleks and Cybermen are sucked into the Void, Rose loses her grip on the lever controlling the breach in the Void, and almost falls in too, but is rescued at the last second by Pete who takes her to his world. The breach is closed one final time, and Rose, realising she can never get back, falls apart while her parents and Mickey watch on, unable to comfort her.

After several months living on Pete's World, and now working for their version of Torchwood, Rose hears the Doctor's voice in her dreams. She easily convinces her parents (Jackie now being three months pregnant) and Mickey to travel with her to find the source of the Doctor's voice – a beach in Norway called Dårlig Ulv Stranden (Bad Wolf Bay). The Doctor has found the final breach and is burning a star just to send Rose a final message. As they say goodbye, Rose's heart breaks and she asks if she will ever see him again. He says there's no chance; once the breach is sealed, that's it. To cross the dimension again would destroy both worlds. She tells him, finally, that she loves him to which the Doctor replies 'quite right, too. And I suppose, if it's my last chance to say it: Rose Tyler...' He doesn't get a chance to finish his sentence; the breach closes and he's left without her, a tear in his eye.

It's unclear how much time passes before we see Rose again, but taking into account the faster-than-normal flow of time on Pete's World, we can assume that more than two years have passed (two years being the time between *Doomsday* and *Turn Left* for Earth Prime). There's a confidence to Rose seldom seen before, and her voice has aged somewhat. Torchwood on Pete's World has created the Dimension Cannon, a device that's able to send people from one world to another. They've also discovered that something's wrong with the timelines: the stars are disappearing and the darkness is approaching. For reasons Rose can't work out, the timelines converge on Donna Noble, and they meet briefly in early 2009 in *Partners in Crime*, before Donna heads off with the Doctor. Neither knows each other at this point. Rose tries to contact the Doctor directly, first on the TARDIS scanner in *The Poison Sky* and later through a television in *Midnight*.

She eventually tracks the Doctor down on Christmas Day 2007. However, she ends up in Donna's World (an alternative branch of reality created by the Time Beetle, which has latched on to Donna) in *Turn Left*. She arrives too late, and the Doctor is dead. Without Donna to stop him, he drowns when he empties the Thames to kill the Racnoss buried in the centre of the Earth. She continues to return at various points over the next couple of years, but it's always in Donna's World and she realises that somehow Donna is the nexus. By this point, Rose has learned all about her, clearly having studied the timelines since she knows about the raffle ticket that Donna will be buying the following Christmas (2008), and she is aware that Jack and his Torchwood team manage to defeat the Sontarans in 2009. She spends some time working with UNIT in Donna's World, although she won't tell them her name, and shows them how to scrape off the surface technology of the TARDIS (found in London, left behind when the Doctor died at Christmas 2007), enabling them to create a primitive time machine using mirrors. She convinces Donna that she has to return to Earth Prime and find a way to make her younger self turn right and head towards her ultimate destiny with the Doctor. Donna does this, and Rose is able to finally cross over to Earth Prime, where she stands over the dying Donna. Rose gets Donna to pass on a message to the Doctor – two words: 'Bad Wolf'. These words warn the Doctor of the impending danger, and signal that Rose is soon to return to him.

Rose is reunited with the Doctor on Earth Prime, which has been shifted to the Medusa Cascade by the Daleks in *The Stolen Earth*, but not before saving Wilfred Mott and Sylvia Noble, Donna's grandfather and mother respectively. She isn't happy about being excluded from the subspace network – which links the Doctor and Donna with Harriet Jones, Martha Jones, Jack, and Sarah – but she does seem to have got over her old hang-up about the Doctor having companions other than her. She uses the Dimension Cannon to deposit her near the TARDIS, and once the Doctor spots her, the two of them run towards each other, their smiles getting bigger with each step. Unfortunately, before the Doctor can reach her, a Dalek appears and shoots him. She's not surprised by the arrival of Jack, who destroys the Dalek, and together they rush the Doctor into the safety of the TARDIS. Their happy reunion is destroyed when the Doctor begins to regenerate. Rose can't believe it: just as she's found him again, he's about to become a new man – a tad curious, given that she witnessed his previous regeneration and knows whoever emerges will still be the Doctor. Still, she's very attached to that particular face. Luckily, the Doctor has his spare hand (cut off by the Sycorax in *The Christmas Invasion* and returned to him by Jack in *Utopia*) nearby and is able to feed all his regeneration into that, thus healing himself. They joke around a little, the Doctor coyly enjoying the fact that Rose came all this way just to find him. Their reunion is short-lived, however, since the TARDIS, its defences ripped away, is transported to the Crucible, the hub of the Dalek fleet massed at the Medusa Cascade. They become captives of Davros, while Jack is apparently exterminated. From Rose's reaction, it's clear that she doesn't know Jack is now immortal, but she strangely doesn't comment or react with surprise when he reappears later alongside Sarah, Mickey, and Jackie. Refreshingly, she enthuses that Martha is 'good' when Martha attempts to hold the Daleks to ransom with the Osterhagen key, while Martha is surprised that the Doctor finally managed to find Rose again, a comment that makes Rose smile. It's the first time she learns that the Doctor has told others about her. Once the Daleks are defeated by Donna and the Metacrisis Doctor, a clone created from the Doctor's spare hand, the Doctor and his companions return Earth to its normal place in space. It's there that Mickey finally takes his leave of Rose – he knows what's coming; Rose has her Doctor. But he's okay with that. Since his gran on Pete's World died peacefully, he walks off and joins Martha and Jack. Rose and Jackie are returned to Dårlig Ulv Stranden on Pete's World, and she finds out the Metacrisis Doctor is half human, specifically the physical part, meaning he can't regenerate, and instead can grow old with her. Rose isn't sure, but when he tells her what the Doctor never could in *Doomsday*, Rose kisses him. The TARDIS leaves, and Rose turns to her Doctor – and her face makes it clear that he's not quite the man of her dreams, but the best that's on offer.

In *The Day of the Doctor*, the Moment, the sentient world-destroyer that the War Doctor intends to use to end the war between the Time Lords and the Daleks, takes the appearance of Rose as someone significant from his past or his personal future (it always gets those two mixed up). The Moment talks him out of activating the bomb by showing him the Tenth and Eleventh Doctors – 'the man who regrets and the man who forgets', respectively. Though the War Doctor doesn't recognise Rose yet (he regenerates into the incarnation who would), he still thanks his 'Bad Wolf Girl' for helping him find a way out of the Time War.

Mickey Smith – **Noel Clarke** (*Rose, Aliens of London/World War Three, Boom Town, The Parting of the Ways* to *New Earth, School Reunion* to *Rise of the Cybermen/The Age of Steel, Army of Ghosts/Doomsday*, and *The Stolen Earth/Doomsday*, plus *The End of Time*)

Hold On (John Lennon and Plastic Ono Band); *Learning to Fly* (Pink Floyd).

Mickey Smith isn't the first companion to not immediately join the Doctor after meeting him (Nyssa, for instance, met the Doctor on Traken but didn't come aboard the TARDIS until the Watcher picked her up in the following serial), nor is he the last (Donna Noble refused the offer before realising her mistake); however, he is the companion who took longest to mull over travelling, initially meeting the Doctor via his on-off-girlfriend, Rose.

Mickey isn't a natural to this life. When Rose's place of work is blown up, he's concerned for her but equally intent on seeing a football match down the pub. He's also terrified of the Nestene Consciousness, cowering away in the corner of a warehouse it occupies (*Rose*) and stammers that 'it can talk' (it's likely that Mickey can't tell what it's saying, though; we only hear alien gurgles and yells until the TARDIS materialises and the Nestene says 'Time Lord' – the first time the species is mentioned in twenty-first century *Doctor Who*). When the Doctor's captured, too, his cowardice kicks in again as he implores Rose to leave him. Then again, Mickey was kidnapped by the Nestene and has spent some time feeling out of his depth and alone. Still, it perhaps says a lot about Mickey and his relationship with Rose that, when he's replaced by an Auton, his girlfriend doesn't realise.

And after Rose ditches him for the TARDIS, Mickey has a rough twelve months. After she disappeared, Mickey tries telling people what has happened, but naturally, no one believes him. Instead, people think he's killed her. Mickey must've been very isolated and spent much of his time researching the Doctor, grimly realising that his name would appear online and in the history books, 'followed by a list of the dead.' He's spent a year looking on every street corner, every day, for the blue box – and when it does come back, no one even tells him (*Aliens of London*). He hears its engines as it temporarily dematerialises and by the time he gets to it, it's gone. His automatic reaction is to head to Jackie's flat, where he does indeed find Rose. 'Someone owes Mickey an apology,' chimes in a neighbour. Rose does apologise, but the neighbour actually means Jackie, who has spent the intervening time hounding Mickey, spreading rumours about him to residents of the Powell Estate (who react by similarly treating him as guilty until proven innocent).

This Mickey, however, has grown considerably. While acquiring knowledge of the Doctor and even UNIT, he's also gained a lot of courage and good ethics. Despite how she's treated him, Mickey seems close to Jackie and he defends her with a baseball bat when a Slitheen comes after her. Seemingly unconcerned about his own safety, he tells her to 'just run; don't look back.' Sadly, Rose begs the Doctor for help because the alien is attacking her mother, showing little concern for her boyfriend.

For much of *Aliens of London/World War Three*, the Ninth Doctor is pretty disrespectful of Mickey, even getting his name wrong. That changes when the Doctor has to rely on Mickey to hack into the Royal Navy and launch a missile at Downing Street. He shows great courage and determination – but also faith in the Doctor, given that this could kill Rose at the same time. Ultimately, Mickey knows the Doctor will do the right thing. Their slightly closer relationship is only strengthened at the conclusion of this story, with Mickey being frustrated over the media's cover-up of the Slitheen attack and the Doctor acknowledges that, while most members of the human race are just idiots, they're not uniformly so. Mr Smith is no longer 'Mickey the Idiot.' He's still worried about Rose, though, so the Doctor asks him to go with them, accepting that Mickey has more than proven himself, not just in doing what needs to be done, but also in his caring for Rose. 'This life of yours, it's just too much,' Mickey admits. 'I couldn't do it. Don't tell [Rose] I said that.' Sure enough, when Rose herself invites him into the TARDIS, the Doctor abides by his wishes and says he's too much of a liability to join them. Rose's invitation feels quite last-minute, like her heart isn't really in it; the Doctor's, however, seemed genuine. Still, it's arguably his refusal that leads Rose into inviting Adam Mitchell along in the next episode.

Unfortunately, when Mickey next meets with the Doctor and Rose in *Boom Town*, he is back to being a spare part. That vacant spot in the TARDIS has apparently been filled by Jack, who he dubs 'Jumping Jack Flash' and, later, 'Captain Cheesecake.' (Jack and Mickey end up getting along well, however: they hug in *Journey's End*, genuinely happy to see each other, and verbally spar when Mickey rushes to catch up to him and Martha Jones, Jack joking, 'Thought I'd got rid of you.') Everyone treats him poorly – including the Doctor, again calling him Mickey the Idiot when he accidentally lets Margaret Blaine away – but none more so than Rose. Despite promising that they can spend the evening and night together, partying around Cardiff (seeing as he's come all the way from London for her, just because she wants to see him on a whim) and getting a hotel room together, she actually runs off at the first opportunity. 'It's always the Doctor,' he laments as she heads back to the TARDIS. 'It's always going to be the Doctor. It's never me!'

She does come back to find him, but he watches from the shadows: now he knows their connection will never be the same again.

This is confirmed when he next sees her, during *The Parting of the Ways*, and she says there's nothing left for her at home. Mickey takes a brief moment, but seems somewhat determined that she's wrong, saying, 'if that's what you think.' Then he does everything he can to help her out, knowing that she might be heading to her death.

Mickey and Jackie are left hanging for some six months, not knowing whether Rose is alive, until the TARDIS drops her back with a newly-regenerated Tenth Doctor (*The Christmas Invasion*). Mickey, now working in a garage, takes it all in his stride. While the Doctor recovers in bed, he goes shopping with Rose and winds her up about her always talking about travelling. He begs her for a normal Christmas, one he's destined never to get: robotic Santas attack, then he's taken to the Sycorax ship, and sees the Doctor properly in action for himself for the first time – Rose saves the day when they first meet; Mickey's on the phone during *World War Three*'s denouement, hangs back when Blaine hijacks the TARDIS in *Boom Town*, and he is stuck in 2006 while the Doctor fights Daleks in the future during the Series 1 finale. His sometimes-girlfriend holds the Doctor's hand as snow (actually, ash) billows romantically across the Powell Estate. He'd be forgiven for hating the Doctor, but when the TARDIS dematerialises in *New Earth*, Mickey gives the empty space a lingering look, questioning whether staying behind is the right decision.

He's rather taken to this life now, eager to call Rose so that she and the Doctor can investigate strange goings-on at Deffry Vale High School. While the Doctor and Rose embed themselves into the school, respectively becoming a teacher and dinnerlady, Mickey's happy enough to continue digging into online records: he's proving himself a decent detective (*School Reunion*). That's surely something Sarah Jane Smith, former investigative journalist and ex-companion of the Doctor's, would approve of. Sarah is looking into Deffry Vale too, and is impressed enough with Mickey to suggest he join the TARDIS crew – something Rose doesn't seem entirely happy about. Her attitude quickly changes and Mickey is excited to explore his first spaceship in *The Girl in the Fireplace*. 'Brilliant!' he enthuses, 'I got a spaceship on my first go!' Indeed, he and Rose make a good team, which is lucky considering the Doctor spends a considerable amount of time away from them during this adventure. Mickey gets a bit carried away, venturing off after killer droids with Rose (despite the Doctor's advice not to), and feeling psyched to see an 'excellent ice gun'… which is, in fact, a fire extinguisher. He realises the gravity of the situation soon enough, and quickly gets his head around decidedly brain-twisting scenarios (not solely that the King of France's wife and mistress are actually good friends, but also that the *SS Madame de Pompadour* spacecraft has time windows open to track the life of its real-life counterpart). Mickey's concerned about the Doctor, but focuses on the practical problems: with the Doctor seemingly trapped in another time, he asks Rose, 'We can't fly the TARDIS without him. How's he going to get back?' This is a companion with strong connections to home; even in his very first trip into time and space, he's thinking of getting back.

You wouldn't guess it from the next serial, however. In *Rise of the Cybermen/The Age of Steel*, he's quite detached from the Doctor and Rose: while they're giggling about an adventure they shared before he joined them, he's been forgotten, pressing down a button on the TARDIS console. Mickey didn't use his initiative and stop pressing the button; then again, this is all new to him, so how could he possibly know how the ship works? It's a mistake that almost costs them the TARDIS: it falls through the Void and ends up in a parallel world, Pete's World, where Mickey ventures away from his friends to look for his gran. The Doctor is caught between his companions running off in separate directions, so Mickey acknowledges the elephant in the room: 'Well, you don't know anything about me, do you? It's always about Rose. I'm just a spare part.'

Rose treats Mickey poorly here too. She tells the Doctor, 'Mickey's mum just couldn't cope. His dad [Jackson] hung around for a while, but then he just sort of wandered off. He was brought up by his gran.' Despite calling her a 'great woman,' Rose also says that she used to slap Mickey as a child. However, she died – 'she tripped and fell down the stairs. It's about five years ago now. I was still in school.' Seeing as Mickey and Rose are the same age, this tragedy befell him at a young age. On Pete's World, Mickey's gran is still alive, and he's genuinely happy to see her... even if she calls him 'Ricky' and still hits him. Nonetheless, there's a real warmth between him and Rita-Anne Smith, and he scolds her for not fixing the carpet on the stairs. 'You're going to fall and break your neck,' he says, grimly. He assures her he'll fix it, which he likely did – later, we find out she died peacefully.

This is an important escapade for Mickey. Quicker than any previous companion, he shows he's outgrown the Doctor. He goes off without him for much of the story, pairing up with Ricky, i.e. his alternative-Earth duplicate, and Ricky's mate (or, according to a deleted scene, boyfriend), Jake Simmonds, to fight off the Cybermen. When Mickey witnesses Ricky's death, he glares at his metallic, emotionless foes, and something seems to change within him; he's essentially seen himself die, staring death in the face, but soon views this as an opportunity. After coming face-to-face with his own mortality, he's full of life. Mickey and Ricky's combative attitude initially extends to Mickey's relationship with Jake, exacerbated by the latter calling him an idiot, echoing the Ninth Doctor's take on Mickey. But he sticks up for himself, asserting that he's not and going one further by proving it. It's actually Mickey who saves the day: he hacks into the Cybus Industries network, learns from the Doctor, and shuts down the Cybermen's emotional inhibitors. Then he manages to steer an air-balloon away from the Cybus factory, shepherding the Doctor, Rose, and Pete Tyler away from danger. Mickey's bravery shines through: he recognises that more Cybermen still lurk across the world and that someone needs to stop them; also, that when the

TARDIS leaves this parallel reality, it can't come back – Rose and the Doctor will be out of his life, forever (or so it seems). Rose is tearful about losing him, so much so she has to go home to be consoled by Jackie (who immediately asks after him, implying they became much closer while Rose was off gallivanting without them), and Mickey is sad yet fully accepting of this new life.

Indeed, he sets off with Jake to take down more Cybermen. He's always wanted to go to Paris. And off they go. Presumably, Mickey returns to see his gran first, at least to sort that carpet.

It's this confident Mickey we meet again in *Army of Ghosts/ Doomsday*. He's crossed over to Earth Prime via the cracks in reality caused by the Daleks' Void Ship, and has integrated himself into Torchwood; it's heavily implied that Mickey works for the institute on Pete's World anyway. He's expecting to battle more Cybermen, so the Daleks' appearance takes him by surprise. The Doctor, on the other hand, isn't too shocked to see Mickey, having already seen Jake and Pete flitting between universes; he says it's nice to see him and Mickey replies, 'And you, boss' – a happy playfulness has quickly developed between them, and the Doctor is especially happy to see him again in *Journey's End* too, cheerily calling his name amid the melee on the Dalek Crucible. Most of *Doomsday* focuses on Rose's departure, meaning *The Age of Steel* is Mickey's real send-off. Nonetheless, he shows up in the Series 4 finale with Jackie, notably to save Sarah Jane Smith from Dalek extermination ('Us Smiths [have] got to stick together'), and point a gun in Davros' face. Over the years, Mickey and Jackie have grown particularly close, and at the end of the story, he admits to Jackie that he's going to miss her more than he will anyone else. She's confused: 'What do you mean? The Doctor's going to take us home, isn't he?' But Mickey's gran has died and now, he's *really* going home: Mickey gets out of the TARDIS on Earth Prime, running after Jack and Martha.

He's with the latter when we last see Mickey. In *The End of Time*, the Doctor saves him and Martha from a trigger-happy Sontaran, the two companions apparently running missions for an unknown agency (or possibly as freelancers). What's more, Martha and Mickey are now happily married.

That Sarah would return seems, in hindsight, to have been inevitable. This had originally been planned for season eighteen, to help smooth the transition from Fourth to Fifth Doctor, but actress Elisabeth Sladen declined the offer. However, she did accept a pilot for a potential series, and so returned in 1981 for *K9 & Company: A Girl's Best Friend*. Although the series didn't transpire, Sarah came back for the twentieth anniversary adventure, *The Five Doctors* in 1983 and later for the *Children in Need* charity crossover with the cast of popular soap opera *EastEnders*, *Dimensions in Time* (1993). Sarah's popularity is beyond question, and she's appeared in many official and unofficial productions beyond the parent show; when it came time to bring an old companion back for twenty-first century *Doctor Who*, Sarah seemed the obvious option. So successful was her return, both on screen and behind the scenes, that when Children's BBC asked executive producer Russell T Davies to create a new spin-off show, the clear choice was one based around Sarah. *The Sarah Jane Adventures* was created, and proved to be the most successful show on CBBC. It ran for four and a half series, cancelled only by the untimely death of Elisabeth Sladen, and featured the Doctor on two separate occasions – Tenth and Eleventh. Sarah herself returned to *Doctor Who* twice more, both times with her adopted son, Luke.

Sarah Jane Smith – Elisabeth Sladen – Continued... (*School Reunion* and *The Sarah Jane Adventures*, plus *The Stolen Earth* to *Journey's End* and *The End of Time*)

It's been over twenty-five years since Sarah heard from the Doctor (Christmas 1981, in *K9 & Company: A Girl's Best Friend*), so she's in for quite a surprise when, in early 2007, she investigates the strange goings-on at Deffry Vale High School in *School Reunion*.

Ostensibly, she's there to do a profile piece on the new Headmaster, Mr Finch, and he introduces her to the faculty which includes the substitute science teacher, Mr John Smith. There's an immediate connection, and she tells him that there's no harm in doing a little investigating while she's there. Smith agrees totally. She also tells him that she once had a friend who went by that name. She has no idea that it *is* the Doctor she's talking to, and once she walks away from him, he carries on looking at her, his face beaming. 'Oh good for you, Sarah Jane Smith.'

That night, Sarah breaks into the school, and finds herself in a utility room adjacent to the gym, where she finds the one thing she never expected to see. The TARDIS! She's beyond stunned, and staggers out. It seems that a part of her wants to run, but as she turns around, she comes face-to-face with 'John Smith'. 'Hello, Sarah Jane,' he says, probably reminding her of those few tender moments of past years, and she immediately knows who he is, greeting him with the same two words she uses upon meeting the Third Doctor in *The Five Doctors* (not that she remembers such an event); 'It's you,' she says, her voice breaking with the shock. 'Doctor. Oh my god, it's you, isn't it? You've regenerated.' The Doctor says he's regenerated 'half a dozen times' since they last met – thus in his fourth incarnation, ignoring the brief meeting between the Fifth Doctor and Sarah in *The Five Doctors*. She thinks he looks incredible, but she believes she looks old, although the Doctor disagrees. Over twenty-five years of fear and hurt escape when she says, 'I thought you'd died. I waited for you and you didn't come back and I thought you must have died.' In a moment of absolute perfection, the Doctor finds himself about to open up entirely about the Time War; 'I lived. Everyone else died.' It's telling of the bond the Doctor and Sarah share that ever since the Time War, the Doctor has been very reticent about discussing it, and any information garnered has been eked out of him. But with Sarah, it seems he's about to pour it all out; that is, until they're interrupted by a scream from Mickey.

There's some initial friction between her and Rose, who does not take well to the fact that the Doctor once travelled with someone else, whereas Sarah is a little hurt to learn that the Doctor has never mentioned her. After showing him K9 (who's not functioned for a long time) they take a moment to regroup in a nearby café where the Doctor repairs the robot dog. In a quiet moment, Sarah asks the Doctor the questions she never got to ask before, including whether she did something wrong, because he just dumped her and never came back. She waited for him. The Doctor responds by saying he doesn't think that Sarah needed him, since she got on with her life. Sarah disagrees: 'You *were* my life.' She says it was difficult readjusting to life on Earth, after having seen so many wonders, then admits that it wasn't South Croydon where he deposited her in *The Hand of Fear*, but it was in fact Aberdeen. 'That's close to Croydon,' he responds jokingly.

After seeing K9, Mickey realises that he himself is the 'tin dog'; the one who stays behind, and he is only called on from time to time (leading to Mickey joining the Doctor and Rose for a while). Sarah also has a revelation or two for Rose. She helps her see that travelling with the Doctor doesn't last forever – there was a time when Sarah and the Doctor were as close as he and Rose, but it came to an end. When the Doctor is tempted by the idea of being able to stop the Time War by using the Skasis Paradigm, it is Sarah who convinces him otherwise: 'No. The universe has to move forward. Pain and loss; they define us as much as happiness or love. Whether it's a world or a relationship, everything has its time. And everything ends.'

One such ending falls to K9, who sacrifices himself to stop the Krillitanes. This upsets Sarah greatly, though she tries to pass it off, and the Doctor comforts her.

She gets to see the interior of the TARDIS and, although she prefers how it was back in her time, she likes it. Finally, she gets to say goodbye to the Doctor, to give her the closure she needs. 'Please, say it this time,' she tells him, not willing to leave without a goodbye again. 'Goodbye, *my* Sarah Jane,' the Doctor says, giving her a huge hug. Turning away from the TARDIS, she fights to hold back the tears, convinced she will never see him again, but he has left her a gift – once again, it's K9, a brand new Mark IV version, and a few helpful tools, including two sonic lipsticks.

She doesn't see the Doctor again until sometime in 2009 (*The Stolen Earth*), but in the meantime, she's not idle. Indeed, her entire life is re-energised and she sets herself up doing her best to protect Earth and help stranded aliens in *The Sarah Jane Adventures*. As seen in a flashback in *SJA: The Lost Boy,* she's sent a crystalline structure by geologists who cannot define it, and it communicates with her via her laptop, telling her that it is a Xylok and can help her to defend Earth. Together, they rebuild her attic in Bannerman Road, Ealing, creating the super computer Mr Smith (likely a nod to the Doctor) which houses the Xylok. It's just as well she has Mr Smith to aid her, since K9 ends up secreted in a safe in the attic, where he is occupied in a long-term attempt to stabilise a black hole – he does return on occasion, however, when the need arises (including in *Journey's End* when he is required to upload the TARDIS base code to Mr Smith). She survives on her late aunt Lavinia Smith's inheritance, as well as using the income she gets from being one of the most prestigious journalists in the United Kingdom (*SJA: The Man Who Never Was*). She has a reputation for being an odd woman among the residents of Bannerman Road, and actively keeps herself to herself, not willing to risk anyone else's life, until a girl called Maria Jackson moves in across the road, and becomes curious about Sarah (*SJA: Invasion of the Bane*). Maria helps Sarah defeat Mrs Wormwood and the Banemother, who are trying to create the perfect human – the Archetype – to assist in their invasion attempt. They rescue the Archetype, a human boy who appears to be about fourteen years old, but is 'born' on the day that he's rescued by Maria and Sarah. Sarah adopts him, with the help of her contacts at UNIT (most likely the Brigadier – *SJA: Enemy of the Bane* makes it clear that Sarah's only real contact with UNIT is either directly with him, or with people he trusts), and calls him Luke. Joined by another teenager, Clyde Langer, the four of them defend the Earth, while

Sarah learns what it is to be a mother. In some ways, she finds fighting against attempted alien invasions easier than being a mother to Luke, an experience she is unprepared for. During 2008, she comes up against rogue groups of Slitheen, twice, as well as meeting Bea Nelson-Stanley, whose late husband once met the Sontarans, and has her first encounter with the Trickster, member of the Pantheon of Discord, who seems particularly interested in altering Sarah's chronology, using her to feast on the Doctor's timeline.

After an apparent Earthquake in *The Stolen Earth*, Sarah is horrified when Mr Smith plays her the transmission coming from a fleet of ships entering the Earth's atmosphere. The sound of the Daleks' voices terrify her to the core. She clings to Luke, the tears falling, saying, 'but he was so young', convinced that their days are numbered. She's later a little surprised, but flattered, when Jack tells her she's looking good during the subspace network conference with the Doctor, and displays Luke proudly, although she never gets the chance to explain the circumstances of Luke's arrival in her life (when the Doctor next sees Sarah in *SJA: The Wedding of Sarah Jane Smith*, he seems to know a lot about Luke, and the other teenagers who work with Sarah, clearly having done his homework at some point after *Journey's End*). Her joy, though, turns to horror again when Davros breaks through the subspace network; during a subsequent confrontation, he thinks it fitting that Sarah should be there to witness the ultimate triumph of his Daleks, having been there at the very beginning (*Genesis of the Daleks*). Sarah agrees, but tells him that she's learned to fight since then, before she and Jack hold him to ransom with a warp star given to her by a Verron soothsayer (probably the same soothsayer who gave her the puzzle box used in *SJA: Whatever Happened to Sarah Jane Smith*). She says a quick goodbye to the Doctor this time, wanting to make haste and return to Luke, but before going, she makes a point of telling the Doctor that, although he acts lonely, he's got the biggest family of them all (i.e. his companions) – reiterating a point she made about herself in *SJA: The Lost Boy*.

During the next year, Sarah and her team continue to defend the Earth, including taking on Kaagh, the only survivor of the attempted invasion in *The Sontaran Stratagem*, who wishes to take Sarah back to Sontar in order that she stand trial in the Doctor's stead. And she comes up against the Trickster twice more: first, in *SJA: The Temptation of Sarah Jane Smith*, he tempts her with a trip into the past, where she meets her parents in the small village of Foxgrove in 1951. Luke follows her there and tries to convince her to let her parents go, even though doing so means their deaths, but Sarah cannot do it; the emotional pull of saving her parents is too much. She also meets herself as a baby, and when she realises the mistake she's made, she's delighted to spot a Police Box and is certain the Doctor has arrived to help her. It is, however, just a normal Police Box, not the TARDIS. She eventually restores the timeline, at great personal cost. The second encounter with the Trickster is at her wedding to Peter Dalton, a man who has died and made an agreement to live only if he can marry Sarah. Peter is the first person she's had a proper romance with since leaving the TARDIS in 1980: no man could live up to the memory of the Doctor. By marrying him, a mesmerised Sarah is willing to give up her life as a defender of Earth, but the Doctor arrives to stop the wedding. It's only her faith in the Doctor that convinces her to do the right thing, and she shows Peter the truth of his 'angel', the Trickster. Peter alters his deal and the Trickster is defeated, once more at the cost to Sarah's emotional wellbeing. After showing Luke, Clyde, and Rani (who has moved into Maria's old house) around the TARDIS, the Doctor and Sarah say goodbye again, in a manner that echoes their first parting in *The Hand of Fear*, and the Doctor tells Sarah not to forget him. She doesn't think anyone will ever do that.

She encounters further Raxacoricofallapatorians on two occasions and has a return match with Mrs Wormwood, who wishes to claim Luke as her son, having been the one who created him. Luke ultimately chooses Sarah. She's reunited with Brigadier Sir Alistair Lethbridge-Stewart, not seen on television since

Battlefield in 1989. He helps her against Mrs Wormwood and Kaagh the Sontaran (and to gain access to UNIT's Black Archive). They've not seen each other in some time, and have a very sweet and respectful relationship.

Following the fiasco with the 'Master race' in *The End of Time*, she has Mr Smith send out a cover story, and very briefly sees the Doctor, who saves Luke from being run over by a car. No words pass between them, but tears glisten in Sarah's eyes: she's sure it'll be the last time she will see this incarnation. The following year, she discovers how right she was when she's informed by UNIT that the Doctor is dead (*SJA: Death of the Doctor*).

She refuses to accept his death, but agrees to go to the memorial service, taking Luke, Clyde, and Rani with her for emotional support. On seeing the casket and hearing how badly wounded he was, Sarah almost crumbles, the doubt setting in. It's only when she meets Jo Jones (née Grant) that she realises that she's not alone in her belief in the Doctor's continued survival – both are certain that, if the Doctor had died, they would both *know*. Shortly after, they meet the Doctor – now in his eleventh incarnation. Sarah recognises him instantly, and helps convince Jo. She seems a little sorry for Jo, especially when explaining to her how many times she's seen the Doctor since they stopped travelling together. 'Oh, he must have *really* liked you,' Jo says sadly, having not seen the Doctor since she left to get married. Sarah shares a look with the Doctor when, later in the TARDIS, Jo mentions him getting into trouble with the Time Lords – Sarah understands about the Time War now, and the pain the Doctor carries within. She shares an amused goodbye with Jo, who tells Sarah to find a good man, then reminisces with her team about how she sometimes does a search for the Doctor's other companions; like her, there are others out there protecting the Earth in their own way.

The last time we see Sarah is in *SJA: The Man Who Never Was*, by which time, she's further adopted a young girl called Sky, K9 has finally come out of his safe, and she continues to have adventures with Luke, Clyde, and Rani.

For forty years, Sarah has been out there, travelling, defending the Earth, but now, she has found much more. As she says; 'I've seen amazing things out there in space. But strange things can happen wherever you are. I've learned that life on Earth can be an adventure, too. But, in all the universe, I never expected to find a family.'

And Sarah's story goes on... forever.

At the end of *Doomsday*, we're briefly introduced to 'the Bride', who's mysteriously appeared in the TARDIS console room mere moments after the Doctor's heartfelt goodbye with Rose. It's an unexpected cliffhanger – a surprise ending kept from everyone beyond those involved. Donna Noble was not created to be an ongoing companion, but rather the complete opposite of Rose, someone who would help the Doctor get over his loss, and pave the way for the new ongoing companion, Martha Jones. Indeed, many other characters were considered for the role of the next ongoing companion, including Elton Pope (previously seen in *Love & Monsters*) and a new companion, Penny (as producer Russell T Davies relates in *The Writer's Tale*, published in 2008). It was only after actress Catherine Tate mentioned to producer Jane Tranter that she'd be interested in returning, that plans were made for the inclusion of Donna in series four...

Donna Noble – Catherine Tate (*The Runaway Bride* and *Partners in Crime* to *Journey's End*, plus *The End of Time*, and *The Star Beast* to *The Giggle*)

Pompeii MMXXIII (Bastille and Hans Zimmer); *I'm With You* (Avril Lavigne).

Donna makes quite an entry. She appears in the TARDIS seconds after the Doctor's farewell to Rose, and is as surprised as the Doctor. She immediately throws him off balance, not giving him a chance to work through his grief, and he can barely answer her torrent of questions. She doesn't accept that 'TARDIS' is a real word and runs to the doors, flinging them open into space. She pauses for a moment, long enough for the Doctor to try and explain things. She spies Rose's coat and assumes the Doctor kidnaps people – but the Doctor snatches the coat off her and point blank refuses to discuss Rose. Throughout *The Runaway Bride*, she's volatile, shouting her way through everything, taking none of the Doctor's nonsense. All she wants to do is get back to the church – from which she was removed abruptly while walking down the aisle to marry her fiancé, Lance. The Doctor isn't sure why she'd want to get married on Christmas Eve, but Donna says she hates Christmas and is looking forward to her honeymoon in Morocco. She's especially sarcastic when the Doctor asks if she has money for a taxi and she points out that, when choosing a wedding dress, she didn't ask about having pockets. Such is her rush that she ends up in a taxi driven by a Robot Santa (of the type last seen in *The Christmas Invasion*), but the Doctor chases her in the TARDIS. While racing down the motorway, she's faced with a simple choice: either leap from the taxi into the Doctor's waiting arms, or continue in the car with the Robot. She's not won over, even when the Doctor tells her to trust him. She asks if Rose did, and the Doctor replies not only that she did but also that she's safe and well – enough to convince Donna to jump.

When they get to her wedding reception, which her guests are enjoying without her, she puts on a show of her own, playing the upset bride until everyone gathers around her, offering sympathy. She then throws herself into the party, until it's crashed by Robot Santas. The Doctor's surprised that Donna keeps on missing the bigger picture: she didn't see the Sycorax ship over London the previous Christmas, nor all the Cybermen in peoples' houses earlier that year (she had a hangover on Christmas Day, 2006, and was scuba diving when the Daleks and Cybermen battled it out in 2007). She begins to accept the Doctor, as we see when he asserts he couldn't get rid of her if he tried. She responds with a simple smirk of agreement.

Donna goes through a particularly tough time, learning that Lance has betrayed her by poisoning her with huon particles for the Racnoss (which is what pulled her into the TARDIS in the first place); she's initially upset, but still regrets his death later on. She gains some perspective when the Doctor shows her the creation of Earth, but her personal tragedy understandably looms large, as she starts to see the darker shades of the universe. For instance, she's smart enough to realise that the Doctor is going too far when he floods the Racnoss' lair (indeed, it's because she is *not* there to stop him that he dies in the parallel world created in *Turn Left*), and she realises that is why he travels with people. He needs someone to ground him, to stop him from going too far. The Doctor asks her to join him, but she refuses. His life scares her, but she does decide that she's going to travel, see more of the world, 'walk in the dust'. Before he leaves, she makes the Doctor promise to find someone, because he *does* need to. In return, the Doctor tells Donna to be magnificent, and she responds with a smile – 'I think I will, yeah.'

For Martha Jones, the producers wanted something a little different from Rose. Someone less emotional and instinctive, someone a bit more educated, and slightly older. The rebound girl, in many ways. She would be, as Russell T Davies says in *The Inside Story*, 'a true twenty-first century girl. She'll have a family, but they're very different from Rose's because there are lots of different ways of approaching it.'

Martha Jones – Freema Agyeman (*Smith and Jones* to *The Last of the Time Lords*, and *The Sontaran Stratagem* to *The Doctor's Daughter*, and *The Stolen Earth* to *Journey's End*, plus *The End of Time*)

Mr. Medicine (Eliza Doolittle); *Same Old Stuff* (The Feeling).

It's immediately clear that Martha has a lot of responsibility resting on her shoulders (*Smith and Jones*). She's the family mediator, sorting through the arrangements for her brother, Leo's party to ensure that her mother, Francine, doesn't have to share the same room as her father's (Clive Jones) girlfriend, Annalise, whom Clive left Francine for. As well as juggling her semi-dysfunctional family, she's studying to be a doctor at the Royal Hope Hospital, and paying the rent for her London flat. She briefly meets the Doctor while on her way to work; he steps out before her, takes his tie off, and wanders away. She doesn't know what to make of the encounter. When she comes across him in the hospital later, having signed himself in as John Smith, she asks him about their earlier encounter. The Doctor has no idea what she's talking about, but her curiosity catches his interest, and his double heartbeat catches hers. After the entire hospital is transported to the moon by an H2O Scoop, she's the only one not to panic, and even attempts to calm people. The Doctor's impressed, and overhears her remark about the windows not being airtight, so it wouldn't matter if she opens them because the air would've been sucked out by now. The Doctor offers to take her out on a veranda to observe the moon; she's up for it, even when he points out that they might die, to which she responds, 'We might not'. Such a positive attitude attracts the Doctor, and over the next few hours, they work together to hold back the Judoon while unmasking the Plasmavore who intends to destroy half of the Earth's population to make her escape. Martha proves her intelligence and bravery, going from being sceptical of the Doctor's claim he's an alien, to realising he's the only one with the knowledge to stop the Plasmavore's tampering with the EMI scanner, and being prepared to sacrifice her life to save him and Earth. The Doctor seems to leave her behind after the hospital is returned, however. But once Leo's party falls apart – because Annalise refuses to accept Martha's story about the moon – Martha sees the Doctor standing on the corner of an alley. He invites her to go with him for one trip, as a thank you. She's initially resistant, until he proves the TARDIS is a time machine by going back to that morning and removing his tie in front of the day-younger Martha. After learning about Rose, Martha claims she's not remotely interested in him, although it's perfectly obvious that she's totally taken with him.

For a while, the Doctor remains oblivious to her attraction, even when she makes snide comments about Rose while visiting London, 1599, in *The Shakespeare Code*. She's a bit wary about stepping into the past, frightened she might alter her own future and wonders if her skin colour might cause a problem. She soon finds out otherwise; William Shakespeare finds her attractive and attempts to woo her by calling her 'a queen of Africa' and a 'Blackamoor lady', which only succeeds in causing Martha some mild offence. Her knowledge of *Harry Potter* helps Shakespeare repel the Carrionites, and he tells her that the Doctor will never be interested in her, likely as a way of gaining her favour instead. Martha is less than impressed with Shakespeare's bad breath.

After their trip into the past, the Doctor suggests another, into the future. He asks where she wants to go, but when she eagerly suggests the planet of the Time Lords, he refuses and instead takes her to New Earth (*Gridlock*). She can tell he's hiding something but doesn't push the issue. However, when she learns he's taking her to places he once took Rose, she realises she's essentially his 'rebound'. She's kidnapped by Milo and Cheen and threatens them with a gun she finds in their car. She's also disgusted to learn that Cheen is on drugs (like much of New New York) while pregnant. She still gets caught up in the raw emotion of the moment and joins the multitude of drivers trapped beneath the city, singing *The Old Rugged Cross*, bringing her to tears. She realises that she's followed the Doctor blindly, that she could die a long way from home; her family would never know. She still has great faith in him, though. The Doctor frees her from the trapped underground motorways, and the pair witness the death of the Face of Boe. When it's time to leave New Earth, she refuses to go: first, she wants to know what the the Face of Boe told him. She makes him explain about the Time War and all he's lost.

Perhaps as a thank you for understanding, the Doctor extends their time together with another trip, this time to the New York of 1930 (*Daleks in Manhattan/Evolution of the Daleks*). She meets a showgirl, Tallulah, who spots Martha's attraction to the Doctor immediately and says it's obvious; Martha responds, 'not to him'. She's repulsed by the pig slaves at first, until she realises they were once human before the Daleks altered them. She's also horrified by the Daleks' callous killing of Solomon, especially after his speech about them all being outcasts and working together. She wants to go with the Doctor when he offers himself up in place of the inhabitants of Hooverville, but he doesn't want her to get injured. Fortunately, he slips her his psychic paper, and she realises he wants her use it to get into the Empire State Building, to find a way to interfere with the Daleks' plans. While the Doctor tries to remove the Dalekanium from the mast at the top of the building, Martha works out how to channel the lightning to defend them against the pig slaves, but is saddened by their death. After reuniting Tallulah with Laszlo, Martha comments there's someone for everyone, and the Doctor replies, 'maybe'.

Much to her disappointment, he returns Martha home in *The Lazarus Experiment*, and this time (unlike *Aliens of London*), it really has only been twelve hours since she left. She truly believes he's simply going to leave her, and when the TARDIS dematerialises from her flat, she's crushed. However, the TARDIS reappears seconds later and the Doctor pops his head out, his attention having been caught by something he heard on TV before leaving.

Martha isn't known for having a social life, and her sister, Tish, is surprised to learn Martha has had two nights out in a row. Despite it only being twelve hours since they last saw her – for Martha, it's been somewhat longer and her perspective on life has changed considerably – Martha hugs her family in a way that confuses them. She's surprised by her mother's frosty reception to the Doctor; in fairness, Martha's never even mentioned him before (but then, they only met a few hours ago from one point of view). Leo and Tish take to the Doctor well, both rather chuffed to see that Martha has a man in her life.

COMPANIONS

When confronted with Tish's interest in Lazarus – an old man who's managed to rejuvenate his body – Martha warns her of the danger. Tish is annoyed, saying that Martha always finds fault with her boyfriends. In this instance, Martha's right: Lazarus' DNA is breaking down and turning him into a nightmarish creature. Martha's family don't understand why she would rush into a dangerous situation to help the Doctor. Francine, in particular, fears for her (a weakness that Mr Saxon's people are keen to exploit). This fear is so strong that, when Francine confronts the Doctor, she slaps him; nevertheless, this doesn't stop Martha from following the Doctor to Southwark Cathedral for a final confrontation with Lazarus. Inspired by Martha's loyalty, Tish also comes along, though she's not there when the Doctor asks Martha to travel with him again. She refuses, telling him that it's unfair for him to take her on 'one more trip'. She won't be a passenger. The Doctor replies, 'If that's what you want', and she takes it to mean that he's going to leave without her, until he says she's welcome to join him on her terms. As they leave together, he goes on, 'You were never really just a passenger'.

It comes as no surprise to learn in *The Infinite Quest* that Martha's heart's desire is the Doctor. When the Infinite grants her wish, she's somewhat embarrassed when the Doctor appears.

While trapped in an escape pod with Riley Vashtee and heading towards a living sun (*42*), Martha holds on to the belief that the Doctor will save her. The Doctor risks his life to do so and dons a spacesuit. 'I'm not going to lose her,' he affirms. As hope slips away, Martha phones her mother, trying to keep things light and to let Francine know that she loves her; this only worries Francine more. Unable to deal with her mother bad-mouthing the Doctor again, Martha hangs up, unaware that the call is being recorded by Mr Saxon's people. The Doctor saves her, and when he's consumed by a fragment of the living sun, Martha doesn't trust anyone else to work on him. He wants to tell her something important, but doesn't get the chance – Martha has no idea how close she is to learning about regeneration.

Using her initiative to save them all, Martha takes command and demands they dump the *SS Pentallian's* fuel. Martha works out that Riley's fallen for her, but all she can say is, 'It was nice... Not dying with you'. The Doctor finally gives her a TARDIS key. Martha calls her mother again, and agrees to come for tea on Election Day. Naturally, they don't get there straight away.

Instead, after a dangerous encounter with the Family of Blood, the Doctor realises he needs to hide for three months – the remainder of the Family's lifespan – until they die. To do this, he puts his life in Martha's hands by transferring his essence into a fob watch via a Chameleon Arch, which can turn a Time Lord into a human. Together, they hide out in a small village called Farringham in 1913 (*Human Nature*). Under the guise of a maid, working for school teacher John Smith, Martha protects and watches over the Doctor, and also has to deal with the prejudices of the time. She finds it hard to remember her 'place', often speaking out when she should neither be seen nor heard. She builds up a good friendship with another maid, Jenny, who thinks that Martha says the strangest things at times. She watches John Smith's budding romance with Joan Redfern, the school nurse, and goes to the TARDIS, which is hidden away and powered down. There, she finds herself saying 'hello' to it like it's an old friend, then bemoans that she's 'talking to a machine'. She runs through a list of instructions the Doctor left her, but typically the Doctor hadn't considered that John Smith might fall in love; a situation Martha doesn't know how to handle either. 'You had to go and fall in love with a human,' she laments, 'and it wasn't me.'

When she discovers the Family has tracked them down, she knows it's time to bring the Doctor back, but the fob watch is missing. To get John Smith's attention, she slaps him; he dismisses her instantly, leaving her feeling like she alone has to keep the Family at bay. She thinks the Doctor is 'rubbish' as a human and has to push him into action. He uses the children of the school as soldiers in its defence, which horrifies her – the Doctor would never condone such an action. Although she feels sorry for Joan,

Martha has no choice but to explain things to her – and uses her medical training to convince Joan that she's telling the truth.

John Smith refuses to accept reality, despite both Martha and Joan telling him he needs to. Smith wonders what the Doctor needs Martha for; she tells him it's because the Doctor is lonely, and that she 'loves him to bits'. Eventually, the Doctor returns, and after a sad farewell to Joan, who can barely look at the Doctor, he returns to Martha, who tries to palm off her revelation of love as an attempt to shake him up. The Doctor seems to accept this, much to Martha's relief, and he thanks her for looking after him.

After an attack by the Weeping Angels in *Blink*, the Doctor and Martha are stranded in 1969, where she has to get a job in a shop to support the Doctor until they get the TARDIS back.

The TARDIS returns to Cardiff, 2008, in *Utopia*, to refuel at the Rift, and Martha mentions that she remembers hearing about the earthquake in 2006. She's oblivious to the reason behind their swift departure from Cardiff, and can only hold tight to the console as the TARDIS is propelled through the time vortex to the end of the universe. She's a little spooked by the idea that the Doctor doesn't know what's out there (even the Time Lords have a limit to their knowledge), and excitedly follows him onto the surface of Malcassairo. There, she spots a body lying in the dust – a man in a World War II uniform. She tries to save him, but the Doctor tells her not to worry. She's surprised that the Doctor knows him, and sad to announce that the man's dead – that is, until he miraculously comes to life before her. She's receptive to Jack's flirting and watches the slightly off-key reunion between him and the Doctor. She's bitter when Jack celebrates the fact that Rose survived the Battle of Canary Wharf, and is unsurprised to learn that Rose is blonde. After learning what happened to Jack, Martha wonders if the Doctor dumps them all eventually.

She's surprised that Jack's carrying a hand in a jar; learning that it's the Doctor's does not help. She builds a quick friendship with Chantho, the assistant of Professor Yana, and is fascinated by the way Chantho speaks, having to start sentences with 'chan' and end them with 'tho'. To do otherwise would be akin to swearing, which Martha gently chides Chantho into doing. She also relates to Chantho's unrequited love for Yana: going unnoticed by the object of one's affection isn't a new feeling for Martha. (Indeed, she discovers that it's something Jack is dealing with too in *The Sound of Drums*.) She's shocked when Jack is resurrected again – the man who cannot die – and is saddened when she hears him and the Doctor talking about Rose affectionately. She's the first to espy Yana's fob watch, and to work out what it means. The possibility scares her, although she isn't sure why, but she rushes off to tell the Doctor that Yana is another Time Lord made human by a Chameleon Arch. She doesn't understand the Doctor's refusal to believe it: the Doctor is not alone, just as the Face of Boe promised. Yana is revealed to be the Master, and locks the Doctor, Martha, and Jack out of the TARDIS as he regenerates. Martha finds she recognises his new voice, but can't quite place it.

They return to Earth using Jack's vortex manipulator, only to discover that they missed the general election – and the Master, calling himself Harold Saxon, is now prime minister (*The Sound of Drums*). The Master blows up Martha's flat, so she calls her mother, fearing for her family's safety. She's then surprised to learn that Francine and Clive are getting back together; this alerts Martha to another trap as her parents wouldn't get back together 'in a million years'. Going against the Doctor and Jack's warnings, she insists on going to see her parents, with her friends in tow. But after seeing Clive and Francine carted away in a police van, she blames the Doctor. Jack reaches through her anger, and commands her to dump the car. Fearing for her siblings' safety, she rings Tish and Leo. Tish is taken into custody while on the phone, and Leo is holidaying. At least one of them is safe for now.

Martha's made a public enemy by the Master, and goes on the run. Seeing the Master humiliate her family, she says she wants to kill him. Unable to do anything but watch as the Master ages the Doctor using his laser screwdriver and Lazarus' technology, she accepts Jack's vortex manipulator and agrees to go on a mission for the Doctor, leaving them behind on the *Valiant* (a UNIT aircraft carrier designed by the Master).

But she promises to return.

In *Last of the Time Lords*, she circumnavigates the world for a year, crossing the Atlantic on her own, travelling from the ruins of New York to the Fusion Mills of China, witnessing the devastation caused by the Master. While she does so, she spreads two stories: a rumour that she's collecting a weapon capable of destroying the Master, and the truth of the Doctor – the story of the man who will save Earth when everything is in place. Upon returning to Britain, she meets Tom Milligan, a medic who's allowed free travel across the UK, and is immediately attracted to him. She comments wistfully that once again she's travelling with a doctor. When the Master learns that Martha has returned, he tracks her down, and Tom sacrifices himself for her. The Master takes Martha to the *Valiant* where he intends to kill her in front of the Doctor and her family. But she laughs at him, and confesses the truth of her mission. The year is reversed, and Martha and her family, caught in the eye of the temporal storm are among the few who remember the Year That Never Was. The emotional fallout is incredible. Martha can only watch as her mother threatens to shoot the Master; the death she's seen is too much for her. This convinces Martha that she needs to remain on Earth, to help her family heal. She also realises that she can't be second place in the Doctor's affections anymore, and so gets 'out' while she can. She leaves her phone with the Doctor, promising that she will be in touch and when she does he better come running. The Doctor is sad to see her go, but he understands.

Sometime after leaving the Doctor, and having qualified as a doctor herself, she's offered a job with UNIT. She tells Jack this in *Torchwood: Reset*, and they both believe it was the Doctor's doing, later confirmed in *The Sontaran Stratagem*. In 2009, she's called in to help Torchwood, and informs Jack that her family is getting better and that she sometimes misses the Doctor. There's an obvious fondness between her and Jack, which intrigues the Torchwood team – even though Jack has been closer to them since his reunion with the Doctor (*Utopia* to *The Last of the Time Lords*), he's still an enigma and they enjoy having someone there who knows him personally. Martha is careful not to reveal much about Jack, seemingly enjoying the mystery, and she particularly bonds with Gwen Cooper and Owen Harper. When Torchwood needs someone to go undercover and infiltrate the Pharm, Martha offers. The team isn't so sure, but Jack is confident: she's certainly been in worse situations. She takes on the alias Sam Jones (a clever in-joke and nod to an Expanded Universe companion of the Eighth Doctor). She's somewhat curious about Jack's private life, and his interpersonal relations with the Torchwood team, in particular Ianto Jones. When questioned, Ianto plays it coy, and offers up little information; just enough to make Martha even more curious than before.

Due to her journeys through time, she's undergone several positive mutations, and so is a perfect incubator for the alien Mayfly. She's saved by Owen, twice: once when he removes the Mayfly from her; and later when Pharm Director, Aaron Copley, attempts to shoot her and Owen takes the bullet. Owen is resurrected by Jack, and he begins to flirt with Martha, but she tells him that she's already dating someone. The difference is, Owen says, he saved Martha's life. Martha says that the man she's dating also saved her life (a reference to Tom Milligan who laid down his life for her during the Year That Never Was, as confirmed in *The Sontaran Stratagem*). Despite her best efforts, while serving as Torchwood's temporary medic (*Torchwood: Reset* to *A Day in the Death*), she fails to find a way to restore Owen's life, but signs him off as fit for duty again. She goes to great lengths to point out that she doesn't want Owen's job – she's just staying on as a favour to Jack. She is aged by the Duroc (Death itself), but is restored when Owen beats it (a third save for Owen!). Before leaving Torchwood, she snogs Jack, explaining that 'everyone else has had a go'. Jack tells her she can come back at any time, and she responds, 'Maybe I will'.

Martha makes good on her promise to call the Doctor back. She summons him to help with a UNIT investigation into ATMOS (*The Sontaran Stratagem/The Poison Sky*). They have a warm reunion, and Martha takes well to Donna, who's now travelling with the Doctor. Donna explains that the Doctor talks about Martha all the time, that he says 'really good things', and Martha realises that the Doctor has told Donna *everything*. Noticing Martha's engagement ring, Donna says, 'Didn't take you long to get over it, though. Who's the lucky man?' Martha tells them about her and Tom. Both the Doctor and Donna are a little alarmed at how involved she is with UNIT, even though the Doctor recommended her (indeed, she has Security Level One clearance, showing how high up she actually is), and Donna asks if he's turned Martha into a soldier – not far from the mark as later revealed in both *Journey's End* and *The End of Time*. Martha points out that she doesn't carry a gun, and that it's okay for the Doctor as he can just come and go: 'I've got to work from the inside. And by staying inside, maybe I stand a chance of making them better.' The Doctor is pleased, thinking that sounds more like the Martha he remembers. Martha tells Donna about the damage done to her family – that if you stand too close to the Doctor, you end up getting burned. 'It wasn't the Doctor's fault, but you need to be careful... He's wonderful, he's brilliant, but he's like fire.' She's cloned by the Sontarans, which the Doctor notices almost immediately. He questions the clone's lack of concern for Martha's family when the ATMOS gas spreads out, a pointer to his suspicions. When Martha is revived, she sits comforting the clone, watching it die and taking her engagement ring back. She wears the Doctor's coat for a short time, and Donna tells her it 'sort of works', but Martha points out that she feels like she's walking around in her dad's clothes. 'Oh well, if you're calling him "dad", you're definitely over him,' Donna jokes. Both Donna and the Doctor want Martha to come with them, but Martha is happy to stay behind. And when the TARDIS takes off unexpectedly with Martha still on board, she screams out for the Doctor to take her back. But it isn't his doing...

Despite this, when the TARDIS lands on Messaline in *The Doctor's Daughter*, Martha finds herself excited about stepping onto an alien world again. She's there when Jenny is created from the Doctor's DNA, but shortly after, is separated from the Doctor, Donna, and Jenny, finding herself a prisoner of the Hath. She wins their trust by using her medical knowledge to tend to a wounded Hath, who quickly bonds with her. The Hath don't use words to communicate, yet Martha is able to understand them – presumably via the TARDIS' telepathic circuits or through her own intuition. When she starts sinking into a bog, the Hath jumps in to save her, though he then dies as a result. Grief overpowers her for a while, but she still manages to make her way across the surface of Messaline to find the Doctor. When Jenny is shot, Martha is the first to realise she's dead, that even though she is made from the Doctor, she's not going to regenerate. She knows that she can't carry on in the Doctor's world anymore, and Donna wonders how Martha can go back to a normal life after seeing all this. Nonetheless, Martha leaves the TARDIS once more and walks towards her house, fingering her engagement ring.

Months later, she is now working in New York for UNIT's secret Project: Indigo as medical director. She seems to be on first name terms with all the staff, and when the Earth is transported to the Medusa Cascade in *The Stolen Earth*, she receives a call from Jack, who's fully aware of the project. The Daleks attack the UNIT base and Martha is forced to use a teleporter even though Jack strongly warns her against it – and she's given the Osterhagen Key by General Sanchez, the ultimate defence of Earth, placed in her hands. Once she's convinced there's little hope for Earth against the Daleks, she travels to Germany and uses the key as ransom; Rose is impressed by her, commenting, 'Oh, she's good!' Martha offers the Daleks a chance to surrender, believing she's doing as the Doctor would, but the Daleks transport her to the Crucible. After the Doctor and his companions turn the tide on the Daleks, Martha helps pilot the TARDIS in towing the Earth back to its proper spatial location, and says her goodbyes to the Doctor once more. She walks off with Jack, who tells her that he's not so sure about UNIT anymore, implying that he wants her to join him at Torchwood (since Owen died, they need a new medic). They are joined seconds later by Mickey.

During the 456 crisis, a suggestion is made for Torchwood to contact Martha (*Torchwood: Children of Earth*), but Jack won't have it, as Martha's on her honeymoon and she deserves to be happy. But when we next see Martha in *The End of Time*, she's working freelance and is married to Mickey – an odd development, since everything points towards her marrying Tom. It's curious, too, considering Martha and Mickey never shared a word during *The Stolen Earth / Journey's End*. Clearly, a lot more happened off-screen after Mickey caught up with Jack and Martha than has ever been mentioned on television.

Captain Jack Harkness – John Barrowman – Continued... (*The Empty Child* to *The Parting of the Ways*; *Utopia* to *Last of the Time Lords*, *Fugitive of the Judoon*, *Revolution of the Daleks*)

Jack's return occurs in 2008 in *Utopia*, seemingly two years after the Doctor leaves him on Satellite 5 at the end of *The Parting of the Ways*. He appears, running across Roald Dahl Plas, Cardiff Bay, towards the TARDIS which has stopped to refuel. The Doctor spots Jack, and with a look of distaste, sets the TARDIS in motion. Jack jumps onto the TARDIS, clinging to it as it travels through the time vortex to the year one trillion, a journey which kills him.

But what is he doing in Cardiff in the twenty-first century and how did he get back there? Jack uses his vortex manipulator to travel back to Earth, getting the dates wrong, and ends up on Earth in 1869. It isn't until 1892, though, when he's shot on Ellis Island and survives, that he begins to question his mortality. A few more deaths show him an unmistakable truth: he's 'the man who cannot die'. He realises that only the Doctor can explain to him what has happened, so he makes his way to Cardiff to situate himself near the Rift, knowing that eventually the Doctor will return there. After waiting six months, he comes to the attention of Torchwood Three (*Torchwood: Fragments*) in 1899. They enlist him for one job and offer him more work, but he isn't interested, until a fortune teller tells him that the Doctor won't return until the centuries turn twice. Realising he needs something to do in the meantime, he agrees to work for Torchwood.

In 1944, he meets and falls in love with a woman called Estelle Cole, but eventually has to leave. He contacts her again at some point before 2007, posing as his own son (*Torchwood: Small Worlds*). In 1975, he dates another Torchwood agent, Lucia Moretti, and has a daughter, Melissa. At some point, Melissa enters a Witness Protection programme under the name of Alice Sangster. He keeps in semi-regular contact with her, and is known to her son (Jack's grandson) as 'Uncle Jack' (*Torchwood: The Children of Earth*).

After a hundred years serving as a field agent for Torchwood, Jack returns on New Year's Eve 1999 to discover that the head of Torchwood Three, Alex Hopkins, killed the rest of the team before committing suicide. As the new head of Torchwood Three, Jack realises he'll need to assemble a new team, and change Torchwood from within, rebuilding it in the Doctor's honour.

By the time of *Torchwood* series one, Jack has taken to wearing a uniform similar to one he sported in *The Empty Child*. It could be suggested that Jack's mode of dress is a constant reminder of why he's on Earth and who he's waiting for.

Not long before the Doctor returns, Jack travels back to 1941 (*Torchwood: Captain Jack Harkness*) where he meets the real Captain Jack Harkness, whose identity he borrowed shortly before first meeting the Doctor in *The Empty Child*. The two Jacks fall in love, but Jack is very aware that Captain Harkness is due to die the next day – they enjoy a romantic dance before Jack returns back to 2008. Shortly after, Jack dies for several days, his life force having fed Abaddon, the son of the Beast (*Torchwood: End of Days*).

At some point, Jack obtains the Doctor's severed hand, cut off by the Sycorax leader on Christmas Day, 2006 (*The Christmas Invasion*), and keeps it in a jar in the Torchwood Hub – he later calls it his 'Doctor detector', which makes perfect sense since it reacts to the presence of the Doctor, as seen in *Torchwood: End of Days*. It's this reaction, and the sound of the TARDIS materialising above the Hub, that sends Jack running towards it.

Jack has now become a much harder character, almost bitter for having to live over a century on Earth just to find answers. He's no idea what happened to him on Satellite 5, or why he can no longer die. During his time in the twentieth century, he even pays occasional visits to the Powell Estate to watch Rose grow up, but is careful to not let her see him. After the Battle of Canary Wharf (*Doomsday*) Jack notices that Rose's name is on the list of the dead, and he finds himself carrying this loss with him for almost two years until the Doctor tells him about Rose's life on Pete's World – a joyous moment for Jack. In *Torchwood: Everything Changes*, Jack enlists police constable Gwen Cooper into Torchwood, and throughout the first series, she serves a similar function to Rose during the 2005 series of *Doctor Who*: in much the same way Rose helps the Ninth Doctor rediscover himself, through her enthusiasm and passion for life, Gwen's own passion for life and people reminds Jack of the man he used to be before he became hardened by Torchwood. He recognises this early on (*Torchwood: Day One*), and tells her to hold on to her life outside Torchwood; it keeps her grounded, something they all need.

In *Utopia*, when Martha steps out of the TARDIS on Malcassairo, she's certain that Jack is dead, but the Doctor tells her not to bother with him. He's aware of Jack's immortality, and when Jack comes-to, he scares Martha. Then, as is his way, he flirts with her while saying hello. But his reunion with the Doctor isn't a happy one: 'You abandoned me,' Jack points out and receives a very blasé response from the Doctor. Jack doesn't understand the Doctor's attitude towards him, but as the three of them race to rescue a man being chased by an angry mob of

Futurekind, Jack remembers the joy of being with the Doctor. 'Oh, I've missed this!' he says, beaming. When Jack attempts to shoot some of the mob, the Doctor stops him, but he doesn't stop the guards of the Silo – they're not the Doctor's responsibility; Jack is. 'That makes a change,' says a very bitter Jack.

Later, the Doctor almost falls into the Silo, but Jack pulls him back and wonders how the Doctor survived without him. Eventually, the Doctor and Jack do talk, and the former explains that he had to run away from Jack because Rose not only brought him back to life, but she brought him back to life forever. Jack is, to the Doctor's mind, 'wrong' – a fixed point in time. Jack admits to being called 'impossible' before. Even the TARDIS tried to shake him off. Jack finds the Tenth Doctor kind of cheeky, and rather enjoys his flirtatious nature, quite a change from the Doctor he previously knew.

After the Master steals the Doctor's TARDIS, the Doctor uses Jack's vortex manipulator to return them back to 2008, just in time to discover that the Master has become prime minister of Great Britain (*The Sound of Drums*). He tries to contact Torchwood, but there's no response, later learning that the Master has sent them on a fool's errand to the Himalayas. After Martha's home is blown up, he takes command of the situation, calming Martha down after she sees her parents being taken into custody. The Master makes him Public Enemy #3 (the Doctor and Martha are #1 and #2), so the three of them go into hiding. Jack reluctantly reveals to the Doctor his association with Torchwood and the Doctor doesn't approve, until Jack convinces him that Torchwood has been rebuilt in the Doctor's honour. Once again, Jack demonstrates his knowledge of the Time Lords and says he can't comprehend how such a society could produce a psychopath like the Master. He learns the truth about the Tempered Schism, a rip in reality, and how young Gallifreyans are brought to look into it at a very young age. Most run away; some go mad.

Jack still has his TARDIS key. The Doctor uses it to create two further perception filters to enable them to wander the streets unnoticed. He's amused by the filters' effects on Martha, and the

Doctor explains that it's like fancying someone and them never noticing you. At this point, Jack realises Martha's attraction to the Doctor. 'You, too, huh?' Jack asks, understanding how she feels. But although Jack loves the Doctor, he's used to not being the most important person in the Doctor's world.

Once aboard *Valiant*, Jack is killed by the Master's laser screwdriver. He recovers in time to realise that the Master has unleashed death upon the planet in the form of six billion Toclafane, ordered to decimate Earth's population. Knowing he can't leave the Doctor alone, Jack gives his vortex manipulator to Martha, insisting she escapes while she can.

He spends the next year bound in the bowels of *Valiant*, constantly tortured and killed, but he still keeps up his humour. He's prepared, knowing the Doctor has a plan – he frees himself and faces several Toclafane to destroy the Paradox Machine the Master has built out of the Doctor's TARDIS. He makes it to the bridge of *Valiant* just in time to prevent the Master from running, and is the one who takes the gun from Lucy Saxon (the Master's abused wife) after she shoots the Master. The Paradox Machine now destroyed, time rolls back a year, leaving Jack one of the very few to remember the Year That Never Was. The Doctor returns Jack to Cardiff Bay, and once again disables the time travel capabilities of Jack's vortex manipulator. The Doctor asks Jack to join him, but Jack admits he had a lot of time to think in the last year and realises he's responsible for the Torchwood team he built and has to return to them. But before he goes, he asks the Doctor how long he'll live, and whether he will age (having spotted the odd grey hair). The Doctor doesn't know. Jack tells the Doctor how he was the first person from the Boeshane Peninsula to enter the Time Agency, and was a poster boy – 'The Face of Boe', they called him.

Going from the evidence on screen, there's fair reason to believe that the Face of Boe is indeed the ultimate evolution of Jack, having lived for billions of years. In *Gridlock*, the Face of Boe tells the Doctor, 'You are not alone', preparing him for the revelation that Professor Yana (YANA, i.e. You Are Not Alone) is the Master (*Utopia*), and of course, the Face of Boe would know because he was there, billions of years younger, as Jack. What causes him to evolve into a giant head in a jar, however, is yet to be revealed. It's heavily implied in *The Pandorica Opens* that River Song purchases Jack's vortex manipulator from Dorium Maldovar, who says it's 'fresh from the wrist of a handsome Time Agent'. Dorium often works with the Headless Monks, who decapitate people, so could it be that River ends up with Jack's manipulator, as well as his squareness gun, and that the Headless Monks are responsible for Jack losing his body in the fifty-first century? Is this the first step towards Jack becoming the Face of Boe? Similarly, we never learn what ultimately kills the Face of Boe, given that Rose brought Jack back 'forever.'

Jack returns to Torchwood, and builds a deeper connection with each member of his team, no longer stand-offish as he has found *his* Doctor and got the answers he needs. Much happens during the second series of *Torchwood*, and Jack learns as much about himself as he does about others. Owen Harper, Torchwood's resident doctor, dies at one point, and Jack brings him back to life – ostensibly to get codes only Owen knows, but Jack later reveals in a quiet moment between the two of them that he just wasn't ready to give up on Owen. It's also clear that Jack is in love with Gwen Cooper, the *facto* leader. It's mutual, but they both realise she needs someone more reliable so Gwen marries her long-term fiancé, Rhys. He also engages in a more open romance with Ianto Jones, and develops a much deeper respect for Toshiko Sato, the technical buff on the team.

Along the way, Jack enlists the help of Martha, who takes over as Torchwood's doctor during Owen's enforced leave. They reminisce over their experiences in the Year That Never Was, and Jack tells his team that he would trust Martha to the end of the world. Jack is also reunited with another former Time Agent, and ex-lover, Captain John Hart (almost certainly an assumed alias, since they exchange dialogue which heavily implies John is wearing someone else's identity, much like Jack is). We meet Jack's brother, Gray, and see flashbacks to Jack's childhood on the Boeshane Peninsula, wherein we discover that his real name is indeed Jack. Blaming Jack for abandoning him, Gray buries him alive in 27AD, in the grounds of what will become Bute Park, next to Cardiff Castle, and Jack spends 1,874 years constantly suffocating, dying, being brought back to life, suffocating, dying, etc., until he's found in 1901 by Torchwood. At his own request, for fear of crossing his own timeline, he's suspended in Torchwood's cryogenic facility until he's revived in 2009, where he forgives Gray and chloroforms him – storing his brother in the deep freeze. By this point, however, both Owen and Tosh are dead as a result of Gray's revenge scheme.

Jack returns to *Doctor Who* once more in the two-part story *The Stolen Earth / Journey's End*, this time with the remainder of his Torchwood team. It takes place shortly after the events of *Torchwood* series two, with Jack, Gwen, and Ianto still dealing with the deaths of Owen and Toshiko. When the Daleks shift Earth across space to the Medusa Cascade, Jack's first port of call is Martha, now working in New York on Project: Indigo. Neither has heard from the Doctor. Martha is surprised to learn that Jack knows of Indigo, a mobile matter transmitter, cannibalised from Sontaran technology. Jack doesn't think it will work, and believes Martha dead when she uses it to escape the Daleks' attack on the UNIT building. Once Harriet Jones enables the subspace network, and Jack discovers that Martha's alive, he's relieved and learns the base code that fixes his vortex manipulator, which he uses to take him to the Doctor. Before he goes, he promises Gwen and Ianto that he will be back – he won't leave them wondering again, as he did in *Torchwood: End of Days / Doctor Who: Utopia*. He's clearly happy to see the Doctor again via the subspace network, then he compliments Sarah Jane Smith on her work with the Slitheen (*The Sarah Jane Adventures: The Lost Boy*) – and flirts a little with her. He destroys a Dalek, which almost kills the Doctor, and helps Rose to get the Doctor into the TARDIS. Despite being the first time he's seen Rose in over two thousand years, Jack doesn't get to share a happy reunion with her, since the Doctor half-regenerates before the TARDIS is transported to the Dalek Crucible. Jack has a blasé attitude to regeneration, once again revealing knowledge of the Time Lords. When confronted with the Daleks and Davros, he intentionally gets himself shot, knowing his 'dead' body will be removed, freeing him to work against the Daleks while the Doctor keeps them distracted. Though the Doctor's age is up for debate, nothing is made of the fact that Jack is probably at least twice the Doctor's age, although clearly with little of the wisdom or experience.

After making his way through the Crucible, tracking human signals on his vortex manipulator (which appears to have almost sonic screwdriver-like abilities), he finds Mickey, Jackie, and Sarah. Mickey calls him 'Captain Cheesecake' while he calls Mickey 'Mickey Mouse' – still, they share a hug, obviously having missed each other. He teams up with Sarah, using her warp star, an explosion waiting to happen. Alas, before the device can be used, the four of them are transmatted to the vault, for a final showdown with Davros and Dalek Caan.

Jack's actually flirted with every companion he's met, from Rose through to Sarah and Mickey, but the only companion to really show an interest in Jack is Donna. As soon as she sees him on the subspace network, he catches her eye, and when the Doctor survives his almost-regeneration, hugs abound and Donna tells Jack, 'You can hug me', but he just laughs it off. Later, when all the companions are helping the Doctor pilot the TARDIS, Donna tells Jack that she thinks he's the best. Once Earth's spatial location is successfully restored and everyone's celebrates, Donna pulls Sarah away from Jack so she can get a hug too. At the end, Jack walks off with Martha and Mickey, hinting that Martha should come with him to join Torchwood.

Whether or not Mickey and Martha worked with Torchwood is never revealed; by the time we return to Jack in *Torchwood: Children of Earth*, he's looking for a new medic. Martha is off on her honeymoon and Jack refuses to interrupt that. In this five-part story, we discover that, in 1965, Jack, under direct order from the government, gave up twelve children as a 'gift' for the 456. These aliens return in late 2009, wanting ten percent of the Earth's children – who are a drug for the 456. Jack finds himself having to confront his own mistakes, and along the way a bomb is planted inside him: it not only blows him up but also destroys the Torchwood Hub. He survives, but is buried in concrete. He's eventually rescued by Gwen and Rhys, and together they seek to find a way to defeat the 456. But the only way to do so is to use the children of Earth against them. Jack is forced to use the only child available to him – his grandson, Steven. As a result, Steven is killed, causing Jack much pain in the process. So much so, in fact, that he cuts himself off from everyone, including Gwen. Alice, his daughter, walks away from Jack, unable to forgive him for killing her son. He spends six months travelling the Earth, trying to run away from his pain, but it's not enough, and so he catches a lift on a cold fusion freighter at the edge of the Solar System. Gwen tries to tell him that he cannot just run away, but a distraught Jack says, 'Yes I can. Watch me.' And he does. Jack is declared dead under the 456 Regulations. By the time the Tenth Doctor next sees him, in *The End of Time*, Jack's drowning his sorrows in an alien bar. The Doctor gets the bartender to pass on a note to Jack, offering an introduction to Alonso Frame (who the Doctor met during *The Voyage of the Damned*).

Jack returns to Earth in *Torchwood: Miracle Day*, seemingly having been monitoring it since discovering that the word 'Torchwood' is being emailed all across the world. He uses malware to expunge all references of Torchwood, before heading back to Wales to save Gwen from assassins, and along the way discovers he has lost his immortality just as, across the globe, humanity discovers that it has become immortal. This turns out to be a result of the Three Families introducing Jack's immortal blood to the Blessing (which runs through the centre of the Earth). Jack and Rex Matheson are able to reverse the effect by introducing more of Jack's blood – which, through transfusion, now runs through Rex

– to the Blessing. The result is as hoped; except Rex joins Jack in the immortal stakes. Perhaps Rex is one of Boekind, mentioned in *The End of the World*. Although he's still plagued by the guilt of his grandson's death, saving Earth once more seems to have helped Jack rediscover himself and he decides it's time to resurrect Torchwood...

Donna Noble – Catherine Tate – Continued... (*The Runaway Bride* and *Partners in Crime* to *Journey's End*, plus *The End of Time*, and *The Star Beast* to *The Giggle*)

By the time the Doctor appears in Donna's life again, over a year has passed, during which time Donna has been seeking out the Doctor by exploring strange events. In early 2008, she visits Egypt in the hope of finding some excitement, but upon returning, she realises that her same old boring life will always be there. She wants to see more, *feel* more. She often sits with her gramps, Wilfred Mott (who, unbeknown to either of them, met the Doctor briefly on Christmas Day 2008 in *Voyage of the Damned*), looking up at the stars. Wilf is concerned about Donna, recognising that she's waiting for something, and so she tells him about the Doctor, adding that she's not waiting for the Doctor to romance her, but rather to show her the true wonders of the universe. Wilf hopes she finds him. Sylvia, Donna's mother, is constantly nagging her to get a proper job, which always riles Donna. In early 2009, Donna investigates Adipose Industries, unknowingly at the same time as the Doctor (*Partners in Crime*). They almost bump into each other on several occasions until one fateful evening when they eventually see each other across an open office. Donna is looking through the glass in a door, while the Doctor is outside the building in a window-cleaning cage. Donna can't believe her luck, and she explains to him, in mime, how she's been looking for him. Once spotted by Miss Foster, they both run and meet up on a staircase. They barely have time for more than a quick reunion before they're on the run again and Donna remarks that she was right; 'It's always like this with you'.

Crop circles, bees disappearing, UFO sightings: she tells him she believes everything now – apart from the story about the replica Titanic almost crashing into Buckingham Palace on Christmas Day (an event the Doctor *was* involved in). Despite all the danger, she's excited by the chase and helps the Doctor stop Miss Foster from breeding more Adipose. As they stand on the roof of Adipose Industries, she finds herself waving as the baby Adipose are transported to the nursery ship, and can't help but laugh. She tells the Doctor that she must've been mad to turn down that offer, and when the Doctor enquires what offer, she says the one he made about joining him.

'Come with me?' he asks, as if he's forgotten, to which she quickly replies, 'Oh, yes please!' The Doctor isn't entirely sure it's a good idea, concerned that things may get complicated again as with Rose and Martha. This time, he just wants a mate. After a little confusion, during which Donna thinks the Doctor wants *to mate*, she realises what he is in fact offering. She unpacks her car, amazed that they should park in the same place, showing the Doctor she has been ready for ages. Before leaving, she places the car key in a bin and rings her mother to tell her where she's leaving it. She then talks to a blonde girl, completely unaware that it's actually Rose. She gets the Doctor to fly the TARDIS past Wilf, who looks through his telescope and sees the pair waving. He's overjoyed that Donna's found the man she's been waiting for.

Their first proper trip together takes her into the past (*The Fires of Pompeii*), though hearing English, she's not initially convinced, thinking that the Doctor has instead taken her to Epcot. He explains how the TARDIS' telepathic circuits translate languages for her, and Donna's amused that she 'just said "seriously" in Latin'. She decides to try some actual Latin, but the stallholder she speaks to tells her that he does not speak 'Celtic'. Realising that they're mere hours away from the eruption of Mount Vesuvius, and thus the death of everyone in Pompeii, Donna wants to warn them all, to clear the town, but the Doctor tries to tell her that they cannot –

this is a fixed moment in time. She won't have it: 'I don't know what sort of kids you've been flying around with in outer space, but you're not telling me to shut up. That boy – how old is he? Sixteen? And tomorrow he burns to death.'

When introduced to Caecilius, the Doctor and Donna are mistaken for a married couple (a reoccurring motif throughout their time together; they are confused for a married couple on four separate occasions). Meeting with the soothsayer, Lucius, is confusing for Donna; he tells her there's something on her back (foreseeing, in part, the events of *Turn Left*). When attacked by a Pyroville, a creature made of fire, lava, and rock, the Doctor defends himself and Donna with a water-pistol – Donna is gobsmacked.

Faced with the dilemma of either dying or erupting Vesuvius themselves, Donna is crushed by the weight of the decision, but learns a valuable lesson: some things cannot be changed. She cries as she makes the decision to erupt the volcano, and continues to cry in the streets of Pompeii as she tells everyone to run to the hills and not the beach. They escape in the TARDIS, but Donna demands that the Doctor must go back: 'You can't just leave them!' She uses the destruction of Gallifrey against him, reminding him why he travels and why he needs someone like her. 'Just someone. Please. Not the whole town. Just save someone.' The Doctor relents and saves Caecilius' family, admitting that Donna is right. He does need someone.

For some reason, Donna thinks she comes from 2008, even though her native time is 2009 (since Wilf met the Doctor the previous Christmas, which was 2008, a year after Donna met the Doctor on Christmas Eve 2007).

Donna gets her first taste of an alien world when they arrive on the Oodsphere in the year 4126 (*Planet of the Ood*). She's stunned by the idea of it, until she steps out into the snow. While the Doctor is showing off his knowledge, she pops back into the TARDIS to get a warm coat and totally misses what he was saying. She's severely affected by the death of Ood Delta-50 – another example of the depth of emotion Donna feels. This might be why she holds and expresses such strong opinions; it's how she deals with her overriding empathy. She's disgusted by the idea of the Ood being treated as slaves, even though the Doctor tries to tell her that it's not so different from her time. After discovering the truth about the Ood, who are born with their brains in their hands, Donna realises that they weren't a threat to anyone and humanity has lobotomised them. She wants to hear the Ood song, the song of captivity, so the Doctor shares his telepathic awareness with her. However, she finds the song too difficult to bear, and is brought to tears. The Ood refer to them as DoctorDonna – another portent of things to come.

In *The Sontaran Stratagem*, Donna is piloting the TARDIS, doing much better than she should. Even the Doctor can't believe it. When Martha's phone rings, Donna is shocked to find the Doctor has one too. What could've been an awkward first meeting with her predecessor is quickly disarmed by Donna's positive attitude, perhaps happy that the Doctor followed her earlier advice and found someone else to travel with in the interim. She's also more watchful than the Doctor, quickly noticing Martha's engagement ring. She doesn't take kindly to being ignored by Colonel Mace of UNIT, and tells him that she'll have the salute that the Doctor scoffed at. She's surprised to discover that the Doctor used to work for UNIT, and that he's technically still on staff since he never actually resigned. Her experience as a temp comes in useful when she roots through the personnel files at the ATMOS factory and learns that not a single member of the workforce has ever been ill. This alerts the Doctor and UNIT to the workforce's conditioning. Martha advises Donna to look in on her family, and Donna takes the advice, although the Doctor believes she's leaving him for good. He tells her of the wonders he wanted to show her, like the fifteenth broken moon of the Medusa Cascade, before he realises she's just popping home for a visit. Returning home, Donna learns she's only been gone a few days; to her, it seems a lot longer and she shares a tearful reunion with Wilf. She tells him everything, and he's extremely happy for her. Sylvia, though, is her usual miserable self, but Donna doesn't bite back this time and merely shares a knowing smile with her gramps. The Doctor is powerless to save Wilf, who becomes trapped in Donna's car, choking on the fumes coming from the ATMOS device. It's Sylvia who saves him with a pickaxe. Donna knows she has to go with the Doctor, but Sylvia doesn't want her to. Wilf, however, tells Donna to leave: 'Don't listen to her. You go with the Doctor. That's my girl!'

The Doctor hands Donna a TARDIS key, which he calls a big moment, but she reminds him that they can get all sentimental after the world's finished choking to death. Donna is accidentally transported to the Sontaran ship high above the Earth, and is full of doubt when the Doctor tells her that she can figure out how to transmat back to Earth. While stranded on the ship, she rings home using the Doctor's phone, and once again refuses to bite at Sylvia's words. She shares a tearful moment with Wilf, certain the Doctor will fix things. Once the Sontaran invasion has been stopped, Donna suggests Martha join them.

As the TARDIS heads off to Messaline, seemingly of its own accord, Donna is shocked to discover that the hand in the jar, which sits near the console, is the Doctor's. Martha points out the hand got cut off and he grew a new one, to which Donna tells the Doctor, 'You are completely impossible'. She's not overly impressed upon meeting Jenny, *The Doctor's Daughter*, who considers the loss of Martha as collateral damage, and calls her 'GI Jane'. She watches the Doctor's reaction to Jenny, and decides he's not a natural father. She's later surprised to learn that he was once, but he lost every member of his family. She works out why the Doctor's so resistant to Jenny; he can't bear the thought of losing anyone else. Donna helps the Doctor accept Jenny, pointing out that she has two hearts. She's certain that, with Jenny around, the Doctor will improve. As Jenny dies, Donna is within earshot when Martha mentions regeneration, but clearly doesn't pay much attention to it (as her shock at the end of *The Stolen Earth* proves). Once they return Martha to Earth, Donna affirms that she's going to be with the Doctor forever.

When they arrive in the 1920s in *The Unicorn and the Wasp*, Donna isn't easily fobbed off by the Doctor's apparent ability to tell the date just by smelling the air, since she's already spied a car nearby. She is dumbstruck at meeting Agatha Christie, who spots that the Doctor and Donna are *not* a couple. Donna gives Christie the idea of Miss Marple and asks to retain the copyright; similarly, the solution to *Murder on the Orient Express*. She's not too impressed with being called 'the plucky young girl' who helps the Doctor out. To save the Doctor from cyanide poisoning, Donna kisses him, producing the shock he needs to stimulate the inhibited enzymes into reversal. Donna's quick thinking helps save Christie, by luring the Vespiform (a giant wasp) into a lake. The Doctor bemoans this loss of life, saying that the Vespiform couldn't help itself. 'Neither could I,' Donna counters.

The Doctor takes Donna to the Library, a fifty-first century repository of every book ever printed (*Silence in the Library / Forest of the Dead*), only to discover the entire planet is empty. He shows her the message he received on his psychic paper. The Doctor has been summoned by Professor River Song, who calls the Doctor 'pretty boy', which amuses Donna. She's disturbed by the idea of nodes that wear the donated faces of dead people. When Miss Evangelista 'ghosts', meaning an echo of her conscious is stored for a few moments after her death, Donna is distraught and talks to her, attempting to ease her pain. She thinks it's the most horrible thing she's ever seen. River knows Donna's fate, coming from the Doctor's future, but will not reveal it. For the first time, Donna has to face the very real possibility that she will *not* be with the Doctor forever. To save her from the Vashta Nerada, the Doctor attempts to teleport Donna back to the TARDIS but instead she's uploaded to the moon-sized hard drive in orbit around the Library. She finds herself living in a false reality, one in which she gets married and has kids. It's only the appearance of Miss Evangelista that convinces her that it's all fake: the park she's in, for instance, is populated by many copies of the same two children – her own. When she's restored to reality, she wonders if her husband 'Lee' was real too, and she tries to find him. He is real, and he sees her a second before he's transported from the Library, unable to call out to her because of his stutter. The Doctor and Donna share a quiet moment, both pretending to be all right, when in truth they have both lost so much; her, a husband and children, and him, River, the only person who know his real name.

While the Doctor explores the planet *Midnight*, Donna stays behind to relax in luxury, enjoying the break from their hectic life. He returns sometime later to tell her about the horror he faced, of the creature that stole his voice, and Donna tries to lighten the mood by telling him she can't imagine him without a voice.

Donna's greatest challenge arrives in the most unlikely way in *Turn Left*. She visits a fortune teller on Shan Shen, who merely distracts her while a Time Beetle, one of the Trickster's brigade, leaps onto her back and changes reality around her. Her mind travels back to a point before she comes into contact with the Doctor: all she has to do is turn right and head to an interview to become Mr Chowdry's personal assistant, instead of the temp job with HC Clements. Her mother bullies her into doing so, and Donna's World is created, a world in which she doesn't meet the Doctor on Christmas Eve, 2007, and isn't there to stop him going too far against the Racnoss. This results in his death. The extensive fallout is felt throughout the following year and a half. During this horrible ordeal, Donna is visited by a blonde girl who won't tell her her name, but insists that Donna is at the heart of everything, that the timelines converge on her. Eventually, Donna agrees to go with the girl from UNIT, and she learns about her real life. She's convinced to go back in time, to prevent herself from turning right, so she can meet the Doctor and fix the timeline. This Donna does, but only by allowing herself to be run over by a truck. As she's dying, the blonde girl tells Donna to give the Doctor a message, and whispers two words. Back on Shan Shen, Donna snaps out of the trance and the Time Beetle falls off her back. The fortune teller can't believe that Donna was strong enough to resist, fearfully asking what she will become. The Doctor is puzzled by the coincidences, as if there is something binding them together. All Donna can remember is the blonde girl. The Doctor wants to know what the girl's name was, but Donna doesn't know, recalling only the message: 'Bad Wolf.'

Donna realises the truth. Rose is coming back – and that has to be good, right? It's the Doctor's happiness that concerns Donna the most; even when the Earth is taken from beneath them, Donna continues to focus on the good. However, she's concerned about her family. The Doctor doesn't have the answers, but decides it is time to visit the Shadow Proclamation. While there, Donna hears a heartbeat echoing around her. She's told by one of the women at the Shadow Proclamation that she is 'something new', that she's sorry for Donna's losses – those yet to come. Donna helps the Doctor when recalling that the bees were disappearing, and learns that some of them are aliens from the planet Melissa Majoria. They track the Earth to the Medusa Cascade, but none of the lost twenty-seven planets are there. For the first time, the Doctor seems to give up, and Donna gets almost hysterical, unable to accept it. 'Don't do this to me. Not now. Tell me, what are we going to do? You never give up. Please!'

She calls the subspace network an 'Outer Space Facebook', and is happy to see Martha again, and particularly likes the look of Jack. When they arrive on Earth, Donna's the first to notice Rose, and encourages the Doctor towards her. She stands, beaming with fondness as the Doctor and Rose run towards each other, then watches in horror as a Dalek appears and shoots the Doctor. She freaks out when she thinks the Doctor is going to die, and panics when no one will explain what's happening. Once again, Rose explains that the timelines all converge on Donna, but Donna doesn't get it: she's just a temp from Chiswick, nothing special. Once the TARDIS has been transported to the Dalek Crucible, the TARDIS locks Donna inside, knowing what's to come. As the time ship appears to burn up at the centre of the Crucible, Donna feels compelled to reach out to the Doctor's spare hand, and a clone Doctor grows – the result of an emergency meta-crisis, a half-human Doctor, created from both the Doctor's hand and Donna. Donna is out of her depth, and somewhat insulted when the Meta-Doctor throws her own mannerisms back at her. Donna reiterates that she's not special, but the Meta-Doctor tells her, 'You really don't believe that, do you? I can see, Donna, what you're thinking. All that attitude, all that lip, 'cause all this time you think you're not worth it… Shouting at the world because no one's listening.' He explains that something has been binding them together for a long time. The truth is revealed when they meet the insane Dalek Caan – who had broken the timelock and delved into the heart of the Time War, manipulating events so the Doctor and Donna would be in the right place, at the right time. After receiving a shot of energy from Davros, the meta-crisis becomes complete and Donna's mind opens up. Donna receives a copy of the Doctor's mind, becoming the DoctorDonna, as the Ood foresaw. Along with the other two Doctors, she disables the Daleks, and returns all the planets to their correct spatial locations. She then helps pilot the TARDIS and Earth back home. While she encourages the collected companions, she pays particular attention to Jack who she calls 'the best' and later pulls Sarah away so she can hug him herself. Even now she is still Donna, regardless of the Doctor's influence.

In a tragic turn of events, she realises that her head is crammed full of too much information: the reason there's never been a Time Lord-human meta-crisis before is because there cannot be one. Donna will die if she goes on. The only way to save her is for the Doctor to put a block in her mind. She knows this means she'll forget everything about him, every single thing she's experienced since Christmas 2007. 'I can't go back. Don't make me go back. Doctor, please! Please don't make me go back.' Wiping her memory, the Doctor takes the unconscious Donna home, to the heartbroken Wilf.

'She was better with you,' he tells the Doctor. Sylvia wants to refute this, but even she knows it's true. The Doctor tells them that she saved the universe, and that 'for one moment, one shining moment, she was the most important woman in the whole wide universe.' In a rare moment of pride, Sylvia tells the Doctor that

Donna is still the most important woman: 'She's my daughter.' Donna awakens, and is back to shouty-Donna, the personality she had before she met the Doctor, who she no longer remembers.

During the Christmas of 2009, Wilf tracks down the Doctor and brings him into close proximity of Donna in *The End of Time*, who is now engaged to Shaun Temple. Wilf tells the Doctor that, 'Sometimes, I see this look on her face... She's so sad... And she can't remember why.' (This is re-enforced later on, in the sixtieth anniversary trilogy – *The Star Beast*, *Wild Blue Yonder*, and *The Giggle* – when Donna says, 'Sometimes, I think there's something missing. Like I had something lovely, and it's gone. I lie in bed, thinking, what I have lost?') Wilf urges the Doctor to go over to Donna, to make her better. 'You need her, Doctor. I mean, look, wouldn't she make you laugh again?' The Doctor wants to, but he knows it would mean Donna's death. If she remembers, her brain will burn and she will die.

When the Master transplants himself across the planet and turns humanity into the Master-race, only Donna is unaffected, and the surrounding chaos makes her start to remember. But the Doctor leaves a defence mechanism, which saves her. She wakes up once the Master is defeated, none the wiser. She gets married in the spring of 2010, and once again is oblivious to the Doctor's presence. He's arrived to give her a wedding present: a winning-lottery ticket. He gives the ticket to Wilf and Sylvia, and tells them he borrowed the pound off Jeffrey Noble, Donna's late father, to pay for the ticket. Donna thinks it's a bit cheap, as presents go, but then remembers there's a triple roll-over prize draw coming up. Wilf and Sylvia look away smiling at the departing TARDIS.

It's evident that Donna remains in the Doctor's hearts, and that she taught him a lot. When the Eleventh Doctor regenerates, his subconscious picks the face of Lobus Caecilius (played by Peter Capaldi) from Pompeii: 'To remind me, to hold me to the mark,' he notes. 'I'm the Doctor, and I save people' (*The Girl Who Died*). The memory of Donna tells him not to give in, to save who he can, resulting in the Twelfth Doctor bringing a young girl called Ashildr back to life.

And fate isn't finished with Donna just yet. She meets back up with the Fourteenth Doctor, who is wearing the Tenth Doctor's face again, after her daughter, Rose, encounters Beep the Meep (with Donna accusing it of being a Martian, as she suspected the Doctor of being when they first met), and an alien spaceship crashes in front of her. 'I don't believe in destiny,' the Doctor says, once more noting the ties that bind them together, 'but if destiny exists, then it is heading for Donna Noble...'

River Song – Alex Kingston (*Silence in the Library / Forest of the Dead, The Time of Angels / Flesh and Stone, The Pandorica Opens / The Big Bang, The Impossible Astronaut / Day of the Moon* to *Let's Kill Hitler, Closing Time, The Wedding of River Song, The Angels Take Manhattan, The Name of the Doctor*, and *The Husbands of River Song*)

Miss Atomic Bomb (The Killers); *Le Temps Fera Les Choses* (Angèle).

River Song is unique among the Doctor's companions: not only do we meet her out of sequence, but the Doctor does too; also, she knows the Doctor's real name, something even Susan might not know. What's more, she is, in a way, the Doctor's wife. Not that he knows this when he first meets her in the Library (*Silence in the Library / Forest of the Dead*), a planet which boasts a copy of every book ever made but which is also strangely abandoned. Indeed, River actually calls him to the Library, knowing how to send a message – 'The Library. Come as soon as you can x' – to his psychic paper which the Doctor seems to think might be a distress call. 'Cry for help,' Donna scoffs, '*with a kiss?*'

Considering she doesn't actually send a specific date for the Doctor to arrive at the destination, River shows considerable foresight (a recurring trait), arranging so that the expedition she's leading also gets there at the same point in time.

The first words she says to the Doctor (from his point-of-view) are 'Hello, sweetie'; his reply is the less welcoming, 'Get out'. In fairness, he has no idea who she is, what her significance to him and his future is, and he's especially concerned that the Library should be thriving, but is instead, for all intents and purposes, dead. He at least compliments her name while trying to get her and the expedition to leave the planet, lest they too fall victim to the 'piranhas of the air', Vashta Nerada. River, though, stands firm, immediately challenging him when the Doctor claims, as a time traveller, to 'point and laugh at archaeologists.' 'Ah,' she says, introducing herself. 'Professor River Song – archaeologist.' She is very au fait with his stubbornness and quirks: when the expedition leader, Strackman Lux, asks the Doctor and Donna to sign non-disclosure agreements, the Doctor rips up the paper and says, 'I don't want to see everyone in this room dead because some idiot thinks his pride is more important'. Quick as a flash, River interjects, 'Then why don't you sign his contract?' Still, she reveals that she didn't sign either, hinting at her high level of expertise: this isn't about pride for Lux (the Library was built by his grandfather to house the computerised mind of Charlotte Abigail Lux, Strackman's aunt, who died when she was a child), so the NDAs are particularly important to him. River's knowledge and experience, then, overrides even that. He needs her.

And she more than proves her worth. River is proactive, at times leading the whole group while the Doctor is otherwise busy. She's clearly badly affected by the Doctor not knowing her, but doesn't let that distract her from the matter at hand. 'This is the Doctor in the days before he knew me,' she opens up to Donna. 'And he looks at me; he looks right through me and it shouldn't kill me, but it does.'

The rug is pulled from under the Doctor once more when he increases the mesh density on a spacesuit using his sonic screwdriver, only for River to reveal that she's got a sonic screwdriver too – and it looks a lot like his. She tells him he gave it to her, and while he says he doesn't give his sonic screwdriver to anyone, she counters, 'I'm not anyone.' She refuses to tell him more, however. She proves an irritating temptation, especially as she has a TARDIS-coloured diary with her, a book in which she writes about all her adventures with the Doctor; it holds the secrets of their future together. She tells him it's against the rules for him to look inside. 'What rules?' He asks. She replies, 'Your rules.' The Doctor becomes increasingly frustrated by her, but can't deny their natural chemistry or her easy charm and heroics.

Still, it's obvious that the Doctor not knowing her wounds River. She compares this incarnation of the Doctor as like looking at a photograph of someone before you knew them, 'like they're not quite finished'. She says he came for her when she called, as he always does, but that this isn't *her* Doctor. 'Now, my Doctor,' she teases, 'I've seen whole armies turn and run away, and he'd just swagger off back to his TARDIS and open the doors with a snap of his fingers.' (This somewhat foreshadows the events of *The Pandorica Opens* and, to a greater extent, *A Good Man Goes to War*.) The Doctor overhears and says no one can open the TARDIS like that. When she says her Doctor can and he counters that he is the Doctor, she cuttingly replies, 'Some day.' It's up to him to prove himself to her.

She's already proved herself, though not solely through her altruistic feats: she figures they don't have time for him not to trust her so she whispers his real name to him. He's immediately fearful and understanding, a suitable gravitas established. Later, he tearfully says, 'There's only one reason I would ever tell anyone my name. There's only one time I could.' While this is teased in *The Wedding of River Song*, the exact circumstances are never truly revealed.

River is a lot like the Doctor, and it's ultimately down to her to save everyone, in the Doctor's place. When the Vashta Nerada attacked a century ago, the computer, i.e. Charlotte, couldn't cope with the number of teleports happening at one time, so saved the data to itself, in its own hard-drive. But now, it's struggling to cope, and needs extra energy to bring four-thousand and twenty-two people back to life. The Doctor is going to sacrifice himself; instead, River, recognising that the Doctor's death would rewrite their time together in his personal future, knocks him unconscious and takes his place transferring her remaining energy into the computer. He wakes up, handcuffed, just in time to see her death.

But the Doctor isn't ready to give up on her. In an example of the Bootstrap Paradox, i.e. when the origin of an idea is a grey area owing to a causal loop, the Doctor realises that the future version of him must've thought about River's death and wanted to avert it, so he gave her his sonic screwdriver – which included a data ghost of River, her consciousness saved in a neural relay, which he then uploads into the Library's hard-drive. There, she has friends (her fellow expedition members who'd been eaten by the Vashta Nerada, plus Charlotte) and a virtual world in which to play – not forgetting every book ever written to read. Of course, the Doctor likely only manages to save her this way because the future version of him remembers doing exactly that. River's timeline gets muddier too, as when she arrives in the Library, she's clearly expecting the Doctor to recognise her, so she's unaware this is due to be her last corporeal adventure with him; however, it's later established that she knows that she's doing to die there, as the Twelfth Doctor takes her for one special night together on Darillium (*The Husbands of River Song*) before she faces her own fate. River is a good liar by necessity, so perhaps this comes into play; alternatively, maybe her timeline is so convoluted, she doesn't know what to believe, or that it, and her memories, change.

Either way, this is far from the last time the Doctor sees the River; nor is it the last time she sees him…

Wilfred Mott – Bernard Cribbins (*Voyage of the Damned, Partners in Crime, The Sontaran Stratagem/The Poison Sky, Turn Left* to *Journey's End*, and *The End of Time*, plus *Wild Blue Yonder*)

The Hole In the Ground (Bernard Cribbins); *Knockin' on Heaven's Door* (Bob Dylan).

The first time the Doctor and Wilfred Mott meet belies the importance each would have on the other's life. The Doctor is transmatted down to Earth on Christmas Eve, where he meets Wilf, who's trying to sell copies of The Examiner newspaper, despite the streets of London being deserted (*Voyage of the Damned*). When the Doctor asks why no one's out Christmas shopping, Wilf says it's because it's not safe, thanks to all the previous alien attacks over the festivities. Wilf is resolute though: he's staying where he is, standing 'vigil'. He displays a patriotic streak, saluting when the news affirms that Queen Elizabeth II is similarly staying in London over the Christmas period to prove there's no danger (he's definitely a Royalist, also saluting the Queen's Christmas Day speech in *The End of Time* and trying to get his family to be quiet and show respect during the broadcast). He believes in the threat from above, but is resolute that it's important he stays put. He's not exactly shocked to see the Doctor suddenly transmatted away again, seemingly accepting this brave new world he's found himself in, then he recognises the danger later on when the replica Titanic spaceship hurtles through the atmosphere towards Buckingham Palace, as he shouts, 'Don't you dare, you aliens – don't you dare!' at the sky.

Wilf is an open-minded, witty, and kind person, who infers that something is wrong with his granddaughter, Donna Noble, in *Partners in Crime*. He admires her individualism, fondly recalling the time six-year-old Donna was told the family couldn't afford a holiday that year, so she took a bus by herself to Strathclyde, and they had to get the police out to look for her. Wilf and Donna are especially close, so it's something of a shame that he missed her aborted wedding to Lance (*The Runaway Bride*) because he had Spanish flu. They clearly spend a lot of time together: he has an allotment and shed from which he stargazes, and she regularly visits him. He seems to use this partly as a way of escaping his daughter, Sylvia; though they obviously get on, she's somewhat overbearing, and Donna similarly runs to her 'gramps' when it all gets too much. 'Was she nagging you?' Wilf asks Donna, straight away recognising why she's joined him. Nonetheless, Wilf is a warm, loving person, full of joy – another reason Donna takes solace with him. He's the one person she opens up to, explaining that she's waiting for the Doctor (though not that he's an alien with a time machine). 'Go and find him,' Wilf implores her. Importantly, Wilf is also the first and only person she actually lets know that she's found the Doctor, asking the Time Lord to fly the TARDIS over Wilf's allotment just as he's looking through his telescope. He's thrilled when he sees her in that blue box – once again, he shouts at the sky ('Go on, gal!') and leaps around in an outburst of joy.

Wilfred can't have seen the Doctor properly through that telescope, however: when they next meet (in *The Sontaran Stratagem/The Poison Sky*), Wilf lets out a surprised, 'Ah, it's you!', which the Doctor reciprocates.

Before this, Wilf learns Donna is back – following her trips to Pompeii and the Ood Sphere – as she visits home and he greets her with a big hug. They've clearly missed each other a lot, tears welling in their eyes. He hasn't told Sylvia where Donna's been, concluding that it's best she doesn't know for now. Still, the dangers of Donna's new life cements themselves when the threat of ATMOS is revealed: these GPS trackers that also keep carbon emissions at zero percent actually mean the Sontarans can control vehicles; their main function, though, is to convert Earth's air into something suitable for the war-loving clones. Wilf gets straight into his car, intent on moving it off the street so it can't, in his mind at least, hurt anyone. 'It's them aliens again,' he notes. He's locked in the car as the air fills with fumes, and it's Sylvia's quick thinking that saves him: forget all this nonsense with the sonic screwdriver; she just uses an axe to smash the windscreen.

Sylvia and Wilf are rather contrasting people, but that works for them: she's put him on the macrobiotic diet, for instance, but she knows he sneaks down to the petrol station to get pork pies because he leaves the wrappers in the car; what's more, she just accepts his rebellious side, and perhaps sees it in Donna too. Father and daughter are both protective of their family, though it comes out in different ways: while Sylvia is bossy and stroppy, she wants the best for them all, urging Donna, for example, to take a well-paying long-term job in *Turn Left* rather than a temp job at H.C. Clements; Wilf, on the other hand, is more proactive, using paste to seal the doors and windows of their house in *The Poison Sky*, trying to stop the Sontaran's gas from seeping in. When Donna is trapped on a Sontaran ship, she calls home, only for Sylvia to take a jibe at her then breaking down and admitting it's just because she wishes Donna were there with them. Wilf takes the phone from her, telling Sylvia that that doesn't help the situation. He checks where Donna is, and if she's okay, before asserting that the Doctor told him he'd look after her. He's amazed by the scale of the the threat, and questions whether one man can fix it. He does, however, believe Donna when she says the Doctor can. 'Yeah, well, if he doesn't,' Wilfred says, 'you tell him he'll have to answer to me.'

Sylvia is scared by everything, finding excuses to hide away, whereas Wilf is accepting and jubilant: having seen the troubles Donna is facing when she goes off with the Doctor, he's still sure that it's the right path for her. He vows to keep her travelling a secret from Sylvia. 'And you go with him, that wonderful Doctor,' Wilf says to Donna. 'You go and see the stars… and then bring a bit of them back for your old Gramps.'

The next time we see Wilfred Mott isn't under the best circumstances: it's in the world created by Donna's decision to turn right (in the ironically named *Turn Left*), a timeline in which the Doctor has died because Donna wasn't there to stop him going too far when confronting the Racnoss. This is a reality plagued by alien incursions, with no one to stop various disasters. Wilf quickly gathers that Earth is given to the whims of extraterrestrials, acknowledging that rhino-like creatures – actually the Judoon, recalling the events of *Smith and Jones* – that stole the Royal Hope Hospital must be aliens. His interjection is quickly passed over by both Donna and Sylvia, but they're more accepting the more invasions and experiments humanity is subjected to; by the time America falls victim to the Adipose (from *Partners in Crime*), Wilf only has to say 'aliens' for the normally-sceptical Donna to agree with him. Wilf remains stoic, maybe putting on a brave face for the sake of his family, channelling the 'wartime spirit' – although Donna argues that there is no war, 'there's no fight; it's just this.' The Nobles become refugees after the crash of the Titanic replica turns southern England into a radioactive wasteland – they were spared, having taken a holiday, prompted by Rose who saw disaster coming. 'God rest their souls,' is Wilf's immediate reaction to the news; he soon realises how lucky they've been: 'I was supposed to be out there, selling papers. I should have been there. We all should. We'd be dead.'

The whole situation makes Donna introspective, realising she's done nothing with her life and saying that she's a disappointment; Sylvia is especially depressed, giving up on life and rolling deeper into her rut. But Wilf is resolute. As they're taken in by the Colasanto family in Leeds, he becomes an important part of the household, keeping their spirits up by organising a cheery sing-song around the piano, initially to Donna's annoyance. It even cheers Sylvia up, and they all join in a chorus of *Bohemian Rhapsody*.

It's with considerable horror that he watches the Colasantos carted off to labour camps, the new UK policy during this time of crisis being 'England for the English.' Donna is naïve about what this really means – until Wilf points out, 'Labour camps. That's what they called them last time... It's happening again.'

Even this doesn't mean he's lost his sense of wonder. He's kept his allotment and telescope (though questions whether he should sell the latter for some quick cash), and continues to enjoy looking at the stars. It's his terror, seeing that stars going out, that prompts Donna to do something, to listen to Rose, who's been telling her she can right this reality.

Fortunately, all the miseries they've gone through are rewritten by Donna averting the timeline. Still, they have some horrors to face, as the Daleks pluck the Earth out of the sky and relocate it to the rift in the Medusa Cascade (*The Stolen Earth/*

Journey's End). When it becomes obvious something terrible is happening, Wilf ventures outdoors with a cricket bat, immediately concluding that it's down to aliens again and telling Sylvia to get back inside: 'They always want the women.' He quickly swaps his bat for a paint gun after he sees the Daleks, figuring that a splodge of paint to the eyestalk would blind them. He does try this, and it's successful for all of three seconds: the Dalek dissolves the paint in an instant, and aims to exterminate both Wilfred and Sylvia. They're saved by Rose, who's wielding a massive gun. 'Do you wanna swap?' Wilf says, ever the joker.

It's just after this that he finally tells Sylvia that Donna's been travelling with the Doctor, though it's implied that she already has suspicions yet she has been trying to overlook the obvious. Wilf implores her to look at everything that's been going on; 'you can't start denying things now.' He nonetheless tries to shield her from as much as he can: while Rose ducks out to find the Doctor, he stays at home with his daughter. It seems he trusts the Doctor to look after her; similarly, that Donna is strong-willed and smart enough to look after herself. It's entirely justified: Donna does save the universe, with some help from the Doctor, and Wilf and Sylvia cheer as the Earth is towed back to its correct point in space.

Their joy doesn't last. The Doctor turns up at their door later on with an unconscious Donna in his arms, begging for help. Wilf is naturally saddened to see his granddaughter in such a state, but he's absolutely distraught to hear that her experiences with the Doctor have been wiped from her memory. 'All those wonderful things she did,' he laments. And despite Sylvia's objections, he tells the Doctor, 'But she was better with you.' His caring attitude extends to the Doctor too: accompanying him to the door, he checks who the Doctor will travel with now, and says that he'll keep an eye out for him. 'But every night, Doctor,' he says, 'when it gets dark, and the stars come out, I'll look up on her behalf. I'll look up at the sky, and think of you.'

Until this point, Wilf is essentially a recurring character, but in *The End of Time*, he finally travels in the TARDIS and helps the

Doctor out as a companion would. He's also responsible for the Doctor's regeneration – it could be argued, in the same vein as Peri and Rose, that, too, makes him a companion!

Like Donna before him, Wilfred actively searches out the Doctor, partly because he's been having bad dreams (of the Master laughing), and partly to see if he can 'fix' Donna. He's a member of 'the Silver Cloak', a group of pensioners who Wilf gets to look for the TARDIS; they do indeed find it, and track down the Doctor. The Time Lord is nervous about Wilf telling people who he is, but Wilf promises that he's only told them he's a doctor. A smirk passes over the Doctor's face – he's obviously pleased to see him. With his fate catching up with him, the Doctor is especially dour while he and Wilf catch up in a café. The Doctor mulls over fate, that both Donna and Wilf were able to find him while innumerable others have failed to. Mott, though, has an ulterior motive: Donna has parked outside the café, and Wilf asks the Doctor to help her. 'Wouldn't she make you laugh again?' Wilf asks, recognising the Doctor's gloomy disposition. The pair part, but the Doctor goes back to the Noble household in desperation: Wilfred is the only link he can find with the Master, and together, they track destiny's convergence to the Naismith mansion. 'You can't come with me,' the Doctor tells Wilf. 'You're not leaving me with her,' Wilf counters, pointing at a seething Sylvia. 'Fair enough,' the Doctor agrees. It's pretty clear he's happy that Wilf's there, though, welcoming him on board the TARDIS (even after Mott says he thought it would be cleaner).

'We've moved!' Wilf says when they materialise at the Naismith mansion. 'We've really moved!' He's seen the TARDIS materialise and dematerialise before, but actually experiencing this shift himself from inside the machine is obviously a highlight in Wilf's life. Sadly, such joy isn't to last: the Master uses a Vinvocci Immortality Gate (i.e. a medical device used to heal entire planets at a time) to transform the human population into duplicates of himself, and Wilf is only spared by a pod with radiation shielding. Donna, too, is spared, thanks to a failsafe the

Doctor placed in her when he wiped her mind. Wilf panics when she phones and tells him that memories of her time with the Doctor are flooding back in. The Doctor has prepared for this too: Wilf is pleased to hear she'll be fine, that 'she'll just sleep.'

That doesn't help Wilf now though: he and the Doctor are seemingly at the Master's mercy, strapped to chairs as the mad Time Lord gloats. The two Vinvocci save them, teleporting them to their ship, which is orbiting the planet. It's a dire situation, but Wilf still finds time to acknowledge how incredible it is: 'I've always dreamt of a view like that,' he says, looking down at Earth. 'I'm an astronaut.' This cheery mindset affects the Doctor too – he says he'd be proud if Wilf were his dad. The feeling's mutual, and Wilf demonstrates his depth of feeling for the Master by showing him his old service revolver. If the Master were killed, the template would snap and humanity would go back to normal: 'Don't you dare put him before them,' Wilf says, then crumbles: 'You take the gun and save your life. And please don't die. You're the most wonderful man and I don't want you to die.'

Wilf's time in the military has left an impression on him. He's kept his gun from that time, but seemingly only for protection: he's never actually killed anyone before, something he's proud of (although when the Doctor notes that Wilf could've shot the Master himself, the old soldier suggests he was too scared). Wilf's morals run strong. When a soldier in *Turn Left* threatens Donna, having sensed something 'on her back', i.e. the Time Beetle from the main reality, Wilf scolds him: 'Call yourself a soldier, pointing guns at innocent women? You're a disgrace. In my day, we'd have had you court martialled!' In many ways, his moral compass is the same as the Doctor's, and while, in *The End of Time*, the Doctor initially turns down the revolver, he does actually take it, and use it to unravel the Master's plot to bring back Gallifrey, not to mention the Time Lords' plan to unravel reality.

Wilf's empathy ultimately leads to the Doctor's regeneration. Wilf helps one of Naismith's employees escape and in doing so, traps himself in the Immortality Gate's control pod which is about to be flooded by radiation. The Doctor rages against the inevitable, and Wilf begs him to just leave him there: 'I'm an old man, Doctor. I've had my time.' That was never going to happen though: the Doctor tells him it's his honour to give his life for Wilf's, and they swap places. After the radiation is channelled through the booth, Wilf, remembering what the Doctor told him about Time Lords being able to change their bodies to avert death, is surprised to see the Doctor still looks the same. But the regeneration has begun and the Doctor goes off to get his 'reward'; he at least promises Wilf that he'll see him again.

And he stays true to his word: on Donna's wedding day, the TARDIS materialises outside the church, and Wilf and Sylvia head over to see the Doctor. Mott is cheery as ever, noting, 'Same old face – didn't I tell you you'd be all right?' He knows otherwise, however. The Doctor gives them a lottery ticket to pass onto Donna as a wedding present, then goes back to his ship.

A tearful Wilf salutes him as the TARDIS dematerialises.

There's much talk about fate and convergence around the Noble family, and the Fourteenth Doctor sees them again in the sixtieth anniversary specials, *The Star Beast*, *Wild Blue Yonder*, and *The Giggle*. How appropriate that the now-wheelchair-bound Wilf meets this Doctor, the one with the same old face as the tenth incarnation; it's as if Wilf's presence reminds the Doctor and us that everything will be all right in the end.

The Tenth Doctor
Expanded Universe

Rose Tyler's first meeting with the Tenth Doctor is also his last time seeing her, i.e. in the episode, *The End of Time*, and the Target novelisation of *Rose* says that the first three months of 2005 don't go as well as hoped so she continues to wait for the 'great year' that the supposedly drunk man promises her on New Year's Eve. (Ironically, while Rose has a great time, Jackie Tyler has an awful year, as her daughter goes missing.)

The veracity of these books has always been ambiguous, with some completely at odds with their TV counterparts; nonetheless, the Target novel of *Rose* adds the most to Mickey Smith's story. Jackie becomes friends with Odessa Smith, Mickey's mother, in the 1980s and regularly meets up with her, plus Sarah Clark, Suzie, and Bev, forming the 'Wednesday Girls.' Jackie learns much about the Smith household as Odessa leans on the group to buoy her spirits after her relationship with Mickey's dad, Jackson, worsens. In 1989, she commits suicide. Mickey is five years old. Jackson isn't really around for him either, as he works as an engineer and part-time singer on cruise ships, finally disappearing completely. This leaves Mickey to be raised by his 'firebrand' grandmother, Rita-Anne, who is so loved by the locals that some three hundred people attend her funeral and Mickey, now in his teens, is carried around on their shoulders 'like a king.' The 2018 *Short Trips* adventure from Big Finish, *Flight Into Hull!*, says Jackie is 'delighted' when Rose and Mickey get together in 2002. We meet another of Jackie's friends, Marge Ellmore, in 2017's *Infamy of the Zaross*, a story which also shows Jackie calling Rose and the Doctor for help, something she later does in the TV story, *Love & Monsters*, and which Mickey does in *School Reunion*.

The novelisation arguably contradicts Rose's feelings towards the regenerated Tenth Doctor as, if the events of Target's *Rose* are adhered to, Rose has already seen photographs of the Doctor's other incarnations in Clive's shed – including 'a man with two suits, brown and blue,' who is, of course, the Tenth Doctor. (Pleasingly, Clive has two sons, Ben and Michael, perhaps an allusion to Michael Craze, who played First and Second Doctor companion, Ben Jackson.)

The Autons attack again in *He's Behind You*, a short story in the 2020 collection, *The Wintertime Paradox*, in which two Nestene duplicates stage a theatre production called *The Saga of the Time Lords* to lure out survivors of the Time War. Rose, too, has been on stage when she was eight, playing Angel Gabriel, but suffered stage fright; as such, she doesn't like pantomimes! At a similar time in her travels with the Tenth Doctor, i.e. just weeks after his regeneration, they encounter the Doctor's oldest enemies again in the 2006 *Quick Reads* novella, *I Am a Dalek*, in which we learn that Rose has some basic first aid training and it's implied she likes *The X Factor* and Kylie Minogue (who later appears opposite Tennant's Doctor in the TV story, *Voyage of the Damned*). She also encounters the 'totally turtley' Ice Warriors in the 2017 audio, *Cold Vengeance*, as well as another Slitheen in *No Fun at the Fair*, printed in the 2006 book, *Doctor Who Files Three: The Slitheen*, with the Doctor gleefully handing her a photo of Rose and the Raxacoricofallapatorian in the Tunnel of Love at the end of the story.

Rose's relationships with both her mum and Mickey are touched upon in the *New Series Adventures* series, and none more so than in *The Feast of the Drowned*. The story examines how the dynamics of not only these relationships are altered by Rose's increasing absences but also her friendship with an old school friend, Kiesha. When Rose returns to find that Mickey and Kiesha have got together, she's unimpressed. Her jealousy surfaces again in the 2007 *Doctor Who Magazine* comic strip, *The Green-Eyed Monster*, when the Tenth Doctor has a group of actors play

Mickey's stunning girlfriends in a bid to flood the psyche of a creature possessing Rose, one that feeds on jealousy. Rose's attraction to the Doctor is directly addressed in the story and in order to further ensure the creature's defeat, the Doctor even fakes a romance with Jackie.

Clayton Hickman comments on *The Green-Eyed Monster* (reprinted in the graphic novel, *The Betrothal of Sontar*) that it was to begin with Rose, in the TARDIS, waking up in bed. However, this was quashed by Russell T Davies who said that in the new series, nobody sleeps in the TARDIS. This is contradicted by the 2011 TV episode, *The Doctor's Wife*, which says that the TARDIS has bunk beds, while in the 2006 novel, *The Stone Rose* – in which Mickey discovers a statue of Rose in a museum – it's revealed that the Doctor has a set of *Winnie the Pooh* bed linens.

The Cat Came Back, a short story in the 2007 *Doctor Who Storybook*, expands on why the Tylers' flat has a cat-flap yet no cat: in a timey-wimey fashion, their old cat, Puffin, was actually originally called Mitzi, sent into hyperspace in the far future before getting stranded and gaining an enhanced intelligence and lifespan. Mitzi proved something of a dictator, living at least ninety years and ruling over a human colony on the planet Phostris, which Mitzi herself terraformed. However, when Mitzi is returned to simply being a normal cat, Rose and the Doctor take her to the Powell Estate, where a young Rose finds her and convinces Jackie to take her in. The newly-named Puffin lives for a further five years.

A cat plays a key role in *A Rose by Any Other Name*, a long-running backup strip in Titan Comics' *Tenth Doctor* series between 2014 and 2016. In this likely uncanonical run, the Doctor tries to heal from losing Rose Tyler by adopting a cat which he also names Rose, and they travel through time and space with K9.

A number of other tales are set after Rose leaves the Doctor in *Doomsday* but before her return to him in *The Stolen Earth* – namely, Big Finish's 2019 boxset, *The Dimension Cannon*, in which Rose immediately volunteers to use the titular device to get back to the Doctor, only to instead end up in other parallel worlds: one is doomed to be swallowed by its sun, where she meets another version of Clive Finch (*The Endless Night*), who she takes back with her; and in another, her parents have a son named Rob Tyler (*The Flood*), and Rose says she thinks the Doctor is a 'one-off,' that there isn't another in the multiverse – don't show her all these *Doctor Who* novels, audios, and comics! On two further journeys, she's accompanied first by Pete then by Jackie.

After returning to 'Pete's World' in *Journey's End*, Rose, the Meta-Crisis Doctor, Pete, and Jackie all join UNIT, an organisation created by President Harriet Jones by combining Torchwood with the Preachers. The Doctor takes on the role of Scientific Advisor with Rose his assistant. While Pete is given the rank of captain, Jackie is the Head of Food Distribution. This also effectively reinstates a deleted scene from *Journey's End* in which the Tenth Doctor gives the Meta-Crisis Doctor a piece of the TARDIS so he can grow his own; it's continuing to do so in *The Siege of Big Ben*, but given this Doctor has a human lifespan, he presumably won't see it reach maturity. His offspring might, however. *The Turning of the Tide*, from *The Target Storybook*, says that Rose falls pregnant with the Meta-Crisis Doctor's child, who they name Mia, according to Titan Comics' *Empire of the Wolf*. In the comic, set over a decade later, Rose is drawn back into N-Space where she meets the Eighth and Eleventh Doctors, and encourages the latter to find someone new to travel with after he's lost Amy and Rory. She gets back to 'Pete's World' three hours after she left. An alternate Rose, a resistance fighter who rebels against Sea Devil rule in *Alternating Current*, further meets the Tenth and Thirteenth Doctors.

Martha Jones makes her debut in the Expanded Universe a month before her first appearance on television, which is appropriate given that she appears in more *New Series Adventures* books than any other twenty-first century companion.

In Terrance Dick's novella, *Made of Steel*, she mentions that she's the cousin of Torchwood Institute employee, Adeola Oshodi, which is later confirmed in *Smith and Jones*. (Her identical cousin?)

When she steps into the TARDIS, Martha is also entering the life of a Doctor who is still very much haunted by the memory of Rose, and, it appears, is in a state of grief. Martha finds Rose's jacket in the TARDIS in *Peacemaker* and the Doctor doesn't cope very well with the discovery at all. Incidentally, in the same novel, Martha mentions that she purchased her own jacket from Henrik's. When the Doctor tells Martha not to be upset if the TARDIS' holograms refer to her as Rose in 2008's *The Many Hands*, there's a sense of how intimidating it is for her living in a post-Rose TARDIS. The Doctor's former companion plays on Martha's mind in *Snowglobe 7* too, as she immediately thinks of her when the Doctor mentions a hotel in Dubai called The Rose Tower.

The 2013 short story, *The Mystery of the Haunted Cottage*, establishes that Martha was an avid reader growing up, ploughing through the *Harry Potter* novels (hence her allusions to it in *The Shakespeare Code*), *His Dark Materials*, and the fictitious thirty-two children's series, *The Troubleseekers*, written by Annette Billingsley, the latter being the first books she read, at the age of eight. In *Wooden Heart* (2007), it's revealed that she, Tish, and Leo lived with their mother after their parents divorced, but *Sick Building* shows some form of familial bonding, as Martha says they always played board games together on Boxing Day.

Martha's time on board the TARDIS is particularly unusual given that much of Series 3 takes place over less than a week; that is, until *Last of the Time Lords*, which fast-forwards a year, then backtracks twelve months. The Expanded Universe gives us contradicting dates, however, as to when these events actually take place. *The Secret Lives of Monsters* (2014) says Martha joined the Doctor on Sunday 4th June, though around this period, 4th June was only a Sunday in, 2000, 2006, and 2017. The 2020 short story, *The Paradox Moon*, says the Toclafane invaded on 23rd June

2007, but this is at odds with the TV continuity, given that, after *Aliens of London*, every story is set a year after its airdate (the Ninth Doctor having brought Rose back too late), until *The Eleventh Hour*. Curiously, *The Last Dodo* features posts from Martha's blog, dated 1st July 2007; so too do *Wetworld*, *The Pirate Loop*, and *Forever Autumn* – the events of the latter take place on Friday 30th October and Saturday 31st October, meaning it's likely 2009. At least the BBC Sounds podcast series, *Redacted*, concludes that the Royal Hope Hospital was scooped up by the Judoon in 2008. Might we infer that the Paradox Machine being destroyed affected history more than we see on TV? Or is this something else we could blame on Series 5's crack in time?

Either way, focusing on the year between *The Sound of Drums* and *Last of the Time Lords*, *The Story of Martha* (2008) sees the character getting a story all to herself. It traces Martha's journey from the Toclafane attack as she arrived on Earth, to her eventual return to the United Kingdom, where a showdown with the Master awaits. This, more than any other novel, provides the reader with a real insight into Martha's courage, determination, and resilience as she tries to survive in a hostile environment in order to spread the Doctor's story to as many people as possible. We learn more background information from this collection: notably, *The Frozen Wastes* says she was inspired to become a doctor after her brother, Leo, pushed her too hard on a swing and broke her arm when she was a child; she then went to hospital and was fascinated to see x-rays. It also says that she was born in 1986, though this is contradicted by *The Torchwood Archives*, which states she was born on 14th September 1984; neither adheres to Freema Agyeman's birthdate in March 1979, but the latter is backed up by an interview with Russell T Davies in *DWM* #373.

Big Finish's 2021 audio anthology, *The Year of Martha Jones*, also covers the twelve months Martha spent venturing across Earth while hiding from the Toclafane. Its first story, *The Last Diner*, includes Martha's mother, Francine, who says she got off the Valiant as the Master has no interest in keeping prisoners around so early on in his subjugation of the planet; Francine is still bitter towards the Doctor, egged on perhaps by the Master telling her the Doctor's responsible for the sinking of Atlantis. (Martha accidentally discovers Atlantis in the game, *Lost in Time*, during which she also meets the Thirteenth Doctor, Liz Shaw, and the Sea Devils.) Nonetheless, Francine correctly deduces that Martha's travels are part of a bigger plot, rather than merely assembling a weapon, though Martha refuses to tell her more – a good thing too, given that she's later revealed to be a clone working for the Master, and that the real Francine is still on the Valiant. We also learn that Martha had a university friend called Holly, who she drifted away from after the death of Holly's mother, but who she finds again during the Year That Never Was. Though Holly turns out to be working for the Master, she renounces him and helps Martha escape in *Deceived*.

Other audio adventures see Martha reuniting with friends old and new. 2008's *Torchwood* release, *Lost Souls*, finds Martha working with Captain Jack Harkness, Gwen Cooper, and Ianto Jones. Martha attends Tosh and Owen's funerals following the conclusion of *Torchwood* Series 2; their passing is also the reason she apparently turns down Jack's offer in *Journey's End* to join Torchwood, Martha finding Cardiff Bay too steeped in sorrow, at least according to the 2020 Big Finish story, *Dissected*. However, that states that Martha didn't attend Torchwood's 2008 Christmas party as she'd just broken up with Tom Milligan, which is at odds with her still being with him in *Doctor Who* Series 4, set in 2009. When Gwen raises the idea of Martha going freelance, Martha hints that she's been thinking about doing so with 'a friend,' who we can infer is Mickey.

Pleasingly, the ebook novelisation of *The Nightmare Man*, its TV counterpart opening Series 4 of *The Sarah Jane Adventures*, establishes that, post-*Journey's End*, Martha and Sarah kept in touch, meeting up occasionally for coffee. Now going by Martha Smith-Jones, she and her husband, Mickey, attend Luke's farewell party as he leaves for Oxford University.

COMPANIONS

In *The First*, a 2007 *DWM* comic, Martha wears the atmospheric density jacket seen on TV in *The Web Planet* during her trip to see the aurora australis in Antarctica, 1915, which shows her and the Doctor's meeting explorer Ernest Shackleton. In *The Last Soldier*, a comic strip in *DWM*, she talks of returning to a planet in her professional capacity only. It tells of a world in which only the very last male and female survivors of a war, each from opposing sides, are able to reproduce. Martha talks about going back to deliver the new arrival. Referring to the war, she states that she sees quite enough fighting at the hospital on a typical Saturday night. Her studious nature comes in handy in the 2007 *Battles in Time* comic, *House Pests*, in which she reads *Tempus Fugit – The Time Travellers' Companion*.

Tesseract, an IDW 2010 comic, sees Martha filling in as UNIT's Scientific Director, while in another 2010 IDW strip, *Don't Step on the Grass*, the reason for Martha's departure from UNIT is established as being the incident involving the Osterhagen key. She's working with UNIT on a strictly temporary basis as a freelancer, and even this is done only as a favour to Malcolm Taylor (UNIT's Scientific Advisor, seen on television in *Planet of the Dead*), who's a friend of hers. In both stories, Martha's marital status is alluded to: *Tesseract* mentions her recent wedding, but Martha doesn't specify the identity of the man she is married to. *Don't Step on the Grass*, however, has Captain Erisa Magambo (featured in both *Turn Left* and *Planet of the Dead*) referring to her as Mrs Smith, which indicates that she's now married to Mickey. Fuelling this allusion is Martha's observation that Matthew is suffering from 'tin-dog syndrome' – a depressed state of mind where the sufferer feels like the least valuable companion. Mickey Smith is, of course, the original victim of tin-dog syndrome in *School Reunion*, but Martha isn't present and wouldn't have known about it unless she found out some other way…

Martha interacts with a few other iterations of the Doctor: in 2011's *The Golden Ones*, she calls the Eleventh Doctor and Amy to investigate the Shining Dawn Corporation, actually a front for the Axons (previously seen in *The Claws of Axos*), in Tokyo. She also takes a brief trip in the TARDIS with the Ninth Doctor in Titan's *The Transformed* (2016), albeit having been changed into a gargoyle; Mickey helps the Doctor undo the transformation. And Titan's *A Little Help from My Friends* (2020) takes place during the period Martha and the Doctor are stranded in 1969 (*Blink*) and reveals that Martha worked for 'a few weeks' at a clothing store called Face Fashion. On one of her shifts, she helps a woman who calls herself Jane Smith, causing Martha to raise an eyebrow – sure enough, this turns out to be the Thirteenth Doctor, and, alongside the Tenth Doctor and future companions, Yasmin Khan, Graham O'Brien, and Ryan Sinclair, they foil an invasion attempt by the Nestene Consciousness and its Autons!

Martha's husband has significantly fewer Expanded Universe appearances, but most important is *The Lodger*, set during Series 2 but a forerunner to the Series 5 episode of the same name. This finds the Tenth Doctor temporarily stranded on Earth in 2007 and living with Mickey Smith while he waits for Rose to come back in the TARDIS after the ship jumps a time track.

The Doctor and Mickey spend some four days together, during which time the Time Lord gains a greater appreciation of Rose's on-off boyfriend, perhaps leading him to offer him a place on the TARDIS in *School Reunion*. As the Doctor shows off his footballing and video gaming skills, Mickey is left increasingly depressed and accuses the Doctor of having stolen Rose from him. Mickey tells his colleagues that Rose has moved to Northampton, and attempts to go on a date with a new girlfriend; instead, the guilt-ridden Doctor sets Mickey and Rose up to enjoy a normal Sunday together. Mickey nonetheless keeps an eye on Jackie, and worries when she goes missing in *Wednesdays for Beginners*, part of 2017's *The Lives of Captain Jack* audio boxset.

Similarly, there aren't too many Expanded Universe tales for

Captain Jack Harkness after his interactions with the Tenth Doctor, though the two were due to meet again in Big Finish's decidedly absent *Absent Friends*, a title that's unlikely to be released.

However, Jack appears in some stories post-*Last of the Time Lords*, around the time of *Torchwood* Series 2, *Children of Earth*, and *Miracle Day*. In *The Beauty of Our Weapons*, from 2008's *Torchwood: The Official Magazine Yearbook*, Jack says he once tried to explore some of Torchwood Three's unused tunnels but turned back after four days as he hadn't packed enough sandwiches; he seemed to be heading in the direction of Glasgow. In 2008, he also makes a webcast series called *Captain Jack's Monster Files*, about alien threats like the Empress of the Racnoss (*The Runaway Bride*), Pyroviles (*The Fires of Pompeii*), Vashta Nerada (*Silence in the Library / Forest of the Dead*), and Vespiform (*The Unicorn and the Wasp*), none of which he's met: we might infer that there's some record of them in the Torchwood files, that there are unseen adventures featuring these aliens, or that he learned of them via the Doctor. These videos are rendered top secret by UNIT. Still, he works in conjunction with UNIT in *Submission* (2011) to investigate a distress signal in the Mariana Trench.

Despite turning down the Doctor's offer to travel with him again, Jack starts feeling lonely in Cardiff, so enquires into the Church of the Outsiders, a religious cult that thinks humanity's future lies in the stars (Big Finish's 2018 audio, *Believe*), but ultimately turns on them after its leader, Val Ross, refuses to take any responsibility for the suicide of one of the Church's members, Davey Russell, who believed he would evolve instead of dying. The deaths in the TV story, *Exit Wounds*, take their toll on Jack, who, in *Expectant* (2019), agrees to be a surrogate father for 'Junior,' the next leader of the Yalnix Empire. He also leaves Owen's position as Torchwood's medical officer open as he expects Martha Jones to take it in *Dissected*, though she turns down this offer.

Following the events of *Torchwood: Children of Earth*, Jack travels the world but is drawn back to Cardiff by *The House of the*

Dead; he believes destroying it will seal the Rift in Cardiff forever. Though intending to do so by sacrificing himself, he encounters the ghost of Ianto Jones, and the pair admit their love for one another for the last time before Ianto instead blows it up. The Tenth Doctor provides Jack a brief distraction from his reverie at the end of *The End of Time*, so *One Enchanted Evening*, part of *The Lives of Captain Jack*, explores his time with Midshipman Alonso Frame, though the pair are separated by a meteor shower that sends their escape pods on different paths. At some point, he bequeaths his vortex manipulator to UNIT, as it's used in the Black Archive in *The Day of the Doctor* (he's said to have the 'latest model' in his encounter with River Song in the 2021 novel, *The Ruby's Curse*, so perhaps he gets a new one), but after *Miracle Day*, Jack goes missing for four or five years, according to the 2015 audio, *Forgotten Lives*, time he's spent investigating the Committee of Erebus (*The Conspiracy*), a group that had infiltrated Torchwood at various points in history. He'd also been held captive on the planet Peritus IV in Omega Centauri, twelve parsecs from the 'central black hole,' by the Evolved, who he'd asked for help against the Committee. In 2017-18's *Aliens Among Us*, a three-boxset audio series, Jack gets back to Torchwood to lead a new crew, alongside Gwen and Rhys, further including former civil servant, St John Colchester (who would later befriend ex-Seventh Doctor companion, Ace); Sorvan sexual psychomorph, Orr; and journalist, Tyler Steele, who goes on to have a relationship with Jack, and is horrified to learn that, in *Love Rat*, Jack is raped and killed by Duncan, a middle-aged man who's infected by an alien parasite. After being resurrected, the parasite spreads to Tyler, and though they find a cure, Tyler calls off their dalliance. During this time, they also encounter a parallel version of Yvonne Hartman (from *Army of Ghosts/Doomsday*).

At the conclusion of *God Among Us*, another three-boxset series from Big Finish (2018-19), Jack goes on the run with some of his peers, but they're split up and he goes missing. This is presumably when he's entangled with the Thirteenth Doctor, though his fate afterwards is unknown.

R&J, from *The Lives of Captain Jack: Volume Three*, entwines part of his life with part of River Song's, however, first meeting her when he's getting a Kronkburger for the Ninth Doctor and Rose. She sees him during the events of *The Empty Child* (as he's waiting for a Time Agent to arrive), *Boom Town* (when he's confined to the TARDIS as the Doctor takes Blon on a date, and Rose goes out with Mickey), and *Last of the Time Lords* (visiting him while he's chained up on the Valiant). 'Professor Hack Jarkness' temporarily replaces Bernice Summerfield as River's lecturer at the Luna University, during which he talks about graffiti providing a means of time travellers to leave messages for one another: in a possible example of the bootstrap paradox, he might be giving River the idea to leave such messages for the Doctor in *The Time of Angels* and *The Pandorica Opens*, something he may have only learned about through her doing exactly that. He goes on to meet her near the start of her lifetime, as a youngster in New York City (*Day of the Moon*), and towards the end, on Darillium (*The Husbands of River Song*). It's also implied that Jack has some hitherto-unmentioned influence on the Twelfth Doctor's era: the pair meet Ashildr, then going under the name Me, as Jack talks about seeing a woman waiting to play chess with someone at the end of space-time (*Hell Bent*) and knock on Orson Pink's capsule, stranded on the last planet in the universe (*Listen*).

R&J adds another interesting caveat, in that it's revealed Jack went to the interment of the Face of Boe – if the implications of *Last of the Time Lords* are to be believed, Jack went to his own funeral!

River Song goes on to have a few adventures with the Tenth Doctor, trying to console him after he loses Donna Noble. In 2020's *Expiry Dating*, she leads him on a merry dance across time and space, luring him to join her at the Apocalypse Vaults, inside the Quantum Vatican, which will one day open to reveal the exact date of the end of the universe. Though her message eventually gets to the Tenth Doctor, it nearly disrupts time by falling into the hands of the First, Fifth, and Sixth Doctors.

Big Finish's 2020 triptych, *The Tenth Doctor and River Song*, further sees them looking into explosive jewels unearthed in London, 1912, an investigation that leads them to 1632 (*Precious Annihilation*); and then on Demonese 2, the most haunted planet in its galaxy (*Ghosts*). River says she was once imprisoned in the Tower of London during Elizabethan Times, and suggests that living as a digital copy would be a worst-case scenario – something which understandably unsettles the Doctor, given that he knows this is her ultimate fate in the Library.

Interestingly, River also has an adventure with Space Security agents, Anya Kingdom and Mark Seven, two people who join the Tenth Doctor for the *Dalek Universe* audio series, albeit before they meet that incarnation of the Time Lord. They pick up River's distress signal from a planet in the forty-first century overrun by Mechanoids (from *The Chase*), only to find her as the *Queen of the Mechonoids* [sic] (part of *The Diary of River Song: Series Eight* in 2021). She uses them to get her into the 'tomb' of war criminal, Annam Henic, who turns out not to have died, but instead has been conglomerated into the Mechanoids. Anya and River see each other again as the former and the Tenth Doctor investigate Kamen Vers, a human-Movellan hybrid and a secret weapon in the war with the Daleks (against the backdrop of the conflict seen in *Destiny of the Daleks* and, briefly, *The Pilot*), in *The First Son*, from 2021's *Dalek Universe 3*. They discover that Kamen's 'mother' is actually River, who's pretending to be an emotionless Movellan but had previously hinted as to her involvement by leaving the Doctor her patented 'hello sweetie' welcoming, a recording sent in a Dalek voice.

Anya Kingdom and Mark Seven, respectively played by Jane Slavin and Joe Sims in 2021, have longer histories than their appearances in *Dalek Universe* with David Tennant. Anya and Mark are first introduced in *The Dalek Protocol* with the Fourth Doctor, Leela, and K9, and Anya travelled with that incarnation of the Doctor for a short time as WPC Ann Kelso. They meet again on the planet Mira in *Buying Time*, during which time Anya is supposed to be looking into the crash of a spaceship but is actually searching for Mark as she believes he's been compromised – indeed, as he's an android, he is sometimes taken over by outside forces, even unwillingly acting against his friends in *The House of Kingdom*. Anya is the sister of Sara Kingdom, the First Doctor companion who died in *The Daleks' Master Plan*, while the origins of android Mark Seven can be traced back to 1966's *The Dalek Outer Space Book*, an annual written by Terry Nation and Brad Ashton, though he's only briefly mentioned and depicted there. You have to turn to *Terry Nation's Dalek Annual 1976* to find Mark's first full adventure, *Terror Task Force*, which details the first appearance of the Anti-Dalek Force in the fortieth century, for which Mark was second-in-command. Mark and Anya team up with the Doctor when he's manipulated in a plot by the Nun, the regenerated form of the Meddling Monk (*The Wrong Woman*), then ending up in the conflict between the Daleks and Movellans. Though Mark Seven is seemingly killed at Beltros Station (*The Trojan Dalek*), he's instead rescued and apparently becomes the basis for the Movellans in *The Triumph of Davros*. Eventually remembering his time with the Doctor, Mark thanks him and says that the Doctor's trying to be a good man makes him so. Mark's memory core is deleted, and Anya joins the Earth Protection Corps.

You wouldn't assume that Donna Noble is a big fan of sci-fi, and yet…

Making her first Expanded Universe audio appearance in 2008's *Pest Control*, Donna repeatedly references *Star Trek* and joins the Doctor in briefly assuming the aliases of Captain Kirk (Donna) and Dr McCoy (the Doctor). You have to wonder if Donna is a bit of a Trekker as, in *The Nemonite Invasion*, a 2009 audio adventure, she says the Doctor's mind-reading skills are very much like Spock's mind-meld. The Doctor comments that he thinks she watches far too much television. You can see his

414

point: she goes on to refer to him as *Joe 90* in the same story and even claims that she and the Doctor are in the employ of *The X-Files* when asked for identification at one point. *Wannabes* (2023) establishes that Donna loves 'the biggest girl band' of the 1990s – no, not the Spice Girls, but Blood Honeys, as she convinces the Doctor to take her to their first ever gig, at a small club called the Tripod in 1996 Dublin. Sylvia, meanwhile, is more of a Beatles fan, as Donna recalls in a 2009 *Doctor Who Official Annual* story that she always said John, Paul, George, and Ringo made the *Most Beautiful Music* in existence. In *The Creeping Death* (2019), the Doctor and Donna are attempting to see a Pink Floyd concert in 1967, though are unsuccessful.

Returning to *Pest Control*, Donna calls one of the centaurs, Firenze, which is also the name of a centaur in the *Harry Potter* series. She appears to be a *He-Man and the Masters of the Universe* fan as she refers to villains as Skeletor at least three times: once to Meng in *The Immortal Emperor*, a comic strip in the 2009 *Doctor Who Storybook*; then again to one of the Sycorax in *The Widow's Curse*, from the *DWM* comic; and again in the 2016 audio, *Death and the Queen*. During the latter, set in the 1780s, Donna's swept off her feet by Rudolph, Crown Prince of Goritania, an area of the French Riviera that she's never heard of. Rudolph even proposes to her and she accepts; however, on her wedding day, it becomes obvious that this is a trap, as the Royal family of Goritania made a deal with the Death-like Mefistoleans to hide their kingdom from the world and ensure peace – resulting in Death coming for Donna. Rudolph could never have handled Donna anyway as he's clearly intimidated by strong women!

In the 2008 novel, *The Ghosts of India*, which finds Donna and the Doctor meeting Mohandas 'Mahatma' Gandhi in 1947, Donna mentions a cousin called Janice who must be a cousin on her father's side as Wilfred Mott, her maternal grandfather, informs the Doctor that Donna is his only grandchild in the TV episode, *The Sontaran Stratagem*. In *The Lonely Computer*, a short story published on the BBC website in 2008, Donna talks about working in telemarketing, and more specifically about the 'primitives' she was forced to work with, one of whom was a Manchester United follower. You can understand this not getting a warm reception from Donna, who's a staunch West Ham United fan.

Beautiful Chaos has become even more fascinating since its publication in 2008, given that part of it is set after Donna comes home in *Journey's End,* but before she and Wilf meet the Fourteenth Doctor, who happens to look like the Tenth Doctor, in the sixtieth anniversary specials. The novel chiefly concerns Wilf remembering a time when his granddaughter came back to visit with the Doctor on the anniversary of Geoffrey Noble's passing – and to celebrate Wilf's achievement: he's discovered a new star and had it named after him. The Doctor is naturally suspicious, and rightly so, as this novel acts as a sequel to the Fourth Doctor TV serial, *The Masque of Mandragora*. The book reveals that Wilf is part of an astronomy club, and he grows close to a woman suffering from Alzheimer's. (Ageing seems to panic Donna as she's aghast when it happens to her first in *The Time Stealer*, from the *Battles in Time* comic, in which she angrily repeats, 'What have you done to me?', then in *The Time Sickness*, from the 2009 *Doctor Who Official Annual*. This could be understandable angst about ageing prematurely, however.) *Beautiful Chaos* further tells us that Wilf was married to Eileen, and *In the Blood* (2016), he affirms that they never shouted at Sylvia when she was a kid. He remembers this time as the most wonderful years of his life.

Donna and Wilf both cameo in the 2018 Target novelisation of *Rose*. She gets drunk after confessing her feelings for her colleague, Rufus – affections that aren't requited, so she gets home at three in the morning and wakes up early the next day, only for Wilf to advise her to go back to bed to get rid of her hangover. As such, she misses the Autons' attack.

In Big Finish's 2016 audio, *Technophobia*, Donna goes on a little shopping spree at Henrik's, perhaps showing that, at least at this point in her travels, she isn't aware that Rose used to work there as she surely wouldn't risk upsetting the Doctor should he see a Henrik's shopping bag. Later, in *No Place* (2019), Donna, Wilf, and Sylvia star in an episode of *Haunted Makeovers!*, a home improvement show that also features a look for ghosts – alongside Donna's 'husband,' the Doctor, going under the familiar name of John. Donna is shown to play the piano, albeit only a little, while Wilf expresses his admiration for the Doctor and his feeling that, when the Doctor's around, everything will turn out okay. (That sentiment seems to bite him on the backside considering what happens to Donna in *Journey's End.* With hindsight, though, Wilf's proved right, given Donna's time with the Fourteenth Doctor later on.) The Doctor also goes by the name John Smith when pretending to be a detective inspector on twenty-second century Earth in 2008's *Pawns of the Zenith*, from the *Battles in Time* magazine, while Donna enjoys some level of authority as Sergeant Donna Noble from the 'Moon Division,' though she no doubt feels irked she's not afforded the same rank as the Doctor.

Big Finish's 2020 boxset, *Donna Noble: Kidnapped!*, shows that Donna had to return home after the events of *Forest of the Dead*, in order to recover from her CAL-induced false reality. In the set's *Out of this World*, Sylvia signs her daughter up to a speed dating event. Donna's accompanied by her childhood best friend, Natalie Morrison (played by Niky Wardley, who also played Eighth Doctor companion, Tamsin Drew), who goes just 'for a laugh.' When they follow a strange alien who Donna initially thinks is the Doctor, Donna and Natalie are kidnapped and taken away in a similarly-taken TARDIS. Though they escape, Donna's attempts to pilot the TARDIS (helped along by the TARDIS Manual, which Natalie finds later on) lead them to the planet Valdacki (*Spinvasion*) then the Middle Ages (*The Sorcerer of Albion*), where Donna is mistaken for Merlin. Funnily enough, then, Natalie essentially becomes Donna's companion in the TARDIS! They find their way back to London, 2009, in *The Chiswick Cuckoos*, where Donna and her friend team up with UNIT's Second Lieutenant Josh Carter (who Donna rather takes a shine to) to defeat the Collectors who've tried to duplicate them. They also rescue the Doctor, who the Collectors have frozen to steal his ship.

Home remains important to Donna as, in *One Mile Down*, she sends a postcard to Wilf from the fifty-first century; here, she also meets the Judoon, perhaps explaining why she's not intimidated by them in the TV story, *The Stolen Earth*. It seems that Donna kept a diary of her travels, presumably so she could share them with Wilf, but her grandfather takes it so her memories don't come back to kill her (2022's *A Short History of Everyone*). The Doctor is similarly concerned at the idea of Donna seeing him again, as in the 2017 Titan Comics story, *Revolving Doors*, he briefly finds himself in her house, but she's distracted by an argument with her mum, so doesn't see him, allowing him precious seconds to make a getaway. She nonetheless remains in the Doctor's mind: he names a mercenary ship he commands during the Dark Times the HMS Donna in the 2020 novel, *All Flesh is Grass*.

In *The Widow's Curse*, Donna proves pretty well-travelled, as she says she's previously seen Minehead, Paris (on a school trip), Lanzarote, the Isle of Wight, Corfu, Crete, Cornwall, the rings of Saturn, the Magellan Clouds, Venus, Mercury, Pluto, the birth of the Earth, the death of the Mestophelix Galaxy, and Skegness. Some of those destinations might've been between *The Runaway Bride* and *Partners in Crime*, seeing as she was inspired by the Doctor in the former Christmas special, but it's doubtful as she only mentions Egypt in the Series 4 opening episode (though doesn't list it in the *DWM* comic). The 2013 short story, *Judge, Jury and Executioner*, published in *The Doctor: His Lives and Times*, explains that she sold her flat to pay for her trip to Egypt, so she had to move back in with her parents afterwards. During this story, Wilf also meets River Song and chats about the Tenth Doctor.

Most significant is Donna's last *DWM* comic appearance with the Tenth Doctor, *The Time of My Life*, which has a holographic version of Donna activated in the TARDIS as Emergency

Program One (last seen on TV in *The Parting of the Ways*). We're treated to a handful of hitherto-unseen adventures, including their trip to see The Beatles play 'My Bonnie' at the Cavern Club, Liverpool (after which Donna asks John Lennon to sign an anachronistic *1* CD, released in 2000, for her mum), before the holographic Donna thanks the Doctor for all he's done.

The Tenth Doctor has a whole host of Expanded Universe companions. Heather McCrimmon was created by Joanne Hall, the ten-year-old winner of a competition to create a companion for the *Doctor Who Adventures* comic strip. In terms of pure story count, Heather became one of the longest-serving companions, but her most interesting attribute is that she's a direct descendent of Second Doctor companion, Jamie, and his Expanded Universe wife, Kirsty. Such is her importance to the Doctor, that just before his tenth regeneration (*The End of Time*), he visits her briefly to save her life, much like he does with the television companions he travels with.

Interestingly, in the fan-written *A Star in Her Eye*, part of *The Fan Gallery* but published during the 2020 official *Lockdown!* event, it's revealed that Heather McCrimmon is the same Heather we see later on in the Twelfth Doctor era, travelling with Bill Potts. Its canonicity is debatable and raises various questions including why the Doctor doesn't recognise her, why they look different, and why Heather from *The Pilot* isn't Scottish. Nevertheless, it's a fun notion, and cyclical, considering Heather's story begins and ends with fandom.

Heather is joined by Wolfgang Ryster, created by Hamish Cough, the twelve-year-old winner of a competition for *Doctor Who Adventures*. A sixteen-year-old exchange student from Austria, Wolfie leaves at the same time as Heather and is there when the Doctor drops by to save his and Heather's life prior to the Doctor's regeneration.

Meanwhile, in *Doctor Who Magazine* comes Majenta Pryce, a companion who seems a forebear of Eighth Doctor companion,

Destrii, in that she's not a native to Earth and travels with the Tenth Doctor somewhat begrudgingly. Majenta is actually introduced a few issues before travelling with the Doctor, as an antagonist in *Hotel Historia* (2008). Majenta owns the titular hotel chain, which is powered by a Chronexus 3000, capable of offering guests time travel (arguably akin to the hotel in 2024 Christmas special, *Joy to the World*). Though she helps the Doctor get rid of the aggressive Graxnix, the hotel is in serious debt after guests lose interest in time travel, owing to the Time War, so it's shut down and Majenta, and her assistant Fanson, are arrested.

We next find Majenta in the *Thinktwice* Orbital Penitentiary, its harsh psychological torture having erased many of her memories. The Doctor manages to restore memories of her meeting him before, then agrees to help her get the rest back. She joins the TARDIS after destroying the Memeovax, creatures that feed on the memories of prisoners. In *Mortal Beloved*, they find themselves visiting Stormlight House, located on an asteroid in the Proxima System, owned by Wesley Sparks, head of Sparktech. The Doctor refutes Majenta's accusation that he brought her there to confront her past, as it turns out that Wesley was once engaged to Majenta, but she vanished on the night before their wedding. In fact, the Doctor is trying to get to Panacea, a healing planet, but ends up in Sydney, Australia, in 2010 (*The Age of Ice*), where they see Fanson again. He betrays the Skith, and then is killed by Ice Shards meant for Majenta. Before he dies, he apologies to her for wiping her memories, wishing that he'd not done so. Despite the Doctor insisting that he's travelling with her purely because he sees recovering her memories as his 'job,' he and Majenta slowly get closer, even trying to watch Agatha Christie's West End play, *The Mousetrap* in *Ghosts of the Northern Line*, and he starts affectionately calling her 'Madge.'

The Intersol intergalactic police finally track Majenta down, having been hunting the members of *The Crimson Hand*, a malicious group of criminals that Majenta left after they started to destroy planets using artefacts like the Key to Time. She'd had to prove herself to be admitted into the band of criminals, and did so by romancing Wesley; Fanson had tried to keep her hidden from the Hand by erasing her memories. Majenta eventually undoes the remaining members of the Crimson Hand, but dies in the process; the Doctor manages to resurrect her, and drops her off to live a happy life without him – she can only remain alive as long as the Doctor remembers her. It seems he does as we see Majenta again in 2016's *The Stockbridge Showdown*, helping the Twelfth Doctor and various other companions like Izzy, Frobisher, and Destrii take down Josiah W. Dogbolter, owner of Intra-Venus, Inc. – leaving Majenta as CEO of the corporation.

Several more comic companions join the Tenth Doctor after he loses Donna Noble. We're introduced to Gabriella 'Gabby' Lucia Fernanda Gonzalez and Cindy Wu in 2014's *Revolutions of Terror*, from Titan Comics' *The Tenth Doctor* title. Cindy is visiting Gabby while the latter works in her father's laundromat in Brooklyn, New York, when all the machines explode and Gabby thinks she's seen a monster. On her way home, Gabby then meets the Tenth Doctor as she's attacked by a psi-form Cerebravore, and the next day, Halloween, he tracks the interdimensional bridge they used to enter this world to her laundromat. After stopping them, Gabby begs the Doctor to let her go with him, seeing it as an opportunity to learn so much about life. Gabby is indeed a hard worker: not only does she cover at the laundromat, but she also helps out at her dad's Mexican restaurant, The Castillo Mexicano, in Sunset Park, and gets straight A's at night school, where she's studying accounting. The Doctor recognises this and gives her a break – 'Just one trip, mind.' Gabby opts to go to the future with this sole opportunity she's been granted, and the Doctor, knowing she wishes to be an artist, takes her to the Pentaquoteque Gallery on Ouloumos (*The Arts in Space*). There, she meets the Doctor's friend, Zhe Ikiyuyu, who uses mathematical equations to create unique sculptures, having trained on Logopolis to understand Block Transfer Computation.

Gabby takes a sketchbook along with her, and does fun

cartoons of her adventures. One interestingly includes the Tenth Doctor telling her, 'No need to worry about the lingo, all taken care of...' while looking at a series of aliens and robots: in the original comic, these include K1 (*Robot*), a Quark (*The Dominators*), an Ice Warrior, Alpha Centauri (from the *Peladon* stories of the Third Doctor era), a Handbot (*The Girl Who Waited*), a White Robot (*The Mind Robber*), and Fifth Doctor companion, Kamelion, though when the story was reprinted in graphic novel format the following year, the latter three had been replaced by characters from *The Arts in Space*. This implies she met and remembers all these beings from the Pentaquoteque Gallery.

The Doctor welcomes Gabby on board the TARDIS officially on a more long-term basis, partly as she possesses some interesting skills with Block Transfer Computation, and partly because he likes her so much!

When she gets back to New York in 2016 – via a battle with *The Weeping Angels of Mons* (during which she takes a shine to First World War soldier, Jamie Colquhoun) – Gabby shows her journal to a disbelieving Cindy (*Echoes*). Together, the three of them unravel a plot by Anubis, the Ancient Egyptian god of funerary rites and guide to the underworld, whose father is Sutekh from *Pyramids of Mars* and, later, *The Legend of Ruby Sunday/Empire of Death*, to use a quantum harvester to be reunited with Osirans in another universe. The Doctor convinces him not to use it, given that its effects would destroy this universe in *Sins of the Father*, and the Doctor promises to find another way for him to follow his Osiran peers. At the end of this story, Cindy turns down a place in the TARDIS, and regrets it, leading her to use Gabby's sketchbook to track them down again in *Cindy, Cleo and the Magic Sketchbook*, and is indeed accepted as the Doctor's companion in *Arena of Fear*. Their first trip to the UK is in *The Wishing Well Witch*, where they visit the West Yorkshire town of Dewbury, and a visit to 1930s New Orleans sees Cindy deeply falling for jazz musician, Roscoe Ruskin (*The Jazz Monster*); she's understandably gutted when he sacrifices himself in *Music Man*, expounded by Gabby's noting how emotionally dependent she is on others in *Old Girl*. During this, however, Dorothy Bell, who's merged with the quantum harvester, helps Cindy deal with her grief by finding a parallel universe in which Ruskin has become a music icon, pulling one of his songs from that other dimension and giving it to Cindy to remember him by.

In this adventure, Anubis is possessed by Sutekh, but manages to pull free long enough to save Gabby, and she returns the favour using her block transfer powers. Dorothy eventually stops Sutekh, and in doing so, rejuvenates Anubis, also wiping his memory. Now going by the more friendly Noobis, he grows close to Cindy when they all stay in the Garden of Osiris, and admits he would like to go travelling with them – a request the Doctor grants.

The Doctor also gets a temporary companion in Cleopatra 'Cleo' Hunsicker, who, in the fake reality of *Breakfast at Tyranny's*, is Cindy's girlfriend. Cleo is a member of the Cult of the Black Pyramid, formed around 3000BC, that believes the Osiran Horus to be a true god and Sutekh a pretender to the throne. Cleo learns the truth, that their gods are aliens, in *Spiral Staircase*, but the Doctor goes on to show her more wonders like the Guild of Unfeasible Mirthcasters and (unfortunately for her) the Ogrons' Poet Group.

Cindy is afforded a reprise from her travels in *Revolving Doors*, which sees her back in Sunset Park while Gabby and the Doctor explore time and space without her for a short time. Nonetheless, after an adventure with clones of Cindy, Gabby is unnerved to consider the one that died could've been the real version of her friend. Still, Gabby considers the lives of all the clones as important, and Gabby, Noobis, and Cindy continue travelling together in *Vortex Butterflies*, although Noobis stays on the planet Aramuko, where he thinks he's found another Osiran, named Siffhoni. The Doctor drops Gabby and Cindy off at a house he owns in Willesden, in north-west London, in 2009, and asks Sarah Jane Smith to look in on them from time to time while he's away. Sarah smartly realises that Cindy loves Gabby, and gives the pair a proper tour of London. The Doctor comes back after realising that a mysterious 'Butterfly' was actually a version of Gabby from the future, seemingly a projection manifested by Gabby's worry that he'll abandon her, as when the Doctor tells her he'll always be there for her, the Butterfly vanishes. He briefly leaves Gabby with Zhe Ikiyuyu so she can get greater control over her block transfer powers; meanwhile, the Doctor and Cindy first visit the spacestation, Mechma Onzlo III, then back to twenty-first century Earth, where they're reunited with Cleo (*The Good Companion*). They also see Noobis again on Aramuko, when they learn that Siffhoni is actually a Time Sentinel, beings that share a clear resemblance to Shayde from *DWM*.

When Gabby is in touch with the Moment (from *The Day of the Doctor*), she recognises the important part companions play in making the Doctor who he is. The Moment slightly messes up, however, by depositing Gabby back into the *wrong* TARDIS – that of the Twelfth Doctor, who she immediately hugs. Despite writer, Nick Abadzis, intending to lead into a Tenth and Twelfth Doctor crossover, Titan Comics cancelled all their non-Thirteenth Doctor lines when Jodie Whittaker's incarnation debuted, meaning that's sadly where we leave Gabby, Cindy, Noobis, and Cleo – for now.

Other Expanded Universe companions include Gisella who appears in several novels. An apparent twelve-year-old girl in charge of the underwater research base at Flydon Maxima, she's revealed to be an android in *The Pictures of Emptiness*. Space Major Jon Bowman, a one-off companion for *Prisoner of the Daleks* is notable for the similarity between his name and Captain Jack actor, John Barrowman. Emily Winter and Matthew Finnegan also join the Doctor for a series of adventures in IDW's *Doctor Who* comics, beginning in *Silver Scream* (2009). Hailing from Hollywood in the 1920s, Matthew becomes jealous of being overshadowed by actress, Emily, whose death the Tenth Doctor averts. Matthew is taken in by the vengeful Advocate, a survivor of the Time War, and travels with her for two years, during which time Emily continues exploring with the Doctor. After Matthew kills himself to stop the Advocate in *Final Sacrifice* (2010), Emily takes on the 'role' of Torchwood operative, Annabella Primavera, the original Annabella having died despite her life never being a fixed point in time, just as Emily's death was. Emily sets up the United Actors in Hollywood in the past, which ultimately led to her and Matthew meeting the Doctor in the first place.

It's through Emily that we meet Barnaby Edwards – named after the founder of New York's Regeneration Theatre, but drawn to resemble his Big Finish contributor namesake, the latter Barnaby Edwards also being a regular Dalek operator since 2005. The fictional Barnaby only appears in *Old Friend*, the last story in IDW's *Doctor Who Annual 2010*. When the Doctor and Emily land in the Shady Grove Rest Home, Barnaby recognises the Doctor despite having travelled with a future unnamed incarnation. His aged companion shares recollections of fighting the Sontarans and the 'Floor Menace,' then apologises for leaving the Doctor; he says he only did so as he'd fallen in love. As Barnaby passes away, the Doctor assures him he was 'one of the best companions ever,' and then refuses to acknowledge that Barnaby has died, insisting he's just sleeping.

The Eleventh Doctor
Matt Smith

*'Amy Pond, there's something you'd better understand about me
'cause it's important, and one day your life may depend on it:
I am definitely a mad man with a box.'*
The Doctor – *The Eleventh Hour*

The Doctor managed to hold off his regeneration long enough to see not only those who had travelled with him throughout his tenth incarnation, but every companion he'd ever had, according to *Death of the Doctor* (*The Sarah Jane Adventures*), in which he says, 'The last time I was dying, I looked back on all of you. Every single one. And I was so proud.' Such was the extent of his self-control that the regeneration energies finally unleashed were enough to explode the TARDIS console and set the ship crashing towards Earth – and the life of young Amelia Pond...

Amelia 'Amy' Pond* and Rory Williams – Karen Gillan and Arthur Darvill (*The Eleventh Hour* to *The Angels Take Manhattan*, *plus *The Time of the Doctor*)

Vincent (Don McLean); *The Sound of Silence* (Simon & Garfunkel).

I Will Wait For You (Matt Monro); *It's Been A Long, Long Time* (Kitty Kallen).

It's Easter 1996 when seven-year-old Amelia Pond (her younger self played by real-life niece of Karen Gillan, Caitlin Blackwood) – who has spent her whole life in the cosy village of Leadworth but never lost her Scottish accent – is praying to Santa, worrying about a crack in her bedroom wall. She asks Santa to send a policeman and is interrupted by the sound of the TARDIS materialising in her garden, breaking the shed in the process. Her home is mysteriously void of anyone else. The Doctor crawls out of the TARDIS and Amelia checks whether he's a policeman, and whether he can help her. But first, he's the one who needs help: Amelia does this in a surprisingly self-sufficient manner, by providing him with a succession of foods he finds disappointing, including an apple, bacon, 'bad, bad beans,' and a simple slice of bread. In the end, he settles on fish fingers and custard.

The Doctor is clearly impressed with Amelia: she doesn't seem scared of anything; that is, apart from the crack in her wall through which she hears voices. She tells him, 'I don't have a mum or dad,' so she lives with her aunt, Sharon, in a suspiciously large house. The Doctor is charmed by the girl, and heads to her room to sort out the crack; he attempts this by forcing it to invert, though not before he gets a warning from the Atraxi on the other side about Prisoner Zero escaping. That's when the TARDIS' cloister bell tolls, and he rushes back to the ship to stabilise it. He explains to Amelia that it's a time machine, and she immediately takes this on board, asking if she can come too. First, he assures her, he has to take a short hop, five minutes into the future. An enchanted Amelia watches the TARDIS vanish. She rushes off to pack a suitcase and sits to wait for him... but seemingly doesn't see him for another twelve years.

Nineteen-year-old Amy is now a kiss-o-gram. She pretends not to know the Doctor at first, trying to marry this new reality with that night, when she apparently gained an imaginary friend, one she's grown to call her Raggedy Man (after seeing him in his wrecked Tenth Doctor clothing). She's angry at the Doctor for not returning – understandably, seeing as, in the meantime, she's seen four psychiatrists (each one dissuaded by her tendency to bite). The Doctor wonders why she calls herself 'Amy' now; he liked 'Amelia', but she considers that name too 'fairytale,' using his own words against him. Nonetheless, that brief night during her childhood is like a fairytale to her: she's made drawings and dolls of the Doctor, scattered around her bedroom. The Doctor obviously holds a special place in her heart. She initially panics at seeing him again: she knocks him unconscious with a cricket bat (whose bat remains a mystery) and when he wakes, pretends to be a police officer calling for backup.

Amy's soon swept up in the wonder of his world, and though he impresses upon her the tight time limit they've got to find Prisoner Zero and bring him to the attention of the planet-threatening Atraxi, she traps his tie in a car door and demands he tell her his true identity. With the help of an apple that young Amelia gave him when he visited over a decade ago, he convinces her of who he really is. Interestingly, Amelia gave him an apple with a smiley face carved into it: 'I used to hate apples, so my mum put faces on them,' she explains. She doesn't tell him what happened to her mum, but then again, she can't even remember.

She introduces her boyfriend, Rory Williams, merely as a friend, something he's clearly not happy about. Rory's surprised to see the Doctor, and reveals that Amy used to make him dress up as him when they were younger. Rory's only real love is Amy, so she's always his priority; still, he's a nurse, so he's caring and conscientious at all times. He's the one who's spotted strange occurrences in Leadworth, namely that coma patients are seemingly strolling around the village (actually, it's the shape-changing Prisoner Zero). He's been badgering his superiors, Doctors Carver and Ramsden, about it to no avail, as the latter exasperatedly says, 'We've been very patient with you, Rory. You're a good enough nurse, but for God's sake...' In the end, it's Rory's photos of Prisoner Zero's disguises that help the Doctor defeat the alien, alongside Amy's memory of seeing Prisoner Zero in her house. When the creature transforms into a young Amelia holding her Raggedy Man's hand, it could be that his presence in her life has always remained strong, as the dream she can't let go of, but the Doctor argues it's actually because she can hear him despite being rendered unconscious by Zero. The alien's parting comment is to inform them that the universe is cracked, the Pandorica will open, and 'silence will fall.' The Doctor then finds new clothes (stolen from Leadworth hospital), while Amy watches, clearly enticed at seeing him getting changed.

Once the Doctor warns the Atraxi off Earth, he rushes off into the newly restored TARDIS, intending on a quick trip to the moon and back, only to instead return at night two years later: 2010. Amy's not impressed, but he soon wins her over again: 'Amy Pond, the girl who waited. You've waited long enough.' Just as they're about to head off, Amy tells him that she has to return by the next day, but she won't tell him why: it's the night before her wedding to Rory.

During her early moments in the TARDIS (*Meanwhile in the TARDIS*), she can't stop babbling, and constantly asks the Doctor questions. She doesn't know what a Police Box is, or how the control room can fit inside a wooden box. She wonders if the Doctor is a 'little slug in a human suit'. To keep her quiet, and show her the splendour, the Doctor casts her outside the TARDIS, to float in an atmospheric pocket.

By the time they arrive on Starship UK (*The Beast Below*), she's calmed down. She takes the news that he's a Time Lord calmly too, only questioning why he looks human ('No, you look Time Lord') and if there are others like him. He sadly tells her that he's the last of his species.

Amy explores the starship, bravely investigating while wrestling with the Doctor's initial argument that they can't get involved. She compares this to being like filming a wildlife documentary, but almost immediately learns that the Doctor involves himself. Separated from him, she comes across an ugly truth, but she votes to forget; it's too much for her, much like it is for everyone else on the starship. When the Doctor discovers the starship is propelled by a huge Star Whale, held captive and tortured by the humans, he's reluctantly ready to put an end to its suffering, but Amy prevents him from killing the whale. Before this, though, the Doctor rages at her, believing she's decided what he does and doesn't need to know on his behalf. She argues that she doesn't even remember doing it, thanks to the voting booth wiping her memory. Nonetheless, her presumptions about similarities between the Doctor and the Star Whale, both lonely creatures who only want to help mankind, hold her in good stead. Amy is a positive presence: she puts up a fight when the Doctor says he'll take her home, a threat that must've been gutting considering she's waited some fourteen years for this and one mistake might've meant she's dumped back home. It's also irrational of the Doctor, considering the mysteries surrounding her life, but you can't blame his anger in the face of mankind's cruelty. Amy doesn't slump into a reverie for long, so her quick mind and gut instincts mean she jumps to a decision without asking for support – instead, she presses a button that could easily doom everyone on the ship. Fortunately, she's right and saves both the Star Whale and her species.

It seems that the Doctor is appreciating the sights of space offered by Starship UK's observation deck, but it could be argued that he's mulling over whether Amy's recklessness could affect their travels. She helps him see her in a better light by effectively showing him that he *needs* someone by his side to give him another viewpoint. A simple hug is then enough to cement her place in the TARDIS.

Amy's worried about returning to Leadworth and her wedding, and she obliquely asks for the Doctor's advice: 'Have you ever run away from something because you were scared? Or not ready? Or just… just because you could?' The Doctor tells her that yes, he did, a long time ago (referring to his leaving Gallifrey).

Amy's surprised when Winston Churchill calls the TARDIS to speak to the Doctor, and is very impressed to meet him when they visit London, 1941, in *Victory of the Daleks*. She doesn't recognise the Daleks, something that worries the Doctor greatly. She's somehow forgotten all the planets in the sky too (*Journey's End*). It's the second concern about Amy's life, which, to the Doctor, doesn't make sense. Amy's worried about the Doctor's reaction to the Daleks, convinced that they are what they claim to be: 'Ironsides', created by Doctor Bracewell, whom Amy takes to, being a 'Paisley boy.' Still, she's not scared to face the Daleks. She's later bold enough to stride up to a Dalek, tap it on its dome, and demand to know if the Doctor's assertions about its true nature are correct, even though the Doctor attempts to hold her back, proving that she still has that reckless streak within her. (Admittedly, the Doctor doesn't try very hard to hold her back, seemingly more interested in what this Dalek will admit to, if anything.) She's suitably exasperated when the Doctor goes to face them on his own, and she's left with Churchill and Bracewell. Her quick thinking means they don't hang around, taking the fight to the Daleks too by using Bracewell's tech, gleaned from the Daleks, to send spitfires into space.

When Bracewell is revealed to be a Dalek-created human replicant, housing a bomb, Amy helps him hold onto his humanity by talking about the idea of 'fancying someone you know you shouldn't.' Saving Earth means letting the New Paradigm Daleks get away to rebuild their empire, something that leaves a bad taste in the Doctor's mouth, but as Amy points out, 'You saved the Earth. Not too shabby, is it?' (Interestingly, the New Paradigm Daleks' eyestalk was measured so they'd be eye-to-eye with with 5'11" tall Karen Gillan, much as the 2005 bronze Daleks lined up with Billie Piper's eye line; however, Amy doesn't meet any of the Paradigm until *The Big Bang*, and then only briefly.)

She seems somewhat caught up in it all, but still notices firstly when Miss Breen, one of the people serving under Churchill, starts crying, her partner Reg having been lost in an attack in the English Channel, and then when Winston steals the TARDIS key from the Doctor's pocket.

One of the most important moments in Amy's life happens when they visit the Delirium Archive in *The Time of Angels*, although she'll have no idea of this for at least another year. It's the final resting place of the Headless Monks, and the biggest museum ever. Amy's less than impressed with visiting a museum: after all, the Doctor has a time machine, so why would he need to visit a museum? Then she works it out: he visits to 'keep score.' She's not sure of the significance of the home box (like a 'black box') they find, or the words, in Old High Gallifreyan, the ancient language of the Time Lords, carved into it, not even when the Doctor points out that 'there were many days these words could burn stars.' (Actually, she looks thoroughly bored by this, unimpressed by the Doctor's grandstanding.) But she does learn that they say, 'Hello Sweetie'.

Amy's carried along by the Doctor's excitement, and when Professor River Song arrives, Amy finds herself highly intrigued by this woman, who seems to know the Doctor so well. River shows an amazing knack for piloting the TARDIS, more so than the Doctor, in fact. Amy wants to know how River can do it, and she explains that she had lessons from the very best, a compliment the Doctor takes but River goes on to hint that it wasn't him who taught her (it's later revealed she learned from the TARDIS itself). Amy watches River and the Doctor compare notes via River's blue book, and the Doctor warns Amy away from it. It's River's diary – 'our diary' River corrects him – and the Doctor explains that he and River keep meeting out of order and that she's from his future. Watching them more, Amy's certain that River is the Doctor's wife from the future, but he actively avoids confirming or denying this point. Even River won't confirm who she is. 'You are *so* his wife,' Amy says, but River simply responds with, 'Oh, Amy... This is the Doctor we're talking about. Do you really think it could be anything that simple?' Amy says yes, but River won't be drawn further into it. River shows a great affection for Amy, which makes perfect sense after later revelations.

Amy is rather clever: when confronted with a Weeping Angel and told not to blink, she figures that winking will help delay the quantum-locked statue, then uses its own 'blipping' image against it. The Doctor is reluctant to heap on too much praise, but River exclaims, 'You're *brilliant.*'

Amy becomes infected by a Weeping Angel when an image of one becomes stuck in her eye. She tries to keep her spirits up, but finds it difficult. In *Flesh and Stone*, the Doctor instructs her to remember what he told her when she was seven, but she doesn't understand (as later revealed in *The Big Bang*, this is a Doctor from some months in their future). Amy shows a massive degree of determination, guts, and faith in the Doctor and River when she's left alone, her eyes shut, surrounded by Angels. She makes her way through the starliner Byzantium, and is finally transmatted away from the attacking Angels by River. The Doctor's so pleased he says he could kiss River; 'Maybe when you're older,' she replies.

The Angels are defeated when the Doctor sends them all through the hungry crack in time that's seemingly following them since he first encountered it in Amelia's bedroom, and River's returned to the Stormcage Containment Facility, where she's imprisoned for killing someone. Amy then wants to return home, deciding that it's time to stop running from her marriage. Arriving in Leadworth, Amy attempts to seduce the Doctor. Though initially oblivious, he rejects her advances, and is determined to make some sense of her kooky life. She tricks him into unlocking visual records of all his past companions in the TARDIS, and is amused by how many women there have been (*Meanwhile in the TARDIS*). She thinks she's got the Doctor's number, especially after seeing Leela in her 'leather bikini,' concluding that the Doctor is, when it comes down to it, just a bloke: 'Every room you walk into, you laugh at all the men and show off to all the girls.' When she mentions Rory, she's still hurt that the Doctor laughs – an 'involuntary snort… of fondness' – though the Doctor might've done this solely to provoke a reaction as he's intent on the pair living happily ever after.

Then again, this Doctor puts his foot in it a lot. Nowhere is this greater on show than in *The Vampires of Venice*, when he jumps out of the giant cake during Rory's stag-do in lieu of a diabetic stripper called Lucy. 'Now then, Rory, we need to talk about your fiancé,' the Doctor says. 'She tried to kiss me. Tell you what though, you're a lucky man. She's a great kisser.' Unsurprisingly, this doesn't go down well, leaving Rory both angry and embarrassed. This appears to be at a local pub, with Leadworth residents invited (including the postman, as seen later in *Amy's Choice*), all wearing red jumpers emblazoned with 'Rory's Stag' and a photo of the couple in a big heart with an arrow through it.

Amy clearly feels awkward about having Rory join her in the TARDIS. Rory takes the interior of the TARDIS in his stride, so when the Doctor starts to explain about transcendental dimensions, Rory shows his understanding of such things. 'I've been reading up on all the latest scientific theories. FTL travel, parallel universes...' Rory's not afraid of some legwork, especially when it comes to anything to do with Amy. It's pretty impressive considering Rory's probably had a few pints by now: certainly his voicemail to her just before the Doctor arrives makes him sound a little tipsy given that he calls her 'smashing.'

The Doctor decides to take Amy and Rory on a date, to Venice in 1580, because he argues that life on the TARDIS 'blinds you to the things that are important... Because for one person to have seen all that, to taste the glory and then go back...? It will tear you apart.' Rory's on the back foot, but instead of primarily worrying about Amy being with the Doctor, he's more concerned that the Doctor is right, that Amy didn't miss him because life among the stars blots out everything else. However, he does feel a little threatened by Amy and the Doctor's close friendship. When they need to go undercover in Rosanna Calvierri's private school, Amy suggests the Doctor pretend to be her fiancé, which annoys Rory as *he* is her *actual* fiancé. Amy doesn't help the situation by suggesting that Rory pretends to be her brother instead. Amy shows considerable courage when she does get accepted into the school, even offering herself up despite the Doctor and Rory telling her no. It seems the Doctor is trying to learn from previous mistakes as he notes that 'this is how they [meaning his companions] go.' He immediately relents, smiling at Amy's determination as she says they don't have another option. Rory is understandably troubled by this, and goes with the Doctor to get her back as soon as possible. He reveals a fragile yet angry side when he and the Doctor are alone, one minute concerned that Amy's travels mean they'll have to cancel the wedding and the next asserting that the really dangerous thing about the Doctor is that he makes people want to impress him. Rory arguably downplays his emotional pain: he knows they've got a time machine, so Amy could travel for ages and still be back in time for their special day, but his mulling over losing their deposits on the village hall and the salsa band likely means he thinks Amy doesn't want to marry him at all.

Nevertheless, they prove themselves to one another. Rory fights Francesco to save Amy, but she ends up saving him instead, which leads to a passionate kiss. Dumbstruck by the embrace, Rory's then dragged back into the action, as Amy doesn't want to leave the Doctor to take down the Sisters of the Water. Rory's already starting to see how easy it is to be consumed by this life.

The Doctor wants to give Amy away at her wedding, but she seems reluctant. Rory realises that Amy wishes to remain with the Doctor, and asks to be returned to Leadworth, but Amy suggests Rory join her and the Doctor. 'My boys,' as she calls them. Rory joyfully accepts.

Amy and Rory find themselves living in a false reality in *Amy's Choice*, a life five years hence, where she and Rory are married, living in Leadworth still, and she's pregnant. When they awake in the TARDIS, Amy reveals that a life with Rory and a baby is not her ideal, but it is Rory's. She doesn't wish to give up her adventures with the Doctor, effectively postponing the wedding but safe in the knowledge that their time travelling capabilities mean it can be the night before their wedding for however long they wish.

In the dreamland, Rory is something of a bumbler who thinks growing a ponytail makes him interesting and gets annoyed at people favouring leaf blowers over rakes. His life there is safe and happy. To the Doctor, it's a nightmare. They can't tell which is a dream and which reality, their memories seeming to fill in the gaps, so when the Doctor tells them to look for any details that don't ring true, Amy and Rory are justified in noting that life on board the TARDIS is ridiculous anyway. The Doctor is afforded a brief glimpse at life in Leadworth – or Upper Leadworth, which is a bit more 'upmarket' as Rory is at pains to point out. They live on the outskirts in an appropriately dreamy cottage with a vibrant but warm kitchen and a picturesque garden. Amy takes some pride in the flowers in their rockery, at least according to Rory. When the Doctor accuses this existence of being dull, Amy pretends to go into labour, just to make the Doctor panic – which he does, arguably more so than Rory. 'This is my life now and it just turned you white as a sheet,' Amy says, 'so don't you call it dull again, ever, okay?'

Rory takes a degree of pleasure when one of his patients, Mrs Poggit who has a dodgy hip, asks if the Doctor is a junior doctor. It seems Rory works in a care home, and is beloved by all Upper Leadworth's residents. When attacked by OAPs, Rory laments that he fixed Mrs Hamill's depression and that Mr Nainby, who used to run the local sweet shop, loved him so much that he used to slip him the occasional free toffee. He's reticent to hit the former with a plank of wood to stop her coming after them, but Amy instructs him simply to 'whack her.'

Back in reality, Amy questions Rory, 'If that life is real, then why would we give up all this? Why would anyone?' She has an unwavering faith in the Doctor, that he'll save them all, but it's actually down to her. The Dream Lord, a dark echo of the Time Lord, tells her that both the Doctor and Rory are merely waiting for her to make a decision, as to which life she wants. The choice, though, is taken from her somewhat, as the Dream Lord forces her hand by killing Rory. The Doctor isn't able to save him, prompting an angry Amy to ask, 'Then what is the point of you?' as she realises she just wants Rory, and would rather die than not have him. Rory can't recall dying, and the Doctor recognises that Amy telling him she'd effectively die for him will change his life. As such, after sharing a kiss, Amy and Rory decide to carry on travelling together, the latter now perfectly content to go anywhere, as long as Amy is by his side.

In *The Hungry Earth*, they arrive in a small mining town in South Wales in 2020. It's interesting to note that Amy dressed for Rio de Janeiro, i.e. wearing a sheer top and shorts, whereas Rory, likely aware of the Doctor's spotty history of getting them where they want to be, is instead in a bodywarmer!

From a distance, the pair spot their older selves who have passed by to wave at them to relive their days aboard the TARDIS. Amy's somewhat surprised to learn that they're still together ten years later. It seems Rory has more faith in them than she does, though perhaps Amy is simply amazed at this glimpse into their future. He's also worried about her engagement ring, certain she'll lose it. Amy, though, retorts that he likes her wearing it, which he does but he is concerned because it cost a lot of money. She returns it to him and he takes it into the TARDIS to keep it safe. Upon stepping out, he's mistaken for a policeman by Ambrose Northover, and her son, Elliot. Rory plays along and pretends to investigate the local graves, which are apparently 'eating people.' He's impressed by Elliot, who quotes Sherlock Holmes by saying that, once you eliminate the impossible, whatever remains, however improbable, must be the truth. Rory agrees: he's seen enough improbable things since Venice.

Trying to rescue Tony Mack, Ambrose's father, from being eaten by the earth, Amy herself is sucked into the ground. Though she wakes up as a prisoner of a Silurian scientist, she manages to free herself, and with Mo Northover, she explores the Silurian city, picking up a weapon along the way. After the Doctor talks the Silurians down, he appoints Amy and Nasreen Chaudhry as representatives of humanity in the initial peace talks (he failed to broker peace at least three times before, but is determined not to make the same mistake a fourth time). As they flee the Silurian city for the TARDIS, Rory is shot by Restac, one of the Silurian warriors. Amy's distraught, but as they spot a temporal crack in time, like the one from Amy's bedroom, the Doctor pulls Amy away but Rory is consumed by it. The Doctor drags Amy into the TARDIS, telling her she needs to hold onto the memory of Rory, but he knows she's going to forget him – just like she forgot her parents and the Daleks. It's a vain attempt since her memory of Rory fades completely, leaving only the engagement ring for the Doctor to find in the TARDIS. Amy spots her future self again and waves, but the Doctor is disheartened to see that it's only Amy.

Rory has been erased from history.

Following this, the Doctor starts being particularly nice to Amy, taking her to Arcadia (likely a planet, though it shares its name with Gallifrey's second city), the Trojan Gardens, and, in *Vincent and the Doctor*, the Musée d'Orsay. She jokes about his recent attitude towards her being suspicious, and he responds that he's always nice to her. 'There's nothing to be suspicious about,' he says. 'Okay,' Amy considers, 'I was joking. Why aren't you?' Upon meeting Vincent van Gogh, Amy starts flirting with him, and Vincent especially loves her hair colour, thinking that they would have amazing babies together ('the ultimate ginge'). She's surprised he doesn't like sunflowers, and is later stunned when she sees 'for Amy' inscribed on one of his famous Sunflower paintings. Vincent understands Amy on a deeper level than she knows herself, recognising 'the song of your sadness' when she's crying; she, however, has no idea why she's crying. That might be further reason for Vincent's attachment to her: as they're leaving, he says that if she tires of the Doctor, she can return for him and they'll get married and have babies 'by the dozen.' She tells him she's not really the marrying kind.

Vincent can't deal with the thought of being alone again, and Amy struggles to come to terms with the artist committing suicide. She begs the Doctor not to remind her of this fact. Vincent charms the pair so much that they break a rule or two of time travel and take him to the future, to 2010, to see an exhibition and celebration of his work. Amy takes a huge amount of delight in seeing him realise how beloved he becomes. After taking him back to his own time, Amy is sure that the Musée d'Orsay will be filled with 'new' works, that they managed to save him from his depression and subsequent suicide. Alas, time is unchanged, so Amy is gutted to think that they've not made a difference to his life. The Doctor argues otherwise, that the outcome might've been the same, but Vincent's days before then were all the better for their meeting, and Amy finally sees that their visit was 'brighter than sunflowers.'

While the Doctor deals with a mysterious flat that shouldn't exist in *The Lodger* (one that holds greater significance from *Day of the Moon*), Amy's trapped inside the TARDIS. From there, she advises the Doctor on how to be a normal, everyday kind of guy: going to the pub, playing football, watching TV... She reveals a sound understanding of the console, though not perhaps how precise things are, as the Doctor implies the pilot's position in front of the console makes a difference to how the zigzag plotter operates.

Once the Doctor has returned, Amy searches his jacket for a pen and finds instead a box containing her engagement ring. She looks at it curiously, having no recollection of it at all. When she confronts him about it in *The Pandorica Opens*, he says it belonged to a friend of his, one who Amy presumes is a woman, and she admits that it makes her feel a strange feeling she can't put a name to. 'People fall out of the world sometimes, but they always leave traces,' the Doctor tells her, as if he's not giving up on Rory's memory. 'Little things we can't quite account for: faces in photographs, luggage, half-eaten meals, rings. Nothing is ever forgotten, not completely. And if something can be remembered, it can come back.'

River Song summons Amy and the Doctor to 102 AD, where she's pretending to be Cleopatra, camped with a legion of Romans near Stonehenge – under which lies the legendary Pandorica, seemingly based on Pandora's Box. (To get there, Amy demonstrates some impressive skills riding a horse, though this sadly isn't seen again; the Doctor, on the other hand, rides horseback again in *A Town Called Mercy* and *The Bells of St John*.) Amy's confused by River's timeline, certain this is River from after their last meeting, but River points out that the crash of the Byzantium (*The Time of Angels*) has yet to happen for her. The Doctor draws attention to the fact that both Romans and the myth of Pandora's Box are among Amy's favourite things, and tells her that they should never ignore coincidences. He tells her that her life doesn't make sense – her house with too many empty rooms, her lack of parents, and her lack of knowledge of the Daleks – one reason he took her with him. When River returns to the Roman camp to secure an army to defend Stonehenge and the Pandorica which sits beneath it, she meets a very special centurion: Rory! She doesn't recognise Rory: indeed, due to later revelations about her, River is an anomaly here, but she seems to be one of the traces the universe leaves of Rory after he's wiped from space-time; so too a photo of him, dressed as a Roman centurion with Amy in her police officer outfit, which River finds in Amy's house in the future after the TARDIS forcibly takes her there.

Rory the Roman is revealed to be an Auton, as are all the other legionnaires, as this is an elaborate trap to seal the Doctor within the Pandorica, assembled aliens believing he's responsible for the TARDIS exploding and leading to Total Event Collapse. The Daleks know the high esteem in which the Doctor holds his companions so well that they based this subterfuge on Amy, not on anything else related to the Doctor, such as Gallifrey.

Amy starts crying again, but doesn't know why, then finally, she remembers Rory. 'How could I ever forget you?' she says, incredulously, determined not to let him go. Nonetheless, as his Nestene Consciousness conditioning takes hold, he begs her to get away from him. Too late: he shoots her, apparently killing her. In the face of space-time having never existed, the Doctor checks Rory is back to his old self in *The Big Bang* by telling him Amy isn't more important than the whole universe; this earns the Doctor a punch as Rory insists, 'She is to me!' Fortunately, Amy is revived using the Pandorica, and one-thousand, eight-hundred, and ninety-four years later, Amelia is once again praying to Santa about a crack in her wall. She, River, and the Doctor are holding onto existence merely as echoes, the last lights to go out – Rory doubly so, seeing as he's sustained only by memories and a physical body made by the Nestene Consciousness, a being similarly erased from history. Rory stands guard over the Pandorica for all that time, inside of which lies Amy, ready to be restored by a living DNA sample in 1996. He becomes the Lone Centurion, an almost mythical being who's awake all that time, content to wait for Amy and ensure she's safe. At some point, the Doctor might've told him how easily he broke *into* the prison-like Pandorica, or perhaps Rory can't bring himself to leave the love of his life, especially after he was responsible for shooting her.

In this aborted universe, devoid of life, Amelia still needs therapy, albeit because she believes in stars, so her aunt worries about her joining 'one of those star cults.' Her psychiatrist assures Sharon that 'there's bound to be a bit of her that feels alone. Amelia's a really good person.' Amelia follows her gut when a mysterious individual, i.e. the Doctor, gets her interested in visiting the Pandorica in the National Museum, and Sharon is happy to take her. The exhibition is accompanied by a video about the Lone Centurion, who it speculates died in a fire caused by incendiary bombs during the London Blitz in 1941. The narrator says that Rory appears 'as an iconic image in the artwork of many cultures, and there are several documented accounts of his appearances, and his warnings to the many who attempted to open the box before its time.'

Amelia hides there, and Sharon is forced to give up the search when the museum closes, leaving the young girl to reawaken the Pandorica after hours. Rory is revealed to be the museum's security guard, and isn't particularly shocked to see a Dalek alive and well; then again, if he works there, he might've recognised the stone relics of various alien species, notably the Cybermen, one of which he fought with a sword when defending Amy in the past. Though he hasn't met the Daleks before now, he likely would've known that they're not of this planet. When revived, Amy's love for Rory is clear, as is her faith in the Doctor: even though she apparently sees him die, she won't accept it and is eventually proven right.

Together, they reboot the universe using the endless power of the exploding TARDIS and the particles inside the Pandorica, but at the expense of the Doctor.

Amy wakes up on her wedding day in 2010, to find that her parents, Tabetha and Augustus, are there and a joyous Rory back in existence. She's sure something is missing though. At their wedding reception, she sees River walk past the hall and begins to cry – sad about a huge loss. River's TARDIS-blue diary reminds her of something, and upon seeing a bowtie and a pair of braces, Amy remembers the Doctor. 'When I was a kid, I had an imaginary friend. The Raggedy Doctor. *My* Raggedy Doctor... I remember! I brought the others back and I can bring you home, too.'. Rory cannot believe that he forgot the Doctor. When the Doctor is restored through memory, one of the guests mutters that he was the 'stripper' at Rory's stag-do, reaffirming that the events of the past couple of decades still happened, but perhaps in a slightly tweaked manner.

Amy and Rory spend the evening having great fun, dancing late into the night, their playlist including 'Crazy Little Thing Called Love' by Queen and 'You Give Me Something' by James Morrison. The Doctor dances too (something River, who stays outside, takes some pleasure in commenting on), but watches on during the slower numbers. 'Two thousand years,' he says to himself, especially happy to see Rory and Amy together again. 'The boy who waited. Good on you, mate.' They seem to leave the reception early so they can travel in the TARDIS again. There's no question in any of their minds whether they'll carry on or stay in Leadworth.

The Doctor's first attempt to give Amy and Rory a wonderful honeymoon fails because the spaceship they're travelling in is crashing into the city of Sardicktown in *A Christmas Carol*. They're stuck on the ship, and call the Doctor for assistance. He eventually finds a solution, and they join him on the planet below, though recognise the sacrifice Kazran Sardick makes in delivering them safely – namely, he has to give up the love of his life, Abigail Pettigrew. The Doctor wants to know why they're dressed in their kiss-o-gram and centurion outfits, but the pair are evasive. Rory asks if the Doctor has any more honeymoon ideas, and in *The Sarah Jane Adventures: Death of the Doctor*, he tells Sarah Jane Smith and Jo Grant that he's left Amy and Rory on a honeymoon planet for a short period.

After their honeymoon, the Doctor returns them to Earth, 2011, where they spend at least two months. At the start of *The Impossible*

Astronaut, they think the Doctor is being intentionally ridiculous, appearing in the most obscure historical stories, as if he is trying to attract their attention. He even shows up in a *Laurel & Hardy* film, ostensibly one of Rory's favourites as Amy comments incredulously that he's watching it again ('I've explained the jokes,' Rory says.) The Doctor lures them to Lake Silencio in Utah, where, joined by River and a stranger called Canton Everett Delaware III who seems to know them in his past, but their personal futures, they see an astronaut ascend from the lake and shoot him before he can regenerate. Amy can't believe he's gone, but Rory helps River make a Viking funeral, burning his body so no other species can take it and learn the secrets of the Time Lords. They then see the Doctor again, two hundred years in his personal past, and follow a trail to 1969, where they do indeed meet Canton Everett Delaware III again, albeit a younger version, freelancing for President Nixon. They encounter the Silents, terrifying creatures that have infiltrated the earth but are completely memory-proof, meaning the second you turn away, you forget them. This allows them to play with the companions' lives to a great extent.

Although no one knows it, Amy is replaced at some point during this time by a Ganger duplicate, while the now-pregnant real Amy is being held at Demon's Run (*The Almost People* and *A Good Man Goes to War*). This Ganger is a live link to the actual Amy, so even Amy thinks she's the real her, experiencing everything she does while adventuring with the Doctor, Rory, and River, but also getting glimpses at the Eye Patch Lady, later revealed to be Madame Kovarian, of the Church of the Silence. Even the Ganger Amy thinks she's pregnant and tells the Doctor as much, though later concedes that she's probably wrong, likely as she doesn't develop a bump during her time being pursued by the Silents and FBI across America.

Amy feels queasy as a result of her encounter with the Silents, likely a reaction of the Ganger's connection to the real, pregnant Amy. When the Doctor is threatened again by an astronaut, revealed to be a little girl inside the huge suit, Amy shoots to protect the Doctor.

Amy, Rory, and River go on the run for three months at the start of *Day of the Moon*, to see how far the Silents have spread out. While investigating the spooky Graystark Hall orphanage with Canton, Amy finds a nursery containing photographs of herself and a baby. She soon works out that the baby is the girl in the astronaut suit.

By accident, Rory overhears Amy talk about the man who is coming for her, who 'dropped out of the sky,' and mentions his 'stupid face'. Rory's convinced she's talking about the Doctor again. He admits to the Doctor that he only sometimes remembers the two thousand years he spent waiting for Amy to be released from the Pandorica, that the period of his other life can be accessed like a door he can open and close. Rory is reluctant to talk about it, but he does remind the Doctor that they were both there when Rome fell: the Doctor isn't the only one with a good grasp of human history now. (Admittedly, the events of Rory's life could be at odds with established history, given how different that starless universe was.) While River and the Doctor deal with the Silents, Rory frees Amy and she tells him that he needs to get his 'stupid face' to safety. It's then that he realises she was talking about him all the time, not the Doctor, and that she was waiting for him to come and rescue her. After River shoots down the remaining Silents, she wonders if her 'old fella' has seen her, and looks back at Rory, who's watching. When the Doctor asks Amy why she told him she thought she was pregnant rather than Rory, she tells him that it's because 'you're my best friend'. Rory's listening in, but Amy knows this and intentionally winds him up over it. As the two of them leave the console room, the Doctor turns back to the scanner, and finds out that the TARDIS can't decide if Amy is pregnant.

In *The Curse of the Black Spot*, Rory's temporarily entranced by an enigmatic Siren, while Amy becomes a swashbuckler, donning a pirate hat and swinging a sword around with a fair level of expertise. She and Rory also get to help steer Henry Avery's ship during a nasty storm. Rory's swept overboard and Amy and the Doctor take a gamble with their lives to get him back by risking the

Siren taking them all (as does Avery, who wants to rescue his son).
When Rory is close to death, he insists that only Amy can save him,
because he knows she won't give up on him. He teaches her CPR
and she crumbles when she thinks it hasn't worked; fortunately, he
wakes up and the pair embrace, realising how close they came to
losing each other.

Later, in the TARDIS, the Doctor calls her 'Amelia'. Amy
points out he only does this when he's worried about her. The
Doctor agrees, but argues that he's always worried about her. It's
a feeling Amy can't help but share, having witnessed the Doctor's
death. Rory reminds her that they agreed he can't know his future.
In a way, the two of them are merely following the rules laid out
by River, though Rory in particular gets on board, aware that the
last time they meddled with time, 'the universe did blow up.'

After receiving a message from an old Time Lord friend, the
Corsair, the Doctor pushes his TARDIS into another universe (*The
Doctor's Wife*). The TARDIS' soul is forced into the body of a
woman called Idris and the ship is possessed by an entity called
House. Together, Rory and Amy flee deeper into the TARDIS.
House plays mind games with them, separating them and feeding
them nightmares. Amy comes across an older Rory, who angrily
tells her, 'Two thousand years I waited for you and you did it to
me again! How could you leave me? How could you do that to *me*?'
Fortunately, she's soon reunited with the real Rory, but the
emotional damage has been done. It's obvious that Amy feels guilty
about Rory's sacrifice for her. We don't see Rory's fears; we might
find out why in *The God Complex*, although a lot of time lapses
between now and then.

When Idris attempts to contact Amy and Rory, the Doctor
suggests she get a message to Amy. 'Which one's Amy? The pretty
one?' She sends a message to Rory. The Doctor is surprised by the
TARDIS' affiliation: 'The pretty one?!' The TARDIS might've been
trying to keep Amy and Rory apart, seeing as they have, until now,
had bunk beds; this might've been the Doctor's decision, however,
as he sees bunk beds as cool. (Either way, we later find out that not

giving them a double bed didn't hold them back on their honeymoon.) They find their way to the previous console room – destroyed when the Doctor last regenerated, although the TARDIS reveals she stores all the console rooms. Amy demonstrates that she's able to operate the console even though she's never seen this particular console before. Rory and Amy can do little but sympathise as the Doctor breaks down when Idris, housing the TARDIS, dies, meaning she can't talk in a traditional manner to him. Amy particularly doesn't know what to do, since she's never seen the Doctor so distraught before.

While the Doctor is distracting himself by working on the TARDIS, Rory tells him something that Idris whispered before she returned her matrix to the TARDIS: 'The only water in the forest is the river,' which makes no sense to either of them. For now...

At the beginning of *The Rebel Flesh*, we see a much more domesticated side to life in the TARDIS, with Amy and Rory playing darts while listening to 'Supermassive Black Hole' by Muse. The pair are competitive as ever, with Rory celebrating a score Amy calls 'Rubbishy, rubbishy, rubbish.' The Doctor wishes to go off and do something without them, intending to drop off Amy and Rory elsewhere to have chips. Amy doesn't want to leave his side, stating that whatever he's up to, she 'personally' – demonstrating she's showing more consideration to what Rory wants to do – would like to go too. In the event, the TARDIS is pulled to an acid-mining factory on a small island: it's the destination the Doctor has in mind, although he wishes to explore it alone for reasons that become clear later. Here, they're introduced to the Flesh, fully programmable matter which can replicate any living beings generally referred to as Gangers. We also get mention of Rory's mum for the first time; as 'You Don't Have to Say You Love Me' plays, Rory says, 'My mum's a massive fan of Dusty Springfield.' Maybe Rory's inherited some of her (admittedly mournful) romanticism.

Amy has a hard time getting her head around things, especially when, in *The Almost People*, confronted by a Ganger-Doctor who she doesn't consider real at all. Rory befriends Jennifer Lucas, who's revealed to be a rogue Ganger, and shows sympathy for her despite Jennifer's increasingly unstable mental state. She's somewhat violent and eventually turns into a nightmarish monster, but Rory typically sees the best in her, giving her a hug and looking pained when Jennifer laments, 'Why did they do this to us? Help me, Rory.' Amy shows a touch of jealousy, and there's definitely a spark between Rory and Jennifer, though it's rather one-sided as Jennifer tells him that she immediately noticed his 'kind eyes' and comments that Amy's a lucky girl. Nonetheless, when the conflict between the humans and Flesh kicks into a higher gear, Rory is drawn away from Amy and the Doctor by Jennifer's scream and his concern that she's on her own.

Once again, Amy sees Madame Kovarian through a non-existent hatch, but this time, she tells the Doctor about it. He calls it a mirage, a time memory, and apparently dismisses it. Still, he's overly concerned with her welfare, encouraging her to breathe, which confuses her. When apologising to the Ganger-Doctor for how she's treated him, she confesses that she saw the Doctor die, and mulls over the possibility that it might've been the Ganger who was killed at Lake Silenco.

She's so certain she knows which Doctor is which, and is surprised to learn how mistaken she is. Giving him a last hug, she mutters, 'I never thought it possible... You're twice the man I thought you were.' When the Ganger-Doctor is about to give his life to save them, he whispers into Amy's ear, 'Push... But only when she tells you to,' leaving Amy none the wiser. As they escape into the TARDIS, Amy convulses in pain, much to Rory's surprise. The Doctor explains that she's feeling contractions and insists that Rory stand away from her. Such is the power of his voice that Rory complies, although he clearly fears for his wife. Amy is beyond confused and 'properly, properly scared,' and the Doctor explains that he had to learn more about the Flesh to block the signal to her Flesh duplicate. The Doctor promises he will find her: 'However hard, however far, we will find you.' He disrupts the signal and

Ganger-Amy dissolves in front of a horrified Rory. The real Amy snaps awake, inside a medical capsule on Demons Run. Madame Kovarian opens a hatch and tells her that the little one is almost ready to 'pop'. Amy is shocked by her own pregnant body and promptly goes into labour.

We see more of Amy's faith in Rory at the start of *A Good Man Goes to War* when she tells the newly born Melody Pond that she knows Rory will come for them – not even an army can stand in his way. Proving her faith, Rory attacks the Twelfth Cyber Legion, just to get Amy's location, blowing up all but one of their ships with the Doctor's aid.

Dressed as the Lone Centurion again, Rory goes with the Doctor on a mission to find Amy, and trace her to Demons Run, an asteroid filled with Headless Monks and 'clerics' from the Church of the Silence. Rory seems to save Melody from Madame Kovarian, and carries her back to Amy; only then, once they're all together as a family unit, can he properly take stock. Looking at Melody, he starts crying and then says he was hoping to be cool in the moment. 'Crying Roman with a baby?' Amy says. 'Definitely cool.' Despite Demons Run effectively being a trap for the Doctor, neither Amy nor Rory hold it against him, with the latter actively encouraging him to say hello to Melody.

Amy also gets a prayer leaf from a kind-hearted cleric called Lorna Bucket: it details that Melody Pond's name in the language of the Gamma Forest natives. It actually reads Melody River, though, as they don't have a word for 'pond,' seeing as the only water in the forest is the river…

During the final battle of Demons Run, Rory heads off to the front line, but Amy makes him promise to let all the others die first. 'You're so Scottish,' he tells her. Kovarian escapes with Melody while the baby in Amy's hands is revealed to be a Ganger and dissolves as pre-programmed to do so. Amy's furious and heartbroken, so she seeks solace in Rory.

When the Doctor tries to comfort her, Amy backs away – the first time there's ever been a distance between them. The Doctor's hurt, but when River arrives, she reveals her secret. The Doctor rushes off to find Melody, and orders River to get Amy and Rory home. Beyond tired and emotionally exhausted, Amy draws a gun on River and demands answers. 'The Doctor will find your daughter. And he will care for her, whatever it takes. And I know that,' River says. 'It's me. I'm Melody. I'm your daughter.' Presumably, there's some bonding time between *A Good Man Goes to War* and *Let's Kill Hitler*, though naturally River has to avoid too many spoilers. She doesn't, for instance, reveal the truth behind Mels, Amy's best friend from childhood. She's been afforded details of Amy's Raggedy Man, and believed them, perhaps a reason they were so close; in fact, she's more extreme with her belief in the Doctor than even Amelia in school, getting into trouble for back-chatting teachers by talking about the Doctor's significance to history. Mels is the first person to notice that Rory and Amy have a thing for each other and points it out, suggesting, 'Seriously, it's got to be you two.' Prior to this, Amy's always thought of Rory as being gay.

When Amy and Rory track down the Doctor, Mels gatecrashes the reunion while on the run from the police. She pulls out a gun, deciding they should use the TARDIS to get away from the present and instead go to kill Hitler. The TARDIS does indeed take them to Nazi Germany, where Rory ends up punching Hitler and storing him in a cupboard. Hitler shoots Mels, however, and they all stand back in shock as Mels starts to regenerate. Amy and Rory didn't need to look for Melody after all; she found them when they were seven years old. She last regenerated in 1969 (at the end of *Day of the Moon*), into a baby, and lived throughout the twentieth century, growing (very, very) slowly, until she found her parents. Paradoxically, Amy reveals that she named Melody after Mels. Now looking like River, although she's yet to *become* River Song, Melody attempts to kill the Doctor with a kiss, her lips layered with poison from the Judas tree. In the TARDIS, the Doctor activates a hologram interface, which initially appears as Rose, Martha, and then Donna. He feels guilty seeing them, and when he asks for someone who he's not yet screwed up, the hologram takes the form of young Amelia – a telling moment for the Doctor.

Using her quick wits while stuck inside the Teselecta, a robot powered by miniaturised people, Amy takes down the whole crew, but thinks she and Rory are going to die. They both say 'I love you' and hug – just as the TARDIS arrives to save them. Both think it's the Doctor; instead, it's River, who's been taught to pilot the ship by the TARDIS itself. They return to see the Doctor die as a result of River's poisoning him, but encourage her to save him. River asks if he's 'worth it,' and although she's arguably unsure what River's about to do, Amy says he is. And so, River gives up all her remaining regenerations to bring him back to life. Amy later says she shouldn't have done it, but the smile on her face says otherwise.

Curiously, in *Night Terrors*, the Doctor takes charge of finding George, a scared boy who turns out to be an alien Tenza who accidentally creates a world of his own fears and banishes Amy and Rory there. He's only prompted, it seems, by his hearing Rory jokingly say to Amy, 'Maybe we should let the monsters gobble him up,' albeit before he meets George. When banished, Rory immediately thinks they're dead 'again,' letting out his frustration after dying in previous episodes like *Amy's Choice*, *Cold Blood*, and *The Doctor's Wife*. (In fairness, Amy dies numerous times too, notably in the next story, *The Girl Who Waited*, and in *The Pandorica Opens*.) George's worries, it seems, include being turned into a peg doll, trapped in a dolls' house, so Amy is soon turned into one, much to Rory's horror. When restored, she asks, 'Was I –?' but is cut off by Rory confirming what happened. Both take it on the chin, however.

After recent events, the Doctor decides it's time for a holiday and takes Amy and Rory to Apalapucia in *The Girl Who Waited*. Amy finds herself trapped in a faster timestream than Rory and the Doctor, simply because she presses the wrong button in a hospital that isolates its patients. She has to outrun the Handbots, who wish to cure her of Chen-7, a disease she doesn't have; any such cure will kill her. The Doctor sends Rory in after her, since he's susceptible to Chen-7 and will die should he enter Amy's timestream. Rory finds Amy, only it's been thirty-six years for her. She tells him, coldly, that she's been waiting for him, longer than she even waited for the Doctor when she was little. She'd given up hope of them coming for her, and blames the Doctor totally. In that time, she reprogrammed one of the Handbots and called it Rory, her own loyal companion.

Rory has to wear special glasses so the Doctor can see and communicate with them; Amy immediately realises this, and calls them ridiculous. Rory states that anything is better than a fez, which makes Amy laugh – the first time she's done so in many, many years. She considers that she's lived through hell. She's clearly just as in love with Rory as ever, flirting and asking for his 'cutest smile,' then explaining, 'I've known you my whole life. How many games of Doctors and Nurses?' Rory starts blaming the Doctor too, suggesting that his recklessness has caused this. He tells him that he no longer wants to travel with him anymore, not after this. While Amy misinterprets Rory's anger as being because he's seen her get older, he retorts that he doesn't care about her ageing – solely that they didn't grow old together.

The Doctor finds a way to restore the timeline, to save younger Amy so she never has to become the twisted older version. Old Amy doesn't like this idea, knowing it'd mean her end, and she refuses to help. She tells them that when she was Young Amy, she remembers that her old self refused to help, and so by doing so, she's ensuring her timeline remains unchanged. Rory stands aside as the two Amys discuss how Rory has always loved them, and how Young Amy needs to be saved *for* Rory. Young Amy says, 'You know when sometimes you meet someone so beautiful, and then you actually talk to them, and five minutes later, they're as dull as a brick? Then there's other people, and you meet them and think, "Not bad, they're okay." And then you get to know them, and their face just sort of *becomes* them, like their personality's written all over it. And they just turn into something so *beautiful*.' At the same time, both versions of Amy agree: 'Rory's the most beautiful man I've ever met.'

This moves Old Amy and she resolves to pull time apart for Rory, but only if the Doctor allows her to travel with them. The Doctor has to agree, but he's lying, knowing that even the power of the TARDIS can't sustain the paradox. Nonetheless, they manage to merge the two timelines, and Rory is a little awkward around Old Amy once he has his wife back. Rory finds himself having to choose between his wives. It tears him apart, but he essentially makes his choice when Young Amy is rendered unconscious, so he has to carry her into the TARDIS while Old Amy fights off the Handbots. The Doctor supports this decision by closing the TARDIS doors on Old Amy. Rory isn't happy with this situation, and stands by the locked TARDIS door while Old Amy is outside, knowing that he could let her in but that they'd have to sacrifice Young Amy. He snaps at the Doctor, 'This isn't fair – you're turning me into you!' Rory is about to let Old Amy in, regardless of the consequences, but Old Amy won't let him. She'd forgotten how much she loved being Young Amy, and Old Amy's last thought is of a boy she knew on Earth, who once learned to play a guitar, just because he'd pretended to be in a band to impress her…

While waiting for her to wake up, Rory wants to know if the Doctor ever thought they could save both Amys, but the Doctor doesn't answer directly.

Rory's disenchantment with travelling continues in *The God Complex*, illustrating how worried he gets when the Doctor becomes friendly with someone: he feels as though he should notify their next of kin. Faced with a labyrinthine hotel and a Minotaur stalking its corridors, feeding on beliefs, Rory never finds his hotel room; it shows him the exit, though he can't leave Amy and the Doctor. In a moment of clarity, he says, 'After all the time I've spent with you in the TARDIS, what was left to be scared of?' The use of past tense is noted by the Doctor, even if Rory disputes this. When seeing a Weeping Angel in one of the rooms of the ersatz hotel, Amy thinks it's for her – somewhat ironic considering later events in *The Angels Take Manhattan*. Instead, Amy's room is number seven, the age she met the Doctor; as such, inside, she sees her fear: sat again on her suitcase, as the young Amelia, looking outside the window at the stars, waiting, waiting, waiting for her Raggedy Man. Much like he did in *The Curse of Fenric* with Ace, the Doctor forces Amy to lose faith in him to stop the Minotaur's food supply. He tells her to stop waiting for him and to start seeing people as they really are. The final straw for Amy is when the Doctor calls her 'Amy Williams.'

The Doctor takes Amy and Rory back to Earth, 2011, and presents them with their new house and a new car – Rory's favourite car. Rory accepts the keys straight away and goes to get champagne. For him, the journey is over. But Amy wants to know why the Doctor is leaving them, and he tells her it's because they're still breathing. Amy doesn't want him to go, but he rhetorically asks her, somewhat prophetically, 'What's the alternative? Me standing over your grave? Over your broken body? Over Rory's body?' Tears are shed and the Doctor leaves, with a sense that he will come back to see them sometime: it seems that, unlike some other companions, he simply can't leave his best friends forever. Rory wants to know where he's gone, and Amy tells Rory that the Doctor is 'saving them.'

The Doctor looks heartbroken and shatteringly lonely in his TARDIS as it dematerialises.

Some two hundred years later for the Doctor, he visits Craig, a man he befriended the previous series in *The Lodger*. The Doctor spends the weekend with him, helping look after Craig's son, Alfie, and defeat an attempted Cybermen takeover in *Closing Time*. While shopping in Colchester, Amy and Rory almost bump into the Doctor, but he stays out of sight and watches them from afar. Amy's now a model for a perfume called Pertrichor, for the 'Girl Who Waited'. He watches her sign an autograph for a little girl, and leaves them to it, smiling sadly.

During *The Wedding of River Song*, we discover that River herself is in the astronaut suit at Lake Silenco, and it's she who killed the Doctor, as part of her conditioning by the Silence, overseen by

Madame Kovarian. But River cheats, and creates a parallel world that is stuck at 17:02 always. In this one-minute world, Amy works alongside River to rescue the Doctor. Even though Amy's never met him, she still knows the Doctor and remembers a lot of their time together, decking her 'office' (on a train) in drawings of Atraxi, the Weeping Angels, the Pandorica, and more. She's even fashioned small TARDIS idols out of wood, echoing her childhood room in actual reality. Yet she doesn't remember Rory – one of her key officers, however, one she trusts more than anyone else, is Captain Williams, always close at hand. Rory is, once more, waiting. As the Silents break out of their water cages, Rory stands his ground, even though his eye drive (an eye patch that enables him to remember the Silents) is tampered with by the antagonists and causes him great pain. The Silents push through a barricaded door and tower over Rory, who's in agony on the floor, having seemingly made sure his love gets away. But Amy rescues him: even in this reality, their bond is as strong as ever.

Kovarian is also a victim of the Silents' tampering with the eye patches, and she begs Amy to help her because the Doctor would. Amy points out that he's not there at the time. Though Kovarian argues that what River has become is because of her, Amy counters that 'she didn't get it all from you, sweetie.' She reattaches the eye patch, and she and Rory saunter away while Kovarian dies in pain behind them. Amy and Rory resolve to get married. The pair then watch while the Doctor marries River in a handfasting ceremony, which requires him to tell her his name (he doesn't, but pretends to). Upon contact, the real world is restored and River kills the Doctor at Lake Silenco.

Back in the real world, Amy's waiting in the back garden for her daughter to arrive. She obviously expects the visit as there's a 'freak meteor shower two miles away,' so has poured them both a drink. When River gets there, they check where in each other's timelines they are – showing that, by this point, they often see each other – and they work out that this River is from just after Amy first met her (*The Time of Angels/Flesh and Stone*). Amy mourns the

Doctor, believing him to be dead, but River mentions that she still has adventures with him, and she tells Amy the secret: he never died at all. The Doctor she shot in Utah was actually the Teselecta.

Rory returns, presumably from work, to find his wife and daughter dancing in joy. When Amy says, 'He's not dead,' Rory knows who she means straight away, and asks if River's sure. 'Of course I'm sure,' she replies. 'I'm his wife!'

But then something occurs to Amy. Now that River and the Doctor are married, she's the Doctor's mother-in-law...

Two years pass before they see the Doctor again. He abruptly turns up at their house on Christmas Day 2013 in *The Doctor, the Widow and the Wardrobe*. Amy's happy to see him, but she is initially a little bitter that he's taken so long to visit them. It's all an act though: her and Rory's happiness is palpable, and of course, he's not shocked that River told them he's really alive. Amy asks the Doctor if he wants to join them for Christmas dinner, and Rory says there's a place set for him at their table. 'But you didn't know I was coming,' the Doctor notes. Amy smiles: they always set a place for him.

When we next see Amy and Rory in *Asylum of the Daleks*, it's unclear how much time has passed, although it's enough for them to drift apart and begin divorce proceedings. Rory clearly doesn't want a divorce, while Amy is bitter and furious with him. Amy, who is still modelling, is actively pushing him away. Both are abducted and taken to the Parliament of the Daleks, where they're reunited with the Doctor. The Doctor suspects something's not right between them, but he doesn't query it for a while, too busy dealing with the Daleks, who want his help. After they're cast down to the Daleks' asylum planet, the first person Amy calls out for is Rory – a notable reaction. Despite having the Doctor back, it's Rory who she looks for when distressed. Rory finds himself alone in the heart of the asylum, surrounded by insane Daleks. He accidentally wakes up the Daleks, but receives help in the shape of a young woman called Oswin Oswald, who's trapped inside her ship, which crashed into the asylum planet some time ago.

Amy finds that she's missed the danger (which makes sense; it has been over two years, at least, since the Doctor left her on Earth at the end of *The God Complex*), and the Doctor asks her what has happened to her and Rory. 'Don't give me those big wet eyes, Raggedy Man,' Amy scolds. 'It's life. Just life; that thing that goes on when you're not there.' Amy becomes infected by the Dalek nanogenes, designed to turn people into Dalek puppets, and her memories and feelings start to get overwritten. The Doctor tells her to hold on to 'scared,' as 'scared' is very un-Dalek. Rory responds favourably to Oswin's flirting; it's a feeling he has not had for some time. Amy seems convinced that their marriage is a lost cause, and when she expresses this to Rory, he's clearly unimpressed. Her aggression hurts him. They finally have it out, while Amy is apparently holding on for her life, and Rory tells her that he believes he loves her more than she ever loved him. This angers Amy, who instructs him to never dare say that again, but then he reminds her how he waited for her for over two thousand years, and it was she who kicked him out. Amy responds by arguing she did that because Rory wanted children, and after what happened on Demons Run she couldn't have any more. She didn't kick him out; she gave him up. After getting all this out, they realise that the Doctor placed his nanocloud bracelet (which prevents the nanogenes from affecting the wearer) on Amy's wrist, and that the Doctor didn't tell them because he wanted them to fix things. Fear of death is a good motivator. The Doctor returns them home, where Amy invites Rory back into the house. He celebrates when he thinks she isn't watching, but she tells him, 'I can see you.' Rory smiles and pretends to be ashamed.

It's another ten months before we come across them again in *Dinosaurs on a Spaceship*, and we meet Brian Williams, Rory's father, who thinks Rory is lucky to have Amy. Once they're transported to 2367, to the Silurian Ark, a ship drawn to Earth but in imminent danger of breaching its airspace and inviting a defensive attack from the Indian Space Agency. Brian finds himself rambling at the Doctor, who initially thinks he's a spy until Rory points out the

Doctor materialised the TARDIS around them. Rory, known for his own rambling, gets this from his father. It's interesting that this is the first time the Doctor's met Brian, meaning the pair weren't introduced to each other at Amy and Rory's wedding or indeed any other intervening time in what's later revealed to be a decade of travelling. Rory is now thirty-one, and Amy is likely the same age.

Amy reveals she is a fan of Queen Nefertiti, but considers the eighteenth-dynasty queen and John Riddell (a twentieth-century game hunter) her companions while they explore the Silurian Ark. She simply won't have them flirting, however: ironic, considering how much she flirts with both the Doctor and Rory. To save the ship from being destroyed, two pilots are needed with the same DNA – it's fortunate that Brian was there changing a light bulb when the Doctor materialised the TARDIS around them! Sharing a quiet moment amongst the chaos, Amy reveals that she can't settle, having given up two jobs recently, always waiting for the Doctor to arrive to spirit her away on another adventure. But she worries that the gaps between visits are getting longer, almost as if he were weaning her off him. The presence of Nefertiti and Riddell concern her – when first seeing them, she wonders if they're the Doctor's new companions. The Doctor promises otherwise: 'Rory and you, you have lives, have each other. I thought that's what we agreed.' She explains, 'I just worry there'll come a time when you never turn up. That something will have happened to you and I'll still be waiting, never knowing.' The Doctor counters that they'll be there until his end, and she jokingly comments, 'Or vice versa.' He struggles with the idea.

Despite these concerns, both she and Rory want to go back home, but not forever, just for a couple of months.

Aiming for the Day of the Dead festival in Mexico, they instead end up in *A Town Called Mercy* in 1870, and find the townsfolk protecting an alien doctor called Kahler-Jex from a cyborg Gunslinger. Handing a hat with a bullet hole in it between them, the trio prove, as ever, simpatico, but their easy convergence is threatened when the Doctor discovers that Kahler-Jex is a mass murderer. He wants to hand him over to the vengeance-seeking Gunslinger to save the townsfolk, an idea that Amy takes issue with. Rory sides with him, perhaps seeing it as the best way to make sure his wife is safe, leaving Amy to wonder what's happened to them. She doesn't believe Rory will let the Doctor take Kahler-Jex's life. Amy won't have it and challenges the Doctor directly, drawing a gun on him to make him listen. This is what happens, she says, when the Doctor travels alone for too long. 'We can't be like him. We have to be better than him.' Her words strike home and the Doctor acquiesces with a simple 'Amelia Pond.'

The Doctor becomes the town's Marshal. Naturally, Amy is his Deputy.

The three of them appear to be the only ones willing to stand up for the repentant Kahler-Jex, holding the townsfolk back from lynching him and throwing him to the Gunslinger. The Doctor tells them it's not about saving Jex's life, but theirs, implying that crossing that line isn't something they could come back from. It's something that Amy apparently reminded him of (and something his next companion, Clara Oswald, does too, in *The Day of the Doctor*).

In a quiet moment, Kahler-Jex realises Amy's a mother, and says, 'There's kindness in your eyes. And sadness. But a ferocity too.' Ultimately, Jex sacrifices himself, Amy's morals seemingly having brought out the best in him.

In *The Power of Three*, Amy and Rory are concerned they have two lives: 'Doctor life' and real life. The two affect one another, as evident in them getting home from their travels with food out of date and having run out of washing tablets. Rory believes they need to make a choice, and Amy agrees – 'not today though,' as the TARDIS arrives.

Amy is now writing magazine articles, while Rory continues to be a nurse. The Doctor is surprised to learn they both have jobs, until they point out that they don't just sit around waiting for him in between visits. Amy explains that for her and Rory, it's been ten years since they first travelled with the Doctor. Not for him, or even

458

for Earth, but for *them*. They're introduced to Kate Stewart, daughter of the Doctor's old friend Brigadier Lethbridge-Stewart, head of scientific research at UNIT – the Doctor's surprised that science now runs the military, and delighted to learn it's Kate's doing. Amy especially likes Kate, relating to her irreverent humour. Amy and Rory realise that they're almost at the end of their time with the Doctor as they are both making commitments months ahead – for the first time ever. Amy agrees to be a bridesmaid and Rory agrees to go full-time at the hospital. 'The Year of the Slow Invasion' shows the Doctor popping in and out of their lives: notably, in June that year, the Doctor arrives for their wedding anniversary and whisks them off to the Savoy Hotel in 1890 as a gift… only to find themselves embroiled in an attempted Zygon takeover. This is the start of their adventuring again, this time for seven weeks (Brian notices as they're wearing totally different clothes from just moments before from his point of view). Amy even accidentally marries Henry VIII. The events of *A Town Called Mercy* might occur during this period, as at the start of their time in Nevada, the Doctor remembers Rory leaving his phone charger in Henry VIII's en-suite.

Amy tells the Doctor that she isn't sure if she can have both lives anymore, because they pull at each other. There was a time – years – when she couldn't live without him, but now she and Rory are settled. They've built a life. The Doctor's been expecting this, and that is why he keeps on running back to Amy: she was the first person he saw in his eleventh incarnation. He tells her that she's seared onto his hearts, and always will be. 'I'm running to you, and Rory, before you fade from me.' Brian helps them decide, telling them that they have to go with the Doctor and save every planet they can. Who else gets a chance to do that? Life will still be waiting for them, and so will he. Amy realises what 'the power of three' is: them. Amy, Rory, and the Doctor. Unbeatable.

A picnic in Central Park, New York, in 2012 (*The Angels Take Manhattan*) goes wrong when Rory finds himself sent to the 1930s by a Weeping Angel and is found by his daughter, River, there posing as Melody Malone – a detective on the hunt for Angels, and whose adventures are chronicled in *Melody Malone: Private Detective in Old New York Town*, a book the Doctor's reading. Amy is now wearing reading glasses and showing some minor sides of ageing, at least according to the Doctor who suggests her eyes are looking 'all liney.' The Doctor nonetheless takes her glasses and finds they improve his eyesight too.

Amy and the Doctor manage to track Rory and River down with the TARDIS, fixing onto the latter's vortex manipulator. But Amy and the Doctor find an old Rory whose timeline has been eaten by the Angels. Amy watches him die, a fact Rory finds very hard to handle. She thinks they can run, but the Doctor cautions that it'd mean they'd have to run *forever*. He says it would take unimaginable power to achieve this, and asks what they've got in their favour. 'I won't let them take him,' Amy insists. '*That's* what we've got.'

River argues that, by escaping, they can create a paradox, and thus poison the Angel's food source. Rory realises the only way to do this is to kill himself. Amy won't let him, but he tells her that he would rather die than not have Amy in his life – that's what particularly frightens him when he sees his older self die, that he did so with surprise and joy at seeing Amy again. As ever, he'll do anything to save her. This time, though, she's not willing to just let him do it, so she says they either go together or not at all. The Doctor and River reach the rooftop just as the pair jump, unable to stop them. They return to the graveyard where the TARDIS stands, happy to have beaten the Angels, but a lone Angel survives. Rory heads back to the ship with them, but stops to point out a gravestone with his own name on. Before they can do anything, the Angel takes Rory, sending him inescapably back into the past.

Beside herself, Amy insists they can take the TARDIS and get him, but the Doctor tells her he can't – one more paradox would rip New York apart. Amy refuses to believe this until River tells her it's true. Unwilling to be without him, Amy realises that there's space on his gravestone for one more name, and she willingly gives herself to the Angel. The Doctor tries to stop her, but River agrees that it's the only way Amy will see Rory again. Amy tells River, whom she calls Melody once more, to look after the Doctor. A distraught Doctor begs her, informing her that if she does this, she'll create a fixed point in time, and he'll never be able to see her again. Amy knows she'll be fine, because she will be with Rory.

'Raggedy Man, goodbye!' The Angel takes her. The Doctor is understandably devastated.

As revealed in *The Bells of St John*, Amy goes on to write children's books as Amelia Williams, and both she and Rory live to an old age in New York's past. Rory dies aged eighty-two, and Amy aged eighty-seven.

The Doctor takes a little comfort in knowing that River, at least, will pop in to see Amy and Rory occasionally using her vortex manipulator. She tells the Doctor not to be alone, but he shirks the idea. River suggests that he'll at least listen to this advice if Amy gives it: as such, she goes back in time to see her parents (off-screen), so that Amy can leave an afterword for the Doctor in Melody Malone's book. It tells him that 'we lived well, and were very happy. And above all else, know that we will love you always.' Then it brings Amy's journey full circle as the Doctor arguably breaks time – or perhaps adheres to events that Amy never dared share with the Doctor – as he goes back to see young Amelia, seven years old, waiting for him to come back for her. Amy's afterword says, 'She's going to wait a long while, so she's going to need a lot of hope. Go to her. Tell her a story. Tell her that if she's patient, the days are coming that she'll never forget. Tell her she'll go to sea and fight pirates. She'll fall in love with a man who'll wait two thousand years to keep her safe. Tell her she'll give hope to the greatest painter who ever lived and save a whale in outer space. Tell her this is the story of Amelia Pond. And this how it ends.'

There's one small coda for Amy. As the Doctor is about to regenerate in *The Time of the Doctor*, he hallucinates and sees his TARDIS console room full of Amelia's drawings. The young girl runs around the space, and by the time she gets to him, she's all grown up. They appear to hold each other's heads in their hands, and Amy says her last farewell: 'Raggedy Man... Goodnight.'

River Song – Alex Kingston – Continued... (*Silence in the Library/ Forest of the Dead, The Time of Angels/Flesh and Stone, The Pandorica Opens/ The Big Bang, The Impossible Astronaut/Day of the Moon* to *Let's Kill Hitler, Closing Time, The Wedding of River Song, The Angels Take Manhattan, The Name of the Doctor*, and *The Husbands of River Song*)

The daughter of Amy Pond and Rory Williams, River Song is something very special to the Doctor and in *Doctor Who* history. She's also, as Madame Vastra says in *A Good Man Goes to War*, 'human plus Time Lord,' which makes her of interest to a few parties. She's conceived on Amy and Rory's wedding night (*The Big Bang*), while they're travelling in the TARDIS. Vastra says the Time Lords 'became what they did through prolonged exposure to the time vortex,' which the Doctor retorts was only after billions of years. Nonetheless, seemingly as the first person conceived when her parents are in the TARDIS, River's DNA has something special in it, so when Amy gives birth, malicious forces, i.e. the religious sect known as the Silence, led by Madame Kovarian, apparently work to strengthen River's bond to the Time Lords. Before this, Amy is kidnapped by the alien Silents – the Doctor suggests this happens just before *The Impossible Astronaut*, which would fit with Amy seeing echoes of Kovarian at the start of *Day of the Moon*; however, it's just as likely she's taken while she's hunting for Silents across America at the start of the latter episode – and her body doubled using Flesh technology (with her mind connected to the Flesh avatar) so the Doctor doesn't find out the deception until it's too late, and so, when she wakes up at the end of *The Almost People*, she's being watched and encouraged to push by Kovarian.

River is born Melody Pond, a little girl whose father, alongside the Doctor, cuts a path through the universe just to find her. As the Last Centurion, Rory and the Doctor destroy the Twelfth Cyber

Legion, a massive fleet of Cybermen, solely to learn where the Silence has taken River and Amy. Amy's faith in Rory is unshaken, and she tells the baby Melody that, 'however scared you are, I promise you, you will never be alone.' Rory and the Doctor assemble a team of friends to get Amy and their baby back, including Vastra, Jenny Flint, and Strax, hordes of Silurians and Judoon, and Captain Avery and his men from *The Curse of the Black Spot*, but when Rory visits an older River in her cell at the Stormcage facility, not knowing who she really is, she turns him down, saying she can't help because this is the day everything changes for them. Indeed, a displaced River does visit Demons Run, the asteroid the Silence is holding Amy and Melody in, at the end of *A Good Man Goes to War*, to drop a bombshell about her true identity. Before this, though, the Doctor, Rory, and co. invade Demons Run and take down the Silence – seemingly. Neither Amy nor Rory hold it against the Doctor that their kooky lives in the TARDIS have resulted in their child being weaponised; indeed, Rory is insistent that the Doctor meets their baby soon after he does. Rory thinks he's saved Melody from Kovarian, but we don't see his immediate reaction to meeting his own child. When he's reunited with Amy, though, he tells her their baby is beautiful and, despite wanting to be cool, starts crying. Rory seems to like Melody's name straight away (we might infer that he and Amy have discussed baby names before, and Amy later says Melody is named after her childhood friend, Mels – who turns out to actually be Melody, in a neat paradox), but when he suggests her surname should be Williams, Amy quips that Melody Williams is a Geography teacher, whereas 'Melody Pond is a superhero.'

Amy takes Melody into the TARDIS; alas, Amy concludes that Melody doesn't like the noise the TARDIS makes and it starts her crying. The Doctor, though, says he can 'speak baby,' so can interpret her cries as meaning she's tired, so he brings out a wooden cot – his own, as it's got the Doctor's real name inscribed in Old High Gallifreyan. Amy is also gifted a prayer blanket, crocheted with River's name in the language of the Gamma Forests.

The legend of Demons Run is fulfilled, though: 'Demons run when a good man goes to war. Night will fall and drown the sun, when a good man goes to war. Friendship dies and true love lies, night will fall and the dark will rise, when a good man goes to war. Demons run but count the cost. The battle's won, but the child is lost.' Melody, as retrieved from Kovarian, is a flesh avatar, so the Silence makes away with the real Melody, so Amy and Rory are left at Demons Run without their baby. River joins them, and tells them that she's their daughter, grown up. While the Doctor goes off to track baby Melody, he leaves River to drop everyone else home using her vortex manipulator. Presumably, she takes some time off-screen to bond with her parents.

Melody is raised at a Floridian orphanage named Graystark Hall (*Day of the Moon*) in the 1960s. Her main caregiver is seemingly Dr Renfrew, though the 'memory-proof' Silents manipulate events – Graystark Hall was due to close in 1967, but Renfrew (whose memory has been altered so that he doesn't believe the actual year) and Melody are still there when Amy and Canton Everett Delaware III visit in 1969. Melody's room is pretty bare, though there is at least a photo of Amy cradling her from Demons Run plus some toys. Melody's childhood must've been a decidedly grim one.

In early 1969, Melody is 'eaten' by an Apollo NASA spacesuit, one she's destined to don again in the future as foretold in the stories about River and the Doctor, and phones President Nixon for help, the suit defaulting to the highest authority in the country. This is enough to attract the attention of the Doctor, Amy, and Rory in *The Impossible Astronaut*, as well as an older River Song, who must either pretend she doesn't know how this all plays out or whose memory of events has been so affected by the Silents that she really doesn't remember every single thing. That's not a huge stretch of the imagination, considering childhood is always a mix of remembrances and not always reliable ones. The spacesuit has been kept in a warehouse in Florida, somewhere on the intersection of streets named Jefferson, Adams, and Hamilton, and near Cape Kennedy, where Melody has seemingly been taken to be trapped inside the suit. This spacesuit is actually an exoskeleton, acting as a life support system, a combination of some twenty different types of alien technology. Inside the suit, you don't even need to eat; it processes sunlight directly, is self-repairing, and has built-in weaponry and a communications system that can hack into anything. With Melody trapped inside, she goes to the Doctor, Amy, Rory, and River, calling for help, but a panicked Amy, not realising it's her future daughter but instead just registering this as the same suit that kills the Doctor, fires a gun. Fortunately, the shot misses, and a frightened Melody, surrounded by Silents with her parents on the run from them, gets out of the suit and flees. The Doctor is enamoured to find out that the girl is 'incredibly strong and running away.' Nonetheless, when Amy and Canton get to the orphanage three months later, in July 1969, a frightened Melody hides and gets away from the Silence and the Silents. She surfaces again six months later, having made it to New York City. It appears that Melody has learned all about regeneration from her kidnappers, likely part of her training to kill the Doctor, and so, when a homeless man in an alleyway checks whether the decidedly-ill-looking Melody is all right, she calmly says she's dying, but can 'fix that. It's easy really.' She regenerates and, we find out in *Let's Kill Hitler*, ends up a toddler. How she survives being on her own as a toddler in New York is unknown.

Melody changes her name to Mels and makes her way to Leadworth, where she poses as a friend of Amy and Rory, and goes to school there. Effectively, they grow up together. She must use some sort of time travel to get from 1970s New York to Leadworth in the 1990s, though, as she's still young when she's learning all about Amy's Raggedy Man. It's also unknown where she's living in Leadworth, how she covers for seemingly not having parents around, and how she affords a life when she's so young. On the other hand, unseen forces might've helped her, be they the Doctor (who can't interfere with established events but would surely have helped Mels from the shadows, considering her importance to him and his other companions) or the Church of the Silence, given that, in *Closing Time*, Kovarian tells an older River, 'You never really escaped us, Melody Pond.'

Still, as she later tells Amy and Rory, 'It all worked out in the end, didn't it? You got to raise me after all.' Mels sticks close to the pair in school: Amelia, i.e. the young Amy, takes her into her confidence and tells her all about what happened to her when the TARDIS landed in her garden (*The Eleventh Hour*). Her relationship with the Doctor is foreshadowed, given that Mels implies the Doctor is 'hot,' even though Amelia shuts this suggestion down by saying he's instead funny. Mels is a troublemaker – 'the most in trouble in the whole school, except for boys' and for Amelia – and repeatedly gets sent to the headmaster's office for suggesting things that happened in the past did so because of the Doctor. (At one point, she even steals a bus.) If it weren't for Amelia's bedroom being covered in dolls and drawings of her Raggedy Man, you'd think Mels was more obsessed with the Time Lord.

Mels is also responsible for Amy and Rory getting together. She suggests that Amy's on the straight and narrow because she's got 'Mr Perfect,' i.e. Rory, to help guide her. 'Seriously, it's got to be you two,' an exasperated Mels says. 'Oh, cut to the song; it's getting boring!' Amy has misinterpreted Rory's not asking her out as him being gay; it's Mels' suggestion that prompts him to say he's not and the penny finally drops. Mels' comment about it having to be those two implies she's not always been certain who her dad was until she saw Amy and Rory's early friendship.

Mels seems to have a good knowledge of when the Doctor's life will intersect with her parents', as she steals a car and follows Amy and Rory (for them, post-Demons Run) to a field where they've baited the Doctor into returning for them. He's been searching the universe for River; instead, she's come to them. She threatens him with a gun and, on the run from the police, suggests, with his TARDIS, they visit Nazi Germany to kill Hitler. Inside the TARDIS, she shoots the console and they do indeed end up in Adolf Hitler's office in 1938, implying the TARDIS pays attention to River. (Later on in the episode, it becomes clear that the TARDIS is especially receptive to her, given that she learns how to pilot it very quickly. 'She showed me how. She taught me,' River tells Amy. 'The Doctor says I'm the child of the TARDIS.')

Mels reveals herself as Amy and Rory's daughter, but, having been shot by Hitler (who Rory locks in a cupboard), regenerates. This new incarnation is impressed with her own hair, her teeth, her general appearance, enthusing that she loves being 'all mature.' She's immediately all over the Doctor, going back and forth on her earlier suggestion that they get married, such is her level of obsession with him. It's an understatement to say this obsession is unhealthy – it certainly is for the Doctor, though, who she kisses and poisons with deadly lipstick. Her conditioning overrules everything at this point. With the Doctor collapsing, she leaves him for Amy and Rory to comfort, while River goes off to explore Berlin on the eve of war. When shot at by Nazis she winds up, River's regenerative energy is enough for her to save herself, a fact she glories in, and she then steals their weapons and a bike. Rory and Amy give chase. At the Hotel Adlon Restaurant, she threatens everyone and steals some of their clothes; by the time a robotic version of Amy, actually the shape-changing Teselecta, arrives, she's happily trying them on and shirking off any responsibility. The Teselecta has banks of data on River, noting that she's a war criminal who kills the Doctor at Lake Silencio, Utah, in the future, and so tortures her as punishment in advance. Amy saves her by taking down the robot using the sonic screwdriver, at which point River is keen to run away again. The Doctor, on the verge of death, arrives there in the TARDIS and stops her from fleeing, then encourages River to save her parents from the vengeful Teselecta's internal Antibodies. On his deathbed, the Doctor tells Amy and Rory's daughter to 'find River' and then whispers something to her, to which she replies, 'I'm sure she knows.' The Doctor passes away, but when Amy asks the Teselecta to morph into River and she recognises herself as the woman the Doctor clearly is infatuated with, River asks her parents whether the Doctor is 'worth it.' Amy says he is and River kisses the Doctor, expending all her future regenerations, eventually dooming herself, to bring him back to life.

When she wakes, the Doctor's taken her to a hospital in the fifty-second century where he leaves her a TARDIS blue diary to chart down all her adventures. Amy, Rory, and the Doctor leave her to heal. It seems that, without the ability to travel in time, River spends at least a few years in that century, so by 5123, she joins the Luna University to study archaeology, telling her lecturer, Professor Arthur Candy (who previously appeared in a few Expanded Universe stories beginning with *Continuity Errors*, similarly written by Steven Moffat, in 1996) that she's doing so in order to find 'a good man.' But by *Closing Time*, it's clear that all this was predestined: Kovarian and the Silents catch up with her, though River apparently can't remember who they are. 'We've been far too thorough with your dear little head,' Kovarian tells her. It's a mystery, then, what River knows from her own experiences and from her research into historical records and the Doctor's timeline. If she does learn the Doctor's future, she'll know that the Doctor is due to die at Lake Silencio, killed by an Impossible Astronaut that rises from the water and shoots him before he can regenerate (though he's also meant to die on Trenzalore in the far future; what's noted down as history, however, is muddied by the Doctor's later plan to wipe every mention of himself from official documents and databases). That Impossible Astronaut is River, sealed inside the suit again by the Silence, who, the Doctor finds out in *The Wedding of River Song* and *The Time of the Doctor*, wants the Doctor dead so he can't answer the question – 'Doctor who?' – asked by the Time Lords on Trenzalore to confirm they and Gallifrey have found a way back to the correct universe after the events of *The Day of the Doctor*. As some of this plays out after Amy and Rory forcibly leave the TARDIS, we never find out whether they know why River was trained to murder him; we can infer that River tells them at some stage after *The Angels Take Manhattan* – that is, if *she* knows, as she's not seen on-screen during *The Time of the Doctor*.

Either way, two versions of the same event happen simultaneously: in one, as seen in *The Impossible Astronaut*, she kills the Doctor, as witnessed by Amy, Rory, an elderly Canton, and an older River, the latter of whom has to pretend she doesn't recognise the spacesuit at all. In another version, as per *The Wedding of River Song*, River causes a paradox by draining the suit's power from within and refusing to kill the Doctor. For a time, at least.

In this paradoxical world, where all of time is happening at once, the Doctor is intent on being with River, solely so that when they touch, time reverts back and she'll once again be trapped inside the suit, killing him. River sets out a plan to bring the Doctor to Area 52, a special containment facility for the Silents and Madame Kovarian, all of whom River, Amy, and their troops (including Rory) have captured, housed inside the Great Pyramid of Giza. River's intention, though, isn't to immediately end the timey-wimey stalemate, but instead to show the Doctor what she's been building. River being the child of the TARDIS comes in handy again, as she's made a signal that's broadcasting to the wider universe, outside their bubble of time, begging for someone to help avert the Doctor's assassination.

It's a significant gesture: River has upset the fabric of space-time just so that the Doctor knows he is 'loved by so many, and so much, and by no one more than me.' He tells her the whole universe is suffering because of her actions, but she counters that she'll suffer more if she's forced to kill him. Their love for each other is extraordinary, so he whispers a secret to her. He publicly declares that he's just told her his real name; in actuality, he's revealed that he's inside the Teselecta, so when time reverts to its normal flow, the one she shoots isn't really him at all. How she learns the Doctor's true name is forever a mystery: she certainly knows it by the time she dies in the Library (*Forest of the Dead*) and when Clara Oswald asks how she knows in *The Name of the Doctor*, River merely says, 'It took a while.' Now on record as the woman who kills the Doctor, River is sentenced to twelve thousand consecutive life sentences at the Stormcage Containment Facility in the fifty-second century. The Doctor reveals that, while she spends her days imprisoned, she spends her nights with him, exploring the universe, and thus making her an actual companion – or, more accurately, a little more than that, seeing as, in the aborted timeline of *The Wedding of River Song*, they got married.

On one of these nights, for her birthday, the Doctor takes her to the last of the Winter Frost Fairs in 1814, where the Time Lord gets Stevie Wonder to perform personally for her. As seen in *A Good Man Goes to War*, she returns to her cell, informing her captors that she's 'breaking in, not out,' implying that they're fully aware that she keeps escaping and coming back. There, she's also visited by her dad, Rory, who doesn't know River's true identity as he asks for her help at Demons Run, a request she's forced to turn down. Another date is to the planet of the *Rain Gods* (a Series 7 DVD extra), while multiple versions of herself show up in the TARDIS in the *Night and the Doctor* scenes included in the Series 7 boxset. In the latter, we see a decidedly sad Eleventh Doctor who intends to take River to the Singing Towers of Darillium: at this point, he knows it will be her last destination before her death in the Library, but she is seemingly unaware. River later says, in the Twelfth Doctor story, *The Husbands of River Song*, that the Doctor repeatedly intended to take her there, but kept chickening out, suggesting that he could never quite let her go.

She and the Doctor compare their diaries to learn where in each other's timestreams they're meeting. In *The Impossible Astronaut*, they confirm that they've visited both Jim the Fish and Easter Island, where River suggests the famous big-chinned statues are modelled after the Eleventh Doctor.

River likely has a lot of foreknowledge of events in Utah – admittedly, it's probably quite patchy given how manipulated her memories are, thanks to Kovarian and the Silence – but she has to play along when the Doctor invites her, Amy, and Rory along to Lake Silencio. How she gets from the fifty-second century to America in 2011 is unexplained. In 5145, River gets a vortex manipulator, 'fresh from the wrist of a handsome Time Agent' (who we might infer is Captain Jack Harkness), which may account for her jumping time periods, but she doesn't actually appear to have it on her during *The Impossible Astronaut/Day of the Moon*; otherwise, her search for the Silents in the latter would've been sped along quite considerably. However she gets there, she has enough time to picnic with her parents and husband on the shore of Lake Silencio before she views a younger version of herself, in the spacesuit, shooting the Doctor and disappearing back into the watery depths. The spacesuit definitely rings a lot of bells, even if her memories have been compromised, so she shows a lot of self-resentment when she fires several shots at the astronaut as it's walking back into the lake. River has to put on an act for a time, though she seems genuinely caught off-guard when, after helping her parents and Canton burn the Doctor's body (actually the Teselecta, with the real Doctor 'barely singed' inside), they encounter a younger Eleventh Doctor, still very much alive. River is so incensed that she slaps this Doctor, and he correctly deduces it's for something he hasn't done yet. The Doctor is more than a little reluctant, or so it seems, to investigate a series of phone calls made to President Nixon (the calls, of course, being from a younger River, aka Melody Pond). He tracks these back to 8th April, 1969, but, realising his companions know more about future events than he does, challenges them. When River asks that he just trusts them, the Doctor retorts, 'Sure. But, first of all, Dr Song, just one thing: who are you? You're someone from my future, getting that, but who? Okay, why are you in prison? Who did you kill? Now, I love a bad girl, me, but trust you? Seriously?' River is visibly hurt by this, and can only utter a thank you to Amy, who finally convinces him.

River has to witness a lot of events from when she was younger from this other point of view. Like the Doctor, then, she is an exceptional liar. Still, there must be a side of her that wants to know more about the Silents, creatures she tracks across America, while the Doctor, Amy, Rory, and Canton chase them down elsewhere. Their travels across the USA take three months, but they finally all meet up again – River, though, refuses to go along with the Doctor's plan to allow Canton to seemingly shoot all his companions dead then bring their 'bodies' to him in a prison complex in Area 51, in order to put the Silents off the truth. Instead, River demonstrates considerable faith in the Doctor by jumping off the fiftieth floor of a skyscraper in New York, landing inside the TARDIS' swimming pool after the Doctor learns of what she's done and pilots the ship to the correct space-time coordinates.

During her investigations into the Silents, we're forced to wonder whether River has a touch of Stockholm syndrome, offering up a slightly different perspective on what we would otherwise infer is a very bleak childhood at the hands of the Silents, who, she says, were 'keeping her safe, even giving her independence.' She's perfectly happy to kill the Silents, however, especially after they've taken Amy hostage for a few days. The Doctor gets Amy and Rory safely back into the TARDIS while River shoots many Silents dead; when Rory watches her from the TARDIS, she rhetorically asks him, 'My old fella didn't see that, did he? He gets ever so cross.'

When the Doctor drops her back at Stormcage, River embraces him in a kiss, which shocks him; for him, it's the first time they've kissed. She realises, then, that this will be the last time for her.

Though she remains flirty with the Doctor in *The Pandorica Opens/The Big Bang*, they don't kiss, which likely means, from River's point of view, these events transpire after *Day of the Moon*.

From the Doctor's perspective, River already warned him, in *Flesh and Stone*, that she'd see them again 'very soon, when the Pandorica opens', something he laughed off because it's a mere fairytale ('Aren't we all?' she retorts). He learns otherwise in the Series 5 finale, in which River actually draws him into an adventure that would lead to the end of space-time. In Stormcage, she gets a phone call from Winston Churchill, who wants to speak to the Doctor; however, the TARDIS has rerouted the call to Cell 426, i.e. River's. Churchill alerts her to a painting by Vincent Van Gogh, which shows the TARDIS exploding, space-time coordinates on its door. She escapes Stormcage using hallucinogenic lipstick (something she's done before/will do again in *The Time of Angels*) and heads to the Royal Collection, 5145, on Starship UK, where she steals the painting. She then heads to the contemporary

Maldovarium to obtain the vortex manipulator. She's already met Dorium, the black market dealer she acquires the device from, albeit when she was a baby on Demons Run and on the day he's beheaded. Unable to reach the TARDIS by phone, River leaves a message on Planet One, the oldest planet in the universe which includes cliffs of pure diamond. The Doctor says the letters are 'fifty feet high, a message from the dawn of time,' meaning River has visited the infant universe. The message reads, 'Hello Sweetie ΘΣ ΦΓΥΛζ' – that is, what River calls the Doctor, the relevant coordinates, and the Doctor's 'college' nickname, ΘΣ, as revealed in *The Armageddon Factor* and explained further in *The Happiness Patrol*. River knows all there is to know about her husband!

In 102 AD, River has a pretty cushy position, using her lipstick once more to trick the Roman legionnaires into thinking she's Cleopatra. When they locate the Pandorica in a vault underneath Stonehenge, it's River who deduces that the signal it's sending out is drawing in a huge number of the Doctor's enemies; faced with overwhelming odds, she's initially annoyed that the Doctor wants to fight, not run, but still goes off to get equipment from the TARDIS after being told to. Instead, the TARDIS is taken, with River inside, to Amy's house in the future. She isn't familiar with the place, but ventures into Amy's bedroom where River realises where she is, owing to all the drawings and toys the young Amelia made. Interestingly, even when alone, River says, 'Amy,' not 'Mum,' though this might be because she doesn't know if anyone's listening in. Her fictions are absolute. She goes back to the TARDIS, calling the Doctor to let him know that the whole thing, including the Romans, is a trap. She sets the TARDIS to dematerialise, but we might infer that it's actually pulled back to the dawn of our solar system seeing as the ship explodes and replaces our sun.

The TARDIS, ever loyal to River, puts itself into a time loop in *The Big Bang*, saving her inside; she likely has been playing out the same sequence of events for around five billion years before the Doctor saves her with the vortex manipulator in 1996, although it's also exploding 'at every point in history,' so perhaps River's loop is perpetual too. It's unlikely she recalls this period; if she does, it's probably only one loop, consisting of a few minutes. All this time, River has doubly been an anomaly: Rory was wiped from time in *Cold Blood*, meaning she was without a father, becoming unexplainable flotsam and jetsam, presumably too important a space-time event to be deleted from existence accordingly. When she sees Rory, now an Auton duplicate, she questions 'the plastic Centurion', then informs him, Amy, and the Doctor that she dated a Nestene duplicate once with a 'swappable head. It did keep things fresh.' When a Dalek attacks, River tells the others to go on without her: though the Dalek initially doesn't believe River will kill it, she tells it to check its records; perhaps knowing that she's the one destined to kill the Doctor, the Dalek begs for mercy. She shoots it anyway. She then realises the Doctor's plan to reboot the universe, using the TARDIS and the Pandorica, but seems deeply upset that, in his last moments, the Doctor wants to talk to Amy, not her, as he doesn't really know her yet. She ultimately saves the Doctor by visiting Amy and Rory on their wedding day, 26th April 2010, her brief appearance – not to mention her now-empty diary left as a wedding present – enough to remind Amy of her travels with the Doctor, helped along by the Doctor's suggestion of 'something old, something new, something borrowed, something blue,' i.e. the TARDIS. The restored Doctor finds River after the ceremony and gives her back her diary. (It's implied in *A Good Man Goes to War* that River is conceived that night in the TARDIS.)

The Doctor asks if she's married and in doing so, accidentally proposes to her. River cheekily says 'yes' before disappearing using the vortex manipulator to presumably return to the Stormcage facility. When we see her in *The Time of Angels/Flesh and Stone*, the Doctor asks if she's engaged and she replies, 'In a manner of speaking.' They're actually referring to Father Angelo, an Anglican marine who refuses to let River out of his sight. It's through him that the Doctor learns of River's imprisonment, which she later tells him is due to her killing 'the best man I've ever known.' She won't tell him any more information, warning of 'spoilers.'

THE ELEVENTH DOCTOR

The Doctor and Amy are drawn to Alfava Metraxis, the seventh planet of the Dundra System, in the fifty-first century, after following the crashing Galaxy class Starliner known as the Byzantium, which the Doctor saves River from. She leaves messages on its home box, one which simply reads 'Hello Sweetie' in Old High Gallifreyan, 'the lost language of the Time Lords,' and another being what's essentially the ship's CCTV, knowing the Doctor would eventually find it and come for her. Indeed, the Doctor and Amy find the home box in the Delirium Archive, the final resting place of the Headless Monks (as seen in *A Good Man Goes to War*) in the one-hundred and seventy-first century, and trace it back to the Byzantium. Notably, this is the first time Amy meets her future daughter; Rory's first time meeting River is in *The Big Bang*, though that's Auton Rory, so in the main universe, the real Rory first interacts with River in *The Impossible Astronaut*. They're au fait with each other, however, so we might infer that they've had off-screen adventures; Rory has memories of his time as the Lone Centurion too, so is aware of River. Amy is wowed by River straight away, chiefly that she can fly the TARDIS – and knows it has blue stabilisers, something the Eleventh Doctor isn't aware of. In fairness to him, this is a new console, but one she's very familiar with. She also winds the Doctor up by suggesting the TARDIS only makes the wheezing noise when materialising because he leaves the hand brakes on. It's entirely possible that, instead, she 'put the engines on silent,' as he does himself in *The Impossible Astronaut*. Even early on in their relationship, River is always up for poking fun at her beloved. It's so early for them that this is Amy's first trip to another planet, and it's Amy, not River, who entices the Doctor to stay. River expounds on this when telling the Doctor that there's a Weeping Angel on the ship, now free to roam Alfava Metraxis. When it becomes clear that the planet is riddled with Angels, River is clearly troubled by Amy being in such great danger, yet her faith in the Doctor is unwavering. Still, it's River who rescues Amy when she's surrounded by Angels, and she deduces the Doctor's 'genius' plan to use the crack in time, caused by the TARDIS blowing up in his personal future but River's past, to erase the Angels altogether.

River is apparently taken back to Stormcage, hoping she's done enough to earn a pardon, but it seems she instead goes to join her mother in 2011, i.e. after Amy has seen the Doctor 'die' in *The Wedding of River Song*. She knows she shouldn't, but River tells Rory and a grief-stricken Amy that the Doctor they saw was actually the Teselecta, so the Doctor isn't dead. When the Doctor sees them again in *The Doctor, the Widow and the Wardrobe*, the Doctor is frustrated but not shocked that River told them. 'She's a good girl,' Amy affirms.

When we next see River in *The Angels Take Manhattan*, we learn that she has indeed been pardoned, though only because the man she killed never even existed anyway – the Doctor's been taking time following Series 6 to delete every mention of himself from history. We also find out that River has a couple of side-hustles away from archaeology: she writes novels and is a private detective. As such, she's written *Melody Malone: Private Detective in Old New York Town*, an account of her time in New York City, 1938, purported to be fiction. The book instigates the Doctor and Amy becoming involved in those very events, after they learn, via the novel, that Rory has been sent back in time from 2012 by the Weeping Angels.

'Hello, Dad,' River says to Rory when he ends up in the 1930s. She doesn't exactly maintain her levity, nor, it appears, her concern for her father, when they're kidnapped by Julius Grayle, who asks them to investigate the Angels and locks Rory up 'somewhere uncomfortable.' Then again, River might just be taking it all in her stride so she doesn't reveal her connection to Rory, her confidence implying that she knows the Doctor will get them all out of the predicament. The Doctor is keen to impress River and takes time to smooth down his hair and check his breath, apparently emboldened by River's own description of Melody Malone as having 'ice in her heart and a kiss on her lips, and a vulnerable side she keeps well hidden.' They're certainly pleased to see each other, although the Doctor's temper messes up their happy reunion as he leaves River to 'change time' and get herself out of the grip of an Angel once he learns this will be his last adventure with Amy and Rory. She can't change history, however, and is forced to break her own wrist to escape the Angel. Her own resentment for his often-whimsical nature comes through when she says, 'When one's in love with an ageless god who insists on the face of a twelve-year-old, one does one's best to hide the damage.' He apologises by using regeneration energy to heal her wrist, which annoys her further as she calls him a 'sentimental idiot' who embarrasses her.

If River seems a little on edge, it's likely due to her recognising the seriousness of the situation. Indeed, when Rory is irretrievably sent back into the past again, she seems to accept Amy's decision to join him without a fuss – in fact, River encourages it, confirming with Amy that it's her best chance of seeing Rory again, and further keeping an eye on the Angel after it touches Amy so that it cannot also grab a heartbroken Doctor. She's doing what Amy wishes: 'You be a good girl and you look after him.' As such, she helps Amy leave one last message for the Doctor via the last page of *Melody Malone: Private Detective in Old New York Town*. The Doctor asks River to travel with him, but she won't; she's adamant that he not travel by himself, and, when mulling over how to get her Melody Malone book published via Amy, says, 'I'll tell her to write an afterword. For you. Maybe you'll listen to her.'

This implies that, while the Doctor can't visit Amy and Rory, River can, likely using the vortex manipulator, which she tells Rory is 'like a motorbike through traffic.'

(Where this all takes place in River's timeline is unknown, though it probably happens after *Flesh and Stone*. Her chronology is muddied by the Doctor kissing her in *The Angels Take Manhattan*, something she implies doesn't happen again after *The Impossible Astronaut*. It's possible something strange happens with time after *The Big Bang*, or, as he only kisses her cheek and hand in *The Angels Take Manhattan*, perhaps their last kiss on the lips still happens in *Day of the Moon*.)

It's interesting to note that in the unfilmed *P.S.*, an additional scene written by Chris Chibnall that follows *The Angels Take Manhattan*, Rory leaves a note for his father, River's grandfather, Brian Williams, delivered to him by Anthony Brian Williams. Amy and Rory adopted Anthony in 1946, meaning River has an adoptive brother too.

River eventually meets the Twelfth Doctor (*The Husbands of River Song*) then the Tenth Doctor (*Silence in the Library / Forest of the Dead*). During the latter encounter, she dies and is 'saved' to the Library's database. It's after this that she has her last adventure with the Eleventh Doctor, albeit as a 'data ghost' in *The Name of the Doctor*, pulled into the real world for a short time by Madame Vastra, Jenny Flint, and Strax. The Sontaran recalls River, from the aftermath of *A Good Man Goes to War*, as having 'massive hair.' He doesn't seem to approve of her for some reason.

Vastra makes a dream-like 'conference call' between themselves, River, and Clara, who meets River for the first time and is shocked to find out the person the Doctor talks about so often is actually a woman. River's mildly infuriated by this, but still looks after the Doctor's latest companion when she realises Clara's being hunted by the Whisper Men in real life. River forces Clara awake, but importantly keeps the 'line' open so she can maintain a connection to contemporary happenings. Clara relays what's happened to the Doctor (who seemingly can't see River), so they follow the trail left by Vastra, Jenny, Strax, and the Whisper Men to Trenzalore, sometime after the wars we see in *The Time of the Doctor*. There, they find River's gravestone, which neither of them accepts as possible. River shows she's still manipulating events by telling Clara it's a false grave, one which leads them away from the pursuing Whisper Men and into the Doctor's final resting place, i.e. the battle-worn TARDIS. River helps gain entry to the ship using its 'key,' which the Great Intelligence, the true villain behind the Whisper Men, says is the Doctor's real name. River seems mildly annoyed that the Doctor isn't willing to say his name even to save his friends. As Clara can hear her, it's possible she learned the Doctor's real name here, though she must've been distracted by the Whisper Men. Thinking the Doctor can't hear them, River fills in some of the blanks for Clara, noting that when she died, the

Doctor 'left me like a book on a shelf. Didn't even say goodbye. He doesn't like endings.' Nevertheless, he's forced to close that particular chapter.

The Doctor plans to step into his own timestream which River views as lunacy, largely because she believes it'll negatively affect him. Still, when he asserts that he has to save Clara, River agrees. (She's quickly protective of Clara, arguing against her stepping into the Doctor's timestream before the Doctor to restore him from the Intelligence's attack. When Clara asks, perhaps rhetorically, if it's the only way she can save him, River relents and nods silently.) The Doctor then reveals that he's been able to see River all this time, and says what they both know: it's time for River to go. He doesn't know how to bid adieu to his love, so she suggests saying it like he's coming back for her. He does: 'See you around, Professor River Song.' And she does similar.

'Goodbye, sweetie.'

Over the past few years, many old companions have left us, actors so well-regarded by the fans. Tributes are always made, usually with an onscreen caption, or in the case of Nicholas Courtney, an acknowledgement of his death via his character in *The Wedding of River Song*, but the only companion to transcend the classic and new series of *Doctor Who* is Sarah Jane Smith, and her death is marked with a very fitting tribute. A new companion for the fiftieth anniversary, named after her: Elisabeth *Clara* Miller (or Sladen, as she is commonly known by the world at large).

Clara Oswald – Jenna Coleman (*Asylum of the Daleks* and *The Snowmen*, *The Bells of St John* to *Hell Bent*, plus *Twice Upon a Time*)

Pumped Up Kicks (Foster the People); *Don't Stop Me Now* (Queen).

Oswin Oswald. Clara Oswin Oswald. Or simply Clara Oswald. She's a mystery, a companion splintered through time and space, with potentially hundreds of her existing to help the Doctor.

In *Asylum of the Daleks*, the Doctor, Amy, and Rory find themselves being helped through a complex full of insane Daleks by Oswin, the Junior Entertainment Manager of the starliner Alaska which crashed onto the Asylum planet. Oswin believes she's still trapped in the Alaska, passing the time by making soufflés, while keeping the insane Daleks outside at bay – all of them 'survivors of particular wars' on Spiridon (*Planet of the Daleks*), Kembel (*The Daleks' Master Plan*), Aridius (*The Chase*), Vulcan (*The Power of the Daleks*), and Exxilon (*Death to the Daleks*). But when the Doctor finally makes his way to her, he discovers the worst possible truth: she is a Dalek!

Due to her exceptional intelligence, she's been fully converted, unlike the rest of the Alaska crew who are converted into a variation of the Daleks' Robomen using air-borne nanogenes. As a result, Oswin creates a dream world in which she's holding back the Daleks. She's horrified to discover the truth, crying, bereft on her imaginary floor, still refusing to break her dream and give in to her conditioning. She has to fight the Dalek instinct to exterminate the Doctor, then lowers the defences of the asylum so the Doctor can destroy the planet. Before he departs, Oswin tells the Doctor, 'Run, you clever boy, and remember.'

The second time the Doctor meets her is in Victorian London in *The Snowmen*, where she's living two lives: as Clara Oswin Oswald, she's a barmaid at The Rose & Crown, while maintaining a secret life as 'Miss Montague,' governess to Francesca and Digby, children of the widowed Captain Latimer. The kids know there's more to her than meets the eye, as they ask her to do her 'secret voice,' meaning she briefly breaks her posh conceit to put on a more cockney accent. This version was born on 23rd November 1866, and meets the Doctor outside the pub as she's mulling over a mysterious snowman that's appeared out of nowhere. She's suitably intrigued by this stranger and follows him, then takes considerable joy in finding how inept Strax the Sontaran (previously seen in *A Good Man Goes to War*) is when trying to wipe her mind using a Memory Worm. The Doctor is suitably charmed by Clara, and, despite trying to keep a low profile, decides to let her keep her memories anyway. Nonetheless, Clara's interest is piqued and she follows him to the TARDIS, which is hidden away on a cloud, the Doctor having sunk into his depression after losing Amy and Rory. She then intrigues the Doctor by leaving an enigmatic warning with Madame Vastra, the Silurian living on Paternoster Row with her wife, Jenny Flint, and Strax. Suitably taken in, the Doctor further investigates an Ice Governess, which has taken the form of the Latimer's previous governess, and together, they hold back the threat of the Great Intelligence. This ends in tragedy, however, as Clara falls to her death.

But before she dies, she again tells the Doctor, 'Run, you clever boy, and remember.' It's enough to convince the Doctor that she and Oswin (who he never saw in person) are somehow the same person.

The Doctor first meets twenty-first century Clara Oswald when she's a young child, playing on the swings in a park, though he doesn't know who she is at that point (as detailed in the webcast, *The Bells of St John: A Prequel*). Unable to locate her again, he spends some time considering his next move while on sabbatical in Cumbria, 1207, and even paints a rather stunning portrait of her (*The Bells of St John*). He's considered a 'mad monk,' and the Abbot there looks at this painting and comments, 'The woman twice dead... If he truly is mad, then this is his madness.' In the event, Clara effectively finds the Doctor, calling the TARDIS thinking it's a 'computer helpline,' having got the number from a 'woman in the shop' (who is later revealed to be Missy, the Master regenerated into female form). This Clara is a nanny, looking after Angie and Artie Maitland, the children of a friend who's passed away, and who we might've seen walking through a 'creepy' graveyard with Clara in the closing moments of *The Snowmen*. Their father, George, is apparently looking for a replacement au pair, but Clara assures him, 'I'm here as long as you need me.' Clara had been inspired by a book called *101 Places to See* to go travelling; however, she stayed with her friend for a week beforehand, and during that time, her friend died. Her sense of obligation means she's stuck around. Clara insists that she's still going to go exploring one day.

To remember the Wi-Fi code, 'rycbar123,' Clara uses the acrostic 'Run you clever boy and remember,' signalling to the Doctor without even realising it. Almost uploaded to the Great Intelligence's data cloud, her mind is returned with the technical knowledge that she receives while in the cloud, meaning she's a bit more tech-savvy once she properly meets the Doctor. She's a bit confused and weary of the Doctor initially, since he's so certain they've met before, but she quickly warms to him and finds herself gladly helping him. After saving her from the Intelligence, he stands guard outside the Maitlands' house, then further entices her by welcoming her into the TARDIS so they can use it to materialise inside a plummeting plane and save it. The TARDIS then takes them back to London the following morning. All this time, Clara hasn't spilled a drop of her drink!

Despite seeing it work, she tongue-in-cheekily insults the TARDIS by suggesting it's simply made of wood. How's she to know it's alive anyway?

Clara is surprisingly accepting that the Doctor is an alien, and is fascinated by the idea of time travel. Nonetheless, she refuses to go away with him at first. Instead, she tells him to come back the next day and ask again. Before he does, however, he wants to find out more about Clara. As such, he revisits her childhood, briefly meeting her in the park as she's kicking a ball along with her parents, Dave Oswald and Ellie Ravenwood. The couple meet when a leaf falls into Dave's face in mid-1981, and he stumbles into the road – Ellie saves him from an oncoming car, and Dave, in return, keeps the leaf, because, as he later tells her, 'this exact leaf had to grow in that exact way in that exact place so that precise wind could tear it from that precise branch and make it fly into this exact face at that exact moment. And if just one of those tiny little things had never happened, I'd never have met you. Which makes this the most important leaf in human history.' It's a succinct example of causal effect, and one that results in Clara's birth on 23rd November 1986 in Blackpool. Sadly, her mother dies, her tombstone reading, 'Ellie

Oswald, beloved wife and mother'; it says that she was born on 11th September 1960 and died on 5th March 2005. Clara clings onto *101 Places to See*, originally her mum's book, while grieving at Ellie's grave.

Clara is, the Doctor concludes, an impossibly normal girl. Indeed, the Impossible Girl.

He returns for her in *The Rings of Akhaten*, and promises to take her 'somewhere awesome.' She's full of questions, including what time is actually made of. They go to the Pyramid of the Rings of Akhaten, a holy site for the Sun Singers of Akhat, a solar system to seven worlds whose inhabitants all believe life in the whole universe originated there. Clara asks if it really did, and the Doctor is elusive, suggesting instead that it's a nice story. While there, separated briefly from the Doctor, she's annoyed that the TARDIS won't let her back in, and is convinced that it doesn't like her (potentially a result of what happens in *The Name of the Doctor*). She takes the plethora of aliens in her stride – including Pan-Babylonians, a Lugalirakush, some Eukanians, a Hooloovoo, an Ultramanta, and a Terraberserker of the Cadonian Belt – even returning a bark at one of them called Doreen, implying the TARDIS's translation circuits aren't entirely playing ball either. Still, she understands most of what's said, enough at least to help Merry Gejelh, the young Queen of Years, find the strength to sing the Long Song at the Festival of Offerings. Her chemistry with children nicely foreshadows her eventual career.

The festival relies on psychometry, i.e. the values of items being decided on their emotional worth, and so Clara gives up her mother's ring, which is of great sentimental value, to help save Merry. It's fortunately returned to her by the people of Akhaten after she helps save them by sacrificing the leaf that brought her parents together, its psychometry mixed in with all the days of potential happiness Ellie never lived to enjoy, overwhelming the 'Old God.' He takes her back home, and there, she remembers seeing the Doctor at her mother's grave when she was younger; when asked why he was there, the Doctor says she reminds him of someone he knew, someone who died. 'Well, whoever she was, I'm not her, okay?' she replies. 'If you want me to travel with you, that's fine. But as me.'

In *Cold War*, the Doctor tries taking her to Las Vegas, but they instead end up stranded in 1983 on the Soviet submarine, Firebird, the TARDIS dematerialising after the Doctor resets the Hostile Action Displacement System (HADS). There, she meets the fearsome Ice Warrior, Grand Marshall Skaldak, and acquits herself well when it is down to her to question him. In fact, she puts herself forward for this task, something the Doctor is initially nervous about. It's implied that they've run through a script of what needs to be said and found out, but things go off-piste when Skaldak gets out of his captured armour and begins hunting down the submarine's crew. She's out to impress the Doctor at first, and asks how she did when questioning Skaldak. He tells her it is not a test... but she did great. When the Doctor tells her to remain where she is, safe with Professor Grisenko, she agrees and the Doctor is slightly shocked by compliance – so many companions before her would always wander off regardless. Clara is scared, plain and simple, but she's still courageous enough to stick with the Doctor, to do right, and is especially pleased when realising that they've saved everyone. 'That's what we do,' she comments, the idea settling itself in her mind.

She's probably afforded quite some time to get used to the Doctor, and to 1983, as the TARDIS has materialised on the other side of the planet. The Doctor hopes the remaining crew of the Firebird will give them a lift...

They go to Caliburn House in *Hide*, ostensibly to uncover the mystery of the 'Witch of the Well' (a being photographed throughout time, and Clara is the one to notice that she never changes her position, even before the Doctor spots this unusual fact). But really, the Doctor wants to consult with Emma Grayling, an empathic psychic, to find out who or what Clara is. He's disappointed to learn that Clara is just a normal young woman. She's suitably spooked by the possibility of a ghost, but encourages the Doctor to double-dare her into venturing into the darkness with him to look into it further. She also provides him with some humanity, telling him to shush when he accidentally touches a nerve despite intending to compliment Emma.

Having seen the entire life cycle of Earth, she confronts the Doctor, thinking that she's nothing more than a 'ghost' to him. The Doctor appears to swerve her accusations by saying she's the 'only mystery worth solving' – it's easy to conclude that he's solely talking about Clara, but he could actually be shining a light on why he's so involved with humanity. She comes away from this experience with the horrid realisation that everything ends.

Still, Clara more than proves herself, overcoming her fear and pushing aside even her own empathy as she tells Emma she has to help get the Doctor back from a pocket dimension. This risks Emma's stability. But Clara absolutely rails against the idea of losing the Doctor completely, effectively arguing they have no choice but to take big chances to retrieve him. Nevertheless, Emma tells her not to entirely trust the Doctor because 'there's a sliver of ice in his heart.'

Her continued belief that the TARDIS doesn't like her is compounded when the voice interface appears as a holographic copy of her ('I'm programmed to select the image of a person you esteem. Of several billion such images in my databanks, this one best meets the criterion'), and they argue about trying to save the Doctor. In the Series 7 DVD and Blu-ray extra, *Clara and the TARDIS*, the ship makes things worse by deleting Clara's bedroom and alters the flow of time in its interior by making multiple versions of Clara appear at the same time. We learn that Clara has a bed there (which, thanks to time running into itself, she sometimes shares with herself) in case she doesn't feel like going back to the Maitland's house after an adventure. The TARDIS appears to want Clara on the back foot as it willingly demonstrates that she's certainly not the first person to travel with the Doctor; when Amy discovered this, it was only because the Doctor mistakenly allowed her access to the databanks. Clara's mistrust in the ship seems further validated by the constant reconfiguring of the internal dimensions when she's lost in *Journey to the Centre of the TARDIS*, constantly finding herself back in the console room. In fact, the TARDIS has been affected by a salvage ship's Magno-grab, pulling them into a time loop, and the ship keeps presenting her with the console room as it deems it the safest part of itself. It's trying to save her. This is actually a result of the Doctor reverting the TARDIS back to 'basic mode,' i.e. shutting down its shields, so that Clara can learn to pilot it. While the Doctor argues that it's important to him that the two of them get along, Clara is less than enamoured with the notion, saying that it's an 'appliance' and refusing to talk to it. In the loop, Clara still has to venture deeper within the ship and finds an expansive, enviable library. There, she finds *The History of the Time War*, a book that includes the Doctor's real name.

Thinking that they're going to die there, the Doctor confronts Clara, convinced she's a trick or a trap for him, but she maintains she's no idea why he keeps meeting her. Indeed, she can't even remember it happening. She admits that she's now scared of the Doctor... but nonetheless appreciates the hug he offers her after he's safe in the knowledge that whatever's happening with Clara isn't her own doing. Time is snapped back to the point before the TARDIS is snatched up by the scavenger vessel, and Clara no longer remembers anything of her time trapped in the TARDIS. Neither does she remember learning the Doctor's name.

In 1893, Clara finds herself a victim of *The Crimson Horror*, but is saved by the Doctor. Once again, he teams up with Madame Vastra, Jenny Flint, and Strax. Jenny, in particular, is confused by the appearance of Clara, having seen her die in *The Snowmen*; all the Doctor can say is 'it's complicated.' Though Clara is kidnapped and put in stasis, when she wakes, she soon gets up to speed and correctly deduces the location of a rocket Mrs Gillyflower has been constructing to spread the crimson horror more widely. She then latches onto the Doctor jokingly calling her the boss. But when she gets home, Clara's confronted by her wards with a series of photos of her travels with the Doctor, including on the Firebird and a picture of Clara Oswin Oswald – who is definitely not her! The kids realise the Doctor is an alien (apparently due to his chin), and when Angie accuses her of going to Victorian London, Clara accidentally replies, 'No, I was in Victorian Yorkshire.' They quickly convince her into taking them on a trip in the TARDIS and the Doctor seems happy enough to comply in *Nightmare in Silver*. They arrive on Hedgewick's World, 'the biggest and best amusement park there will ever be'… but too late. It's closed down and is being used by a punishment platoon to train soldiers after the Cyber-Wars. Nonetheless, they discover a hidden legion of Cybermen there and the Doctor is partially converted. When 'Mr Clever,' i.e. the Cyber-Planner tries to take over the Doctor's mind, attempts to trick Clara using flattery and a hint of romance, Clara realises and says, 'even if that was true, which it is obviously not, I know you well enough to know that you would rather die than say it.' She doesn't, however, correct Artie when he calls the Doctor 'Clara's boyfriend.' Clara further develops a sweet relationship with Porridge, who eventually reveals himself to be the Emperor, hiding from his responsibilities. Porridge even invites her to stay and marry him, though his mixed-up worldview likely means he does so because he doesn't want to be lonely, not that he loves her.

Clara shows considerable guts when fighting off an untold number of Cybermen, and does well to organise the troops and weapons in the face of overwhelming odds. She's grown a lot in the short time she's been travelling with the Doctor already.

But she really proves herself in *The Name of the Doctor*, in which she witnesses Vastra, Jenny, and Strax being abducted by the Great Intelligence's Whisper Men. She's worried when she sees the Doctor's tears, his reaction to learning that the Intelligence is trying to lure him to Trenzalore, the planet of his final resting place. 'No point in telling you this is too dangerous?' the Doctor says. And Clara simply responds, 'None at all. How can we save them?' When they do get to Trenzalore, it's a ruined battleground with an older TARDIS standing sentinel over the wrecked desolation: its dimensional transcendentalism has got out of hand at the end of its life and deep within is the Doctor's grave. This, however, is like a tear in space-time, his timestream rippling like a crack in fabric; he describes it as 'a tear in the fabric of reality. That is the scar tissue of my journey through the universe. My path through time and space from Gallifrey to Trenzalore.' They can only gain access to it, and thus save Vastra, Jenny, and Strax from the Whisper Men, by revealing the Doctor's real name. He refuses to do it, even when the Whisper Men threaten to stop Clara's heart – some secrets are just too big. A data-ghost of River Song, who Clara meets at a dream-like 'conference call' but who follows them unseen to Trenzalore, says his name, though only Clara might've heard it; it's unlikely, however, as she never mentions it and at the time is on the verge of death.

Clara discovers that she was born to save the Doctor – jumping into his timestream and splintering herself throughout his lives in an effort to undo the damage caused by the Great Intelligence who did similar. Versions of Clara meet all eleven Doctors, and Clara laments, 'I don't know where I am... Sometimes, it's like I've lived a thousand lives in a thousand places. I'm born, I live, I die. And always, there's the Doctor. Always, I'm running to save the Doctor again and again and again. And he hardly ever hears me. But I've always been there.' Indeed, she appears on Gallifrey at the moment the First Doctor and Susan leave on their travels. It's Clara who tells the Doctor which TARDIS to take: although it's broken, it will be much more fun.

The Doctor rescues her from his timestream, but not before she meets the War Doctor, a hitherto unknown incarnation who fought in the Time War. They meet again in *The Day of the Doctor*. Clara and the Doctor are taken to the National Gallery by Kate Stewart and UNIT, to investigate figures disappearing from inside secret paintings in their Under Gallery. Clara is now a schoolteacher at Coal Hill School, regaling her class with a quote by one of her favourite historical figures, Marcus Aurelius: 'Waste no more time arguing about what a good man should be. Be one.' Called to the TARDIS by the Doctor, she takes a motorbike there and drives straight in, the ship's doors opening automatically for her. She's clearly been travelling with the Doctor for some time as she can close the TARDIS doors by clicking her fingers, much as the Doctor learned to do in *Forest of the Dead*. Still, she doesn't quite believe that the Doctor works for UNIT (he's still on the payroll, in fact, and demands a desk), tongue in cheekily saying that he could never have a job anyway. When they find the painting with conflicting titles that eventually join into one, i.e. 'Gallifrey Falls No More,' Clara immediately recognises the Doctor's anguish at recalling the last days of the Time War; indeed, he tearfully grabs her hand for support.

The Eleventh and Tenth Doctors end up in 1562, entertaining Queen Elizabeth I, the former having got there via a dimensional portal in the Under Gallery, leaving Clara in London, 2013, with Kate. In the past, the two Doctors join up with the War Doctor and are imprisoned in the Tower of London: though Kate realises that the Eleventh Doctor has left scrapings in its walls to tell them the activation code for UNIT's vortex manipulator, it's Clara who uses it to escape as she learns Kate has been replaced by a shapeshifting Zygon. Back in 1562, Clara rescues the Doctors... by simply opening the cell door, which wasn't locked in the first place – not that the clever old Time Lord ever thought of that!

Clara pays particular attention to the War Doctor. When the Tenth Doctor tells Kate later on that what he did on the day he ended the Time War was wrong, 'just wrong,' the War Doctor looks at his invisible companion, the stellar weapon known as the Moment; however, as no one else can see her, it appears to Clara as if he's suddenly looking at her. It's almost as if he's unconsciously asking her to take note.

After introducing herself, Clara says he looks so young; that is, despite this incarnation being physically more aged than the others. She says she knows due to his eyes. Indeed, she's the only one who realises he's not destroyed Gallifrey yet. She says that 'her' Doctor talks about the end of the Time War all the time, and that he regrets it: 'I see it in his eyes every day. He'd do anything to change it.' The War Doctor thinks the Tenth and Eleventh Doctors are so courageous because he made the decision to destroy Gallifrey. Off-screen, Clara must've convinced the Tenth and Eleventh Doctors that they need to follow him back into the Time War, so they all find themselves hovering over a big red button on the Moment. The imagery of the trio poised like this makes Clara cry as she couldn't imagine him ever doing it – despite what he's told her in the past, it's unthinkable to Clara that the Doctor could wipe out so many people. This really affects the Eleventh Doctor, who stops them all eradicating all the Daleks and Time Lords in one fell swoop, and instead finds a way to end the Time War without such immense amounts of blood on his hands.

Clara impresses them all. The Tenth Doctor kisses her hand goodbye, and the War Doctor departs by saying, 'And if I grow to be half the man that you are, Clara Oswald... I shall be happy indeed.' 'That's right,' she jokingly retorts. 'Aim high.'

Clara swiftly becomes at ease with travelling in time and space (*The Time of the Doctor*). The next time we see her, she's phoning the Doctor for help cooking the Christmas dinner in the TARDIS. The Doctor suggests exposure to the time winds will mean the turkey will 'either come up a treat, or just possibly lay some eggs.' He complains about her misusing the TARDIS for such events, like missing birthdays, restaurant bookings, and TV shows ('please just learn how to use iPlayer'). A lot falls on Clara, however: this seems to be the first time she's cooked the Christmas Day meal for her whole family. Her worrying dad emails her instructions and phones her at the time the turkey needs to go into the oven, and her dad's new partner, Linda, easily rubs everyone up the wrong way, even saying she's made a list of potential boyfriends for Clara. Her gran, however, is largely content, except for Linda's choice in Christmas crackers: they don't have jokes inside; they have poems. It turns out that her gran does fancy the Doctor, though perhaps because Clara introduces himself as her boyfriend... while he's accidentally naked.

But while the turkey's cooking inside the TARDIS, Clara gets embroiled in the Doctor's investigation into Trenzalore, a planet which is beaming out a mysterious signal to all time and space: 'Doctor who?' Handles, a Cyberman head the Doctor's accompanied by, suggests the signal hails from Gallifrey. Though the Doctor asserts otherwise, Clara entertains the possibility as she says he thought he'd saved his home planet at the end of *The Day of the Doctor*. The pair venture down to Trenzalore, initially with no protection from whatever's going on there, then the Doctor calls in the TARDIS, which is piloted there by Handles responding to the Time Lord digging out his TARDIS key. They happen upon a truth field in a town called Christmas, where Clara introduces herself as 'an English teacher from planet Earth, and I've run off with a man from space because I really fancy—' before shushing herself up. Nonetheless, she can't help also admitting that she has a bubbly personality that masks her being a bossy control freak.

Inside the town's clock tower, they discover the crack in time, a structural weakness in the fabric of the universe left over from when the TARDIS exploded (*The Pandorica Opens*), through which the Time Lords are trying to return home to the right dimension. Realising that if they return, the Time War will rage anew, especially with so many alien spaceships circling Trenzalore, the Doctor sends Clara back to the TARDIS supposedly to charge up his sonic screwdriver; instead, the TARDIS takes Clara home, and by the time she disembarks and realises what's happened, the ship is dematerialising.

It doesn't get back to Trenzalore for three-hundred years – as Clara is clinging to its shell. 'I was in space,' a dumbstruck Clara utters. Protecting her from the Time Vortex throws the TARDIS off, meaning the Doctor has been stuck on the planet all that time, and as such has aged. The Doctor says he's furious with her for returning as he thought he'd saved her. Nonetheless, their reunion is joyous, as they hug and the Doctor shows her around his new home in the clock tower. They watch the very brief sunrise which quickly gives way to sunset. The air ominous, Clara implores the Doctor to change the future and escape his destiny – they both remember finding his grave on Trenzalore in *The Name of the Doctor*. The Doctor argues that his staying there saves lives, but Clara responds, 'What about your life? Just for once, after all this time, have you not earned the right to think about that?' He relents and admits he, too, has been torn by this very argument. When Tasha Lem, Mother Superious of the Papal Mainframe and head of the Church of the Silence (the cult believing that silence must fall when the question – Doctor who? – is asked, here on Trenzalore), calls for the Doctor to meet with her to discuss the 'Siege of Trenzalore,' Clara accompanies him and is almost killed. 'I'm not afraid,' says Clara, defiant until the end. The Doctor, though is afraid for his companion, and, when the Daleks attack the planet in earnest, he tricks her once again by sending her back to her own time using the TARDIS. Brandishing the cooked turkey, Clara heads indoors, heartbroken.

It's far from the last time she sees the Doctor. The TARDIS comes back for her, piloted by Tasha who thinks the Doctor now needs a friend by his side. Clara finds an old-aged Doctor in the clock tower some five hundred years after she was forced to leave him.

He's naturally shocked but happy to see her again. He's less than enamoured with the Christmas cracker she's brought from home, preferring one with a joke inside. He is, however, too weak to pull the cracker without her assistance. When the Daleks push onwards with their final assault, he asks Clara to stay hidden inside: 'I'll be keeping you safe. One last victory. Allow me that. Give me that – my Impossible Girl. Thank you. And goodbye.'

It seems Clara is more accepting of the Doctor's fate now, seeing him so ancient and battle-worn. Yet she rushes over to the crack and begs the Time Lords for help, suggesting the question they're asking is wrong: 'His name is the Doctor. All the name he needs. Everything you need to know about him. And if you love him, and you should, help him.' They do, giving him a new regenerative cycle.

Returning to the TARDIS after the Daleks have been repelled, Clara puts the ship's phone back in its cradle (foreshadowing events at the end of *Deep* Breath). She's pleasantly surprised to see the Eleventh Doctor restored to his youth again, albeit temporarily, and is tearful when the Doctor starts musing over how everyone changes in time. Dropping his bowtie to the floor, the Doctor regenerates. The Doctor, then, owes not just his life to Clara, but all his lives.

The Eleventh Doctor's last companion is his most unusual in more than one way – not only is Handles a Cyberman head, but he also only sticks around for one festive episode. What makes him a companion? Apart from the TARDIS, he stays with the Doctor longer than anyone else…

Handles – Kayvan Novak (*The Time of the Doctor*)

En livstid i krig (Sabaton); *Radio Head* (Talking Heads).

The Time of the Doctor opens with the Doctor on a spaceship, waving around a Dalek eyestalk as 'proof of courage and comradeship.' He quickly realises the mistake when the ship turns out to be a Dalek ship, and he calls for Handles, his new companion, to transmat him back inside the TARDIS. He scolds the Cyberman head for plonking him down there, but Handles plainly states that he didn't indicate a preference in which ship he should be teleported to.

Handles isn't afforded a proper introduction, but the Doctor tells Clara that he's 'just a bit of a Cyberman,' and goes on to explain, 'The organics are all gone, but there's still a full set of data banks. Found it at the Maldovar market.' Handles accompanies the Doctor on a trip to a Cyberman ship orbiting the planet Trenzalore, though the Time Lord uses the disembodied head to deflect their fire, then helps translate the signal coming from Trenzalore – 'Doctor who?' – and suggests it actually hails from Gallifrey.

Handles has no intuition. When the Doctor answers a phone call from Clara to the TARDIS, it comes via the ship's exterior handset. He asks Handles to remind him later that he's got to patch the telephone back through the console unit, and Handles repeatedly asks when. The Doctor replies, 'Just pick a random number, express that number as a quantity of minutes, and when that time has elapsed, remind me to patch the telephone back through the console unit.' He's left inside the TARDIS while the Doctor and Clara are asked to investigate the planet by Tasha Lem and her Papal Mainframe, but reacts to the Doctor calling for the ship using his key while on Trenzalore. Handles, apparently somewhat integrated into its matrixes, can loosely pilot the TARDIS.

Clara is unwittingly sent home away from the Siege of Trenzalore, after a crack in time reveals the Time Lords trying to get back into this universe. But after taking Clara back to the twenty-first century, the TARDIS doesn't return for three hundred years – during which time, Handles is the Doctor's devoted companion. The two are left defending a town called Christmas from threats like the Daleks, Silents, Cybermen, Judoon, Sontarans, Terileptils, and Slitheen.

It seems that the Doctor tries to get replacement parts whenever part of Handles needs fixing, likely from Tasha and from the aftermaths of failed invasion attempts. Though he's the head of one of his enemies, the Doctor has grown to love Handles and needs him by his side as a friend. Nonetheless, the Doctor admits that it's a struggle to find the right equipment and Handles frequently says he's developed faults.

When Clara does return, having grabbed hold of the TARDIS exterior, she finds Handles in the clock tower that he and the Doctor have called home for some three centuries. Together, they wait for the sunrise to light up Christmas: daylight on Trenzalore, however, only lasts a few minutes, so they have to time it right. The Doctor places Handles affectionately on a cushion. Though Handles argues that comfort is irrelevant, the Doctor moves him slightly, and Handles relents that this is indeed a more comfortable vantage point. But Handles is on his last legs. The Doctor encourages him to see one more dawn, but he simply can't make it. His last message to the Doctor is a reminder: 'Urgent action required. You must patch the telephone device back through the console unit.'

As Handles' lights go out, the Doctor thanks him and says, 'Well done, mate.'

As the sun sets on them, the Doctor says, 'Everything ends, Clara. And sooner than you think.'

The Eleventh Doctor
Expanded Universe

Amy Pond makes her Expanded Universe debut in the *New Series Adventures* book, *Apollo 23* (2010), which sees her and the Eleventh Doctor don spacesuits like the ones seen in the TV serial, *The Moonbase*, while visiting a secret military base on the moon called Base Diana.

And so, when trying to impress Amy by telling her that the Doctor has taken him to the moon, Rory gets the response, 'been there, done that,' in 2011's *Heart of Stone*, a two-in-one book also featuring *Death Riders*. The Doctor's approach is criticised somewhat in the latter when Rory observes that without his sonic screwdriver, the Doctor would simply resort to smashing controls with his shoe. In the same story, Amy steals the Doctor's catchphrase of 'Geronimo!' leaving him feeling quite indignant at having missed out on an opportunity to use it; the catchphrase actually gets far more usage in the Expanded Universe than it does in the television series.

Amy's early *NSA* appearances occur before *The Time of Angels*, given that she refers to her wedding dress, one she 'might never wear,' in *Night of the Humans*, and *The Forgotten Archive* ends with them heading for the Delirium Archive. However, in the former, they visit the flat planet, Gyre, contradicting the implication in *The Time of Angels* that Amy's not been to a proper planet before; and in the latter, Amy remembers penguins in the Nile, as seen later in *The Big Bang*. We might blame some inconsistencies on the crack in time at least. Rory then joins the *NSA* range in *Nuclear Time* (2010), in which he compares a quiet town to the one in *Texas Chainsaw Massacre*.

Like Tegan and Donna before them, Amy and Rory aren't

slow in coming up with a reference to popular culture. One particularly memorable moment is when Rory notices that the Cemar, in the 2011 novel *The Good, the Bad and the Alien*, look just like meerkats. He turns to Amy and says 'simples' referencing the real-world comparison website character, Aleksandr the Meerkat. In 2012's *Terrible Lizards,* Rory also mentions that he prefers *The Land That Time Forgot* to *Jurassic Park*. And Rory reveals himself as a fan of *The Goon Show* in the comic, *The Upper Deck* (2011), as they go to 1959 to watch the cast record a show.

Doctor Who itself even gets a mention: in the 2011 *Doctor Who Magazine* comic story, *The Professor, the Queen and the Bookshop*, Amy reads a copy of *Shada*, the 2012 *Doctor Who* novel. She's also revealed to be a fan of the 1960s, especially The Beatles, in *Forever Dreaming*, and *The Child of Time* tells us that she likes *Pride and Prejudice*.

The interesting relationship between the Doctor, Amy, and Rory, and all its tensions, affections, and teasing, is further explored in the Expanded Universe. Nowhere is this greater examined than in *Dead of Winter* (2011), in which the power dynamics are shaken up and Rory's desire to be looked up to by Amy, as she has her Raggedy Man, is made clear.

The Forgotten Army tells us that before she moved to Leadworth, Amy grew up in Inverness, Scotland, which is also the home city of actress, Karen Gillan. According to the 2011 audio drama, *The Gemini Contagion*, Amy didn't see the point of learning French at school as she never believed she was ever going to go anywhere other than Leadworth (how wrong could she be?). Meanwhile, a young Rory was largely seen as a geek at school and shunned by other kids, apart from Amelia, Mels, and, according to *The Glamour Chase* (2010), Alec, who used to hang around underneath a willow tree. The pair's imaginations would transform it into the USS Enterprise or a labyrinth Indiana Jones would explore. Alec, however, died at a young age of a heart attack, and Rory helped his family process their grief. This might've influenced his career decisions.

In the 2020 webcast, *The Raggedy Doctor by Amelia Pond*, Amy confirms that Rory has always been her best friend, and that she only told him and Mels about the Doctor. The feisty Amelia wasn't always fair to Rory, however: she forgot all about him when playing hide-and-seek and blind man's buff (Mrs Angelo from *The Eleventh Hour* found him wandering about in her garden); and when he was nine, she melted his Action Man in the microwave, according to *I, Rorius*. In that 2021 audio, part of *The Lone Centurion: Volume One*, it's revealed that Rory once had a labrador called Bernard. He's also a collector of Match Attax cards, and supports Leicester City and Leeds United, as per 2012's *Extra Time*, which shows the trio attending the 1966 World Cup.

The King's Dragon features the first reference in any *Doctor Who* media to Rory's family. Both Amy and Rory mention his grandmother and the especially impressive gravy she used to make. In the 2013 short story, *Nothing O'Clock*, Amy notes that her parents haven't met yet when she and the Doctor arrive in 1984, but trails off as she can't remember much else about them. Amy also visits her parents, who are only seen on TV in *The Big Bang*, in the 2011 novel, *Borrowed Time*. In *Doctor Who Adventures'* *Power of the Mykuootni* (2011), she recalls her father taking her camping in the Scottish Highlands.

Other Expanded Universe stories follow the repercussions of events in the TV series. In *The King's Dragon* (2010), Rory confronts the Doctor about having kissed Amy in *Flesh and Stone*, and the Doctor retaliates, mentioning Lucy, the stripper from Rory's stag do. In *The Glamour Chase*, they're still trying to get to Rio de Janeiro, placing this sometime before *The Hungry Earth*, and the Doctor refers to Rory's waiting two thousand years for Amy (*The Big Bang*) in *The Way Through the Woods* (2011).

Most significantly, *The Lone Centurion* audio series from Big Finish examines what happened to Rory while he was guarding the Pandorica. *Gladiator* explains what happened when the Pandorica is taken to Rome in 118 AD, as mentioned in *The Big Bang*: Rory is forced to fight in the Colosseum (and his idea to fake his own death is soon unravelled), setting in a chain of events that leads to the death of 'Caesar,' who is likely Hadrian. However, historical records note that Hadrian actually died some two decades after this, so Rory questions whether time is further altered by the TARDIS exploding. Sure enough, Caesar's wife, Augusta, becomes empress in *The Unwilling Assassin*, and after her death, Rory becomes the new emperor in *I, Rorius*. He reveals he had a childhood interest in Roman times, possibly inspired by Amy's fascination with it, and concludes that this might be an alternate timeline given that he never read of Augusta's or the Lone Centurion's reigns in history books. Rory also has to think quickly in explaining his plastic anatomy and why he survives being 'killed' by a fellow gladiator, telling people his heart is on the wrong side of his body. Despite being employed first as a bodyguard then a pacifist assassin, he also has to find ways of adhering to the Hippocratic Oath.

Home still calls to Rory: he frequently talks to a statue he's had made of Amy ('Well, the proportions cannot be right – no woman has legs that long!'), and ponders over whether they'll ever have kids. He's adamant that Amy would do a better job as an immortal Pandorica guard than him, but he learns a lot about life and himself while waiting, including how far he'll go to protect his fiancée, and how his morals will be tested. He nonetheless gains a fair degree of confidence, standing up for the rights of the poor and not fearing death too much, given his immortality.

The next we hear of Rory, in *The Once and Future Nurse* (in 2022's *The Lone Centurion: Volume Two*), he's a nurse's apprentice in Camelot, embracing his caring ways and career but being criticised for being a little too good. During the story, he meets King Arthur, and Guinevere, as well as Sir Lancelot (who has a crush on Rory, not that he realises), and the manipulative Merlin, who sees Rory as a worthy foe, even unsuccessfully torturing him. Still, he soon curries favour in court so by *The Glowing Knight*, a retelling of the Arthurian legend, *The Green Knight*, Rory is now Sir Rory. By the time he and Lancelot get back from a quest set by Guinevere, Merlin has brainwashed Camelot (*The Last King of Camelot*), meaning Rory has to join the resistance alongside King Arthur and Guinevere. At the end of the story, Lancelot assures Rory that he'll be remembered.

(*The Constant Warrior*, a short story published in *The Brilliant Book 2011*, also tells us that Rory helped King Harold Godwinson in the Battle of Hastings, met Samuel Pepys and escaped the Great Fire of London, and was depicted in political cartoons opposing the rise of the Nazis. He mulls over the weight of his memories with the Doctor in *Visiting Hours*, from *The Wintertime Paradox* collection. In this, he also visits River in Stormcage – an annual festive tradition that Amy misses out on this time as her mother is ill – and recalls that he was bullied at school by Raymond Chettery... who Amy punched in retaliation.)

Amy's audio adventures began almost immediately, *The Runaway Train* being first given away with *The Daily Telegraph* in April 2010. She goes back to Scotland, albeit Orkney, 2025, in *The Ring of Steel*, and *The Hounds of Artemis* reveals Amy, like her future daughter, keeps a diary (though this is a classic storytelling technique employed by various Expanded Universe ranges). Rory joins the AudioGO brand in *The Eye of the Jungle* (2011), he has to travel two thousand years into the past with the Doctor in *Sleepers in the Dust* (2012) to find a cure for an infected Amy, and *Blackout* (2011) somewhat foreshadows their leaving as it takes them to New York City in 1965 (somewhere they also go to in the comic, *Dinosaurs in New York!*, published the same year).

The Eleventh Doctor era's association with the Weeping Angels is strengthened in 2011's *Touched by an Angel*, which interestingly contradicts *The Angels Take Manhattan*, that aired over a year after the book's release: in the novel, the Angels feed off paradoxes, something that poisons them in the TV episode. Perhaps these Angels work differently as they're a different clan or they're from a different point in their evolution. The Doctor also implies they can only feed like this if they're not directly involved in the paradox. The novel further foreshadows Rory's eventual fate, as the Weeping Angels displace him in time; fortunately, in *Touched by an Angel*, he's not sent too far back, so waits around to meet up with the Doctor and Amy again. 2023's *The Angel of Redemption* – a book of poetry that begins by ruminating on the origins of the Angels then goes on to explore their relationship with the 'lonely god', with New York, and with London – explains that Amy changed this Weeping Angel, the last left in the Big Apple, making it feel like it had a crack in its stone, stressing on its own loneliness then horror at being able to observe its own species' cut-throat nature. One of the Angels also appears, alongside a Dalek, Cyberman, and an Ood, in the Prestige Stamp Book celebrating *Doctor Who*'s fiftieth anniversary, a page with the working title, *Doctor Who and the Last Stand*. Upon seeing them all, the Doctor and Amy rush back into the TARDIS, meaning the foes end up attacking each other, something that essentially happens in *The Day of the Doctor* too, albeit solely the Daleks. As it turns out, Amy does a great Dalek impression: in *The Silent Stars Go By*, a longer-than-usual 2011 *Doctor Who* novel featuring the Ice Warriors, Amy tries to describe the Daleks, saying, 'Ras-py voiced a-liens who talk like this and yell "ex-ter-mi-nate".'

As with *Touched by an Angel*, the game, *Blood of the Cybermen*, contradicts events on TV, as Amy's travelling without Rory, likely placing it sometime during Series 5; however, she's also unfamiliar with the Cybermen in *The Pandorica Opens*. Nevertheless, this PC and Mac title is important for being the second in *Doctor Who: The Adventure Games* (2010-11), a series of free-to-download games, commissioned for BBC Online by BBC Wales Interactive, but cancelled after five releases. Significantly, these feature Matt Smith, Karen Gillan, and Arthur Darvill voicing their respective roles, with gameplay also based on their tracked movements, lending the range a large deal of credibility. While *City of the Daleks* finds the Doctor and Amy on Skaro, *Shadows of the Vashta Nerada* sees Amy meeting the flesh-eating 'piranhas of the air' introduced in River Song's first story, *Silence in the Library / Forest of the Dead*;

Rory joins them for *The Gunpowder Plot*, which not only introduces these companions to Guy Fawkes but also sees them meeting the Rutans, the shape-changing rivals to the Sontarans. Rory sees a member of the Silents in 1605, but naturally forgets all about it. Amy further encounters the Autons and Nestene Consciousness in *The Christmas Trap*, a 2011 purchasable level in *The Mazes of Time* iOS game. Another 2010 title, *Evacuation Earth*, for the Nintendo DS, shows that Amy is quite a whizz on computers, something she later demonstrates by quickly getting up to speed in *Dinosaurs on a Spaceship*.

Reflecting some of the tensions of early Series 6, the short story, *The King in Glass*, part of 2018's *Twelve Angels Weeping*, sees Amy going sunbathing on Gauss Electra, in order to give the Doctor and Rory some bonding time without her; the two guys head to a Coronation party on the planet Numina Vitri, only for it to be crashed by the Zygons. Amy suggests they give it another go, so in IDW's *The Doctor and the Nurse* (2012-13), she leaves the Doctor and Rory in a pub in 1814. It feels a little mean to them both, and undermines their relationship which is otherwise pretty convivial, that the Doctor waves around the idea of instead taking the TARDIS a few hours into the future so they don't have to suffer small talk until Amy returns. Naturally, this trip in the TARDIS goes wrong and they end up in 1812. Even though there's a war between the Royal Navy and the USA going on, Rory is content enough to wait two years for his wife. The Doctor isn't, so they again use the TARDIS to fast-forward to 1814. It's enough for Amy to conclude, 'No more "boys nights".'

Things get better between them, but they don't entirely gel: Rory actually slaps the Doctor in *The Cornucopia Caper*, a 2012 comic strip in *Doctor Who Magazine,* after which the Doctor states that he's been slapped by angry brides, angry mothers, and angry archaeologists.

Honeymoon Horrors, from *The Brilliant Book 2012*, published in 2011, details Amy and Rory's various attempts to honeymoon. They first go to see *Romeo and Juliet* at the Globe Theatre on 13th

January 1605, but Rory mentioning the Doctor results in them hiding from King James I's troops in a hotel wine cellar; the Gardens of Zul-Thep on 9th July 3104, where they're besieged by giant killer bees; Arizona in 1881, where Wyatt Earp shoots at Rory (who also suffers a 'cactus accident') and Amy fends off lecherous cowboys; and a beach on Drago 14, where acid-spitting squids melt Rory's Terry Pratchett book. He can't get another as it's been out of print for some four hundred years. Amy then considers a brochure for a romantic space-cruise courtesy of Solaris World Holidays, especially when she sees a photo of herself and Rory on said promo brochure! This also gives a name to the ship seen in *A Christmas Carol*: the Thrasymachus. It names the planet as Ember, and says Sardicktown's tourist attractions include Miss Garglespike's World of Pins, the Duckchester Tanneries, the Scratchington Fish Market, Dr Henry Fizzog's Museum of the Macabre, and, at 91 Throttleby Lane, the offices of Sardick, Sardick & Sons, presumably inside Sardick Towers.

The book features *A Silent Influence*, which tracks Amy across North Dakota, South Dakota, Washington, and Idaho while searching for the Silents (i.e. at the start of *Day of the Moon*), and Rory watched *The Illustrated Man* in California.

Later, in *Hypothetical Gentleman* from IDW in 2012, the Doctor takes Amy and Rory to the Great Exhibition in 1851 as an anniversary gift, possibly expanding on the sequence in *The Power of Three*.

Both Amy and Rory feature in a huge number of comic strips, primarily in *Doctor Who Adventures*, with Amy debuting in the second part of 2010's *Attack of the Space Leeches!*, and Rory in *First Foot First*, the latter of which, released in December 2010, taking them to Edinburgh Castle on New Year's Eve. As a brief snapshot of their journeys, *Booked Up* takes Amy to the Library (unbeknown to her, the place her daughter would lose her life and gain a new digital existence in *Forest of the Dead*); astronauts in *The Lunar Tyk* arrive on the moon in 2039 to already find the Doctor and Amy there; Amy is sent careering through time, notably visiting Ancient

Rome, in *Random History* (2011); the titular companion in *Rory's Story* pretends to be 'the scourge of a thousand worlds,' aka the Doctor, and sees off a terrifying alien using a whisk; they meet a golden Roman Centurion in 39 BC in *Golden Slumbers*; they return to a warped Leadworth in *Dino World*; the trio repeatedly meet the Space Service's *Agent 99*, eventually giving him a lift in the TARDIS in *The Secret Star Trail*; they encounter Silurians that, for the first time in *Doctor* Who history, can travel *Faster Than Light* (2012); they show off their skills on unicycles in *Le Tour de Death*; and, on the *Planet of the Rorys*, the titular character has his DNA used as a template for a species – they all bow down and worship Amy...

Ghosts of the Never-were confirms that they sleep together in the TARDIS and that, post-*The Doctor's Wife*, were granted a double bed instead of bunk beds. *Samurai's Secret* is one of numerous trips to Japan for Amy, the others including the 2011 audio, *The Jade Pyramid*, and the *DWM* story, *The Golden Ones*.

In the latter, Martha Jones calls the Doctor and Amy into a UNIT briefing in Tokyo, where they uncover an invasion attempt by the Axons (from *The Claws of Axos*).

There are, of course, various allusions to and mentions of previous companions. In the 2012 novella, *Magic of the Angels*, Amy dons a sparkly catsuit once worn by Zoe Heriot, the Second Doctor's companion, while the Doctor wears the Third Doctor's outfit; and in the graphic novel, *The Only Good Dalek* (2010), the Doctor establishes his credentials with the guards at Station 7, actually agents of the Space Security Service, by mentioning he's worked with Sara Kingdom and her brother, Bret Vyon. In the 2011 *DWA* comic, *If You Go Down to the Woods Today*, the Doctor tells Amy that there'll be no pets on the TARDIS... except 'perhaps a robot dog,' alluding to K9. Missy even meets a young Amelia, who's still waiting for her Raggedy Man to return, in *Fairies at the Bottom of the Garden*, part of the 2023 audio boxset, *The Eighth of March: Strange Chemistry*. This shows Amelia's ultimately altruistic nature as she turns down Missy's offer of becoming her companion if she helps open a dimensional rift for her. Her memories are wiped of this adventure, but we find out that Amelia has stood up to a bully named Fran at school, and that her Aunt Sharon has a partner called Conor.

In *The Glamour Chase*, the Doctor accidentally insults his future wife, and Amy and Rory's future daughter, River Song: when talking about history's greatest archaeologists, he mentions Howard Carter, Indiana Jones, Marcus Scarman (*Pyramids of Mars*), and Enola Porter – at least he does name-check his former companion, Bernice Summerfield, though!

Perhaps the most poignant piece of biographical information is given in the 2012 *DWM* comic, *Imaginary Enemies*, the final story to feature Amy and Rory, and the only one to include Brian, Rory's dad. At the story's close, the reader is presented with a series of images representing the later years of Amy and Rory's life after *The Angels Take Manhattan*, where they were trapped back in time by the Weeping Angels. Rory is pictured as a doctor, suggesting that he took his medical career further. It's clear he does this out of love for the job too, as River gave the royalties of *Melody Malone: Private Detective in Old New York Town*, and its prequel, *The Angel's Kiss*, to Amy and Rory so they could buy a home, according to the novel, *The Ruby's Curse*. River intends to publish more Melody Malone stories, but Amy suggests she hand over the reins to her mother, now publishing books as Amelia Williams, as she's too close to the subject matter. In 1969, Amy and Rory are interviewed by journalist, Chrissie Allen (published as *The Girl Who Never Grew Up*, in the 2013 anthology, *Summer Falls and Other Stories*). By this point, Rory has created the Williams Wonder Beds to help patients in hospital. Amy says her next book is about a little girl, lost in New York City, who intends to change the world using her magical powers, alluding to Melody in *Day of the Moon*.

River's Expanded Universe likely starts in the hospital seen at the end of *Let's Kill Hitler*. The 2012 PlayStation 3, PlayStation Vita, and PC game, *The Eternity Clock*, sees her add her first entry into her TARDIS-blue diary, using a pen secured by the nurses from an antique shop. The title also includes River meeting various other incarnations of the Doctor (even trying to find the First Doctor on Totter's Lane, but being scared off when she hears Susan approaching), and singing karaoke with the Doctor and Jim the Fish in the forty-eighth century.

Audio tales pick up her story at the Luna University, with an adventure in the 2018 set, *The Diary of River Song: Series Three*, that sees her investigate the legend of *The Furies*, mythical creatures Madame Kovarian used to scare a young Melody with. This reveals that River has numerous proto-Time Lord clones, H-One, H-Two, O, and Brooke, the latter of whom briefly travels with the Fifth Doctor. *The Lady in the Lake* adds more clones to the mix: Tarn, Lake, and Lily. Kovarian conditioned them all not to kill her, which explains River not doing so in *The Wedding of River Song*. Nonetheless, River takes pleasure in knowing the Church of the Silence 'washed their hands' of Kovarian after the Battle of Demons Run, and uses her and her clones' psychic link, granted to them by the TARDIS, to send taunting messages into Kovarian's mind. Still, *Student Bodies*, a short story in the prose collection, *Twelve Angels Weeping*, details the Silents infiltrating the university in December 5124; at some point before this, River acquired hallucinogenic lipstick, and is almost expelled when attempting to use a stolen vortex manipulator to travel into her future to ask herself for help writing essays. She only avoids expulsion when arguing it's impossible to plagiarise herself.

River also tries to wriggle out of being imprisoned for murdering the Doctor in *Whodunnit?* – in which she further sees the Fourth Doctor and steals the TARDIS from 107 Baker Street, a residence used most frequently by the Eighth Doctor – from *The Diary of River Song: Series Four* (2018). She pleads not guilty, saying she only did so to save the universe. Obviously, she still ends up in Stormcage, but frequently escapes, including having a *Picnic at Asgard* (in 2016's *The Legends of River Song*) with the Doctor. In that short story, River confirms that, one day, she'd like to have a child. She's in contact with Father Octavian (seen on TV in *The Time of Angels/Flesh and Stone*), with the latter sending her a holy relic. It's possible River and the Doctor visit Asgard more than once, as Steven Moffat's Target novelisation of *The Day of the Doctor* implies she had a picnic there with the Tenth Doctor, as does dialogue in *Silence in the Library*. It also suggests that River found a therapy robot, which had been accidentally let loose inside the TARDIS by the Ninth Doctor, and used it to wipe the Eleventh Doctor's memories of how many children died on Gallifrey on the last day of the Time War.

She's also well aware of Gallifrey's history of atrocities: in *River of Time*, we learn that she wrote a paper about the Racnoss ruins on Arcnoy Twelve, as she includes them in a list of species the Time Lords' Fledgling Empires wiped out, alongside the Great Vampires (*State of Decay*), Narlok, and other races lost to the past. River helps defeat the Qwerm, who'd allied themselves with the Time Lords during the ancient Time Wars but turned against them as they feared betrayal themselves.

River has a good knowledge of the Last Great Time War. In fact, she comes off worst from an encounter with the War Master in 2019's *Concealed Weapon*, as he picks off River's colleagues on a deep space exploration mission; he makes her forget him in the end, so she's unaware that this incarnation of the Master fought in the conflict.

When Professor Bernice Summerfield, one of her lecturers at Luna University, says she thought the Doctor would find an elaborate means of averting the conflict, River retorts, 'Who's to say that someday he won't?' (*Lies in Ruins*, in 2019's *The Legacy of Time*). River, Bernice, and the Eighth Doctor find themselves on a ruined planet which Bernice thinks is the remnants of Gallifrey following the war. River helps the Doctor come to terms with this after he's apparently given the power to bring his home back using the Matrix, which River argues would make him a god, bringing him out of his reverie by reminding him who he really is. By this point, she's learned that 'Gallifrey' is, in reality, a projection created by a TARDIS, and she holds his hand as Gallifrey disappears from him.

River becomes a teacher herself in the opening story of 2019's *The Diary of River Song: Series Six. An Unearthly Woman* takes us back to London in October, 1963, where it's implied River meets the policeman from *An Unearthly Child*. River is wearing her mother's police outfit and goes by WPC Pond; when the officer doesn't believe her, she uses her eau de forget perfume to knock him out. Next, she's teaching Susan's class in Coal Hill School, and raises some eyebrows after referencing events in the 1970s. She also meets Ian Chesterton (who isn't too impressed by her not tidying up after lecturing as a supply teacher in his room, Class C3) and Barbara Wright, then briefly the First Doctor, albeit after she's attacked by a creature from another dimension that's drawn to her proto-Time Lord scent. When River finally admits to being a time traveller, Susan automatically trusts her, sensing an 'air of family' about River – indeed, Susan is her step-granddaughter – and helps her see off the creature. River reveals she only came to 1963 after learning of a bounty put on 'young Time Lords' at the Maldovarium. Susan offers for River to travel with her and the Doctor, but she has to turn it down. (River further helps a much older Susan rebuild London after the Daleks' invasion of Earth in *Dead Man Talking*, in 2023.)

River eventually returns to that period, spending a few months in 1962 and 1963 after her vortex manipulator stops working so acts as governess to Thomas Mortimer and becomes a *Friend of the Family* (2023). During the time River's looking into a mystery involving the Mortimer household, something she's drawn into when a Luna University trip to an anomaly at their home uncovers pages torn from her diary. We find out that River's grasp on time travel still occasionally needs assistance as she has to draw a timeline of events so she can keep track of when she's present in the past and future.

Various stories see River spending time with her parents,

possibly even living with Amy and Rory: in *Pond Life*, a back-up strip in a 2014 issue of Titan Comics' *The Eleventh Doctor*, River comes downstairs in a plunging black dress while her parents are canoodling, only for Rory to scold her, 'You're not going out dressed like that! Amy, tell her she's not going out dressed like that.' They're similarly not impressed in a 2015 comic when the Doctor and River turn up on a *Double Date* with Amy and Rory.

Carnival of Angels, from *The Diary of River Song: Series Seven* (2020), acts as something of a prequel to *The Angels Take Manhattan*, as it sees River, as Melody Malone, opening up her Angel Detective Agency with now-former-student, Luke Sullieman. In 2012, the BBC took the unusual step of releasing *The Angel's Kiss: A Melody Malone Mystery*, rare as it was actually seen in the show, although there were differences between these editions. Collected in *Summer Falls and Other Stories* (2013), another book partially seen on TV in *The Bells of St John* and notable for being a favourite of Clara Oswald, its dedication reads 'To My Daughter,' i.e. from Amy to River, while the latter's bio, attributed to Melody Malone, says she 'might be married,' casting further ambiguity on her partnership with the Doctor due to it happening in an aborted timeline.

The 2012 book, *Horror of the Space Snakes*, lists a few places the Doctor has taken River while she's supposedly been locked up, including Paris, New York, Amsterdam, Cersis Major, and the planet Talusia. Steven Moffat's Target novel, *The Day of the Doctor*, indicates that River once cloned herself – making for quite the birthday celebration and quite a headache for the Doctor!

Aside from her frequent escapes, River is also forcibly removed from Stormcage. In *The Bekdel Test*, which opens *The Diary of River Song: Series Five* in 2019, River wakes up as the 'most valued' prisoner in the Bekdel Institute but tells its director, 'A prison hasn't been built that can hold me.' Indeed, she does get out, with the help of a reluctant Missy, who says she's jealous that River is the one who managed to kill the Doctor. The Master, at an earlier point in his timeline, employs River to apparently transport an expanding sun and its planet, temporarily contained by dimension condensers, across the universe (*Rivers of Light*, which closes 2021's *The Diary of River Song: New Recruit*), but her vortex manipulator malfunctioning means she's instead separated from the condensers when she crashes to Earth. She sends the Third Doctor on a wild goose chase and tricks the Brigadier into employing her as Liz Shaw's assistant. The pair work together on several missions, eventually recovering the condensers and trapping the Master. Though the Third Doctor isn't involved, River also travels, in 2022's *Peladon* boxset, to the titular planet he visited at least a couple of times: in *The Poison of Peladon*, she goes undercover as a high priestess and befriends the delegate from Alpha Centauri. The Doctor's love of that world is enough for River to stick around, even when she's falsely arrested for attempted murder. Queen Thalira recalls learning about women's liberation from Sarah Jane Smith, a name that River knows, so we can infer she's met the Third and Fourth Doctor companion at some point (the Doctor has no doubt talked about her at any rate).

River goes on to meet Kate Stewart, the Brigadier's daughter, in *The Power of River Song*, from the 2019 set, *UNIT: Incursions*, and implies that there was some flirtation between her and the Brigadier as she says, 'We'll always have Cromer.' In this, a body is found at Exousia Solutions' new power station, and the company's director, River, is the main suspect – though it turns out that River has been replaced by the Battle-Queen of the Wampeerix. Kate lets River go after she helps a time-displaced Osgood get home from first 1972 then 2091. At some point, River meets Ann Bishop, née Travers, whose history is linked with UNIT on TV through *The Web of Fear.* in *Pure History*, a *Lethbridge-Stewart* short story from the 2019 collection, *The HAVOC Files: The Laughing Gnome*, Ann recognises a vortex manipulator as being the same or similar to one worn by River.

River meets many other companions, including the Eighth Doctor's audio assistants like Charley Pollard and Liv Chenka in

Companion Piece (during which she's interrupted by a rogue Time Lord known as the Nine as she's trying to retrieve the body of Katarina drifting in space following *The Daleks' Master Plan*). The story also features Jamie McCrimmon, Adric, Romana II (who River pretends to be in *Someone I Once Knew* and *Emancipation*), Jo Grant, and Leela – the latter of whom River meets and gets on well with in 2019's *The Eighth of March*. In that audio story, River proves adept with any TARDIS as she opens Leela's with a click of her fingers. She encounters Captain Jack Harkness in *R&J*, falling for him while also being on the run from Javic Piotr Thane, i.e. Jack from a past when he's still working for the Time Agency. She takes over the organisation to get him off her back. She also moves into the Powell Estate and helps her neighbour, Jackie Tyler, wash a duvet while they chat about River's dilemma, having to choose between two men (meaning the Doctor and Jack). She and Jackie later visit a health spa run by the titular crystalline beings in *Harvest of the Krotons*, part of the 2023 set, *The Orphan Quartet*.

The 2023 book, *Rebellion on Treasure Island*, causes a slight continuity issue in that it's set shortly after *Cold War* and, though River knows of the Doctor's new companion, Clara doesn't know River – this contradicts *The Name of the Doctor*, which shows their first meeting, as Clara apparently didn't realise until that point that River is a woman.

It's through River that we also meet one of the Eighth Doctor's companions, though not a fully-fledged one as Ria, played by Alexandria Riley, only briefly features in *Lies in Ruins*. An android the Doctor built himself, Ria was irreparably damaged by scavengers where she and the Doctor find River and Bernice. Ria was notably named after a character from the fan-made *Audio Visuals* cassettes between 1984 and 1991, a range extensively worked on by Big Finish's Nicholas Briggs.

After being pardoned for killing the Doctor, River returns to Stormcage in 5147 for the novel, *The Ruby's Curse* (2021), significant as it's written by actress, Alex Kingston. She retreats to her old cell for some peace and quiet. There, she gets to know Ventrion, who she gives her vortex manipulator to when raiders attack the facility and they have to flee. With help from Captain Jack Harkness, she makes her way to 1939 where she finds a parcel from Amy containing the final manuscript for *The Ruby's Curse* and her vortex manipulator. The former included both instructions for destroying a powerful device known as the Eye of Horus and an AI that calls itself Melody Malone. With its help, she manages to fend off an attack from a Silent, and stop the Eye of Horus, but at the cost of Melody's life. This prompts River into questioning whether she's in the Land of Fiction (from *The Mind Robber*), showing she's either experienced it before or chatted to the Doctor about it. We learn that she's been involved with the Sensorites and Ood too, as Ventrion recognises her name from an archaeological paper called *Concomitant Development on the Ood Sphere and the Sense Sphere*.

River, of course, meets numerous other incarnations of the Doctor. In *Suspicious Minds*, from *The Legends of River Song*, she even mentions that she went back in time to see the Doctor's first three incarnations meet (i.e. *The Three Doctors*), but was saddened to learn most of those events happened in Omega's anti-matter universe. In the following short story, *A Gamble with Time*, she's very enthused with the idea of having two Doctors around at the same time, something which she does later experience...

Interestingly, when she encounters the Seventh Doctor in *The Unknown*, the opening story in *The Diary of River Song: Series Two* (2016), she doesn't know him, owing to a paradox affecting her memory. These lapses don't affect her ability to pilot the TARDIS, implying it's innate, and she still has some recognition of the name 'Doctor,' without knowing why. She then meets the Sixth Doctor in *World Enough and Time* (the audio story with the same name as the 2017 TV episode) when trying to infiltrate the corrupt Golden Futures, only to find her husband is working on bringing down the company from within as its director. After doing so, they find themselves in London, on 26th November 1703, with River sharing a cell in Newgate Prison with novelist, Daniel Defoe, and the Doctor present twice: both the Seventh and Sixth Doctors are there too, drawn into a paradox around Isaac George and Sarah Dean, a couple the Sixth Doctor is trying to save (*The Eye of the Storm*). While the Sixth Doctor is more trusting of River, the Seventh Doctor goes so far as to handcuff her and leave her to be arrested for attempted theft. He realises she's up to something dubious later on, as he refuses her attempts to erase his memory of these events, using first spiked food and drink then her lipstick. Instead, she knocks him out and gets the TARDIS to help blank out what's transpired.

It's notable that, while the Doctor is content to meddle with people's lives, River prefers to lay out the whole situation to Sarah and Isaac, and trust that they'll do the right thing: they do, embracing the paradox together and being wiped from existence to save Earth. It's implied that River resents being manipulated by Kovarian and the Church of the Silence when she was younger so she doesn't want to take this option here. (Still, when given the opportunity in *Animal Instinct* to help an alien species by changing their DNA, River jumps to do so, before being held back by Luke Sullieman, who points out it's not her decision to make.)

Elsewhere in the boxset, we meet Rachel Burrows – played by Alex Kingston's daughter, Salome Haertel – an android adopted by her parents, Lisa and Emmett, as they couldn't have human children themselves; River spends an evening and the next day getting to know the Burrows family as, in the future, she learned that Rachel is the last survivor of a deadly signal broadcast at *Five Twenty-Nine*. She can't avert it, though, so Lisa and Emmett are killed and Rachel is left deactivated. River later reactivates her and leaves her on the spaceship Saturnius. Feeling a sense of obligation towards her, River eventually returns to teach Rachel about being immortal in 2021's *The Diary of River Song: Series Eight*. In the set's *A Brave New World*, Rachel persuades River to leave her help colonists on the ship, Armis 20, but while she gets close to one of them called Aaron, she's manipulated by two others and is forced to navigate the vessel for almost five hundred years, with her memory temporarily expunged. She gets it back in time to call River for help saving the colonists from zombie electric eels, and stays with Aaron to build a new life there.

The following set, *The Diary of River Song: Series Three*, sees River repeatedly meeting the Fifth Doctor.

In *The Lady in the Lake*, her life changes as she learns of her clones, the first 'batch' consisting of Lake, Rindle, Tarn, Wadi, Creek, Stream, and Beck. Following the events of *A Good Man Goes to War* and *The Wedding of River Song*, Kovarian created a second lot of Proto-Time Lords, one of whom, Brooke (Joanna Horton), goes on to travel with the Fifth Doctor alongside, for a short time, River, who doesn't know anything about Brooke, completely unaware of who she really is. In a visit to Vienna in 1791 (*A Requiem for the Doctor*), River discovers that Brooke has been sent by Kovarian to kill the Doctor, but she counteracts Brooke's poisoning him. In the subsequent story, *My Dinner with Andrew*, she wipes Brooke's recent memory and suggests she's killed the Doctor. This is further complicated when River goes to meet Kovarian and tries to convince her that Andrew Edwardson, who has an uncanny resemblance to the Fifth Doctor (and is played by Peter Davison), is actually the Doctor, only for the real Doctor to walk in. Brooke eventually kills the Doctor – in anger, River shoots her, only for her to regenerate – but regrets it and uses a vortex manipulator to rewrite time so that it's Andrew that she murders. Brooke 2, notable for being played by Mels actress, Nina Toussaint-White, further features in *The Furies* and *The Wife of River Song* (2023).

Her history with the Doctor is altered by the Discordia, a predatory species able to take the form of its prey's fears, so that when the Fourth Doctor sees her in *Someone I Once Knew* (from *The Diary of River Song: Series Four*), he says he's known her since his first incarnation. This is undone so the status quo is reverted to, meaning the Doctor can't remember her, but during the process, River thinks the Doctor is dead; interestingly, while this does naturally upset her, it also makes her more determined and loyal, ferociously batting away interest from the lecherous General Dante.

Somehow, River meets the Thirteenth Doctor, at least according to a short story called *The Guide to the Dark Times*, or *The Time Lord Victorious?*, included in the *Doctor Who Official Annual 2021*, written by River. This starts with her detailing her stealing the Black Scrolls of Rassilon from Gallifrey, ancient texts that contain forbidden knowledge from the Dark Times. River calls herself 'one of the most dangerous people who ever lived' and describes the Doctor as her 'on-off husband and occasional wife.' As River doesn't recognise that there can be subsequent incarnations after the Eleventh Doctor until *The Husbands of River Song*, *The Guide to the Dark Times* perhaps takes place after her last night with the Twelfth Doctor on Darillium, but before the events of *Silence in the Library*.

Indeed, in the 2022 book, *A Short History of Everyone*, she writes about the Time Lord from the afterlife, and is surprised that the Thirteenth Doctor is a woman. The canonicity of annuals is always debatable, though in the *Doctor Who Official Annual 2018*, River and the Doctor are said to have made a home during their last night together, listing it as 'Flat 40, Singing Towers View, Darillium.'

After being saved to the Library, *Firewall*, from the 2022 boxset, *Two Rivers and a Firewall*, follows River's afterlife, when she's apparently married to Proper Dave who was killed by the Vashta Nerada in *Silence in the Library*. She's hunted by a computer virus installed by Alan, a hacker taking revenge on River as he believes the Doctor killed his parents.

The Death and Life of River Song: Last Words (2024) adds an interesting coda to River's afterlife – more specifically, a new lease of life. Possibly. This finds the memories of River wrenched from the Library's database and uploaded into a clone body, after thousands of years of her digital existence. She's desperate to get back to the Library, but instead has to track down a missing scientist, Dr Balthazar, at the behest of billionaire, Garrison Clay. River experiences the solar apocalypse on Earth, seeing the hand the less-privileged were dealt in contrast to those lucky enough to escape, as per the Fourth Doctor story, *The Ark in Space*. At this point, she's still writing in her diary and mourns her previous life.

After some ten thousand years in the Library, River still pines for her lost love, the Doctor.

Most of Clara Oswald's Expanded Universe adventures feature the Twelfth Doctor. In fact, before 2023, Clara only appears in one novel with the Eleventh Doctor: *Shroud of Sorrow* (2013), an anniversary title that takes place on 23rd November 1963, the day of the very first episode of *Doctor Who*. This book also features Totter's Lane with many references to *An Unearthly Child*. The novel includes a smorgasbord of references and recollections, including many companions like Jamie McCrimmon, Jo Grant, Nyssa, Grace Holloway, Amy and Rory, and the Brigadier (though when the Doctor disguises himself as the latter, he goes by Colonel, Lethbridge-Stewart's rank when the Second Doctor first met him in *The Web of Fear*). *Shroud of Sorrow* somewhat pre-empts Clara's later developments, almost as if she's trying to emulate the Doctor so early on in their time together. Here, she's still the Impossible Girl, so much about Clara remains a mystery, though we hear about a deceased friend of the family she calls Uncle Reuben, this being a term of affection rather than hinting at any familial connection. The Doctor is similarly troubled by Clara's rushing into danger in the 2018 short story, *Clara and the Maze of Cui Palta* (from *The Day She Saved the Doctor: Four Stories from the TARDIS*), which is set after Clara has a stressful day looking after Angie and Artie Maitland.

Clara appears in a short story called *Into the Nowhere*, reprinted in the 2015 *Time Trips* anthology, in which she recalls attending Sunday school with a 'nice lady teacher.' Though this tale is set after *The Day of the Doctor*, it's interesting for highlighting just how afraid Clara is, something hinted at in earlier TV serials like *Cold*

War and *Hide*. We also find out that Clara can only sometimes remember her other lives and what she learned when she stepped into the Doctor's timestream, most often with events coming to her in dreams.

Another short story, *Normality*, from *Heroes and Monsters Collection* in 2015, is set largely in Coal Hill School, and Clara admits the Doctor might've had a hand in her getting a job there. It says that Clara is uneasy about heights owing to a trip with her father to a tower block near Stockport when she was nine years old. The block had a restaurant on the top and some boys jokingly stomped around on its glass floor. Clara is further inspired to look after kids when she finds a tome in a second-hand book shop with an inscription reading, 'There's no larger responsibility than great potential.' She's juggling being a nanny and travelling alongside the Doctor with her studying to be a teacher. Judging that George Maitland was coping better now after the death of his wife, Clara was happy to get a job at Coal Hill School.

Normality then fleshes out Courtney Woods' class, noting students named Joshua Adams, Tommy Breare, Mackenzie Brooks, Chiana Holden, Zehra Jalindra, Sam Kaye-Jones, Liam Mannings, and Kelly Squires. Clara's travels clearly influence her teaching as, for one lesson, she takes her English class outside and teaches them about microscopic tardigrades, trying to instil in them the sense of wonder so vital in literature.

It's not until *Rebellion on Treasure Island* that we get another full-length novel with the Eleventh Doctor and Clara, over a decade after the previous book with the pair; in the intervening years, Clara has featured extensively with the Twelfth Doctor in books. Nonetheless, this confuses the timeline as they've apparently just left the *Firebird* submarine seen in *Cold War*, yet it features Madame Vastra, Jenny Flint, and Strax, who, in *The Crimson Horror*, are confused by seeing Clara for the first time since seeing her Victorian counterpart die (*The Snowmen*). Clara also says the Doctor has spoken of meeting other Claras, something she doesn't learn about until *Journey to the Centre of the TARDIS* before forgetting and remembering in *The Name of the Doctor*. If the story does occur early on in Clara's travels with the Doctor, he's been very forward about his past, having already talked about River Song two or three times. As is, we learn most about Jenny Flint from the book, including that her parents ran a freak show, and that she ran away from home, working at a match factory, and living on the streets until meeting Madame Vastra.

Origin Stories (2022) includes *Clara Oswald and the Enchanted Forest*, which shows a fourteen-year-old Clara getting chips with her best friend, Asharim, before going to a Halloween party dressed as a vampire, i.e. a sparkly dress, holey tights, and a pair of red Doc Martens. The 'loveliest, most thoughtful boy' in Year 10, Gem, also dresses as a vampire. In frustration with her mum, this youthful Clara lets the 'most important leaf in human history,' i.e. from *The Rings of Akhaten*, drift away on the breeze. With the Doctor's help, she gets it back, and, not wanting to change time, he wipes her memory of their meeting.

Away from prose, Clara meets a few historical figures including Jane Austen in *False Coronets*, the final story in 2018's *The Eleventh Doctor Chronicles*, who she later says is a 'phenomenal kisser' (in *The Magician's Apprentice*). In IDW's 2013 comic story, *Dead Man's Hand*, she encounters Calamity Jane and inspires Oscar Wilde to write *The Picture of Dorian Gray* and the short story, *The Happy Prince*.

In *A Wing and a Prayer*, Clara's *DWM* comic debut, she meets Amy Johnson and lies by telling her that she's a teacher; by the time she sees Johnson again in *The Blood of Azrael*, she's fulfilled that dream. While *A Wing and a Prayer* seems set early on in their travels, the subsequent strip, *Welcome to Tickle Town*, appears to take place after *Nightmare in Silver*, given Clara's reservations about amusement parks. Then, in the following *John Smith and the Common Men*, Clara is said to have lived 'so many lives, on so many worlds.'

John Smith and the Common Men is notable, as the fiftieth anniversary celebration comic, for featuring numerous allusions to the past and including false reality versions of Harry Sullivan, Jamie McCrimmon, the Brigadier, and Ace. These happen in the hellscape, a dream created by a mind parasite, which fashions the Doctor into 'Smith' and Clara into a fired nanny, similar to her Victorian splinter.

The Heist, from *Twelve Angels Weeping*, reveals Handles' backstory: he's one of twelve Cybermen modified by Dorium Maldovar to patrol his Maldovarium. The Cybermen are beheaded by the appropriately named Kiz the Head-Taker, who, with two accomplices, attempts to steal from Dorium and props a door open with Handles to aid their escape. When he's moved, the thieves are trapped. Dorium then gives Handles his name.

Handles appears in the short stories collected in the 2014 anthology, *Tales of Trenzalore: The Eleventh Doctor's Last Stand*, in which the Cyber-head is tasked with looking after Christmas' clock tower then hears of the Doctor's adventures fighting off the Ice Warriors, Krynoids, Autons, and the Mara.

Finally, the Twelfth Doctor confirms Handles' status in *The Mondas Touch* (from the 2017 book, *Myths & Legends*) when he notes that he was a 'great companion.'

Not to be outdone by his past selves and their predilection for strange comic companions, the Eleventh Doctor travels for a time with a robotic Tyrannosaurus Rex called Kevin in the pages of IDW's *Doctor Who* comic, first appearing in *When Worlds Collide*. He accompanies Amy and Rory on a couple of adventures, but his appearance makes things a little difficult! On the other hand, when his usually polite manner falls away, he's able to scare any antagonists with a few roars, leading Amy to jokingly comment, 'You know, I kinda miss the "running away lots" part.' He further laments that he can't reach any of the TARDIS controls due to his short arms. After the Doctor makes him an exoskeleton, Kevin leaves to become the security chief of a space station in *Space Squid*. The Doctor is also joined by another shapeshifter (following on from Kamelion and Frobisher) by the name of Decky Flamboon in *Doctor Who Adventures* – another result of a create-a-companion competition, this time by Mitchell Collett. Decky's natural form is a lizard as seen in his first appearance in *Meteorite Meeting* (2012). He's trying to get home to Sirus but can't find his way; when they eventually get there in *The Tail of Decky Flamboon* the following year, they repel an invasion and find Decky's people spread across the planet's three moons.

The Doctor's companions from Titan Comics' *Eleventh Doctor* title are a similarly kooky bunch, though the first, Alice Obiefune, doesn't seem so. In fact, she seems very normal, but finds perhaps an unusual level of joy in seeing a Kharitite (a colourful creature that becomes attracted to Alice due to her grief) wandering down the street in 2014's *After Life*. And that's exactly why Alice is so taken in with the Doctor's world initially: she's suffering through a severe bout of depression brought on by the death of her mother, Ada. Her father, Ijezie Uwaebuka Obiefune, died when she was little, meaning Ada brought Alice up, though the engraving on her dad's tombstone – 'The world is complex, do not lose hope' – sums up their family well. Nonetheless, Alice has a lot to cope with, as she's laid off from her job as a library assistant and evicted from her flat, and she finds Citizen's Advice lacking: though she knows she should sort all these responsibilities, she can't help but take up the Doctor's offer to travel with him. (She clearly still loves her job, as she later, in *First Rule*, dreams of being a librarian and shelving books by Enid Blyton, Roald Dahl, CS Lewis, Spike Milligan, and JK Rowling.)

He wants to show her the untouched beauty of Rokhandi, but arrives too late, and they're instead greeted by an unwelcome theme park created by SERVEYOUinc in *The Friendly Place*. This story introduces the Entity, a giant telepathic being that's abused and tortured by SERVEYOUinc. In *Whodunnit?* and *The Sound of Our Voices*, we then meet Entity's mind, Autonomous Reasoning Center, ARC for short, which initially tries reaching out to SERVEYOUinc personnel but accidentally puts them into comas before learning how to speak. The Doctor recognises ARC's attempts to make contact and his helping to wake up the comatose crew, so invites him onto the TARDIS.

In 1962 (*What He Wants...*), they also encounter a twenty-something musician called John Jones. It's Alice's idea to see him, as Jones was one of her mum's favourite artists, notably an album called *Abanazar's Madness*; it turns out, however, that he's rubbish – indeed, when he joins them on the TARDIS and wants their honest opinions, he has to then ask for them to be a little less brutal. Jones and ARC get on particularly well, the former seeing ARC's shifting form as meaning he might be able to play guitar.

Things get grimmer for the companions as, when Alice returns to her own time to sort out issues with her solicitors, she's soon met with the Talent Scout, an employee of SERVEYOUinc who terrifies ARC and who feeds on Alice's grief when taking the form of her mother (*The Eternal Dogfight*). Jones, too, is suffering, his nerves making him eat an unhealthy amount. ARC's fear soon turns him violent, meaning he uses his body (which the Doctor describes as like a 'big glob of stuff') to expand and consume people and things. He then curls up into a ball until the Talent Scout has gone. Alice doesn't immediately recognise that this Ada isn't really her mum; she finally sees through the Talent Scout's deception in *The Infinite Astronaut*, as Alice recalls her mother, in June 1982, telling her that, no matter how much it hurts, you have to speak up when something is wrong. To stop SERVEYOUinc, the Doctor purchases fifty-one per cent shares in the company and becomes its chief executive in *The Rise and Fall*, but this role corrupts him, egged on by the Talent Scout's promise to bring back the Time Lords in *The Other Doctor*. His companions are able to get him back from the brink. In an effort to get him back on side, Alice even dresses like the Doctor, and later tells him that she's come to terms with her mother's passing. The Doctor now plans to bring ARC and the Entity together again, but his first attempt sees ARC merge with the TARDIS and the foursome being manipulated by the Talent Scout (*Four Dimensions*). As Jones is offered his chance at stardom, we learn that his stage name is Xavi Moonburst, with allusions to David Bowie as Ziggy Stardust constantly being highlighted. Jones' species is never entirely explained, though the Doctor offers that he's a 'human chameleon,' capable of mirroring emotions and changing his persona to accommodate. In the end, ARC manages to fight back against the Talent Scout, with Alice's help.

Jones merges with the Entity in *The Comfort of the Good* – as does ARC, all becoming one being, saving Jones from what he thinks is his own death. Instead, ARC encourages him to write more, and Alice, who continues to travel with the Doctor after Jones and ARC have left, tells him he can become the prog rock legend he's always dreamt of being. 'I forgive you for being a right mardy cow occasionally,' Jones says to Alice, summing up their playful relationship. 'And for taking ages in the bathroom.'

The Doctor then gets two new companions, the Squire and Abslom Daak – the 'Dalek Killer' who debuted in backup strips of *Doctor Who Weekly* in 1980 – and are chased by *The Then and the Now*, a Time Lord legend actually created by the War Doctor during the Time War. The Squire is eager to reminisce about her time with the Doctor, a period he'd rather forget. Nonetheless, the Squire travels with the Eleventh Doctor for a short while, and acts as the War Doctor's companion. Alice becomes a bit fed up with her 'best friends forever' attitude towards the Doctor. Still, the Squire clearly suffered during the war, having nightmares of seeing a Kaled mutant outside its Dalek casing. In *Pull to Open*, she shows her history with the TARDIS, calling it a loyal and valorous friend; Alice, however, who's had various troubles with the ship in the past, retorts that it's more like a 'time-caravan.' Alice later sees the Time War herself, battling alongside the War Doctor as his temporary companion.

Abslom Daak, meanwhile, is only there to get the Doctor: after being forced to abandon his raison d'être as he couldn't find any more Daleks to kill, he takes on a job to bring the Doctor to a court tribunal. Instead, he's forced to help the Time Lord, and becomes uneasy bedfellows with him. River Song doesn't exactly approve, telling the Doctor that they're going to have to have a long chat about his 'TARDIS-entry vetting' in *Physician, Heal Thyself* when she sees Daak. When the Squire is eventually revealed to be planted there by the Volatix Cabal, a Dalek society of mutants, she has to subdue an angry Daak by shooting him twice. She still saves the lives of her friends many times before the revelation, fighting against the Daleks; rescuing the Doctor, the Master, and Alice from the Time Lord prison, Shada; and even aiding River Song's escape from Stormcage (in stories like *The Then and the Now*, *The Judas Goatee*, and *The One*).

Despite battling against her origins, the Squire caves into her Dalek conditioning in *Gently Pulls the Strings* and River is forced to kill her. Daak ends up in the Time War, content to kill as many Daleks as possible in the ultimate conflict against them.

Titan Comics' 2017 run opens with *Remembrance*, which sees the Doctor and Alice track down John Jones' last album. Playing a song called *Whitestar* reveals secret space-time coordinates Jones left for them – taking them to his funeral, which understandably upsets Alice. She quickly comes to realise that the Doctor's seeming lack of mourning is solely because, as a seasoned time traveller, he experiences death differently. They then encounter *The Scream*, a member of the Silents in a white suit forgotten by even its own species. The Scream desperately wants to be remembered, so creates its own 'Sapling,' formed from the memories of the Doctor and Alice. However, this Sapling has his own sentience and wants to learn from his 'progenitors.' First, Alice saves him from the Scream, then the Doctor refuses to kill him, despite the Sapling begging the Doctor to do so, and thus prevent him fulfilling his genocidal destiny. As the Sapling joins them and marvels at the TARDIS' transcendentalism, the Doctor explains that it 'starts to feel a lot smaller as it fills up with passengers' (*The Tragical History Tour*).

Their journeys take them to a planet to see an old friend of the Ninth Doctor's called Plex (*The Promise*); the Ood-Sphere

(*Time of the Ood*), where they play chess with Ood Sigma; and a Memory Ark in the Antrozenus Zone, normally a quiet place that the Doctor takes them to so they can discuss the Sapling attempting to sacrifice himself for the greater good, something the Sapling argues is akin to the Doctor trying something similar at the end of the Time War (*The Memory Feast*). Alice later recalls 'spending six months playing mum with the Sapling.'

With Titan Comics focusing solely on its Thirteenth Doctor output from 2018, *The Eleventh Doctor* ends with *Hungry Thirsty Roots*, in which the Sapling has to hold the dying TARDIS together as Alice discovers the Scream has been following them. The Doctor discovers the Sapling is mnemomimetic, meaning he can turn their memories into fruit, eventually creating 'The Doctor's World', made up of his memories. Across three series of adventures, Alice leaves a lot of happy memories for the Doctor and comic readers, her character perhaps summed up best when she tells the Doctor, 'Life is finite. Mum. Me. Even you. So let's have some fun while we can.'

Several books see the Eleventh Doctor travelling alone, though in some, he gets temporary companions. In 2012's *Dark Horizons*, he meets Princess Freydis of Trondheim, Norway, and her Viking protector, Henrik. The Doctor rescues Freydis (who thinks he's the mischievous Norse god, Loki) from a burning ship that is carrying her to her marriage to twelfth-century Icelandic king, Gissar Polvaderson, and they find themselves in the Scottish village of Lowith. Henrik is one of the Viking settlers there, and he proves particularly adventurous and heroic, saving fellow Nordic passengers on another passing ship before it, too, can burn to ash, then, when Freydis is taken by more Vikings, travelling in the TARDIS to save her. Freydis marvels at the TARDIS, pondering whether she has reached Valhalla. Henrik also dons the spacesuit that first appeared in *The Impossible Planet / The Satan Pit* to save the Doctor from drowning. After advising all the villagers and rescued crew on how to get home, the Doctor offers for Freydis and Henrik to travel with him, but they turn him down.

In *The Dalek Generation* (2013), the Doctor is aided by Sabel, Jenibeth, and Ollus Blakely, siblings whose parents killed themselves to stop important information about the Cradle of the Gods, a powerful monument that the Daleks intended to use to make 'a billion Skaros.' Jenibeth, however, is abducted by the Daleks, converted into their puppet using nanogenes, and is held captive for some ninety years. Nonetheless, Jenibeth resists the Daleks and helps hold them off when the Doctor sets the Cradle to self-destruct. Though Jenibeth dies, it's only temporary, as the Doctor also uses the Cradle to revert Sabel, Jenibeth, and Ollus back into children, and revive their parents. They're left with no memory of the Doctor, who's content to saunter off. The Doctor is similarly helped to defeat the titular threat in the 2013 book, *Plague of the Cybermen*, in which Olga Bordmann, a nineteenth-century schoolteacher in the village of Klimtenburg, uses lightning to battle a Cyber-fleet in a local castle. Coming so close to death obviously makes things clearer for Olga, as when the Doctor goes to leave in the TARDIS, he sees that she's now holding hands with her long-time friend, Klaus, and the pair seemingly live long, happy lives together.

Another Expanded Universe companion, Valarie Dee Lockwood, played on audio by Safiyya Ingar, has her time on board the TARDIS linked to the Daleks and Cybermen. *The Inheritance*, from 2022's *Geronimo!* boxset, opens with Cyberneticist, Valarie, working on her mother's leg on Research Rig 6 in the fifty-fourth century. Valarie and Patricia 'Pat' Lockwood live together at 49 Gibson Avenue on the rig, and meet the Doctor there as he wants to use her plasma cutter to disable a bomb. Both Valarie and Pat have neural interfaces and universal translators, and have had several limbs replaced by cybernetic parts, as have many of their peers. They're infected by the Darinthian Blight, which also takes the lives of Valarie's friends, Daniel and Simone Simpson, and though the Doctor saves Valarie, Pat passes away. The Doctor leaves a note for the hospitalised Valarie saying he'll be back in ten minutes; instead, he returns two weeks later – in which time Valarie has organised her mother's estate as well as her funeral – and invites her to travel with him and find Clara Oswald.

Despite her recent life being mired in tragedy, Valarie is a joyful assistant for a time, enthusing about how much her mum would've enjoyed the carnival when her first trip in the TARDIS takes them to Venice in the late eighteenth century (*The House of Masks*). Valarie hasn't even heard of Venice and rarely attends parties, so this is a particularly happy occasion for her. She quickly develops a warm bond with the Doctor: when he tells her about his wiping out the Daleks and Time Lords in the Time War (or believing that he did, anyway), he offers to take her home, should she feel uncomfortable with him. Valarie tells him he's not the monster he thinks he is and offers to be a friendly ear if he ever needs to chat about his past. However, they soon come to blows, firstly about the web of time (*The Galois Group* in 2023's *Short Trips: Volume 12*) then about the Doctor manipulating her in *Curiosity Shop*; in the latter, she's left scared and alone, being forced to sell her parts for money and food, unbeknown to her to the Doctor in a plot to stop a greater war. She gets them all back, but questions whether she even knows the Doctor, especially when she discovers a statue of the Eighth Doctor in *Broken Hearts*. She decides to carry on travelling with him, but she's determined that he won't hurt her again.

After a trip to Lapland in the 1890s (*Spirit of the Season*), during which they find a malicious Clara splinter and a manifestation of Patricia, conjured by Valarie's memories, Valarie vows to her mother that she won't put off her relationship with Roanna, last of the Medrüthians, who they met in *The Yearn*, part of *All of Time and Space* (2023). The Doctor has previously tried to bring them together by suggesting to Valerie that she could invite Roanna along. Valarie said she didn't know enough about her, but from *Spirit of the Season*, we can infer that she was just too nervous. Nonetheless, Valarie gave Roanna the TARDIS phone number, and they parted with a kiss.

Their first date is to Chicago's World's Fair in 1893 (*All's Fair*, from *Everywhere and Anywhere*), but it's wrecked by the appearance of Hayden, Valarie's future husband, while an older Valarie is on life support and dies in the course of the episode. Valarie and Roanna hold onto their relationship and agree to carry on dating, despite finding out that it's actually Roanna who is destined to put Valarie on life support, albeit not on purpose: an infected Roanna drains her cybernetic components, leaving her too weak. This glimpse of her mortality makes her fall back on the hope of an afterlife, and in *Sins of the Flesh*, the Doctor voices his concerns about losing her, given that he's recently parted from Amy and Rory. She's then confronted with Rebirth Organisation, a conversion therapy group that sees victims encased in 'redemption suits' that 'cure' them of their sexuality – by changing them into Cybermen. Valarie is rightly horrified, and her anger gets the better of her as she rips the head off a Cyberman using her enhanced strength granted by her own cybernetic upgrades; she reveals that she studied the Cybermen in university, and uses her components, which the Cybermen adapt for themselves, to stop them.

In *Didn't You Kill My Mother?*, Valarie and the Doctor go head-to-head with an artificial intelligence called Arabella Hendricks, who had been responsible for infecting the rig with Darinthian Blight, thus killing Valarie's mother, and for murdering the older Valarie who'd been on life support. Valarie nonetheless spares Hendricks, not wanting to let her mum down. *Daleks Victorious* then takes them to Medrüth, where the Daleks are attacking, but the New Paradigm exterminates Hayden and destroys the planet. Roanna escapes, and she and Valarie get engaged in *The Last Stand of Miss Valarie Lockwood*, but Roanna is also killed by the Daleks. (The story also reveals that Valarie was born on 6th October 5324.) Determined to get her happy ending, Valarie changes time, so she can save Roanna and defeat the Daleks in *Victory of the Doctor*, which rounds off the 2024 boxset of the same name. The Doctor is best man at Valarie and Roanna's wedding, telling them that he'll miss them but that he's now going to take some time away from the hassles of the universe and quietly contemplate how he can find Clara. This nicely segues into *The Bells of St John*.

In keeping with the Eleventh Doctor's imaginative mind, he has an imaginary companion named Bob. This non-companion doesn't appear in *Houdini and The Space Cuckoos*, a 2012 short story published on the BBC website. The Doctor chats to Bob, which we're told is short for Robert or Roberta, as a way of talking his way through a problem. This shows that the Doctor is better when he's not alone, that is, having someone to explain things to and help him find his way out of situations – like being trapped in a glass box filling with water, as happens in the tale.

And speaking of the Doctor blurring fictional lines, no mention of the Eleventh Doctor's Expanded Universe companions is complete without acknowledging his very special companions – the entire crew of USS Enterprise NCC-1701-D, including Captain Jean-Luc Picard, Commander William Riker, Lieutenant Commander Data, Counsellor Deanna Troi, Lieutenant Commander Geordi LaForge, Lieutenant Worf, Doctor Beverly Crusher, and Guinan. They all appear to help the Doctor, Amy, and Rory combat a combined army of Cybermen and Borg in the pages of IDW's *Doctor Who/Star Trek: The Next Generation* crossover extravaganza, which boldly goes where no comic has gone before.

As he first appeared in *The Name of the Doctor*, it's pertinent to note that the War Doctor has Expanded Universe companions too. First comes Cinder in the 2014 novel, *Engines of War*, whose family are killed in the Dalek invasion of her home planet, Moldox, when she is seven. This leads her to a life as a Dalek hunter as part of the resistance, though she's just as critical of the Time Lords, initially being prepared to kill the Doctor when he crash-lands on Moldox. Instead, she decides life there isn't worth living, so escapes it in the TARDIS, and the two uncover the Daleks' plot to make a temporal cannon capable of wiping out Gallifrey. Her judgment of the Time Lords is justified as they take her captive and torture her with the mind probe to verify her and the Doctor's story. Though the Doctor rescues her, they further learn that the Time Lords intend to wipe out Moldox. They manage to stop them, and vow to travel together when they've dealt with the Time War; however, Cinder sacrifices herself by taking a shot meant for the Doctor and she dies in his arms. He spends some three days searching for the remains of her family, then buries them all together. It's all too much for him and he says, 'No more.' It's implied Cinder's death leads the Doctor back to Gallifrey to use the Moment in *The Day of the Doctor*.

In *The Innocent*, part of 2015's Big Finish boxset, *Only the Monstrous*, Cardinal Ollistra (played by *Blake's 7's* Jacqueline Pearce) works with the War Doctor at some point after trying to tempt the Eighth Doctor into the Time War. A high-ranking, heartless politician, Ollistra has mixed feelings about the Doctor, calling him an embarrassment to his species one minute and the next telling soldiers that, 'The Doctor is worth a hundred of you *people*.' When she hears the Doctor might've been killed, she attends his funeral largely as she doesn't quite believe it – a belief that is, of course, correct – but nevertheless admits that the universe feels more dangerous with him gone. Ollistra and the Doctor have an interesting partnership, far removed from a typical Doctor-companion relationship (not least because they don't travel together consistently); in *A Thing of Guile*, from 2016's *Infernal Devices*, the Doctor is even Ollistra's prisoner, despite him having just saved Gallifrey. In this story, Captain Solex of the Time Lord's Chancellery Guard, and Jared, Co-ordinator of the Celestial Intervention Agency, briefly travel with them, though both are killed, the former while defending the Doctor. It's a fate similarly shared by Ollistra: in *Splinters* (from 2022's *Tenth Doctor, Classic Companions*), Fourth Doctor companion, Leela says she's one of the Time Lords who has now 'gone,' presumably lost to the Time War.

Another friend of the War Doctor likely died in the Time War, though Ollistra casts doubt on her fate: the Doctor met Rejoice, played by Lucy Briggs-Owen, in *The Innocents* as she nurses him back to health over about a hundred days following his detonating the Daleks' Time Destructor. Rejoice's devotion is enough for him to stick around to stop an invasion by the Taalyen, but even though she travels briefly in the TARDIS, he refuses to take her on as a companion for any significant length of time. *The Heart of the Battle* reveals that Rejoice went on to become leader of her planet's Keskan Collective, and tried to negotiate her people's surrender to the Taalyens (who have teamed up with the Daleks), only to be seemingly killed. Ollistra isn't sure whether she did die here, but her people remember her as a symbol of hope.

As far as we know, Time Lord commander, Veklin (Beth Chalmers), also introduced in *The Innocents* doesn't die in the Time War, and acts as another on-off companion to the War Doctor who she frequently butts heads with – understandable as she's so loyal to Cardinal Ollistra. In return, Ollistra gives her many high-profile tasks, including keeping an eye on Eighth Doctor companions, Liv Chenka and Helen Sinclair (*Songs of Love* and *The Side of the Angels*); transporting Leela to the War Rooms on Gallifrey (*The Last Days of Freme*); and picking up the Doctor's granddaughter, Susan, and First Doctor companion, Ian Chesterton, so they can negotiate an alliance with the Sensorites (*Sphere of Influence*). Veklin works alongside the Doctor numerous times, notably as part of a bigger taskforce in *The War Doctor Begins 2* (2021), and trying to rescue Davros and ascertain his true motives when he sends the Doctor (retro-regenerated into his seventh incarnation) a message asking for help in *Once and Future: A Genius for War* (2023).

In an aborted dimension, the Doctor gets a rather unusual companion: the Master. The War Master retro-regenerates into a young Asian boy, seen in *Fast Asleep* (2016), who ditches the name Master in an alliance with the Doctor, Alice, and the Squire (*The Organ Grinder*). They fight the Daleks, as well as the Cyclors, who have formed an alliance with the Daleks. It's notable that a robotic

Master travelled with a parallel Ninth Doctor, played by Richard E Grant in webcast, *Scream of the Shalka*; though it languished in continuity hell for a few decades, this version of the Doctor, and by extension the Master, was given some credibility as a hologram of him was seen in the Fifteenth Doctor TV episode, *Rogue*.

Finally, the War Doctor is accompanied by former Eighth Doctor companion, Fey Truscott-Sade, in *DWM*'s 2018 comic, *The Clockwise War*, actively taking her on as a companion again. Recruited to the British Intelligence forces in 1933, Fey is serving during the Second World War when the Doctor picks her up, leaving her human peers to think she died in 1944. Instead, she fights alongside the Doctor and the Sisterhood of Karn, with the Daleks calling her 'Haruk Za,' which translates to 'The Death of Light.' Though Fey is seemingly killed, she instead finds herself in the college dormitory of her future nephew, Alexander Truscott, via the Dreamspace. Alexander turns her against the Time Lords as she recovers and temporarily expunges Shayde from Fey's mind. Fortunately, the Doctor is able to find Fey again, entering her Dreamspace using her favourite childhood book, *Peter Pan*, and Shayde sacrifices his life, and their shared memories of their bonding, to save Fey – who the Twelfth Doctor leaves in a hospital in London. When his companion, Bill Potts, asks why he doesn't say bye to Fey, he replies, 'I never say goodbye... Not to the people I want to see again.'

The Twelfth Doctor
Peter Capaldi

'*Between here and my office, before the kettle boils, is everything that ever happened or ever will. Make your choice.*'
– The Doctor, *Smile.*

Clara Oswald – Jenna Coleman – Continued... (*Asylum of the Daleks* and *The Snowmen, The Bells of St John* to *Hell Bent*, plus *Twice Upon a Time*)

Despite Clara having had a great deal of experience with regeneration (not only conversing with the War Doctor and Tenth Doctor in *The Day of the Doctor,* but also seeing all his incarnations when being split apart by his time stream in *The Name of the Doctor*), she struggles, arguably more than most, with the Doctor changing his face this time around. She's immediately on the back foot when confronted with the Twelfth Doctor at the end of *The Time of the Doctor*, still dealing with a great deal of grief from her brief time on Trenzalore, and perhaps even more unnerved by the Eleventh Doctor's assertion that he won't forget a single second of his time, swiftly being undone by the Twelfth Doctor's post-regenerative haze clouding his memory so much so that he can't remember how to fly the TARDIS!

When they arrive – via the late Cretaceous period, accidentally bringing a tyrannosaurus with them – it's on the banks of the Thames in the 1890s. The Doctor (and/or the TARDIS) seem to know Clara will need help, so they take her to the Paternoster Row gang (Madame Vastra, Jenny Flint, and Strax), whom she met in *The Crimson Horror*. They welcome her, give her some contemporary clothes, and let her stay for a few nights. She's still ostensibly concerned about the Doctor, telling him he has to lie down as he keeps passing out. When he's unconscious, however, Clara's concerns bubble over and she asks Jenny how they can 'fix' him, meaning change him back. She's worried the Doctor isn't someone she likes anymore. Still, she's the one who realises the Doctor's sleep-talking is actually him translating the dinosaur's roars of anguish.

Clara tells Vastra that the TARDIS had gone haywire and the Doctor was 'gone'; she's then cynical about the Silurian calling his regeneration a 'renewal,' arguing that he looks older, not renewed. She appears embarrassed by Vastra's assertion that Clara flirted with the Doctor (and vice versa), and then rails against her asking Clara whether she's judging the Time Lord for trusting her with an older appearance. 'How dare you?' Clara says, before revealing that her only pin-up poster on her bedroom wall when she was fifteen was of Roman emperor and philosopher, Marcus Aurelius (who she quotes in her lecture in *The Day of the Doctor*). 'I'm not sure who you think you're talking to right now, Madame Vastra, but I have never had the slightest interest in pretty young men,' Clara tells her. 'And for the record, if there ever was anybody who could flirt with a mountain range, she's probably standing in front of you right now. Just because my pretty face has turned your head, do not assume that I am so easily distracted.' This implies that Clara has a good level of self-awareness, though it's not entirely accurate: she sees herself as being romantically interested in the Eleventh Doctor not because he looks youthful but because he's an extraordinary person; from her reaction to the Twelfth Doctor, however, that comes across as a half-truth. She does at least know she's an outrageous flirt though!

When the Doctor disappears to investigate disappearances across London and a mysterious Half-Face Man, Clara is determined to find him again, panicking slightly when Strax implies she's been abandoned there. Strax reads her subconscious and finds 'deflected narcissism, traces of passive-aggressive, and a lot of muscular young men doing sport.' At this point, she's twenty-seven years old, with an 'enviable spleen,' though he warns her of fluid retention at a later age.

Clara's sharp enough to unravel clues that she thinks the Doctor has left her in a newspaper, and so tracks him down to Mancini's restaurant. The pair are clearly glad to see one another, though there's underlying resentment: Clara admits to being extremely cross with him, partly for running away and partly for his leaving such a cryptic trail for her to find. However, it quickly becomes obvious that he didn't leave the ad in the newspaper, but thought she did. Each is happy to oblige the other. Nonetheless, when the Doctor implies Clara's an 'egomaniac, needy, game-player,' she initially thinks he's talking about himself. She still places great trust in the Doctor, and against considerable odds, they find themselves in the larder, ready to be harvested by cyborgs led by the Half-Face Man, and the Doctor seemingly leaves her: he escapes while she's locked in – that is, despite him having the sonic screwdriver which could easily have got her out of the predicament. 'There's no point in them catching us both,' he says, hightailing it. Fortunately, it's all part of the Doctor's ad-hoc plan, with the Time Lord disguising himself as a cyborg and rescuing her. When the Half-Face Man asks where the Doctor is, Clara realises something vital: 'Where he will always be. If the Doctor is still the Doctor, he will have my back.'

This seems to be undermined by the Doctor disappearing again after taking down the Half-Face Man and his peers. She returns to Paternoster Row, presuming she's stuck in Victorian London. Vastra knows differently, albeit only because Clara really knows the Doctor is coming back for her: she's changed back into her twenty-first century clothes. Sure enough, the TARDIS materialises and Clara runs on board.

Yet when the TARDIS arrives in twenty-first century Glasgow, she asks if she's home and the Doctor implies the TARDIS can be just that if she wants it to be. She apologises and says, 'I don't think I know who you are anymore.' Their conversation is cut short by her iPhone ringing: a call from the Eleventh Doctor, still on Trenzalore. 'I think you might be scared,' the Eleventh Doctor acknowledges. 'And however scared you are, Clara, the man you are with right now – the man I *hope* you are with – believe me, he is more scared than anything you can imagine right now and he needs you.' This is the Doctor knowing firstly that Clara won't deal very well with his regeneration (so we should infer that he thinks she'd struggle with his changing at all, no matter the next incarnation's appearance), and secondly, that he, in the future, would find the transition hard too and would need his trusty companion by his side.

The Eleventh Doctor says a proper goodbye to Clara, but she doesn't do the same: instead, she turns to the Twelfth Doctor, who she thinks has been listening in. He argues that he doesn't have to, implying Clara still doesn't see him as the same man; after he implores her to 'just see me,' she takes a closer look, thanks him for phoning, and hugs him, finally having come to terms with his regeneration. He doesn't exactly hug back, but they go off for coffee.

Into the Dalek implies the Doctor went to get their drinks but vanished before he could return for her, already a recurring theme in their partnership. Seeing as she left her family on Christmas Day to go to Trenzalore (*The Time of the Doctor*) then reappears in Scotland seemingly at a later date (it's certainly not 25th December in the end scene of *Deep Breath*), it's unexplained how and when she gets back home properly and what happened to her dad, nan, and Linda in the interim. When the Doctor arrives at Coal Hill School to pick Clara back up three weeks after he left, she greets him with a simple 'Where the hell have you been?' She's nevertheless taken in by his asking her whether he's a good man and they travel to the Aristotle, a ship fighting a war against the Daleks but which also contains a 'good' Dalek. After investigating, they find this Dalek is faulty, so Clara scorns the Doctor because she sees his mood as self-congratulatory: 'I mean, there's a little bit of you that's pleased. The Daleks are evil after all. Everything makes sense. The Doctor is right.' Instead, she shows him that the real lesson is that a good Dalek *is* possible.

(She's so angry at the Doctor that she slaps him, something that she does quite regularly. She did so to the Eleventh Doctor in *Nightmare in Silver* – admittedly to snap him out of his being the Cyber-controlled 'Mr Clever' – then to the Twelfth Doctor first in *Into the Dalek*, in *Listen* – albeit on the back of his head – and finally in *Last Christmas*. In *Kill the Moon*, she also threatens to slap him so hard, he'd regenerate.)

After dealing with the Daleks, Clara concedes to the Doctor that she's not sure whether he's a good man or not: 'But I think you try to be and I think that's probably the point.' Yes, she's pretty accurate there, but it's quite a cutting remark, considering she's aware he's recently given up a thousand years or so of his life solely because he couldn't let the Daleks burn Trenzalore. She's witnessed him being a good man plenty of times, but perhaps she's only saying it so this new incarnation continues to prove himself. After all, her faith in him apparently spurred the Time Lords into granting him a new regenerative cycle at the end of *The Time of the Doctor*.

We're also introduced to Danny Pink, a maths teacher also working at Coal Hill who plays an important part in Clara's story. There's obviously an attraction between them, but Danny repeatedly messes up his opportunities – when Clara essentially invites him to a leaving-do for someone called Cathy, he turns her down but later realises he should've said, 'I wasn't going, but I am now, because you're going to be there, and suddenly it seems like the best idea ever' – even when Clara implores him to change his mind. It's Clara's insistence, following him to his classroom and watching him berate himself without his realising she's there, that results in them eventually going on a date together. (A woman named Journey Blue on the Aristotle seems to have a momentary crush on Clara as she calls Danny Pink a 'lucky fella' based on the smile the thought of him elicits.)

Unwittingly, Clara learns a lot more about Danny Pink during the date, one which the Doctor interrupts, unseen by Danny, and accidentally piloting the TARDIS to a children's home in Gloucester in the 1990s, where he grew up (*Listen*). Danny was born Rupert Pink, but didn't like his forename so changed it when he got older; Clara is sad to learn that it's partly the Doctor's fault after he puts him to sleep with dreams of being 'Dan the Soldier Man' following a scary incident at the home. Before this, Clara leaves a warm impression on Rupert, comforting him about the monster under his bed. Considering she's a complete stranger, the young boy must've instantly trusted her, given that he must've invited her in off-screen. Clara asks the Doctor to take her back to her date with Danny, after her earlier self walked out on him. She joins Danny again in the restaurant and apologises to him, asking that they start the date over. So how does Clara view herself? Sometimes literally: watching herself go, she seems particularly enamoured with her appearance, then tells Danny, 'I'm a bit tricky, sometimes a bit up myself, and I do not like my surname... Also, I mouth off when I'm nervous and I've got a mouth on me.'

When Clara messes up and reveals she knows he was born Rupert Pink, it's Danny's turn to walk out. The TARDIS is waiting for Clara anyway, though inside, she finds the Doctor and a guest: Colonel Orson Pink, a time traveller from the twenty-second century who also happens to look exactly like an older Danny. As Clara has left a psychic trace of herself in the TARDIS' telepathic circuits, the Doctor posits that Orson is related to Clara. Though he comes from around a century in her future, the Doctor instead finds him in an experimental capsule in the *distant* future – on the very last planet in the almost-dead universe. Orson is nonetheless terrified of something he thinks is waiting for him outside, but Clara shuts him inside the TARDIS, promising that nothing can get through its doors. She's obviously freaked out and intimidated by this man, who resembles the maths teacher she's just been on a date with. He is somehow connected to Orson and gives her a family heirloom, a toy soldier without a gun which she set up in Rupert Pink's bedroom to patrol the space under his bed. 'Supposed to bring good luck,' he says. 'What were the chances of you two finding me?'

Under the impression that the capsule may be under attack, the Doctor angrily tells Clara to get back into the TARDIS too, threatening that if she doesn't do as she's instructed, she'll never travel with him again. She reluctantly joins Orson in the TARDIS, but only after telling the Doctor he's an idiot. Though they don't find out what exactly happened outside, Orson helps bring an unconscious Doctor into the TARDIS and a panicking Clara sets the ship into motion.

Clara then proves vital in the Doctor's story: the TARDIS dematerialises and she ends up in a barn on, it's later revealed, Gallifrey; probably the same barn she visited previously with the Eleventh, Tenth, and War Doctors in *The Day of the Doctor*. There, she finds a little boy who's scared of the dark – a boy who, it at least appears, is actually the Doctor in his youth. Hiding under his bed, Clara imparts some wisdom she paradoxically learnt while travelling with the older Doctor: 'You're always going to be afraid, even if you learn to hide it. Fear is like a companion. A constant companion, always there. But that's okay, because fear can bring us together. Fear can bring you home. I'm going to leave you something, just so you'll always remember, fear makes companions of us all.' (She's echoing what the First Doctor tells Barbara Wright in *The Cave of Skulls*, episode three of *An Unearthly Child*.)

She leaves the young Doctor with the toy soldier, 'so brave, he doesn't need a gun.'

At the episode's conclusion, she visits Danny's flat and the pair make up and make out. We never find out how she knows where Danny lives exactly – nor the true heritage of Orson Pink (who they drop off back home), especially given what later happens to Danny.

Their next dates go much better than their first, even if Clara's life with the Doctor seems to divide her (*The Caretaker*). She and

Danny go to the pub after school, and one morning, he turns up at her flat as they've agreed to go running. He begins to notice some strange things – including that she's suddenly very tanned after a visit to a desert planet and that, following a trip to see the Fish People (from *The Underwater Menace*), she's wet and has seaweed on her shoulder – but she tries to hold her conflicting days together. While she once relents that she can't keep doing it all, she then determinedly tells herself she's 'got it all under control.' That all goes wrong when the Doctor goes undercover at Coal Hill School to stop the threat of the robotic Skovox Blitzer, and meets Danny. The Doctor can't seem to compute that Danny, a former soldier, is now a maths teacher, instead thinking he teaches PE. Aware that she's dating someone at the school, the Doctor thinks it's Adrian, a fellow English tutor who bears a passing resemblance to the Eleventh Doctor. Still, the Doctor doesn't want Clara involved in his plan to trap the Skovox Blitzer, knowing she'd object to his luring it to the school after hours. And indeed she does kick up a fuss, but eventually relents and tries to help him out. The Doctor's plan is undone by Danny, earning him more scorn from the Time Lord, and even further when he learns that Danny, not Adrian, is going out with Clara. Danny's horror at the Doctor's alienness is Clara's immediate concern, but she then has to deal with the Doctor's disapproval. The two most important men in her life are at odds, and though Danny eventually helps defeat the Skovox Blitzer, it's clear neither likes the other.

The Doctor and Clara still have fun together though. At her request, the Doctor takes her to Sherwood Forest, circa 1190, to meet one of her childhood heroes, Robin Hood, in *Robot of Sherwood*. The Doctor is adamant that Robin is merely fictitious, thinking the appearance of the famed archer and his Merry Men is some sort of trap; Clara, on the other hand, is overjoyed and echoes Robin's enthusiasm to see Maid Marian too. When a shocked Robin asks if she knows her, Clara happily replies, 'I have always known her.' She's less than pleased to meet the Sheriff of

Nottingham, though he's more than a little enamoured with her; she uses this to her advantage, tricking him into revealing his plans. Still, her disassembling is turned on its head when Robin interrogates her and learns the truth about the Doctor. After the Doctor says she shouldn't have told Robin anything about his past, the Earl of Loxley counters, 'Once the story started, she could hardly stop herself. You are her hero, I think.'

Danny remains a distraction, however. About to go on a date, Clara is first tempted in by a mysterious call received on the TARDIS telephone in *Time Heist*, and drawn into a plan to seemingly rob the Bank of Karabraxos, the most secure financial facility in its galaxy. Of course, it turns out to be a plan concocted by the Doctor and the bank's manager, Director Karabraxos, to save the alien psychic Tellers held hostage by the corporation. Still, their track team includes the augmented Psi, whose apparent death seems to affect Clara badly – partly because he sacrificed himself to save her life. She's relieved to find out neither he nor the mutant Saibra are actually dead.

The Doctor clearly sees his relationship with Danny Pink as a game of one-upmanship, as he initially tries to tempt Clara away from him by promising trips to the Satanic Nebula, the Lagoon of Lost Stars, and Brighton, then, at the end of the episode, secretly boasts, 'Robbing a bank. Robbing a whole bank. Beat *that* for a date.'

Nevertheless, her life is getting more complicated as she has to reconcile travelling in the TARDIS with her home life. Clara also has an interesting relationship with Courtney Woods, a trouble-making student who, on Clara's first day at Coal Hill, challenged her to expel the whole class due to their disruptive behaviour. It's Courtney's calling her bluff that teaches Clara never to start with the ultimate sanction – a lesson she used when facing the Half-Face Man. Courtney, though, is something of a bully, graffitiing 'Ozzie loves the Squaddie' around the school and even muttering it to Clara behind her back. Nonetheless, Clara's appalled to learn the Doctor's flippant attitude to her student has made Courtney give up trying. The Doctor apparently called her 'nothing,' making Courtney doubt her overall significance. In *Kill the Moon*, Clara tells the Doctor he must make it up to her... so he invites Courtney into the TARDIS for a trip to the moon in 2049. Things go badly for them all when the Doctor discovers the moon is actually an egg, one that's breaking apart while the creature inside hatches. Even worse, the Doctor leaves Clara and Courtney, as representatives of mankind, to make the decision whether to let it break free (the potential side-effect being it destroys Earth) or kill it before it can be born. Clara initially thinks rationally, factoring in that 'there would be no tides. But we'd survive that, right? They've knocked out the satellites; there's no internet, no mobiles – I'd be fine with that.' Still, she doesn't realise the practicalities of the situation, given she has little knowledge of Earth during this time period (the Doctor has already warned that 'the tides will be so high that they will drown whole cities'). Clara and Courtney are trying desperately to avert having to make the decision between killing a baby or potentially killing humanity. One life versus billions.

Clara is particularly horrified that the Doctor literally leaves them to it, disappearing with the TARDIS without giving any advice or imparting any knowledge of the future. So instead, Clara makes an appeal to Earth, broadcasting a signal to ask humankind to make a decision for them. It seems she believes in democracy, but when humanity votes to save themselves, leaving Clara to activate the bombs placed across the moon, her morality comes to the fore and she instead deactivates them. Though it all turns out for the best and the Doctor returns for them, dropping them back home, she's furious at the Doctor and tells him not to come back. In her anger, she wants him to be lonely.

(Despite how the Doctor's time with Courtney turns out, he still meddles in Clara's work life later on: in *The Woman Who Lived*, she chides him about his helping a Year Seven student called Evie Hubbard with an 'imaginary' interview with Winston Churchill. 'You basically cheated,' Clara says, but is largely unconcerned and rather pleased her pupil is awarded an A.)

At some point, the Doctor and Clara come to an understanding, so they venture to the Orient Express in space for their last trip together (*Mummy on the Orient Express*). Clara, still angry at him, is nonetheless trying to reel her emotions back in, and appears both shocked and gutted when the Doctor makes it clear that, if it really is their last trip, she won't see him again. 'You're going to come round for dinner or something, aren't you?' she asks. 'Do you do that?' Though the Doctor says he does, they both recognise the lie and toast their last hurrah. Clara reaffirms that she hated the Doctor for weeks after the events of *Kill the Moon*, and the Doctor implies she made that very obvious. She recalls going to a concert where the singer said, 'hatred is too strong an emotion to waste on someone that you don't like' (the singer in question possibly being the Michigan-born Sixto Rodriguez, so we could infer that Clara is a fan of blues, soul, and jazz).

Clara certainly takes to the Orient Express, sporting a vintage dress and hairstyle, and being taken in by their lavish surroundings. She calls Danny, now firmly her boyfriend, and asks, 'So, what are you saying? Just because he brought me somewhere cool, I shouldn't dump him?' Danny notes that Clara and the Doctor aren't going out, so she can't 'dump' him regardless. By the end of the adventure, she's rescinding her earlier remarks, lying to both the Doctor and Danny. She maintains that she's not travelling with the Doctor anymore, and tells the Time Lord that it was Danny's idea that she stop anyway; now, however, Danny's fine with her exploring time and space. The Doctor is eager to accept this lie.

Significantly, she ends her phone call to Danny by telling him she loves him – while she's actually looking at the Doctor.

Her time on the Orient Express gives Clara a new perspective, so she can fully appreciate the Doctor's point of view, and his alienness. 'Sometimes, the only choices you have are bad ones,' he tells her, 'but you still have to choose.' This lesson holds her in good stead in *Flatline*, in which the Doctor is locked inside a miniature TARDIS and Clara takes on the mantle of being the hero. She can't contain her laughter when she sees the tiny TARDIS with an even tinier Time Lord trapped within, and cheekily asks if his passing her the sonic screwdriver and slightly psychic paper means she's not him. If the Doctor is to be believed, Clara's not considered the implications of the TARDIS' transcendentalism as he tells her, 'It's always lighter. If the TARDIS were to land with its true weight, it would fracture the surface of the Earth.' She investigates a series of disappearances in Bristol, becoming friends with Rigsy, a local graffiti artist who's been ordered to do community service, painting over his own street art. She introduces herself as the Doctor, specifically Doctor Oswald, but when Rigsy asked what her doctorate's in, she quips, 'Well, I'm usually quite vague about that. I think I just picked the title because it makes me sound important.' Rigsy takes her to the flat where the most recent missing person lived, and the police get involved; thanks to the psychic paper, the police officer trusts Clara immediately, even when she retrieves a massive sledgehammer from her small bag (actually from inside the TARDIS). She nearly scares Rigsy off by mulling over the possibility of a shrink ray miniaturising people, but throws the youngster in at the deep end by doing something the Doctor is reluctant to do: showing him the TARDIS with the Doctor inside. It does the trick.

While battling creatures from a 2D universe, Clara gets a call from Danny (he calls her 'hon' and tells her he's managed to secure the bench they regularly meet at) and has to pretend everything is fine, maintaining her lie – though the Doctor, listening in, realises Danny doesn't know she's still travelling with him. The Doctor doesn't particularly scold her, instead congratulating her because lying is a vital survival skill. Indeed, when the beings, which the Doctor christens the Boneless, turn on the community service group, Clara has to save them, and does so by lying to them. 'Give them hope,' Clara encourages herself,

'Tell them they're all going to be fine.' She knows she can't save them all, and takes on the responsibilities the Doctor carries with him. She remains optimistic for a while, until it becomes apparent that the Boneless do wish them harm. Unable to contact the Doctor, it's Clara's wits that save them all, as she tricks the Boneless into pouring their dimensional energy into the TARDIS, restoring it and the Doctor so he can expel them. However, after Clara seeks the Doctor's approval, asking him to confirm she was a good Doctor, he counters that she was an exceptional Doctor but 'goodness had nothing to do with it.' Later, in *Death in Heaven*, she feels confident enough to declare herself the Doctor, pretending in order to delay the Cybermen from killing her. She goes into *a lot* of detail, saying, 'Where to start? I was born on the planet Gallifrey, in the constellation of Kasterborous. I'm a Time Lord, but my Prydonian privileges were revoked when I stole a time capsule and ran away. Currently pilot a Type 40 TARDIS. I've been married four times, all deceased. My children and grandchildren are missing, and I assume, dead. I have a non-Gallifreyan daughter created via genetic transfer.' This is a lot of detail, and she expounds on it even further by noting that 'she' doesn't even have a doctorate, except one from Glasgow University, though she accidentally graduated in the wrong century (as per *The Moonbase*). Some of this is common enough knowledge for companions generally, but knowing about the Doctor's qualification and Jenny from *The Doctor's Daughter* is a deep level of insight. The Doctor's shared a lot with her during their travels... or maybe she can still remember some of what she learned when in his timestream in *The Name of the Doctor*.

She takes on the role of a leader in *In the Forest of the Night* too, though this arguably comes even more naturally seeing as she's overseeing a school trip to the fictitious London Zoological Museum. Students under her and Danny's purview include the troublesome Bradley and Samson, inquisitive Ruby, and the vulnerable Maebh Arden, who's found her way to the Doctor in the TARDIS. Meanwhile, the world has been taken over by trees, so Clara and Danny have to navigate this green maze to get the kids back to their parents. Danny presumes Clara has called the school to keep them updated on the field trip; he's disappointed to learn she's actually been in touch with the Doctor, and she defensively says, 'I can't stop him calling me, can I?' The pupils are all aware of Clara and Danny's fondness for each other – Ruby especially, as she's the one who notices more than the other students and who seems to look up to Clara. Whenever she spots something strange, Ruby immediately turns to Clara and informs her about it. In return, Clara is receptive and interested, but Ruby's obviously been stung by a bit of feedback she previously gave that noted that Ruby's got no imagination. Ruby adores her though, and when Clara disappears with the Doctor, the young girl tells off Danny – her teacher! – by saying, 'You let her go off with some randomer into the forest. You're supposed to be madly in love with her.'

Yet the difference between Clara and Danny is striking here. He's more interested in looking after the children (which she concedes is 'actually very attractive') and argues, 'I don't want to see more things. I want to see the things in front of me more clearly. There are wonders here, Clara Oswald. Bradley saying "please"; that's a wonder. One person is more amazing, harder to understand, but more amazing than universes.' Meanwhile, Clara's excited to take up the Doctor's proposal to see the sun's coronal ejections and geomagnetic storms.

In fairness to Danny, he takes the news that she's still travelling with the Doctor very calmly. It doesn't seem to bother him much at all. He just wants to know the truth.

In *Dark Water*, Clara decides to do the right thing and open up to Danny, though she doesn't want to do so while he's in the same room. She calls him so she can tell him the truth about her travels; he says he's on his way to her flat, so presumably Danny intends to visit Clara but she wants to pre-empt him. She's noted down things she needs to talk about on Post-It notes on her bookshelves including: 'Impossible Girl' (Series 7); 'Robin Hood'

(*Robot of Sherwood*); 'Rupert Pink' and 'Dan, Dan the Soldier Man' (so she really does intend to come clean about the events of *Listen*); 'Miniature Clara' (*Into the Dalek*); 'Vastra' and 'Jenny' (*The Crimson Horror*, *The Name of the Doctor*, and *Deep Breath*); and 'Maisie' (*Mummy on the Orient Express*). The majority of the notes comment on people, so we might infer that it's the individuals Clara remembers more so than events. Notably, she's underlined 'Lying' and 'Truth'.

Interestingly, her shelves also include a photo of her father holding her as a baby (*The Rings of Akhaten*); a Hyperscape Body Swap Ticket the Eleventh Doctor hoped to use to get them into the Royal Albert Hall (*Doctor Who at the Proms* 2013); a statue of a parent frog and its offspring; another of an owl (which could be a cookie jar or wax melter for tea lights); a photograph of a horse and another of Danny in a deerstalker; an elaborately detailed hand-fan; a vase; an Encyclopaedia of World Facts; a 2012 Time Out guide; *Augustus John: The Biographie* by Michael Holroyd; a compact Atlas; *Drop Dead Gorgeous* by Anna Cheska (appropriately about a woman whose husband dies unexpectedly); *The Heart-Shaped Bullet* by Kathryn Flett; *The Pyramids and Sphinx*; *Notorious: The It Girl #2* by Cecily von Ziegesar (set at a boarding school); *Himalaya* by Michael Palin; and further books on the menopause, mysteries from across the world, Prague, and the poet, John Milton. Clearly, Clara has a diverse range of interests but most notable are art, history, and travel.

But even more interesting is a never-explained note that read 'Three months.' Is this the amount of time she's been lying to Danny about travelling in the TARDIS? Has she and Danny been dating for three months? Or was there a time she disappeared for that amount of time from her perspective, but which seems less from Danny's? Whatever she intends to tell Danny, she doesn't get to: she tells him she loves him then that she'll never say those words to anyone else again because 'those words, from me, are yours now.' The last thing Danny says to her is 'I love *you*. Clara—'

He's then run over by a car and is killed. She arrives at the scene of the incident just in time to see paramedics taking his body away.

Naturally, his passing hits her hard. It seems she's most affected by the fact his death was 'boring,' that he didn't go out with a grand exit. She seems almost impassive as her gran checks she's okay, relays her condolences, and implores her to cry. Clara, however, has a plan, and phones the Doctor, putting on a happy-go-lucky act. Instead, she tries to blackmail the Doctor into taking her back in time to undo Danny's death. In her view, the Doctor owes her that. Clara is incredibly duplicitous here, something we can only really put down to grief – she seemingly uses 'sleep patches' to knock the Doctor out and then systematically destroys the seven TARDIS keys until he'll agree to help her. With all the keys apparently gone, she breaks down in tears and tells him, 'I'd say I'm sorry but I'd do it again.' Not only does she think she's cut off their means of travel and forcibly expelled the Doctor from his home, but she's also stranded them on a volcanic planet. Her anguish is so great that she's effectively given up her life and betrayed her best friend. She also can't know that the Doctor can still open the TARDIS with a click of his fingers – but does know all his secret hiding places. (This flies in the face of her later assertion that 'he is the closest person to me in this whole world. He is the man I will always forgive, always trust. The one man I would never, ever lie to'; in fairness, this might be a lie to throw the Cybermen off guard.)

Fortunately, the Doctor has actually tricked her: he used one of the sleep patches on her, revealing that they actually induce a dream-like state, and is interested in seeing how far Clara will go for her lost love. When Clara's out of this dream, she misinterprets the Doctor's sentiment, fully accepting what she thinks is him kicking her out of the TARDIS. He does highlight that she betrayed him and let him down, but wants to help her nonetheless; as he tells her, 'Do you think I care for you so little that betraying me would make a difference?' The Doctor's then more practical, saying, 'I need sceptical, clever, critical... We're here to get your boyfriend back from the dead, so buck up and give me some attitude.'

Their investigation into the afterlife to look for Danny Pink's soul takes them to 3W at St Paul's Cathedral, where they meet Missy, the Master regenerated into female form, and many bodies being converted into Cybermen – including Danny. She gets in touch with Danny's consciousness via 3W's technology, but has to interrogate him to check his veracity. Danny can't remember the name of the restaurant they went to in *Listen*, but gets her birthday correct. (The Cybermen have information about Clara anyway, knowing she was born on 23rd November 1986 and her parents are David James Oswald and Elena Alison Oswald.) Still, he sacrifices her belief in him when he realises that, if he gives the right answers and confirms it's really him, Clara will kill herself to be reunited with him.

Despite the whole world suffering, when Danny is downloaded back into his body, now mostly converted into a Cyberman, she won't leave his side. He's in pain and Clara wants to help. The Doctor warns that, if she does by activating his emotional inhibitor, he'll be fully converted into a Cyberman and so will try to kill her. It's not even a difficult decision for her though: her overwhelming urge is to help him. This might partially be guilt, as Clara says Danny's hurting because *she* hurt him. The Doctor begs her not to activate his inhibitor, but Danny points out that, once she does, he'll know the plans made by the Cybermen and Missy – who, it's revealed, is the woman in the shop who originally gave Clara the TARDIS number in *The Bells of St John* – so he relents and gives Clara the sonic screwdriver to finish the job. As she does, she laments that it feels like she's killing him, and reiterates that she loves him. Danny – as a Cyberman – refuses to hurt Clara, though, because, as the Doctor says, love isn't an emotion; 'love is a promise.' Indeed, Danny then proves himself by burning all the Cybermen and sacrificing himself. Though the Doctor thinks he can get back from the afterlife created by Missy, Danny instead sends back a boy he accidentally

COMPANIONS

killed in combat as a soldier, and Clara is tasked with tracking down his parents. Her teaching skills no doubt come in handy here; notably, she does all this without the aid or knowledge of the Doctor, seeing as they part ways – he thinks she's settled down with Danny; she thinks he's going back home to Gallifrey. Each thinks they're saving the other.

Actually, they're reunited in the dream states of *Last Christmas*. Somehow, the Kantrofarri, colloquially known as Dream Crabs, have latched onto both the Doctor and Clara at separate points in time, and linked them as 'time travel is always possible in dreams.' Interestingly, the Doctor is seemingly taken by the Dream Crabs at the same volcanic place Clara thought she took him to in her own dream at the start of *Dark Water*, though why is never explained. Most notably, Clara sees Danny again in her slumber. Her idyllic life consists of warm days by the fire in what could be a cottage (it's certainly not her flat at any rate), with Danny dressed as Santa Claus. For Christmas, he's got her tickets for the Indian Orient Express, a painting they saw in Paris, and permission to own a cat. Their trip to France might've happened before Danny's passing or solely in the dream. This is the last time we see Danny, but his heroism has clearly stuck with Clara as even the Dream Crab-induced Danny is keen to stop her dreaming so she can save herself from the Kantrofarri.

This being a dream within a dream, Clara's warm reality is spent travelling in Santa's sleigh with Father Christmas and, for a time, the Doctor. She seems content to escape reality. The Doctor, however, saves her, seemingly too late: he arrives sixty-two years after she left the TARDIS, though he tries to not notice that she's aged. This dreamed-up Clara taught in every country in Europe, learned to fly a plane, and turned down a plethora of marriage proposals. These fake memories show her passion for exploration and for teaching, plus hint at some desire to be with other people after Danny's death. This, too, is a dream – a good thing too, seeing as the Doctor wants her to continue travelling with him. When he wakes and finds the real Clara, she checks that she's young and happily accepts his offer to go with him.

By the time we next see her, presumably after several months, she's more jovial, announcing to her students that Jane Austen is an 'amazing writer, brilliant comic observer, and strictly among ourselves, a phenomenal kisser.'

Clara is still working at Coal Hill School, and she demonstrates a decent enough knowledge of social media in *The Magician's Apprentice*, signalling that she's come a long way since having little technical proficiency in *The Bells of St John* – then again, the hashtag she suggests her students look for, #ThePlanesHaveStopped, isn't exactly catchy enough to go viral. Still, she's seen as an expert and is called away from classes by UNIT who she makes her way to by motorbike (as previously seen in *The Day of the Doctor*) when Missy enacts a time-lock to freeze the skies. Clara happily goes head-to-head with her on Kate Stewart's behalf, backed up by snipers and extra UNIT troops, all apparently under her control. When Missy baits her about Danny's death, Clara doesn't rise to it, but her misjudged words lead the rogue Time Lady to murder a couple of UNIT personnel before Clara can stop her. She quickly realises that Missy needs her to find the Doctor. Together, they do locate him, in twelfth-century Essex, and follow him there using a vortex manipulator.

Despite being part of a large crowd, the Doctor notices Clara almost immediately and plays *Pretty Woman* on his guitar to show her as much. Her loyalty to him means she also recognises a rare expression on his face, i.e. shame, and then she volunteers herself and Missy to go with him when he's taken to Skaro by Colony Sarff (not that Clara is aware that Skaro is the Daleks' home planet yet).

While the events around Danny's death are still close to home, Clara is manipulative, albeit for altruistic purposes, using that tragedy to blackmail the Doctor: he knew Missy was alive despite them seeing her apparently being killed in *Death in Heaven*, choosing to send his confession dial, a Time Lord's last will and testament, to her instead of Clara – she's more angry that he kept this a secret, not that she didn't receive the dial, informing that he has to come back from seeming certain death to make it up to her. (It's a tactic Clara uses again, in *Before the Flood*, telling him he has to break the rules of time travel because 'you owe me. You've made yourself essential to me. You've given me something else to be. And you can't do that and then die. It's not fair... I don't care about your rules or your bloody survivor's guilt. If you love me in any way, you'll come back.') She has a complex relationship with Missy, in fact. When both Clara and Missy are exterminated by Daleks, Missy reroutes the energy from their weapons to their vortex manipulator, meaning Missy saves the Doctor's companion. This might be Missy's own confession: to her, best friends fight all the time, and she spends a fair amount of *The Witch's Familiar* goading Clara, even tying her up and threatening to eat her unless Clara can help her rescue the Doctor from the middle of the Dalek city. Clara clearly hates her, though, and threatens, 'You won't survive turning your back.' It's a glib comment, but Missy challenges her on it, giving her the opportunity. Yet Clara can't commit murder, though why she won't kill Missy isn't elaborated on: can she not bring herself to kill someone, or has she recognised the odds being so against her that she will need Missy's help?

Things get worse when Missy takes a huge amount of joy in locking a terrified Clara inside a Dalek (reflecting *Asylum of the Daleks*), using her as bait to enter the city via the Dalek sewers. Their attitudes to their dynamic are best summed up in Clara maintaining that they're not a team, and Missy countering that they are because 'every miner needs a canary.' Indeed, Missy's sick ideals mean she relishes the notion of the Doctor killing Clara by mistake when he's unaware Clara is still trapped inside the Dalek armour. Clara's call for 'mercy' instead makes it through the Dalek's translators. This isn't a huge shock, given the Doctor's unwavering belief that he can save her, demanding the Daleks bring her back, despite him having seen her apparently die at their hands/suckers. His anger at the thought of her being dead is enough, Missy says, to compel him to 'burn everything.'

They experience a mutual joy when they're reunited, alive and well and back in the TARDIS once more. Still, it's a shame that this is the last time Clara and Missy appear on-screen together.

The Doctor and Clara get separated quite frequently, including by time, space... and death. Their time apart proves how in sync they really are. In *The Girl Who Died*, they first get to spend two days together as prisoners of a Viking longboat, then they are forced to help a ninth-century village defend itself in less than a day. They nevertheless get to show how much they know each other and their level of trust, as Clara is transmatted to the spaceship of the war-like Mire alongside a young girl they've only just met called Ashildr. As the Mire disintegrates their prisoners to harvest their adrenaline and testosterone, the Doctor fears they'll do the same to Clara. However, aside from his initial worry, he doesn't seem too concerned. He focuses on trying to convince the Viking village – who believe the Mire are gods – confident that Clara will figure out a way to escape. And she does, noting that the Mire have detected her advanced technology (i.e. sonic sunglasses) and saying, 'I'm not from around here, and it's highly unlikely I will have come alone. You see, you haven't killed us because killing us would start a fight you didn't come here to have, and you're not sure you can win.' Unfortunately, Ashildr unwittingly stokes the flames of war, so the Mire promise to return the next day to slaughter the village. Though his good mood is quickly extinguished by this news, the Doctor is still overjoyed to see Clara again, hugging her so tightly, he lifts her into the air. The Doctor is keen to leave them to it, after advising the villagers to simply leave so the Mire has no target. He even gives Clara a fair argument that, if a small human settlement, now devoid of warriors thanks to the Mire killing them in the ship, beats the Mire, word will get out and Earth will be seen as a target of strategic value. Yet Clara is able to change his mind, challenging him to save the Viking children based solely on his hearing a baby cry.

When Ashildr expresses her concerns, Clara tells her, 'He

hasn't got a plan yet. But he will have, and it will be spectacular.'

Sure enough, they manage to expel the Mire largely through humiliation, but the cost is Ashildr's life: she dies of suspected heart failure, but the Doctor won't give up on her and gives her a piece of technology from inside the Mire's suits, irreversibly resurrecting her and turning her immortal. When the Doctor meets Ashildr again, in London, 1651, Clara is still at home but Ashildr, whose memory is failing from the weight of her recollections, nevertheless remembers her, she suggests purely as Clara is the Doctor's weakness (*The Woman Who Lived*). She changes her mind, however, saying that she'll watch for the Doctor's companions because 'Someone has to look out for the people you abandon. Who better than me? I'll be the patron saint of the Doctor's leftovers.'

The Doctor and Clara are separated again in *The Zygon Invasion/The Zygon Inversion* when she's kidnapped and replaced by a Zygon Commander called Bonnie. We find out a little more about Clara's home life, namely that she still lives in her flat and she's a force for good in her community: she knows Sandeep by name, and searches for his parents back at his home, number Fifty-Two, though she could also know him from school. When the Doctor leaves her some one-hundred and twenty-seven missed calls, he gets annoyed at her voicemail message, 'Hi, this is Clara Oswald. I'm probably on the Tube or in outer space. Leave a message!' We can infer that she often uses the London Underground despite owning a motorbike. After this, she's taken by the shape-changing aliens and becomes the face of the Zygon resistance. They've clearly identified Clara as being key to their plans, as the Zygon base can be accessed through the lift in her block of flats.

From *The Zygon Inversion, Listen, Time Heist, The Caretaker*, and *Dark Water*, we get a good look around Clara's flat. It's largely a mix of modern IKEA-like products and vintage furniture, including a rattan settee with a mix of colourful cushions, electric fire, photos and art on most walls, ornate lamps, a triplex mirror (which the Doctor says is because her face is so wide), a double bed layered with plush cushions and a sunflower quilt, a large vanity table covered in jewellery, a plastic white bookcase covering a whole wall in her living room, and a rocking chair. Clara's flat acts as a something of a safe space, as when she's taken over by the Zygons, her dream takes her there – it's now much more sinister, however, with its windows and door shut off and the TV veering between static and, when it's useful to Bonnie, a look at what's happening in the real world. Clara finds she can influence those events too, proving what a strong character she is. She undermines Bonnie by texting the Doctor to tell him she's still alive, something Bonnie isn't even aware that her body's doing. Bonnie gets so infuriated by Clara holding back some of her memories of UNIT's Black Archive and the Osgood Box(es), that she confronts her, both in the dreamscape and in person, with the inanimate Clara trapped in a Zygon pod.

Indeed, the Doctor has trusted Clara with all the information about the deal made after *The Day of the Doctor*, right down to the intricacies of the alien settlement, as the real Clara tells her alien counterpart that this war would 'twenty million Zygons against seven billion humans.' And Clara has full access to the Black Archive, all its personnel simply waving her on – which is admittedly a little curious, given that, when we last saw the repository of hidden artefacts, Kate Stewart made it TARDIS-proof: she'll trust Clara, but not the Doctor...

Presented with the chance to undo the human-Zygon ceasefire, Bonnie is talked out of it by the Doctor, and he only knows she's changed her mind as he recognises the look on her face. He suggests his not activating the Moment in *The Day of the Doctor* was because 'I let Clara Oswald get inside my head. Trust me, she doesn't leave.' Once Clara is released, her and the Doctor's next trip takes them to the Le Verrier space station, in orbit around Neptune, in the thirty-eighth century, where they apparently find a group being attacked by Sandmen, creatures made of human sleep dust (*Sleep No More*). Clara is tired enough that a Morpheus Pod automatically pulls her in and gives her forty winks in seconds. She's unnerved by the Le Verrier: it's dark and she fears something is watching them – as is the case, or so it would appear at least. She's further fearful of the Doctor mentioning a Great Catastrophe happening to Earth, but the Doctor doesn't explain further, so we can infer he still keeps important future events from her. Nonetheless, they have a convivial air between them as they have a sarcastic exchange about calling extraterrestrial pirates 'space pirates.' (Later, in *Hell Bent*, he relents and calls Gallifrey 'Space Glasgow'.) However, as the whole transmission is a trap concocted by the Sandmen's creator, Gagan Rassmussen, we can't say for certain that anything we find out about Clara is real.

Most significantly, Clara and the Doctor are, in Series 9, separated by death, be it apparent or delayed. In *Under the Lake/Before the Flood*, the Doctor seemingly dies but is instead cut off from his companion by over a hundred and thirty years. He's forced to leave Clara in the underwater mining facility known as The Drum in 2119, while he takes the TARDIS to investigate why the area was flooded in 1980. As he's in Краснодар (pronounced, 'Krasondar'), a mock Soviet town built in Caithness, Scotland, and used to train soldiers during the Cold War, Clara has to lead the charge against a plethora of ghosts, surrounded by people she doesn't know.

Before this, they integrate themselves in with the Drum's crew, partly as the group work for UNIT and so have read the files on the Doctor. His attitude initially puts them at odds, but Clara has, at some stage, recognised his abrupt manner and tried to correct it by giving him a series of cards to read from (one of which says, 'It was my fault, I should have known you didn't live in Aberdeen,' an allusion to Sarah Jane Smith). They all work beautifully together, rounding up the ghosts so they can try to get to the bottom of their appearance, learning that they're all saying the same words – the dark, the sword, the forsaken, the temple – which act as coordinates towards the Fisher King's resting place under the water. The Doctor investigates by taking the TARDIS back to 1980, but Clara is cut off from it and is horrified to see the Doctor's ghost suddenly appear, implying he died in the past. The Doctor's phone call from history doesn't reassure her, seeing as he tells her she's got actual proof that he now has to die. She then panics when the ghosts steal her phone so she can't give the Doctor any updates, and concocts a plan to get it back, risking their lives. Clara doesn't take the Doctor's apparent death well at all. He tries to remind her that no one can escape it forever, so she gives him an angry, tearful plea to 'die with whoever comes after me. You do not leave *me*.' This at least shows she's fully aware that, whatever happens to her, the Doctor will go on to travel with someone else. Yet the Doctor is willing to do what he shouldn't: he learns that Clara is going to die shortly so determines that he's changing history purely to save Clara. And he does, with the Doctor's ghost only being a hologram.

After the death of a loved one, a member of the crew mourns and asks what he should do next. Clara, with Danny Pink still on her mind, says that he has to keep going because 'there is a whole world out there; a galaxy, a life.'

Throughout their time together, the Twelfth Doctor expresses concerns about what travelling with him has done to Clara. In *The Girl Who Died*, he notes her enthusiasm for turning the villagers into fighters and says, 'Oh, Clara Oswald, what have I made of you?' At the start of *Under the Lake*, she's still loving every second, enthusing about 'monsters, things blowing up,' then asking if they can 'go back to that place where the people with the long necks have been celebrating New Year for two centuries? I left my sunglasses there. And most of my dignity.' Later, inside the TARDIS, he warns her that she needs a hobby (or maybe a new relationship) because she's getting too involved and daring in the face of death: 'Look, there's a whole dimension in here, but there's only room for one *me*.' He argues that he has a duty of care towards her, speaking in terms a schoolteacher will no doubt resonate with. Her times in school, though, appear to get fewer and more far between; by the time of *For Tonight We Might Die*, the first episode of the spin-off, *Class*, the Doctor notices that 'Oswald. C.' has been added to Coal Hill's Roll of Honours memorial board of the dead. From the point of view of any other teachers or students, Clara just goes missing, presumed dead, her last visit to contemporary Earth being in *Face the Raven*.

It's during this adventure that her behaviour is noticed by Rigsy, who calls the Doctor and Clara to Earth to help him deduce why he has a tattoo on his neck that's counting down. Risking her life by hanging outside the TARDIS, Rigsy says she shouldn't be enjoying that as much as she is; the Doctor tells him it's an ongoing issue. Things spiral further out of control when it's revealed that the tattoo is ticking away the minutes until his death, and Clara, so sure that she and the Doctor can undo it, takes the countdown.

The Doctor's feelings for Clara are so overwhelming that he first threatens Ashildr, now known as Mayor Me of the hidden Trap Street, with exposing all the refugees taking shelter there if she doesn't undo the damage done by her luring him there with said tattoo, before Clara insists he step back from this ultimatum. It's her own fault and cannot be avoided. She asks the Doctor to not watch her die, but he can't help seeing her being run through by a Quantum Shade that takes the form of a raven. She dies in a surprisingly violent manner, arms up either side of her and screaming as her life dissolves into smoke before her body falls helplessly to the ground.

We don't find out what happens to her corpse, but Ashildr presumably takes it away, while Rigsy adds some graffiti as a tribute to her on the TARDIS exterior.

The Doctor's grief is so overwhelming that, when he's trapped inside his own time-looped confession dial, he spends an estimated four and a half billion years trying to escape so he can undo her death (*Heaven Sent*). Throughout that time, he talks to an imagined version of Clara, who largely resides in a dreamed-up TARDIS console, the place his mind wanders to when he starts to lose hope and a grip on life. Ultimately, his time in the confession dial leads him back to Gallifrey, where he uses Sector Fifty-Two's Extraction Chamber seven to freeze time on the point of Clara's death (*Hell Bent*). This is a fixed point, however, so the Doctor and Clara then have to run from the pursuing Time Lords, with the Doctor believing that this will avert her passing. Instead, she learns that this is a living death, unable to hear her heartbeat in her ears anymore simply because her heart no longer beats. Climbing through the Gallifreyan cloisters, Clara realises with horror how far the Doctor's come for her, not just surviving the 'torture chamber' that is the confession dial, but also shooting his old friend, the General, and forcing him to regenerate. They have a heart-to-heart, before Clara distracts the Time Lords (telling them that the universe hates them, but none more than she does) so they can both get away in a stolen TARDIS. Scared of the Time Lords' promise of time fracturing if she's saved, Clara tries to persuade him to let her die. The Doctor is distracted by talk of the mysterious hybrid noted down in Time Lord and Dalek lore as a being capable of threatening all of space-time – which Ashildr implies is the Doctor and Clara together, a partnership that results in each pushing the other too far.

Meanwhile, Clara, who hears their talk, uses the sonic sunglasses to tamper with the neural block the Doctor's taken from Gallifrey: this technology makes someone forget all about another, so when she and the Doctor use it, neither knows who will forget who.

The neural block erases the Doctor's memory of who Clara is, but before he passes out, he asks Clara for a simple smile, one he says he'll never forget. As she must leave the Doctor, Clara knows her death waits for her in her past and her future, but until then, she travels with Ashildr in the stolen TARDIS, returning to Gallifrey 'the long way round.'

There's one final caveat to the Doctor forgetting Clara – in that, he actually doesn't. He's aware that he travelled with a girl called Clara, but can't recall her face, so when he does meet her again, apparently in an American diner that the Eleventh Doctor visited with Amy, Rory and River in *The Impossible Astronaut*, he doesn't recognise her at all. He doesn't see Rigsy's mural to her. And he seems only vaguely aware of the diner dematerialising, it turning out to be the stolen TARDIS. Then, in *Twice Upon a Time*, when faced with the Testimony, glass people who collect memories on individuals' deathbeds, a remembered copy of companion Bill Potts proves to him the importance of memory by bringing back his recollections of Clara. He can't help but smile as he realises she's back in his head.

In the end, Clara learns that she can't be the Doctor. But by taking the TARDIS, running away from Gallifrey, and exploring all of time and space, she comes very close.

River Song – Alex Kingston – Continued... (*Silence in the Library/ Forest of the Dead, The Time of Angels/ Flesh and Stone, The Pandorica Opens/ The Big Bang, The Impossible Astronaut/ Day of the Moon* to *Let's Kill Hitler, Closing Time, The Wedding of River Song, The Angels Take Manhattan, The Name of the Doctor,* and *The Husbands of River Song*)

River Song's last adventure with the Doctor before she meets the Tenth Doctor in the Library (*Silence in the Library/ Forest of the Dead*) is also her first with the Twelfth Doctor. It's an inauspicious start: when her employee, Nardole brings the Doctor to her on Mendorax Dellora, she doesn't recognise her husband, seeing as this is the first face of his new regenerative cycle. She cheerily informs him later on that the Doctor 'has his limits,' and produces a wallet detailing his first twelve faces in order, including the War Doctor (*The Husbands of River Song*). She remains certain that she would know the Doctor instantly due to her spotter's guide; River even knows he's in the vicinity as this is the 'closest intersection with the Doctor's timeline' and Mendorax Dellora, yet can't immediately conceive of his having a regeneration she doesn't know about. Instead, she believes the Doctor is a surgeon that she has also employed to remove the Halassi Androvar, the most valuable diamond in the fifty-fourth century, from the head of her 'husband,' the cyborg King Hydroflax. The Halassi have tasked River Song with getting it back after Hydroflax led a raid on their vaults in which the Androvar was caught in an explosion and became lodged in his head as shrapnel. But River actually intends to sell it to the highest bidder. Before that, though, she's got to get it out of his cranium – a considerable task given that Hydroflax is widely worshipped for his brutal, dictatorial rule and that he's known as 'the Butcher of the Bone Meadows.'

Naturally, River Song demonstrates considerable guts, arranging to kill Hydroflax while being surrounded by his worshippers and genetically engineered warrior monks, armed with sentient laser swords. When the plan goes wrong, she and the Doctor remove Hydroflax's head and spirit it away, River doing so in a slightly more breezy fashion than the Doctor. Then again, she is the one with a plan, albeit one that relies on the Doctor being there: again, so certain is she that he'll turn up. Sure enough, after leaving Nardole behind to face the wrath of Hydroflax's robotic body, she greets another co-conspirator, Ramone, who's found the TARDIS, though not its owner, who River's given the codename of 'Damsel', i.e. 'Damsel in Distress,' seeing as, Ramone says, 'he needs a lot of rescuing.'

Despite River and the Doctor getting on well, laughing raucously at the ridiculousness of the situation, the Doctor is constantly on the back foot. His hints about who he really is fall on deaf ears, and he admits, 'I can't approve of any of this, you know, but I haven't laughed in a long time.' The situation might not be ideal, but River's presence is still enough to get the Doctor out of his post-Clara reverie. Yet not only does River greet Ramone with a kiss (and says that they're married but she wiped Ramone's memory of their wedding when he was being annoying), but she also drops the revelation that she often steals the TARDIS without the Doctor knowing. It is a time machine she's got a key for; she can easily get it back to him without him realising it has ever gone. That's her plan this time too, giving the Doctor, still pretending to be a random surgeon under her employ, a chance to enthuse about the TARDIS being bigger on the inside. River displays a cavalier attitude, arguing that things would be simpler if they simply shot Hydroflax in the face. She also places considerable trust in her mysterious 'surgeon,' a man who's quickly got to grips with the workings of the TARDIS, and so asks him for advice in flying the ship. It won't dematerialise as it's registering Hydroflax as being both inside and out; River might be a child of the TARDIS, but in some ways, the Doctor still knows more about the craft than she does.

When the king's body, now sporting the heads of Nardole and Ramone in place of Hydroflax's, catches up with them and enters the TARDIS, they relocate to the space cruise ship, Harmony and Redemption, all part of River's plan: she's made friends with the Maître d', Flemming, who agrees to deadlock the baggage hold (which conceals the TARDIS and Hydroflax's body) after she says to him, 'Do you remember that time I was transporting dragon eggs?'

The company River seems to keep when the Doctor isn't around surprises the Time Lord. The Harmony and Redemption is reserved for mass murderers, so River's chosen buyer of the Halassi Androvar is a criminal named Scratch. To prepare for the sale, she uses a perfume-like spray to change her clothes, from what's effectively combat gear to a golden dress. 'Not bad for two hundred, eh?' she says to the Doctor, attributing her age to an augmented lifespan. While waiting for Scratch, River and the Doctor have a chat, the two having a warm relationship even though the former still hasn't cottoned on to the latter's true identity. Nonetheless, River is very trusting of her 'new' friend, and informs him that it only took a week to get Hydroflax to fall for her while she posed as his nurse, and implies that being in love is 'the easiest lie you can tell a man.' She also shows him her TARDIS blue diary and looks sad about it, explaining that 'the man who gave me this was the sort of man who'd know exactly how long a diary you were going to need.'

As it happens, however, the sale – one hundred billion credits – doesn't all go according to plan, as Scratch reveals, firstly, that the whole place is filled with his colleagues, and secondly that they represent the Shoal of the Winter Harmony who are retrieving the Halassi Androvar for their king... Hydroflax.

In response to the former, River tells Scratch, 'Please do assume that I have also taken precautions, and don't do anything that might make me cross and kill you'; the latter revelation, though, truly catches her off-guard.

Indeed, River has taken precautions, so when she and the Doctor are taken prisoner, it's a strategic move. Still, she doesn't predict Flemming's betrayal to help Hydroflax, nor him starting to read from her diary, something that initially infuriates her. He comments on the Pandorica; picnic at Asgard, the crash of the Byzantium (from *The Time of Angels / Flesh and Stone*, which he thinks they made a movie about), and Jim the Fish ('well, we all know Jim the Fish!'), before learning that she's just visited Manhattan – the latter implies this takes place, for River at least, shortly after losing her parents, Amy and Rory, in *The Angels Take Manhattan*, although it's more than likely that it could simply be a trip she's taken to visit them after they were displaced in time by the Weeping Angels. Flemming is intent on capturing the Doctor, not knowing he's right in front of him, and wants to use River as bait. She, however, assures him that, while she loves him, the Doctor doesn't love her back. Hydroflax's scans show that she isn't lying, which surprisingly shows that, despite the Doctor marrying her (in an aborted timeline), she truly believes he isn't truly in love with her. She explains that, 'When you love the Doctor, it's like loving the stars themselves. You don't expect a sunset to admire you back. And if I happen to find myself in danger, let me tell you, the Doctor is not stupid enough, or sentimental enough, and he is certainly not in love enough to find himself standing in it with me!'

The Doctor finally reveals himself with a simple smile. River accepts his new face in an instant.

With him at her side, River's confidence returns, aided, no doubt, by the timely arrival of a meteor storm crashing into the Harmony and Redemption: River had learned of the ships' demise from reading a book called History's Finest Exploding Restaurants, meaning she can get dinner for free. She tells Flemming that, as an archaeologist, she simply dug up the Harmony and Redemption, but as the wreck would be on Darillium, a planet she delayed visiting, that's likely just a clever line; similarly, a clever line, when River recognises the planet they're heading for *is* Darillium, the Doctor counters, 'Always good to know where we're going.' As the ship crashes, the pair hide inside the TARDIS where River is rendered unconscious.

When she wakes up, the Doctor has decided to fast-forward to when there's a restaurant looking out on the planet's Singing Towers, destined to be the last night the Doctor and River spend together. The Doctor, now in a new suit as River said in *Forest of the Dead*, gives her a new sonic screwdriver, one she showed off in her aforementioned introductory tale, as a Christmas present, replacing a sonic trowel she'd earlier threatened King Hydroflax with.

River admits that she often looks up stories about them and that she worries. 'Please don't,' the Doctor reassures her, though he, too, is tearful. Nonetheless, River appears scared of her death and argues that the Doctor always finds a way around it, touching upon a time the Eleventh Doctor considered taking her to Darillium (in the 2011 mini-episode, *Last Night*). He says that not everything can be avoided – he knows that his tenth self ultimately saves her to the Library's database, but as far as she knows, this is her last night with the Doctor.

Fortunately, as the Doctor happily tells River, one night on Darillium lasts twenty-four years...

River, of course, has a lasting effect on the Doctor: he keeps a photo of her on his desk, alongside one of Susan, at St. Luke's University (*The Pilot*) and words from her diary stay with him as he faces the Cybermen in *The Doctor Falls*, on the verge of his death. The diary entry concludes: 'Goodness is not goodness that seeks advantage. Good is good in the final hour, in the deepest pit. Without hope, without witness, without reward. Virtue is only virtue in extremis. This is what he believes, and this is the reason, above all, I love him. My husband. My madman in a box. My Doctor.'

Though Nardole appears a couple of episodes before Bill Potts, the two are linked through the Twelfth Doctor's time as a tutor in Bristol. They have adventures separate from each other too, with Nardole in *The Husbands of River Song* and *The Return of Doctor Mysterio* and with Bill in, for instance, *Smile* and *Thin Ice*.

Bill Potts and Nardole – Pearl Mackie and Matt Lucas (*The Husbands of River Song* to *World Enough and Time/ The Doctor Falls*, plus *Twice Upon a Time*)

Reach (S Club 7); *Pupille* (Madame Monsieur).

The Chain (Fleetwood Mac); *Do You Love Me Yet?* (Nothing But Thieves).

Nardole is one of the more unusual companions to travel with the Doctor. Not only do we not see him join the TARDIS properly, but we also don't find out a great deal of backstory while he's (sometimes unwillingly) exploring time and space – not even his species or how he cheats his apparent death!

Also unusually, Nardole's first interaction with the TARDIS is his knocking on its door while looking for 'the surgeon' (*The Husbands of River Song*). The Doctor, taken in by this odd request, follows Nardole to a flying saucer on the human colony of Mendorax Dellora – inside of which, the Doctor meets Nardole's employer, River Song, who doesn't recognise him. It's Christmas Day in the year 5343, and River's trying to retrieve a valuable diamond from inside the humanoid head of the cyborg, King Hydroflax. Nardole swiftly realises his mistake and panics that the Doctor will mess everything up, a fair worry given that Hydroflax is a tyrant and the saucer is surrounded by his subjects.

While the Doctor and River get away, they don't seem to register that Nardole has been captured by Hydroflax's robotic body, which gathers information on River by 'uploading' Nardole, i.e. chopping off his head and attaching it to its own body. Nardole, still very much with a mind of his own, is naturally resistant, but is seemingly accustomed to being dismembered; his main objections appear to be that he never gave Hydroflax permission and that, now propped on top of a large, flying android torso, he's afraid of heights.

Using Nardole's memories, Hydroflax tracks down another of River's associates, Ramone, who's taken back by Nardole apparently aiming a gun at his own head, this instead being the king's body, Nardole's actual body, it's fair to infer, being left behind in Hydroflax's saucer. Now with Ramone's head also added to a shuffling library of faces within Hydroflax, they track down the TARDIS and make their way inside. The TARDIS transports them all to the spaceship, Harmony and Redemption, a place for mass murderers to kick back and relax, so Nardole is effectively locked in the baggage hold. When he's next seen, he's called upon to confirm that River is a known consort of the Doctor – 'I think so, yeah' – before being lowered back within Hydroax's 'whiffy' torso. Though the Harmony and Redemption crashes on Darillium, the Doctor saves Nardole and Ramone as part of Hydroflax's body and they act as a waiter at the restaurant that looks out on the planet's Singing Towers. River is happy to hear they survived, though Nardole stays inside the robotic body as he's off-duty and having some 'me time.'

Somehow, the Doctor repairs Nardole, cutting him out of Hydroflax's body and gluing his head back on (*The Return of Doctor Mysterio*). Nardole argues that the Doctor only did this because he was worried he'd be lonely after River died. However, River must've grown close to Nardole and recognised his usefulness as she gave him her diary and instructions to follow the Doctor, according to *Extremis*. (How he does this is unknown, given his lack of time travel technology at that point, though the planet he follows the Doctor to could be in the same time period.) Nardole comes across as a composite being, someone who, he reveals in *The Doctor Falls*, can't even remember when or where he was born because he was instead 'found,' and who once swapped his face (*Oxygen*) – at least twice, given he says in *World Enough and Time* that he was once blue. In *The Lie of the Land*, Nardole reveals he learned to practice the Tarovian neck pinch (earning the rank of Brown Tabard in the martial art), though can't perform it properly with his left hand, considering that it's not his original hand. Whether the body the Doctor makes for him is the one we saw in *The Husbands of River Song* or not is unknown too: if so, the Doctor had to swap out his lungs with some human ones he found cheap (*The Pyramid at the End of the World*) and some of him is metal, implying he's a cyborg: a screw falls out of him in *The Pilot*, although it's seemingly an unimportant component as he sneakily kicks it away with his heel to hide it from Bill Potts.

However he did it, the Doctor is clearly important to Nardole. He's a somewhat reticent adventurer, but is nonetheless the Doctor's cheerleader, literally pumping his fist in the air in triumph when the Doctor effectively tells the attacking Harmony Shoal in *The Return of Doctor Mysterio* he'll stop them. ('Don't do that,' the Doctor scorns afterwards.) Nardole's been affected by his time on Darillium too. At the end of the story, he calls the Doctor 'very brave and he's very silly and I think, for a time, he's going to be very sad. But I promise, in the end, he'll be all right. I'll make sure of it.' This is a marked departure from the Nardole of old, at least if we take to heart what Nardole says in *The Doctor Falls*, i.e. 'If there's more than three people in a room, I start a black market. Send me with [humans to look after], I'll be selling their own spaceship back to them once a week.'

He does live among humans for a time, though we don't find out whether he spends his evenings in the TARDIS or somewhere on St Luke's University campus.

In *The Pilot*, he meets Bill Potts, who he welcomes to the Doctor's office after the Time Lord sets himself up as a lecturer while tasked with guarding Missy in the vault underneath the university. Bill charms first the Doctor then eventually Nardole: though she works at the university serving chips at the café there, Bill pretends to be a student so she can sneak into the Doctor's lectures. He notices her especially because whenever she doesn't understand something, she smiles, in contrast to most others whose reaction is typically to frown. There's some friction when Bill misunderstands why the Doctor calls her to his office, believing he's accusing her of something and putting her down by cheekily asking whether she wanted to go to university to serve chips and nothing more. He quickly quashes that, though, by offering her private tuition. He knows how good she is already, telling her that if she ever gets anything less than a First on her assignments, their arrangement is over. He's also pretty tough with her, informing her that she has to be there at six every weekday and that she must never be late. Bill's very receptive to this, and is enthusiastic about her classes. She tells her foster mum, Moira, that he's 'like a foster tutor,' which Moira sees as a concerning relationship, advising her foster daughter to keep an eye on men. 'Men aren't where I keep my eye, actually,' Bill retorts under her breath.

Indeed, Bill develops a crush on a fellow pupil at St. Luke's: Heather, who has a 'defect' in her eye that makes her iris look like a star. Heather takes Bill to a cordoned-off area of the university to see a mysterious puddle that turns out to be sentient and later engulfs Heather, converting her into its 'pilot.' Bill turns to the Doctor for help straight away, and disbelieves that the TARDIS is bigger on the inside – similarly that the doors, which she sees as made of wood, can stop the pursuing Pilot from getting inside. In fact, she first thinks it's a 'knock through' then an elevator, before finally realising its alien origins.

Nardole comes across as a mix between focused and haphazard. He's pretty strict with the Doctor, frequently reminding him that he's got a duty to carry out, but he typically bumbles on behind him when they're wandering the campus or heading to the vault. Either way, the Doctor trusts a decidedly scared Nardole to run 'interference' when they visit 'the deadliest fire in the universe,' materialising during the conflict between the Daleks and Movellans (from *Destiny of the Daleks*). Nardole's attitude means he's more than familiar with not just the Daleks but also this exact warzone, as he begs the Doctor to go 'anywhere but there.' Still, he isolates all the Daleks using the sonic screwdriver, without the Doctor's help, something most companions can't do. He's set the vault security as 'friends only,' which, presuming it uses similar technology and psychic connections as the TARDIS, says a lot about Bill seeing as she is admitted with no hassle.

Both Heather and Bill are heartbroken when the latter has to turn down Heather's offer to travel with her through time and space by converting her into the curious substance Heather's become. The Doctor thinks she's fine, and Nardole thinks he knows the Time Lord too well: 'That's the Doctor for you,' he states. 'Never notices the tears.' Bill, however, says she doesn't think the tears left on her face are her own, implying they're Heather's, who goes off to travel without Bill. In doing so, Heather pre-emptively saves Bill's life, as per *The Doctor Falls*, so all of Bill's time with the Doctor is essentially delaying her journeying with Heather.

The Doctor goes to wipe Bill's memories of what's just happened, it seems as if it would otherwise compromise the security of the vault, but Bill realises and tries to stop him. 'This is the most exciting thing that's ever happened to me in my life. The *only* exciting thing!' she pleads. 'Okay, [let me remember] just for tonight. Just one night. Come on, let me have some good dreams for once.' He's won over by her asking him to imagine what it would feel like if someone did it to him, not knowing this is what's happened with Clara. Looking at photos of River Song and Susan he keeps on his desk, he initially lets Bill go... then goes after her, telling her to join him as his companion for a while.

At the conclusion of *The Pilot*, Nardole is disapproving of seeing Bill in the TARDIS and warns the Doctor about disappearing; Nardole – who Bill calls 'little fella' – grumpily says he'll make tea for the Doctor but not for 'any *human.*' He's momentarily tricked by the Doctor into thinking he's merely taking the TARDIS up to his office to skip the stairs, and, when the Doctor and Bill get back from an adventure in 1814, both dressed in period clothing, Nardole instantly twigs what's happened and is furious about the Doctor breaking his oath to guard Missy. And rightly so: Nardole later shows that he plays a key part in looking after the vault, being very familiar with its systems and being perturbed by Missy's knocking, something he says is new – clearly, Nardole is particularly vigilant, taking his duties far more seriously than the Doctor. We learn in *Extremis* that Nardole was there when the Doctor supposedly witnessed Missy's 'execution' and helps the Doctor move her to the vault in question. Presumably, he aids the Doctor in getting the vault to Earth too, though acknowledges that Bill has a valid point when she questions why they put something they don't want people being too curious about in the middle of a university. Nardole's orders come from the Doctor himself, and when he realises the Doctor's thinking about travelling again following a lecture about space, he tries to sabotage the TARDIS by removing its fluid link. The Doctor says he's docking Nardole's pay for this, so he must provide for his companion (presumably his university pay is decent, and he doesn't need to spend out on bed and board).

In *Smile*, Bill immediately thinks the Doctor will cave to Nardole's request, but he instead asks her whether she first wants to go to the past or future. She chooses the future, to see whether it's 'happy.' It's largely not, as when they arrive on Gliese 581d, where the last vestiges of mankind have fled after solar flares have ravaged the earth. (She questions if they can call for help from the TARDIS, but later suggests to the Doctor, '"Advice and Assistance Obtainable Immediately." You like that... You don't call the helpline because you *are* the helpline.') Bill is horrified to learn this, but finds considerable solace in saving the population from the Emojibots that have misinterpreted their orders and kill anyone who isn't always happy. She is both overjoyed and almost disbelieving when she asks the Doctor, 'Did you just – well, did *we* just jumpstart a new civilisation?'

Bill's a particularly emotive companion, absolutely revelling in her travels and also acknowledging its horrors as soon as she faces up to them. When she learns the Doctor stole the TARDIS, she cheekily says, 'What if I steal it from you?' She loves the Emojibots and marvels at smelling a rosemary plant while 'twenty light years from home,' one such bush also being outside the student union back in Bristol. She says her brain's overloading and also realises that the Doctor has really high blood pressure when he tells her he has two hearts. She soon finds something she doesn't like about the Doctor: his relationship with death. In *Thin Ice*, she's tearful to see him regarding life so carelessly, and to learn that, not only has he killed, but also that he can't even remember how many he's killed. She holds his suggestion that he's moved on with some contempt. Nonetheless, she appreciates him more when he takes care of some homeless kids and his violent reaction when Lord Sutcliffe is shockingly racist to Bill. She appreciates the Doctor's powerful verbal defence of everyday human life arguably more than his punching Sutcliffe in the face.

Not all the trips in the TARDIS are to far-flung times and places: Bill asks the Doctor to help her move her stuff from Moira's to a gloomy house she's sharing with five other students, Shireen, Felicity, Harry, Pavel, and Paul, in *Knock Knock*. Shireen is Bill's friend, and Bill quickly gets to know the others (with Paul taking a fancy to Bill, though he soon realises that's never going to happen) – all except Pavel who is eaten by the house before the rest of them arrive. Detecting something strange going on, especially when he meets the creepy Landlord, the Doctor, who Bill tells the others is her grandfather, stays for the first night, much to Bill's annoyance. To her, this is the part of her life he can't be involved with; he thinks otherwise. And it's a good thing too, seeing as all her friends are engulfed by the wood sprites known as Dryads, and it's the Doctor who manages to bring them back. While the Doctor is taken by the alienness of the threat, Bill's humanity shines through, so she figures out and implies to him the true nature of the Landlord and his 'daughter' (actually his mother, considering the human lifespan).

Nardole enthuses that, 'You don't have to go to outer space to find monsters. There's plenty of things that want to kill you right here on Earth!' He'll try anything to keep the Doctor safeguarding Missy, and is aghast when he discovers the Doctor has given her a piano to occupy her time.

Still, Nardole warms to their adventures, reluctantly joining them on a trip to space station Chasm Forge in *Oxygen*, NASA Vehicle Assembly Building at Kennedy Space Centre, Florida, then Mars in *Empress of Mars* (though this doesn't go according to plan, as Nardole runs back to the TARDIS to get equipment to rescue Bill but it instead mysteriously dematerialises, returning him to Earth), and Scotland in *The Eaters of Light*. The latter he particularly takes to, especially considering their investigation into The Devil's Cairn, actually an inter-dimensional temporal rift, means the Doctor is trapped inside for two days, so Nardole ingratiates himself with the locals. Nardole has a good sense of time, going on to note the exact number of hours and minutes the Doctor's been gone. He's also been looking for Bill during that time, though unsuccessfully. He's adamant the Doctor will come back, staying by the cairn with some Picts and telling them stories about his trips to the Mary Celeste and RMS Lusitania. He sports a bobble hat and dressing gown but adopts some local colours, painting his face to fit in, and seems to enjoy his time in the second century, even if his initial reaction to Scotland is by calling it 'damp.'

Rather bizarrely, given that, early in their relationship, the Doctor acknowledges she's full of questions, it's very late in their journeys that Bill finally asks why she can understand other languages (i.e. thanks to the TARDIS' translation circuits). Her time in Scotland is pretty scary, even if it was her idea to investigate what happened to the Ninth Roman Legion, who suddenly vanished. Bill thinks she knows all there is to know about them, given that she read all the material she could and got an A* in her subsequent project about them. Instead, she's knocked unconscious by the Eater of Light but taken to an underground cave to recover by the last surviving legionnaires. One of them, Lucius, falls for Bill, but she has to tell him she's a lesbian; he suggests most of his friends are bisexual, which Bill thinks is particularly 'modern.' 'Hey, not everyone has to be modern,' Lucius says. 'I think it's really sweet that you're so restricted.' The Romans can still surprise the historically-literature Bill.

Both Bill and Nardole are shocked to see Missy carrying out chores for the Doctor in the TARDIS when they get back. Bill says they can't trust her, and Nardole argues, 'Sir, I must protest in the strongest, most upset terms possible.' The Doctor largely ignores them.

The Doctor and Nardole have a fun relationship, as they trust each other (even though the Doctor pushes this trust to its limit when it comes to Missy). He's not afraid to stand up to the Doctor, however. After the Time Lord is knocked out so he can't sacrifice his life to stop the Eaters of Light, Nardole warns, 'I know you're inclined to bear a grudge, so just remember, I know about ten per cent of your secrets – the dark secrets. And I'm the only one in the TARDIS who knows where the tea cakes are.'

Nevertheless, after the Doctor's blinded in *Oxygen*, it's Nardole, not Bill, he trusts with the secret. Nardole helps him day to day, explaining events in *Extremis* and *The Pyramid at the End of the World*, proving indispensable: despite the Doctor using his sonic sunglasses to detect certain things, Nardole must point out who people actually are, what's on screens and books (including the Veritas, which holds a truth so devastating that anyone who reads it commits suicide), and notable events like lights and portals in the Vatican's Haereticum, a library of forbidden knowledge. *Extremis* is technically out of continuity, occurring in a computer simulation, so what we learn about Nardole and Bill is arguably invalid; however, considering the Truth Monks create an accurate artificial prediction, the companions would still likely act as they do in the fake world; certainly their relationship with the Doctor goes accordingly, given how we see them interact throughout the rest of the series. During the simulation, Bill goes on a date with Penny (who we later see in *The Pyramid at the End of the World*), implying she's trying to get over her experiences with Heather. Bill also appears to be helping Penny get over an unseen hurdle, as she tells her that, whatever happens between them, it's nothing to feel guilty about. Perhaps Penny has only recently come out as a lesbian, so the more confident Bill is showing her the way. Saying that, Moira, upon meeting Penny, is still clueless as to Bill's sexuality, joking, 'Here's me thinking that she dragged some poor, terrified man home!' Bill concedes that her dates are 'rare and special,' and is annoyed at the Doctor for messing this one up by dropping the Pope off in her bedroom.

When separated from the Doctor, Bill and Nardole stick closely together, and the latter understandably panics when they realise the simulation and eventually vanish. The fake Doctor sends this file, all the data collected during *Extremis*, to the real Doctor, to warn him of the Truth Monks. And he would've stopped their invasion if it weren't for Bill, who is horrified to learn the Doctor's been lying to her about his sight.

This could be driven by guilt too. The Doctor sacrificed his eyesight for her in *Oxygen*, in which they find themselves victims of capitalism on Chasm Forge, where the oxygen is rationed and paid for. The zombified crew are out to kill them, thus saving their oxygen supplies, which naturally freaks Bill out. She's totally on board with Nardole's suggestion to ignore the station's distress call in favour of returning to the TARDIS, but when they're cut off from it, they've no choice but to be continually on the run from the crewmates. Though the Doctor disassembles the corporation's cutthroat plan, killing the resource-heavy yet ineffective miners only to replace them to cut costs, it comes at a considerable cost: it appears Bill dies and joins the zombie horde – we never find out

how she felt during the short time she's neither dead or alive –
and the Doctor is exposed to the emptiness of space when he gives
Bill his oxygen helmet to save her but blinding himself in the
process. Until *The Pyramid at the End of the World*, Bill believes he
gets his sight back thanks to the sonic sunglasses; alas, when she
finds out the truth, she makes a deal with the Monks to save him,
yet putting Earth under their rule. Bill acts as the Monks' anchor
to the planet, her very presence maintaining the illusion via a
psychic link that the aliens have always been there, helping
humanity along (*The Lie of the Land*). Missy says that killing Bill
would make the Monks lose their grip on the planet, but the
Doctor absolutely refuses to, despite Bill's insistence that they do
it for the greater good.

This also appears to be the will of the Doctor, whose regular
broadcasts across the planet act as propaganda for the Truth
Monks. Living under their reign, Bill refuses to believe the
Doctor's gone against his altruistic ways, even when she and
Nardole track him down and he keeps up this lie. Bill admits it's
been a struggle clinging onto reality and feels abandoned by her
friends after some six weeks of having no communication. When
he tracks her down, she lashes out at Nardole, even though he's
been recovering from bacteria he ingested in *The Pyramid at the
End of the World*, something he says would've killed a human
being. Nardole's been in touch with the Doctor, however,
concocting a plan to make sure Bill's not been corrupted by the
Monks.

What saves them is Bill's mum, the love of whom overpowers
the Truth Monks' propaganda machine, forcing them away from
Earth. Bill's knowledge of her mother partly comes from the
Doctor: when she brings the Doctor a Christmas present in *The
Pilot* (a rug, which he puts in his office, the corner underneath the
TARDIS, which confuses Bill who was previously told he needed
a crane to move his 'box'), he sadly says he's not got her anything.
However, when she gets back to Moira's, her foster mother has
conveniently found an old shoebox filled with photos of her birth

mum. Previously, Bill had not had any photos of her mother, not even knowing if she looked like her. Bill is suspicious when she sees the Doctor in a mirror in one of the photos. This is before she learns about the TARDIS, and she can't explain what she sees. Crucially, she never asks, at least on screen, to visit her parents, so perhaps this is sacred ground for Bill, too important to risk... or perhaps the Doctor has warned her off, given his recollections of Rose Tyler meeting her dad in *Father's Day*.

Either way, the Doctor taking photos of her deceased mum so Bill has some knowledge of her life is one of the most thoughtful things he's done for a companion.

That's likely why he trusts Bill and Nardole to come with him to test Missy, who seems to have redeemed herself after many lives of villainy. Even Nardole is forced to hold some faith in Missy in *Empress of Mars*, after the TARDIS mysteriously takes him back to the vault while stranding the Doctor and Bill on the red planet in 1881. There, Bill meets the Ice Warriors, including their Ice Queen, Iraxxa, plus some Victorian pioneers. She reveals that she's a fan of *The Terminator* and *The Thing*, but seemingly hasn't read *Robinson Crusoe*. Bill doesn't seem especially panicked about the TARDIS disappearing, likely trusting that either the Doctor or Nardole will get them out of this situation, and appreciates Iraxxa deferring to her advice based on them both being women surrounded by men; when an officer called Godsacre laughs at her notion that a woman could be a police officer, Bill says she's 'going to make allowances for your Victorian attitudes because, well, you actually are Victorian.' In fact, Bill deals with everything well: when the Doctor asks for a distraction, Bill immediately volunteers. Still, she's on the back foot when the TARDIS comes back, piloted by Missy.

World Enough and Time takes an overly enthusiastic Missy (posing as 'Doctor Who,' while the actual Doctor initially stays in the TARDIS to monitor events) and her two reluctant companions to Floor 0000, the flight deck of a Mondasian colony ship that's reversing out of a black hole. Due to this, the time dilation effect means the top deck that they arrive on moves more slowly to the rest of the universe. When a crewmember worries about corpse-like creatures coming for fresh meat, i.e. Bill, he shoots her, cutting a gaping hole in her chest. This is particularly gutting seeing as the Doctor somewhat betrays Bill's faith in him: she admitted previously that Missy really scares her, and asked him to promise he won't let her die. It's actually the creatures that appear to save her, taking her to the other end of the ship, where time runs faster, fitting her with a chest unit that keeps her alive. The Doctor leaves a psychic message in her mind to wait for him as he intends to take the lift down, alongside Missy and Nardole, to follow her. When Bill wakes, months later, she's on Floor 1056 with a helper called Mr Razor, and the Doctor and co. are still on Floor 0000. She befriends Razor, who shows her around the hospital she's staying in, though the sight of the corpse-like creatures sitting around freaks her out – not as much as hearing one of them repeatedly exclaim he's in pain. Bill says she's sorry, not being able to bear this and so turning his volume down. Bill's been trying to escape the hospital though, as she knows there are multiple locks. She also demonstrates how well she knows the Doctor: she can view the upper floor on a TV screen, and happily tells Razor, 'See he's raising that eyebrow? That's his sarcasm face. He's making a joke.'

She largely remains positive, knowing the Doctor is coming for her and believing he can fix her. We don't know exactly how long she's separated from her friends, but Razor, now revealed to be the Master, pre-Missy, estimates it as some ten years in *The Doctor Falls*. Two hours before the Doctor gets there, however, Razor lures Bill into a trap and she is fully converted into a Cyberman.

As Missy and the Master attack, Nardole runs away, seemingly out of cowardice, but his unwavering dedication to the Doctor means he's actually locating a shuttlecraft to escape Floor 1056 as it's taken over by Cybermen. The Master and Missy try to convince him that the Doctor's dead so they need to leave early, but Nardole is adamant, and this pays off when a converted Bill rescues the Doctor and all of them plough through the ceiling to get away from the Mondasian forces. Nardole's true feelings for Bill shines through when he joyously says, 'Bill's back.' Despite her looking like a Cyberman, he stays true to his friend. Even when the rest of the colonists are shocked and scared by Bill's presence, Nardole tries to view her simply as she was – that's certainly how Bill sees herself, unable to come to terms with her transformation. Looking in a reflection, though, Bill is confronted with the truth, which immediately makes her angry then upset, afraid everyone will always be scared of her. She wins a small victory when the Master tries to rile her up. She simply informs him that she's not upset inside. However, she is, and actually cries, not something a Cyberman should be able to do. When the Cybermen come for the rest of the colonists, the Doctor, Nardole, and Bill are determined to defend them; Nardole rigs it so that the floor will explode on the Doctor's command, but both he and Bill are seemingly content with dying here. The Doctor instead tasks him with looking after the colonists as they flee to the other floors, something which he isn't pleased with and tries to drag Bill along with him. She refuses and he realises with great sadness and a touch of anger that he can't think of what to say when he leaves them. 'You'll think of the right words later,' Bill says.

'You're wrong, you know; quite wrong,' he retorts, before taking the elevator to a different floor. 'I never will be able to find the words.

Nardole goes on to live with the colonists on Floor 502, and realises that one of them, Hazran, rather fancies him. It's implied he spends his days with them all, defending them against repeated Cyberman attacks but still happily making a family. In some ways, the kids there see him as the kids on Trenzalore did the Eleventh Doctor.

As the Doctor is apparently killed by the Cybermen, he blows the floor up, leaving a wounded Bill stumbling through the piles of cybernetic bodies to find his. Her grief is overwhelming, and calls forth Heather, who left her tear with Bill in *The Pilot*, ready to save her at just the right time, by transmogrifying her into the alien substance so they can travel the stars together. Before doing so, they take the Doctor back to his TARDIS and leave his body there, at peace. Bill won't believe he's gone forever: 'Because one day, everyone's just going to need you too much. Until then... It's a big universe, but I hope I see you again.'

And she does, albeit after travelling the universe and settling down again on Earth with Heather, Bill's atoms rearrange again so she can become human. Only the memory of Bill meets the Doctor again in *Twice Upon a Time*, but as she argues, 'A life is just memories. I'm all her memories, so I'm her.' The Doctor still sees a division, but this version of Bill becomes hugely important to *Doctor Who* lore, given that she meets the First Doctor too and says to him, 'You dash around the universe trying to figure out what's holding it all together, and you really, really don't know?' She reiterates, 'You're amazing, Doctor. Never forget that. Never, ever.'

In their last moments together, and worried that the Doctor is refusing to regenerate, Bill calls the memory of Nardole too. They tell him they respect him enough to allow him to choose whether to regenerate or not, but leave him with a hug.

Like Amy, Rory, River, and Clara before them, Bill and Nardole are afforded full lives before the inevitable: yes, they die, but they're allowed to live first.

The Twelfth Doctor

Expanded Universe

The Target novelisation, *The Zygon Invasion*, adds a bit more context behind the Series 9 story, though its canonicity is debatable, especially given that it calls the Doctor's companion 'Clara Oswin Oswald,' her middle name taken from *Asylum of the Daleks* and *The Snowmen*, but which contradicts *The Bells of St John*. It states that, at this point, Clara is twenty-eight years old, meaning she's been travelling with the Doctor for a much shorter duration than implied on TV, especially as many months seem to pass during Series 8. It also adds that Clara's father and aunt were replaced by Zygons, and suggests that there was a duplicate of Danny Pink named Clyde (with Clara's being called Bonnie).

Elsewhere in prose, one of the initial three *New Series Adventures* novels of the Twelfth Doctor era, released in 2014, unusually is largely companion-lite: *The Blood Cell* finds the Doctor imprisoned on an asteroid in deep space, so Clara doesn't feature all that much. However, when the Doctor's sonic screwdriver is broken, it reveals Clara has a spare that she smuggles into the prison (indeed, the 2016 comic, *Clara Oswald and the School of Death*, confirms she has one), as well as the lengths she'll go to to help the Doctor, despite this still being early on in her relationship with the Twelfth Doctor. She says her nan, whom we saw in *The Time of the Doctor* and *Dark Water*, uses a mobility scooter. She then meets with the Paternoster Row gang again in *Silhouette* then demonstrates the lock-picking skills she learned from Jenny Flint in *The Crawling Terror*. Various sources show that Clara is very fond of hot chocolate, including the novel, *Deep Time*, and *The Fractures* (both 2015) from Titan Comics.

Titan's *Twelfth Doctor* comic shows the Doctor and Clara come up against sentient stars called Hyperions in *Terrorformer* and *The Hyperion Empire*, respectively from 2014 and 2015. In the former, Clara implies she's tried locking the Doctor out of her flat as she comments that his sonic screwdriver doesn't work on the deadbolts at her property (he instead prefers to land his TARDIS inside), and in the latter comic, we learn that she teaches her first-year class tae kwon do, something not seen on TV! In an unusual, yet nice example of synchronicity, *Terrorformer* sees her overdressed for the tropical vistas of Isen VI, sporting skiing gear for an apparent Yeti hunting expedition, *while The Eye of Torment*, the first Twelfth Doctor strip in *Doctor Who Magazine* and published around the same time as the Titan Comic, finds Clara underdressed for the icy climates of the sunship, Pollyanna.

Rather surprisingly, 2015's *The Swords of Kali* (sometimes called *The Swords of Okti*, after complaints about the representation of the Hindu goddess of death and rebirth) establishes that Clara was the model for the Mona Lisa, sitting for Leonardo Da Vinci in Florence, 1505, although it's perhaps fitting given her cheeky smile as she happily exclaims, 'Right now, I do know something no one else does.' This is also the only contemporary Titan Comic to include a cameo from Danny Pink. *DWM* includes a post-death Danny in *Spirits of the Jungle* (2015), though this turns out to be a false version of her deceased boyfriend harvested from Clara's memory to gain her truth; she realises the truth when this version of Danny doesn't remember the name of his favourite primary school teacher, saying that everyone recalls that and implying that she does. At its conclusion, she says she's had 'enough goodbyes' with Danny and can't face any more. He still looms large, though, as Clara relates to a woman called Jess Collins about lost boyfriends in the following tale, *The Highgate Horror* (which also sees Clara sporting the same jacket Jo Grant wore in *The Three Doctors*), then sees him as a hallucination in *Witch Hunt*, which she's concerned is a prophecy of her own upcoming death. On a lighter note, she's accused of being a witch, so counts Katy Perry, Nicki Minaj, and Taylor Swift as among her coven.

In *Gangland* from Titan Comics, Clara says her dad is a fan of boxing, especially the fictional Sonny Lawson. In *Unearthly Things,* she affirms her love of libraries and suggests she might've forgotten getting lost in a massive repository of books (perhaps alluding to *Journey to the Centre of the TARDIS*). She then meets the Toymaker in *Relative Dimensions* and the reimagined Sea Devils in *Clara Oswald and the School of Death*, during which we also find out her voicemail message is, 'Hi, it's Clara. I'm either banging my head against a brick wall trying to teach Class 2B Shakespeare, or, y'know, out saving the universe,' which she changes in time for *The Zygon Invasion*, and further implies she's on leave from Coal Hill School. Clara also likes to put extra effort into her teaching: at the beginning of *DWM*'s 2014-15 strip, *The Instruments of War*, set shortly after *Flatline*, she asks the Doctor to take her to the 1641 Frost Fair as some of her students are doing a project on it. Instead, they end up in the Sahara Desert in 1941, opposing the Sontarans. Field Marshal Rommel and his cohorts are a lot different to Clara's previous experiences with the race, i.e. Strax. And in *The Fourth Wall*, Clara battles the Boneless again as they deconstruct comic book conventions.

Clara and the Doctor repeatedly encounter members of the Winter family in a quadrilogy of 2015-16 audio adventures, *The Gods of Winter*, *The House of Winter*, *The Sins of Winter*, and *The Memory of Winter*, all taking place after *Last Christmas* considering Clara's angry over the death of Danny Pink: the second of these sees Clara happily surprised that printed books are still around in the twenty-fifth century, and tells us that she used to visit National Trust properties when she was a child.

Most significant, though, is *DWM*'s 2015 comic, *Blood and Ice*. During this, we see various other versions of Clara, i.e. those splintered through the past and future by her jumping into the Eleventh Doctor's timestream in *The Name of the Doctor*. This begins with the Doctor and Clara meeting Winnie 'Oswin' Clarence, a research graduate at the Snowcap University, Antarctica, in 2048, who rescues them both from a helicopter crash. Though Winnie is shocked when she overhears the pair discussing how Clara's echoes exist through time, she comes to terms with it and tells Clara that she feels she almost knows the story already, so we might infer that all of Clara's splinters have some unconscious recollections of their other selves.

Aside from modern-day Clara, Winnie, Oswin Oswald (*Asylum of the Daleks*) baking a soufflé, and Clara Oswin Oswald from *The Snowmen*, we see splinters who are: an Egyptian Pharoah, a member of *The Happiness Patrol*, a police officer, a visitor to the Library (*Silence in the Library/Forest of the Dead*), an Atlantian (*The Underwater Menace*), a Tudor monarch, a Morestran (*Planet of Evil*), and a Guardian of *The Ark*. Though it's previously believed that all these splinters died saving the Doctor, Winnie is evidence that some survived and lived full lives after encountering him. This relieves Clara of some substantial guilt which might've held her back from embracing her dreams, as she enthuses, 'I can think about them now. I don't have to shut them out! I don't have to think of a million deaths, a million women in fear and pain, because of me... They have lives. They have futures!'

The Expanded Universe fits in a lot of extra adventures for River Song between *The Husbands of River Song* and *Silence in the Library/Forest of the Dead* – years' worth of adventures, especially if we go by the comic event, *The Lost Dimension* in which she finds portraits of the Third, Ninth, Eleventh, and Twelfth Doctors. Surprisingly, her time with the Doctor on Darillium hasn't been fleshed out to any great extent, though *R&J*, the concluding tale in *The Lives of Captain Jack: Volume Three* (2020), partly takes place during that period and sees Captain Jack Harkness falling head over heels for her. In return, she initially thinks he's one of the stupidest men she's ever met. Still, when he sees her at the restaurant on Darillium, he learns that she's married to the Doctor and he's resigned to never measuring up.

The 2021 *Missy* comic, *The Master Plan*, perhaps takes place during this time too, as River is briefly tricked into thinking Missy is another incarnation of the Doctor, although River is still in Stormcage, so its placement is unknown. We nevertheless learn that the facility also houses the Master (specifically Roger Delgado's incarnation, who the Third Doctor regularly checks on via videocall, this being during the Doctor's banishment to Earth), a Cyberman, a Raxacoricofallapatorian, a Skithra Queen (from *Nikola Tesla's Night of Terror*), Krasko (*Rosa*), and two prisoners who are linked to River, i.e. a Silent and Dorium Maldovar. Stormcage's staff include Sea Devils. Missy and River's relationship is further muddled by the former's appearance in Big Finish's *The Bekdel Test*, from the 2019 set, *The Diary of River Song: Series Five*, in which Missy comes after Professor Song as she's apparently annoyed someone else has killed the Doctor before she can (though she later admits that she knows the Doctor is alive, Missy hailing from after the Eleventh Doctor's faked death at Lake Silencio). Upon meeting Missy, River deduces she's either the Rani, Romana, or the Monk, before correctly guessing her true identity. Missy's seemingly sincere condolences expressed in *Extremis* fly in the face of her calling River the 'rebound girl' who the Doctor has settled for, which might somewhat account for River's uncertainty about the Doctor loving her in *The Husbands of River Song*. Here, we also find out that River knows Venusian aikido, presumably having learned it from the Third Doctor.

River meets another Master in *The Lifeboat and the Deathboat* (2019), specifically the one in Bruce's body from *The TV Movie*. She even stays with him for a while as he and his companion, Alison, rescue her from the time vortex when her vortex manipulator burns out; he pretends to be a man named Daniel who's travelling to the Triassic Era, and while River rails at his deception, they eventually work together against a criminal called Kaliopi Mileska, before River goes to find someone to repair her vortex manipulator.

Another audio story, *The Two Rivers*, from *Two Rivers and a Firewall*, chronicles River at multiple stages of her life death – sort of. In it, she accompanies Professor Dern on an archaeological dig to the grave of... River Song! She recalls giving up her regenerations in *Let's Kill Hitler*, so that doesn't explain why the tomb's statues of this deceased River don't look like her; nor does her previously having clones like H-One, H-Two, and Fifth Doctor companion, Brooke (in *The Furies*). Instead, she learns that this is a Melody Pond from an alternate reality in which she did actually kill the Doctor, then the Silence at Demons Run, before exploring the universe in a stolen TARDIS.

In the 2017-18 comics, *The Parliament of Fear* and *The Phantom Piper*, the Twelfth Doctor might still be mourning River as he intends to take Bill Potts to New Asgard in the seventy-sixth century – perhaps like a 'greatest hits' tour, seeing as he and River had a picnic there at some point off-screen – then talks about spending time on Darillium in an effort to get Alan Turing to propose to a colleague called Ranesh.

There's a distinct dearth of Expanded Universe adventures for Nardole; there are fewer stories in other formats for Bill Potts, at least compared to, say, Martha Jones, another companion who primarily only stayed for one series. Nonetheless, Nardole and Bill do show up in a few novels, audios, and comics.

Having only seen them briefly in *The Pilot*, Bill gets to properly meet the Daleks in the 2022 audio adventure, *Emancipation of the Daleks*, as well as a second Bill, around twenty years older, who visits her younger self while at university, somewhat foreshadowing her ageing while waiting for the Doctor in *World Enough and Time*. During the Big Finish story, we learn that Bill used to dream about her birth mother when she was younger, which ties into a conversation with her in *The Lie of the Land*. Things get slightly messier in a 'timey-wimey' fashion thanks to *Inflicting Christmas*, a short story from the 2020 collection, *The Wintertime Paradox*, as Bill recalls a date that was interrupted by the Pope: this happened in the simulated world of *Extremis*, so we have to infer that either the Doctor told her about it at some point afterward or this also happened in the main *Doctor Who* continuity.

While *Emancipation of the Daleks* seems to take place later on in Bill's travels, two 2017 novels, *Diamond Dogs* and *The Shining Man* occur earlier, perhaps soon after *Thin Ice* seeing as Bill recalls events from the TV episode in the latter book. The novel also shows that her mum plays on her mind a lot: her phone's PIN is even her mother's date of birth. *Diamond Dogs* finds Bill on Kollo-Zarnista Mining Facility 27, the crew of which are extracting diamonds from Saturn's atmosphere. A later *DWM* comic strip, *The Soul Garden*, though also from 2017, says that Saturn is actually Bill's favourite planet in our solar system. While on one of its moons, Titan, Bill and the Doctor don atmospheric density jackets previously seen in *The Web Planet*. Fewer stories seem to take place later on in Bill's time in the TARDIS, though *The Wolves of Winter* from Titan Comics occurs after *Empress of Mars* as she recognises the Ice Warriors, and *Harvest of the Daleks*, from 2018's *The Many Lives of Doctor Who*, hints that the Thirteenth Doctor era is just around the corner. So too does *Tulpa* from *The Road to the Thirteenth Doctor*, in which the Doctor and Bill are called to help UNIT by Kate Stewart (who Bill previously met in the 2017 comic book event, *The Lost Dimension*).

From these, we can infer that, even when Nardole began regularly travelling with the pair, Bill and the Doctor still went off on adventures without him. Nonetheless, he makes his only contemporary novel appearance in 2017's *Plague City*, during which Bill says Nardole is like the Doctor's 'bodyguard.' Building on his fondness for Scotland from *Eaters of Light*, Nardole wears a Tam O'Shanter, kilt, and Sporran, when the trio visit Edinburgh, 1645, and jokes he has Scottish ancestry, hailing from the clan 'MacNardole.'

In *I Am the Doctor*, from the *Doctor Who Official Annual 2018*, Nardole dons the Fourth Doctor's scarf, jacket, and hat, and demonstrates an awareness of the Shadow Proclamation (though he invokes Article 2367, when only two-thousand, three-hundred, and sixty-six exist). *Girl Power!*, part of the 2018 collection, *The Missy Chronicles*, explains a little of how the early dynamic between

Nardole, Missy, and the Doctor worked, namely that Missy would request items, Nardole would make a list, and then get them for her if the Doctor approved, which he almost unwaveringly would – even when Nardole raised concerns about her activities. *The Target Storybook*'s *Pain Management* expands on this further by showing Nardole, Bill (who wants to see Led Zeppelin and Nirvana live), the Doctor, and Missy, the latter begrudgingly in psychic handcuffs, visiting concerts in the past. And in the 2019 *Short Trips* story, *Dead Media*, from Big Finish, Nardole has taken the TARDIS to the Eurovision Song Contest in 1974 to see ABBA perform.

The Shining Man and *The Soul Garden* imply Bill is a Marvel fan, as she enthuses about Doctor Strange, though whether that's the comic book character or the MCU film is unknown, then Iron Man in the 2018 comic strip, *The Clockwise War*.

In *The Great Shopping Bill*, a 2017 story from Titan Comics' *The Twelfth Doctor* series, the Time Lord takes Bill and Nardole to the Übermarket, which boasts 'everything you'll ever need under one sky,' so they can get a new relative dimensional stabiliser (something seen in various TARDIS consoles) for Missy's Vault. During that story, we learn that Bill has some experience of *Rick and Morty* and has sat the Doctor down to watch *Back to the Future*: mainly spending the time criticising its approach to time travel, but it's clearly made an impression as he later exclaims, 'Great Scott!' (Nardole is aware of *Desperate Housewives* too, according to the 2021 audio, *The Nightmare Realm*. The Twelfth Doctor also briefly gets another companion, albeit for one 2023 audiobook only, *The Ice Kings*: Professor Irene Hyde is a fellow lecturer at St. Luke's University whom he takes back to 1806, to the trading ship Favorite, whose crew is slowly being picked off one by one.)

Bill and Nardole reveal themselves to be *Star Wars* fans in the following comic story, *A Confusion of Angels* (2017-18), during which they meet the Weeping Angels and Heavenly Host (from *Voyage of the Damned*), as well as Detective Inspector Margaret Ag-Kris Therur-Ford Jingatheen from Raxacoricofallapatorius, who is wearing the skinsuit of Margaret Blaine, this being Blon Fel-Fotch Passameer-Day Slitheen, given a second chance at the end of *Boom Town*. Seeing the latter, Nardole explains, 'Oh, green! Nice. As it happens, I've never been green. Blue, yes. Green, no…'

Most significantly, the 2018 Target novelisation – its canonicity debatable, as previously noted – of *Twice Upon a Time* expands on what happened to Nardole after he was left on the colony ship towards the conclusion of *The Doctor Falls*. The Cybermen apparently attack a couple more times, with Cybermats in particular attacking every spring of Nardole's later life, but their threat is largely stunted. During that period, Nardole marries six times, at one point with two women at the same time, and eventually passes away at the age of seven-hundred and twenty-eight. The same book says that Bill and Heather explore the universe together before the former wants to return to being human, suggesting the alien fuel that has transformed Heather can also transmute 'pilots' and their passengers back into their original species. In the 2020 webcast, *The Best of Days*, Bill takes a break from her time with Heather so she can study again at St. Luke's University (and Nardole keeps in touch with her, joyously telling her that he broke his legs on the banana meadow but rather enjoys being carted around in a wheelbarrow by the kids), and Heather demonstrates her omniscience by telling her they'd be back together in four months, two weeks, and three days. The pair buy a house on Earth and adopt cats, and as Bill dies of old age and the two share a kiss, she said that Heather could carry on travelling without her, from which we might infer that either Heather doesn't turn human or can transmute back into her alien form. (Either way, we don't find out if Heather takes up Bill's suggestion.) This implies that Bill was accepting of death at the end.

Pleasingly, both companions live happily ever after.

Hattie Munroe, Jata, Gaz, Maxwell Collins, and his aforementioned sister, Jessica Collins all join the Twelfth Doctor as comic-exclusive companions.

THE TWELFTH DOCTOR

The latter two live in Brixton with their parents, Lloyd and Devina, who fell in love on the 1948 ship, Windrush. Jess meets the Doctor and Clara in 1972 while hunting for vampires in *The Highgate Horror*, but her boyfriend, Dave, is killed and Jess risks her life to save her new friends. When the vampiric Corvids are defeated, Clara tries to console Jess, who's mourning Dave, by telling her, 'As long as we remember, they'll have all the peace they deserve.' When the Doctor is then trapped in 1972, six months after his previous visit, while his TARDIS repairs itself following *The Pestilent Heart*, Jess is naturally shocked to learn he can't remember Clara (thanks to the event of *Hell Bent*). Nonetheless, she allows him to stay with them in Brixton and the Doctor spends time getting to know each member of the family. In doing so, he becomes good friends with Maxwell, a comic book fan who especially likes Spider-Man and Hulk (*Moving In*).

Jess is an art history student, so the Doctor is keen to regale her with tales of his seeing artists like Picasso and Boucher, and take her to meet Monet and Renoir. He can't without the TARDIS, so instead, he wants to show her the universe through her love of paintings. As such, he takes Jess and Maxwell to the National Gallery, but are confronted by hunters, Skadi and Tarquel, who kidnap Maxwell (*Bloodsport*). The Doctor values him and Jess (who is also being hunted) so much that he offers his life in exchange for theirs. After Skadi and Tarquel's defeat, the Doctor sticks around to experience Christmas with the Collins household in *Be Forgot*: even though the Time Lord still isn't a fan of the festivities, the family's community spirit seems to affect him, so much so that he delivers Christmas cards with Jess, helps Devina cook, and plays the guitar for a street party during which Maxwell excitedly shows off his present: a new bike.

The following year, tragedy seems to strike once more in *Doorway to Hell*, when Jess, Devina, and Lloyd are taken and used by the Master, and Lloyd is aged to death (akin to Sara Kingdom) while defending them. Separated from his family, Maxwell is then aged by a time storm, and is horrified to be reunited with them only to see his father die. Fortunately, the effects are reversed and Lloyd is resurrected.

Though the Master insinuates that it's the Doctor doing them harm, they stay true to him, with Jess arguing, 'We're the Doctor's family!' Nonetheless, when the Master is defeated, the Doctor has to leave them: 'I fooled myself into thinking I could stop for a while – but death is always snapping at my heels.' He leaves Maxwell with the best of his comic book collection, and Devina tells him he's forever welcome at their table; his departing words to Jess remind her that art is a window into the universe. We see Jess again in 2003, working at the National Gallery, showing students paintings, including John Constable's *The Hay Wain*, which now includes the Twelfth Doctor waving at her from the TARDIS.

Hattie Munroe, meanwhile, is a bit more rock 'n' roll, being the lead in a band called the Space Pirates, playing at *The Twist* (also the name of Titan Comics' 2016 story that introduces her) in the fortieth century. The Doctor steals her bass guitar, prompting her to follow him into an investigation into the murder of local councillor, Idra Panatar. After finding the culprit, the Doctor invites Hattie to join him in the TARDIS, and the pair spend a fair amount of time having jam sessions in the ship; in 2017's *Beneath the Waves*, he even implies Hattie should meet and play the spoons with his seventh incarnation.

The Doctor mainly takes Hattie with him so they can play music together. Still, when he drops her back home for a short time, he comes back to provide her with a brief respite from the media after her career garners a lot of attention.

(Coincidentally, Grant, Lucy, and Jennifer from *The Return of Doctor Mysterio* briefly travel with the Doctor in Titan's *Ghost Stories*, as they try to track down three other Hazandra gemstones like the one that gave Grant his powers. Grant adopts Jennifer, but he and Lucy don't have children of their own as they think their lives too impractical. Even when Grant's crystal is removed, he keeps his Ghost abilities as it has already bonded and transformed his DNA.)

THE TWELFTH DOCTOR

Arguably, the Twelfth Doctor's most unusual companion is Jata, who appears in six comics between 2016 and 2017 in *Doctor Who Adventures* and is important for being created and written exclusively by Seventh Doctor era producer, Andrew Cartmel. Jata joins the Doctor in *From the Horse's Mouth* – indeed, this companion looks like a white horse with a star shape on its brow, but is actually an alien. Jata left his native Osumare in an Alnitak Class Q7 starship, but crash-landed in Wyoming, America, in 1899, and was forced to make the best of 'this barbaric world,' living with Clint Currie, a dumb small-time crook whose bounties increased considerably after Jata started working with him in exchange for food. The Doctor arrives three months later and foils Currie's plot to rob a train. With the criminal arrested, the Doctor agrees to take Jata back home, but instead go on numerous detours, including to a school in the twenty-first century where the students had been turned into mindless zombies (*Fear Buds*), and to the human colony of Bode 215 in *Night of the Worms*, where Jata expressed his love of apples and a distaste for humans, asking if humanity has messed the planet up yet. In *Royal Wedding*, he also reveals that his species can fly and sprouts impressive wings to carry the Doctor away from trouble.

Jata doesn't get a proper goodbye as his last appearance comes in *Killer App* before being replaced by a one-off companion called Gaz in the Twelfth Doctor's last *DWA* strip, *A Cold Snap*. Jata does at least warm to mankind somewhat, offering contemporary schoolchildren free 'pony rides' to cheer them up. Gaz, meanwhile, meets the Doctor in Blackpool in 1976, and together they stop an invasion by the bear-like S'Qwatch. The Doctor takes to calling him Gaz-better, as his real name is Gary but says he 'likes Gaz better.'

Away from comic books, the Twelfth Doctor gets a few new assistants on audio, including Chicago-born Alex Yow and her brother, Brandon, the first companions exclusive to the *New Series Adventures* audio range.

In their first appearance, *The Lost Angel*, Brandon visits his sister, an aspiring photojournalist seeking her big break, in Rickman in upstate New York, when they witness her landlord being displaced in time by a Weeping Angel. The Doctor agrees to take them on one quick trip, but instead, they venture deep inside the TARDIS when it comes under attack, and discover the lost world of Ultacan, quarantined inside the ship (*The Lost Planet*), then find themselves separated when the Spanish galleon the TARDIS lands on in July 1588 is destroyed in a freak storm and the Doctor experiences a degeneration cycle, running back through his previous eleven incarnations (*The Lost Magic*). Their last adventures come in *The Lost Flame*, which takes them to Escalupia, a medical hub for the First Great and Bountiful Human Empire, via Karn (from *The Brain of Morbius*).

Big Finish's *The Twelfth Doctor Chronicles* also gives the Twelfth Doctor a new companion: Keira Sanstrom, a trainee Time Agent, played by Bhavnisha Parmar, whose curiosity leads her to dismantle her vortex manipulator while assigned to Calandra in *Flight to Calandra*, part of *Timejacked!* (2021). She can't reassemble it, so she manipulates Calandra's Science Bureau in order to get to Earth and blackmail the Doctor into assisting her, the Time Lord being the stuff of legend at the Time Agency. She finds him at St Luke's University in Bristol and disassembles Nardole to obtain the Doctor's help; after fixing issues she's caused on Calandra, they make their way back to Bristol, only to find it's been drastically changed (*Split Second*). Following a mix-up with two Keiras (*The Weight of History*), the Doctor leaves her but promises to watch how she gets on in future. Instead, she calls him in to help her and the Time Agency take down the Quartermaster, one of the most notorious weapons dealers in the universe, in 2024's *You Only Die Twice*, a boxset which takes the pair from a party on a private sun (*Sunstrike*), to a time-looped Austria in 1677 (*Never The End Is*), before digging into the Time Agency itself.

Finally, *When the Wolves Came*, from the *Doctor Who Official Annual 2015*, is significant for being the first licensed short story to feature the Twelfth Doctor, and for giving us a temporary, one-shot companion of sorts in Simon, a boy struggling to survive in twenty-second century Bedfordshire, likely during *The Dalek Invasion of Earth*. The TARDIS is stuck there for several months and gives Simon shelter from the wolves roaming the wrecked county. Pleading for help, Simon connects to the TARDIS telepathic circuits and so holograms of the Doctor and Clara help him pilot the ship back to them, and in doing so, saves them from Aaraanandal slime beasts. In return, the Doctor delivers him safely away from Bedfordshire. In a way, then, Simon is more like the TARDIS' very brief companion than the Doctor's!

The Thirteenth Doctor
Jodie Whitaker

*'You want to know the secrets of existence? Start with the
mysteries of the heart. I can show you everything if you stop
being afraid of what you don't understand.'*
– The Doctor, *The Witchfinders*.

Ryan Sinclair – Tosin Cole (*The Woman Who Fell to Earth* to
Revolution of the Daleks)

Cheap Thrills (Sia); *Pura Vida* (Izïa).

Ryan Sinclair's life has been mired in tragedy, and we first meet
him in *The Woman Who Fell to Earth* as he's delivering a
message about the greatest woman he's ever met – who he says is
'smart, funny, caring, special' – to his followers on YouTube.

Ryan's nan, Grace, is on a train with her husband, Graham,
when the power cuts and they're locked in. She phones Ryan, only
to be attacked by an electrical creature. Ryan, hearing his nan in
distress, races to the train, alongside probationary police officer,
Yasmin Khan, or just 'Yaz', for short; the pair went to school
together but drifted apart, and have only now met again after Ryan
calls the police about a weird purple pod in the woods. Ryan is
understandably close to Grace, but less so Graham, who Ryan
refuses to call his grandad and scoffs at their encouraging him to
ride a bike. Having dyspraxia and a lack of self-confidence, Ryan
can't grasp the technique and in frustration even throws his bike off
a hill.

He's quite open-minded, however, and, after seeing the Doctor
crash through the train carriage roof and the electrical monster affect

the vehicle, he is quick to suggest it's all down to aliens (he later confides in Yaz that he truly believes the Doctor is an alien too). After the Doctor saves them, he and Grace take her back to their house. The Doctor borrows Ryan's phone and reformats it in order to use it to track alien activity. He laments that all his data is on there. 'Not anymore,' the Doctor says, dismissively.

Ryan blames himself for them all getting infected by DNA bombs, and the trail leads to Tzim-Sha, a Stenza warrior whom the Doctor defeats – but at considerable cost, as Grace is killed.

Ryan's YouTube video, then, turns out to be a eulogy for the woman who raised him after his mother died in 2012 and his father abandoned him. (In retrospect, his phone's data being erased must've been difficult for Ryan, seeing as it stored all his photos and texts with Grace.) 'It's like the best people get taken first,' he says. Just as upsetting for Ryan is the fact his dad doesn't attend Grace's funeral. He still feels an obligation to the Doctor, and helps as she makes a transmat – which she uses to accidentally teleport herself, Ryan, Graham, and Yaz into deep space.

They're rescued and taken to the planet Desolation, where they compete in the final Rally of the Twelve Galaxies, a race to *The Ghost Monument*, i.e. the TARDIS (which he initially dismisses: 'Didn't look all that'). 'We're on an alien planet, Graham,' Ryan enthuses, showing the pair have already grown closer since Grace's passing. He's also particularly pleased to find out Yaz is still alive, them having been separated for a short time. While there, Ryan has his time to shine, displaying skills learned from playing *Call of Duty* while firing at SniperBots. The Doctor claims she doesn't like guns, but later tells him, 'You're amazing... Think of what you've gone through to be here, and you're still going. I'm proper impressed.'

Ryan's consistently amazed at being on another planet, and at the TARDIS when they finally get there, proclaiming it 'awesome.' His mood takes a downturn when the TARDIS takes them to 1955, and Ryan sees a white woman dropping a glove; he hands it back to her, only for her husband to slap him – this is the racially segregated Montgomery, Alabama, and Ryan is on the receiving end of some horrendous discrimination throughout (*Rosa*). He gets confused about who Rosa Parks actually is, but enthuses about Martin Luther King, asserting that he's 'not totally ignorant. I just got confused by the whole bus thing.'

Still, Ryan is more than up to the task of standing up for himself. When waiting for food at a restaurant, a waitress tells him, 'We don't serve negroes.' Ryan replies, 'Good, because I don't eat them.' He also finds Rosa inspirational, saying he'll be okay there for a few hours, considering Parks has to live in that era. He later confides to Yaz, 'I'm having to work so hard to keep my temper, every second here. I could've slapped that guy back there as soon as we arrived.' He's got a hang-up about the police, but Yaz argues against his preconceptions, including his belief that nothing changes, despite Parks' bravery. It's meeting Martin Luther King that seems to change his mind: he can't stop shaking his hand, forgets to serve the coffee Parks asked for, and later thanks her, telling her he does now believe things will get better.

He's still happy to get home (*Arachnids in the UK*), though doesn't want to break away from the group just yet, accepting Yaz's offer for them all to go back to her place for tea. There, Ryan takes a liking to Yaz's sister, Sonya, though this might be deflection seeing as there's clearly some attraction between him and Yasmin: in *Rosa*, he says that a boy in Year 10 whose bedroom Yaz crept into 'was punching well above his weight'. Still, it appears to be reciprocated, as Sonya is pleased to hear Ryan and Yaz are just friends (and later, in *Spyfall: Part One*, she asks for Ryan's number, though Yaz refuses to share it).

We get hints that Ryan might be starting to regret not being closer to Graham too: his grandad goes off home and Ryan asks the Doctor if she thinks he should've gone with him. 'You know him better than me,' the Doctor says, to which Ryan replies, 'Not much.' Ryan's especially annoyed to read a letter from his dad saying he can come to live with him, seeing as he's his *real* family; Ryan's realising that family's made up of the people who look after you, and Graham's proved himself. He's more understanding in the next episode, explaining to Yaz that, aged thirteen, he found his mum on the floor after she'd died from a heart attack and that everyone says Ryan looks like her; he admits that his dad might've found that hard. Still, Graham and Ryan want to spend more time together, telling the Doctor that they want to carry on travelling with her and Yaz. Their relationship is cemented further when the pair help deliver a baby in *The Tsuranga Conundrum*; Graham suggests Ryan's learned his bedside manner from Grace while he himself takes on this considerable challenge after watching every episode of *Call the Midwife* – he concedes that he looks away during the squeamish parts. Despite this, Ryan refuses to give Graham a celebratory fist bump.

Ryan's time working in a warehouse is another reason he doesn't want to go back to his normal life. In *Kerblam!*, he says he and his co-workers used to mess about by putting stuff in the trainers they used to pack up, so is initially unconcerned to see 'help me' on the back of a parcel's packing slip delivered to the TARDIS, figuring it's someone mucking about. So he's pretty annoyed about travelling across the universe, only to end up working undercover in another warehouse – this time, Kerblam!, the biggest retailer in the galaxy operating from the moon of Kandoka. He's also creeped out by the robotic TeamMates that make up ninety percent of the workforce; still, the foursome meet humans there, and Ryan connects with Kira as he tells her, 'Takes me a while to learn things physically. Get there in the end, but just some stuff takes me a bit longer. Luckily, I had mates who covered for me in the beginning.' She, too, had a wobbly start at Kerblam! and feared the system would fire her. When she later goes missing, Ryan leads the charge to find her, though is fairly unfazed by her death.

And while Ryan's eye has been rather wandering during his travels, the tables are turned in *The Witchfinders* when King James I takes a liking to him. He tries to use this to his advantage when the King thinks the Doctor is a witch and attempts to drown her; his begging, 'Please, Your Majesty' seems to make James cave and raise the dunking stool. When the monarch tries to recruit him as his protector, Ryan turns down the offer but tells him he'll be keeping an eye on him regardless, having seen the King's bloodlust and obsession with witches.

It seems that Ryan has got used to death, and he bonds with Graham because the latter is struggling so much to move on from Grace. In *It Takes You Away*, when they meet the Solitract, a being who lures in victims by taking on the faces of the dead, Graham seemingly comes face-to-face with Grace again and believes this strange creature really is his deceased wife – that is, until Ryan is in danger and 'Grace' apparently doesn't care. Ryan and Graham admit how much they both miss her, and Ryan finally calls Graham 'Grandad'. In *The Battle of Ranskoor Av Kolos*, Ryan affirms that they're family and that he loves him.

This familial connection is strengthened when Ryan's dad, Aaron, turns up at their door on New Year's Day 2019 (*Resolution*). While Graham's instinct is to shut him out, Ryan lets him in and then goes for a coffee with him. Aaron is something of a 'Del Boy', having given up working on rigs and now trying to flog a microwave to strangers in the café. Ryan isn't fooled, and doesn't forgive his father, admitting that he'd felt lonely, abandoned, and undeserving of love. Ryan accuses him of hiding from his responsibilities and tells Yaz that he doesn't want him there. Still, when Aaron is taken over by a Dalek mutant and he's nearly sucked out of the TARDIS into a supernova, Ryan saves him and appeals, 'Dad, I'm here for you. I forgive you. I love you, Dad.' Even the Doctor proves forgiving, offering Aaron a trip in the ship – it's for the best that Aaron turns it down, but checks that Ryan will call him as soon as he gets back.

As is, the group works well together. In *Spyfall*, Ryan and Yaz go undercover at technology giant, VOX, and interview its creator, Daniel Barton, while the Doctor and Graham search for the missing MI6 Agent, O; it says a lot about their relationship that Graham trusts Ryan to go on this dangerous mission without him and the 'Doc'. Yaz is teleported away by the Kasaavin and Ryan can do nothing but run – he at least apologises and contacts the Doctor, though his initial reaction to what's happened to Yaz undermines his later reassuring her that he'd never let anything happen to her. He somewhat makes up for it by helping to land a plane that Agent O, aka the Master, has trapped them all in. Ryan also reacts quicker than Yaz after realising Barton can track them all by their smartphones and quickly smashes his own and Yaz's. The pair have become closer, though Ryan's eye drifts somewhat in *Orphan 55* when, after recovering from an attack by the Hopper virus, he meets fellow patient, Bella. He tries to impress her, fumbling up two perhaps dream jobs and merging them by telling her he's a 'pilot surgeon – I'm a surgeon for pilots.' The feeling is mutual: she accuses him of acting stupid so that girls reply to all his questions; he tells her he's not trying to chat her up, and she responds, 'Shame.' He also tells her that his mum died 'eight years ago', putting into question how long he's actually been travelling in the TARDIS. He's uncomfortable when the Doctor and particularly Yaz start to notice his growing attraction to Bella, though he makes it more obvious when he and Bella are forced to say goodbye (with a parting kiss) as she effectively sacrifices herself while the others get away. It's heavily implied she and her father, Kane, are dead: despite Graham trying to assure him that she'll be okay, Ryan counters, 'How are they going to be okay? No oxygen, no help…'

Later, the events of *Orphan 55* come back to haunt him when the Eternal, Zellin, causes Ryan to have a nightmare about his experience there, as well as his old friend, Tibo, who, in the dream state, appears aged and says he's waited all his life for Ryan to come back (*Can You Hear Me?*). Ryan's time in the TARDIS has strained this friendship, so much so that Tibo is surprised to see him again at all, considering he's been receiving the silent treatment for months now. In that time, Tibo has grown lonely, and let parts of his life fall apart – something Ryan notices when playing a game of FIFA with him. Ryan tells Tibo the truth about his travels, but it's clear he feels some guilt: he encourages Tibo to go to group therapy sessions, and admits to Yaz that their new life unsettles him: 'We're getting older, but without them; missing out bits of their lives... We'll have changed; they wouldn't have. It's like we're living at different rates.'

The Doctor's recent behaviour doesn't help. At the start of *Fugitive of the Judoon*, the companions confront her about her being distant, and she explains she's worried that the Master is still out there. Ryan does try to comfort her later on, telling her that whatever happens, she's got the three of them; the Doctor throws this back in his face, however, by saying they don't even know her, 'not even a little bit.' Ryan disagrees and hints that he's trying to embrace the present in his life, noting, 'Whoever you were in the past or are in the future, we know who you are right now.' This could show his attitude towards his history with his dad, Graham, and Grace. It would seem his time as a vlogger could come back to confront him in *Praxeus* when he meets another YouTube star, Gabriela Camara, half of travel vlog duo, Two Girls Roaming. But Ryan doesn't recognise her and doesn't bring up his own channel, so perhaps he really has moved on from that life.

The tension comes to a head in *Ascension of the Cybermen / The Timeless Children* when truths about the Doctor's past lives come to light and Ryan and his peers must try to help her battle through these revelations. He and the Doctor are separated from Graham and Yaz, and though his gut reaction is to find them again, he instantly refocuses when the Doctor highlights the dangers that they're in as they help a group of humans escape the last of the Cybermen. He gets a bit travel sick when flying at warp speed, and shows that the Doctor's distaste for weapons has rubbed off on him, initially turning them down before being told he has no choice.

Ryan pulls out all the stops in trying to defeat the Cybermen, fighting his nerves to throw a bomb at a group of Cybermen. His lack of self-belief swiftly turns on its head afterwards when he jumps the gun in boasting 'You come for humans, you come for me, Ryan Sinclair! We defeated the Cybermen. Well, me. Technically, it's me.' (Naturally, there are more Cybermen behind him.)

Despite her attitude towards her companions of late, the three reaffirm that they're here for the Doctor after she learns that her memories of her early lives have been expunged and that Time Lord society is essentially based on child abuse – and that she was the child in question. Nonetheless, Ryan realises that, to stop the Master and the Cybermen, someone has to sacrifice themselves as the rest use a reprogrammed TARDIS to get them back to Earth in the twenty-first century: while Yaz is resistant to the idea of the Doctor staying behind, Ryan perhaps values Yaz more and seizes the chance to get home.

Ryan seemingly honours the Doctor's wishes, that they go on to enjoy their lives to the fullest, but stays loyal to Yaz, who, in turn, stays loyal to the Doctor by largely refusing to leave the TARDIS in case it can get them back to her (*Revolution of the Daleks*). Ryan, Graham, and Yaz don't find out the Doctor is still alive until ten months later, when they're trying to stop the production of defence drones that are, in reality, Daleks. In that time, the Doctor's moral compass has clearly stuck with them. Graham confronts Jack Robertson, who appears to be responsible for the Dalek drones, and Ryan praises him: 'I like that whole "whatever you're doing, we're going to stop you" vibe. Very Doctory.' He channels this himself later on, saying he wants a word with Robertson, and goes with Graham and Captain Jack Harkness to blow up a Dalek Death Squad spacecraft. (Admittedly, this is both brave and stupid, considering Captain Jack can come back from the dead. Still, it is Ryan who detonates the bombs and destroys the Dalek craft.)

Ryan obviously isn't very happy with the Doctor, though it's initially uncertain whether that's because she's been gone ten months without letting them know she's not dead, or because he's actually come to enjoy life back home and she threatens that safety.

They have a discussion about what's happened since the last time they saw each other. Ryan has spent the time reconnecting with his dad (who is now back on the oil rigs) and his mates, and adds that he did nonetheless miss the Doctor. She tells him about what happened to her on Gallifrey, and questions who she even is now. Ryan explains that she'll always be the Doctor, but dismisses her conclusion that it's 'same Doctor, same Ryan'. He instead suggests that change is scary but good, and that she should learn about the memories taken by the Time Lords: 'Confront the new or the old. And then everything will be all right.' He resolves to look after the planet when the Doctor isn't around, and leaves the TARDIS with Graham, the Doctor and Ryan parting with a hug and thanking each other for being good friends.

Together, Graham and Ryan plan to use psychic paper to gain access to sites in Finland and Korea where suspected aliens have surfaced. By the time Graham meets the Doctor again in *The Power of the Doctor*, Ryan is exploring Patagonia, apparently by himself; however, it's clear, from his once more calling Graham 'Grandad' at the end of *Revolution of the Daleks*, that things have changed a lot for Ryan.

Yasmin Khan – Mandip Gill (*The Woman Who Fell to Earth* to *The Power of the Doctor*)

I Will Wait (Mumford & Sons); *New Year's Day* (Taylor Swift).

Yasmin Khan's life is changed forever when she appeals to her senior, Ramesh Sunder, for more interesting policing work than settling parking disputes (*The Woman Who Fell to Earth*). As a nineteen-year-old probationary police officer in Sheffield, she wants to challenge herself, and that's exactly what happens. She's called to 'something different', i.e. Ryan Sinclair's reporting that he's found a giant purple pod in the woods. Though they don't immediately recognise each other, Yasmin clocks his name and recalls that they went to Redlands Primary school together.

Yasmin initially has a caring and no-nonsense approach to policing, and, when she overhears Ryan's phone call, in which his nan, Grace, tells him their train has stopped and that something weird is going on, she races off with Ryan to investigate further. On the train, they meet the Doctor, an eccentric woman (who's somewhat surprised by the fact Yasmin refers to her as 'madam') who falls through the carriage roof, the TARDIS having dropped her off in mid-air before dematerialising. Yasmin tries to assert her authority here, telling the Doctor, 'I need you to do as I say. This could be a potential crime scene.' The Doctor subverts this by asking for her name, and while the probationer initially replies, 'PC Khan, Hallamshire Police', she soon relents: 'Yasmin Khan. Yaz to my friends.' It's not long before they're all calling her Yaz.

She intends to send a report to her station about the incident but is held back by the Doctor's insistence that, first, she needs actual facts about what happened on the train. As you might expect, Yaz begins to interview one of the witnesses, a crane operator called Karl, and wants to view CCTV footage of the incident. She deals with facts, so doesn't entirely buy into Ryan's belief that whatever electrical creature attacked the train was an alien, though she can't think of an alternative.

Yaz uses her initiative and drives the Doctor, Graham O'Brien, Grace, and Ryan to the woods to see the alien pod she was called in to investigate; then, after the Doctor faints and Grace and Ryan take her to their house, Yaz checks in with her colleagues to see if there have been any other out-of-the-ordinary incidents that night, to no avail. Still, she gravitates back towards the Doctor and co. When it turns out they've all been laced with DNA bombs, she follows them all while tracing the aliens responsible, and assures Ryan it's not his fault, despite Graham blaming him. Her and Ryan quickly develop a bond and take each other into their confidence, with both confessing that they do now believe the Doctor is an alien. Yaz is protective of her community – one reason she's training to be a police officer – and asserts, 'This is my home, and I'm not having it being an alien battleground.'

They find Tzim-Sha of the Stenza and the Doctor defeats him after a face-off at the top of a crane; Yaz and Ryan demonstrate considerable guile by climbing to the top with the Time Lord they've only just met. PC Khan must feel a sense of duty or companionship for them as she attends Grace's memorial service, and helps the Doctor choose some new clothes at a charity shop. With Ryan and Graham, she's then accidentally teleported into deep space by the Doctor.

They're taken to the planet Desolation and compete in a race to *The Ghost Monument*, which turns out to be the TARDIS. Yasmin is quick to trust the Doctor, checking she can get them all home again but is nonetheless confident. This pays off, as they do make it to the ship, which immediately amazes Yaz; so too is the idea it's a time machine, and she's enthusiastic about stepping into the 'real life 1950s' (*Rosa*). That is, until it turns out they're in Montgomery, Alabama, at a time during racial segregation. Her police training kicks in when Ryan is abused, telling his attacker to step back. She's then amazed to meet Rosa Parks, reminding Ryan that Year 4, 5, and 6 school classes were named after inspirational people – and they were in Parks'. She's shocked when he doesn't recognise her historical significance, though doesn't know that Parks and Martin Luther King knew each other. Yaz takes some racial discrimination on the chin, not quite believing that a waitress in a local café thinks she's Mexican then joking with Ryan that she'll use him as a piñata.

Yaz is thoroughly optimistic throughout their experience in 1955, admitting to Ryan that, 'I get called a "Paki" when I'm sorting out a domestic, or a terrorist on the way home from the mosque... But they don't win, those people. I can be a police officer now because people like Rosa Parks fought those battles for me. For us.' Her faith is strengthened further when she chats with Parks and realises that they're all a part of this story.

The Doctor manages to get them back home in *Arachnids in the UK* and Yaz seems genuinely pleased to be back. When she learns the Doctor is going to travel on her own, though, she offers them all to go back to her flat in the Park Hill estate for tea. She introduces the Doctor and Ryan as her friends and her sister, Sonya, shows mock surprise that she has any mates at all. Her father, the conspiracy-loving Hakim, says Yasmin never brings any friends around, and Sonya suggests she's married to her job. Yaz appears close to her family, and as soon as she sees her mum, Najia, she gives her a big hug – which Najia suggests is odd seeing as they only saw each other a few hours ago. She finds the Doctor weird, questioning why Yasmin hasn't mentioned her before, then asking whether Yaz and the Doctor are dating (which we might infer means Yaz is secretive about her relationships and perhaps sexuality). Still, Yaz is quick to take on the Doctor's offer to continue travelling in the TARDIS, telling her, 'I love my family, but they also drive me completely insane. I want more. More of the universe. More time with you. You're like the best person I've ever met.'

It's this closeness to her family that prompts Yaz to ask the Doctor to visit the historical Punjab and see her 'Nani', Umbreen, when she was younger (*Demons of the Punjab*). This is prompted by Umbreen giving Yaz – her 'favourite granddaughter' – a broken watch which she says must never be fixed. She doesn't elaborate, despite Yaz asserting that she wants to know: 'Your life's our heritage.' The TARDIS takes them to 17th August 1947, the exact date the watch was broken, and Yaz is surprised to see it in the possession of Prem, a young Hindu man whom the young Umbreen intends to marry. The wedding ceremony is the following day, right at the time of the partition of India.

Yaz is upset about Umbreen keeping this part of her past hidden. She is also nervous about the Doctor officiating the marriage, and is certainly conflicted about Prem. Nevertheless, she initially rejects the idea of Prem having to die, though she is quickly won around by the Doctor's insistence that he has to in order for Yasmin to exist. Yaz wants to stick around anyway, to look after Umbreen, to make sure she's okay, likely concerned not only about how she'd deal with his death but also with the partition. She's understandably emotional at the ceremony, saying she always cries at weddings. Yaz helps her grandmother tie a rope between herself and Prem, noting it's 'a Hindu thing', to which Umbreen replies, 'Now it can be our thing; if we want it to be.' Prem responds by doing 'a Muslim' thing, giving her the watch as a madr; it promptly smashes and Umbreen says it's perfect, symbolising their 'moment in time' together. After Prem gives his life for Umbreen to get away during such a turbulent time, Yaz heads back to contemporary Sheffield and asks her nani if she's really happy with her life; she says she is, then offers to tell her granddaughter the story of the watch; Yaz, however, is content and suggests she tells her the tale another time.

She's a natural investigator, noticing things in *Kerblam!* that even the Doctor doesn't: firstly, that there's a cry for help on the back of a parcel's packing slip; then that Dan Cooper, a warehouse worker she befriends, is one of numerous people who have gone missing; and that, as the whole place is automated, it makes little sense that Warehouse Executive, Jarva Slade, relies on a clipboard to keep select things out of the System. Indeed, the Doctor calls her and Ryan the 'greatest detectives in the galaxy'. Yaz obviously connected with Dan during her brief time working there: at the end of the episode, when it's apparent that Dan is dead, she asks the Doctor if she can take his 'Dad' pendant back to his daughter, to tell her 'how much he loved it; how much he loved her.' This also comes across as a sort of penance, as Dan saved Yaz's life by switching scanners with her and saving her from a robotic Kerblam! Man. She also quickly gravitates towards Willa in *The Witchfinders*, showing herself to be approachable and able to befriend the locals, no matter the time period they end up in. And while the Doctor automatically looks for something physically wrong with Willa, Yaz is smart enough to recognise that she's overcome by the same fear and dread that Yaz faced in school, when a girl called Izzy Flint turned the whole class against her and she had to live through a 'year of Hell.' This awakened something within her, a desire to stand up against bullies like Flint when she grew up, likely inspiring her to become a police officer.

This is later expanded upon in *Can You Hear Me?*, in which Yaz recalls the mental health crisis she suffered just three years before meeting the Doctor. She'd intended to run away, but Sonya called the police, fearing that she'd hurt herself. Officer Anita Patel found her at the side of a road and bet her that, in three years' time, things would improve. After being forced to relive those experiences in a dream, but realising how much better her life is now, Yaz visits Anita to give her that money.

As far as her family is concerned, Yaz's career is taking off. At the start of *Spyfall: Part One*, she's told everyone, including her boss, that she's on secondment (i.e. travelling in the TARDIS). Sunder thinks this is really undercover work, but insists she has to come back to finish her probation. Indeed, she's excited by the idea of going undercover, posing as a journalist called Sofia Afzal, for the Doctor: she and Ryan are instructed to spy on Daniel Barton, creator of VOR, and it's clear she's dug into him before – Ryan says VOR is just a search engine, but Yaz further explains it's comprised of 'web apps, social, global mapping, advertising, scientific and medical research, robotics, data polling, [and] human analytics.' She takes to this legend better than Ryan, who, posing as photographer Logan Jackson, rather fumbles his introduction, meaning Yaz has to cover for him. When Barton leaves the supposed press interview early, the two companions are gutsy enough to carry on snooping around his office, though this backfires when a Kasaavin appears and transports Yaz elsewhere. She later admits to Ryan that she was scared because she thought she was dead. She bonds rather well with missing MI6 agent, O, who they find in the Australian outback – there's even a little bit of flirting – until it's revealed he's actually the Master. He strands them on a plummeting airplane (rough going for Yaz, who, in *Kerblam!*, said that she had never liked rollercoasters...), though the Doctor intervenes in a timey-wimey fashion and helps them land it.

After the Doctor's showdown with the Master, we get the first instances of tension between the three companions and the Time Lord as they tell her they know very little about her; she answers a few questions, but the Doctor doesn't want to take them to Gallifrey (it having been destroyed by the Master), somewhere

Yaz is notably keen to visit. It's something that leaves the Doctor in, according to Yaz, a 'mardy mood' (*Orphan 55*), and there's more friction in *Fugitive of the Judoon* when the Doctor tells her companions that they don't really know her. It's Ryan who immediately steps up and tells her she's wrong; Yaz is a bit more passive in the confrontation, simply agreeing with Graham when he says they're family now, but nevertheless tells the Doctor not to talk to Ryan in such an abrupt fashion and assuring the Doctor that they'll be there for her, no matter what's coming. Yaz has a strong sense of duty, perhaps more so than even the Doctor, and this seems to drive her into following the Doctor into danger. So she takes responsibility for the Doctor – in *Fugitive of the Judoon*, she doesn't seem quite as shocked as the others to see Captain Jack Harkness, instead telling him, 'You have to get us back there; the Doctor needs us' – and for those whose lives their travels have affected (she does CPR on Percy Shelley in *The Haunting of Villa Diodati* after the Doctor shows him a vision of his own death).

Yaz is generally sure of herself too: she and Graham go on a solo mission to Hong Kong to investigate curious energy readings in *Praxeus* and, when fired at, she holds up a control panel to defend herself, which she soon deduces is important to them – important enough that they won't risk hitting it when attacking – so she stays behind to look into it further while her peers go to meet with the Doctor. She's also gutsy enough to follow aliens wearing hazmats to an unknown destination via their teleport. Her bravery could be due to her police training, or the trust the Doctor places in her.

Given her scolding Ryan over Rosa Parks, Yaz obviously has a decent amount of historical knowledge, but doesn't know the lead protagonist in *Nikola Tesla's Night of Terror*. That at least means she's not intimidated by his genius and reacts to him empathetically, spurring him on when she realises what a genius he is – perhaps this is why the Doctor trusts her to stay with him while she goes to meet Thomas Edison (someone Yaz is less enamoured with). Yaz's respect and empathy for Tesla is clearly mutual. When the Queen of the Skithra threatens to kill Yaz if Tesla doesn't do what she wants, he appeals, 'She's my assistant! I need her!' When they save the day using Tesla's doomed Wardenclyffe, Yaz is sure the future will change so the scientist is better remembered; sadly, the Doctor says this isn't the case. 'That's not right. People should know,' Yaz argues, her appreciation of modern life seemingly turned on its head, and Yaz concludes that he shouldn't give up, 'whatever anyone says.'

Her historical knowledge is put to the test again in *The Haunting of Villa Diodati*, when she and her friends meet Mary Shelley, Percy Shelley, and Lord Byron. It's definitely the former she's most excited about, seeing as the TARDIS lands on the night that inspired Mary to write *Frankenstein*. She seemingly wants to challenge the Doctor's rules – don't mention the book, don't interfere in events, and don't snog Byron – but it's actually the Time Lord who stretches her own rules by pushing for Mary to start writing. Yaz is quick to point this out, even though the Doctor has a good excuse (i.e. that something is wrong with history as Byron hasn't tasked his peers with writing a ghost story). Yaz's no-nonsense approach comes to the fore throughout: when she finds Claire Clairmont trying to pick a door lock to find letters that might reveal Byron's feelings for her, Yaz suggests, 'Or you could try asking him.' Interestingly, she ditches this straightforward attitude when it comes to her love for the Doctor, which she keeps hidden for much of their adventures together. She also acts as an anchor for the Doctor, trying to keep her more excessive and careless side in check; Yaz is the one who remembers Captain Jack Harkness' warning them of the Lone Cyberman, Ashad, from *Fugitive of the Judoon*, and is willing to risk Earth, suggesting to the Doctor that Ashad's threat to 'tear this reality' and leave the planet 'only in shreds' is just a bluff. When things go from bad to worse, the Doctor says she can drop her companions home to 2020, but it's Yaz who immediately volunteers them all to go with her to stop the Cybermen. When they're split up in *Ascension of the Cybermen/The Timeless Children*,

Yaz keeps a positive attitude: against overwhelming odds, she says to Graham, 'Me and you together? No one else stands a chance.' Indeed, they prove a good team. They save a Gravraft full of refugees from the Cybermen as the ship drifts powerlessly through space with the idea of rerouting the last of the life support systems to the propulsion units; they save Ryan and move about the Cyber-Carrier ship freely by disguising themselves as Cybermen; and later on, Yaz laughs at her friend and says, 'You've come a long way, Graham O'Brien.' Graham thinks she's the best person he's ever met; she says it's the nicest thing anyone's ever said to her. She tells him, 'You're not such a bad human yourself either.' When he scoffs at this, she retorts, 'Mate, I'm from Yorkshire. That's a love letter.'

It's a shame, then, that Graham leaves in *Revolution of the Daleks*; it's obvious that they're staying in touch. When the Doctor is imprisoned and believed dead, Yaz stays vigilant around the TARDIS, hoping they can get back to her, and it's Graham who pulls her out of this reverie. When Graham leaves alongside Ryan, they share a group hug and Graham tells Yaz to keep doing humanity proud. Yaz tells him she'll miss him, and then off she and the Doctor go, ostensibly to the Meringue Galaxy.

Conversely, Yaz is initially quite dismissive of Dan Lewis, the next person to step on board the TARDIS – she immediately shuts down his suggestion that the TARDIS isn't a 'ship' and tells him to shut up when he jokes about having a mate with another craft that's bigger on the inside – though this could be because she's reflecting the Doctor's panic over the Flux. Fortunately, they quickly grow closer, with Yasmin essentially becoming Dan's guide through his crazy new life on board the TARDIS. She rescues him from Karvanista of the Lupari (*The Halloween Apocalypse*) and the Doctor defers to her to check if Dan's okay following the Flux, a force that destroys half the universe and flings the TARDIS trio back to the Crimean War. In *War of the Sontarans*, the second chapter of *Flux*, they're separated from the Doctor (with the latter promising Yaz that she'll find her, making it apparent that her extended absence between *The Timeless Children* and *Revolution of the Daleks* upset Yaz), Yaz ending up in the mysterious Temple of Atropos with pilot, Inston-Vee Vinder, and Liverpudlian philanthropist, Joseph Williamson.

It appears that it's wanting to find Yaz that makes Dan accept the Doctor's offer to travel in the TARDIS with her at the conclusion of *War of the Sontarans*; before this, when the Doctor and Dan see each other again, they're both immediately concerned with Yaz's whereabouts. When they do find her, she's being held hostage by two Ravagers, Swarm and Azure, but the Doctor manages to get herself, Yaz, Dan, and Vinder away by trapping them in a time storm (*Once, Upon Time*). Here, Yaz pictures herself back on duty as a police officer, but her peer is on-off replaced by the Doctor, both a sign that Yaz's mind is on the Time Lord and that the Doctor is trying to rescue her and Dan from the storm. Meanwhile, Vinder might feel something more for Yaz as she appears in place of his superior military officer in his storm-induced vision. Next, Yaz recalls reluctantly playing a video game with her sister, Sonya, the latter only doing so to impress a boy. Sonya says, 'I'm going to learn to be ace at this, so the next time I'm in a room with him, he's going to look at me and think, "who's the sexy girl with the nimble fingers?"' Is it a coincidence that, following this sentiment, Sonya turns into the Doctor? Still, after trying to discover the memories hidden from her during her time as the 'Timeless Child', the Doctor isn't pleased to be pulled back to the Temple and reunited with her companions – and even less so when they escape in the TARDIS, only for a Weeping Angel to take control of the ship via Yaz's smartphone. Yaz believes the Angel is stalking her. The Doctor is able to get rid of the Angel, but not before it powers down the TARDIS, stranding them in the 'cursed village' of Medderton, where they're split up.

Yaz and Dan spend a lot of time together, primarily in *Village of the Angels* and *Survivors of the Flux*. In the former, they're sent back to 1901 by the Weeping Angels, where they meet Eustacius

Jericho and Peggy, more victims of the moving statues. Despite the odds, Yaz firmly believes in the Doctor, telling them, 'I've got a friend, and she'll sort this. She'll save us. She always does.' That belief is arguably shaken a little when she witnesses the Doctor being turned into an Angel and subsequently disappearing.

The Doctor has prepared for this eventuality and leaves them a holographic message to find out details of an upcoming battle for ownership of the earth. *Survivors of the Flux* reveals that this mission has taken Yaz, Dan, and Jericho three years. Yaz tells this hologram that she misses her, and Dan affirms that they'll see her again. And they do, in *The Vanquishers*, using Williamson's tunnels that lead them back to 2021. The Doctor greets Yaz with a big hug, and when the Doctor asks if she's okay, Yaz replies, 'I am now.' Dan interjects and says, 'We went all over the world. [Yaz] was amazing. She *is* amazing.' Together, they thwart attempted invasions from the Sontarans, Cybermen, and Daleks, and stop the Flux from destroying the rest of the universe.

After inviting Dan to join them on their travels in time and space, the Doctor apologises to Yaz for keeping details of her past to herself. 'I want to tell you everything,' she says.

While facing Daleks in a time loop (*Eve of the Daleks*), between getting exterminated, Dan confronts Yaz about her feelings for the Doctor, feelings Yaz initially denies then admits she's not told anyone about, not even herself. Dan says he realised that Yaz was in love with the Doctor during their four years together, watching the way she reacted to the Doctor's hologram when they were travelling the globe. Dan suggests she just be honest and tell her.

By *Legend of the Sea Devils*, Yaz still hasn't aired how she feels. The Doctor, Yaz, and Dan are enjoying journeying together, with the latter two developing something of a sibling bond. (For one, Yaz has convinced Dan to dress up as a pantomime pirate, complete with hook.) Nonetheless, there's something between Yaz and the Doctor, so they finally confess their feelings for each other. It doesn't go as Yaz would've hoped, however: while the Doctor does have feelings for Yaz, she says, 'Well, dates are not something I really do, you know. I mean, I used to. Have done. And if I was going to, believe me, it'd be with you. I think you're one of the greatest people I've ever known, including my wife' – that catches Yaz by surprise, so River Song seemingly has never come up in conversation before now – 'but the point is, if it was going to be anyone, it'd be you. But I can't.' After they've defeated the Sea Devils, the Doctor feels Yaz needs more of an explanation, so explains she can't fix herself to anything, anywhere, or anyone because 'sooner or later, it'll hurt.' This is enough for Yaz for now, and by the time of *The Power of the Doctor*, she and Dan are still trying to give the Doctor something she wished for at the conclusion of the previous episode: 'I wish this would go on forever.'

Though Dan leaves at the start of *The Power of the Doctor*, Yaz soon meets representatives of her future in the form of ex-companions, Tegan Jovanka and Ace. The Doctor forgets to make introductions, so Yaz concedes that she's 'the only one here who doesn't really know what's going on.' Ace explains, and Yaz takes this on board with ease, likely showing that she'd already mulled over the fact that the Doctor has travelled with many others. Still, the Doctor's abruptness has affected her, and she complains that she can't keep running from place to place with no explanation. The Doctor says she doesn't have time, so Yaz counters, 'Make time', then points out the seemingly disparate elements (Cybermen, Daleks, and the Master) all at play, implying that something greater is going on.

Despite sometimes rubbing up against one another, Yaz always remains loyal to the Doctor. When the Master steals her body, it's Yaz who sticks with the dangerous Time Lord, just so she can later help reverse the process. It's also Yaz who braves fire from Qurunx to retrieve the Doctor and carry her back to the safety of the TARDIS. But it's too late. The Doctor knows she's going to regenerate. Now it's just the two of them, as Yaz has already dropped everyone else off – she's proved adept at piloting the TARDIS, so we can infer that the ship likes her, likely owing to her travelling so long in it. Nevertheless, the Doctor tells Yaz, 'Oh, I have loved being with you, Yaz. And I have loved being me. I think I need to do this next bit alone.' So, after an ice cream while sitting on the TARDIS roof, the Doctor drops Yaz off, ready to attend a meeting of former companions.

There, Ace asks if the Doctor is okay. 'Of course she's okay.' Yaz replies. 'She's the Doctor.'

Graham O'Brien – Bradley Walsh (*The Woman Who Fell to Earth* to *Revolution of the Daleks* and *The Power of the Doctor*)

A Sadness Runs Through Him (The Hoosiers); *Wonderful Land* (The Shadows).

Graham O'Brien's time with the Doctor is punctuated by three main things: his largely secret fears of his cancer returning; his care for his grandson, Ryan Sinclair; and his optimistic spirit. The latter two are on show the first time we meet him in *The Woman Who Fell to Earth*, as, with his wife, Grace, he's trying to help Ryan ride a bike. Though Ryan falls off, throws his bike off a hill, and gives up on himself, Graham's encouragement is unwavering. He cheers him on, and then, when Ryan admits defeat, says, 'Mate, you rode it for a second' (though he looks somewhat dejected when Ryan tells him to stop calling him 'mate').

Indeed, later on, as Graham and Grace are on a train together without Ryan, Graham's insecurities and concerns come to the fore as he asks his wife, 'Do you ever think he's going to call me "Grandad"?' He soon has more things to worry about as the train stops, the lights turn off, and they're attacked by a tentacled electrical being. Ryan gets into the train with probationary police officer, Yasmin 'Yaz' Khan, and the foursome – plus crane operator, Karl – are saved by the Doctor who has plummeted through the roof after the TARDIS deposited her in the air above Sheffield before dematerialising.

Despite, or perhaps because of, all the weird things he's seen,

Graham is eager to get away from the train, not believing Ryan's theory that it's due to aliens: 'There's no such thing as aliens,' he asserts. 'Anyway, even if there was, they ain't going to be on a train in Sheffield.' Still, his insistence they get away is overruled by Grace who simply states that they're not leaving the Doctor, seeing as she saved them and that there are too many questions left to answer about the evening's events.

When the Doctor passes out, Grace and Ryan take her back to Grace's house, while Graham asks around at the bus station where he used to work to see if there have been any other strange happenings that evening. He goes home and when the Doctor wakes, she discovers they've been infected by DNA bombs; Graham is now more up for chasing the alien culprits, though he's annoyed at Ryan for bringing the trouble to their door. 'I suppose you'll be blaming this on the dyspraxia as well,' he scorns Ryan, in a rare harsh moment. 'Can't ride a bike, started an alien invasion.' It's pretty clear that he's lashing out in panic. They track Tzim-Sha of the Stenza to a construction site and he and Grace work to help the Doctor from the ground while Ryan and Yaz head up a crane after the Doctor. Grace admits she's enjoying it and, though he says otherwise, it's clear Graham is rather taken in by the excitement of the evening.

That enthusiasm doesn't last, however: Tzim-Sha is defeated, but Grace is killed while trying to follow Ryan. 'Promise me you won't be scared,' she says to Graham before she dies, 'without me.' Graham gives a tearful eulogy at her funeral, explaining that Grace showed him life had more to offer him and revealing that he thinks he should've been the one who died. When the Doctor questions him further in private, he tells her he had cancer three years ago and is in remission; Grace was his nurse and they fell in love.

Graham accompanies Ryan, Yaz, and the Doctor to an industrial unit where the latter lashes up a transmat to help her locate the TARDIS. Graham, alongside his grandson and Yasmin, are unwilling travellers as the Doctor accidentally teleports them to deep space. They're swiftly rescued and find themselves on their first alien planet: Desolation (*The Ghost Monument*). Graham largely approaches this with resignation, happy that they're all still alive and keen to get home sharpish, while putting his faith in the Doctor because she's their best bet... and only option. He's also the first to notice that they can understand and speak to aliens despite the language barrier, and, when they reach their destination, to question the TARDIS' transcendentalism. He's less impressed that the Doctor has little control over the ship, and, when she says it's her ninth attempt to get them home, he corrects her: it's actually their fourteenth try (*Rosa*).

Once he learns that the TARDIS is in 1955, Graham's thoughts turn to seeing Elvis live. But the reality of the situation becomes clear when it turns out they're actually in Montgomery, Alabama, where racial discrimination is rife. Graham is suitably appalled, first when Ryan is attacked then at the general attitude held by the locals. It seems he's learned a lot from Grace about Rosa Parks, whom they meet while there, as he scorns Ryan for not knowing who she is: 'Your nan would have a fit right now.' In fact, the first thing Grace did upon learning Graham was a bus driver was checking he wasn't like 'James Blake the Snake', i.e. the bus driver who Rosa Parks stood up to (a harsh and surprising first comparison, considering Graham and Grace met when the former was undergoing cancer treatment).

Graham takes the whole ordeal to heart. He's ashamed to learn Ryan has to sit at the back of the bus and that any black person has to give up their seat for a white person at that time. He seems more affected than even Yaz at the fateful night, specifically because the Doctor can't let him get off the bus, as that would mean there are enough seats for white people without Rosa having to give up hers. 'I don't want to be part of this', Graham laments.

He's considerably cheerier when the Doctor gets them all back to Sheffield again in *Arachnids in the UK*, but turns down Yaz's offer of tea in favour of going home and trying to pick up the pieces of his life, post-Grace. Nonetheless, he sees her ghost there and says he has so much to tell her, implying that he does believe in some sort of afterlife, but not that she's always with him; he associates her with home and still wants time to talk to her memory. He accepts that the grieving process is going to take time, and wants to travel in the TARDIS with the Doctor, Yaz, and Ryan: 'I don't want to sit around my house waiting for it to go away, because that house is full of Grace and it makes it so much harder. But being with you and seeing all these things out there... it really helps.'

He grows closer to Yasmin as well: in *Demons of the Punjab*, they bond over how amazing they both find visiting the historical events, and, when she's hurt about her nan not telling her about her past, Graham advises Yaz, 'that girl in there, she ain't your nan yet. It's only later she'll decide how to tell it. And I honestly don't know whether any of us know the real truth of our own lives, because we're too busy living them from the inside. So just enjoy it, Yaz. Live this moment and figure it out later.'

It's something of a surprise that he takes a rather laid-back approach when watching a woman be murdered in *The Witchfinders* too: while Yaz and Ryan are appalled, Graham reminds them that the Doctor doesn't want them interfering. Still, perhaps Graham's initial attitude is due to his familiarity with the witch-hunts and resignation that they can't change what's happened; he immediately recognises that they're in Lancashire and recalls that he went on the Pendle Witches Walking Trail. Naturally, the Doctor nonetheless drags them all into the action and is accused of witchcraft herself. Graham, on the other hand, takes on more of an authoritative role when King James I thinks he's the Witchfinder General, though he claims all of them have their areas of expertise. (In *Spyfall: Part One*, the head of MI6 confuses Graham for the Doctor too; so does Captain Jack Harkness in *Fugitive of the Judoon*, offering up a 'have we met?' when Jack kisses him.)

It's clearer that Graham, Ryan, and Yaz have been travelling with the Doctor for some time and the team has gelled further:

Graham at least now knows that he needs to bring food along because it doesn't seem to cross the Doctor's mind at all. For instance, on their trip to Norway (a place Graham's particularly excited about seeing, having discussed a holiday there with Grace) in *It Takes You Away*, he comes armed with a cheese and pickle sandwich – which he offers up to Hanne, a young girl left on her own in a cabin in the woods by her father, Erik. Here, they encounter the Solitract, an energy being comprised of its own universe that lured people into its own plane by taking the form of the deceased. Though he initially rejects it, Graham soon grabs at this chance to seemingly be with Grace again, and talks to the Solitract (which has taken Grace's face and seems to share her memories) about all he's seen and done. They connect over a frog necklace that both Graham and Ryan accidentally bought Grace as a Christmas present, and which Graham carries with him as a reminder.

'I'm lost, Grace,' Graham tells her. 'I miss you. All my life, I was looking for you. Then I found you and I was so happy… And then I lost you.'

Graham connects with Grace so quickly and deeply that he refuses to believe the Doctor when she explains none of it is real. As the Solitract's reality collapses, it's 'Grace's' refusal to help Ryan that convinces Graham that the Doctor is right, and the Solitract banishes him from that dimension. Graham is relieved to see Ryan is all right, and the pair talk about how much they both miss Grace. Graham's loyalty and love for his grandson is rewarded when Ryan finally calls him 'Grandad.'

The Doctor knows Graham still blames himself for Grace's death, however, and is worried at his need for vengeance after they meet T'zim-Sha again (*The Battle of Ranskoor Av Kolos*). Graham obviously has a lot of respect for the Doctor and her morals, so he takes her to one side and says quite honestly that he does intend to kill the Stenza warrior for what he did; the Doctor responds by telling him to go back to the TARDIS, which he, of course, refuses to do. He wholly accepts that if he murders the alien, the Doctor won't let him travel with her again, but he rejects the Time Lord's claim that, if Graham were to get his revenge, he would be the same as T'zim-Sha. It's ultimately Ryan who wins Graham around: despite a few precarious moments, Ryan reminding Graham to be the better man has an effect, as does his telling him, 'We're family. And I love you.'

While Graham explains to the Doctor he couldn't go through with it because he's weak, the Doctor counters that he's one of the strongest people she knows.

Graham is less than enamoured with the Doctor when she crushes one of his chairs with the TARDIS when returning them all home in *Resolution*. And his mood only gets worse when Ryan's dad, Aaron, arrives at their door. Graham answers the doorbell, sees who it is, and immediately shuts the door on him. Ryan is slightly more forgiving, bringing him into the house then trying to reach some sort of accord by taking him out to a café while Graham and Yaz help the Doctor track down a Dalek. Back at his house, though, Graham has to spend a bit of one-on-one time with Aaron and reveals that Grace saved a lot of Aaron's childhood drawings and toys. 'Why didn't you come, Aaron?' he asks. 'Not for your mum or for Ryan, but for yourself?' It's further up to Graham to explain the TARDIS to Ryan's baffled father (a far cry from *Revolution of the Daleks*, in which he and Ryan agree it's more fun if the nasty would-be politician Jack Robertson never gets an explanation for the Ship; Graham doesn't like Robertson at all, asking at one point for him to 'Give us one good reason why we should save your life', which is hopefully a joke, bearing in mind his moral dilemma with T'zim-Sha).

In *Spyfall*, Graham is especially excited about getting his hands – or feet, in the case of shoes that fire lasers – on some MI6 gadgets. He goes off with the Doctor to find missing agent, O, who they find hiding out in the Australian outback. Graham and O get on pretty well, with the former saying that he doesn't really know how long he's been travelling with the 'Doc'; we also learn that Graham didn't believe the Doctor's tales of being a man before, until O confirms their validity. Graham has faith in the Doctor, even when Agent O turns out to be the Master and the Kasaavin kidnap her. While Yaz is worried, Graham is sure she'll be all right (and is rather pleased when he finds himself back in his 'manor', Essex). Nevertheless, after the Master has been defeated, it's actually Graham who first confronts the Doctor about not sharing anything with them. She opens up a little, but refuses to take them to her home planet; unbeknown to the three companions, Gallifrey has been effectively destroyed by the Master after he uncovered the secret of the 'Timeless Child'.

The foursome are ready for a holiday, and it's Graham who accidentally teleports them to the Tranquillity Spa on the planet, *Orphan 55*. While Yaz is keen to find the pool, and the Doctor and Ryan are uneasy settling into this 'all-inclusive' break, Graham is extremely happy to sunbathe under the fake sky of the complex's dome. He's understandably annoyed when chaos ensues, and his concern immediately turns to where Ryan is. 'It ain't the aliens that are going to kill me,' Graham says when he finds him, 'it's worrying about you.'

Indeed, Graham proves a decent judge of character and a cooling agent in arguments, but isn't afraid to speak his mind: when he and his peers accuse the Doctor of being distant in *Fugitive of the Judoon*, Graham realises how often she tries to divert their attention from finding out more about her. He assures her they're only enquiring because they care for her. This consolatory demeanour comes to the fore in *Nikola Tesla's Night of Terror*, too, when he breaks up an argument between Tesla and Thomas Edison – though he also recognises that he once had a supervisor whose temperament was much like the latter's. (He also makes a solid quip in calling them AC/DC.) In *Praxeus*, Graham further brings together DI Jake Willis and astronaut, Adam Lang, a married couple who had drifted apart when the former didn't attend the launch of Lang's shuttle when it headed to the International Space Station. While Willis doesn't understand what Lang would see in him, Graham first jibes, 'So you were quite the catch, then', and then helps him realise his mistake by saying, 'I don't think he's the one you're punishing.'

Despite proving good counsel for everyone else, Graham's own calls for help are left unanswered in *Can You Hear Me?*, during which the Eternal, Zellin, forces him to have a nightmare about his cancer returning. Later on, he admits to the Doctor that the thought terrifies him, but she can't tell him anything reassuring, instead saying that she's too socially awkward. It's especially horrible and hard to reconcile, bearing in mind that the Doctor has previously given hints at other people's futures (in *The TV Movie*, for instance), gone to futuristic hospitals to help solve problems (*Let's Kill Hitler*), and even found cures in the TARDIS itself (*The Almost People*). Graham passes this off, laughs, and jokingly comments that he's glad they had this conversation; nevertheless, one can't wholly escape the notion that this will continue to eat at him and that he's merely burying his feelings for the sake of keeping the peace. The next time we see him, he's fortunately in good spirits, donning a cod nineteenth-century accent in *The Haunting of Villa Diodati* and jibing the Doctor, 'It is a truth universally acknowledged... that one's driver will park one's carriage imprudently too far from whence one is going.' She later unsettles him by refusing to deny the existence of ghosts; Graham's thoughts on the afterlife apparently wavering between the notion creeping him out and giving him comfort, given that he's quite recently felt Grace's presence.

Ascension of the Cybermen underlines Graham's relationship with Yasmin when the two are separated from the Doctor and Ryan. They fight to get back to them, with the pair showing their adaptive skills in staying alive against the odds, even risking oxygen starvation – this shortly before Yaz agreeing when Graham states he was 'born careful.' In *The Timeless Children*, too, Graham demonstrates he's inventive, suggesting that he, Yaz, and their new friends escape the Cybermen by disguising themselves as them. Then he confides in Yasmin that, 'I think you're such an impressive young woman. Never thrown by anything. Always fighting… You said to the Doc that you thought she was the best person you'd ever met. But you know what, Yaz? I think you are.' He goes on to explain that while the Doctor has a sonic screwdriver and time machine, Yaz has thrived without them, and done the human race proud. She tells him it's the nicest thing anyone's ever said to her. This might sound like something of an insult to Ryan (who is at least absent during this scene), but Graham and Yasmin have spent a lot of time together during their travels, and he clearly has a strong relationship with her on a different level to the one he has with his grandson. He obviously has trust and affection of the Doctor as well, but he doesn't say anything much when she's going to sacrifice herself as he, Yaz, and Ryan head home in a stolen TARDIS.

Her go-get-'em approach has rubbed off on Graham though: ten months after they last saw her, he and Ryan are investigating security drones that are ostensibly Daleks, and encourage Yaz to join them (*Revolution of the Daleks*). When the Doctor and Captain Jack Harkness find them on Earth, Graham is more wary of Captain Jack, who calls him a 'silver fox.' As with his friends, he's pleased that the Doctor isn't dead, but unlike Yaz, he doesn't want to continue travelling. The pull of family is too strong, so Graham leaves the TARDIS with Ryan, despite his grandson saying he can go on without him. Graham's initial departing joke to the Doctor goes back to his earlier scepticism about UFOs: 'Doc, I was wrong: we do get aliens in Sheffield.'

By the time we next see Graham, in *The Power of the Doctor*, he and Ryan aren't travelling together. The latter is in Patagonia while Graham is investigating curious volcanic activity in Bolivia. There, he comes up against the Daleks again and meets former Seventh Doctor companion, Ace. Graham tries to tell Ace he's 'Arnold Palmerson, rig inspector', but his psychic paper immediately disassembles the subterfuge. That's how he gains Ace's trust, but it seems he doesn't need any reassurance about her allegiance: he's (understandably) 'wowed' by her in a matter of seconds.

While Ace sets to blowing up the Daleks, a plan he can fully get behind, Graham's already planned a route out of the volcano – something which isn't ultimately needed when the TARDIS materialises to save them. Joined by Fourth and Fifth Doctor companion, Tegan Jovanka, Kate Stewart of UNIT, Yasmin, and space fleet pilot,

Vinder, they pilot the TARDIS together.

Graham doesn't get to say a proper goodbye to the Doctor this time. Yaz drops him home to Croydon as the Doctor prepares to regenerate. At some point afterwards, he meets up with Yaz as he and fellow companion, Dan Lewis, are trying to find a support group for friends of the Doctor who have left the TARDIS. He begins the meeting, enthusing that it's the perfect place to talk about his travels in time and space because no one else would ever believe such amazing things.

Captain Jack Harkness – John Barrowman – Continued... (*The Empty Child* to *The Parting of the Ways*; *Utopia* to *Last of the Time Lords, Fugitive of the Judoon, Revolution of the Daleks*)

It takes a while for Captain Jack Harkness to meet the Thirteenth Doctor. Before he does, he attempts to transmat the Doctor to a spaceship he's stolen, but fails due to the Judoon interfering. Instead, he scoops up Yaz, Ryan, and Graham, the latter of whom – his 'silver fox' – he initially thinks is the Doctor (*Fugitive of the Judoon*). He's trying to get a warning to the Doctor, to beware the Lone Cyberman and not give it what it wants, a warning she must ultimately ignore or risk Earth being destroyed. It's never explained on TV how Jack knows about the Lone Cyberman. Still, he gets on well with the other companions, notably his 'favourite' Ryan who accuses him of being cheesy, and the Doctor later sums him up as an 'old friend' yet doesn't expand on this.

This belies their relationship, of course: when Jack hears rumours that the Doctor is imprisoned in the Judoon's maximum security facility seventy-nine billion light years away from Earth, he gets himself imprisoned too, and it takes him nineteen years to finally get the cell next to her (*Revolution of the Daleks*). He uses a temporal-freezing gateway disinhibitor bubble to smuggle in his vortex manipulator, and they use it to escape to the TARDIS. Jack likes the ship's new look and asks where his room is. The Doctor says he never had a room, to which he replies, 'I had a suite with its own cocktail lounge.'

Jack still misses his time with the Doctor, and subtly notes that he wishes the Doctor never changed. He also mentions Rose when explaining to Ryan, Yaz, and Graham that he can cheat death. He takes to Yaz and the pair go off together to investigate a Dalek farming facility in Osaka. They bond over the Doctor's attitude towards companions and being left behind: Jack infers that Yaz thought the Doctor wouldn't come back, says something similar happened to him (i.e. at the conclusion of *The Parting of the Ways*), and tells her that it's a 'hard way to live. Being with the Doctor, you don't get to choose when it stops... Enjoy the journey while you're on it. Because the joy is worth the pain.' His reassuring her is quickly reversed when Yaz deconstructs his character; looking for praise or amazement at his squareness gun, Yaz instead suggests he's rather insecure. And he is, certainly when the Daleks are there – noting that 'you never forget your first death,' Jack is especially trigger-happy around the Daleks and, with the help of the Thirteenth Doctor's companions, blows up the SAS Dalek ship.

Given his belief that it's not up to the companions when their adventures stop, it's ironic that, at the end of this story, it's Jack who effectively decides to leave the Doctor. He doesn't get a proper send-off but his departure hints that Torchwood might still be around as he talks about Gwen Cooper seeing off a Dalek with a moped and her son's boxing gloves. Jack tells the Doctor he's going to stay on Earth for a while to catch up with Gwen. He does, however, promise to call the Doctor sometime.

Dan Lewis – John Bishop (*Flux: The Halloween Apocalypse* to *The Power of the Doctor*)

Raindrops Keep Fallin' on My Head (B. J. Thomas); *You'll Never Walk Alone* (Gerry and the Pacemakers).

Daniel 'Dan' Lewis isn't the luckiest of companions. Nonetheless, he remains a generally happy, funny chap who puts others before himself. In some ways, he's always on the periphery, looking on and noticing, for instance, Yasmin Khan's feelings for the Doctor, while apparently having come to terms with his own relationship status.

The Halloween Apocalypse, the first part of the *Flux* season, sets Dan up as someone likeable and enthusiastic. We meet him as he's acting as a tour guide, taking visitors around the Museum of Liverpool. This is in an unofficial compactly: Diane, who actually works at the museum, sees him out, warning him that if he continues to dupe people, he'll be banned; he protests, 'I am official. Official Scouse. Just think of me as a free exhibit – just a little bit livelier than the others... I make your punters happy. What's the point of being alive if it's not to make others happy?' Still, Dan and Diane are clearly friends (for one, she knows he's always late) and promise to meet for Halloween drinks that night. His altruistic attitude is further demonstrated by his working at the Jenning Street Food Bank, but refusing to take anything back for himself, despite him barely having anything to eat at home. He tells his fellow volunteer, Wilma, that his 'numbers' are coming up on Wednesday, claiming to be lucky. Wilma, however, knows he's only saying this to pacify her: Dan doesn't even play the lottery. That night, he also gives his last bits of food to some trick-or-treaters.

His next Halloween visitor is Karvanista, a Lupari officer begrudgingly assigned to protect Dan. The member of the dog-like species tries to hypnotise Dan, but it doesn't work, perhaps owing to Dan's overly rational mind concluding that it's a prank. Instead, Karvanista kidnaps Dan using a 'stun cube', which the Doctor and Yaz trace. The two save Dan (with the Doctor echoing what she first said to Rose Tyler: 'Nice to meet you, Dan. Run for your life'), taking him with them in the TARDIS to investigate the Flux, which Karvanista claimed to be saving Dan from. Dan takes the TARDIS in his stride, joking that he had a friend with a similar ship – 'I think his was a bit bigger, actually.' Yaz isn't impressed and tells him to shut up. Fortunately, their friendship develops quickly, likely due to them being flung together thanks to the Flux, a destructive force primarily made up of antimatter that annihilated half the universe.

Earth is shielded from the Flux, but the Doctor, Yaz, and Dan black out and wake up in the Crimean War, except the British Empire isn't fighting Russians – it's fighting Sontarans (*War of the Sontarans*). The trio are separated, however, when Yaz is transported to the Temple of Atropos and Dan back to 37 Granger Street in Anfield, Liverpool, where he lives. Or lived: his property was effectively destroyed during the events of *The Halloween Apocalypse*. There, Dan discovers more Sontarans, and the troops following him are surprisingly knocked out by Dan's parents, Eileen and Neville. They explain that the Sontarans began invading Earth the day Dan disappeared; though this was only two days ago, Neville says it 'already feels like a month.' His parents have a fun relationship, sometimes argumentative but only in a joking sort of way: Neville claims he suggested fighting back against the Sontarans, and Eileen corrects him, noting that Neville thought they'd be gone by the weekend anyway. Dan's mum suggest Neville normally just sits at home and complains about events; he counters that he was Wallasey's 'Junior Boxing Champion in 1966' (something Dan and Eileen chime in on, showing it's something he regularly brings up). It's clear to see where Dan gets his sense of humour from. When they split up, Neville gifts his son a wok, after explaining that you can take down Sontarans by hitting the probic vent on the back of their necks. Otherwise, he uses his initiative, infiltrating the docklands where the Sontarans originally invaded from, remembering that the 'potatoheads' spoke about Temporal Command (though he mistakes this for 'Tempura Command'), and recording all he's seen on his phone, especially for the Doctor.

Dan has already identified the Doctor as Earth's best defender. The Doctor similarly entrusts Dan to save Liverpool from the Sontarans, which he does with the help of Karvanista.

When the Doctor and Dan are reunited, she offers to take him in the TARDIS with her. After a brief pause, he agrees, though it might be so they can find Yaz together. When they do, she's at the mercy of two Ravagers, Swarm and Azure; though the Doctor is able to rescue her and get them all away, including pilot Inston-Vee Vinder, they're trapped in a time storm.

Diane is obviously on Dan's mind. He unsuccessfully tries to ring her when he gets back to Liverpool in *War of the Sontarans*, and in *Once, Upon Time*, the time storm makes him relive conversations with her, notably about their respective love lives. He enquires about a boring 'not-date' which made Diane fall asleep while eating pizza, and she then questions why he's not already married with kids. 'It nearly happened, once – fifteen years ago? Lost count now,' he tells her. 'I was engaged to get married. Two days before, she changed her mind... Said she'd been thinking about it properly. Couldn't bear spending the rest of her life with me, so thought she could do better.' Dan admits that he really loved her. Before they can bond on this revelation, Dan's guilt over missing having coffee with Diane comes to the fore as she, or at least the fake bioform Passenger form resembling her, tells him that she waited for him.

Once he and the others have got back to the Temple, Swarm and Azure announce that they have Diane captive, and Dan understandably tries to rescue her, only to be scolded by the Doctor who effectively pulls rank. They get away in the TARDIS, and, in *Village of the Angels*, end up in Medderton, a place policed by Weeping Angels. Dan and Yaz are sent back in time, and Dan defers to Yaz's experience, asking whether she's seen anything like Medderton, a village on the edge of space, before. When she says no, Dan bombards her with questions until she tells him to stop. He's panicking but keeps a cool head when, at the episode's conclusion, he and Yaz witness the Doctor being temporarily turned into an Angel and 'recalled' to the mysterious Division, an organisation set up during the early days of Gallifrey.

So far, Dan has spent a lot of time separated from his fellow travellers, but he at least grows closer to Yaz in *Survivors of the Flux*, who he later calls 'amazing'. When we next see them, it's 1904, three years after he and Yaz were stranded in the past with

Eustacius Jericho. They've spent the intervening time following hints left via a holographic message from the Doctor, detailing an upcoming battle for Earth caused by the Flux. During this period, Dan is enthused to meet philanthropist, Joseph Williamson, whose tunnels are a local tourist attraction. He seems sure they're a way to get back to the Doctor, especially when he finds out their central chamber has doorways leading off to other times and places. Sure enough, in *The Vanquishers*, one leads to 2021, where they are indeed reunited with the Doctor and meet Kate Stewart, formerly of UNIT and now leading the resistance against the Sontarans. They stop the Sontarans, Daleks, and Cybermen invading, and save Diane from Swarm and Azure; it's Diane's idea to use the 'endless matter' of the Ravagers' Passenger forms to contain the rest of the Flux and save the universe.

But what's good for the universe is bad for Dan. Diane's experiences mean she turns down Dan's offer to go for a drink at a restaurant called the Rivera. Dan's once more been acting as an unofficial tour guide in Liverpool Museum, this time extolling the virtues of Joseph Williamson and his tunnels. Diane's reaction seems to hit hard, and he leaves the place feeling dejected. Luckily, the Doctor and Yaz are waiting outside, offering for him to travel with them – something he gladly accepts.

Romance looms large in Dan's head, and in *Eve of the Daleks*, he and Yaz have a conversation about the latter being in love with the Doctor. His advice? Tell her. 'Look, I took way too long to tell somebody that I liked them, and then... the universe ended and everything got messy,' he says. 'I wouldn't want that to happen to you.' He later confronts the Doctor, and refuses to accept the Doctor doesn't know what he means: 'I think you do. But for some reason, you pretend to me – and to her – that you don't.' Dan has recognised the Doctor's uneasiness around such matters. But it appears his losing those he loves has blinded him to the Doctor's reluctance.

Nevertheless, the three seem happy travelling together. In *Legend of the Sea Devils*, Yaz has convinced Dan to dress up like a pirate in a pantomime, their relationship is almost like brother and sister.

Though Dan's more experienced in life, Yaz's time in the TARDIS means she's also a step ahead of him sometimes. That doesn't stop them from getting separated again, as Dan wanders off to comfort Ying Ki after the death of his father. Ying Ki plans to get revenge by murdering Zheng Yi Sao, aka the 'pirate queen' Madam Ching, who he believes is responsible. It's not a plan Dan agrees with, and he protests, 'Nobody said anything about killing!' This reluctance eases, however: he slashes at numerous Sea Devils with a sword. Perhaps he's quickly come to terms with murder, especially when motivated to stop them from getting to the Doctor and Yaz, or he sees a distinction between human life and the Sea Devils' lives. Either way, his time in the TARDIS has reinforced what – or rather *who* – he misses, and as soon as he can, he phones Diane. It goes to voicemail, so he says, 'I've been having all these mad adventures, and I can't tell anyone, and I just felt like telling you. I know we're not at where we were at, but...' Diane, much to his surprise, does pick up and tells him she's missed him too. It seems a date is still on the cards.

Dan's still travelling with the Doctor and Yaz in *The Power of the Doctor*, albeit not for long. While attempting to board a bullet train speeding through the Toraji system, Dan jokingly complains that he's got a date to get to. He soon has more things to worry about: the train is being attacked by Cybermen, and although the TARDIS trio stop them, Dan nearly spins off into space and fears suffocation. The Doctor drops him home, ready for his date with Diane and intending to pick him up the next day. But Dan tells her he doesn't want to go with her anymore: 'All this is amazing, and I've had the most incredible time. But it's not my life. And my life's far from perfect, but... I need to get back to it. I need to attack it. And I can now... 'cause I've been with you.' The Doctor lets him go without a proper goodbye (or restoring his house, shrunken during the events of *The Halloween Apocalypse*, meaning he'll need to sleep back at his parents' house), something which stings him as he asks Yaz if he's upset her. Yaz tells him she's just bad at goodbyes and the pair depart as friends, Dan promising to call her.

Indeed, he sees her again a month later, alongside Graham, Ian

The Thirteenth Doctor
Expanded Universe

There's not a wealth of Thirteenth Doctor stories in other mediums just yet, though *Doctor Who Magazine*'s comic is a stalwart and a few novels were released here and there. Titan Comics also had a Thirteenth Doctor title with a second volume primarily to pair the Thirteenth and Tenth Doctors up.

Yaz, Ryan, and Graham feature in all the Thirteenth Doctor books released between 2018 and 2021, and we learn a few nice little details about the trio.

The Good Doctor (2018) expands on their travels by telling us they've experienced singing waterfalls made of pink crystals, a unicorn sanctuary on a lost moon, and the Big Bang (but *which* Big Bang?); Ryan has previously been to Crete – where he dropped his phone in the bath while taking nude photos of himself – while Graham's youthful trips were more conservative, i.e. to Margate and Whitstable.

It also includes a delicious meta-reference when the Doctor says Graham looks like 'him from that game show', meaning *The Chase*, hosted by actor, Bradley Walsh. Graham is more of a *Pointless* fan. *The Good Doctor* is a significant tale for Graham, who is worshipped as the titular character by the people of Lobos after they stopped a war six hundred years before. Graham is uneasy being seen in such a light, but his hatred of racism means he's ultimately denounced, and it's up to the Doctor to broker peace again between the human colonists and the dog-like species, loba. A bay is instead named after Graham.

The novel further reveals that Graham attended school in Chingford, near the border of Essex, and that Yaz's best friend in primary school was Poppy Hillman; they stayed friends until secondary school when someone Poppy knew called Yaz an 'Islamist terrorist'. While Yaz generally rises above bigotry, she's hurt that it cost her a friendship. At this point, it appears her best friend became Aisha, who she went on a camping trip with, at least according to *The Secret in Vault 13*. The 2018 children's book also says Ryan 'borrowed' Graham's car (without permission) to impress Alison Mayer, and Graham's a keen plantsman – though his favourite plant, a begonia he nicknamed Vera, died after he forgot to water it before going to a trip to Blackpool. This is perhaps due to his grandfather having an allotment, which we learn about in *The Romanov Project*. During this 2023 audio, Graham also asks himself 'What would the Doctor do?', echoing Yaz having written 'WWTDD' on her hand in the TV episode, *War of the Sontarans*.

Yaz's police work is referenced a few times. In *Gatecrashers*, a short story from 2019's *The Target Storybook*, Yaz talks about domestic abuse cases and investigates the murder of the alien, Iz. She commands respect in Titan Comics' *A New Beginning* (2018-19) by claiming she and Ryan are 'Time Cops'. In *The Shadow Passes*, a 2020 online short story in which the friends have to shelter in a bunker for three weeks with the locals of Calapia, it's revealed that Yaz studied criminology. She also pretends to be a time agent in *A Little Help from My Friends* (2020), and the 2021 short story, *Black Powder*, set after Graham and Ryan's departure in *Revolution of the Daleks*, opens with Yaz confronting a man with a gun on Bonfire Night.

2018's *Combat Magicks* establishes that Graham is a fan of Ray Harryhausen movies, while *Molten Heart*, released the same year, says that he formed a bond with Ryan over films, notably the latter's love of *Lord of the Rings*. (Yaz is more of a *Harry Potter* fan, claiming to be Bellatrix Lestrange in the 2019 comic, *Herald of Madness*, calling someone a 'muggle', and mentioning Hogwarts.) Ryan gets to meet one of his heroes, Bruce Lee, in the *Doctor Who Magazine* comic, *The White Dragon* (2020-21), but is aghast that he can't warn the martial artist that he's only got a year to live.

Instead, Lee mentors Ryan a little, and is impressed with his progress, leaving him with a neat bit of advice: 'If you love life, don't waste time... Time is what life is made up of.'

Many expanded universe stories for the Thirteenth Doctor rely on nostalgia. The TARDIS team meet Berakka Dogbolter, daughter of recurring *DWM* villain, Josiah W. Dogbolter, in 2018-19's *The Warmonger* (which also tells us that Yaz learned a degree of leadership at school through a lesson about command presence) and in *Mistress of Chaos* later that same year; come up against the Nimon (from *The Horns of Nimon*) in 2020's *The Maze of Doom*; and experience *The Power of the Mobox* (2019), the Mobox having first appeared in the 2002 Eighth Doctor comic, *Uroboros*. (In the latter, Ryan affirms his wish to be James Bond, pre-empting his suiting up in the following year's *Spyfall*, and Graham says he wants to meet The Beatles. He's understandably disappointed when the Doctor says she's already 'used up all the dates,' contradicting the 2024 TV episode, *The Devil's Chord*.) A Draconian from *Frontier in Space* turns up in the 2020 short story, *The Simple Things*; we properly meet the Corsair – a character only previously mentioned in the TV story, *The Doctor's Wife* (2011) – in the 2019 Titan Comic, *Old Friends*; and Missy stars in *The Wonderful Doctor of Oz*, a 2021 mash-up with Frank L. Baum's *The Wonderful Wizard of Oz*. Indeed, Yaz watched *The Wizard of Oz* when she was younger and wanted ruby-red shoes for school, though she ended up with black lace-up ones instead.

Yaz and Ryan even have an adventure with the Second Doctor, albeit when they were much younger! *The Myriapod Mutiny*, from the 2022 collection, *Origin Stories*, details their Year 7 trip to the Natural History Museum, where they help the Second Doctor defeat the insectoid Myriapods, something they seemingly forget about.

But the most significant nostalgia fix comes in Titan Comics' *A Little Help from My Friends* and *Alternating Current* (2020- 21), in which they meet the Tenth Doctor alongside, respectively, Martha Jones and Rose Tyler. The former takes place in 1969, during the time the Tenth Doctor and Martha are stranded thanks to the Weeping Angels in *Blink* – sure enough, Graham, Yaz, and Ryan all help him battle them, though these events are contradicted by *Once, Upon Time* in which Yaz doesn't recognise the Angels. During this, they further confront the invading Nestene Consciousness and its Autons. Pleasingly, Graham immediately identifies the Tenth Doctor as the same person they know because he's got a 'dramatic coat' and does 'the running bit.' That comic concludes back in 2020, with the companions eager for a break from their adventuring – only to find London invaded by Sea Devils, ostensibly a result of a paradox caused by the two Doctors meeting. Yaz, Graham, and Ryan meet Jackie and Pete Tyler in *Alternating Current* and then travel back to 1903, when history changed as the Skithra successfully kidnapped Tesla and Edison (i.e. rewriting the events of *Nikola Tesla's Night of Terror*). There, they see the Tenth Doctor again, with an alternative version of Rose Tyler, one who grew up on a conquered Earth. The trio are somewhat on the back foot when confronted by this incarnation's angst compared to the Thirteenth Doctor's, something they'll have to get used to given the upcoming (for them) 'Timeless Child' revelations.

Very few stories were released between *Revolution of the Daleks* and *The Halloween Apocalypse* to chronicle Yaz's time with the Doctor without Graham and Ryan, but Big Finish amends this oversight with *The Thirteenth Doctor Adventures* from 2025.

Unsurprisingly given the nature of the *Flux* storyline, most of Dan Lewis' expanded universe adventures take place between *The Vanquishers* and *The Power of the Doctor*. Still, more Earth-based tales should be expected, set during the period he, Yaz, and Jericho are stranded together in the past, working to get back to the Doctor (*Survivors of the Flux*).

It's Behind You!, his first comic strip in *Doctor Who Magazine*, sees the Doctor take her companions to the pantomime, only for her to accidentally bring real versions of fictional characters into being. This includes Captain Hook from *Peter Pan*, and Dan crosses swords with him, pre-empting or perhaps inspiring his look in *Legend of the Sea Devils*. The Doctor undoes her mistake using her three wishes granted to her by a genie, and Dan's giving nature kicks in as he suggests giving free ice cream to all the kids enjoying the pantomime. Dan obviously gets on well with youngsters, which we might infer is a desire to have a family – he's close to his parents so family means a lot to him, and, in the next strip, *Hydra's Gate*, he quickly connects with Sidney Bird, an evacuee from 1942, and they spend much of the story together. In *The Everlasting Summer*, his paternal side comes out when he looks after a young Beeling, a species of large bee-like aliens with offspring about the size of a human baby. Seeing this small creature – who he nicknames 'Stripe' – as helpless, Dan takes refuge in the TARDIS. (Sadly, we never see him getting his own key, neither on screen or in multimedia stories; nonetheless, he has one here.) At the end of the comic, he's happy to surrender Stripe to his own kind as they plan to care for and raise him properly as part of their community.

Dan's seen some amazing things, and in *Hydra's Gate*, Dan's sense of wonder is still present, as he hopes a genie can help him out (no such genie does). That magic seems to persist, though, as he appears to become something of a soothsayer in *Fear of the Future*, as the TARDIS lands on a beach, and he first sees Yaz apparently drowning and then a man falling off a cliff. Alas, it's the Doctor's fault: Dan's sunglasses, ones he found in the TARDIS, are actually Preventacles, capable of telling the future to prevent accidents. Dan smashes them up, concluding that they don't need help finding trouble...

It's also worth noting that, while the Thirteenth Doctor doesn't have any expanded universe exclusive companions, the so-called Fugitive Doctor, introduced in *Fugitive of the Judoon*, does: Taslo, whose only appearance comes in Titan Comics' *Origins* (2022), set before the TV episode. She's a Time Lady who's freshly graduated from the Academy, and now works for the Division. Taslo and the Doctor are sent on a mission by the Time Lord High Council to stop a cult apparently planning to destroy Gallifrey. The Doctor learns the truth: this 'cult' is made up of rejected Time Lords who are clearly peaceful people. This gives Taslo an interesting moral dilemma, as she tries to equate what she's experiencing with what she's been told by the Division (and a desire to impress the organisation). As such, the Doctor has to talk her out of carrying a gun with her; Taslo nonetheless takes seven knives with her and kills some of the colonists. By the end of the story, though, she refuses to shoot the Doctor, telling her that enough people have died today, and secretly hands her details of where bombs designed to wipe out the 'cult' are stashed. We end Taslo's tale (for now) with the companion in prison.

Just before her pairing with Taslo, it seems the Doctor has been on a mission with another companion – a Weeping Angel. As it's established on TV that the Division can recruit agents no matter the species, this is an intriguing possibility, though not one expanded upon yet in other media.

The Fourteenth Doctor
David Tennant

*'I fought all those battles for all those years, and now I know what for.
This. I've never been so happy in my life.'*
– The Doctor, *The Giggle*.

Donna Noble – Catherine Tate – Continued... (*The Runaway
Bride* and *Partners in Crime* to *Journey's End*, plus *The End of Time*,
and *The Star Beast* to *The Giggle*)

For Donna Noble, a lot has changed since she stopped
travelling with the Doctor; equally, not a lot has changed.

You'd expect more to have altered, given that the Tenth
Doctor left her a winning lottery ticket on her wedding day. But
when we meet her again, in 2023's *The Star Beast*, the Noble family
live in a relatively modest house (albeit in London, so still bought
using some of the money from the triple-rollover), her husband
Shaun Temple is a taxi driver, and her daughter Rose sells
handmade toys online to make a bit of cash for the household.
Donna gave the rest of her £166 million winnings to charity
because 'there are places out there where people are in danger and
in pain and fear. And I could help. It just felt like the sort of thing
he' – meaning the Doctor, a part of her memory subconsciously
gnawing at her – 'would do.' (She later says this was caused by a
infracutaneous retrofold memory loop, i.e. she wanted to be like
the Doctor.)

The TARDIS brings the Fourteenth Doctor to see Donna in
Camden. He helps a mysterious woman carrying boxes before
realising it's actually Donna, carting around crafting purchases

for Rose (whose name initially surprises the Doctor). Though he's a stranger to her, Donna nonetheless treats him like someone she knows, joking, 'Word of advice: you can wear a suit that tight up to the age of thirty-five and no further', not something you'd typically say to a man you've just met. Still, she's dismissive of the Doctor and Rose seeing a spaceship crash overhead (once again, she misses such a big event happening, as she did the Sycorax in *The Christmas Invasion*, and Dalek and Cyberman invasion of *Army of Ghosts/Doomsday*). It's left to the Doctor to investigate, but he does so by getting a lift in a taxi, coincidentally driven by Shaun. The Doctor subtly tries to find out how life's treated Donna by posing as a friend of Nerys.

It's clear to the Doctor that meeting Donna again has something to do with his tenth face returning, and he tells UNIT Scientific Adviser Shirley Anne Bingham that Donna's his best friend in the universe, someone he absolutely loves. He's seen her family, but is unsure whether she's really happy...

Back at the Noble household, Donna is frustrated when kids who know her trans daughter at school are deadnaming her. Rose doesn't seem bothered and goes to put her craft items in the shed, while Donna and Sylvia have a catch-up. The latter has made them a tuna madras, ostensibly feeling like she has to help out as Donna's lost her job again; Sylvia is also unsure about what's considered sexist, having called Rose 'gorgeous', and Donna sympathises. She then starts mulling over the reported spaceship and how her grandad, i.e. Wilfred Mott, used to talk about aliens a lot before Donna lost her memories. Her mother says she had a breakdown, but Donna confesses, 'Sometimes, I think there's something missing. Like I had something lovely, and it's gone... I should be happy. I should be really happy. But some nights, I lie in bed thinking, "What have I lost?"'

Meanwhile, out in the shed, Rose has come face-to-face with Beep the Meep, a cute-looking furry creature who is being hunted by the Wrarth Warriors. Ignoring the 'keep out' sign on the shed door (Donna says they don't keep secrets in that house, ironic given the burden Sylvia carries), Donna barges in and also meets the Meep, causing her to freak out and accuse it of being a Martian. Her mind quickly turns to selling the 'mad Paddington' bear for £1 million.

The Doctor has tracked the Meep to the Noble household, and Sylvia understandably panics about Donna seeing him. She passes him off as 'the skinny man,' but questions his having two hearts. It's not long before his manic life fully intrudes when UNIT soldiers, controlled by the Wrarth Warriors, rush into the house and start blowing things up, including making a huge hole in the wall. They escape in Shaun's taxi, but Donna already appreciates the Doctor's handy work (as does Sylvia who thanks him for saving their lives).

When true intentions are revealed – that the Meep is one of a maniacal species intent on conquest and the Warriors are there as its captors – Donna is most offended by the Meep calling Rose a 'weird child', and scolds herself for giving away the lottery money, given that it could've afforded them a new life in Monte Carlo or Switzerland, away from danger. Did the subconscious part of Donna not want to travel in case the Doctor returned? Or was it the Donna of old's mindset, not wanting to see the world without the Doctor? Either way, she's by the Doctor's side when the Meep takes them to its ship, a craft that would use the whole of London as fuel if it takes off. When the Doctor is cut off from the controls, he's reluctantly forced to unlock Donna's memories. She stops the Meep and falls to the floor, seemingly ready to say goodbye. But she doesn't die: instead, the metacrisis energy is shared between Donna and Rose – who chose her own name and has subconscious memories of the TARDIS (expressed through the shed) and the aliens they met, which she turned into toys. Those toys curiously include the Daleks (*The Stolen Earth/Journey's End*) and Judoon (*The Stolen Earth*), as well as creatures she never met like the Cybermen, Atraxi (*The Eleventh Hour*), and the Lupari (*Flux*), so the DoctorDonna was an ongoing connection between them all.

With her memories back, Donna is torn between going with the Doctor and staying with her family; she reaches an accord by taking one quick trip in the TARDIS to see her grandad, Wilf.

But she spills tea onto the new TARDIS console, sending it bounding around time and space in *Wild Blue Yonder*. In doing so, they accidentally give Isaac Newton the word 'gravity', which he mishears as 'mavity', thus Donna and the Doctor change a small aspect of history (though the word itself existed since at least the early 1500s, so it's impossible to think Newton didn't know it before that). Donna then says she thought Newton was 'hot' and the Doctor agrees, leading Donna to suggest she always thought he was... bisexual – presumably: she's cut off, but she knew he wasn't gay considering she recognised his emotions for Rose Tyler when she first heard about her in *The Runaway Bride*.

Her accidental spillage means the TARDIS drops them off on a spaceship at the very edge of the universe, then dematerialises thanks to the HADS. Donna struggles with the concept of nothingness; the Doctor explains it's a limitation of twenty-first century language, as the universe contains everything so everything can't have an edge. Though visions of the Flux drag the Doctor down, Donna's positivity seems to inspire him too. Later, she refuses to believe another being's accusation that the universe is loud with 'war and blood and fury and hate'. 'We are more than that,' Donna argues. She doesn't retain any of the knowledge gained through the metacrisis, admitting that it's too much – 'like looking into a furnace' – but at least has memories of her time in the TARDIS. As such, she wants to know more about what's happened to the Doctor in the intervening years, but he stays tight-lipped.

Donna admits to the Doctor that she's worried about how long her family would wait for her if she can't get back to her own time. She thinks Rose would eventually grow up and move on, but Shaun would stay in the alleyway, ever the devoted husband, as would Wilf, who'd sit there with a sleeping bag and Thermos, calling the Doctor every name under the sun. She wonders what her mother would do, but doesn't come to any conclusions. She soon expands on her relationship with Sylvia: Donna was born in Southampton as they were visiting Donna's Auntie Iris, an aunt who refused to travel to Chiswick despite Sylvia being heavily pregnant. To Donna, that meant her mother always saw her as a 'problem' child.

It becomes clear the ship isn't empty as two beings, apparently from beyond the universe, take the Doctor and Donna's forms, testing their trust in each other. They open up to each other, with the Doctor admitting he's missed her all those years – that is, at least over a thousand years, considering his time on Trenzalore (Even though his isolation in the confession dial might account for a few billion years, he experienced loops of around two weeks). Their trust is ultimately stretched to the limit when the TARDIS reappears and the Doctor must choose which is the real Donna to take with him. He initially chooses the wrong Donna, but swiftly corrects his mistake.

They return straight to Camden where they're joyously reunited with Wilf. The celebrations don't last long, however. In *The Giggle*, the world has gone mad as everyone is obnoxious and violent, thinking themselves in the right (including the government; 'no change there then', intones Donna). UNIT picks the Doctor and Donna up, and the latter is introduced to Mel Bush, who calls herself one of the Doctor's companions. 'Don't say "companion",' Donna replies. 'That sounds like we park him on the seafront at Weston-super-Mare.'

Donna's attitude and expertise impress Kate Stewart straight away – enough for her to not only offer her a job at UNIT but also to accept Donna's counterbid of £120,000 a year (up from Kate's £60,000 offer) plus five weeks' holiday. Travelling with the Doctor naturally means you're especially valued, hence Mel having such a cushy gig too. When they're alone in 1925, locating the source of a TV signal put there by the Toymaker, Donna questions why the Doctor's never mentioned Mel; initially, this appears like she's coming to terms with the Doctor moving on from people so quickly, but apparently not, given that she's previously witnessed his infatuation with Rose Tyler and met previous companions. Indeed, she's actually worried about his health, that he never seems to slow down enough to chat about old times. She's the one who realises why the Fourteenth Doctor looks like the Tenth, to tell him that he's wearing himself out. This only gets worse when the Toymaker starts teasing the Doctor about the fates of his previous companions. An encounter with a ventriloquist dummy in an ever-shifting house freaks Donna out and, when the Doctor challenges him to a card-cutting game, she believes the Toymaker will cheat.

Chasing the Toymaker back to 2023, Donna shows off her temping skills once more, as well as a fair degree of technical acumen, working with UNIT and Mel. At UNIT, the Toymaker takes control of the Galvanic Beam, i.e. a massive gun, and forces the Doctor to regenerate – sort of. Mel and Donna rush to his side, with the latter telling the Toymaker, 'He's not dying alone. You can do what you like to me. I'm going to be with him.' She knows he's not exactly dying, but she still recognises the pain the Doctor goes through each time. This is unlike any other regeneration, though: the Doctor instead bi-generates, splitting in half with the Fifteenth Doctor growing out of the Fourteenth. Donna stays emotionally attached to the Fourteenth Doctor, however, and when he asks how many have died thanks to the Toymaker, Donna assures him it's not his fault.

After the Toymaker's defeat, the Fifteenth Doctor expounds on what Donna's been saying: the Doctor needs a break, needs to *stop*. The Doctor confesses he doesn't know how, to which Donna replies, 'Well, I can tell you. Because you know what I did when you went flying off in your blue box, spaceman? I stayed in one place, and I lived day after day after day.' She admits that it drives you mad, but equally, that 'that's the adventure.' So, as the Fifteenth Doctor goes travelling in his TARDIS, Donna suggests the Fourteenth Doctor comes 'home', and Donna seems content with staying too – for her family, and because, when she sees the

Fifteenth Doctor in the TARDIS, she says, 'I'm not doing that again,' shutting the door metaphorically and physically on trips into time and space.

Still, the journeys aren't entirely behind them: the Fourteenth Doctor accidentally lets slip that he's taken Rose – who he calls his niece, while Sylvia is the 'evil stepmother' – to Mars and Mel to New York during the Gilded Age. Donna, it would seem, hasn't indulged in that life again; at least, not yet.

By the time the Fifteenth Doctor returns to UNIT in *The Legend of Ruby Sunday*, Rose is working at the London HQ and Donna is still on staff, though not available to battle Sutekh.

Wilfred Mott – Bernard Cribbins – Continued... (*Voyage of the Damned, Partners in Crime, The Sontaran Stratagem/ The Poison Sky, Turn Left* to *Journey's End*, and *The End of Time*, plus *Wild Blue Yonder*)

We barely see Wilfred during the sixtieth anniversary specials, but he remains a presence in the Fourteenth Doctor era.

In *The Star Beast*, we learn that Wilfred, now aged ninety-four, is in sheltered accommodation as he can no longer manage the stairs (indeed, when he returns, he's in a wheelchair). The Noble family wouldn't be able to afford it, if not for Kate Stewart of UNIT, who is paying for it because he's an 'old soldier.' When Donna gets her memories back, it's the draw of seeing Wilf that makes her want to travel in the TARDIS with the Doctor again. Sylvia complains, but Donna counters, 'Oh, but imagine his face, Mum. Oh, he would be so happy. All those secrets Grandad kept for years. He thought I'd never remember. And to see the Doctor one last time?'

In *Wild Blue Yonder*, we learn that Donna's primary school choir sung The U.S. Air Force song at a Christmas concert every year until Wilf complained that it may sound fun and jaunty, but it's actually a piece about going to war.

It's not until the very end of this episode that the Doctor and Wilf see each other again. After their time at the edge of the universe, the TARDIS drops the Doctor and Donna back to Camden where they find a world gone mad. Most of the Nobles have sheltered away, but Wilf has remained vigilant, on the lookout for the Doctor. 'Now nothing is wrong, nothing in the whole wide world!' enthuses the Doctor. 'Hello, me old soldier!' They immediately hug and Wilf says he never lost faith. He describes seeing him as 'springtime.'

At the start of *The Giggle*, UNIT takes charge and makes sure Wilf is safe, away from the machinations of the Toymaker.

When the Fourteenth Doctor effectively retires from travelling in time and space, we see him having dinner with the Noble family – all except Wilfred, who is busy entertaining himself by shooting moles. The Doctor tells Donna not to worry: he's given the moles their own forcefield.

The Fourteenth Doctor

Expanded Universe

Considering the Fourteenth Doctor's first full adventure, *Liberation of the Daleks* (2022-23), was actually a comic in *Doctor Who Magazine*, it's perhaps curious that we don't spend much time with him and Donna in expanded media.

An untitled comic strip ran in *DWM* #598, set between *The Star Beast* and *Wild Blue Yonder*. This sees the out-of-control TARDIS take the Doctor and Donna to various times and places including the Western Front in 1917, the Battle of Hastings in 1066, and one December in the 1970s, when Eric Morecambe and Ernie Wise are filming one of their ever-popular Christmas specials (probably 1971 given Glenda Jackson is mentioned). Donna's souped-up phone still connects to the Internet of 2023, and she displays her knowledge of the TARDIS again, noting it has a laundrette, disco, and library.

So what did Donna recall of her time with the Doctor before her memories returned? The Target novelisation of *The Star Beast* says that she believes Lance, her fiancé from *The Runaway Bride*, simply vanished on their wedding day. Her family has banned science-fiction, something which is perhaps contradicted by the aforementioned untitled comic strip which suggests Wilf is a *Star Wars* fan. It also expands on Donna's childhood, suggesting she was really close to her parents: when she was two, she'd go into her mum and dad's room for a hug every morning, and when she was ten, she wandered away from Sylvia to help another child find his mother; for this, she got an award from the manager and her photograph in the Little Heroes section of *The Herald* newspaper. *The Star Beast* further names the Nobles' house as 23 Bachelor Road.

Interestingly, the Target novelisation of *The Giggle* reveals that the Fourteenth Doctor didn't settle down with Donna and family

– instead, he gets his own place in the countryside, and Wilfred Mott goes to visit him for picnics!

The Doctor doesn't get a companion, per se, in *Liberation of the Daleks*, but there is Lieutenant Georgette Gold, who's taking a PhD in Dalek Studies. She learns about the Doctor and the Space-Time Telegraph (as seen in the TV story, *Terror of the Zygons*), and sends out a distress call to lure him in, so she can quiz him for her degree. The Doctor is immediately disgusted by the Dalek Dome, an exhibit about the Kaled race, but Georgette defends it. The Dalek Dome includes psychoscapes based on Dalek history, fuelled by the memories of twelve Kaled mutants harvested from a crashed Dalek saucer by humans, including Georgette. She's clearly smart, but her morals are questionable, arguably skewed by her time in the military.

Her early acquisition of those mutants means there's also a psychoplasmic construct (effectively a copy) of her called Georgy Gold. When Georgy is captured by fellow constructs that purport to be Daleks, they come to the conclusion that the Doctor can stabilise them, i.e. make them all real – and Georgy is desperate to hang onto this life, so much so that she lures the Doctor into the Daleks' trap. She realises too late that the Daleks won't let anyone else live, but nonetheless manages to free Georgette and others from their control, before being exterminated. The Doctor values Georgy and tries to stop her being killed; stepping between the Daleks and Georgy, he forgets that their weapons only work on fellow constructs, so it passes straight through him to exterminate her. Georgy's sacrifice obviously affects Georgette too, who goes to rescue the Doctor.

Together, they stop the Daleks' invasion, but Georgette has seen the true face of the Kaled race now: a true expert in Dalek Studies. She asks the Doctor if the mutants powering the Dalek Dome should be destroyed – but the Doctor bitterly leaves the decision to her, and, despite her pleas for him to stay with her, disappears in the TARDIS.

The Fifteenth Doctor
Ncuti Gatwa

> *'We've got to keep the pace up; otherwise, nothing would get done.*
> *Dying defines us. Snow isn't snow until it falls… We all melt away*
> *in the end, but something stays. Maybe the best part. A sad*
> *old man once told me, what survives of us is love.'*
> – The Doctor, *Boom*.

Before meeting the titular character in *Joy to the World*, the 2024 Christmas special, and his next companion, Belinda Chandra (Varada Sethu) in the 2025 run of stories, the Fifteenth Doctor meets a girl whose heritage plays an important role in her story…

Ruby Sunday – Millie Gibson (*The Church on Ruby Road* to *Empire of Death*)

It's a Mystery (Toyah); *Ruby* (Kaiser Chiefs).

In her own words, Ruby Sunday is still waiting for her life to begin.

She was born around 2pm on Christmas Eve, 2004, but was left by her mother at *The Church on Ruby Road* in Manchester, and was soon fostered by Carla Sunday. She doesn't know who her birth parents are; the identity of her mother is a particular fixation, perhaps given that this mysterious hooded figure was seen walking away from the church that evening. As such, around Christmas 2023, she applies to be on a TV show presented by Davina McCall, which uses a DNA sample to find someone's birth family. She tells Davina that she considers Carla the 'best mum in the world' and that they moved down to London from Manchester to look after Ruby's bedridden gran, Cherry, as they couldn't afford home care. She also admits that her A-level results weren't great – Ruby seems to be more creatively-minded than academic, seeing as she plays keyboard in a band with singer, Trudy, Clark (on guitar), and drummer, Big Jim. They play gigs at pubs around London, featuring their 'usual set' of Christmas tracks, implying they've been together for numerous years at this point. (Later, she keeps up with an impromptu song-and-dance routine with the Doctor, and in *Space Babies*, the following episode, one of the first things she spots in the TARDIS is its jukebox.)

Ruby doesn't have any particular hopes for who her mother is; she just wants 'the truth.' After a brief search, however, the TV show finds that there are no DNA matches on file, so it's ultimately fruitless. Ruby is understanding but struggles to believe her birth mother has never had a blood sample taken or similar. That's just one example of the bad luck Ruby faces that festive period – but there's at least one bit of good luck: her running into the Doctor.

The pair meet briefly in a nightclub, the Doctor drawn to her run of bad luck, caused by obsessive and malicious goblins. She drops her drink and the Doctor miraculously appears to catch it, joking that he's from health and safety, 'gin and tonic division.' Though Ruby believes she's just clumsy, the Doctor informs her she's not, that it's worse than that, but then vanishes.

Ruby is a compassionate, thoughtful, and responsible youngster: Carla tasks her with getting the shopping in before Christmas (though she dropped the eggs, and she cheekily notes, it's 'a really big problem because the shops close for all of one day'); she cares for Cherry as soon as she gets home; and she's joyous when hearing they're fostering another baby, despite being told at the last minute, on Christmas Eve. Baby Lulubelle, a name they all hate, is staying with them for a few days as her mother can't cope and the family is 'too complicated.' It's Ruby who notices the nappies are for six-month-olds, not Ruth Lyons, the social worker who provides said nappies. Clearly, Ruby is used to having a lot on her plate and has got used to spotting the minutiae – indeed, we see a gallery of Polaroid snaps on the fridge, all photos of the children Carla's fostered over the years, with a new picture of Lulubelle added to it. Still, it's Carla who ventures out to get more supplies, leaving Ruby to look after Lulubelle and Cherry. Things get out of hand when goblins kidnap Lulubelle, and Ruby has no qualms about hopping onto the building's roof and leaping onto a ladder suspended from the goblins' ship. She immediately recognises the Doctor when he does the same, following her into the ship: the Doctor has obviously left quite the impression on her.

The Doctor posits that the goblins felt the coincidence of it being both Ruby's birthday and Lulubelle's, so have 'weaved' Ruby's story recently, resulting in the slew of bad luck, all to make the baby, to them, a tastier meal. (Another coincidence, perhaps, is Ruby living in an attic flat at 3 Minto Road, the same street where a new pizza shop opened back in 2005, mentioned in *Rose*.) They get Lulubelle back in time for Carla's return, and she's introduced to the Doctor. While shopping, Carla's counted up the number of kids she's fostered: Lulubelle's the thirty-third. 'I had some of them for days, some for weeks, some for years, but only one of them stayed,' she says, turning to Ruby. 'And you made my life. You absolutely made my life. You can wonder about your parents, but I wonder who I'd be without you.'

She soon finds out: the goblins go back in time and steal Ruby from the church on Ruby Road, so nineteen-year-old Ruby vanishes and Carla turns cold and dismissive, telling the Doctor she only fosters because there's money in it. This goes to show how Ruby's enthusiasm and help fuel Carla's love of fostering.

The Doctor undoes the damage by going to 2004 and saving Ruby from the goblins; there, he also sees Ruby's mother, though not her exact identity. In 2023, Ruby works out that the Doctor is a time traveller from his earlier mentions of Harry Houdini, then rushes to the TARDIS, where the Time Lord is waiting for her.

Showing off in *Space Babies*, the Doctor briefly takes Ruby one hundred and fifty million years into the past. Ruby panics about the butterfly effect, showing she's got some knowledge of cause and effect, but something the Doctor poo-poos. Amazed at seeing prehistoric Green River, Wyoming, Ruby does, in fact, step on a butterfly and she's transformed into the arrogant Rubathon Blue of the fifty-seventh Hemisphere Hatchlings, before the Doctor revives the butterfly and Ruby is back to normal with no recollection of her metamorphosis. Next, they arrive on a space station orbiting the planet Pacifico del Rio in the year 21506, and Ruby quickly figures out that the TARDIS works similarly to a matter transporter, 'like in *Star Trek*,' which accounts for her awareness of scientific theory and sci-fi. She takes a lot on board in a very short space of time, including the TARDIS' chameleon circuit, that she can now (with the sonic screwdriver's help) phone Carla a few minutes after they left her, and that the Doctor's people are all gone. She's nevertheless amazed that the human race survived and 'went to the stars.' Ruby's experiences with her foster siblings later prove useful when it turns out the space station is manned by babies (she learns their names particularly quickly), but is concerned when she learns it's a 'baby farm' and that there's a monster on the loose; fortunately, her worry that they're being bred just to feed the Bogeyman is disproved.

Ruby thinks about her family a lot – she's worried that looking after these babies will take years and delay getting back to Carla – and not solely her parentage… though when she does think about the Christmas night she was abandoned, snowflakes appear around them, seemingly out of thin air, a phenomenon the Doctor can't explain. He later concludes that the snow is a warning, telling him not to interfere in the past, hence him refusing to take Ruby back to see who her mother really is. It's not until *The Legend of Ruby Sunday* that he suggests the snow 'means that that night is so raw and so open, the last thing that I should do is take a time machine back there… Time has tides and hollows and secrets, and this fixed point on Christmas Eve is the wildest I have ever seen.'

It could be the rawness of time around Ruby's lineage that

the Maestro in *The Devil's Chord* picks up as the elemental being says there's 'a hidden song deep inside her soul' (it's a variation of Carol of the Bells, rearranged by Samuel Pegg as the Shepherd's Bell Carol, sung by the choir on the night Ruby is left there in *The Church on Ruby Road*) and that 'the Oldest One' was there too.

Songs are obviously important to Ruby. At the start of the episode, she asks the Doctor to see The Beatles. She explains that Carla had a friend called Clare who had every Beatles album on vinyl; Ruby used to listen to them all after school when she was ten years old, and it's clear she loves the spirit of the 1960s, as she swiftly dons '60s clothing.

Curiously, Ruby has a greater knowledge of the Doctor than we may expect from what we see on TV; in *The Devil's Chord*, he plans to run and hide from the Maestro, and Ruby counters that he never does that – despite him doing exactly that when faced with the Bogeyman in the previous episode. When he says he doesn't know what to do in the face of the Maestro, she also says that's unlike him, that he always knows what to do, again in contrast to *Space Babies* in which the Doctor finally works out the truth behind the Bogeyman but not before Ruby suggests its real origin.

Fortunately, the Doctor can't run in the next episode, *Boom*, and he works out what's happening without Ruby's help. Unfortunately, that's because Ruby is unconscious at the time.

This is Ruby's first time on another planet. Kastarion 3 is a warzone with 'good trees, great mountains, [and] rainbow crystal,' and Ruby is rightly amazed, even if she was hoping for a beach instead. She doesn't get time to properly digest it. The Doctor steps on a landmine and it's up to Ruby to firstly investigate the source of a scream, and then help the Doctor escape, showcasing her bravery in extreme circumstances. In doing so, however, she gets shot and is on the verge of death when the Doctor stops the war, effectively disabling the landmine and forcing an automated ambulance to revive her. Once more, her empathy for children shines through, as she's particularly concerned for Splice, a young girl whose father died on the battlefield but who remains upbeat about it, happily telling Ruby that her dad isn't gone; he's just dead. Ruby confides that she finds this attitude sweet but not a great comfort. 'Dying defines us,' the Doctor replies. 'Snow isn't snow until it falls.' For now, that appeases her.

We might infer that family is such an important part of Ruby's life that she would otherwise struggle with loneliness. But *73 Yards* shows Ruby without company, and she copes admirably. The TARDIS lands in Wales, somewhere Ruby's visited twice before – once to see the DJ, Shygirl, in Cardiff and once when she was sixteen years old, to the Mumbles, due to a boy whose heart she broke. Before she can find out more about their surroundings, she steps into a fairy circle, the Doctor vanishes, and she's being watched by a woman who always remains exactly seventy-three yards away from her. She's clearly on the back foot: when she finds a nearby pub in Glyngatwg, she asks if she can pay for drinks on her phone – a fair question considering she doesn't know the year – but the locals take her for naïve and spin her a yarn about the legendary Mad Jack. They suspect she's just like other outsiders who think they're 'all witches and druids.' Still, when one of them goes to talk to the enigmatic woman following Ruby, he screams and runs away; later, when the landlady rings him to find out what happened, he says to ask *her*, though we're unsure whether he means Ruby or the woman. Either way, the landlady of the Y Pren Marw pub lets Ruby stay there for a short time between Ruby's vigils by the TARDIS, waiting for the Doctor to return. How long Ruby waits is unknown, but the landlady eventually gets resentful of her customer and Ruby heads home to London. It's notable that Ruby knows it's 2024 and Carla is at home for her, but for a while, she instead remains certain that the Doctor will come back for her and won't leave the Welsh town until forced to (though this could be desperation as the mysterious woman won't leave her alone and the Doctor would surely have the answers she's looking for).

Still, Ruby hates the notion of losing Carla. When she explains the situation to her mother, Carla approaches the woman and chats to Ruby on the phone so she can hear what's being said; instead, Carla listens to the woman then looks at Ruby in disgust and runs away. All Ruby can do is give chase and plead for her to come back. Carla bitterly tells her, 'Even your real mother didn't want you' and issues her with an injunction as a parting gift.

By the following year, Ruby is making ends meet by taking a job at Kleinermann's, and she's tried to learn as much as she can about the woman following her, including her exact distance and that she has a perception filter so few spot her without Ruby pointing her out. Kate Stewart of UNIT, however, has training to see through such things, and so she sees the woman when she meets up with Ruby and chats to her about the Doctor going missing and the increasingly supernatural threats UNIT has to face. This is the first time Ruby and Kate meet, and the latter assures her she can both help with the current problem and offer her a job with the taskforce. Alas, Ruby is soon shunned by Kate and UNIT when they talk to the woman, and over the years, Ruby grows more isolated. She gets into a relationship with a man named Frank, but his suggestion of going to New York falls on deaf ears – Ruby previously explained to Kate that she won't move abroad as this woman has a weird hold over her, as if severing that connection might kill one or both of them. So instead, her boyfriends think there's always someone else, implying Ruby won't grow too attached to anyone or tell them about the woman for fear of them doing what Carla did. This includes Sanjay who says she's difficult to talk to because it's like she's elsewhere. As her fortieth birthday passes, she breaks up with a guy called Rufus, though she admits that the relationship was never going to work out. It feels like Ruby is just going through the motions and can't commit, almost as if she uses people. During that break-up, she learns of a politician the Doctor warned her about, Roger ap Gwilliam, nicknamed Mad Jack. Ruby's got used to the supernatural now and, perhaps informed by her experiences with the goblins in *The Church on Ruby Road*, thinks the coincidence is too great, so she joins Gwilliam's campaign team, donating £1000 of her savings for the cause.

Getting ever closer to the now-elected Prime Minister, she admits to Marti Bridges, a fellow volunteer, that he gives her the creeps and Marti calls him a monster, hinting that he sexually assaulted her. Ruby demonstrates she can focus on what might be seen as the bigger picture, essentially allowing Gwilliam to abuse his power in order to stop him getting a nuclear arsenal. At just the right time, however, Ruby tells Marti, 'I'm sorry I took so long, because I think I'll only get one chance and I had to make sure I was right. But I wish I could have helped you. I'm so sorry.' Using the mysterious woman to her advantage, she gets Gwilliam to resign, though it's again unknown what she said to him to make him literally run away.

The Doctor doesn't reappear, despite Ruby believing he would after scaring off Gwilliam, so she spends the rest of her life waiting. Curiously, we never hear about her getting in touch with any of her thirty-two foster siblings, so she remains alone: you'd think at least a few of them would be there for her across those lonely decades.

Forty years later, the woman is still following Ruby, who returns to the clifftop to see the TARDIS one last time. She laments that she never saw Carla again and never made it snow again either. By 2089, Ruby is on her deathbed, telling her nurse that she's never been alone, despite no one ever growing close to her. Once the nurse leaves, the woman is no longer seventy-three yards away: she's now at the end of her bed, facing away. Ruby recognises that the woman has given her hope that her previous life can be attained again, that the Doctor will come back; indeed, as she flatlines, Ruby comes to realise the old woman is actually herself and she's transported back to 2024, where she witnesses herself and the Doctor get out of the TARDIS and avert the timeline by not stepping into the fairy circle. But her development is undone when the timeline is reset – or so it would seem, as now,

Ruby thinks she's been to Wales three times before. And later, in *Empire of Death*, she recalls that the TARDIS has a perception filter that extends to around seventy-three yards away, hinting that her subconscious has somehow clung to this other life. Still, we learn much about Ruby, notably how patient and seemingly heartless she can be (albeit for the right reasons), how she can distance herself from people and perceive the juxtaposition of being both alone and having someone there for you, and how strong a connection she has with the Doctor despite not spending a great deal of time with him.

She's also quick-thinking: in *The Devil's Chord*, she gets access to the EMI Recording Studios, i.e. Abbey Road Studios, by posing as a tea trolley lady; in *Boom*, she works out that she needs to hand the Doctor a counterweight instead of throwing it for him as that risks setting off the landmine; and in *Dot and Bubble*, she poses as a systems administrator to gain information from users of the titular social media network, including the immediately resistant Lindy Pepper-Bean, who Ruby charms by admiring her top. She manages to get Lindy to turn the Dot and Bubble off to look at the real world and spot that her friends are going missing, taken by the slug-like Mantraps. This is quite an achievement: without the Bubble guiding her, Lindy even struggles to walk, meaning that society's reliance on it is extreme. Later, when the Doctor and Ruby have helped Lindy escape with a few of her peers, Ruby can't immediately compute why Lindy refuses the Doctor's offer to get away from the Mantraps in the TARDIS. The Doctor quickly realises that society is racist and says he doesn't care; he just wants them safe. Ruby, however, is rightly disbelieving and disgusted.

When we next see her and the Doctor, it's in happier circumstances: the TARDIS has dropped them off in Bath, 1813, and the pair has fully embraced the extravagances of the era by dressing in period clothing (*Rogue*). Ruby is obviously a *Bridgerton* fan and is drawn in by the Duchess of Pemberton's poshness. Ruby admits she can't waltz, so it seems her musical inclinations don't extend to the dance floor (though she later says that she gets over breakups by going dancing). Nonetheless, the Duchess is impressed by her and tries to find her a suitor; it's the Doctor who instead finds one for himself, in the form of a bounty hunter called Rogue.

Ruby shows her gutsy nature throughout. When told she should be admired in silence, i.e. not speak back, she counters that, 'If you spoke to me and the girls like that on a Friday night down at the Spinning Wheel, then we'd rip you a new one, mate'; as she befriends Miss Emily Beckett, Ruby mentions another feisty friend, Bex, who, it seems, previously tied a man to a lamppost for not going out with her. Ruby appears to inspire Emily: 'This life may seem small, but there are horizons out there, and adventures and mountains to be climbed.' When Emily is revealed as a shape-changing Chuldur, Ruby pretends to be her and infiltrates the aliens. She does such a good job that even the Doctor is fooled for a while, and he traps the Chuldur, including Ruby, in a triform device that'll transport them all to an empty dimension. He has no choice but to send them there with Ruby, or risk the Chuldur destroying the city – and Ruby accepts this, happy to give her happiness and her life for the city. Fortunately, Rogue sees how close they are and instead sacrifices himself so the Doctor and Ruby can continue to travel together. Though the Doctor puts on a brave face, Ruby tells him, 'Doctor, you don't have to be like this,' and gives him a hug.

They've grown so close that the Doctor has shared details of his granddaughter, Susan, and the Time Lord's family looms so much in Ruby's mind that she instantly thinks of Susan when learning of Susan Triad, a woman whose face, it appears, has been following them through time and space (*The Legend of Ruby Sunday*). The Doctor dismisses this, but the possibility still nags at him. UNIT has already been looking into Susan as her company, Triad Technology, is set to announce the public release of something important. In fact, UNIT has Mel Bush going undercover at the organisation. UNIT also volunteers to help

Ruby find her birth mother by using a Time Window to create a version of events based on CCTV captures of Ruby Road on Christmas Eve, 2004. Ruby brings Carla to UNIT in order to experience this important time with her, and while the Doctor is distracted by seeing the TARDIS there (as seen in *The Church on Ruby Road*) and mulls over the links between time and memory, Carla realises that Ruby's birth mother is crying as she gives away her daughter. Carla helplessly tells this image, 'I took her in, darling, and she's safe, and she's wonderful.' Ruby pleads for time to change as she sees her mother turn her back on her and walk away. When a sinister presence connected to the TARDIS makes itself felt, Ruby initially panics that it's come for her mum, then worries that she and the Doctor are its real targets. Sure enough, this is Sutekh the Destroyer (originally from *Pyramids of Mars*), luring the Doctor in via one of his 'angels of death,' Susan Triad.

In a way, Ruby's birth mother saves all of creation. Sutekh has essentially been piggybacking on the TARDIS and has seen so much – while he destroys much of the universe in *Empire of Death*, he keeps the Doctor, Ruby, and Mel alive in order to learn the answer to the puzzle he hasn't solved: who Ruby's mother is. Discovering that, in 2046, new Prime Minister Roger ap Gwilliam made it compulsory for every UK citizen to give a DNA sample, the Doctor heads there to get details about Ruby's lineage.

After defeating Sutekh and undoing the damage he's done, they discover who Ruby's parents are. Her mother, now aged thirty-five, is Louise Alison Miller, and her father is William Benjamin Garnet, both fifteen at the time Ruby was born, though Louise kept her pregnancy a secret. Louise moved to Coventry when she was eighteen, got a degree, and became a nurse. Ruby is amazed but baffled that Sutekh was fascinated with an ordinary person; the Doctor explains Louise was important because they thought of her as such: 'We invest things with significance, so while the whole of creation was turning around her, it made her sheer existence more powerful than Time Lords and gods. In the end, the most important person in the universe was the most ordinary: a scared little girl, making her baby safe.'

When Ruby meets her birth mother, Louise apologises and embraces her. Ruby insists that she has nothing to be sorry for, and thanks her for leaving her somewhere safe. Carla and Cherry gel with Louise too, the former enthusing about the hundreds of photos she'd got to share, notably one from when Ruby dressed up as David Bowie when she was ten.

Having found her family, and about to meet her dad, Ruby decides to leave the TARDIS – albeit temporarily as the Doctor promises he'll come back to see her after her Earth-bound adventures have settled down a bit. The Doctor tells her she's changed him, changed the way he talks about family, and that she's made his life bigger and better. As he leaves, Ruby simply says, 'I love you.'

Melanie Bush – Bonnie Langford – Continued... (*The Trial of a Time Lord* to *Dragonfire*, plus *The Power of the Doctor*, *The Giggle* and *The Legend of Ruby Sunday/Empire of Death*)

Mel's reintroduction is somewhat unheralded on screen, her meeting the Fourteenth Doctor while fighting off the Toymaker in *The Giggle*, meaning there's very little time to mull over their connection. She'd previously been seen as part of the companions' support group at the end of *The Power of the Doctor*, so she has chatted to numerous other former peers. There, Kate Stewart offered them all a role working with UNIT, an offer Mel has obviously taken up. We learn that she hitched a lift with a Zingo back to Earth, though even the Doctor doesn't know what a Zingo is. She's then part of both the UNIT family and that of the Nobles, attending a gathering of Donna, Sylvia, Rose, and the Doctor, the latter of whom calls her 'Mad Auntie Mel.' Indeed, the Fifteenth Doctor enthuses to Ruby that she'd love Mel because she's 'bonkers.'

By the time the Fifteenth Doctor arrives at UNIT HQ in *The Legend of Ruby Sunday*, however, Mel isn't there: Kate's assigned her to an undercover role in a media team, so she can stick close to

COMPANIONS

Susan Triad of Triad Technologies. Susan clearly values Mel's input: after a rehearsal for a big speech, she looks for Mel's reassurance and asks her to just call her Sue. As Mel finally meets the Fifteenth Doctor, they share a big hug and she connects with Ruby almost immediately, helping her in the search for her mother. When Ruby's foster mum arrives, Ruby trusts Mel with making sure she's safe, and Mel opens up: 'I lost my family to the most terrible things, but the Doctor helped me.' Mel also has knowledge of Susan, the Doctor's granddaughter, though it's uncertain how: UNIT (or at least Kate) doesn't seem to know until Ruby mentions this, and Mel doesn't arrive until after that happens; perhaps they have a catch-up off-screen, or the Doctor did talk about Susan while with Mel in his sixth or seventh incarnation. Either way, she gets the Doctor in to meet Susan Triad, who they discover is a vessel for Sutekh the Destroyer.

The Doctor is understandably concerned with saving Mel from Sutekh's sand cloud of death that starts to emanate from Triad, but it's Mel who initially saves the Doctor by making a quick getaway on the back of her Vespa scooter (*Empire of Death*). They head to UNIT HQ and then into the TARDIS – that is, a memory TARDIS, made up of various previous console rooms. Mel recognises footage of the Fourth Doctor as the same man she's with now, meaning she's either encountered that incarnation at some stage, or, more likely, has pored over all of UNIT's files about the Doctor since returning to Earth. Nonetheless, the episode implies Mel's had numerous off-screen adventures with the Doctor as she acknowledges that Skaro is the home of the Daleks, these being a planet and species she never encountered on TV.

In *Tales of the TARDIS*, the Seventh Doctor describes the memory TARDIS as 'a special place where old friends come together to share stories, to remember, and to confront difficult truths'; appropriately, then, inside the makeshift ship in *Empire of Death*, Mel fondly touches the Sixth Doctor's clothes. Mel says travelling with the Doctor was the 'best time of my life' but has forgotten about meeting Albert Einstein (in *Time and the Rani*). She

656

admits to the Doctor that she's exhausted, but doesn't give up on finding Ruby's mother amid the chaos of Sutekh's attempt to destroy all life.

Still, this could be due to Sutekh himself, a god who's obsessed with finding out who Ruby's biological mum is, and who's also killed Mel and is possessing her body to manipulate the Doctor. Fortunately, Mel is resurrected and continues to work for UNIT once Sutekh has been defeated. And if it weren't obvious already that Mel still adores the Doctor and vice versa, the Time Lord revealed his true feelings for his former companion when he thought she was dead, saying, 'I loved you, Mel.'

Anita Benn – Stephanie de Whalley (*Joy to the World*)

Goodbye (Spice Girls); *Auld Lang Syne*.

Anita might not have travelled in the TARDIS, but she does spend a year with the Doctor and nonetheless travels in time.

Anita is a receptionist at the Sandringham Hotel, London, where she checks in Joy Almondo and takes her to her room. She leaves her there to collect towels, but when she comes back, she's faced with both the Doctor (proffering a ham and cheese toastie and a pumpkin latte) and the Silurian, Melnak. Anita takes this in her stride, apologising to Joy and assuring her nothing like this has ever happened before. Joy's taken to the Time Hotel via a door that's usually locked, and the Doctor is also locked out: the next time he can get back to the Time Hotel – and his TARDIS – is Christmas Eve 2025, so he asks Anita if he can stay in the room for the next year. He makes money by doing jobs around the Sandringham, essentially becoming the handyman.

Over this period, he and Anita become close, spending Christmas and New Year together and chatting about the meaning of Auld Lang Syne. She recognises that he misses someone, and he briefly mentions Ruby Sunday. He fixes Anita's satnav (when she says it doesn't take her where she wants to go, he replies, 'Ah, but it takes you where you need to go'), turns her car blue, and makes the hotel's microwave dimensionally transcendental. He misses his ship: when she visits him in his room, she finds models of the TARDIS, and after she says she likes them, he replies, 'They like you too. I can tell.'

And so, they set up a regular night together – 'Chair Night', where they sit in his room and chat. Their favourite evening of the week. With him, she celebrates the clocks going forward in the spring and laments them going back in autumn. They play board games, they share takeaways, and he entrusts her with stories of his travels (Anita deems the idea of the Weeping Angels 'rubbish'). Still, he hasn't explained about the Time Hotel as she admits she has 'no idea' what he's talking about. Similarly, she doesn't take much notice of his talk of Guy Fawkes on Bonfire Night, apparently being content that he's not the Doctor's boyfriend. Indeed, she hints at romantic tragedy, which might account for her attachment to the Time Lord.

The Doctor is a source of great joy to Anita, and, at Christmas 2025, she's aghast at the thought of him leaving without saying goodbye. The Doctor tells her the last year has been 'amazing', all thanks to her: 'Everyone who knows you is so lucky.' He's sad about leaving, but Anita tells him never to be alone at Christmas because she'll always be waiting at the Sandringham for him.

She's wrong, however: soon, someone from the Time Hotel arrives and offers her a job, saying that she comes highly recommended by an old friend. Anita gets a Christmas card that simply reads, 'For Auld Lang Syne.'

In a timey-wimey way, Anita Benn might've been working at the Time Hotel for a while: earlier on, the Doctor passed a shop there called 'Mr Benn's Any Era Clothes.' While this is likely an allusion to the book and TV series, Mr Benn, it could also mean that Anita finds romance again…

The Fifteenth Doctor
Expanded Universe

U nderstandably, out of the four Target novelisation released in 2024 adapting that year's run of stories, *73 Yards* adds the most to Ruby's story (though *Space Babies* highlights Ruby's closeness to Carla amid talk of finding her birth mother). We learn how reluctant she is to leave the TARDIS and is concerned it's died, and how she became a small and brief part of the Glyngatwg community. Carla abandoning her results in Cherry being evicted too, and Ruby's gran dies two years later; Cherry hasn't changed her will, though, leading to a legal dispute which Ruby fortunately wins, meaning she can now afford her own flat – a property on the Powell Estate, where Rose Tyler used to live.

Most notably, however, Ruby visits UNIT and meets Ace, who works there on a freelance basis. The extraterrestrial threats dry up without the Doctor to battle them (in contrast to, say, *Turn Left*), forcing UNIT out of business; UNIT Tower becomes The Unit, a multi-purpose location combining a shopping centre with apartments. UNIT perennial favourite, Osgood, is its concierge.

Back in the main timeline, Ruby and the Doctor face the Cybermen at the Sanctum Shopping Centre, the last mall on Earth, in Titan Comics' *Everyone Must Go!*; go Bigfoot hunting in a National Park in North-West America, in the audio adventure, *Sting of the Sasquatch*; experience the 'true Eden' of the Gardens of Kubuntu on the planet Yewa (in the novel, *Eden Rebellion*); and seemingly lose themselves in the audio story, *On Ghost Beach*.

The 2024 novel, *Ruby Red*, happens early on in the Doctor and Ruby's adventures. She shows great excitement about medieval Estonia, as well as great amazement at a futuristic distress call hailing from there – the Doctor has to explain to her about spaceships crashing through history. She's concerned about invaders getting into the TARDIS, so she hasn't yet discovered how impenetrable it is. Nonetheless, when aliens attack, she immediately tries to get back into the resistant TARDIS, so Ruby knows it's a safe space and she dreams of its 'cosiness.' She's clearly getting used to the ship being alive: it takes her a few moments to recognise that, when the Doctor places his head on its door, he's actually listening for a response to their dilemma. Later, when asked how long it usually takes to fly the TARDIS, Ruby shows her inexperience by admitting she doesn't know because she's 'always been inside it before...'

Ruby's further amazed at how quickly the Doctor can fit in and take charge, though she quickly blends into time periods on TV, perhaps most notably in *Rogue*. (The Doctor makes her feel more at home by taking her to the titular city in the *DWM* comic, *Mancopolis*, and she recalls her childhood in Manchester: if nothing else, she remembers it raining a lot there!)

The following novel, *Caged* (2024), seems to take place early in Ruby's travels too, or at least early enough for her to still marvel at what she's experiencing. She loves remembering that she travels in time and space, and doubly that they're on a planet no one has ever set foot on before, but is keen to bring that wonder back home: Ruby recalls seeing an online filter that would show what the night sky in London would look like without light pollution. 'I don't think I'd realised how vivid it was. How different it must have seemed, to our ancestors,' she says, further remembering her desire to find out the name of each star. She's also amazed to see shooting stars, something she'd only experienced once or twice before, and later on demonstrates how well she's adapting to this new life by taking a stand against apparent antagonists when the Doctor is on another planet entirely.

The Brigadier/
Kate Stewart

Nicholas Courtney/
Jemma Redgrave

> *'I just do the best I can.'*
> The Brigadier – *Battlefield*

Brigadier Sir Alistair Lethbridge-Stewart. No book about the Doctor's companions would be complete without an entry for the Brigadier – even though he was not technically a companion, he is the one character who transcends the entire series, and almost every Doctor, in one medium or another. He's also met many *Doctor Who* companions, and his relationship with them is as interesting as his with the Doctor. The Doctor's oldest friend...

Alistair Gordon Lethbridge-Stewart – Nicholas Courtney (*The Web of Fear* to *Terror of the Zygons* and *Mawdryn Undead, The Five Doctors* and *Battlefield* plus *Enemy of the Bane*)

I Sustain the Wings (Glenn Miller); *Now and Then* (The Beatles).

When we first meet the Brigadier, he isn't even a *brigadier*, but rather a colonel in the Scots Guard. While the Great Intelligence is planning an assault on London with its robotic Yeti in the 1968 story, *The Web of Fear*, Colonel Lethbridge-Stewart takes control of the armed forces and bumps into the Doctor while searching the London Underground.

They don't have the most auspicious of starts. The Doctor meets Lethbridge-Stewart off-screen, so it's not until episode three that we're introduced to him; the Doctor explains to Victoria that the colonel 'popped out from nowhere' while he was wandering around the

London Underground. Alistair is immediately suspicious of them – not helped by Victoria mistakenly telling them that Professor Travers believes the Doctor is responsible for the Yeti's return. Lethbridge-Stewart doesn't initially grasp the threat they're facing, so once back at headquarters, he seems happy enough to accept Travers vouching for the Doctor, and by extension, the Doctor saying Waterfield is one of his staff. With little more evidence of the Doctor's innocence, he even admits that he's dependent on Professor Travers, Anne Travers, and the Doctor. He's placing the fate of London – 'England itself perhaps' – in the hands of relative strangers.

He's then happy enough to accept Victoria at face value too. This establishes a common theme when it comes to Lethbridge-Stewart's relationships with companions: if the Doctor trusts them, so does he. It's a gambit that works out rather well for him, perhaps demonstrating what a good judge of character he is. Conversely, the colonel is met with some level of distrust for much of the serial, especially as his ammunition party was all killed – except for himself and Evans, the driver. The Doctor briefly takes him into his confidence, explaining his theory that there's a traitor in their midst before Lethbridge-Stewart realises this could be an accusation. But he doesn't hold it against the Time Lord, nor his companions. Despite not having been formally introduced (at least on screen), Lethbridge-Stewart trusts Jamie to pass on the message that he's trying to retrieve the TARDIS.

It's a remarkable leap of faith: if this information were to fall into the wrong hands, the enemy could learn of his taskforce's general position, heading from Goodge Street to Covent Garden; he'd barely met the young Scotsman, and in his eyes, this could potentially give the Great Intelligence a tactical advantage. Alistair's bravery isn't rewarded: his men are massacred by the Yeti, but the Doctor, Jamie, and Victoria are all pleased to see him return. From that point onwards, the foursome come together more as a unit. Lethbridge-Stewart identifies which parties can actually help the situation ('Evans, when I want your opinion, I'll ask for it'), orders Jamie to accompany him on a scouting mission through the tunnels, and takes his advice on how to proceed.

Sadly, he doesn't have many scenes with Victoria. Nonetheless, we see the colonel at his gallant best here: he doesn't really know Victoria and Travers, but he still tries to get them back from the Intelligence. Lethbridge-Stewart shows himself to be a trusting man, open to ideas, but not one to suffer fools gladly. He's not particularly harsh to Evans, considering the driver is willing to desert them at the first opportunity; as his superior in this emergency military matter, Alistair could've been a lot tougher with him. Still, he doesn't put as much faith in him as he does the time travellers. After defeating the Great Intelligence, Lethbridge-Stewart considers the Doctor a hero, but the Doctor disappears after he learns that a reporter wants to make him a household name.

It's some four years before they meet again, by which time UNIT (the United Nations Intelligence Taskforce) has been formed to counter alien threats, and Lethbridge-Stewart has been promoted to Brigadier and Commander of the United Kingdom branch of UNIT.

(Interestingly, the Thirteenth Doctor episode, *Survivors of the Flux*, takes place before this, in 1967, at which point UNIT has already been established and Colonel Lethbridge-Stewart is heard off-screen. We might infer that the machinations of the Grand Serpent have altered UNIT's already slightly convoluted history...)

UNIT is investigating the strange goings-on at International Electromatics, run by industrialist Tobias Vaughn. The Doctor and Jamie stumble into things there and are spotted by UNIT surveillance, and brought immediately to a reunion with the Brigadier. It's a happy meeting, and the Brigadier immediately enlists the Doctor's help to prevent *The Invasion* of the Cybermen. As soon as he learns that Zoe has entered International Electromatics, Lethbridge-Stewart is happy to provide backup, while the Doctor, Jamie, and Zoe take charge. He's already realised it's best not to underestimate them. Indeed, for the first three episodes, UNIT does very little, based largely on Lethbridge-Stewart's trust of these relative strangers. And he clearly holds such faith in high regard: he places his taskforce on a pedestal, blusteringly asking his superior, 'If you can't trust a UNIT force, who can you trust?'

The reverence Lethbridge-Stewart shows to the Doctor and Jamie is extended to Zoe and Isobel Watkins. He does irk them by telling the latter she can't be expected to go into the Cybermen-infested sewers because it's 'a job for my men.' In return, she says he's bigoted, anti-feminist, and idiotic, and he inadvertently spurs the pair on to venture into danger.

Still, it's unfair on the Brigadier: he may be somewhat a product of his age (as are we all, lest we forget), but his general attitude tells us he's protective of the pair, rather than thinking them inferior – after all, he knows they're capable after learning of their escapades in the International Electromatics building. Indeed, the Second Doctor displays this same concern when he learns that 'those crazy kids' – as the Brigadier calls them – have gone in search of Cybermen. Alistair immediately lists their recovery as 'a top priority alert' and the Doctor subsequently entrusts their safety to his capable hands. Zoe and Lethbridge-Stewart soon get over this minor grievance, and, in a time of high pressure (with an invasion in full swing and seconds to calculate a counterattack), the Brigadier relies on Zoe utterly. There's an absolute trust in her to complete seemingly impossible computations in record time. She asks for just thirty seconds and he grants her this, despite advice from Major Branwell. Naturally, his confidence in her pays off.

Sometime later, the Brigadier is trying to draft Liz Shaw into being UNIT's scientific advisor (*Spearhead from Space*). He talks about the Doctor as an expert on alien life, unaware that the Doctor is about to fall into his life in a rather permanent way. Freshly regenerated by the Time Lords and exiled to Earth, the Third Doctor is not initially accepted by the Brigadier, who doesn't believe it's the same man, even though the Doctor knows him. He gradually warms to this new Doctor, who is somewhat brusque towards the Brigadier, dismissing him with a wave at one point. Once the first Nestene invasion is defeated, the Brigadier asks the Doctor to stick around in case they should try again. The Doctor becomes UNIT's Scientific Advisor, with Liz now serving as his assistant.

It's easy to see the great respect the Brigadier has for Liz: for one, he keeps her on at UNIT as he enlisted her skills before he knew the Doctor was back on Earth, and in spite of her vocal scepticism about alien life. His jibe in *Terror of the Autons* that the Doctor only needs someone 'to pass you your test tubes and to tell you how brilliant you are' is purely to win over the Doctor, and apparently paraphrasing Liz herself. The high regard he holds Liz in is apparent, through the responsibilities he places on her and through their chemistry. He frequently defers to her when circumstances get the better of him. *Doctor Who and the Silurians* is especially notable for the great burden placed on her shoulders. When the Doctor is kidnapped by the titular creatures, she has to rifle through his notes and provide the vaccine to a plague set to wipe out the whole of humanity.

The Doctor remains for several years, even after his exile is rescinded, and over time an extremely strong friendship is developed between the two men. It takes some time, however, since the easy companionship the Brigadier and the Second Doctor enjoyed is gone, replaced by a Doctor who is less forgiving of the Brigadier's military mindset. One of the most notable early examples of them clashing was at Wenley Moor in *Doctor Who and the Silurians*. Once the Doctor has successfully beaten the Silurian plague, he wishes to broker a peace between humanity and the Silurians (the original owners of the Earth), and as soon as his back is turned, the Brigadier sets off charges and destroys the Silurian hibernation settlement beneath the moor; to the Doctor, this approaches genocide, or at the very least murder. Their relationship remains strained for a short while afterwards, but still stranded on Earth, the Doctor continues in his role as scientific advisor. It's perhaps a sign of Liz's appreciation for the Brigadier (or her position in UNIT) that she sticks with Lethbridge-Stewart after the Silurian dilemma. In fact, some of her comments afterwards indicate that, though she's not in agreement with this course of action, she does at least understand it. She empathises with the fact he's had to kowtow to his orders from the Ministry. Her skating over the issue, when the Doctor mentions it in the following episode, implies she's trying to keep the peace and move past their grievances.

In *The Ambassadors of Death*, Liz is held hostage for a considerable time, but the Brigadier doesn't give up hope. After all she's been through, Alistair still trusts her to keep a level head and her characteristic moral judgment when working with Professor Cornish to arrange the safe return of human astronauts in exchange for three irradiated creatures from Mars Probe 7. It's an even greater responsibility than an international incident – she's cooperating with an alien intelligence, and they've all seen the power the ambassadors wield.

(Liz's and the Doctor's scientific leanings rub off on the Brigadier: in *Day of the Daleks*, he makes it quite clear that he doesn't believe in ghosts, a fact the Doctor enjoys mocking before explaining his scientific rationale behind such things. This kind of insight slowly changes the Brigadier's ideals about science versus military might, as reflected in the 2012 episode, *The Power of Three*, when his daughter, Kate, tells the Eleventh Doctor that her father drove into her that 'science leads.')

That isn't to say the Brigadier isn't at loggerheads with Liz and the Doctor. Liz still maintains a cool demeanour and sure-footedness; Lethbridge-Stewart displays a similar self-assurance on most occasions, yet sometimes gives in to impatience or frustration.

The greatest example of their butting heads comes in *Inferno* – and it's not even *our* Liz and Brigadier. In a parallel world, we meet the Brigade Leader and Elizabeth Shaw. This Lethbridge-Stewart is a military man through and through: he's demanding, ruthless, and something of a dictator. Meanwhile, Elizabeth's nature is slightly more akin to Liz's. She's as sceptical of the Doctor's stories as her alternate incarnation was of the Brigadier's recollections of aliens. But eventually, she gives into her curious side, her sheer open-mindedness – so much so that, with the apocalypse looming over them, she destroys the establishment she loves by shooting the Brigade Leader. At what must surely be the end of her life, she takes a chance and goes against everything she's believed in. In contrast, the Brigade Leader has revealed a selfish streak, desperate as he is to save his own hide. By the time we return to more familiar surroundings, Earth is still in danger. It nonetheless comes as a relief to be back on an uncondemned world, back where the 'good guys' are in charge.

Similarly, in *Inferno*, the Doctor decides he's leaving Earth, having seemingly got the TARDIS console working again. He makes a point of saying he won't miss the Brigadier, but when the console sends him to a nearby rubbish tip, he returns with his tail between his legs. The Brigadier takes great pleasure in reminding the Doctor of his harsh words before agreeing to help. This pretty much encapsulates their relationship for the next couple of years – two men who have a grudging respect for each other, but are not quite friends yet. One almost suspects the Brigadier's assigning of Jo Grant to the Doctor is an act of spite: faced with an agent he doesn't know what to do with, he simply palms her off onto the Doctor. When the Doctor wants rid of her, the Brigadier refuses to accept the responsibility of telling her, and says if he wishes to 'sack' Miss Grant, he'll have to tell her himself. The Brigadier has already seen Jo's potential and charisma, knowing she'll win the Doctor around. Indeed, her arrival mellows the Doctor and smoothes relations between him and the Brigadier.

Jo becomes more of a friend to her peers than an employee of UNIT. Lethbridge-Stewart sometimes has to remind her that she is his subordinate, but their respective ranks are rarely heavily enforced, except when there's concern for her safety. He sees her as someone to aid the Doctor, rather than someone to carry out his own instructions. This is, in essence, the Brigadier playing matchmaker. In *The Dæmons*, even the Doctor pulls her up on this, albeit in a tongue-in-cheek fashion: after insulting the Brigadier himself, he turns to his companion and scolds, 'Jo, the Brigadier is doing his best to cope with an almost impossible situation. And since he is your superior officer; you might at least show him a little respect.'

Jo gets away with a lot – right from the off, in fact! There's a great deal of understanding and warmth extended to her: despite her being hypnotised by the Master and carrying a bomb into the heart of UNIT, she's accepted into this tight squad. Then, when she's recovered, she disobeys orders straight away and heads off to help the Doctor; more astonishingly, she's not disciplined (although we might infer that she would've been if the occasion had ended badly). Their unity is tested very early on. Their trial by fire comes when the

Doctor appears to abandon Earth to its fate in *The Claws of Axos* after finally getting the opportunity to explore time and space again. Lethbridge-Stewart's forces are overwhelmed, but Jo's attention is purely on the betrayal, not that she sees it like that. She refuses to believe the worst of the Doctor. While the Brigadier falls back on his characteristic pragmatism, she's consumed by worry for the Time Lord. We never really learn whether the Brigadier truly believed the Doctor had deserted them; he's far more concerned with the safety of those still stood by his side.

She has heart, and actually, she *is* the heart of this UNIT family: she's someone everyone else feels compelled to look after, and who could (and often does) get away with anything. In return, Jo seems to hold the disparate elements together; in much the same way as Liz acted as a cushion between Alistair's militaristic tendencies and the Doctor's general pacifism, they remain loyal to Jo. Still, Jo strives for her own independence and tries to prove herself whenever she can. Lethbridge-Stewart suffers the consequences of her actions but rarely infringes upon them; for many of her unauthorised excursions, she could be stricken off the taskforce, but that thought doesn't seem to cross his mind at all. In *The Green Death*, his tenderness for her bookends the serial. She's determined to fight against Global Chemicals, no matter the repercussions to her career. By pure chance, Alistair's on his way over to Llanfairfach anyway, so he offers her a lift. Let's call it… serendipity.

He also recognises her hyperbole in threatening to resign from UNIT, almost treating it as a teenage tantrum; clearly, he knows her too well to accept such a suggestion is serious. Nonetheless, his accepting that she's leaving to get married later on is surely a further indicator that Lethbridge-Stewart holds Jo, and the opinions she holds which are typically averse to his own, in high esteem. And even though it means their little unit (small 'u') is breaking apart, the Brigadier's genuinely elated at the news that Jo's found love.

It's little wonder Jo and Lethbridge-Stewart are so close: aside from the former's ability to charm anything that moves, they spend a lot of time together, much of it off-screen. A car journey from

London to South Wales is around three and a half hours, and we must presume very little of that was small talk about the weather. They have shared a lot of experiences. They've faced the end of the world more times than either could probably have imagined when signing up. Still, by the time Jo leaves, the Doctor and the Brigadier's friendship is strong enough to keep the Doctor attached to UNIT, even though he has no reason to remain behind anymore.

The Doctor's next companion has little to do with the Brigadier, at least initially, but the two nonetheless formed a solid friendship over many years. The Brigadier doesn't even meet Sarah Jane Smith in her first serial, so it's Sergeant Benton who recognises Sarah from photos of captives in *Invasion of the Dinosaurs*. When she and the Doctor vanish, UNIT has to cope with an emergency situation, in which eight million people have to be evacuated out of central London. The Brigadier's reaction to seeing the Doctor again – exasperated yet glad – is understandable. Once more, Sarah's association with the Doctor affords her certain privileges: she's granted information about the crisis, despite being a journalist, someone a top secret organisation shouldn't share information with. In fact, her integration into this tight team is remarkable, considering she occupies a very different place to Jo, with a more inquisitive attitude than her predecessor. Vitally, Sarah's not part of UNIT. Any benefits she enjoys come as a concession of her co-operation – and undoubtedly something more. In effect, she earns an unofficial place on the team because the Brigadier likes her. They are perhaps diametrically opposed: one works for the establishment in a top secret capacity; and the other believes in freedom of speech, of expression, and of the press. The pair nonetheless share a genuine warmth, which is especially obvious when the Fourth Doctor returns to Earth with Sarah and Harry in *Terror of the Zygons*, and they share a laugh about the Brigadier's kilt.

Indeed, the Brigadier and the Doctor have a similar sense of humour. In *Planet of the Spiders*, the Doctor discovers, via the latent telepathic abilities of Professor Clegg, that sometime ago the Brigadier had a tryst with a woman called Doris in Brighton, where she bought him a much-loved watch. The Brigadier takes the Doctor's ribbing well, but is clearly embarrassed by such private information being revealed. The Brigadier is also there when the Doctor undergoes his third regeneration; his reaction is a far cry from his protracted acceptance of the Third Doctor. He merely raises an eyebrow and says, 'Well, here we go again.' And he's more amused than annoyed when the newly-regenerated Fourth Doctor departs abruptly rather than give an address at Buckingham Palace.

It's in *Terror of the Zygons* that we discover that the Brigadier is of Scottish descent, of the Clan Stewart, and he proudly wears a kilt while in Scotland. While the trip feels somewhat like a holiday, the Brigadier further realises – seemingly before the Time Lord – the jeopardy he and the Doctor have left Sarah in, when it comes to light that the Duke of Forgill is an alien, and he rushes to her aid. In return, she immediately wants to alert the Doctor and the Brigadier to the dangers she and Harry Sullivan have uncovered, knowing the two are best equipped to deal with the threat.

In contrast to Sarah, Harry *does* work for the Brigadier, though he's given a similar free rein. Then again, even before joining Sarah and the Doctor on their travels, Harry demonstrates an intuition and independence that marks him apart from some of his fellow UNIT employees. This could be because he's employed as a surgeon, allowing him some flexibility due to a different degree of expertise. Nonetheless, it remains paramount for anyone under the employ of the military to obey orders. He's clearly risen through the ranks and obtained a high level of respect from his peers – notably the Brigadier. When the Third Doctor falls into a coma in *Planet of the Spiders*, the Brigadier calls for Dr Sullivan, which is immediately indicative of the esteem Harry is held in. Post-regeneration, Lethbridge-Stewart places the Doctor in Harry's personal care, a great responsibility considering the last time the Time Lord changed his face, he acted erratically (more so than usual). When Sarah questions whether he's the right person to look after the Doctor, the Brigadier is adamant about his abilities: 'Young Sullivan? Oh, he's a very fine chap. First class doctor.'

The Brigadier and Harry click straight away, likely due to their similar attitudes: both are devoted and loyal, have strong moral compasses, and hold stereotypically 'English' beliefs. When Sarah comments on the latter, Lethbridge-Stewart jovially replies, 'You may not have noticed, but I'm a bit old-fashioned myself.' His confidence is somewhat undermined by the sight of a tied-up Lieutenant Sullivan locked in a cupboard by the Doctor. Still, he's swiftly forgiven and put back in charge of the alien's health. He remains receptive to his ideas, particularly his suggestion that they need an inside man at Think Tank in *Robot*, and entrusts this risky task to Harry himself.

But the Brigadier is practical: he knows his friendships with Harry and Sarah can't be a priority over the safety of the world. When Miss Winters issues threats to Lethbridge-Stewart regarding her hostages, he simply states that it won't deter him. However, Harry becomes akin to Lethbridge-Stewart's right-hand man afterwards, so it's a shame we seldom see this partnership develop. By the end of *Robot*, the Doctor is keen to escape Earth again, and he takes Sarah and an unwitting Harry with him. We never find out the Brigadier's position on Sullivan shirking his responsibilities at UNIT for a flight through time and space, although he's naturally perturbed by the TARDIS dematerialising at the story's conclusion.

We could infer that, if the Brigadier were desperate for Harry's return, he'd have activated the Space-Time Telegraph earlier than he did. Instead, he does this when several oil rigs are attacked in *Terror of the Zygons*, alas the only other serial in which the Brigadier and Lieutenant Sullivan are seen together. As soon as Harry's back on terra firma, he reverts to his military ways, referring to the Brigadier as 'sir' and adhering to the status quo, because this is seemingly how he likes it. Sarah gets a warmer greeting than Harry – indeed, hers is warmer than even the one he gives to the Doctor – but, once more, it feels more like they're instantly settling back into their respective ranks rather than there being any animosity between the pair. Equally, the Brigadier's been dealing with face-changers long enough not to have any antipathy for Harry after a Zygon had copied him.

It may be due to the Zygons' comparative inability to accurately copy the personalities of those whose visage they steal, but the Brigadier doesn't appear very suspicious of anyone in particular during the serial. Their cloning of the Duke of Forgill, Sister Lamont, and the Caber is effective because they're unknown quantities – Mr Huckle provides an explanation for the Duke's frosty temperament ('He owns just about everything in this part of Scotland, except our shore base, and frankly, he doesn't like us. Not one little bit'). Yet the cloned Harry is singularly driven to recover the Skarasen signalling device, so the deception is glaring.

Harry later declines the Doctor's offer of a return trip to London via TARDIS, instead content with an InterCity train ride back to the capital city, presumably alongside his boss. Plenty of time to catch up on all each had missed.

Shortly after, the Brigadier seems to become heavily involved in the bureaucracy of UNIT business, spending an increasing amount of time away from direct command of UNIT UK. When the Doctor returns in *The Android Invasion* and *The Seeds of Doom*, UNIT is being commanded by two replacements while the Brigadier is away in Geneva.

The Brigadier leaves UNIT in 1976, and is replaced by Colonel Crichton (as seen in *The Five Doctors*). He moves on to teaching A-level maths at Brendon Public School in 1977, though everyone carries on calling him 'Brigadier.' He meets Tegan and Nyssa in *Mawdryn Undead*, during the Queen's Silver Jubilee and becomes involved in an adventure which sees him losing much of his memory – particularly in connection with the Doctor. When the Fifth Doctor arrives at Brendon in 1983, the Brigadier totally fails to recognise him, despite the Doctor reminding him of their time at UNIT and his ability to regenerate. Eventually, the Doctor jogs the Brigadier's memory, and he accompanies the Doctor on a ship stuck in a warp ellipse. There, he meets his younger self from 1977 and as they touch hands the Blinovitch Limitation Effect shorts out the time differential, causing the 1977-Brigadier to lose all memory of the Doctor. While at Brendon Public School, one of his pupils is Vislor Turlough, a character who the Doctor comes to trust but who the Brigadier never places much responsibility in. In many ways, Lethbridge-Stewart acts as an audience-identification figure. The Doctor remains suspicious but seemingly optimistic about Turlough, whereas viewers have witnessed his deal with the Black Guardian. The Brigadier, then, reflects this scepticism.

However, he does seem ruder than the last time we met him, going so far as telling a student, 'If you took more regular exercise, Ibbotson, not only would your body be less disgusting, but you'd enjoy a healthier imagination.' This version of the character is distanced from any other time we see him, including in *The Web of Fear* when he could've been an enemy agent.

Much of this Brigadier's attitude can be dismissed as differentiating between the pre- and post-Blinovitch Limitation Effect Lethbridge-Stewarts.

Then again, the Brigadier has a very different connection to Turlough than he does to any other regular character: he's his tutor. Arguably this puts as much responsibility on his head as when he was serving in UNIT. It's an obligation he takes seriously. In the face of all Turlough has done, he's still concerned about his student when Vislor is keen to travel to Mawdryn's ship via the transmat capsule. Though the Doctor cheekily tells the Brigadier to set an example by staying behind on Earth, Lethbridge-Stewart's curiosity gets the better of him. His accompanying Turlough is somewhat akin to supervision on a school trip... though the Brigadier appears more fuelled by a need to be with the Doctor again.

His distrust of Turlough rarely wanes, although his association with the Doctor grants him a little leeway. Nonetheless, time has not been kind to the Brigadier. Not only has he suffered considerable memory loss, but the education system has also ground him down: 'In thirty years of soldiering, I've never encountered such destructive power as I have seen displayed here and now by the British schoolboy,' he tells the headmaster. His disposition is comparatively reasonable, even if a modern audience might arch an eyebrow hearing Alistair check whether the headmaster has 'flogged that young man to

COMPANIONS

within an inch of his life.' That suggestion aside, we might expect Lethbridge-Stewart to be harsher, given Turlough stole and subsequently crashed his unique 1929 Humber – and the Brigadier once more demonstrates his solid judge of character in seeing through the boy's lies.

He's similarly astute with Tegan and Nyssa. He meets both in emergency circumstances: Tegan finds him tending to the garden in Brendon Public School as she's looking for a doctor. He keeps calm when he learns there's been an accident involving one of the pupils at the school, which can probably be put down to his military training.

Still, he's learnt about life beyond national service, and that seems to have opened his world up just as much as travelling in the TARDIS did for the Doctor's other friends. This could be why he's content to potter around in the grounds of the school, to teach maths, and offer support to his students and fellow staff. Nonetheless, the pre-Blinovitch Brigadier is certainly the same man as the one we left in *Terror of the Zygons*. He's determined to help people in whatever little ways he can. This means keeping Tegan temperate (to some extent anyway), and evenly assessing the details of the accident.

Obviously, his ears prick up when he hears about the Doctor again. From then onwards, he's more at home: he tries to take charge when he can, assuring Tegan and Nyssa that he knows all about regeneration, insisting he'll accompany them in the TARDIS, and ordering them to both stay there for their own safety. The Doctor's presence gives him the courage to travel in the potentially dangerous transmat capsule, but it's the promise of adventure that spurs him on when he's with Tegan and Nyssa. Let's not forget that they're strangers, and the only familiar element to him (in that time zone) is the TARDIS, which could easily transplant him into more danger – yet his instinct is to trust the Doctor's companions. More so than that, he wants to take charge. Is this because he wants to actively engage in the adventure again? Does he automatically think his experience is greater than theirs, qualifying him for more danger? Or is this an almost paternalistic nature kicking in, not wanting to put them in any more trouble than they're already in? It's probably all of the above.

While attending a reunion at UNIT HQ, the Brigadier is visited by

674

the Second Doctor, who's 'bending' the Laws of Time in *The Five Doctors*. They are both time-scooped to the Death Zone on Gallifrey where they have to find their way to the Dark Tower and Rassilon, the single greatest figure in Time Lord history. There, the Brigadier is reunited with other incarnations of the Doctor (the Fifth, Third, and First, the latter of whom he saw in *The Three Doctors*) and is reacquainted with both Sarah and Tegan. He strangely ignores Turlough, however. He also takes great pleasure in flooring the Master with a single punch – 'how nice to see you again' – no doubt taking out years of frustration at being beaten by the Master so many times during his UNIT days.

It's many years before the Brigadier meets the Doctor again, in a piece of flam called *Dimensions in Time*. Giving the Doctor a helicopter ride to the Greenwich Meridian, he fails to spot that he's picked up the Third Doctor but is dropping off the Sixth. The Brigadier does say, however, that he's having trouble keeping up with all the Doctors. At some point before the 1990s, he gives up teaching and leaves UNIT permanently, and marries Doris. He's called out of retirement by Geneva, being told that the Doctor is back. Doris doesn't want him to go, but the presence of the Doctor is the deciding factor.

In *Battlefield*, the Brigadier throws himself into the events at Carbury and rather enjoys the adventure. After reading the report of Brigadier Bambera, he assumes his replacement is a man and is a little surprised to discover that *Winifred* Bambera is a woman, although he doesn't let respect for the fairer sex get in the way. His awkwardness around women is emphasised in his initial bad handling of Ace (his chivalrous tendencies backfiring with Ace just as they did with Tegan, whereas the cooler Nyssa willingly accepts his aid in the same vein in which it was intended in *Mawdryn Undead*), who he implies is just the latest in a long line of companions of the Doctor. He's not wrong, but unintentionally downplays the importance of the Time Lord's friends. He tries to comfort Ace, offering her a blanket after she rises from the depths of Lake Vortigern holding Excalibur. 'Just call me the latest one,' she says, using his own words against him, 'and I can get my own blanket.'

Fortunately, they soon bond over her love of explosives, and work together to blow up King Arthur's spaceship. There's no malice remaining between the pair, and despite their differences, they naturally continue to fight side-by-side with the Doctor. That is, until the Brigadier puts a spanner in the works – Lethbridge-Stewart's courageous efforts against the Destroyer, stealing the silver bullets and knocking the Doctor unconscious, elicits an outraged 'you scumbag' from Ace. The Doctor has faith in the Brigadier, but that good grace doesn't extend to Ace. You can't exactly blame her: she's barely spent any time with Lethbridge-Stewart, and, unlike the audience, can't see the similarities between the two of them. Both are more inclined towards violence, and both would sacrifice themselves for the Doctor. He single-handedly stands down the Destroyer, armed with only his faithful revolver and silver bullets. The Destroyer asks if the world can do no better than the Brigadier, to which he replies, 'Probably. I just do the best I can,' and pumps bullets into the creature. He's redeemed in Ace's eyes when the Doctor laments his death… only to discover that the Brigadier has survived the ordeal. The Doctor states that the Brigadier was supposed to die in bed, but the Brigadier waves this away. 'Have a little faith,' he tells the Doctor.

'I'm getting too old for this sort of thing,' the soldier tells Ace. 'He's all yours from now on. I'm going home to Doris.' (The line does make you question whether Ace's possessiveness over the Doctor played a part in her dislike of Alistair. She'd met Mel Bush in *Dragonfire*, so knows she *is* just the latest in a long line of companions, meaning she shouldn't have been so irked by the Brigadier's 'the latest one' comment.)

By the end of *Battlefield*, Ace and Alistair have bonded and she's happy enough to go off on a jaunt with her new mates, Shou Yuing, Bambera, and Doris Lethbridge-Stewart. It seems the Brigadier has proven to Ace what an important character he is in the life of the Doctor. The Brigadier has gelled with the Seventh Doctor already and seems more than happy to spend time with his friend while the others head off. (Indeed, an old hand at regeneration by now, the Brigadier isn't even slightly fazed by the Doctor's new appearance, recognising him immediately. 'Who else would it be?' he asks with a smile.)

Over the following years, the Brigadier is made a Commander of the British Empire and becomes Sir Alistair. Shortly after this he takes on a position as UNIT's special envoy, and is often sent overseas, especially to Peru, where he tends to get stuck quite a lot. This is evident in *The Sontaran Stratagem* when the Sontarans attempt to turn Earth into a cloning planet. The Tenth Doctor bemoans the lack of his presence. Shortly after returning from Peru, he's debriefed by Major Kilburne and visited by a very old friend, Sarah Jane Smith (*The Sarah Jane Adventures: Enemy of the Bane*). Although they haven't seen each other in a long time, they've kept in contact and the Brigadier often pulls strings at UNIT whenever Sarah needs help (in such stories as *SJA: Invasion of the Bane* and *SJA: Revenge of the Slitheen*).

In fact, the Brigadier is the first person Sarah thinks of when she learns the location of the Tunguska Scroll, and he's immediately receptive to helping her. There are no minor pleasantries, no passing the time of day: these are two friends back in the swing of things in an instant. Most touchingly, his loyalty is to Sarah, not UNIT. The taskforce might've consumed much of his life, but as he points out to Major Kilburn, he's now retired (though UNIT remains an occasional employer, hence his trips abroad for the organisation). It's clear that Lethbridge-Stewart is tired of the politics, yet can't quite give it up entirely. That certainly doesn't stop him from using his position (and reputation) to go under the radar and help Sarah in retrieving the Scroll from the Black Archive. This is the first time we see the vault – for its subsequent appearances in *The Day of the Doctor* and *The Zygon Inversion*, it relocates to UNIT HQ, then the Tower of London – so its security isn't as tight as you might expect.

In retrospect, Sir Alistair's undermining of UNIT is a big leap for the character, given the reverence the Archive has since been held in. Essentially, it's a betrayal. He's always had a deep respect for the establishment, but he hides a rebellious streak too; it surfaces here and the catalyst is Sarah. The pair seem to egg each other on: Sarah tells him her visit isn't a social call, and he replies that he 'would almost be disappointed if it were.' He's not put off by the odds and doesn't immediately question why she needs access or gets defensive. Her explanations presumably happen off-screen, but even so, he sticks with her throughout the security breach.

Sarah and Alistair have never shared a great deal of screen time.

Nonetheless, their relationship has built over the intervening years, and it's probably best summed up by Sarah herself: 'The truly marvellous thing is to share the wonders that the universe brings us with good, true friends – the people we can rely on, no matter what; the people we love.'

By the time of Sarah's wedding and, later, when a faux funeral for the Doctor is arranged, the Brigadier is back in Peru and thus unable to attend.

Tragedy strikes at some point around 2012 when the Eleventh Doctor makes a phone call to speak to the Brigadier, only to discover the old soldier died peacefully in his bed, as the Seventh Doctor had previously anticipated. The nurse to whom the Doctor speaks informs him that the Brigadier always talked of the Doctor, and kept a small glass of brandy ready for him. The news hits the Doctor hard, and is enough to convince him to face his own apparent death in *The Wedding of River Song*.

Their long-standing friendship inspires his own daughter, Kate Stewart, who goes on to be a lead scientist in UNIT (now renamed the UNified Intelligence Taskforce), and she forces the old organisation to reform with scientists taking the lead and not the military.

It's sad that the next time we see the Brigadier, he is apparently a Cyberman, everyone in their graves having been converted in *Death in Heaven*. He saves his daughter when Missy blows up a UNIT plane and Kate's sent hurtling towards the ground; the Brigadier as a Cyberman seemingly catches her, brings her safely to the ground, and briefly meets the Twelfth Doctor.

Before this, though, the Doctor shows the respect he has for the Brigadier. After the Doctor moans about people saluting him, Kate explains, 'Do you know, that was always my dad's big ambition, to get you to salute him just once?' The Doctor simply replies, 'He should've asked,' implying he would happily have done so. Indeed, he does, albeit when the Brigadier has been converted into a Cyberman, before the latter flies off.

It's worth noting that we meet the Brigadier's grandfather too. In *Twice Upon a Time*, time stops around Archibald Hamish Lethbridge-Stewart (played by comedy actor and occasional *Doctor*

Who writer Mark Gatiss) as he serves at Ypres in December 1914. There, Archibald meets the Twelfth and First Doctors. He's lifted out of his timestream by the Testimony, creatures that catalogue lives on their deathbeds; indeed, Archie is supposed to die here, but their intervention means he's accidentally deposited in Antarctica in December 1986, where the two incarnations of the Doctor are about to regenerate. Archie charms both versions of the Time Lord, so much so that the Twelfth Doctor decides to shift time completely, albeit only by a few hours, meaning that Archie is instead unfrozen during the Christmas Armistice, when troops from both sides of the First World War agree to a temporary truce. This saves Archibald's life.

Although Archie is forced to forget events that occurred when his timeline was frozen, he still has some recognition of the Twelfth Doctor, saluting him in No Man's Land.

Before this, however, Archibald accepts that his time has come, and he regrets not being able to make it back home to see his wife. He asks the Doctor if he'll look in on his family from time to time; when he reveals himself as a Lethbridge-Stewart and the First Doctor agrees to check on his family, the Twelfth Doctor says, 'You can trust him on that.'

And so, although Brigadier Sir Alistair Gordon Lethbridge-Stewart has passed, his name and his legacy lives on...

Kate Stewart – Jemma Redgrave (*The Power of Three, The Day of the Doctor, Death in Heaven, The Magician's Apprentice, The Zygon Invasion / The Zygon Inversion, Survivors of the Flux, The Vanquishers, The Power of the Doctor, The Giggle, 73 Yards,* and *The Legend of Ruby Sunday / Empire of Death*)

Run for Cover (The Killers); *Wichita Lineman* (Glen Campbell).

Kate Stewart – having initially dropped the 'Lethbridge' so as not to curry favour – finally meets the Doctor in *The Power of Three* sometime after her father's death. (In the apocryphal video/novel *Downtime,*

COMPANIONS

she previously meets Sarah in 1996, and we learn Kate also has a son, Gordy, named after her father. It's important to note that none of this is referenced in the parent show.) She explains why she changed UNIT, what her father taught her, and how he had 'learned that from an old friend'. Here, she's introduced as UNIT's Chief Scientific Officer, but she's ostensibly in charge – by *Survivors of the Flux*, she's called the Head of UNIT, and in *The Legend of Ruby Sunday*, she informs Sutekh that she's 'Commander-in-Chief of the UNified Intelligence Taskforce.' Nonetheless, she still must answer to someone higher up, likely the United Nations, as, when the cubes arrive on Earth in *The Power of Three*, she tells the Doctor, 'I've recommended we treat this as a hostile incursion.'

It's a role Kate's obviously found difficult, admitting to the Doctor on their first meeting that UNIT was generally resistant to her 'adapting' the taskforce; she remains cheery, however, and downplays that period of her life, instead enthusing that she'd hoped the detected spike in Artron energy at the Ponds' house would indeed be the Doctor. (At some point during or after *The Power of Three* but before *The Angels Take Manhattan*, Kate 'screens' Amy and Rory and welcomes them to the Black Archive, as seen in *The Day of the Doctor*. Kate's perhaps fallen behind on the Doctor's companions, given she didn't automatically register that this Artron energy was at the Ponds' residence.)

Kate is focused primarily on the Doctor during *The Power of Three*, but she gets on well with Amy: when the latter is shown into the Tower of London and asks whether they're there because they know too much, Kate jokes that she's got officers trained in beheadings, alongside 'ravens of death.' Amy tells the Doctor she likes her. Aside from after bursting into their house, Kate doesn't really interact with Rory; however, almost a year passes during the episode, so it's possible they talk more off-screen. Given the Black Archive wipes people's memories, it's even possible that Amy and Rory have been to UNIT HQ before.

You can still tell that she comes at things from a distinctly human angle (which is entirely understandable), as when the cubes start counting down, she questions whether it's doing so in minutes. 'Why would it be minutes?' the Doctor points out. Kate is arguably more emotive than her father too: after people across the world start having cube-induced heart attacks, Kate reports that to the 'Secretary General' that their best hope lies in relying on each other.

In actuality, their best hope is, of course, the Doctor. When they part, she tells the Doctor that he really is as remarkable as her father said, and pecks him on the cheek. 'A kiss from a Lethbridge-Stewart – that's new!' the Doctor says, beaming.

By *The Day of the Doctor*, it seems Kate has a second-in-command, or at least someone she appears to trust absolutely: Petronella Osgood, UNIT's new scientific advisor, who is bold enough to answer Kate's personal smartphone, apparently recognising the ringtone as one set exclusively for calls from the TARDIS. We might infer that the Doctor and Kate have been in touch off-screen, albeit not alongside Clara it initially seems – the Doctor has to explain to her that he used to work for UNIT. Nevertheless, it becomes clear that Clara has been to the Black Archive before but has had her memories wiped, something which is largely skipped over as pretty standard for someone living this kooky lifestyle.

Acting under instructions from Queen Elizabeth I (that is, a sealed order Kate gives to the Doctor, plus, presumably, additional orders directly to UNIT carried throughout history by royalty, especially as Kate later notes that 'Elizabeth told us where to find [the painting, Gallifrey Falls], and its significance'), Kate brings the TARDIS – and with it, the Doctor and Clara – to the National Gallery, where mysterious creatures, soon revealed to be shape-changing Zygons, have somehow escaped from various paintings in the enigmatic Under Gallery. Kate knows her way around, so has been to this area before, but across the years, no one seems to have deduced that the painting's two names actually combine to form one: 'Gallifrey Falls No More.'

Though there are some silly mistakes and missteps, Kate knows what she's doing. She shows how much she studied UNIT's files when the Eleventh Doctor is confronted with the Tenth Doctor and the War Doctor in another time-zone; Kate immediately recognises the precedent and calls Malcolm (a member of UNIT we previously met in *Planet of the Dead*) to look for 'one of my father's incident files. Codenamed "Cromer." Seventies or Eighties depending on the dating protocol.' This references both *The Three Doctors* and UNIT's dating controversy. Kate's not intimidated by the Doctor's brusqueness either. When he tries to tell Osgood what to do, the scientific advisor defers to Kate, despite being in total awe of the Time Lord. Furthermore, when the Doctor is taken to the Tower of London in the past, Kate instantly recognises his convoluted yet genius plan and tells her team they're looking for a string of numbers left there from around 1550. As her father did, Kate instinctively trusts the Doctor's companions, taking Clara with her to the Black Archive (though safe in the knowledge that her mind will be wiped afterwards) where they intend to use Captain Jack Harkness' vortex manipulator to get back to the Doctor.

Things are a little muddier here, though: this isn't the real Kate, but a Zygon duplicate with her memories. Osgood finds the real Kate, strung up in Zygon machinery, and while you'd think this would put her on the back foot, she gets straight back on the horse and confronts the alien invaders.

She then demonstrates considerable bravery, or 'human stupidity' in the Doctor's eyes, by threatening to detonate nuclear warheads placed twenty feet below the Black Archive in order to stop the Zygons. Considering the bounty within the Archive, Kate reckons it's worth destroying London to save the world. Fortunately, it's not a decision she's forced to make, instead reaching an agreement with the aliens; nonetheless, it's a potential solution somewhat reminiscent of the Brigadier's blowing up the Silurian base (*Doctor Who and the Silurians*).

Indeed, Kate is a little bit of her father, a little bit of the Doctor. This is no more evident than in *The Zygon Invasion/ The Zygon Inversion*, during which some the Zygons that are living among the human race (as agreed in the negotiations following the fiftieth anniversary episode) rebel. Osgood, now acting as a bridge between the two races after the death of the Zygon version of her in *Death in*

Heaven, is kidnapped, and Kate hits panic stations, sending out a distress signal to the Twelfth Doctor. She calls the ceasefire an 'impossible situation,' and intends to bomb a Zygon settlement in Turmezistan as she views the treaty as having been comprehensively violated. The Doctor talks her down from this position and Kate instead goes to Truth or Consequences, New Mexico, to search for Osgood. There, she's attacked by a Zygon but shoots it, deferring to her father's advice of using 'five rounds rapid' (from *The Dæmons*). Kate demonstrates considerable guile and guts by then pretending to be a Zygon and infiltrating the rebellious splinter group, but later, upon revealing herself, apologises to the Doctor for the bloodshed, knowing he doesn't approve.

This culminates in Kate and a Zygon that's impersonating Clara with their fingers hovering over unmarked buttons in the two Osgood boxes in the Black Archive: one button is said to release gas that turns Zygons inside-out; another would detonate the nuclear warhead underneath them all. So sure is she that the Doctor will side with the human race over the Zygons, Kate asks the Doctor to tell her which is the button she should press. Still, she seems a bit bitter that the Doctor set all this up. Kate's militaristic mindset is at the fore, and then she shows a willingness to step back from the brink. She witnesses the Doctor's own PTSD, his raging over the pain war inflicts on people, and closes the box. 'I'm sorry,' she says to the Doctor, unable to bring herself to push either button. The Doctor remains a massive influence on her, just as much as the Brigadier was. Still, Kate is empathetic, particularly showing care when it comes to her colleagues. Is that what ultimately stops her from using the Osgood Boxes? Does her maternal side kick in? Or can she never truly bring herself to kill so many, so violently? It's never explored; it is, however, a decision she keeps making, as the Doctor reveals the human-Zygon ceasefire has broken down fifteen times in the past and each time, he makes Kate forget. Whatever stops Kate does so repeatedly.

It's not the first time she's met the Twelfth Doctor. That happens in *Death in Heaven*, when UNIT surrounds St Paul's Cathedral as

Cybermen pour out of it. Kate confidently introduces herself as a 'divorcee, mother of two, keen gardener, outstanding bridge player.' She instantly recognises the Doctor, quips about his grey hair, and promptly tranquilises him. Kate later explains, 'In the event of an alien incursion on this scale, protocols are in place. Your co-operation is to be ensured and your unreliability assumed. You have a history.' This last remark might refer to *The Claws of Axos*, during which the Doctor seemingly abandons humanity to the Axons, again showing that Kate has studied her dad's files in depth.

She certainly alludes to Brigadier Lethbridge-Stewart a lot, and has a portrait of him on Boat One, the aircraft designated for the President of Earth. When the Doctor suggests the human race's answer for anything is to elect an idiot, Kate cheekily retorts, 'If you say so, Mr President.' She has a fun relationship with the Doctor, even if it's sometimes a little fraught in the face of alien incursions.

Kate has a brush with death when Missy blows up Boat One and Kate is pulled out of the fuselage. The Doctor and Clara are overjoyed to see her, and while still half in slumber, Kate begins muttering about her father – now a Cyberman who's caught and saved his daughter.

Sadly, the next time Clara talks to Kate, UNIT's on the back foot and reacting to things in a decidedly dumb fashion. In *The Magician's Apprentice*, Missy stops airplanes mid-flight and someone at UNIT calls Clara to come over to the Tower of London. Though we don't know who exactly, it's someone who dimly suggests sending a helicopter to collect her. 'Think it through,' Clara scolds. Would she speak like this to Kate? Or was it simply a UNIT lackey? Either way, it seems Kate's not fully thought through the implications of Missy's actions, as she's shocked when Clara points out that the planes might be running out of fuel; then again, she might be humouring Clara as Jac, another UNIT employee, informs the latter that the planes are 'frozen in time,' something Jac will have surely already told her superior officer. Later, when Missy kills two UNIT soldiers, Kate holds back her troops by telling them not to fire in retaliation, recognising that they need Missy alive to, firstly, find the Doctor, and secondly, unfreeze the aeroplanes. Still, she's apparently placed in

Clara a great level of trust, as Clara tells Missy the snipers trained on the Time Lady will only kill her on Clara's command. Clara might be lying, but Kate clearly values her enough to potentially hand this control over.

After *The Zygon Inversion*, UNIT's funding is withdrawn (*Resolution*). By this time, though, Kate's recognised the machinations of the Grand Serpent, a being intent on destroying UNIT from the inside, and is railing against it (*Survivors of the Flux*), telling him, 'This taskforce has been many lifetimes' work for me and my family. I will not let it be sabotaged from within.' In 2017, she informs Osgood that she has to go dark and so goes off the grid.

When she meets the Thirteenth Doctor, Yasmin Khan, and Dan Lewis in the Williamson Tunnels in 2021 (*The Vanquishers*), Kate is initially suspicious of the latter pair, but quickly scans them for residual Artron energy and so realises they've been in the TARDIS. Kate's now the leader of the Human Resistance Against Sontaran Occupation, and is further proving a thorn in the side of the Grand Serpent. Indeed, he's become quite obsessed with her, repeatedly asking others where she is. She's clearly got under his skin, and though he tracks her down, he's caught off guard by pilot, Inston-Vee Vinder, and they strand him on an asteroid. When it's time to bid adieu to the Doctor, Kate says she likes this incarnation and hopes she meets her again.

And she does, in *The Power of the Doctor*. By then, Kate's been busy rebuilding UNIT, and in doing so, she makes the organisation very public – going so far as to erect a giant skyscraper at London's heart, acting as UNIT HQ. She's also taking on freelancers as aides, including former companions, Tegan Jovanka and Ace, on whom she forces a reunion with the Doctor. 'I'm rebuilding our intelligence networks with people who understand the problems Earth faces from personal experience,' Kate tells the Doctor. 'It seemed pretty clear where to start.' In some ways, then, she's doing what her dad did before her: keeping on people who know the Doctor. Kate, though, is taking on companions after they've travelled in the TARDIS; the Brigadier actively introduced people like Liz Shaw, Jo Grant, and

Harry Sullivan to the Doctor. Later, when attending a meet-up of former companions, Kate says she intends to offer many of them jobs at UNIT.

Following her reviving the taskforce, Kate is very much in charge on a global scale, informing the Doctor that they've a UNIT base in Naples and that she can arrange local support, and later telling invading Cybermen that she's called in reinforcements from across the globe (although this is likely subterfuge). She's not afraid to make a tough call either, locking down UNIT HQ in order to contain the threat, but also identifying Tegan and Ace as key to the Doctor's success and so helping them break lockdown. Tegan feels such guilt for accidentally bringing the Cybermen into the base, and it seems a loyalty to Kate, that she risks her life by staying behind anyway. Kate's ultimate plan is to sacrifice herself by blowing up the building. She acts as bait for the Cybermen, keeping them away from Tegan while the latter gets to the structural termination system in UNIT HQ's basement. Kate even offers herself up as someone with great strategic value; in return, the Cybermen must agree to let her soldiers go. (It's a request the Cybermen pretend to adhere to, but instead go back on their word, obviously upsetting Kate when she finds out what's happening to her troops.) Whether this is a genuine offer or a delaying tactic is unknown, as Kate escapes first the Cybermen then the building being levelled.

She's then afforded her first trip inside the TARDIS, helping to pilot it alongside the Doctor's companions. Yes, Kate's studied all the UNIT files, but is still amazed at its being dimensionally transcendental and astonishingly asks, 'How is it bigger on the inside?'

By the time of *The Giggle*, she's rebuilt UNIT HQ and is now going by 'Lethbridge-Stewart,' seemingly a considerable milestone, except her father's influence has always been obvious in previous stories. Kate clearly values the Doctor's companions, having given Mel Bush a job, offering Donna Noble one (and immediately granting her a salary of £120,000 a year), and shouldering the fees for putting Wilfred Mott into sheltered accommodation (as per *The Star Beast*). What's more, once they've dealt with the threat of the Toymaker, she gives Donna's daughter, Rose, a job at UNIT too. She's expanded her team further, first taking on Shirley Anne Bingham, then, by the time of *The Legend of Ruby Sunday*, Morris Gibbons, as scientific advisors, as well as a robot called the Vlinx. The Fourteenth Doctor seems proud that Kate's ushering in a more public era of UNIT; meanwhile, she seems prouder of the Galvanic beam, which she says is able to pick off a pebble on the moon. Kate recalls fighting 'robots and insects and Yetis and clones,' alluding to various off-screen adventures, including taking on the Great Intelligence, the alien being whose second appearance came in the Brigadier's introductory tale, *The Web of Fear*. Despite facing a terrifying elemental force, Kate's as focused on the danger to her staff; after the Toymaker's been trapped by the Fourteenth and Fifteenth Doctors, she wants a list of names of the deceased, presumably so she can offer her condolences personally. Indeed, this is a Lethbridge-Stewart more in touch with her emotions, as she hugs the Doctor and, in the parallel future of *73 Yards*, tells Ruby Sunday that she adores the Time Lord – not that she'll tell him that face to face. She's fine about disobeying him, though, as she later admits to making a Time Window, something he expressly forbade in the Seventies. (She's also noticed that the perils facing Earth are becoming more supernatural, hence her binding the Toymaker in a ring of salt.)

This empathetic Kate gels well with the more personable Fifteenth Doctor, who tells his companion in *The Legend of Ruby Sunday*, 'We love Kate. I knew Kate's dad. He was the best of men.' She's also more clued in, taking the Doctor by surprise by saying she'd already worked out that 'S Triad', the company UNIT is keeping an eye on, is an anagram of 'TARDIS.' Kate's further got a file devoted to Ruby Sunday following the events of *The Church on Ruby Road*, so she's more on the ball now than she was when it came to Amy and Rory. She doesn't know about Susan, however, saying to the Doctor, 'My father, he'd tell me stories about you when I was a kid. He'd sit there in the firelight, telling tales of the Doctor, his eyes... shining. But he never ever mentioned a granddaughter.' It seems curious that the Brigadier didn't relay any anecdotes from during *The Five Doctors*, but we might infer the timelines being out of sync, owing to the multiple incarnations of the Doctor being present on Gallifrey, affected his memories too. The Doctor then opens up to her, explaining that, as a Time Lord, he can have grandchildren without having kids just yet. His willingness to walk into an obvious trap prompts her to give him a hug. She's largely right about the nature of the trap too: in a rather poetic turn of phrase, she explains that the enigmatic Susan Triad might be nice now but can easily change, as 'a caterpillar doesn't know it's a butterfly, and a phoenix is just a bird until it burns.'

Her romantic mindset stays with her to the end; that is, her death at the hands of Sutekh the Destroyer who she and her taskforce face up to in *Empire of Death*. 'This is me signing off, with thanks and love. And please send this monster back into hell,' she says to the Doctor. 'Because I have to hope that the birds will sing again. There will be birds.'

Fortunately, the Doctor brings her back to life, alongside the rest of the planet, and all Kate can remember about the afterlife are 'echoes.' In this life, though, she's reunited with her soldiers, most notably Colonel Christofer Ibrahim, whose hand she takes following Sutekh's defeat, and who she goes into battle with for *The War Between the Land and the Sea*.

Kate might've started out as a leader of UNIT who believes that 'science leads,' but quickly changes into someone who values people more than anything else.

UNIT's story has otherwise been explored in a spin-off, *The War Between the Land and the Sea*; on audio (most notably in a series of Big Finish sets featuring Kate Stewart and Osgood); and prominently in novels, novellas, and short story collections in the *Lethbridge-Stewart, The Benton Files*, and *UNIT* ranges.

Beginning with *The Forgotten Son*, the Brigadier's backstory is greatly added to across some forty novels in his own series, which introduces a number of original characters like Bill Bishop, Samson Ware, and Alistair's nephew, Owain, and brother, James, the latter of whom died when they were both youngsters. *Moon Blink*, which began the second series of *Lethbridge-Stewart* books in 2016, was even written by Sadie Miller, the daughter of Sarah Jane Smith actress, Elisabeth Sladen.

The Lethbridge-Stewart legacy also lives on in the titular lead of *The Lucy Wilson Mysteries*. Lucy is the granddaughter of the Brigadier and as such, faces familiar aliens such as the Borad and Bandrils from *Timelash* (*The Ballad of the Borad* and *The Bandril Invasion*, respectively), the Great Intelligence (*Avatars of the Intelligence*), and the Rutans (*The Keeper of Fang Rock* and *The Children of January*).

To read more about these Candy Jar stories, UNIT: A Legacy in Doctor Who *by Baz Greenland is a great source of information. It's available from www.candycarbooks.co.uk and all major retailers.*

To listen to a Companions Spotify playlist, scan the QR code above.

Afterword

As a lifelong *Doctor Who* fan, the role of the Doctor's companions has changed quite a lot for me since I first started watching the show back in the 1970s.

In the early days, the companion seemed to be there to guide us, to give us the sense we could trust this mysterious Doctor to look after us, as well as our little planet – to ensure no harm would befall us, from the non-stop cavalcade of scary creatures intent on invading our tiny corner of the universe. The companions were there to ask the questions we could not. To educate and inform. And to assure us that everything will be okay.

Liz Shaw, Jo Grant, and Sarah Jane Smith were my first companions as a young viewer.

As I grew older, things started to change over just how I felt about them. Elisabeth Sladen was my first crush, and I was devastated when Sarah left at the end of *The Hand of Fear*. It felt as if we'd been abandoned and it took some time before Leela and then Romana earned a place in my heart, just as Tom Baker and his flashing grin did after Jon Pertwee hung up his cape. But the companions all managed to find a way into my emotions, one way or another. It's just something you allow and invest in as a viewer.

I'm always willing to give that chance, to open up my imagination, and to get carried along with the journey, wherever it leads. Because after all, isn't that the point?

Colin Howard

UNIT: A LEGACY IN DOCTOR WHO

UNIT: A Legacy in Doctor Who explores the rich history of the United Nations Intelligence Taskforce – and later Unified Intelligence Taskforce – from its inception under producer and writer Derrick Sherwin, through the UNIT family days of Jon Pertwee's Doctor, all the way to the Kate and Osgood era of recent years.

With UNIT featuring in numerous other media like Reeltime Productions, Big Finish audio, and the *Lethbridge-Stewart* range from Candy Jar Books, the legacy of UNIT – and its importance to *Doctor Who* extends beyond its television appearances.

The book features exclusive interviews with writers and actors John Levene and Sophie Aldred, and explores the development of UNIT, its importance in the *Doctor Who* mythos and the actors that brought these iconic characters to life – from Nicholas Courtney's stalwart Brigadier Alistair Lethbridge-Stewart to Jemma Redgrave's courageous Kate Stewart.

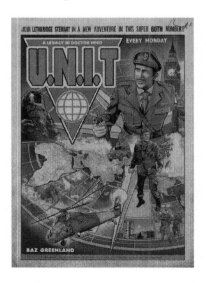

References

TV
Doctor Who (BBC Television, 1963- 2025)
The Sarah Jane Adventures (Children's BBC Television, 2008- 12)
Torchwood (BBC Television, 2007- 10)

Magazines
Doctor Who Magazine (Marvel, Panini, 1979- 2025)
Doctor Who comics by IDW (2007- 13)
Doctor Who comics by Titan Comics (2014- 25)
Vworp Vworp! fanzine (2010- 24)

Audios
Doctor Who audios (BBC Audio, Big Finish, 1996- 2025)

Books
The Comic Strip Companion by Paul Scoones (Telos Publishing, 2012)
The DisContinuity Guide by Paul Cornell, Martin Day, and Keith Topping (Virgin Publishing, 1995)
Doctor Who novels (Virgin Publishing, BBC Books, 1991- 2025)
Doctor Who: The Encyclopaedia by Gary Russell (BBC Books, 2012)
Doctor Who: The Inside Story by Gary Russell (BBC Books, 2006)
Doctor Who: The New Audio Adventures – The Inside Story by Benjamin Cook (Big Finish, 2004)
Doctor Who: The Television Companion by David J Howe & Stephen James Walker (BBC Books, 1998)
The Encyclopaedia of the Worlds of Doctor Who by David Saunders (Knight Books, 1989)
A History of the Universe by Lance Parkin (Virgin Publishing, 1996)
Inside the Hub by Stephen James Walker (Telos Publishing, 2007)

I, Who 1, 2 & *3* by Lars Pearson (Mad Norwegian Press, 2003)
UNIT: A Legacy in Doctor Who by Baz Greenland (Candy Jar Books, 2024)
The Black Archive: The Pandorica Opens / The Big Bang by Philip Bates (Obverse Books, 2020)

Websites
The Doctor Who Companion (thedoctorwhocompanion.com)
The Doctor Who Reference Guide (drwhoguide.com)
Chrissie's Transcripts Site
(http://www.chakoteya.net/index.html)
Hogan Reviews (hoganreviews.co.uk)
TARDIS Data Core (tardis.wikia.com)
The Time Scales (thetimescales.com)

Acknowledgements

Andy

It's always said that no book is written by one person. This is doubly true of this book. I had the help and support of some great people, and they deserve thanks for their help, because without them this book would not be half the book it is.

For help with research and answering my barrage of questions, I thank *Doctor Who* experts (in no particular order), David Howe, Gary Russell, Paul Scoones, Paul Simpson, John Dorney, Joe Lidster, David McIntee, Justin Richards, Keith Topping, Martin Day, Mark Michalowski, and Steve Lyons.

Special thanks go to the team at Candy Jar Books for going beyond the call of duty in putting this all together: Shaun Russell, Hayley Cox, Richard Kelly, Jake Rudge, Rose Wildlake, Terry Cooper, Rebecca Lloyd James, Charles Lax, and Justin Chaloner.

Personal thanks for general support and interest goes to my family, as ever, and Phillip Archer, Jay Hartman, Katie Riggs, Jolene Ferries, Jack Adams, Lukus Therneau, Tom Webster, Luke Spillane, Owen and Damien (our very own Russell Howard) Moran, Rebecca Flower, Elizabeth Medeiros, Kristian Barry, Gareth Starling & Jason Godden, Merlin Cryer, Christian Mansell, Tom Sanford, Jon Cooper, James Beale, John Davies, Steve Roberts, Trudi Topham, JR Southall, Christopher Bryant, Sharon Bidwell, Prakash Bakrania, and Simon Williams.

And, of course, special thanks go to Joseph W Quintana; you will always be 'so much more'.

Philip

Firstly, I want to thank Shaun and Andy for asking me to take on this project. It's been years in the making, but I certainly enjoyed it. It's pretty mad to consider how much *Doctor Who* there now is across all its mediums. And look at the fantastic cover! *The* Colin Howard has created a cover for my *Doctor Who* book! How insane is that?! Cheers, bud.

Of course, a special thanks to Mum and Dad – always the first people to read and edit my work. Thank you to my sister and brother, Kay and Paul, and to my other half, Tabi. Thank you all for your love and support.

All my friends have been hugely encouraging of my career, so thank you to each and every one of you. Especially to the kind folk who bought *100 Objects of Dr Who* and made it a success. Thanks, too, to my wonderful team at *The Doctor Who Companion*: running the site is a pleasure because of its contributors. Special thanks go to the lovely Bar Nash-Williams (our resident Liv Chenka expert) the also-lovely Colin Burden, a fellow Eighth Doctor aficionado, and the equally-lovely Jordan Shortman, whose *Doctor Who* novel knowledge puts the rest of us to shame.

Is it too grandiose to thank Russell T Davies and Steven Moffat? I know you'll never read this, but this book is a result of you properly introducing me to *Doctor Who* and making me love it. Sorry about that.

And finally, thank you to you, dear reader. You've been very patient as the page count of this tome spiralled out of control. I hope you think it's worth it. It's pretty ironic that the final words I wrote for *Companions* were: 'Everything ends, Clara. And sooner than you think...'

Coming Soon from Candy Jar

TEN YEARS IN THE MAKING

Just Sarah:
More Than Fifty Years of a Doctor Who Companion

On 15th December 1973, Sarah Jane Smith joined the Doctor on his travels and became one of the most loved companions throughout its initial twenty-six-year run. In 2006, she returned *to Doctor Who*, which led to her own spin-off series, *The Sarah Jane Adventures* – the most successful show on CBBC.

Half a century on from *The Time Warrior*, this essay collection celebrates not just this cherished character but also the remarkable person who played her, as well as those lives she touched.

Just Sarah: More Than Fifty Years of a Doctor Who Companion includes a guide to Sarah's adventures in the TARDIS and beyond; examinations of her relationship with the Doctor; a look at the horror tropes in tales like *Planet of Evil* and *The Brain of Morbius*; recollections of Sladen's other roles (often for Third Doctor producer, Barry Letts); warm memories from artists, Colin Howard and Martin Geraghty; and much more.

Plus, of course, why she's not Sarah Jane Smith – she is *just Sarah*.

For more information on Candy Jar's range of books, visit
www.candyjarbooks.co.uk